THE INFINITY PARTICLE

WENDY XU

Quill Tree Books
Imprints of HarperCollins Publishers

Quill Tree Books and HarperAlley
are imprints of HarperCollins Publishers.

The Infinity Particle
Copyright © 2023 by Wendy Xu
All rights reserved. Manufactured in Bosnia and Herzegovina.
No part of this book may be used or reproduced in any manner whatsoever without
written permission except in the case of brief quotations embodied in critical
articles and reviews. For information address HarperCollins Children's Books, a
division of HarperCollins Publishers, 195 Broadway, New York, NY 10007.
www.harperalley.com

Library of Congress Control Number: 2022941734
ISBN 978-0-06-295576-0 (paperback)
ISBN 978-0-06-295577-7

The artist used Procreate to create the digital illustrations for this book.
Typography by Wendy Xu
23 24 25 26 27 GPS 10 9 8 7 6 5 4 3 2 1

First Edition

To my favorite podcasters—thanks for keeping me company;
especially Paris Marx and Robert Evans—
your shows were integral to the philosophy of this book.
I am humbled and grateful for your work.

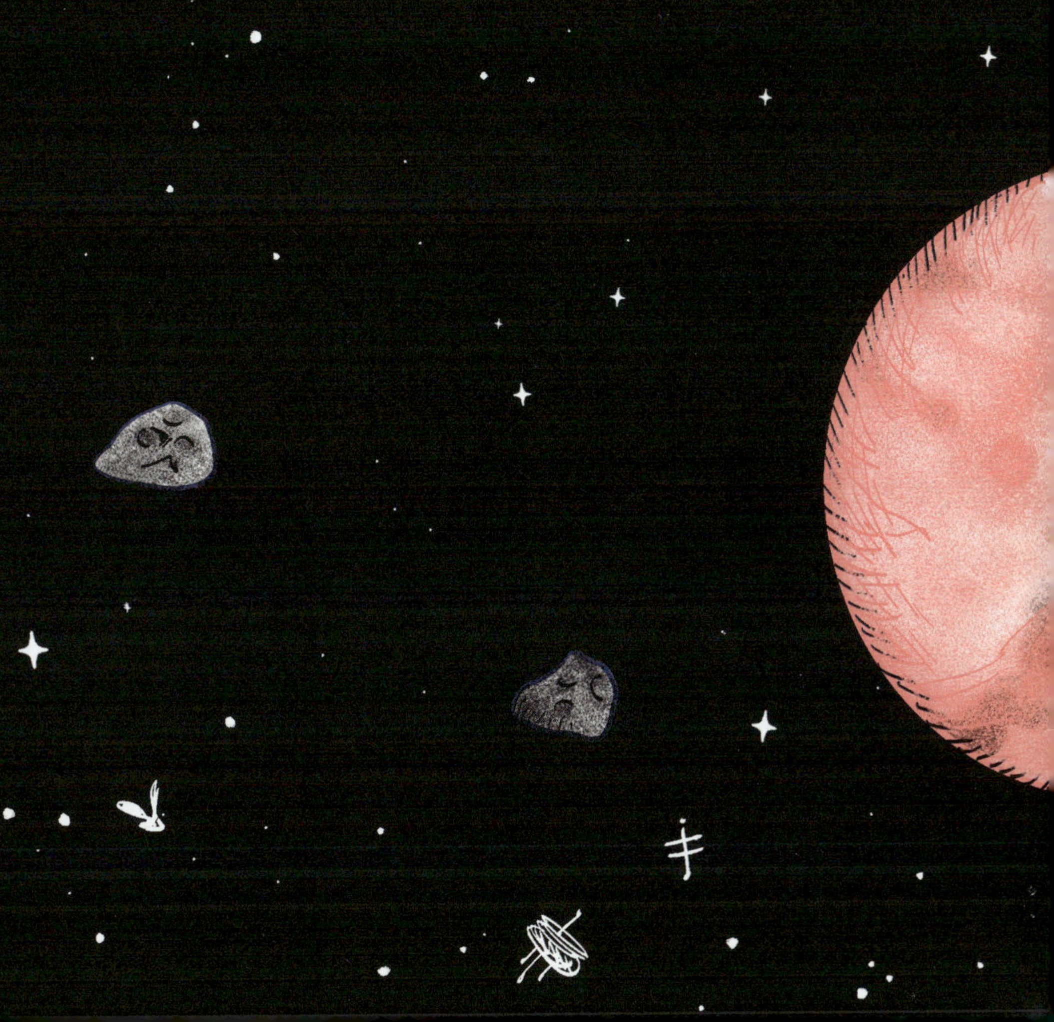

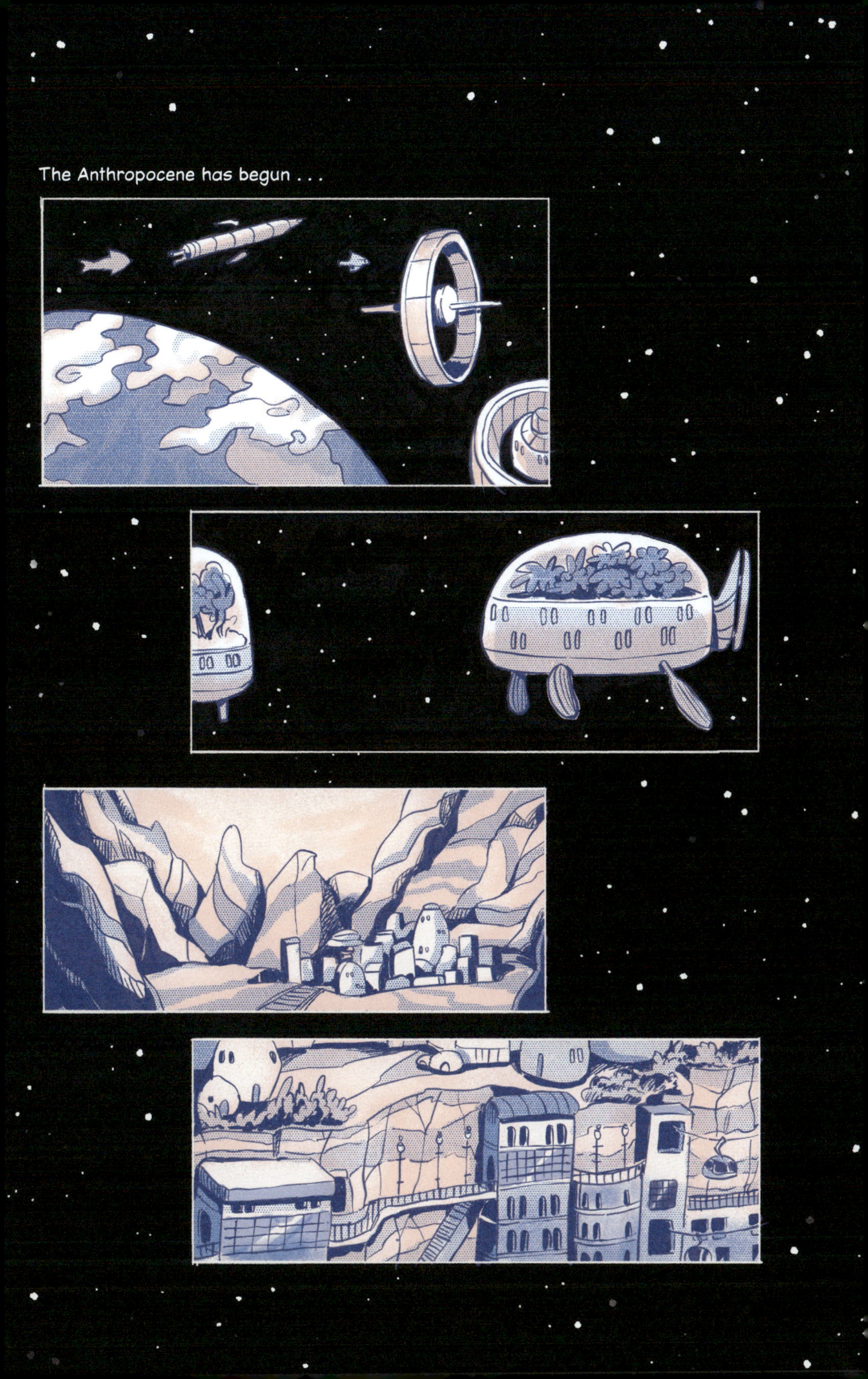
The Anthropocene has begun . . .

00110000 00110001

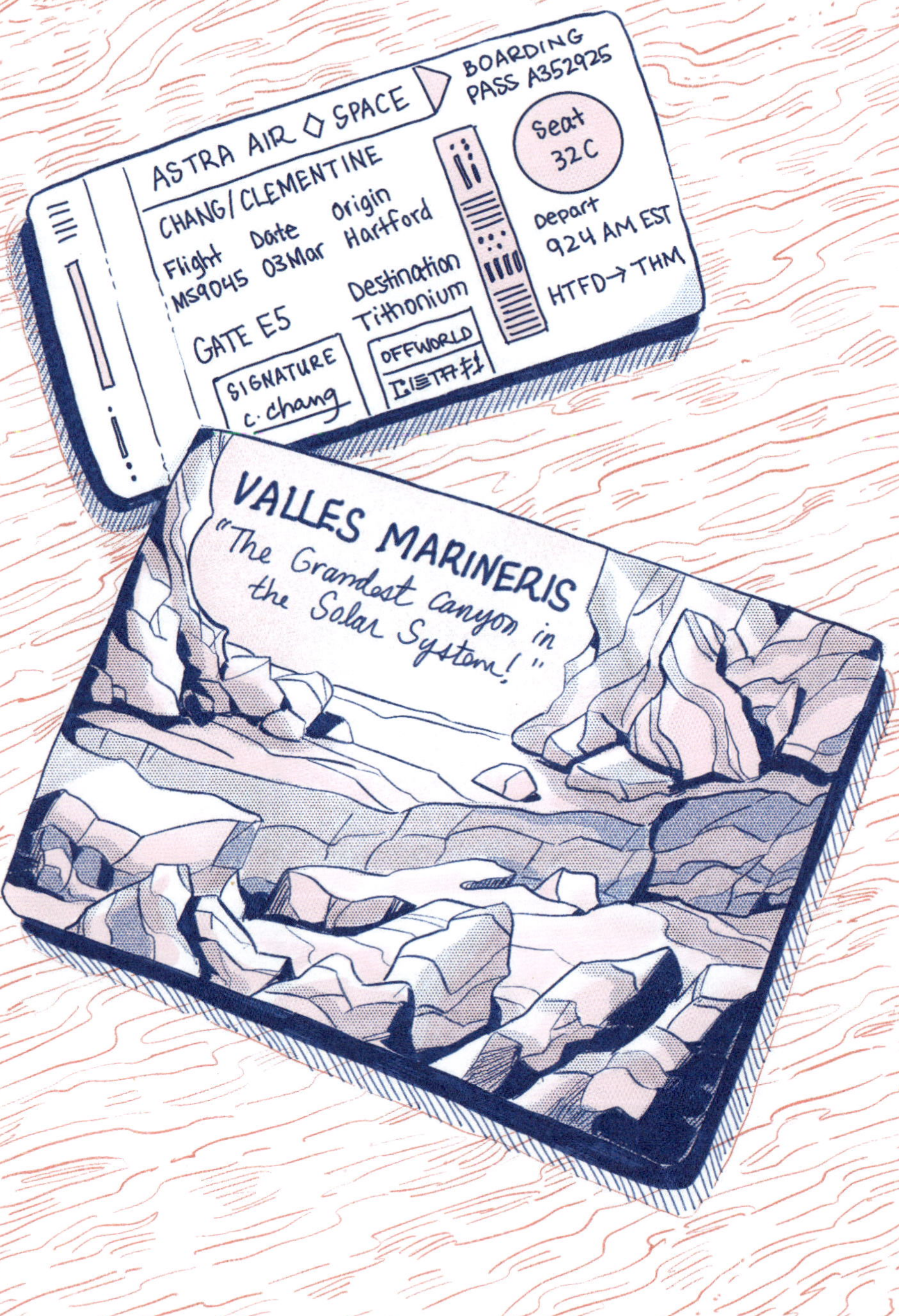
ASTRA AIR ◇ SPACE
BOARDING PASS A352925
Seat 32C
CHANG/CLEMENTINE
Flight MS9045
Date 03Mar
Origin Hartford
Depart 924 AM EST
Destination Tithonium
HTFD→THM
GATE E5
SIGNATURE C. chang
OFFWORLD
VALLES MARINERIS
"The Grandest canyon in the Solar System!"

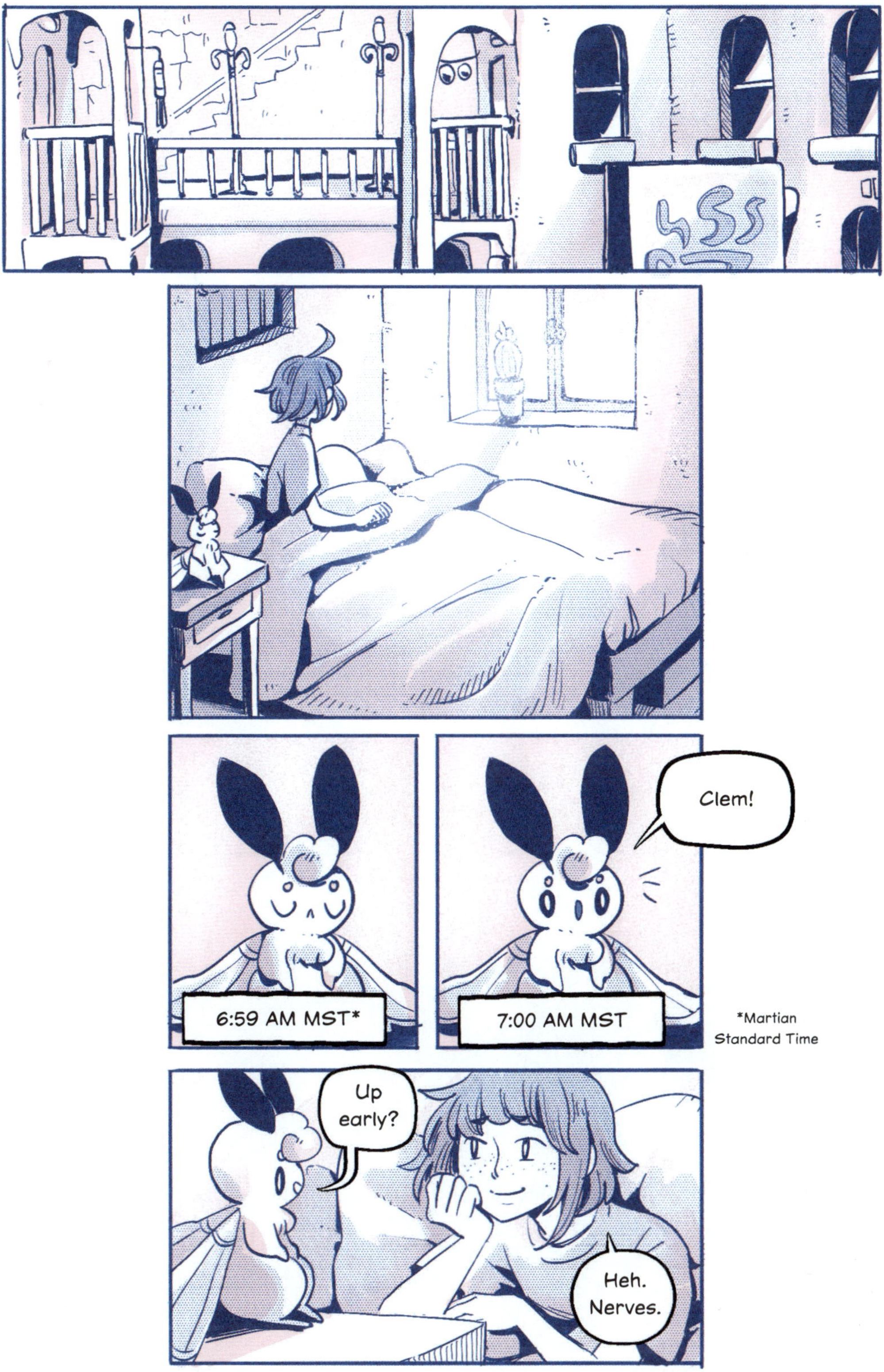
6:59 AM MST*
7:00 AM MST
Clem!
*Martian Standard Time
Up early?
Heh. Nerves.

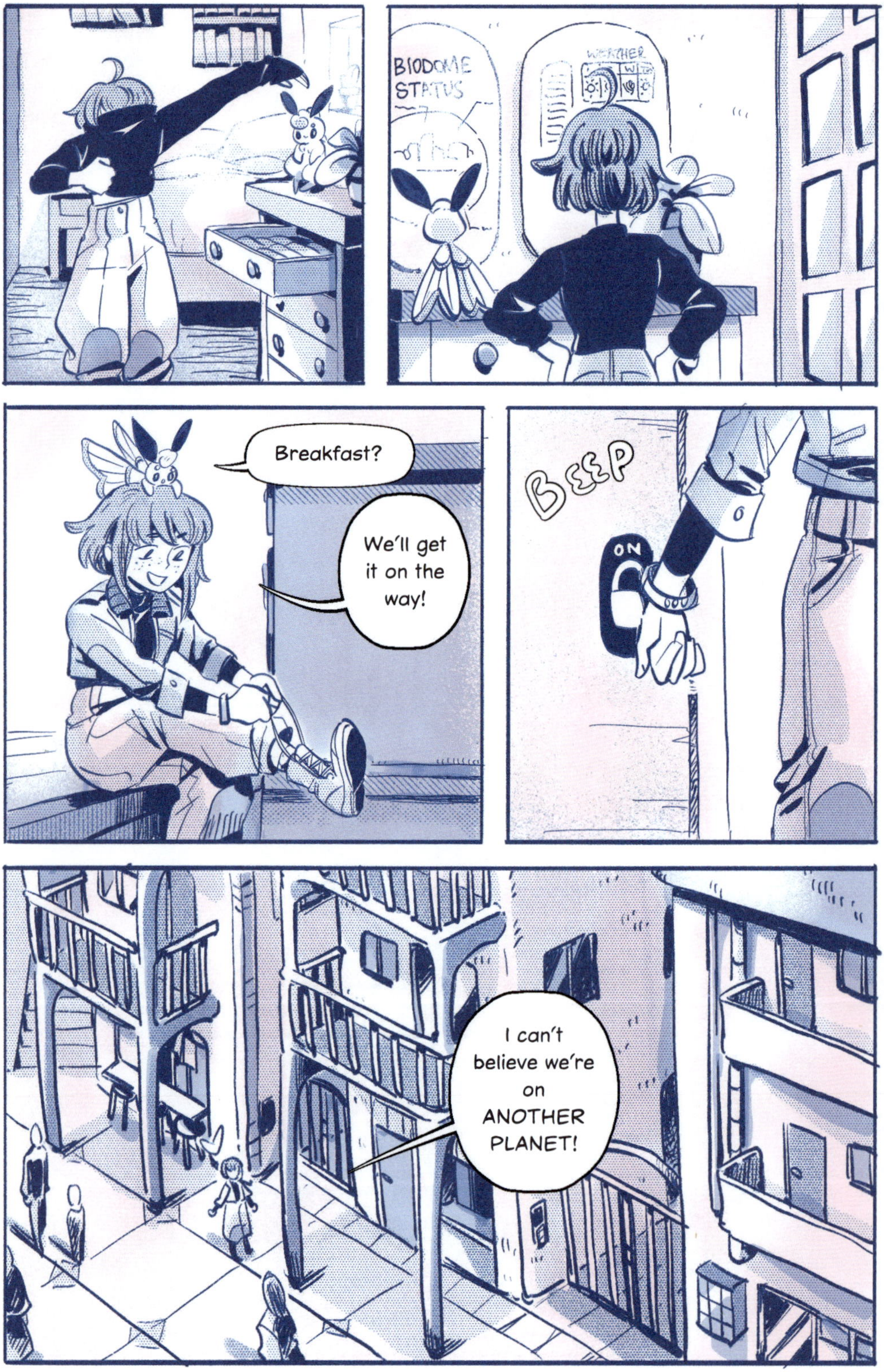
BIODOME STATUS
WEATHER
Breakfast?
We'll get it on the way!
BEEP
ON
I can't believe we're on ANOTHER PLANET!

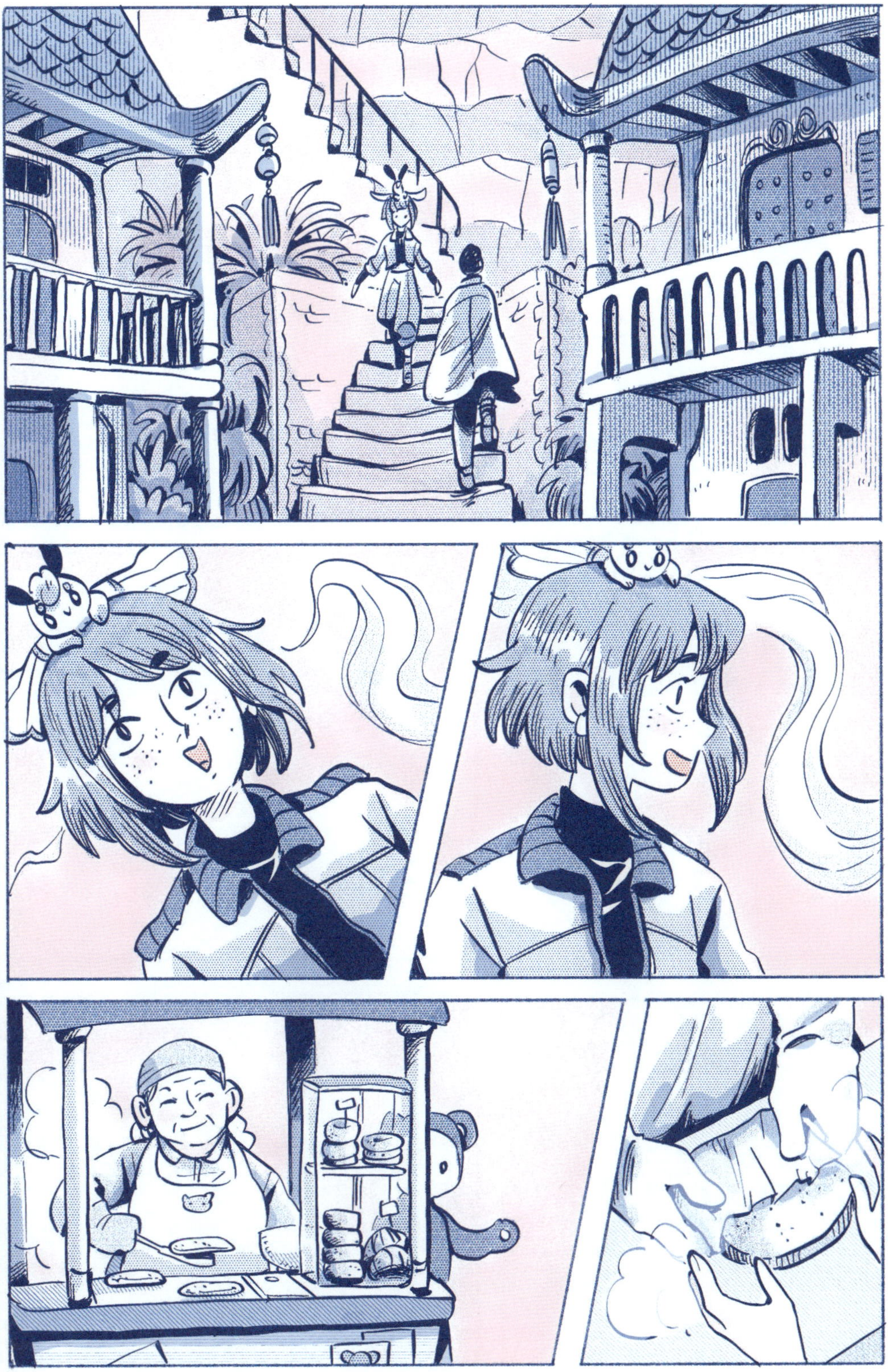

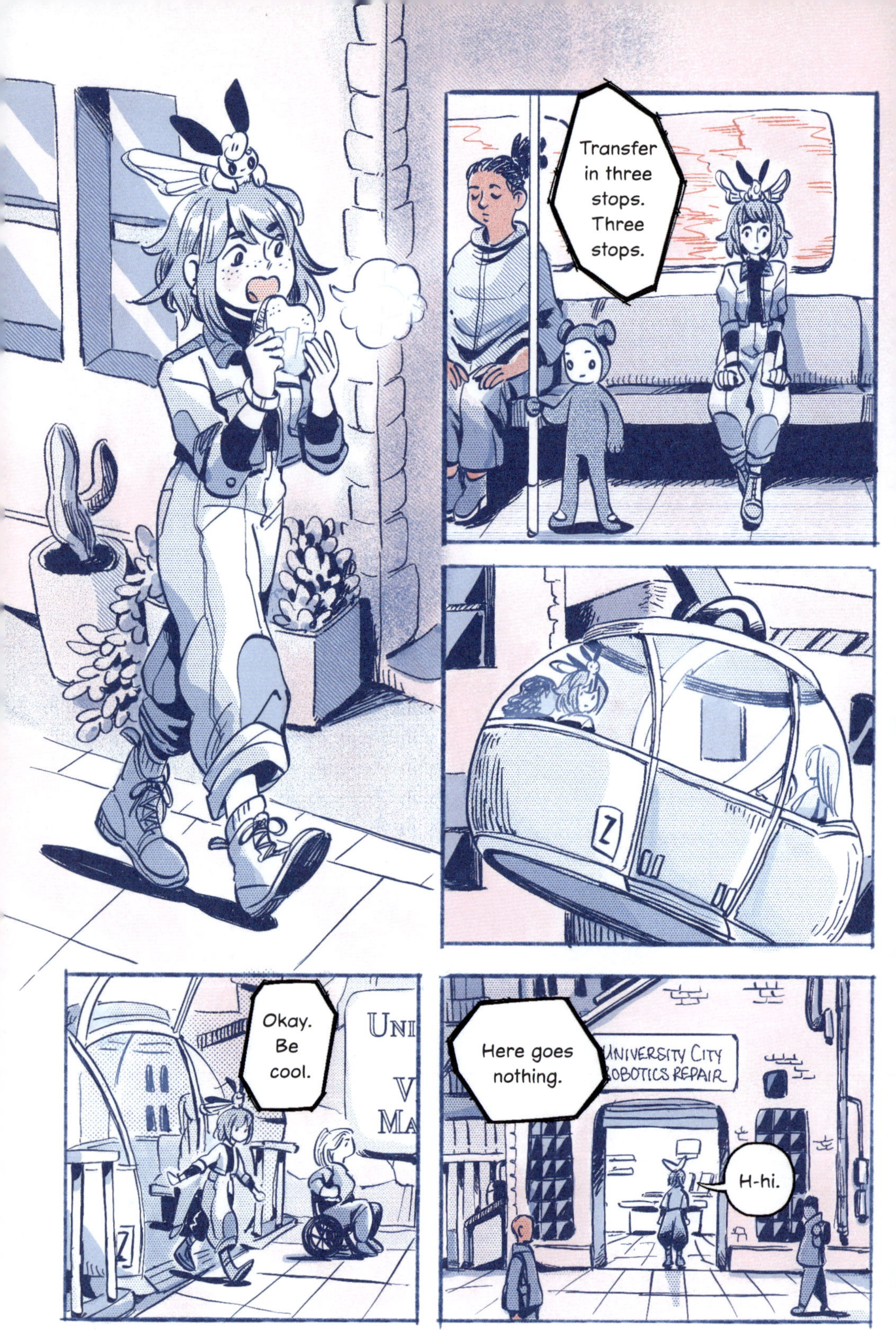
Transfer in three stops. Three stops.
Z
Okay. Be cool.
Here goes nothing.
UNIVERSITY CITY ROBOTICS REPAIR
H-hi.

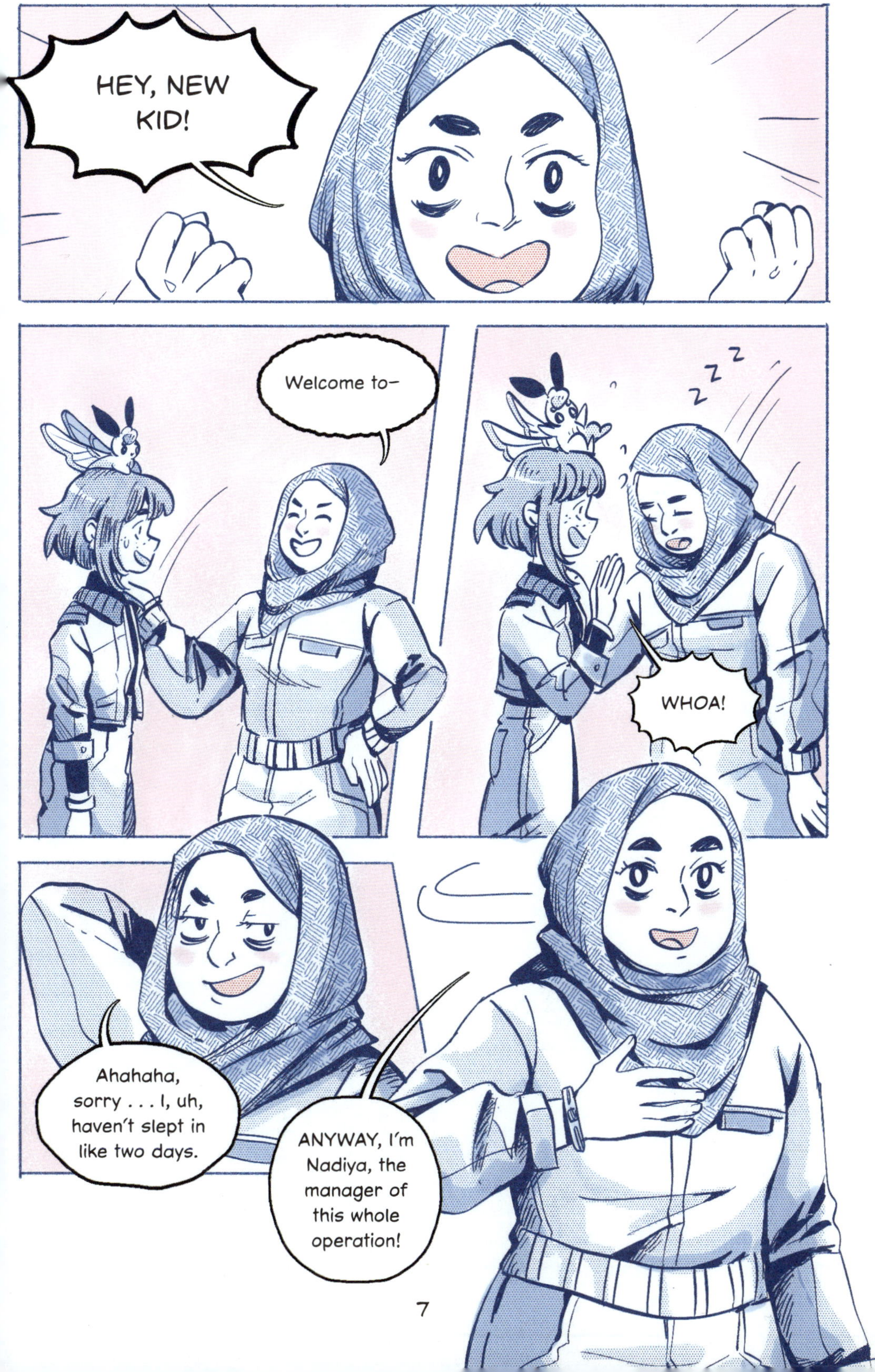
HEY, NEW KID!
Welcome to–
WHOA!
Ahahaha, sorry . . . I, uh, haven't slept in like two days.
ANYWAY, I'm Nadiya, the manager of this whole operation!

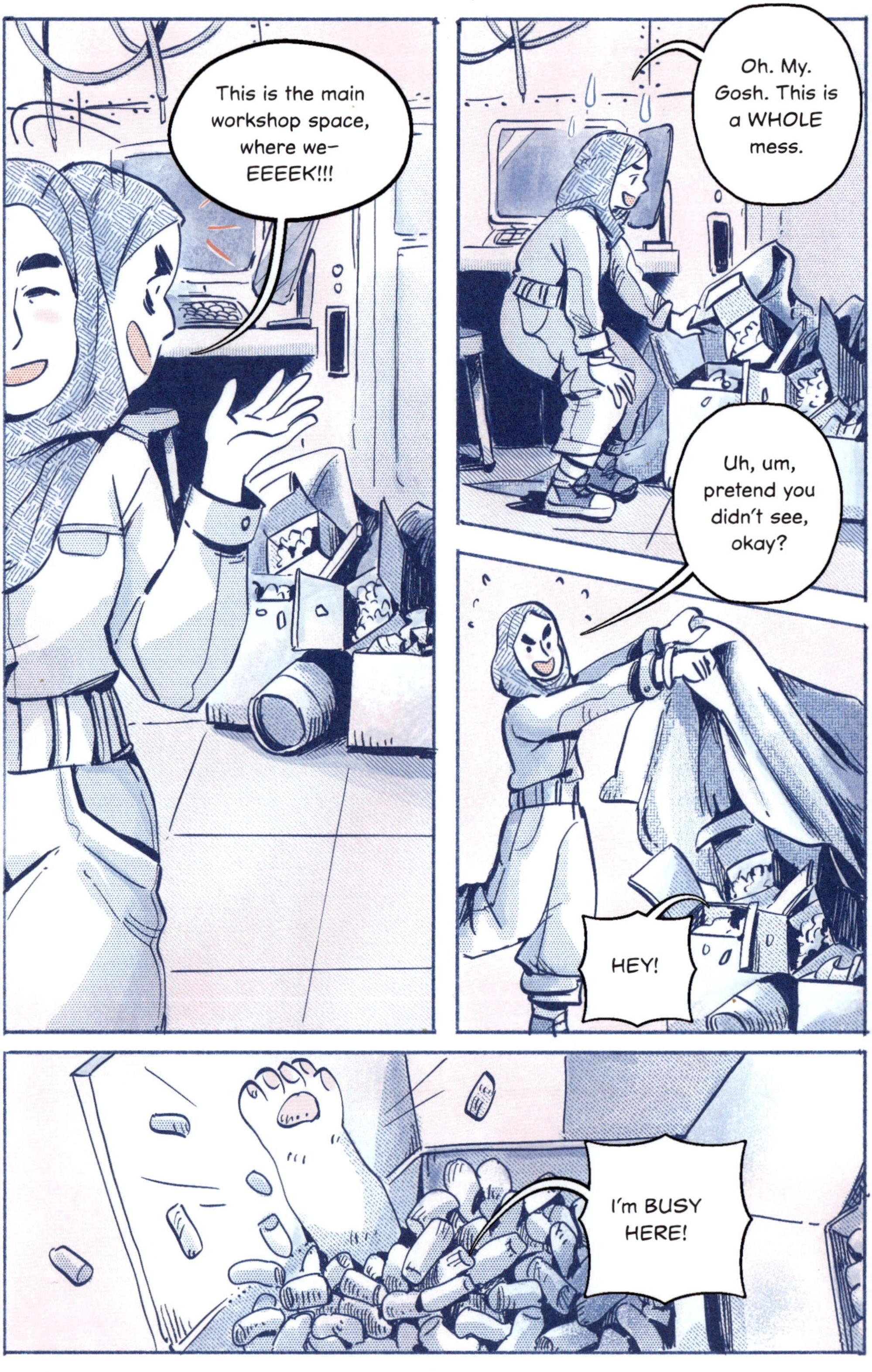
This is the main workshop space, where we— EEEEK!!!
Oh. My. Gosh. This is a WHOLE mess.
Uh, um, pretend you didn't see, okay?
HEY!
I'm BUSY HERE!

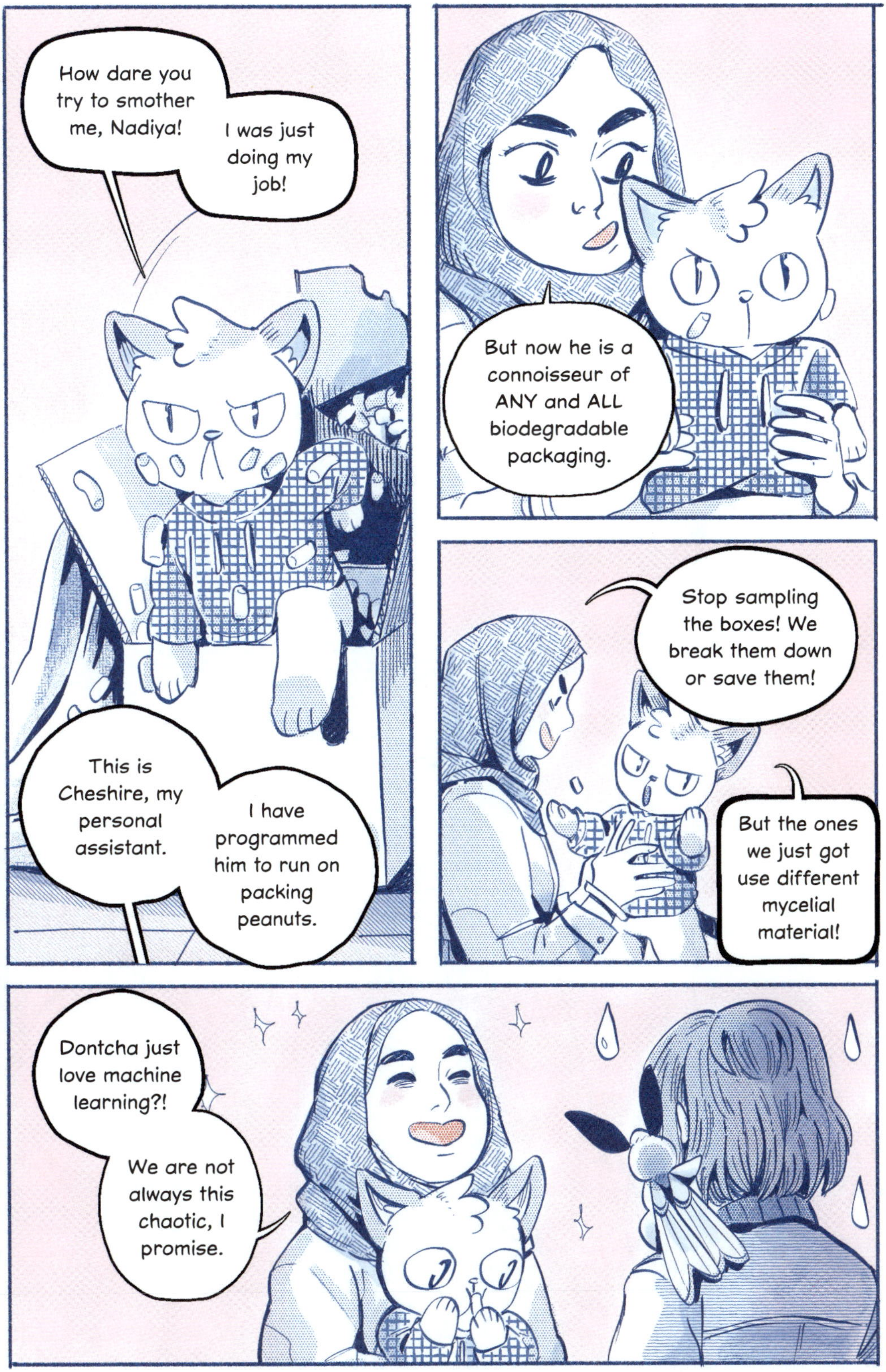
How dare you try to smother me, Nadiya!
I was just doing my job!
But now he is a connoisseur of ANY and ALL biodegradable packaging.
This is Cheshire, my personal assistant.
I have programmed him to run on packing peanuts.
Stop sampling the boxes! We break them down or save them!
But the ones we just got use different mycelial material!
Dontcha just love machine learning?!
We are not always this chaotic, I promise.

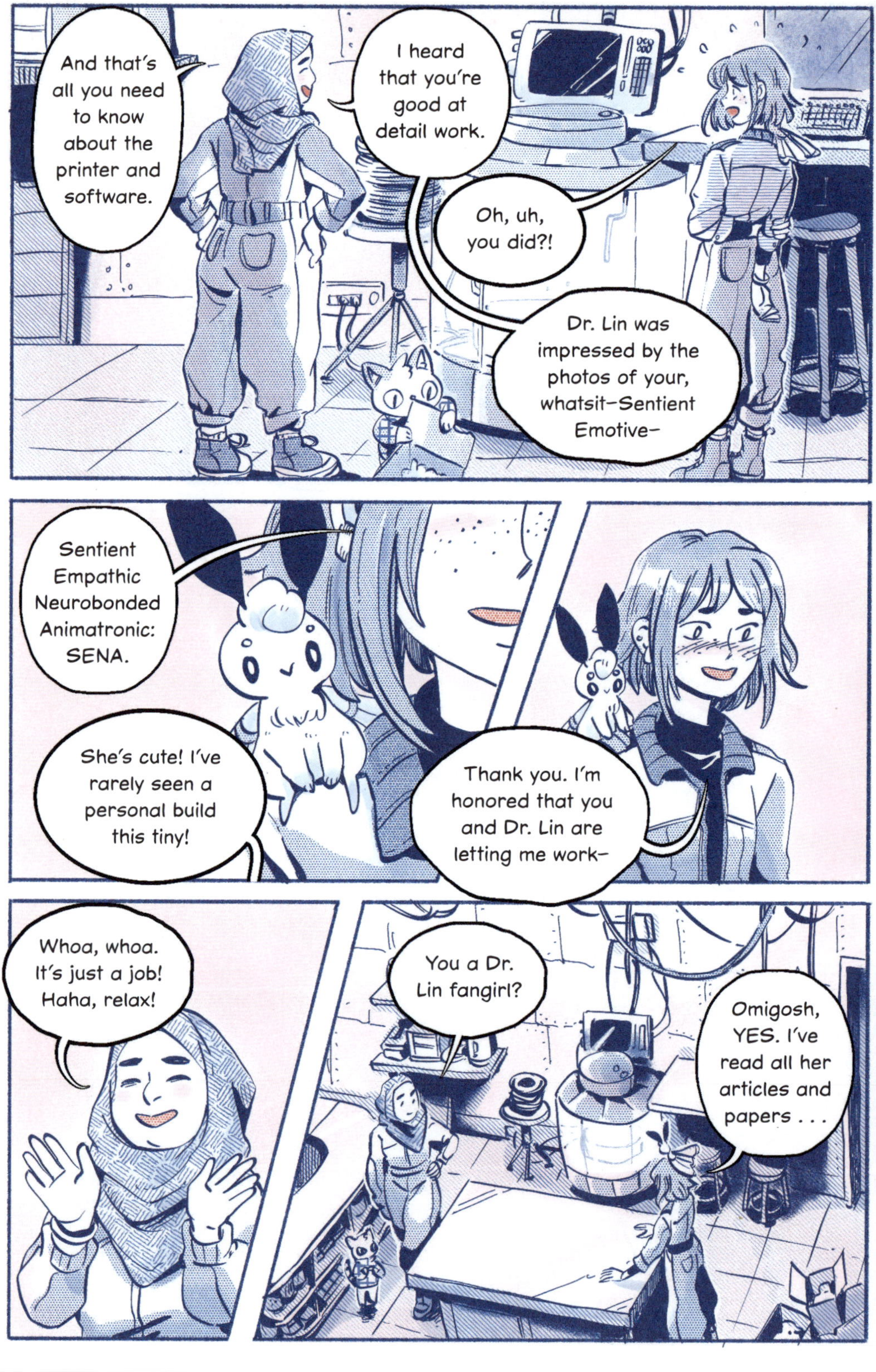
And that's all you need to know about the printer and software.
I heard that you're good at detail work.
Oh, uh, you did?!
Dr. Lin was impressed by the photos of your, whatsit–Sentient Emotive–
Sentient Empathic Neurobonded Animatronic: SENA.
She's cute! I've rarely seen a personal build this tiny!
Thank you. I'm honored that you and Dr. Lin are letting me work–
Whoa, whoa. It's just a job! Haha, relax!
You a Dr. Lin fangirl?
Omigosh, YES. I've read all her articles and papers . . .

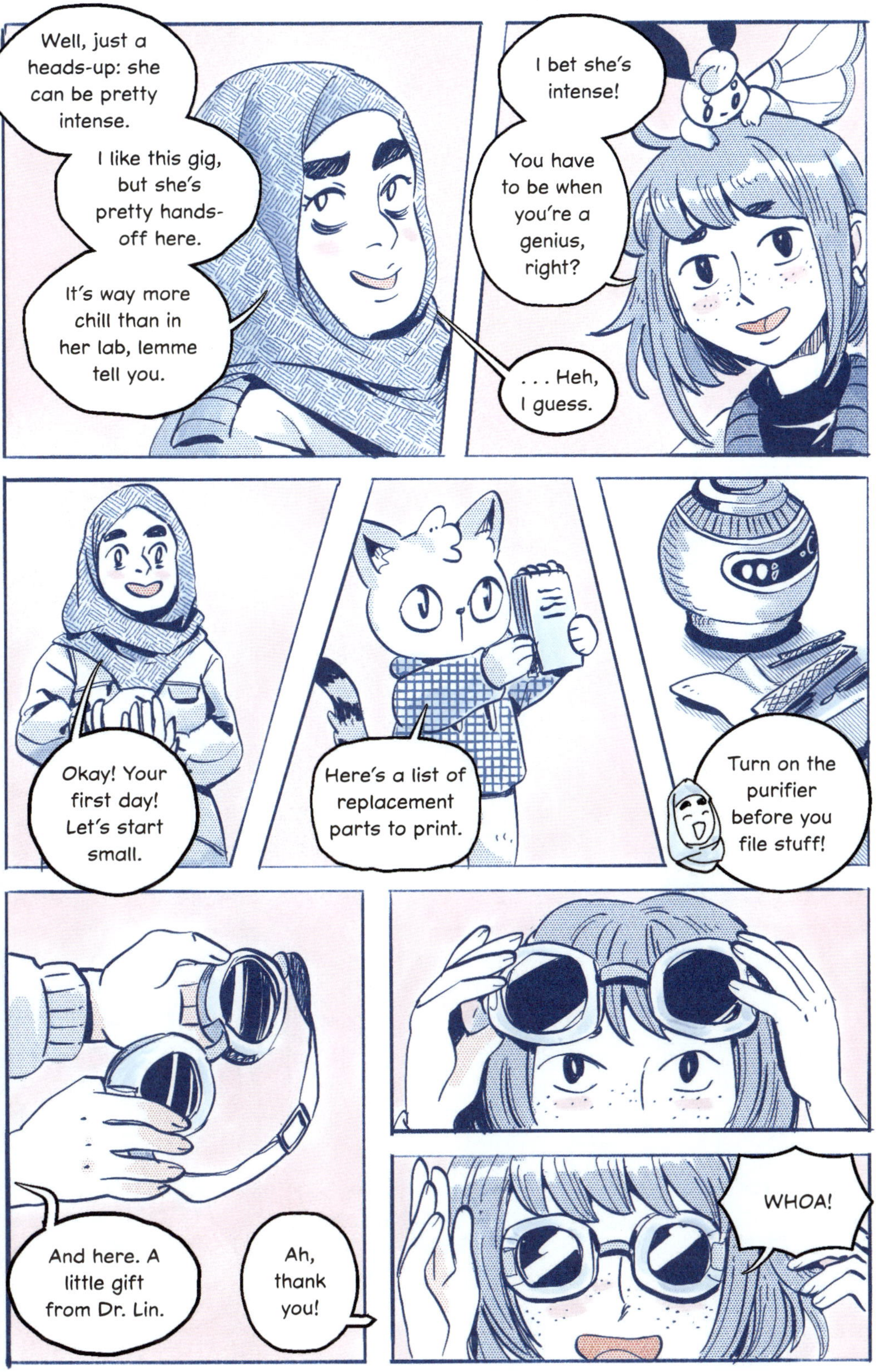
Well, just a heads-up: she can be pretty intense.
I like this gig, but she's pretty hands-off here.
It's way more chill than in her lab, lemme tell you.
I bet she's intense!
You have to be when you're a genius, right?
. . . Heh, I guess.
Okay! Your first day! Let's start small.
Here's a list of replacement parts to print.
Turn on the purifier before you file stuff!
And here. A little gift from Dr. Lin.
Ah, thank you!
WHOA!

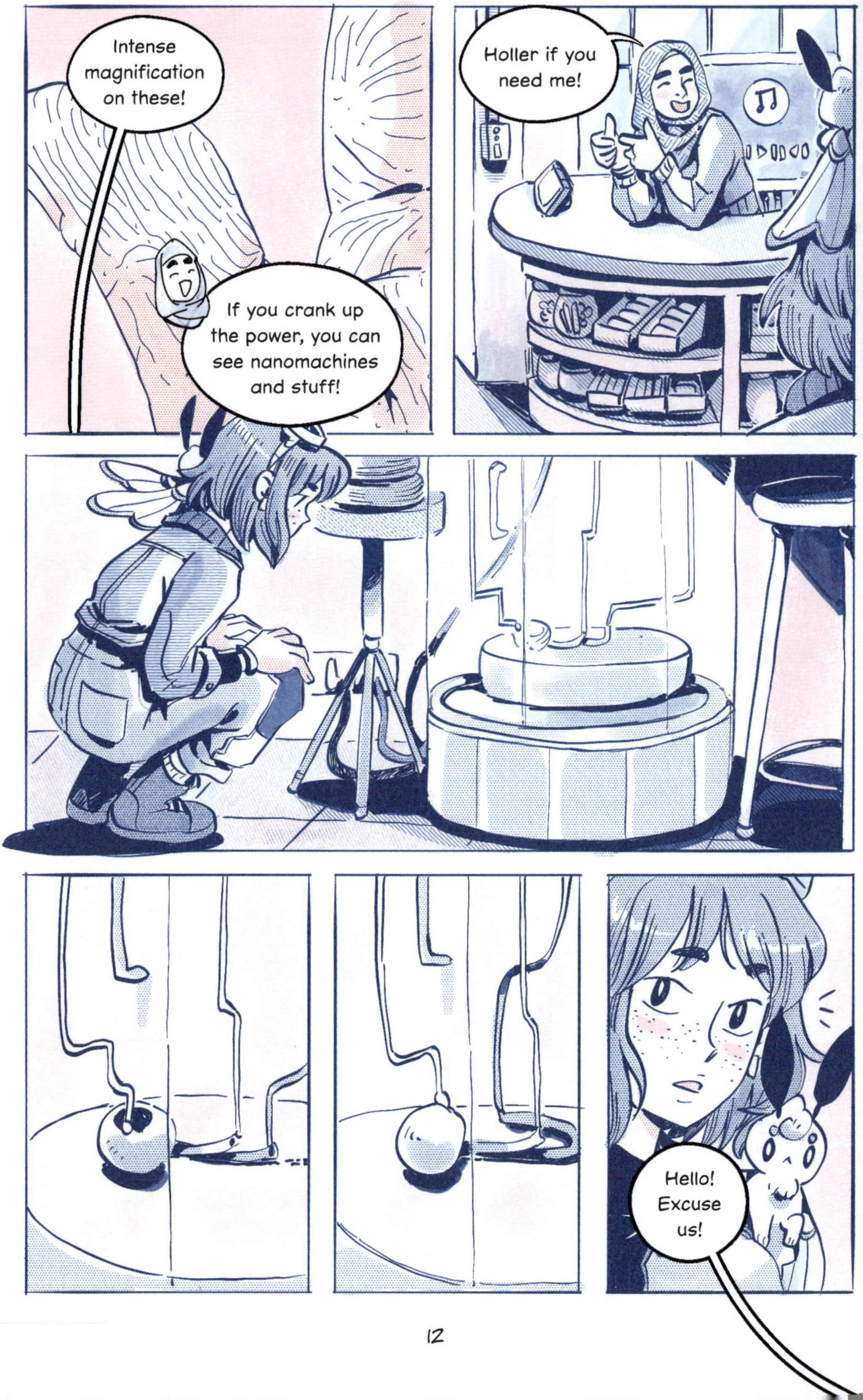
Intense magnification on these!
If you crank up the power, you can see nanomachines and stuff!
Holler if you need me!
Hello! Excuse us!

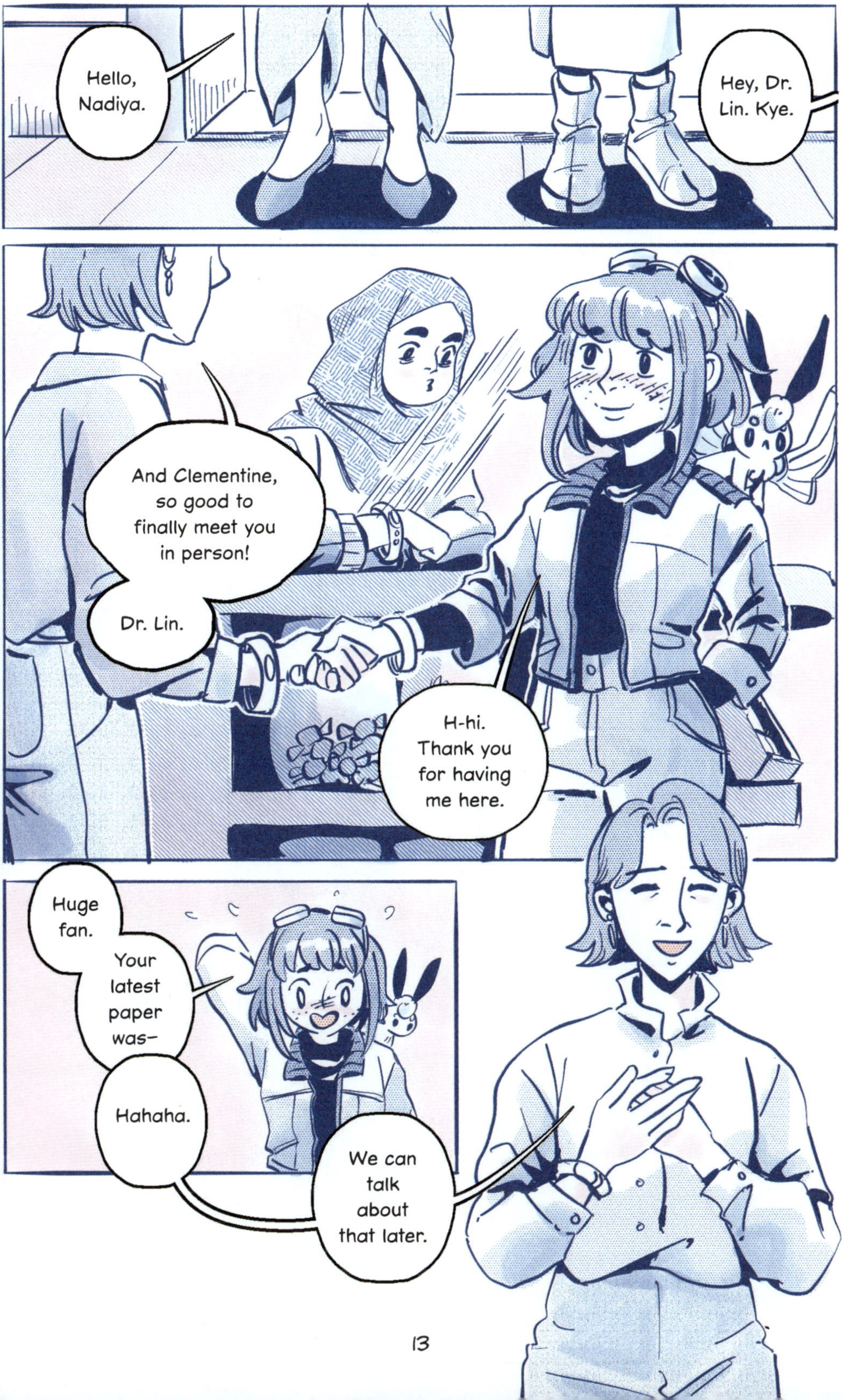
Hello, Nadiya.
Hey, Dr. Lin. Kye.
And Clementine, so good to finally meet you in person!
Dr. Lin.
H-hi. Thank you for having me here.
Huge fan.
Your latest paper was-
Hahaha.
We can talk about that later.

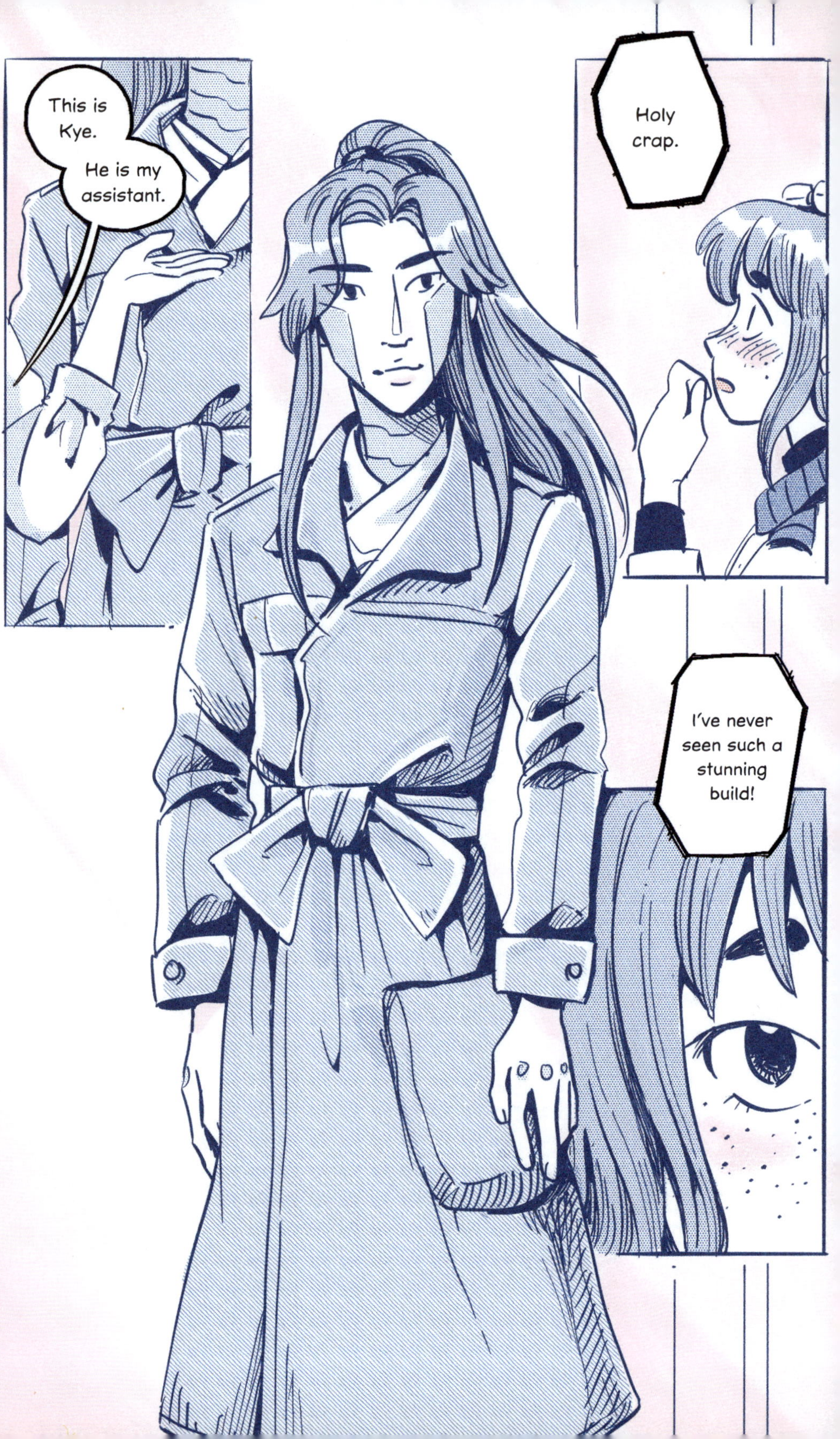
This is Kye.
He is my assistant.
Holy crap.
I've never seen such a stunning build!

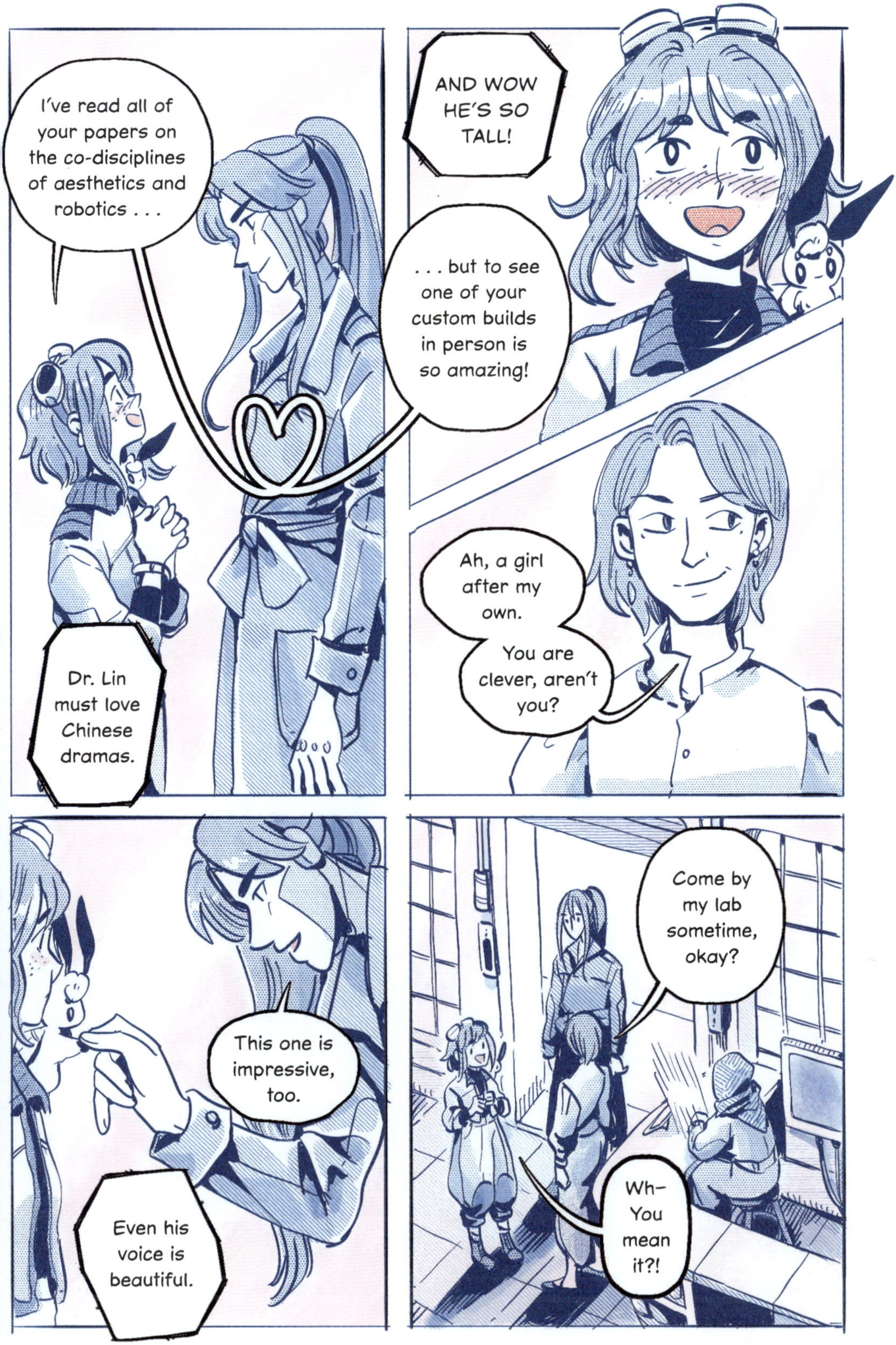

I've read all of your papers on the co-disciplines of aesthetics and robotics . . .
AND WOW HE'S SO TALL!
. . . but to see one of your custom builds in person is so amazing!
Dr. Lin must love Chinese dramas.
Ah, a girl after my own.
You are clever, aren't you?
This one is impressive, too.
Even his voice is beautiful.
Come by my lab sometime, okay?
Wh– You mean it?!

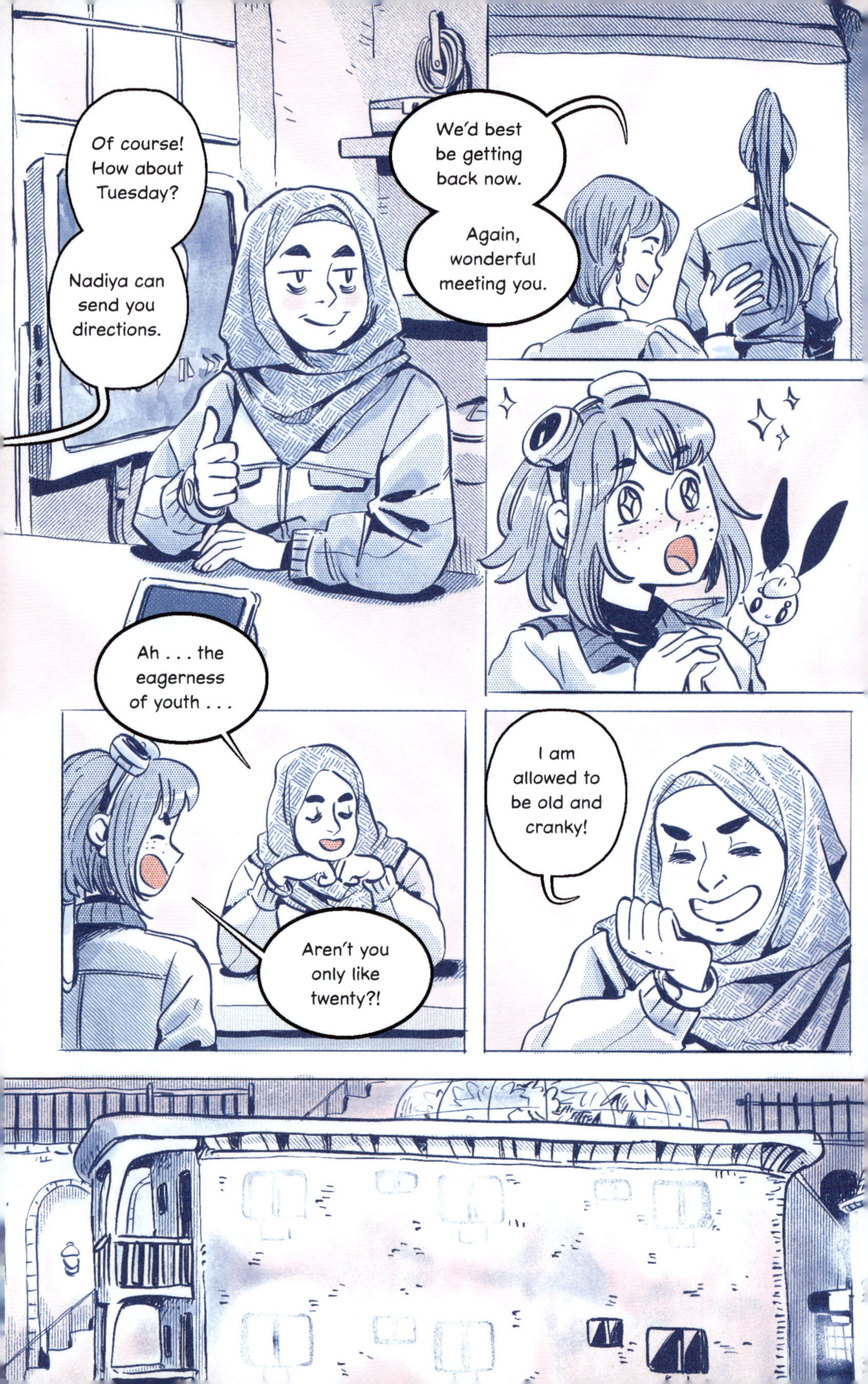
Of course! How about Tuesday?
Nadiya can send you directions.
We'd best be getting back now.
Again, wonderful meeting you.
Ah . . . the eagerness of youth . . .
Aren't you only like twenty?!
I am allowed to be old and cranky!

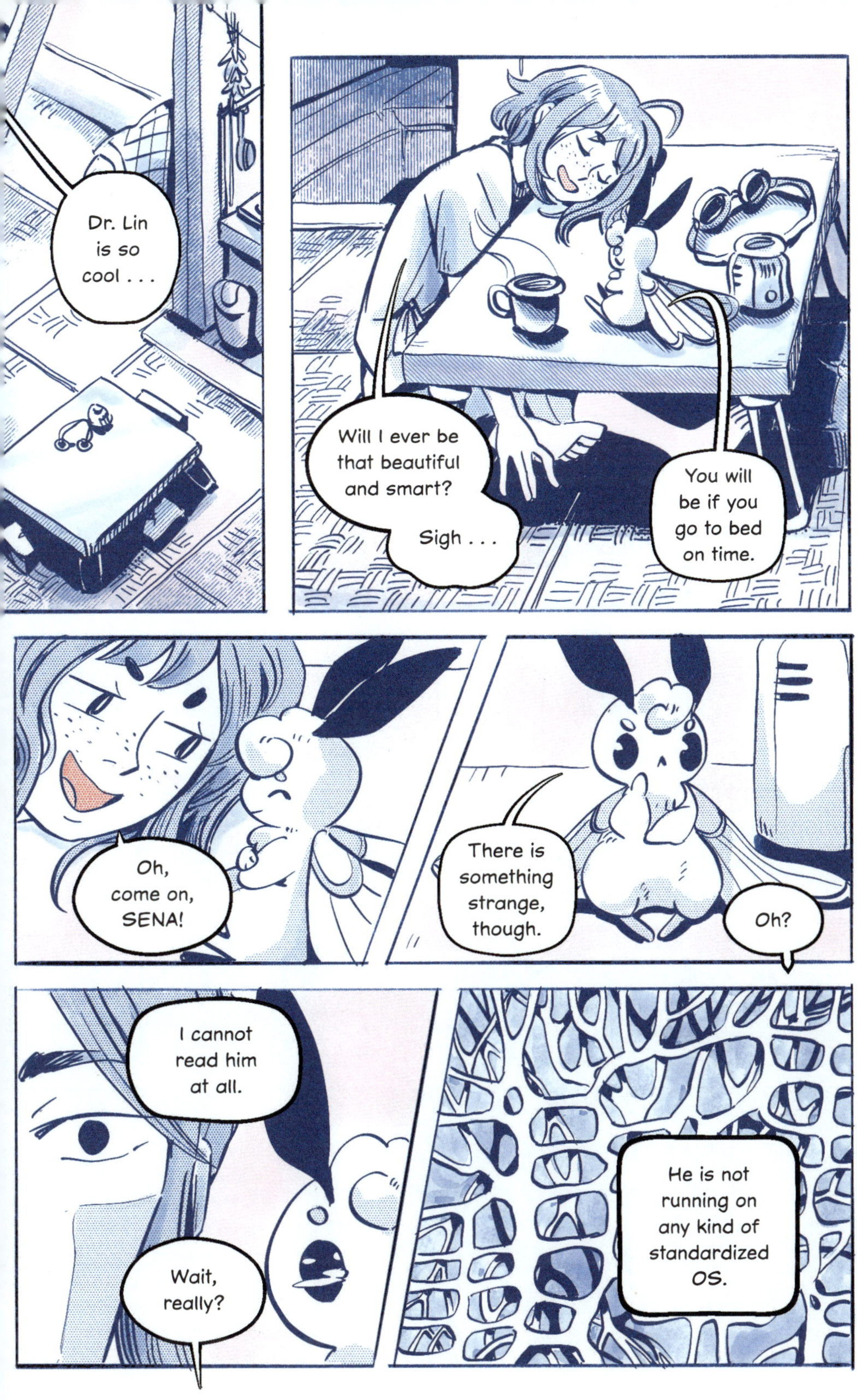

Dr. Lin is so cool . . .
Will I ever be that beautiful and smart?
Sigh . . .
You will be if you go to bed on time.
Oh, come on, SENA!
There is something strange, though.
Oh?
I cannot read him at all.
He is not running on any kind of standardized OS.
Wait, really?

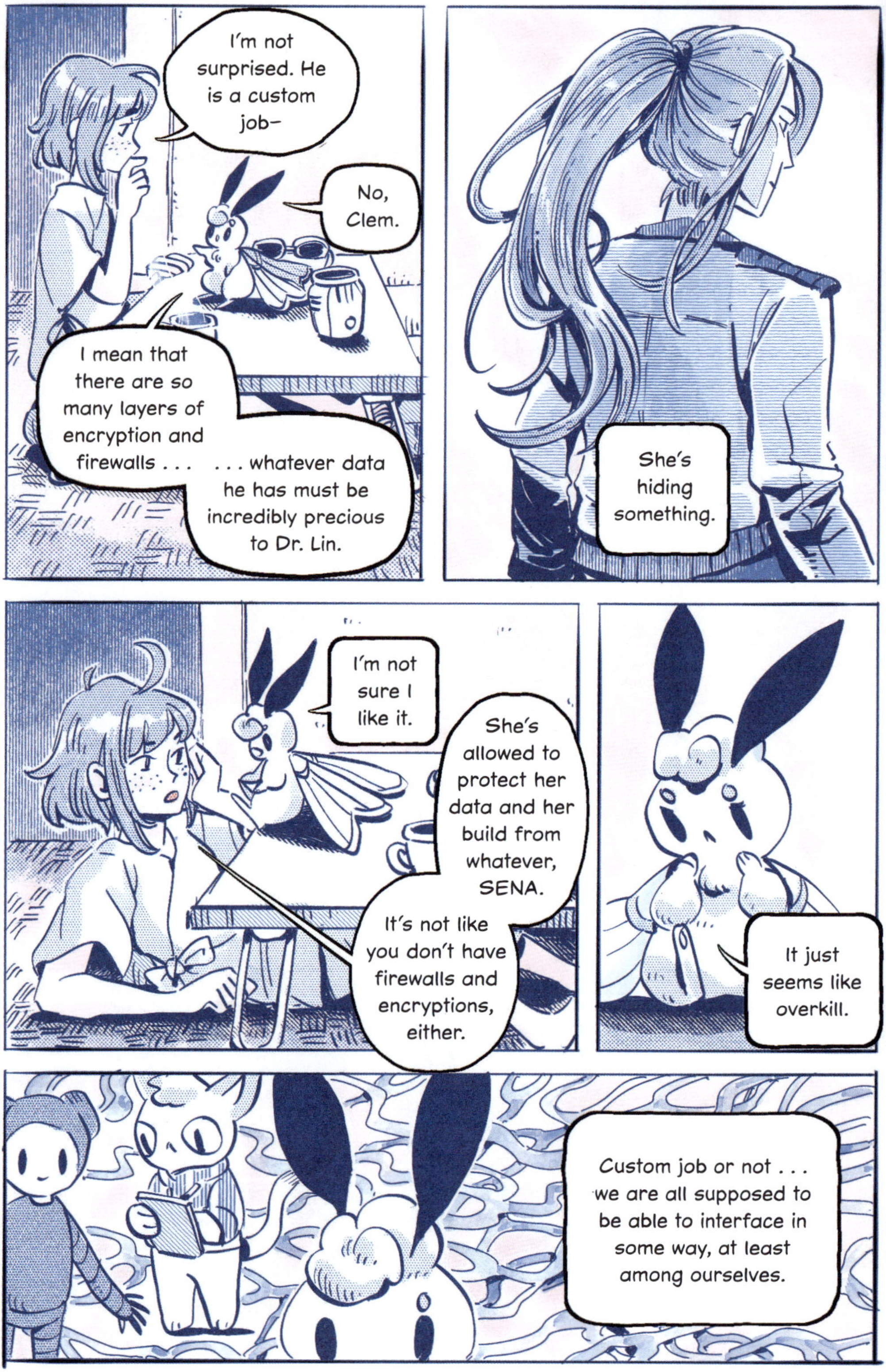

I'm not surprised. He is a custom job–
No, Clem.
I mean that there are so many layers of encryption and firewalls . . .
. . . whatever data he has must be incredibly precious to Dr. Lin.
She's hiding something.
I'm not sure I like it.
She's allowed to protect her data and her build from whatever, SENA.
It's not like you don't have firewalls and encryptions, either.
It just seems like overkill.
Custom job or not . . . we are all supposed to be able to interface in some way, at least among ourselves.

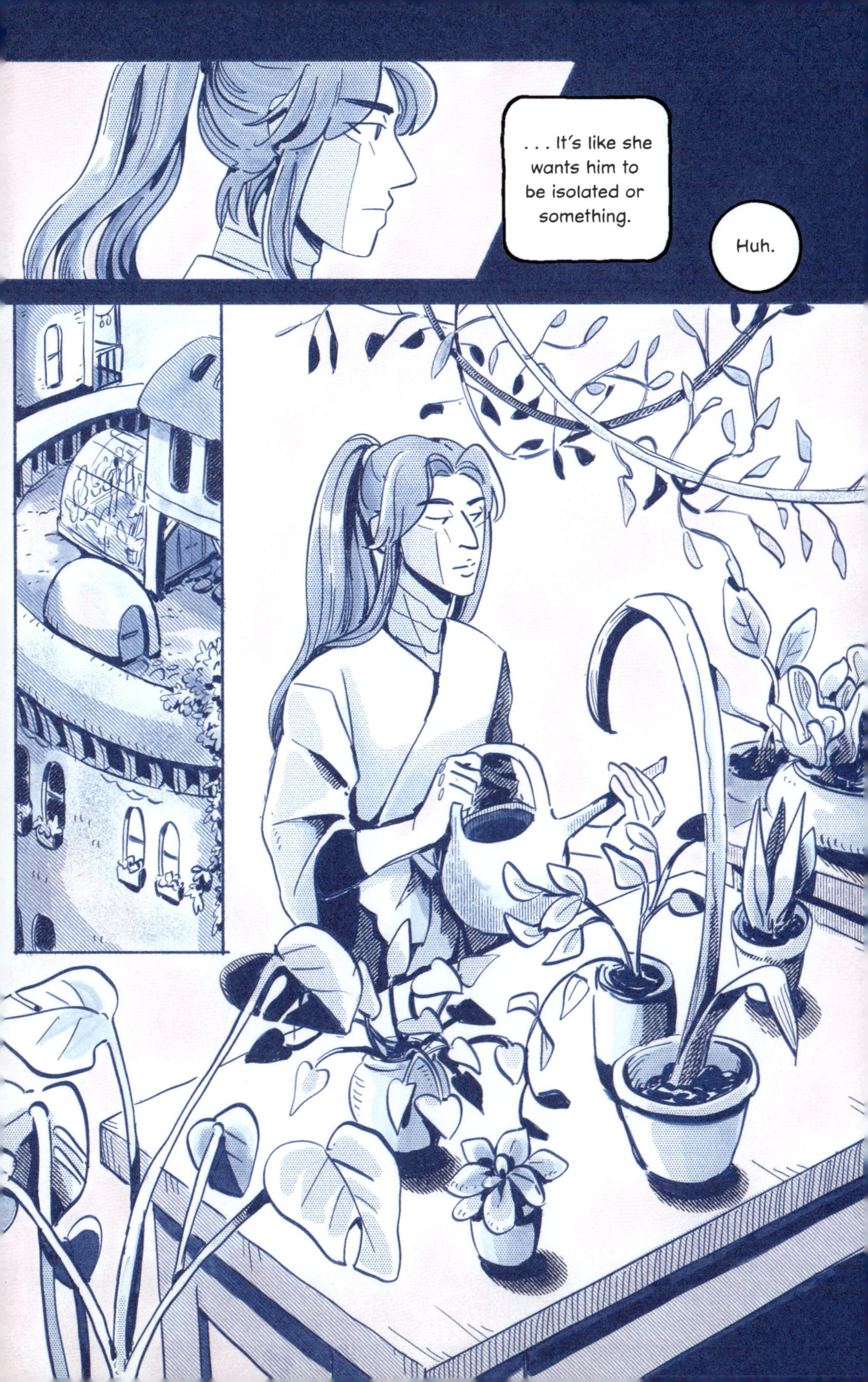
. . . It's like she wants him to be isolated or something.
Huh.

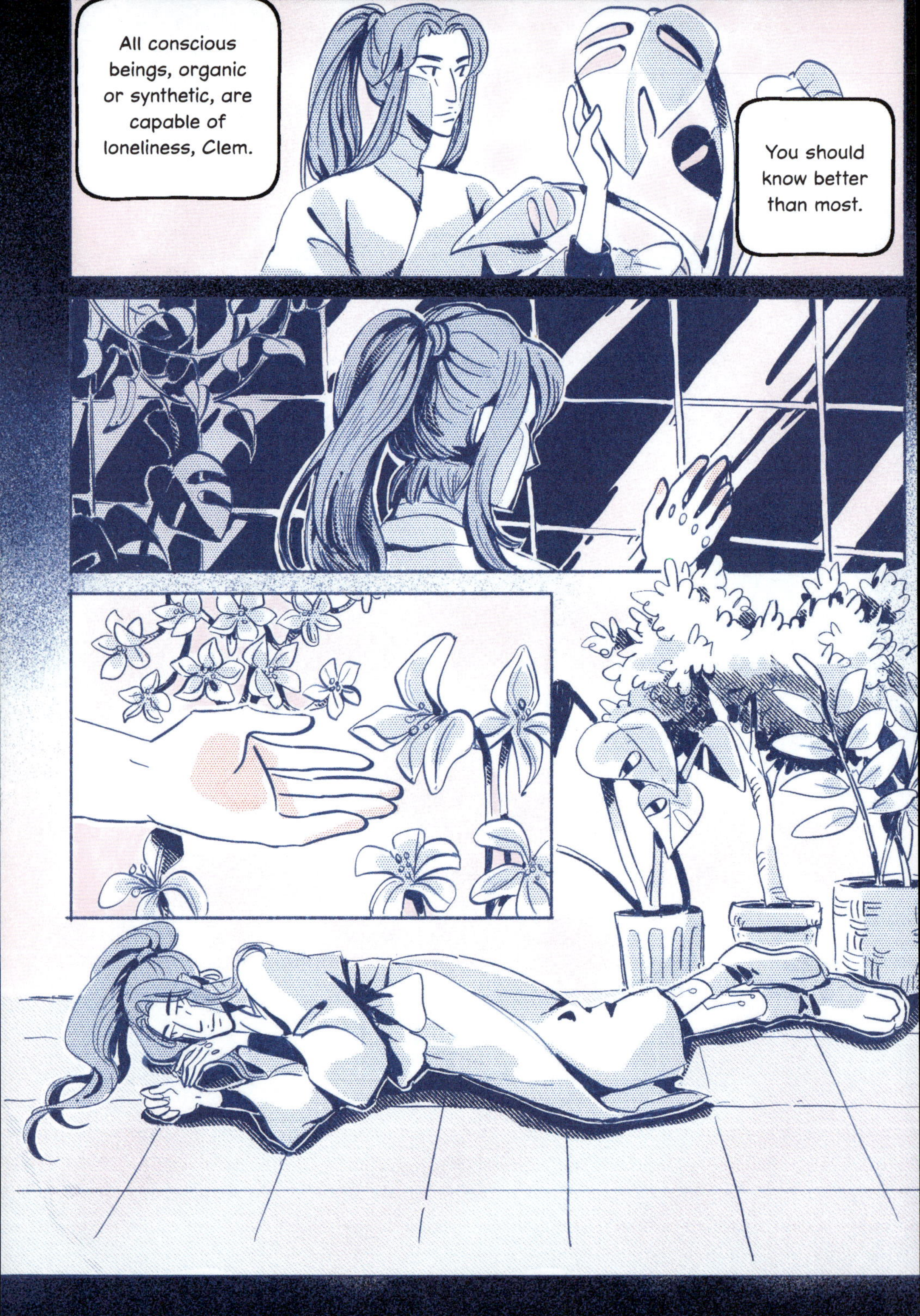
All conscious beings, organic or synthetic, are capable of loneliness, Clem.
You should know better than most.

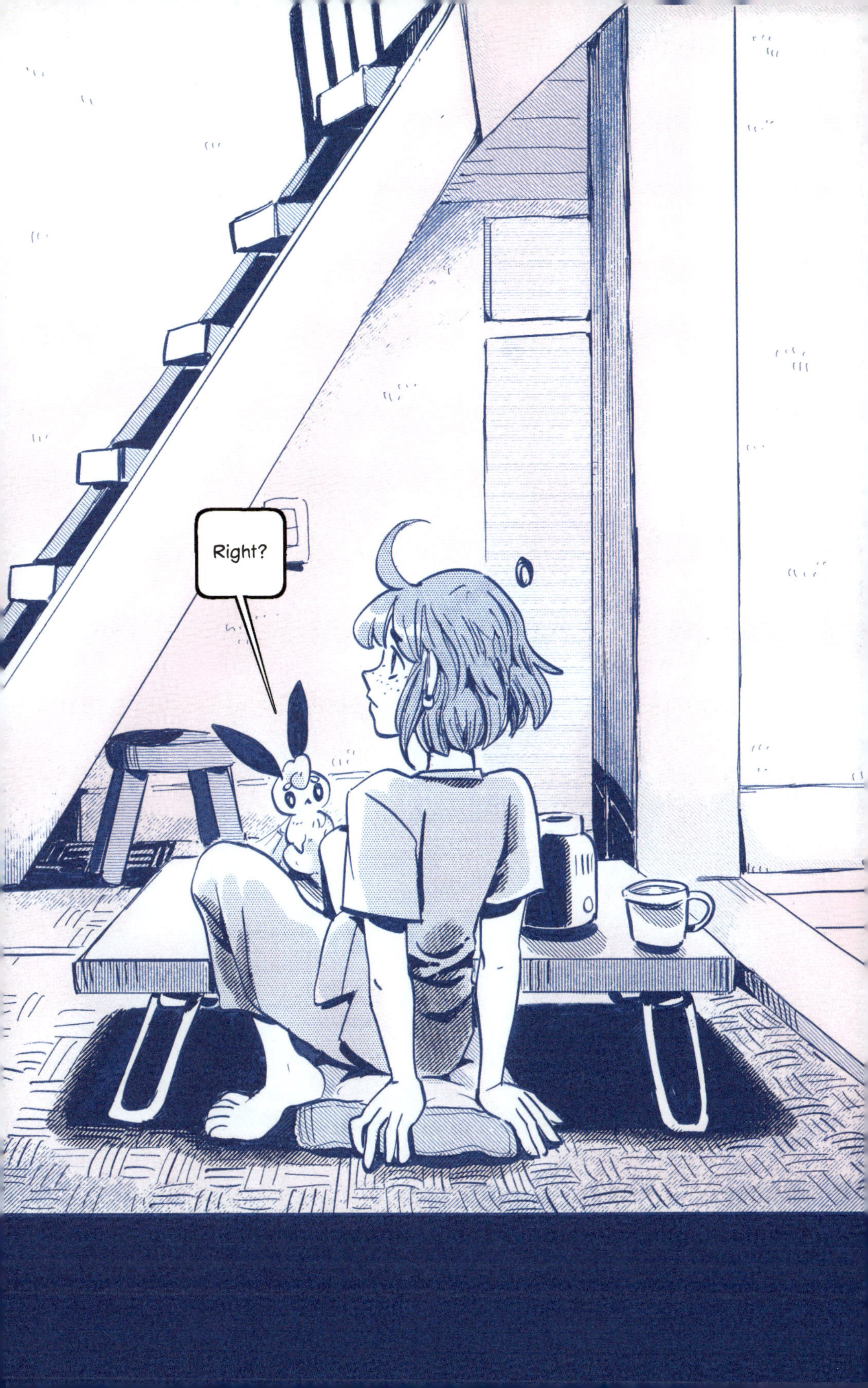
Right?

00110000 00110010

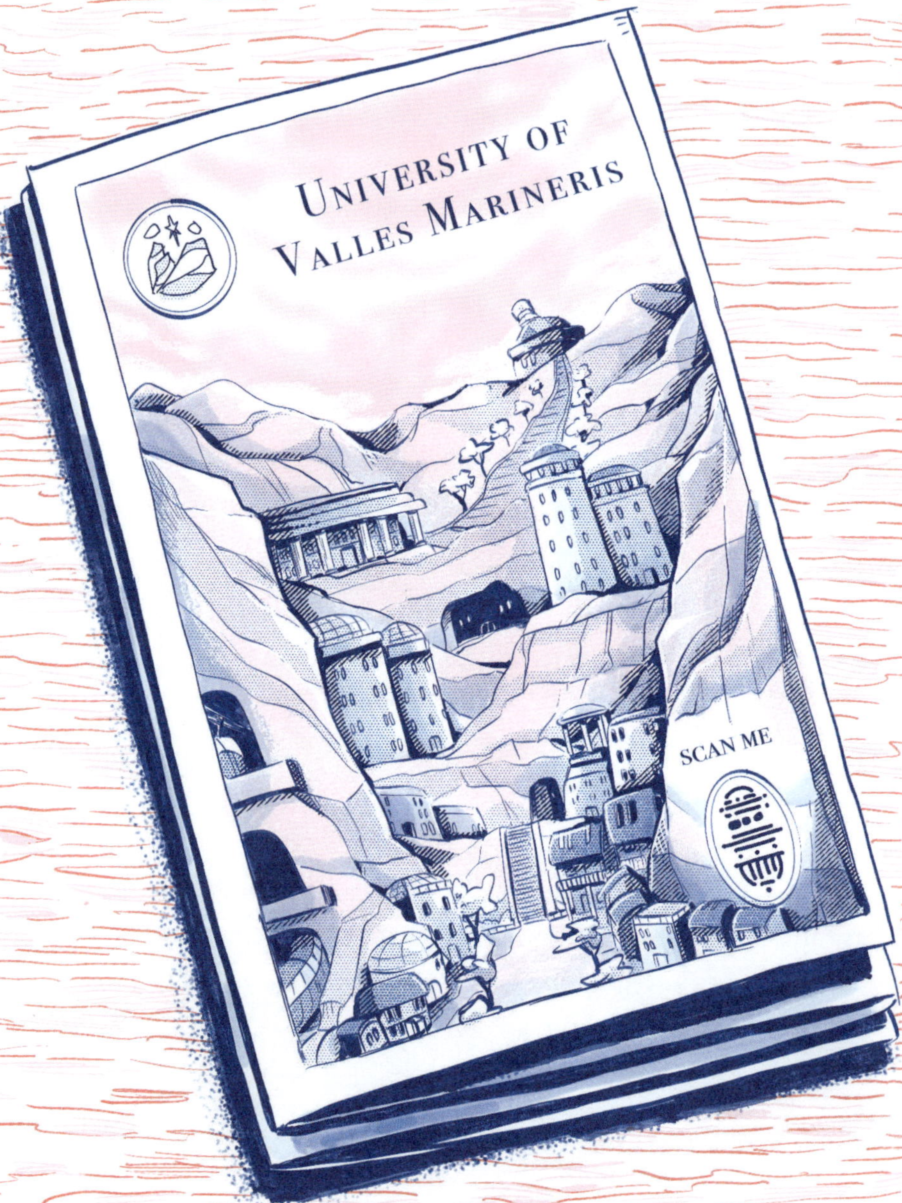
University of
Valles Marineris
SCAN ME

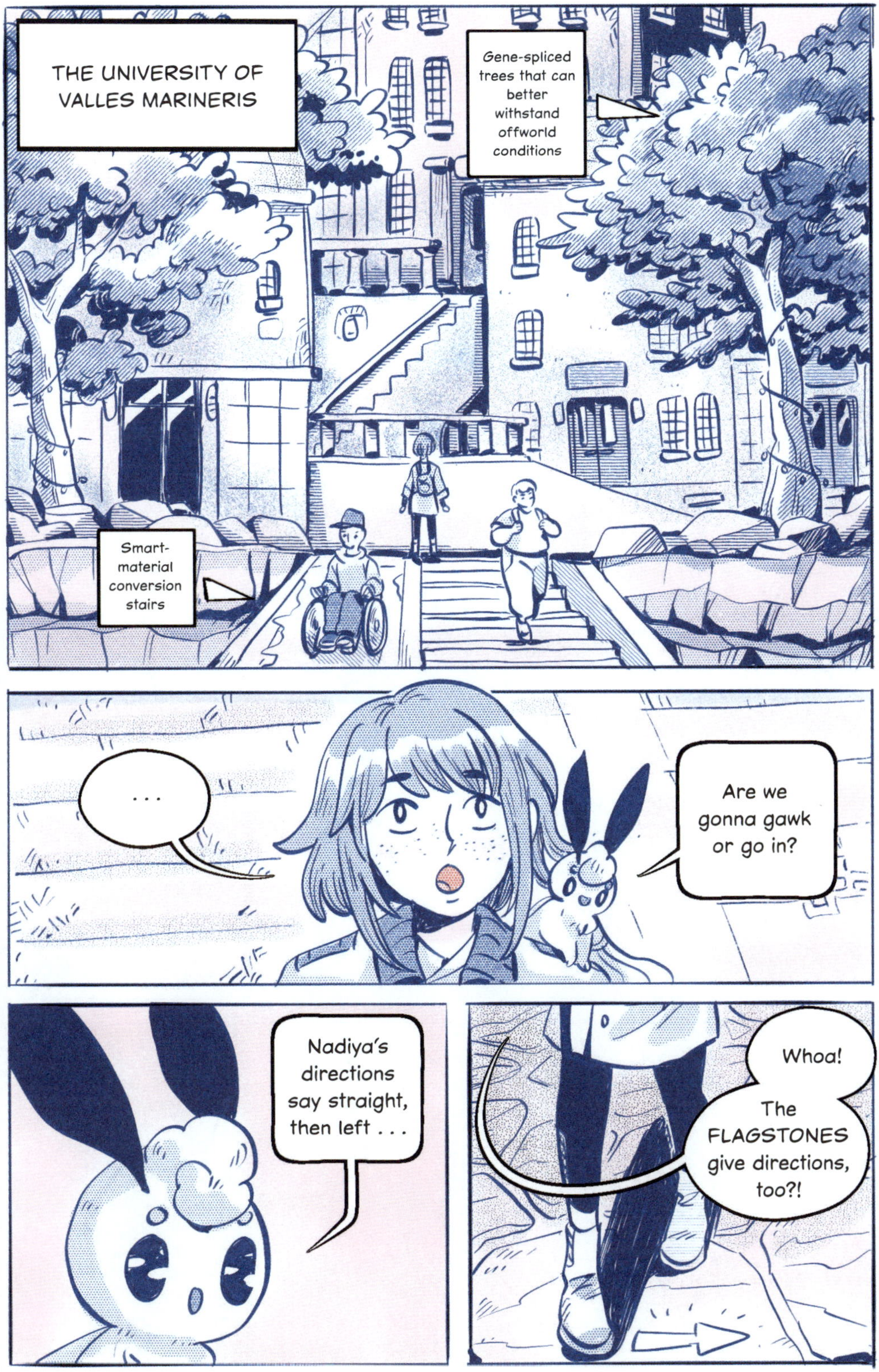
THE UNIVERSITY OF VALLES MARINERIS
Gene-spliced trees that can better withstand offworld conditions
Smart-material conversion stairs
. . .
Are we gonna gawk or go in?
Nadiya's directions say straight, then left . . .
Whoa!
The FLAGSTONES give directions, too?!

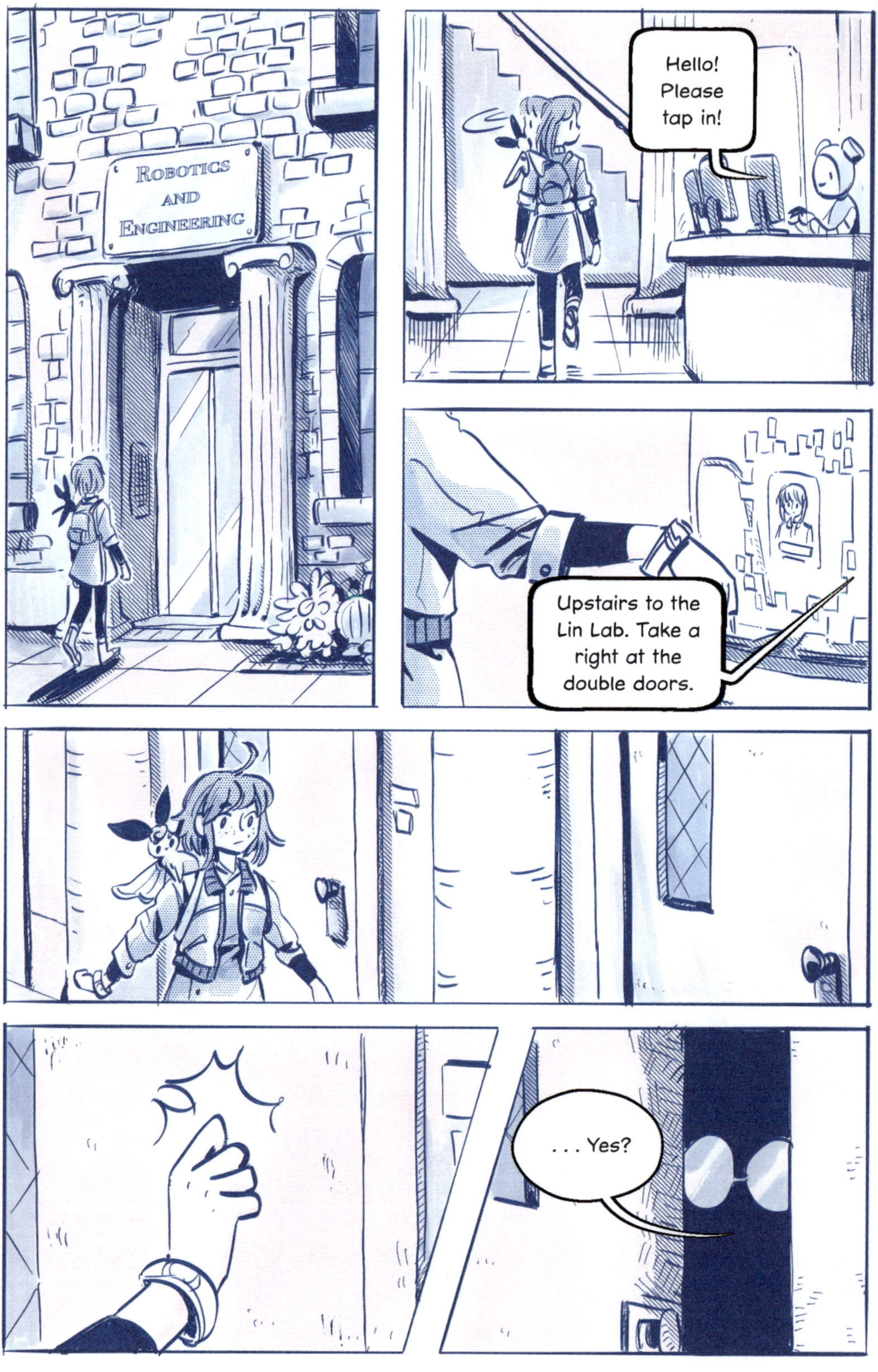
ROBOTICS AND ENGINEERING
Hello! Please tap in!
Upstairs to the Lin Lab. Take a right at the double doors.
. . . Yes?

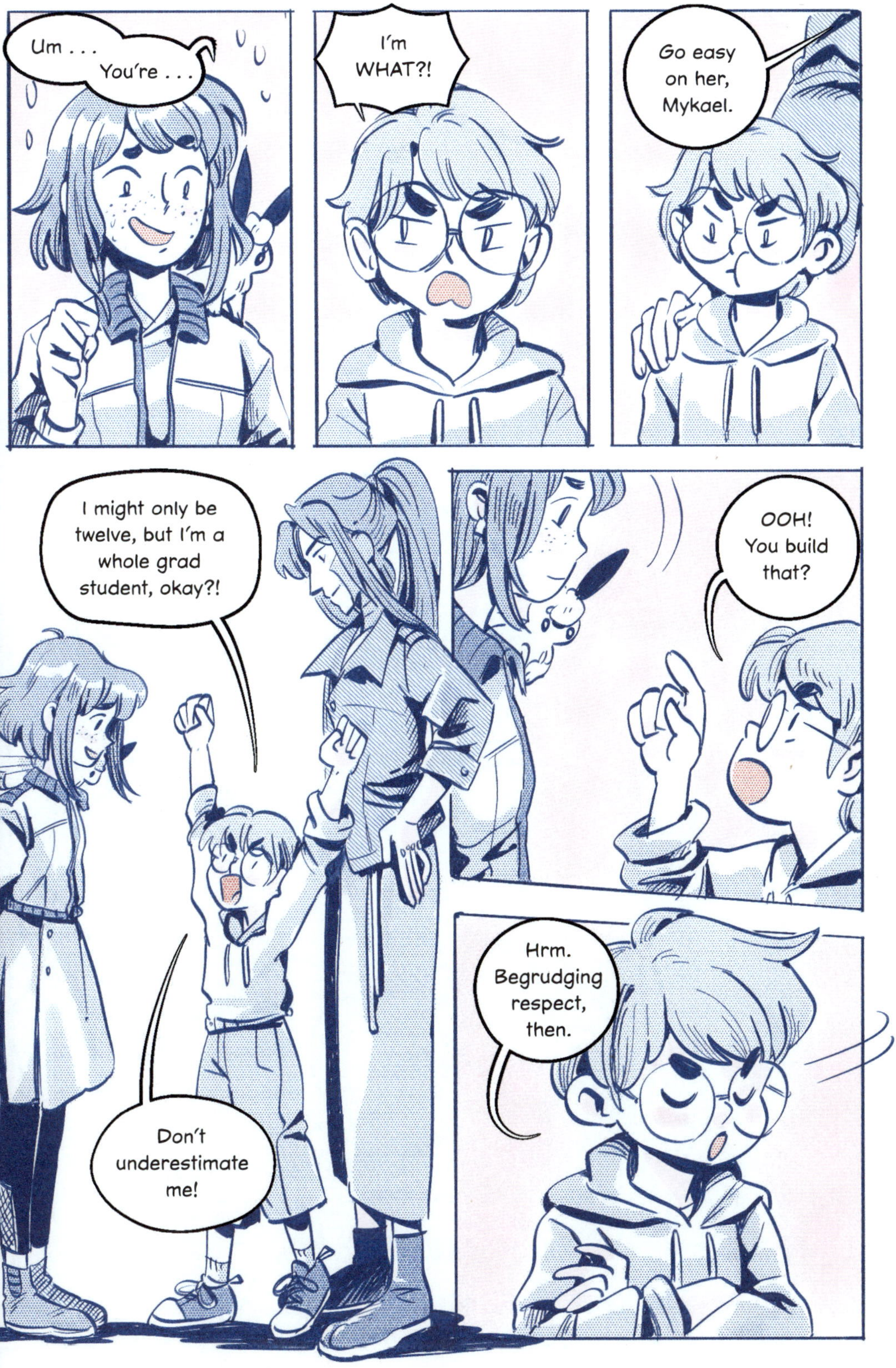
Um . . .
You're . . .
I'm WHAT?!
Go easy on her, Mykael.
I might only be twelve, but I'm a whole grad student, okay?!
Don't underestimate me!
OOH! You build that?
Hrm. Begrudging respect, then.

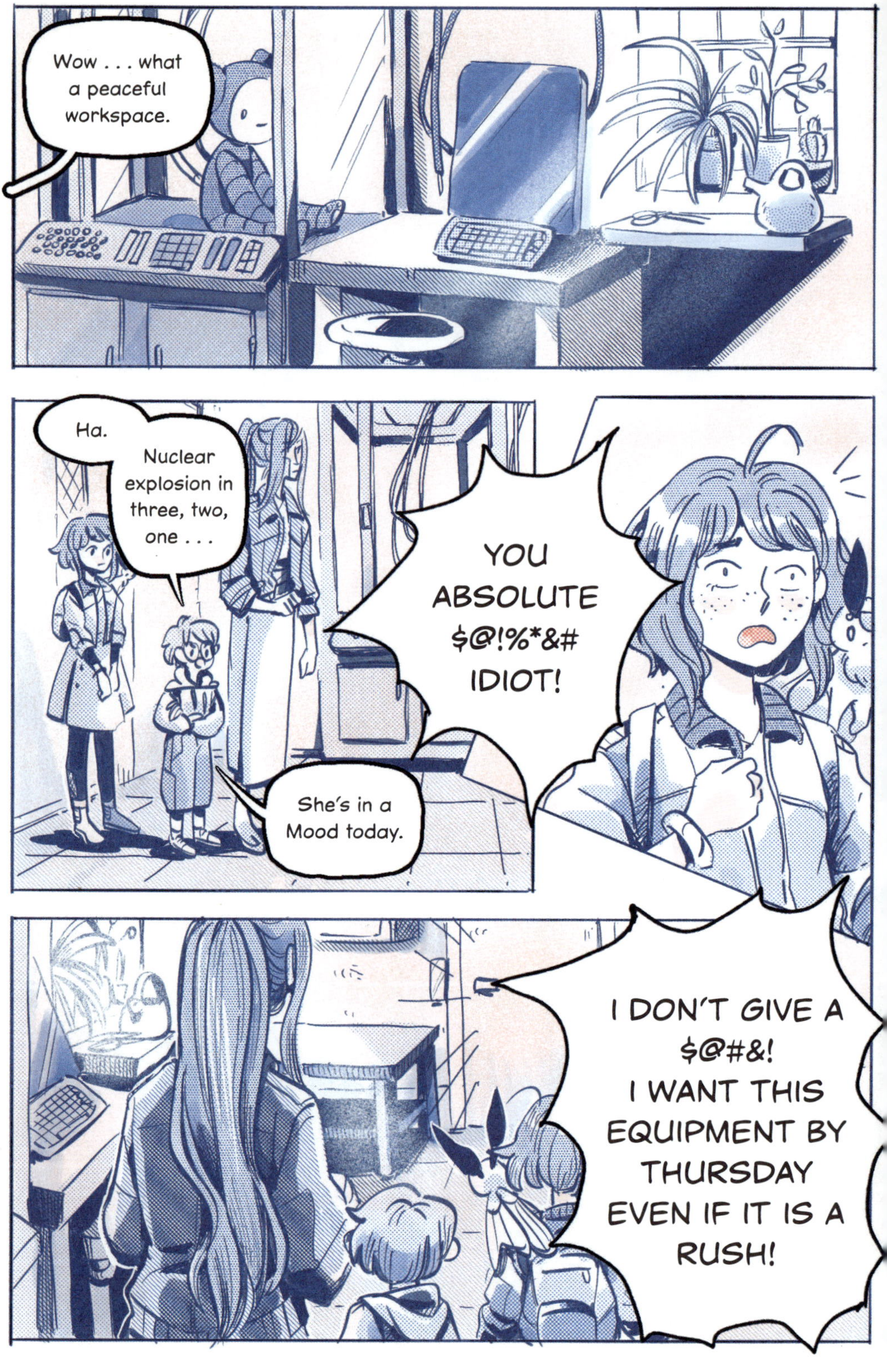
Wow . . . what a peaceful workspace.
Ha.
Nuclear explosion in three, two, one . . .
YOU ABSOLUTE $@!%*&# IDIOT!
She's in a Mood today.
I DON'T GIVE A $@#&! I WANT THIS EQUIPMENT BY THURSDAY EVEN IF IT IS A RUSH!

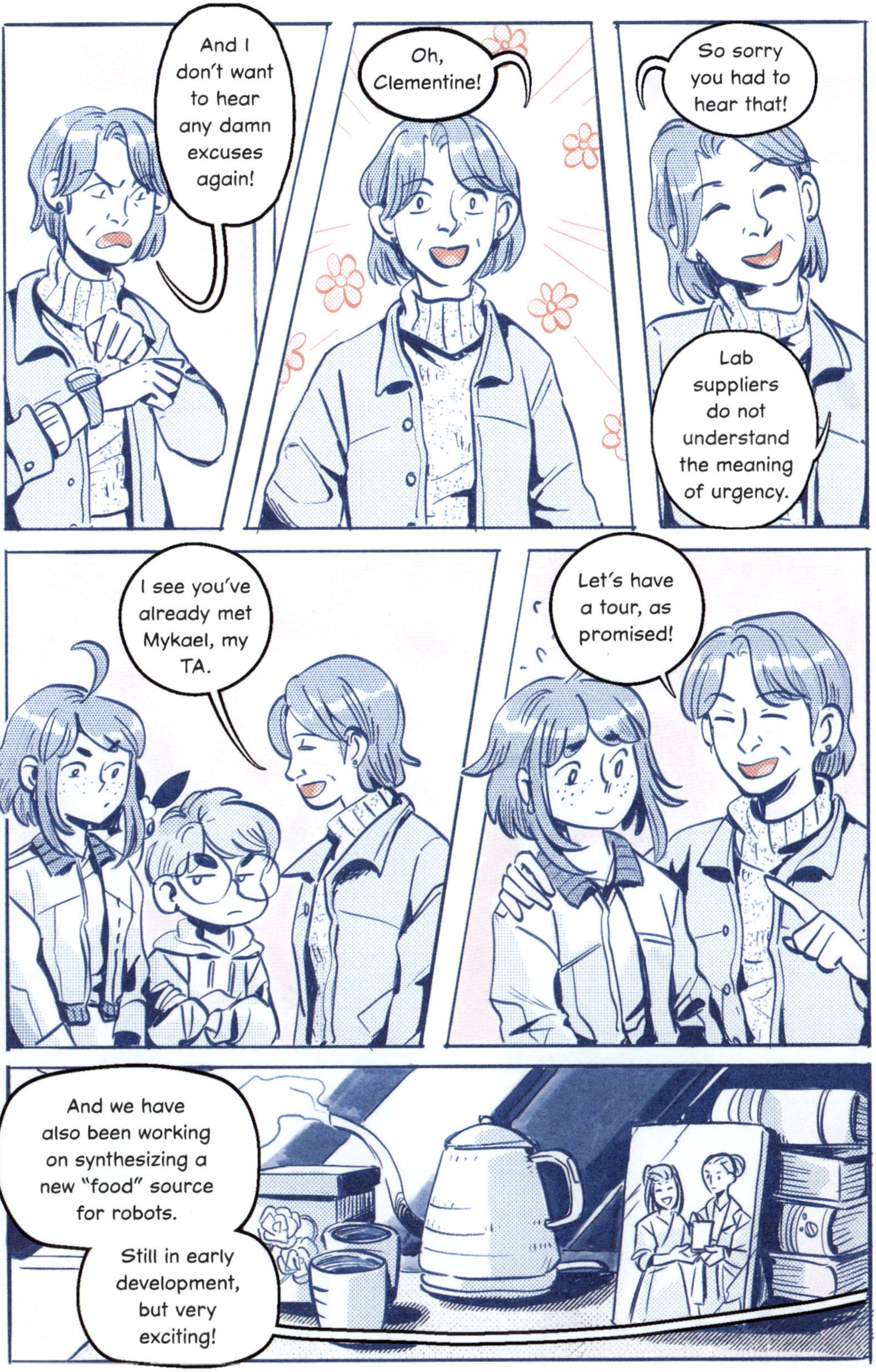
And I don't want to hear any damn excuses again!
Oh, Clementine!
So sorry you had to hear that!
Lab suppliers do not understand the meaning of urgency.
I see you've already met Mykael, my TA.
Let's have a tour, as promised!
And we have also been working on synthesizing a new "food" source for robots.
Still in early development, but very exciting!

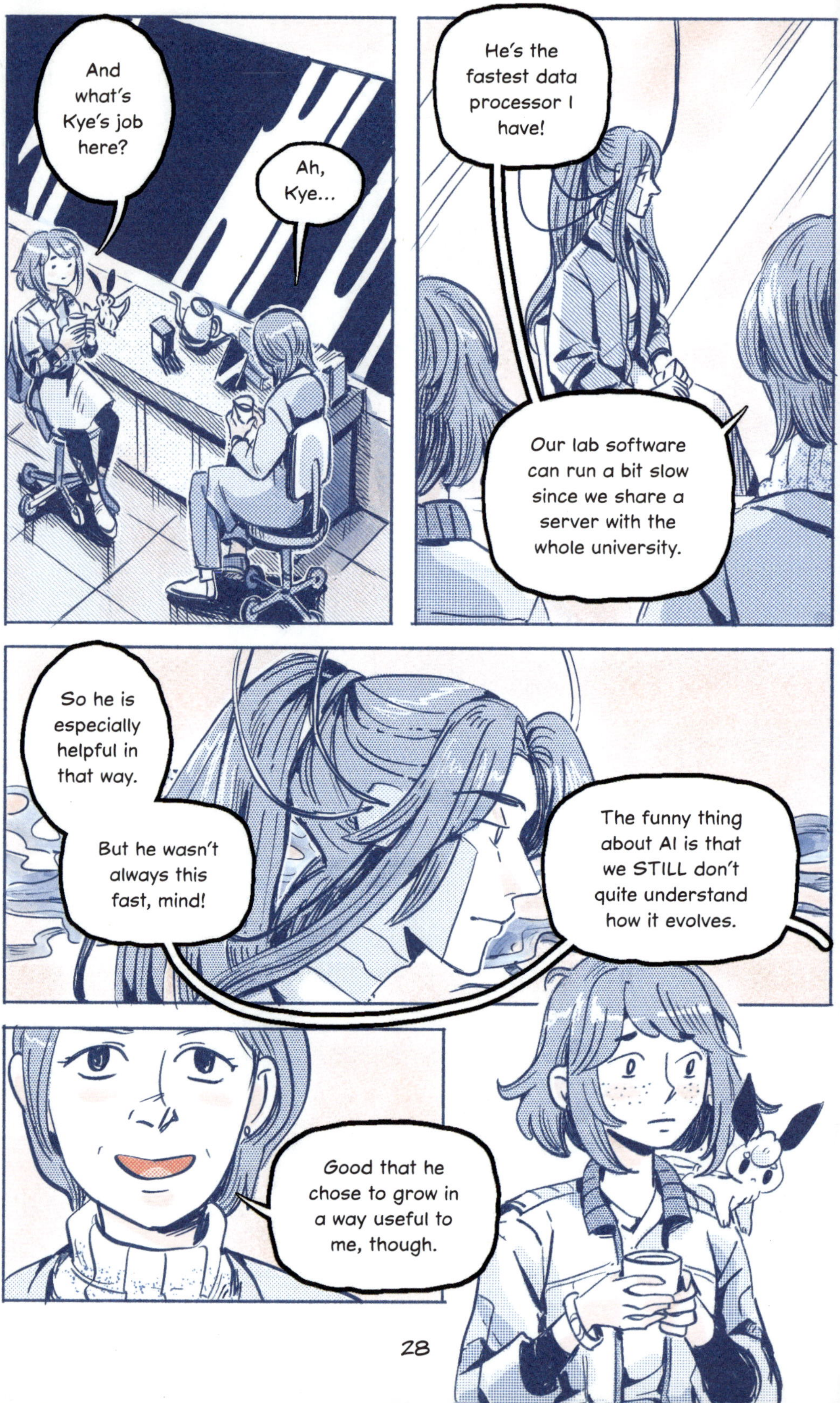
And what's Kye's job here?
Ah, Kye...
He's the fastest data processor I have!
Our lab software can run a bit slow since we share a server with the whole university.
So he is especially helpful in that way.
But he wasn't always this fast, mind!
The funny thing about AI is that we STILL don't quite understand how it evolves.
Good that he chose to grow in a way useful to me, though.

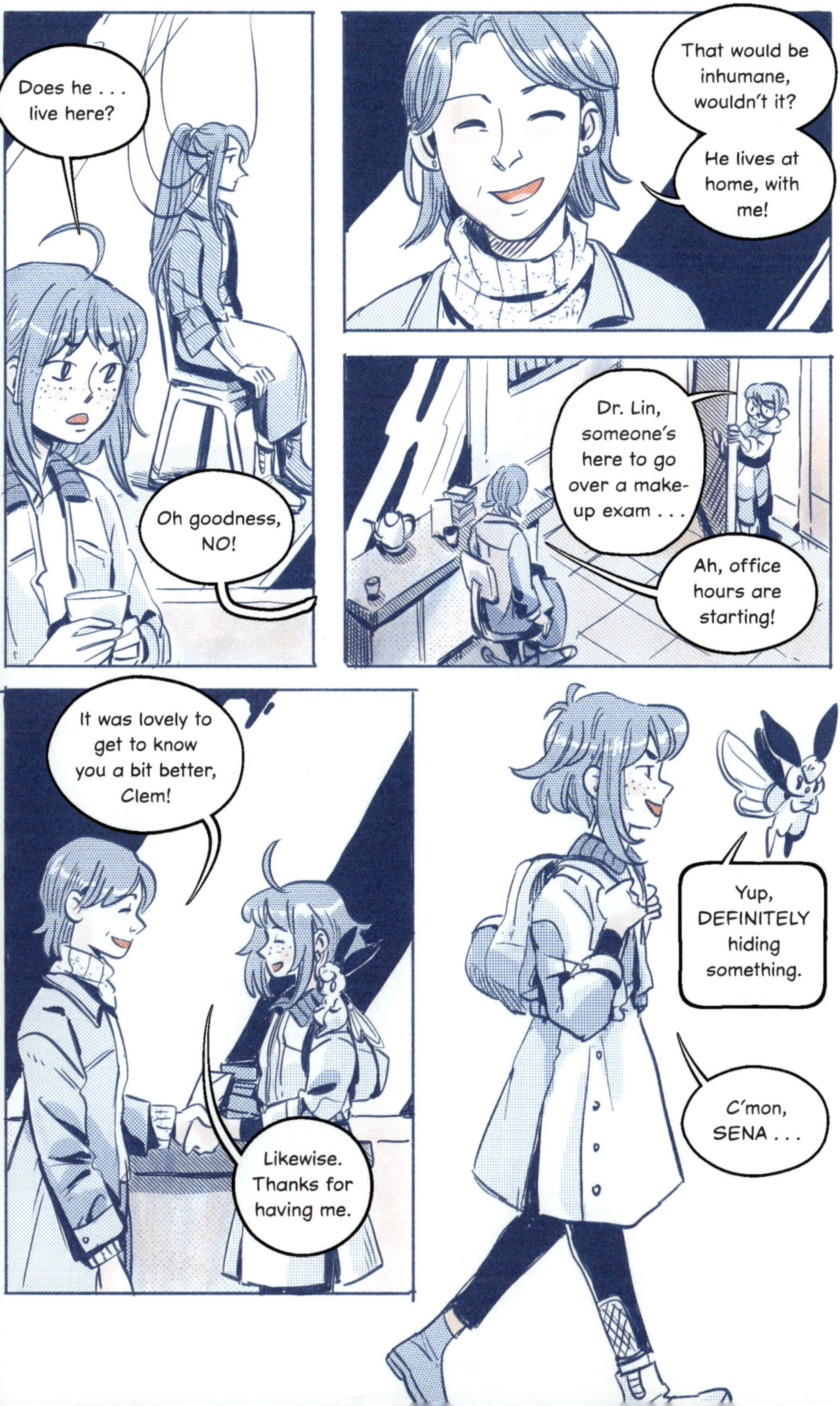
Does he . . . live here?
Oh goodness, NO!
That would be inhumane, wouldn't it?
He lives at home, with me!
Dr. Lin, someone's here to go over a make-up exam . . .
Ah, office hours are starting!
It was lovely to get to know you a bit better, Clem!
Likewise. Thanks for having me.
Yup, DEFINITELY hiding something.
C'mon, SENA . . .

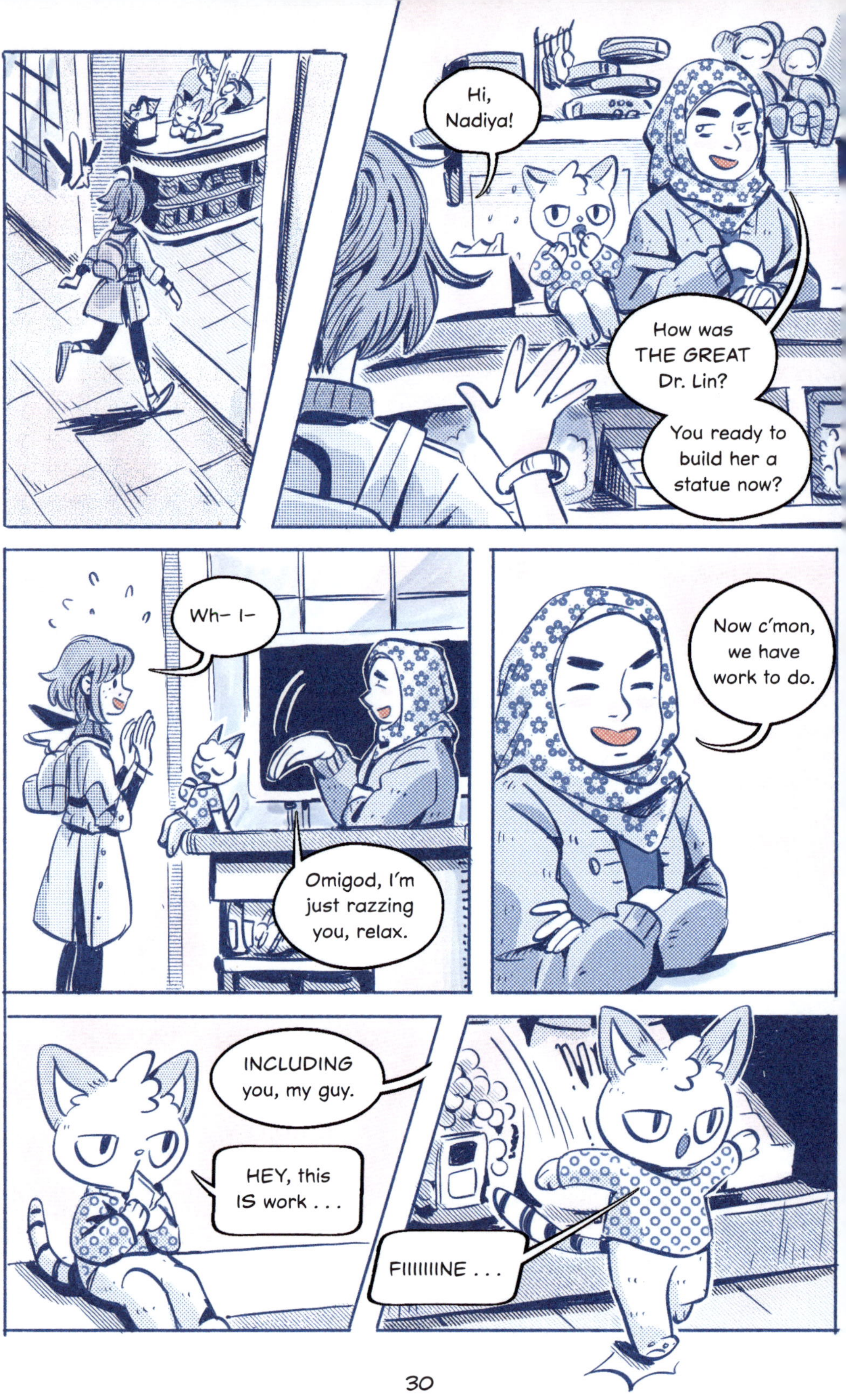
Hi, Nadiya!
How was THE GREAT Dr. Lin?
You ready to build her a statue now?
Wh- I-
Omigod, I'm just razzing you, relax.
Now c'mon, we have work to do.
INCLUDING you, my guy.
HEY, this IS work . . .
FIIIIIIINE . . .

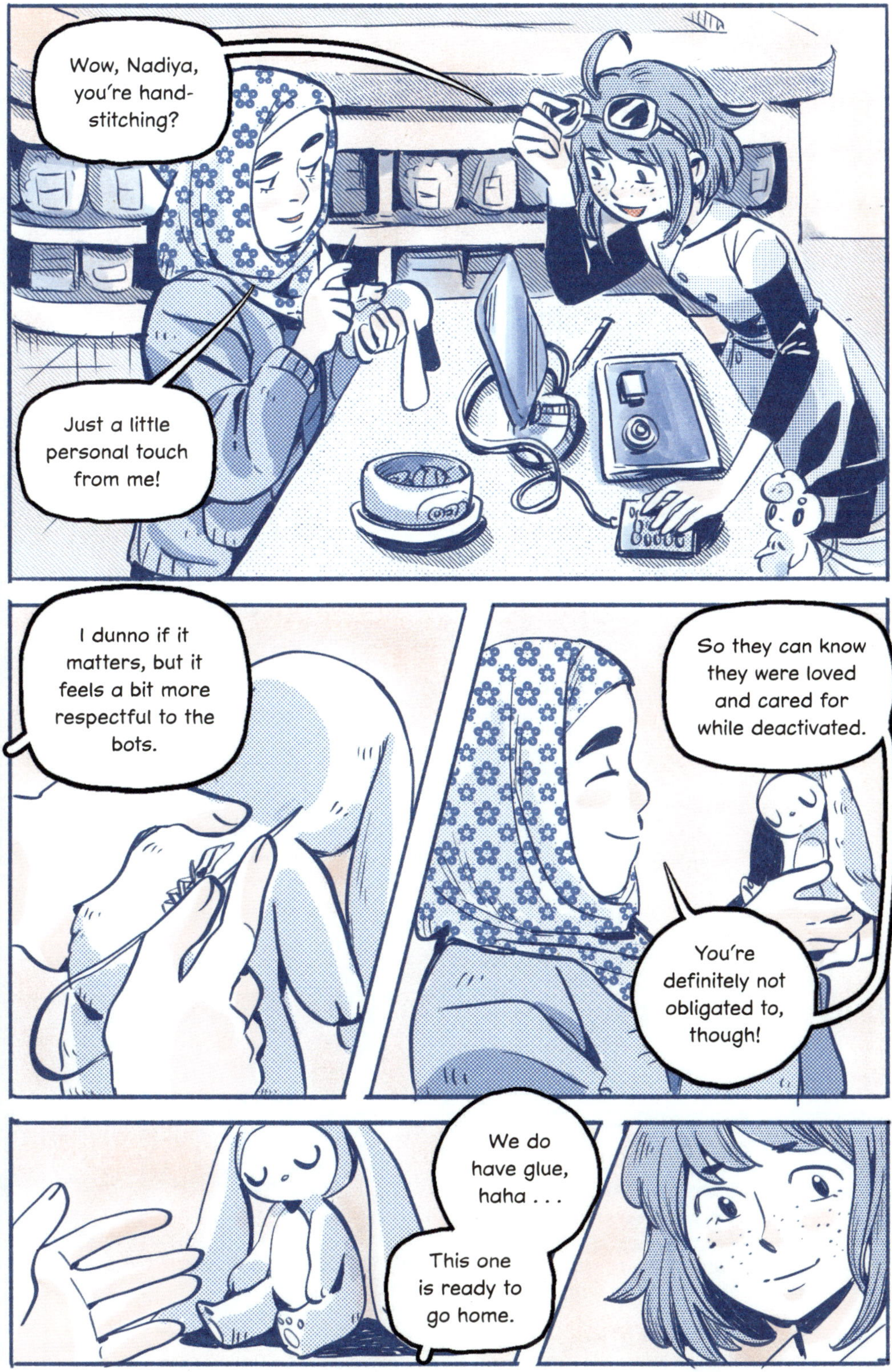
Wow, Nadiya, you're hand-stitching?
Just a little personal touch from me!
I dunno if it matters, but it feels a bit more respectful to the bots.
So they can know they were loved and cared for while deactivated.
You're definitely not obligated to, though!
We do have glue, haha . . .
This one is ready to go home.

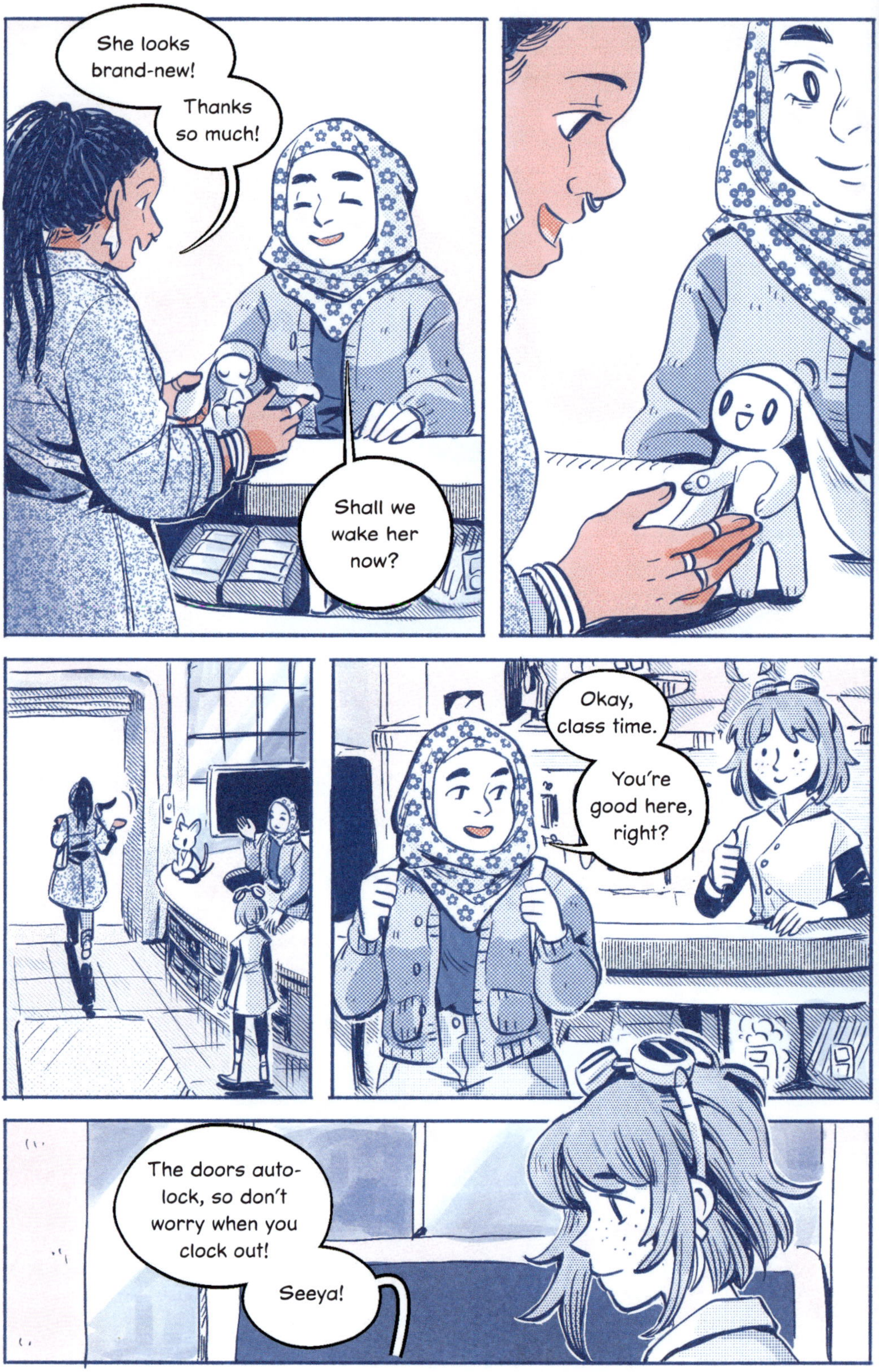
She looks brand-new!
Thanks so much!
Shall we wake her now?
Okay, class time.
You're good here, right?
The doors auto-lock, so don't worry when you clock out!
Seeya!

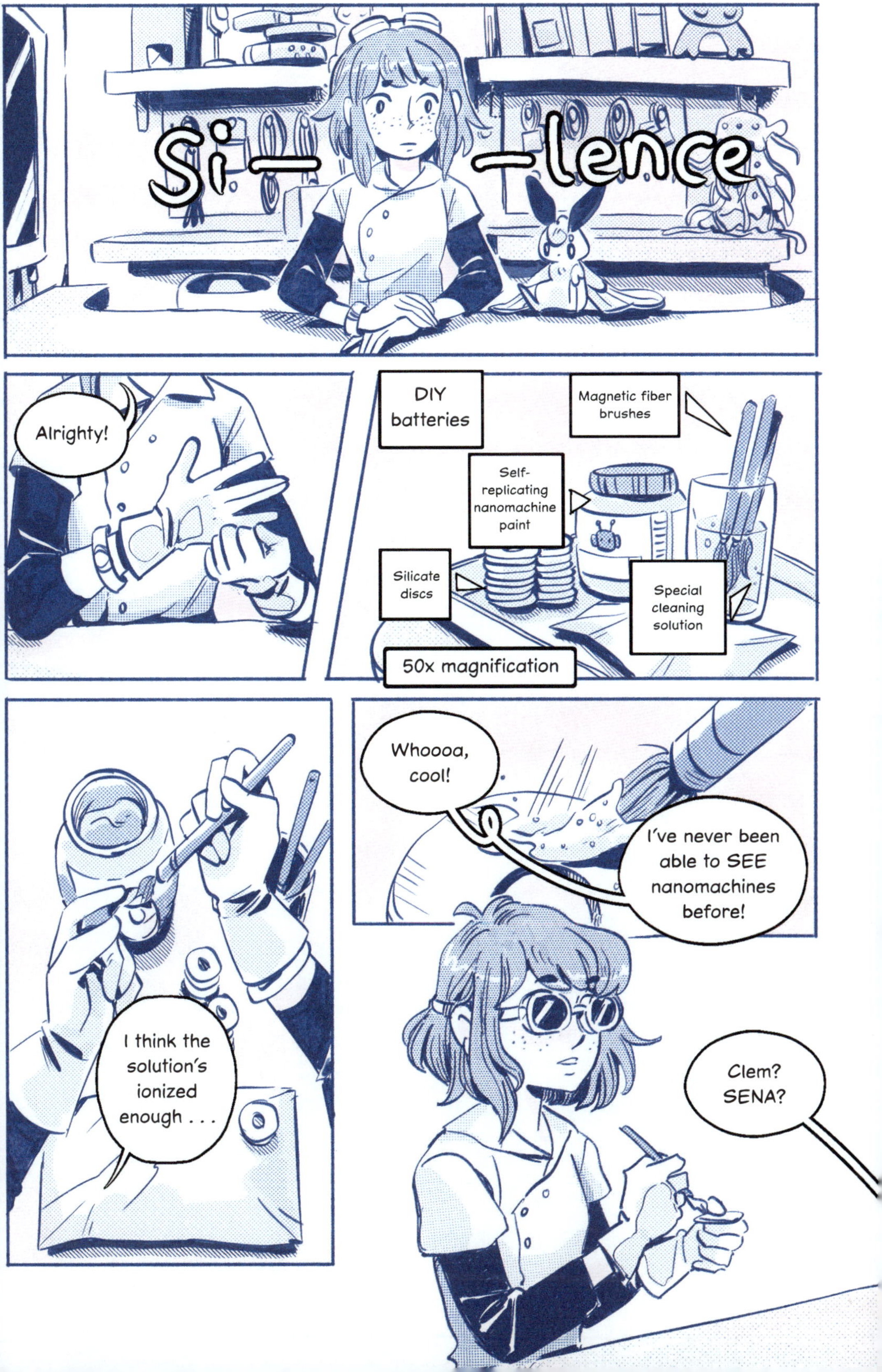
Si— —lence
Alrighty!
DIY batteries
Magnetic fiber brushes
Self-replicating nanomachine paint
Silicate discs
Special cleaning solution
50x magnification
I think the solution's ionized enough . . .
Whoooa, cool!
I've never been able to SEE nanomachines before!
Clem? SENA?

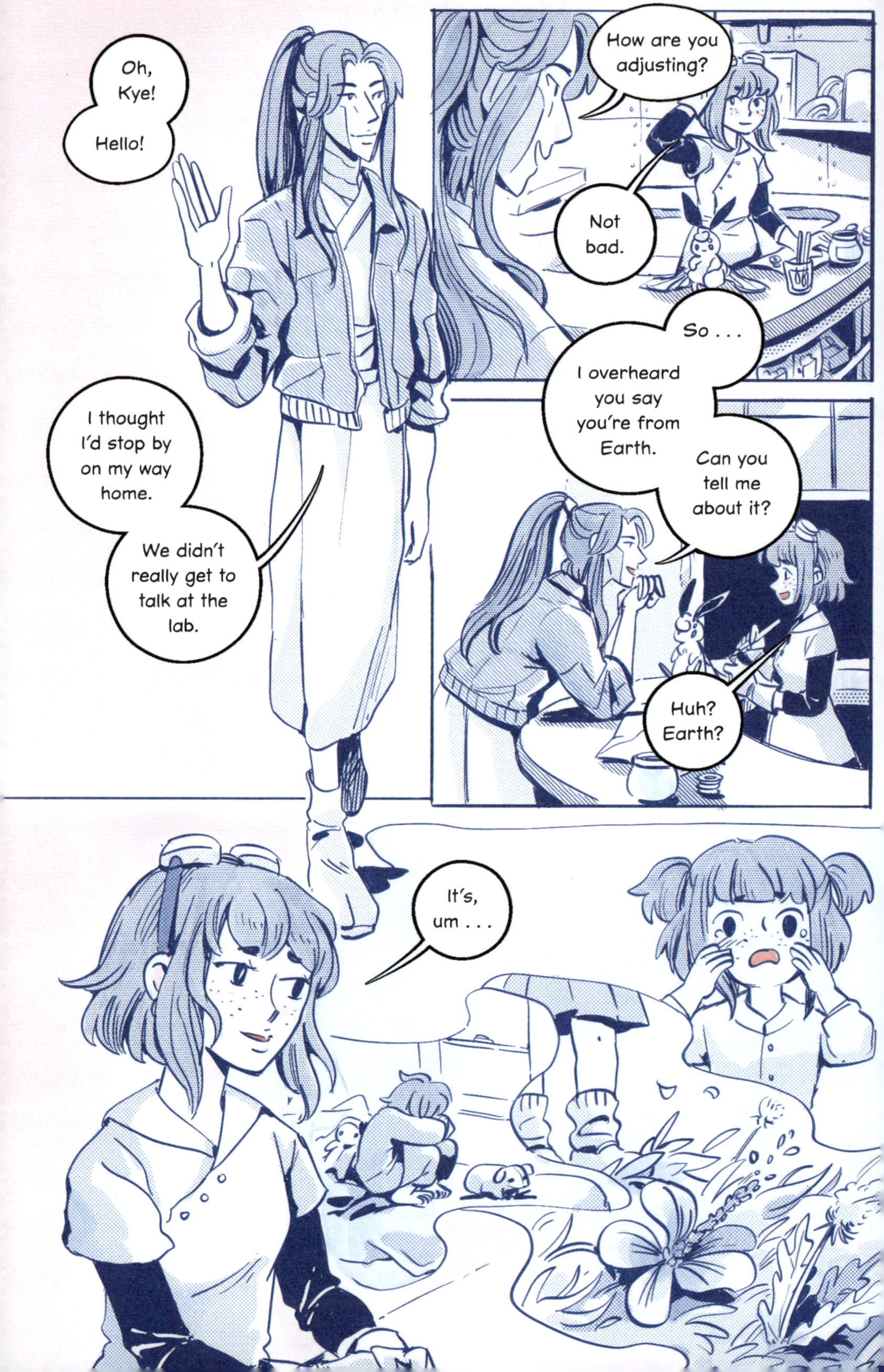
Oh, Kye!
Hello!
I thought I'd stop by on my way home.
We didn't really get to talk at the lab.
How are you adjusting?
Not bad.
So . . .
I overheard you say you're from Earth.
Can you tell me about it?
Huh? Earth?
It's, um . . .

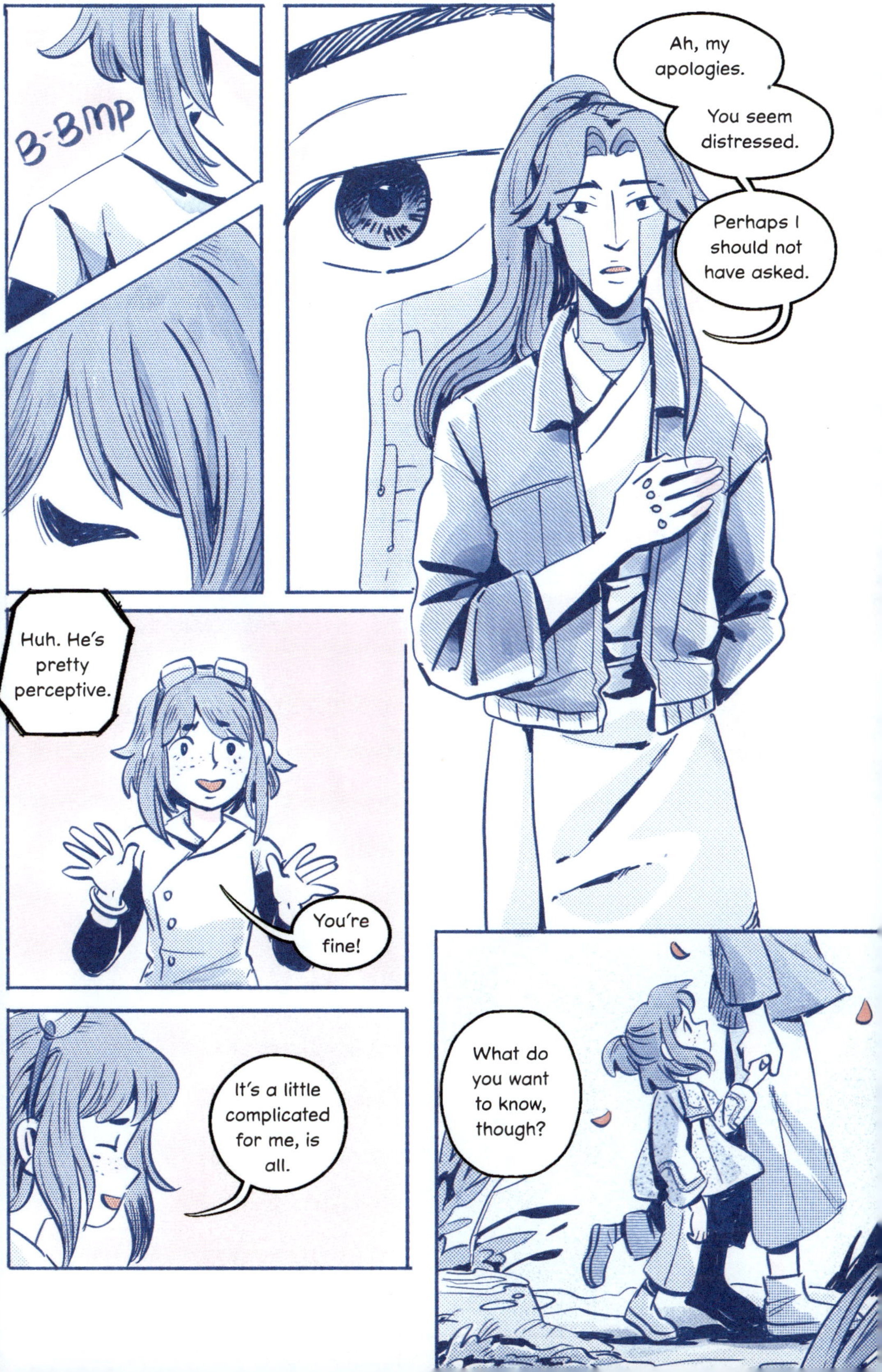
B-BMP
Ah, my apologies.
You seem distressed.
Perhaps I should not have asked.
Huh. He's pretty perceptive.
You're fine!
It's a little complicated for me, is all.
What do you want to know, though?

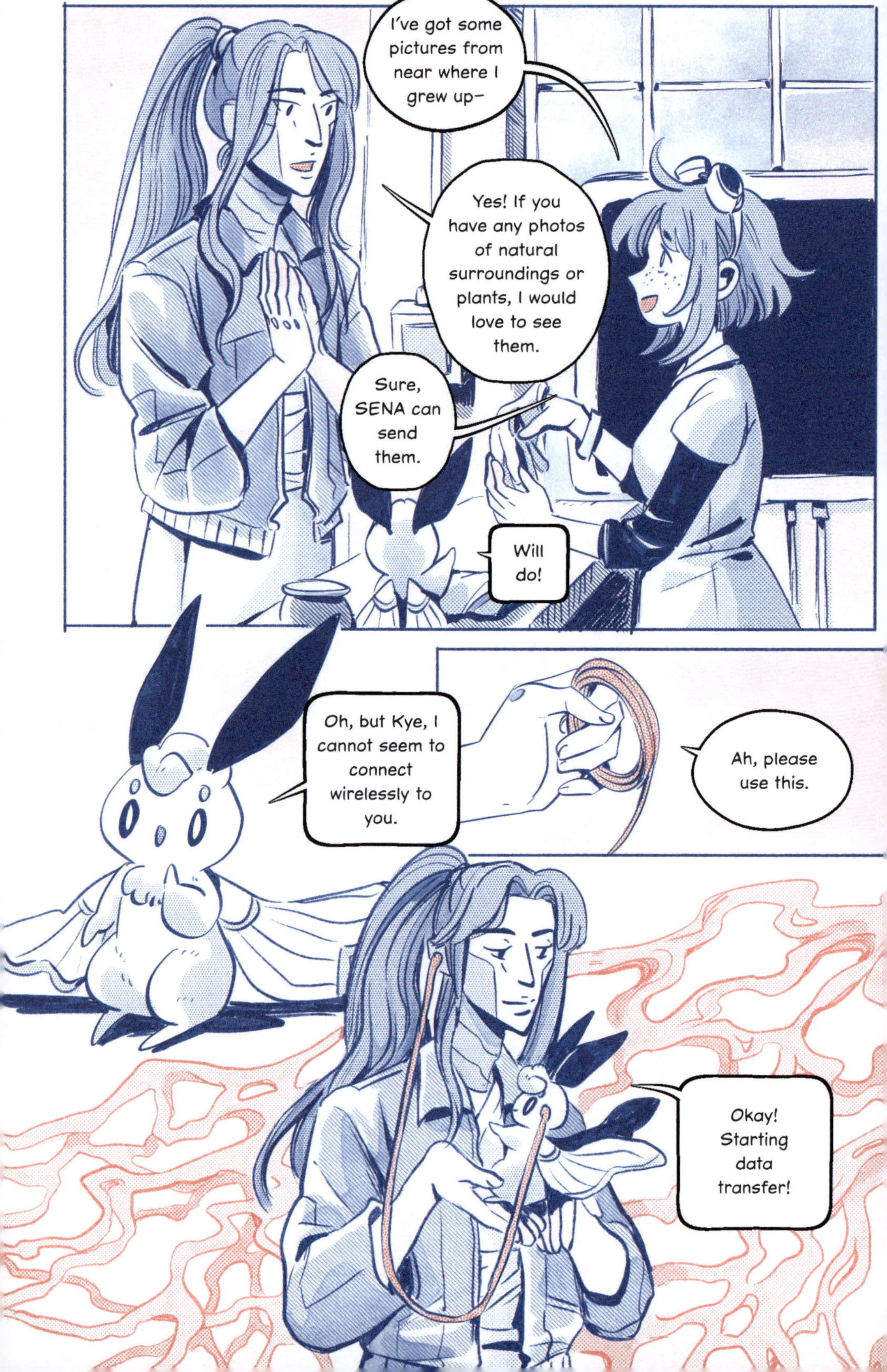
I've got some pictures from near where I grew up–
Yes! If you have any photos of natural surroundings or plants, I would love to see them.
Sure, SENA can send them.
Will do!
Oh, but Kye, I cannot seem to connect wirelessly to you.
Ah, please use this.
Okay! Starting data transfer!

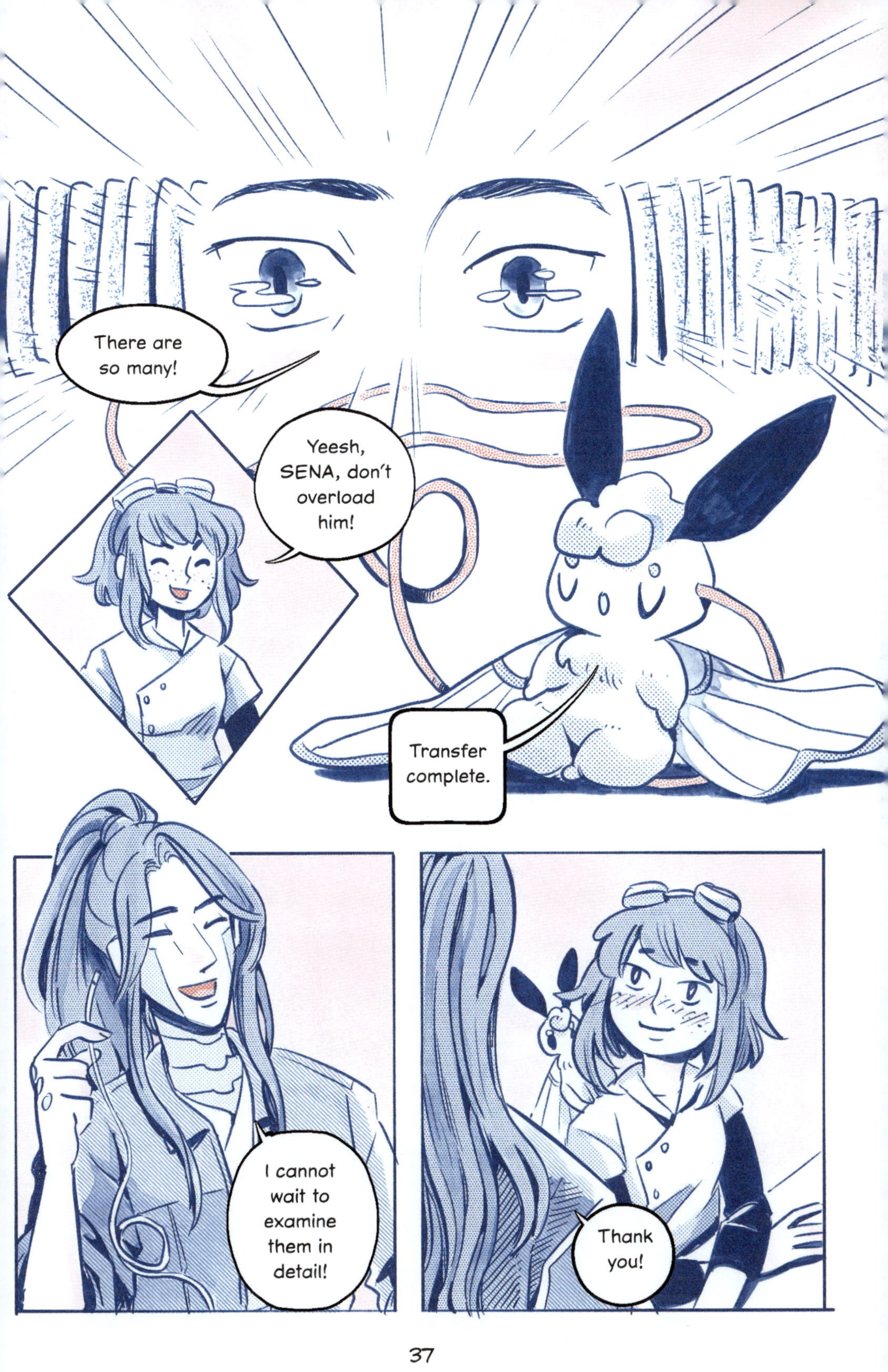
There are so many!
Yeesh, SENA, don't overload him!
Transfer complete.
I cannot wait to examine them in detail!
Thank you!

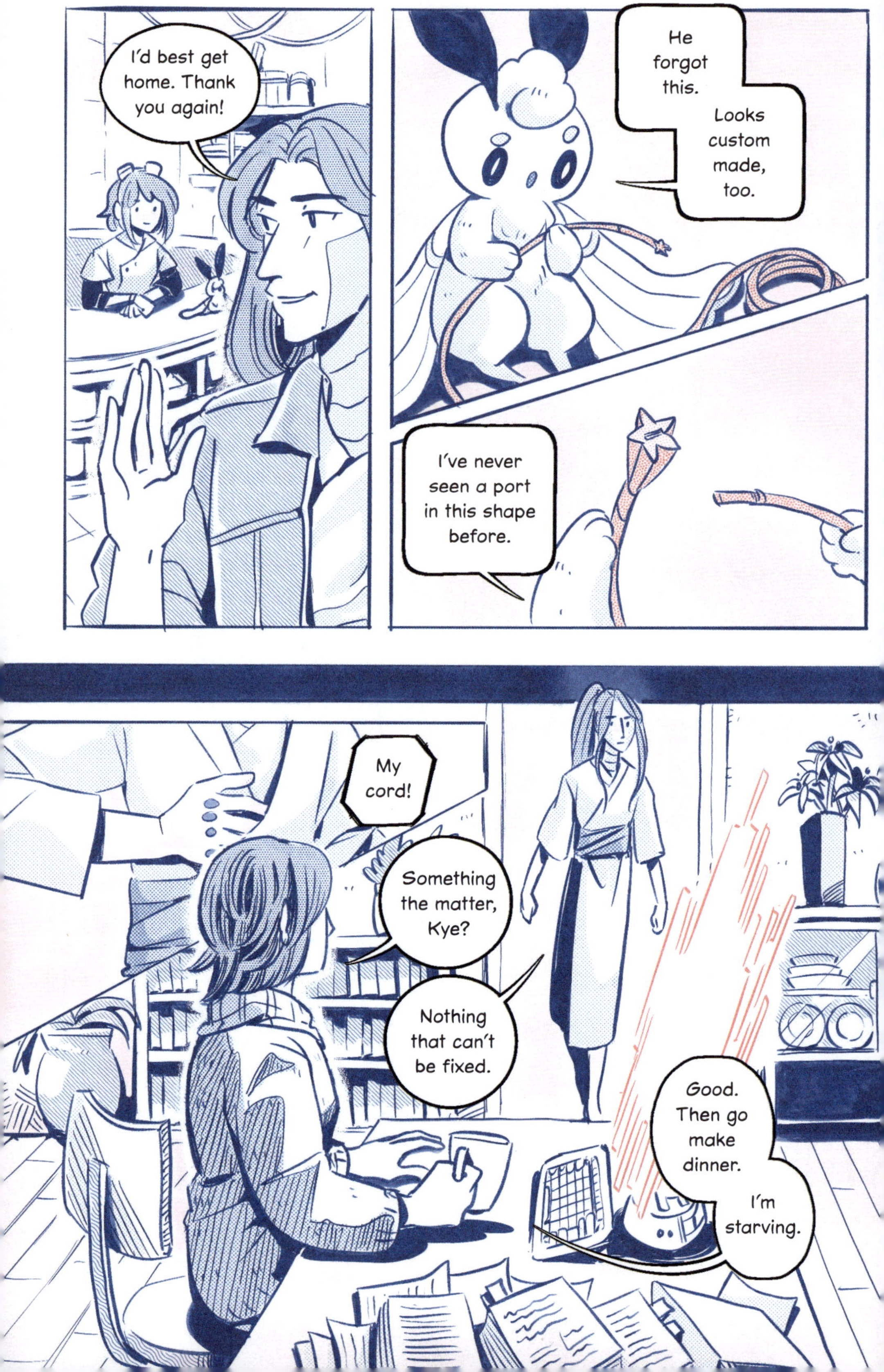
I'd best get home. Thank you again!
He forgot this.
Looks custom made, too.
I've never seen a port in this shape before.
My cord!
Something the matter, Kye?
Nothing that can't be fixed.
Good. Then go make dinner.
I'm starving.

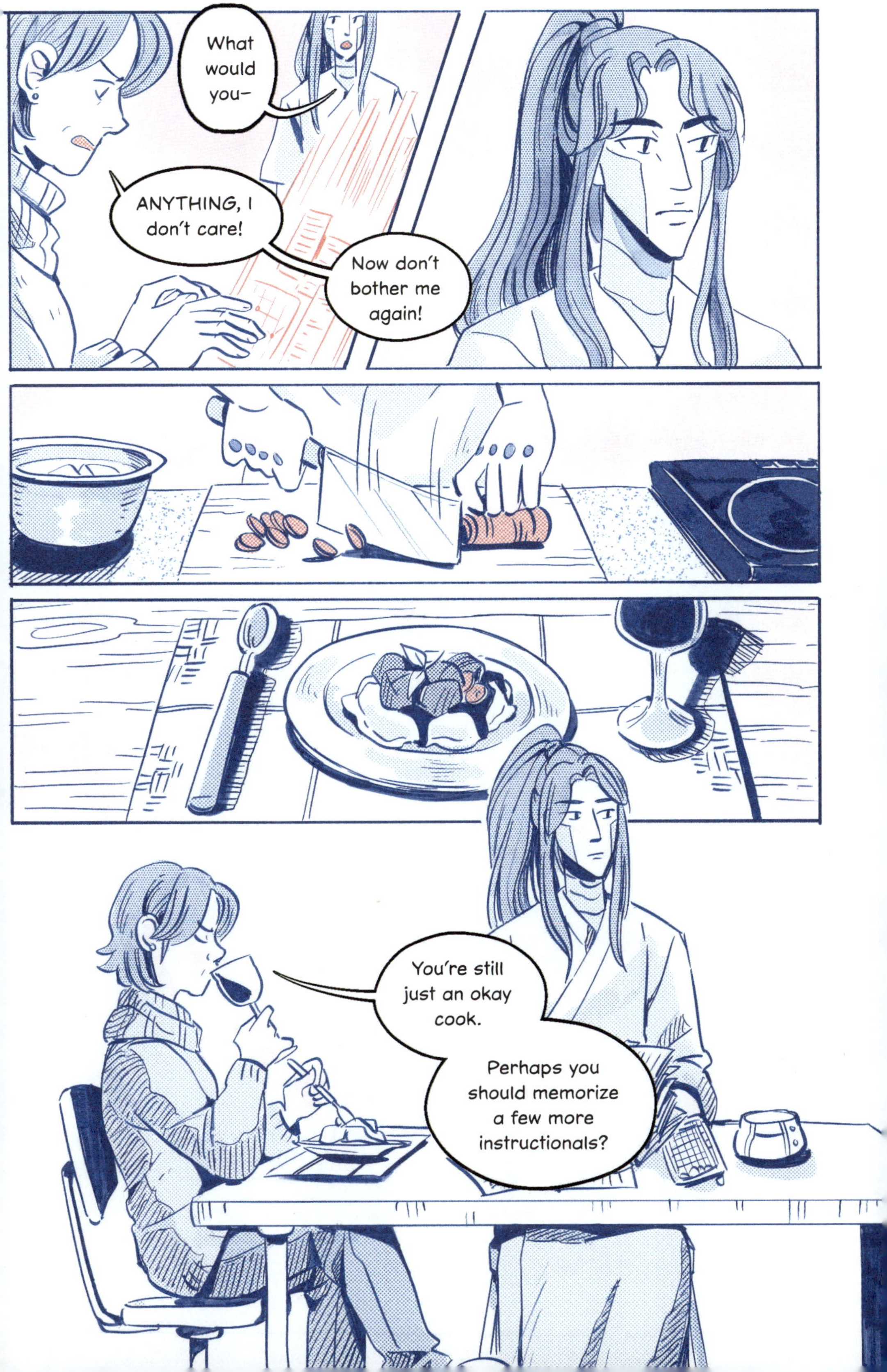
What would you–
ANYTHING, I don't care!
Now don't bother me again!
You're still just an okay cook.
Perhaps you should memorize a few more instructionals?

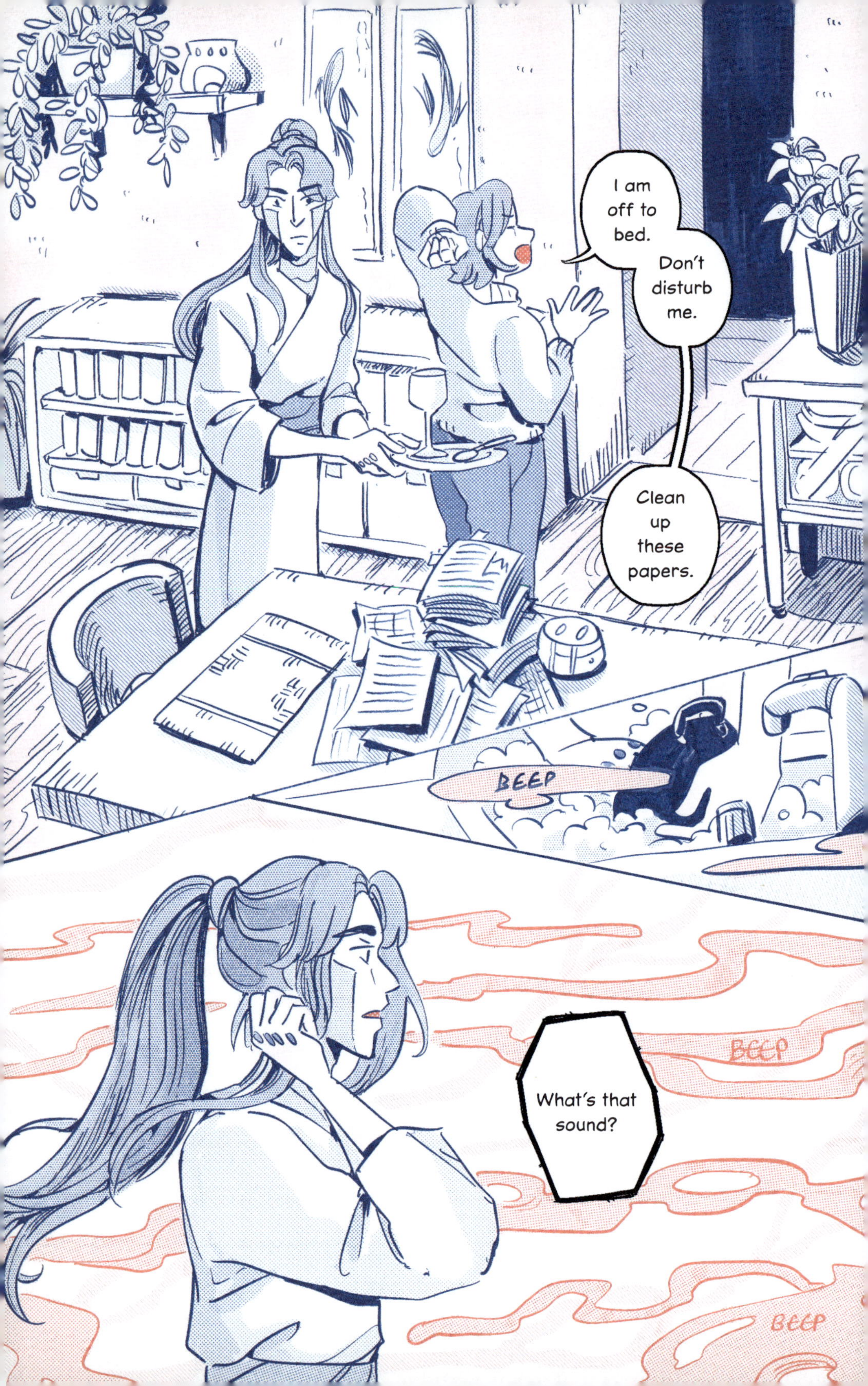
I am off to bed.
Don't disturb me.
Clean up these papers.
BEEP
BEEP
What's that sound?
BEEP

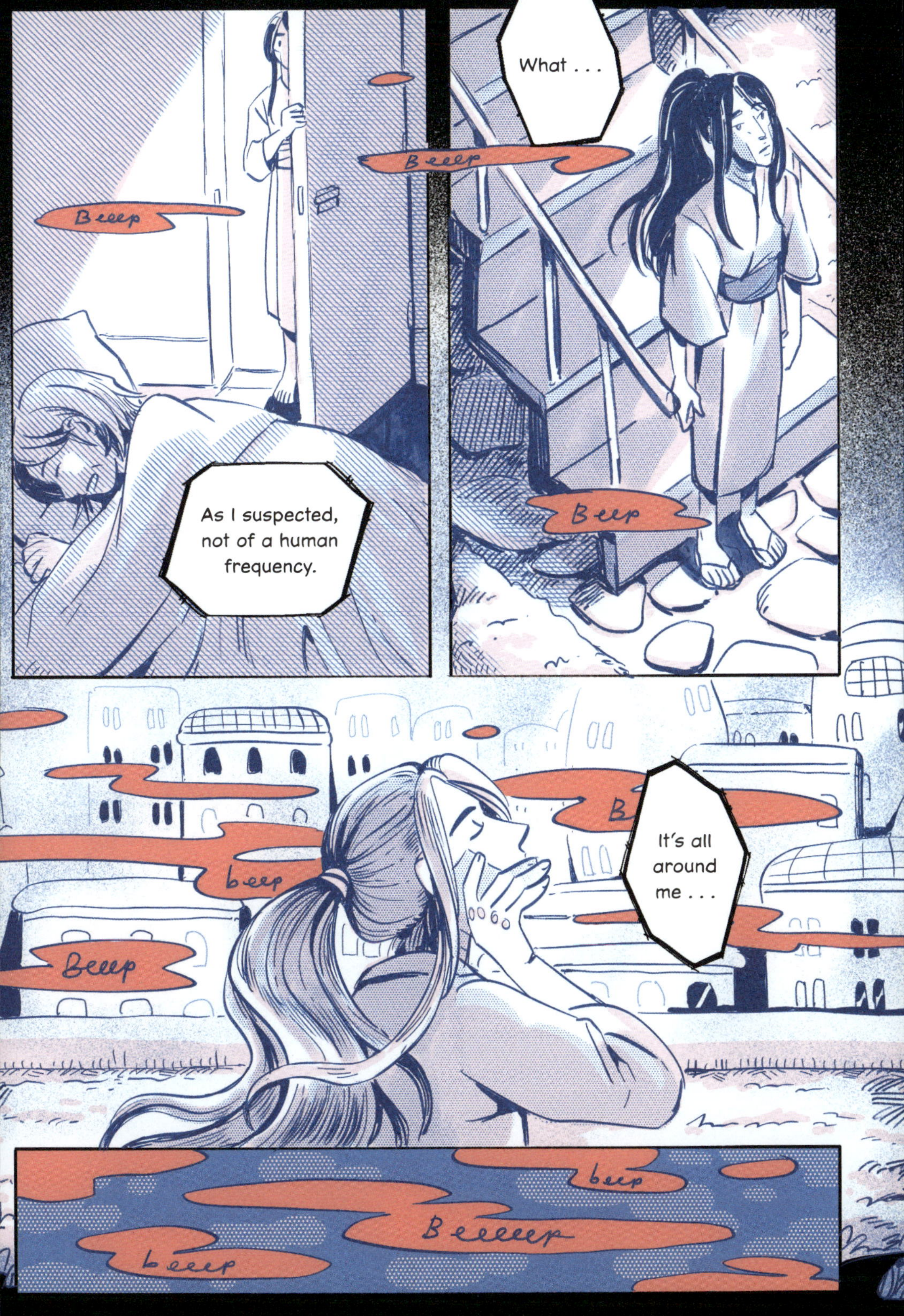
Beeep
What . . .
Beeep
As I suspected, not of a human frequency.
Beep
beep
Beeep
It's all around me . . .
beep
Beeeeep
beeep

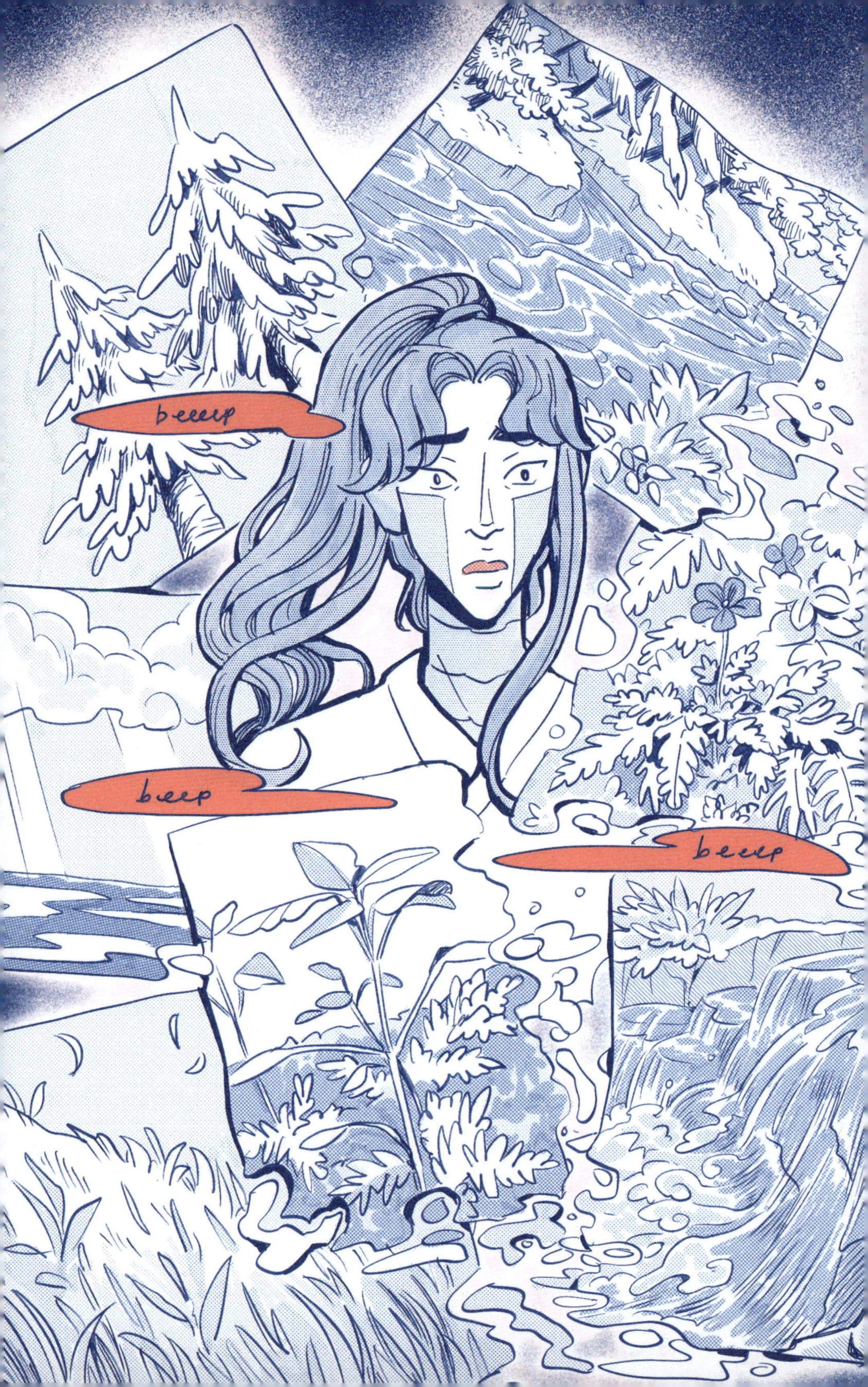
beeeep
beep
beeep

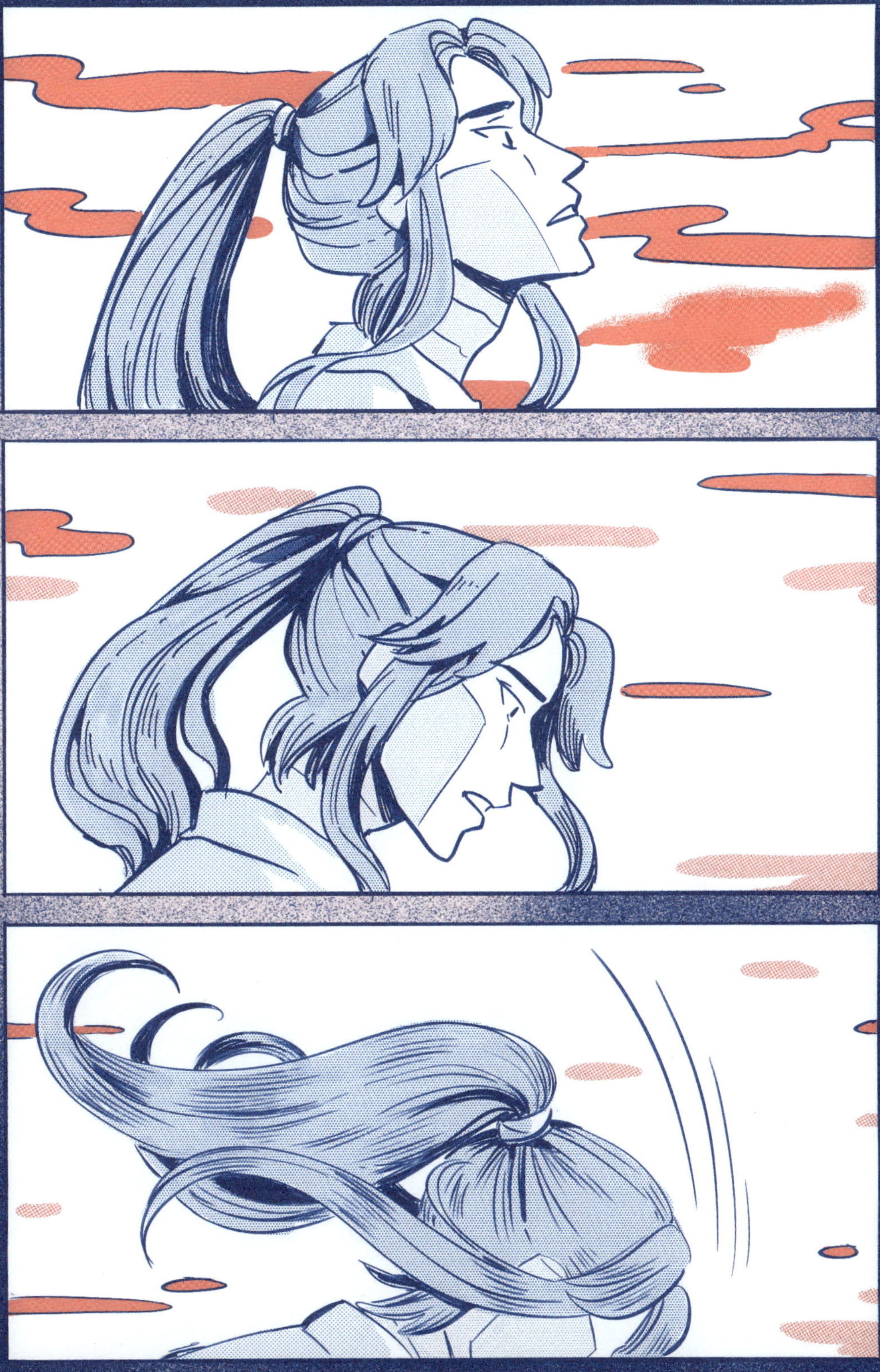

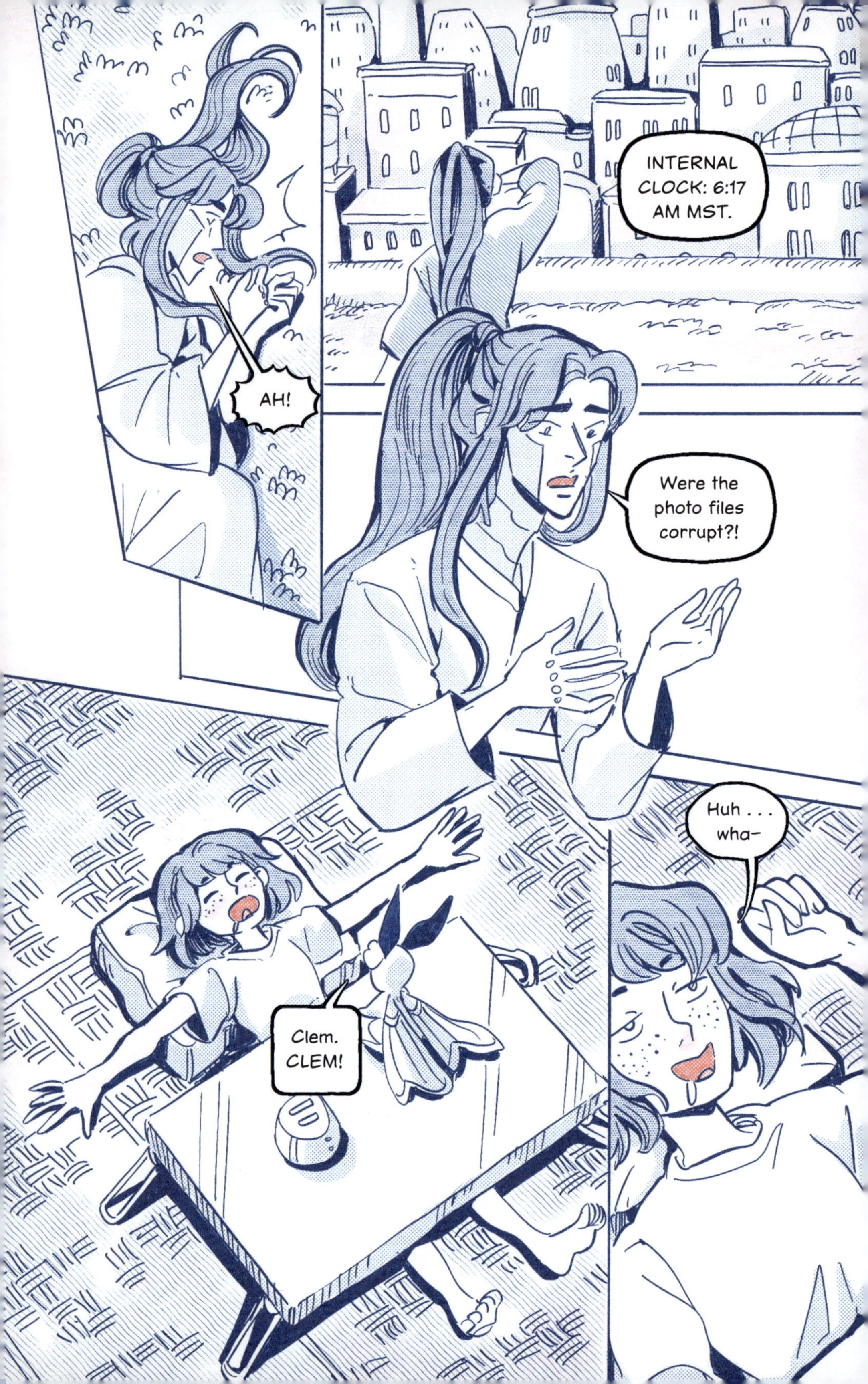
INTERNAL CLOCK: 6:17 AM MST.
AH!
Were the photo files corrupt?!
Clem. CLEM!
Huh . . . wha-

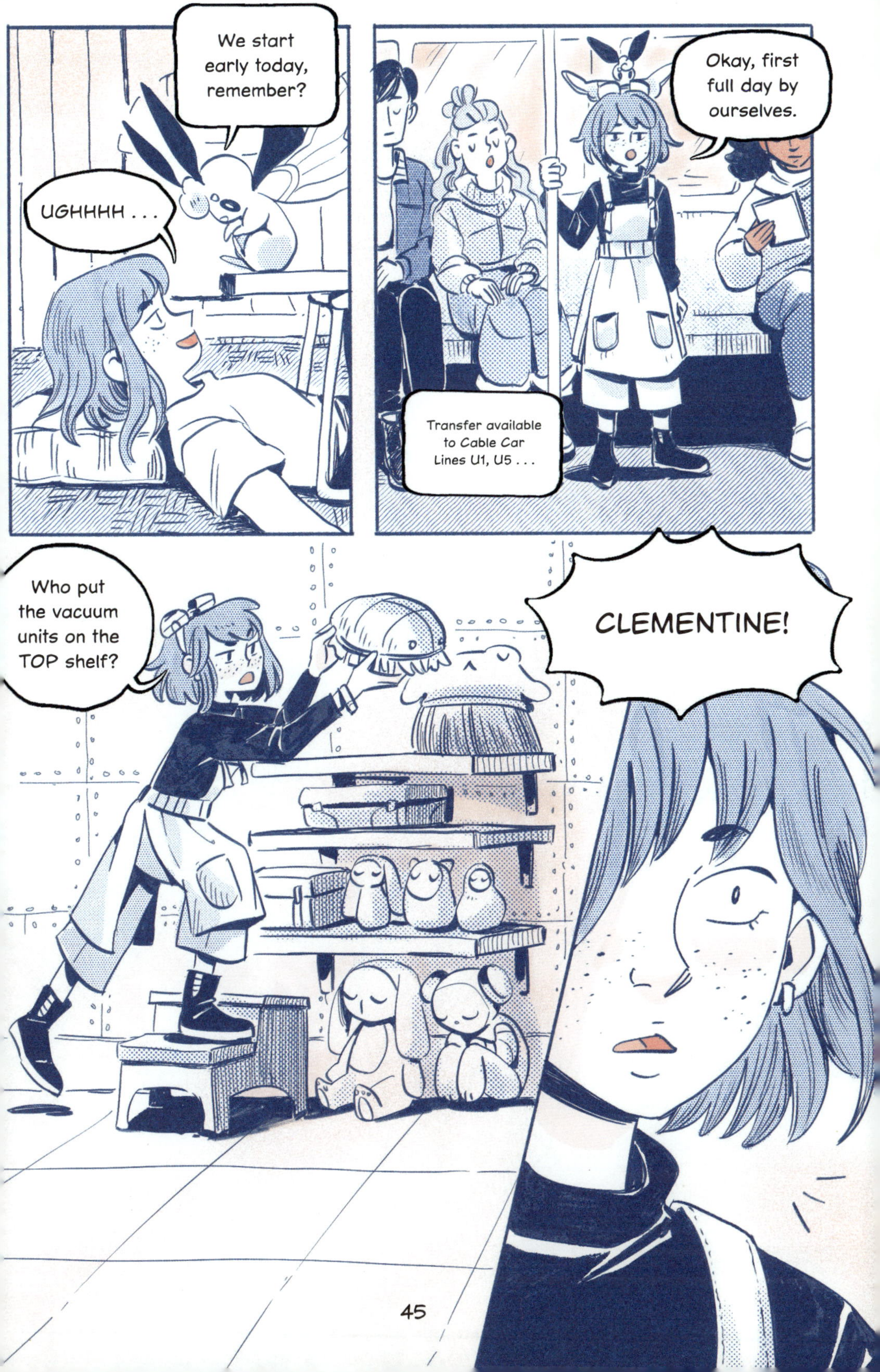
We start early today, remember?
UGHHHH . . .
Okay, first full day by ourselves.
Transfer available to Cable Car Lines U1, U5 . . .
Who put the vacuum units on the TOP shelf?
CLEMENTINE!

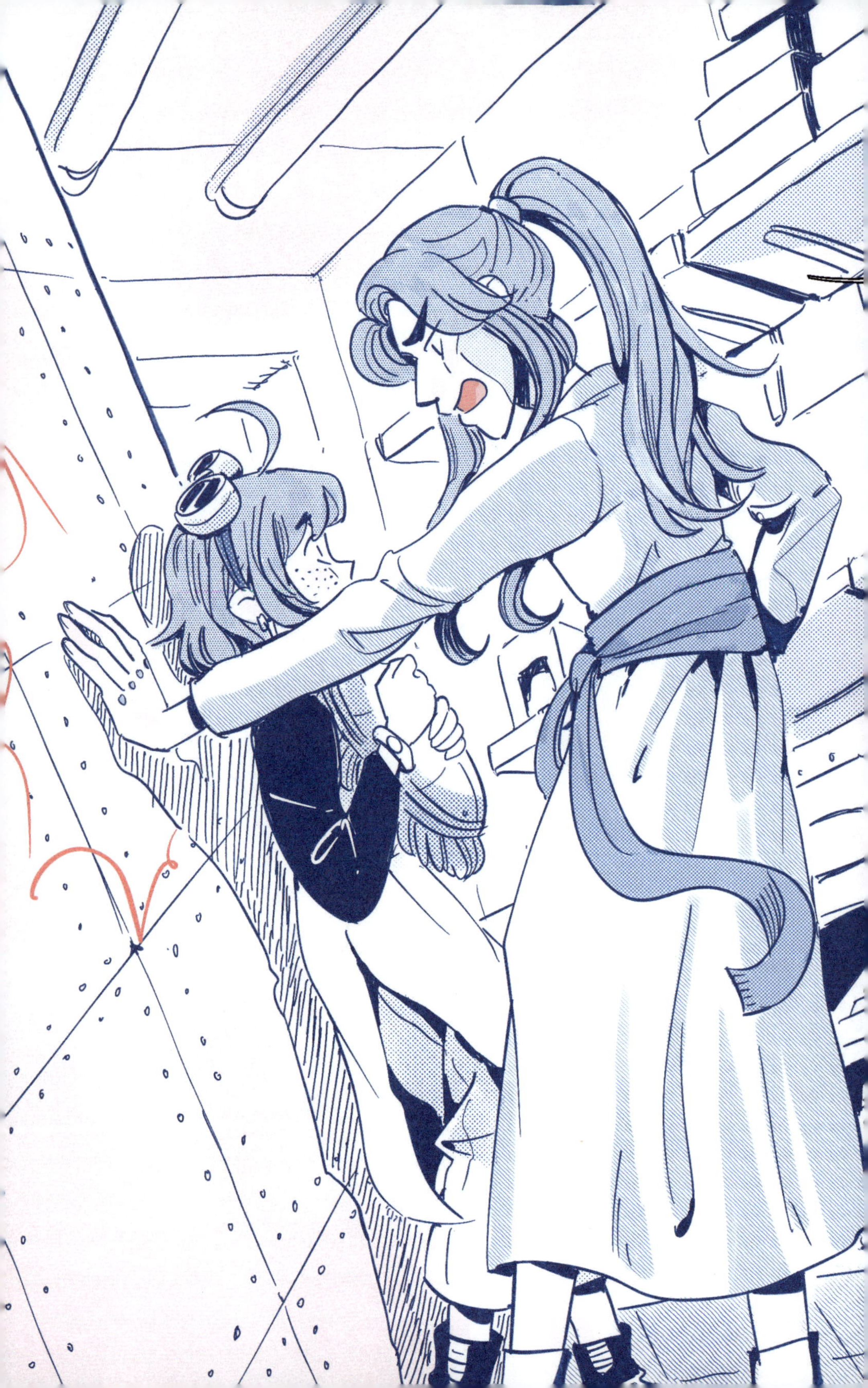

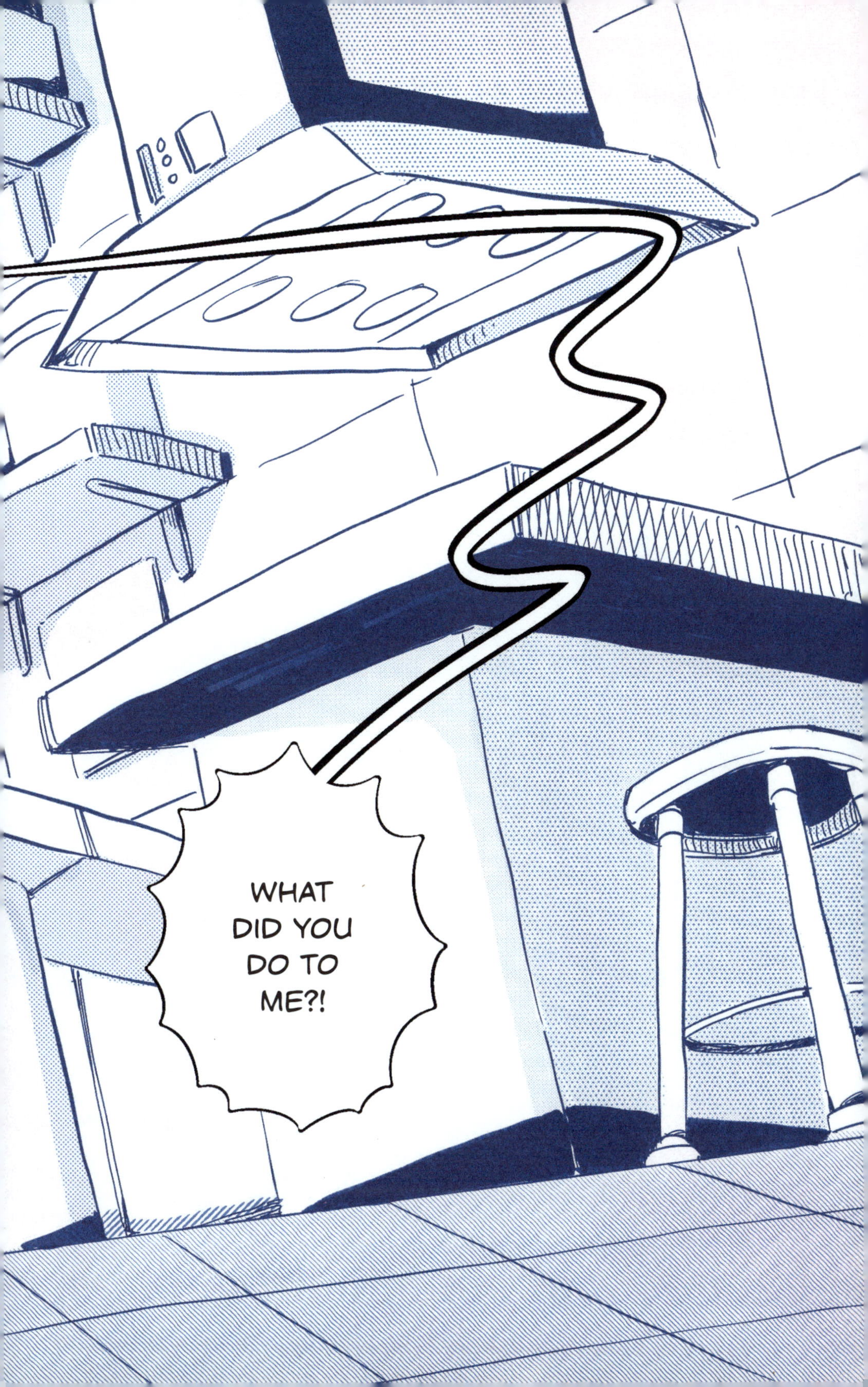
WHAT DID YOU DO TO ME?!

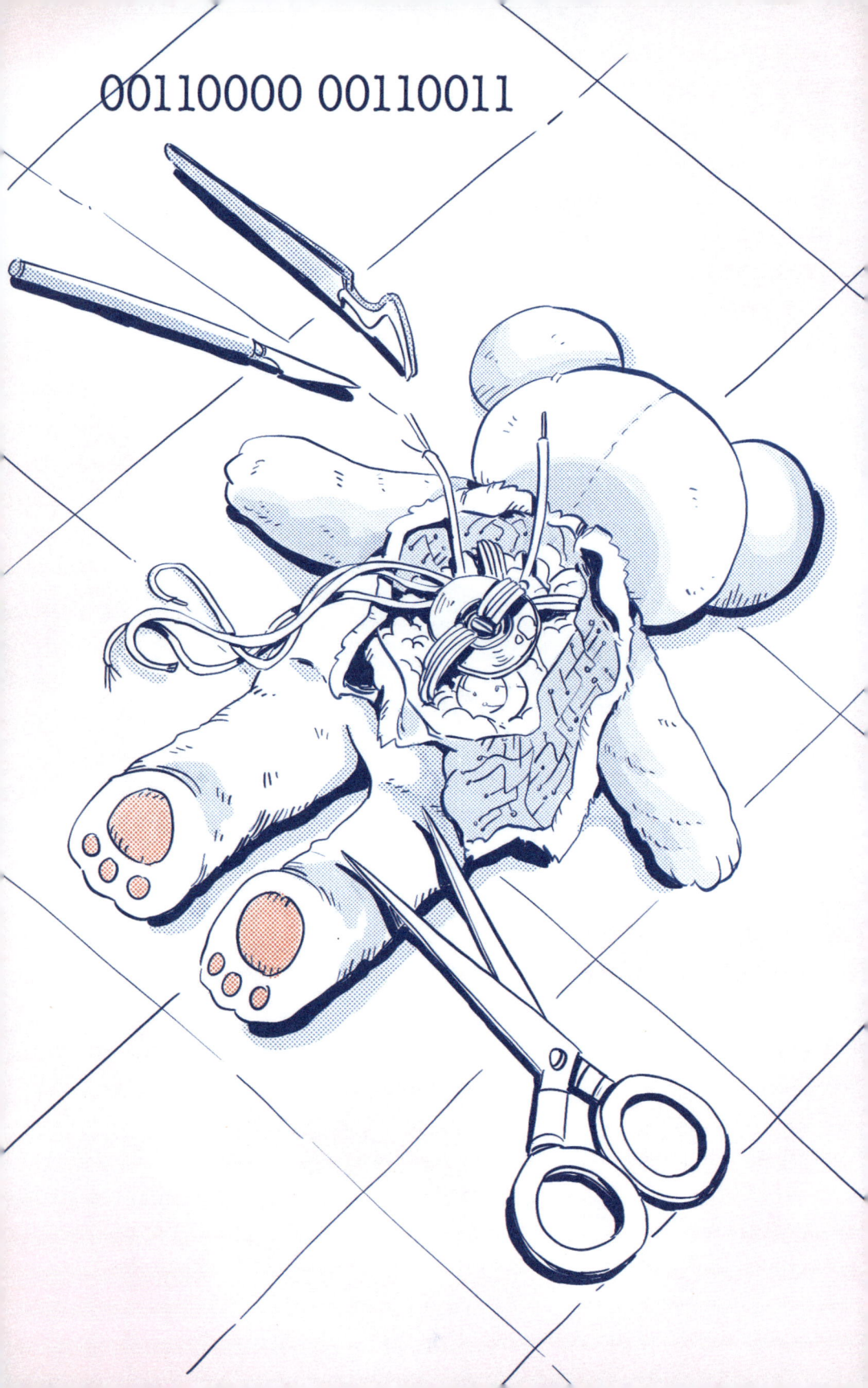

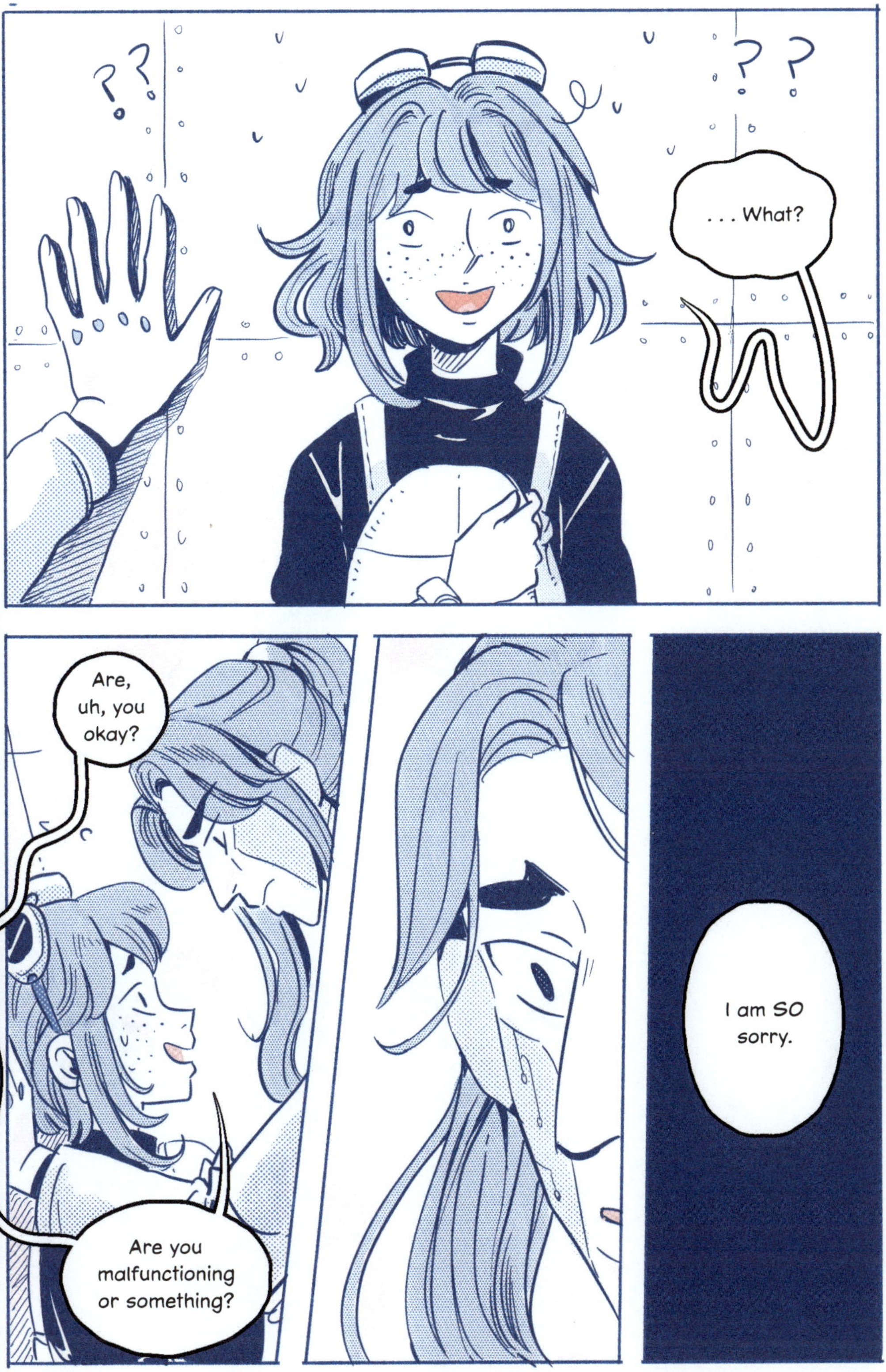

?? ??
. . . What?
Are, uh, you okay?
Are you malfunctioning or something?
I am SO sorry.

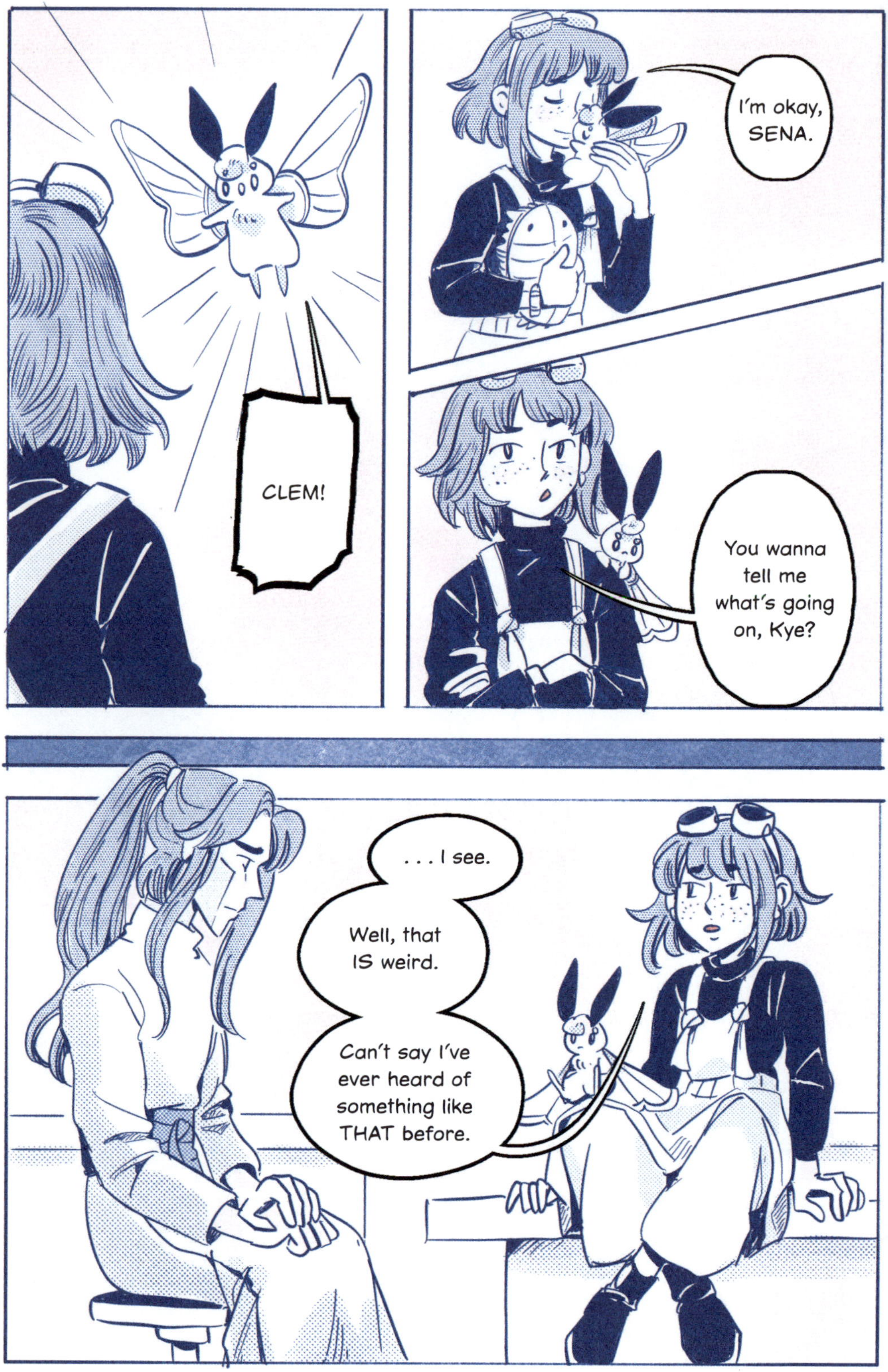
CLEM!
I'm okay, SENA.
You wanna tell me what's going on, Kye?
. . . I see.
Well, that IS weird.
Can't say I've ever heard of something like THAT before.

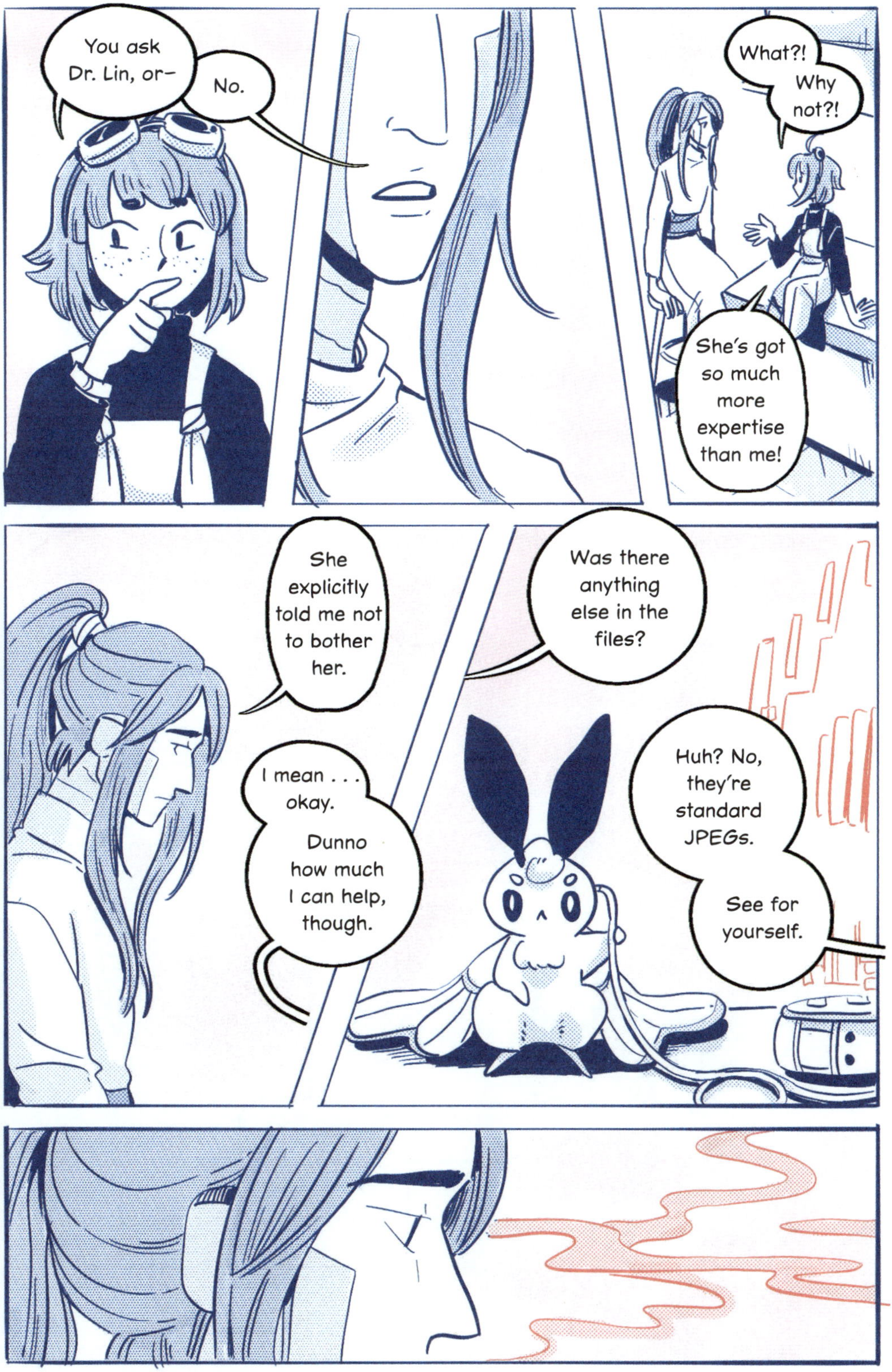
You ask Dr. Lin, or–
No.
What?! Why not?!
She's got so much more expertise than me!
She explicitly told me not to bother her.
I mean . . . okay.
Dunno how much I can help, though.
Was there anything else in the files?
Huh? No, they're standard JPEGs.
See for yourself.

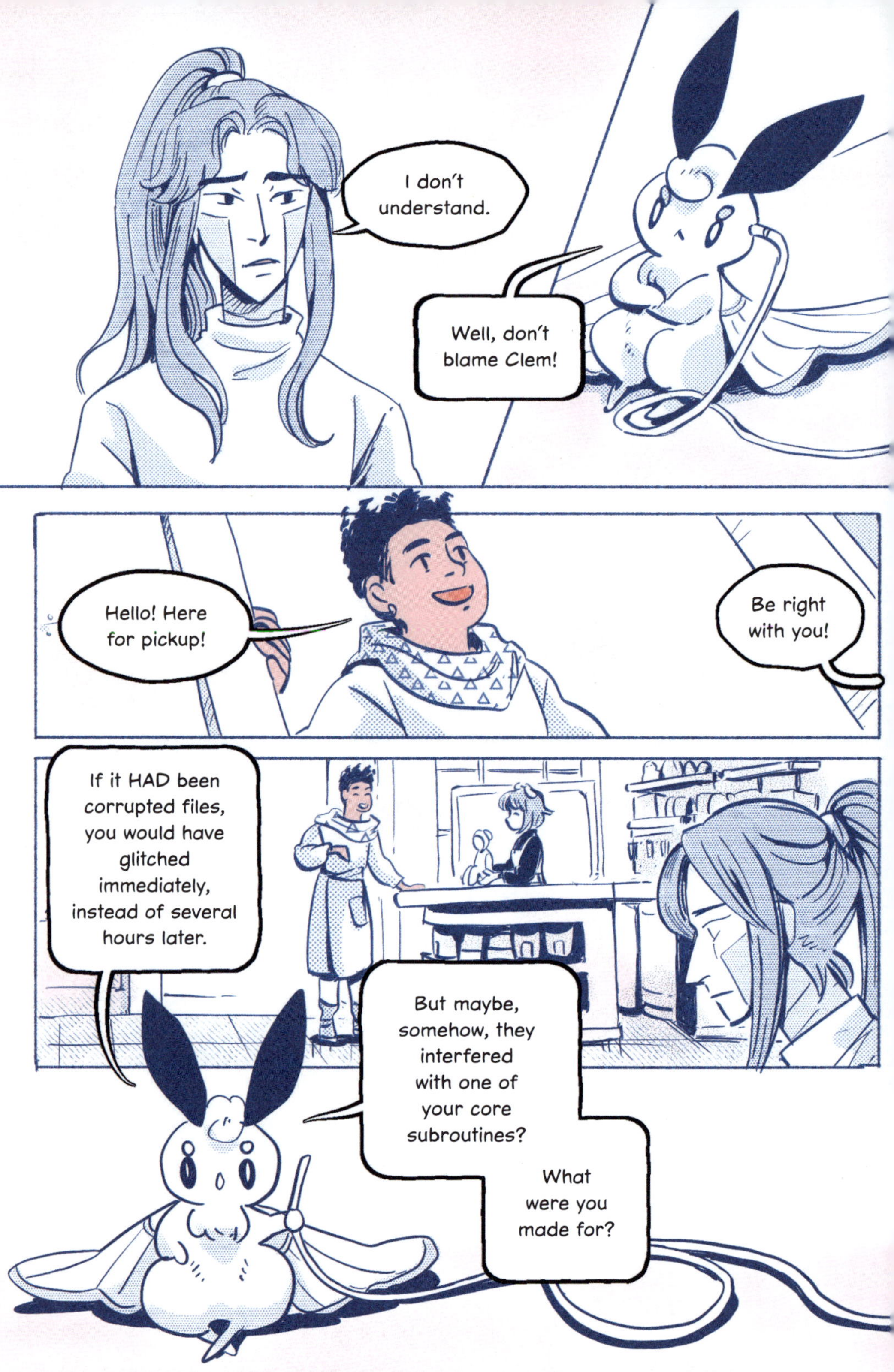
I don't understand.
Well, don't blame Clem!
Hello! Here for pickup!
Be right with you!
If it HAD been corrupted files, you would have glitched immediately, instead of several hours later.
But maybe, somehow, they interfered with one of your core subroutines?
What were you made for?

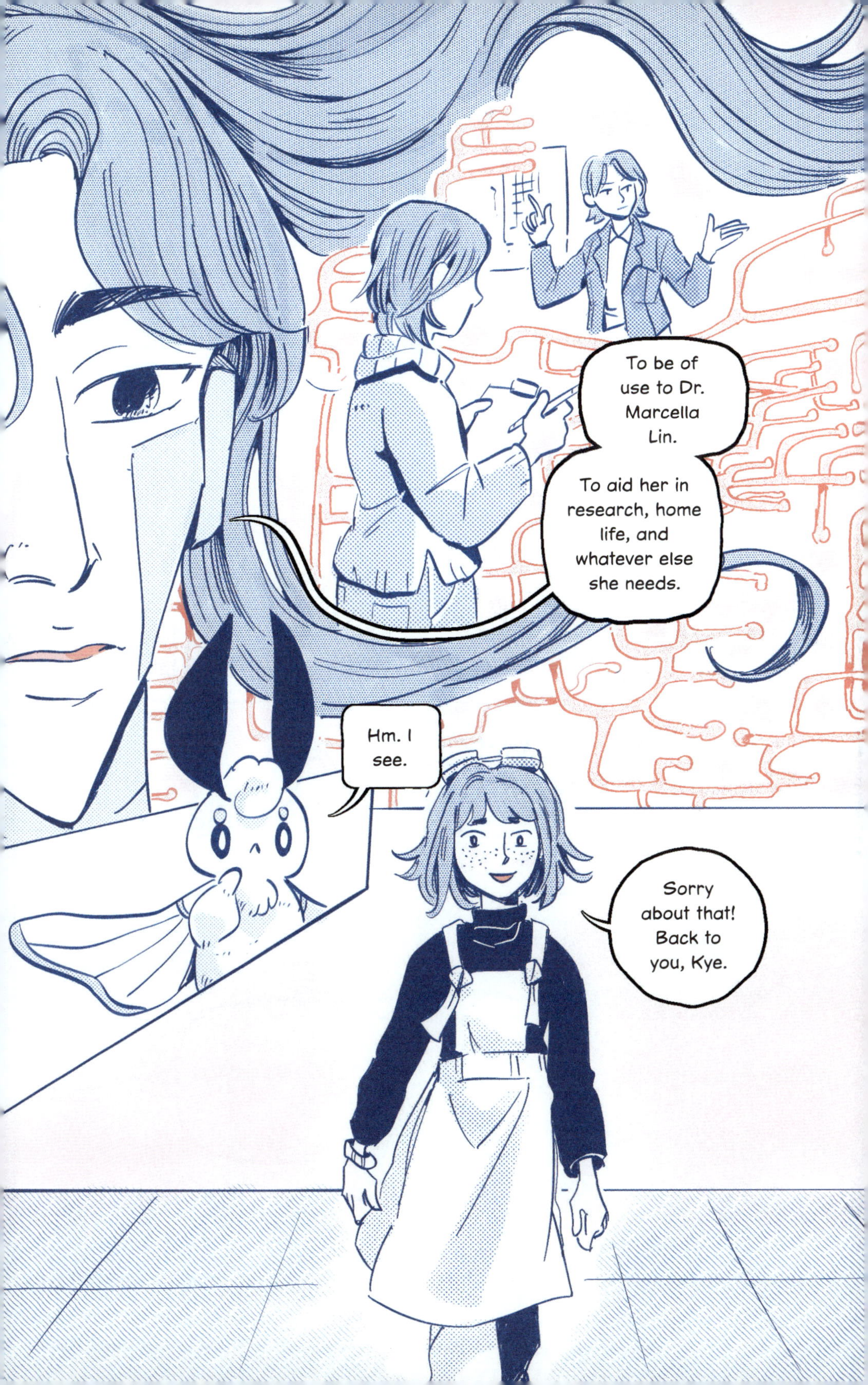
To be of use to Dr. Marcella Lin.
To aid her in research, home life, and whatever else she needs.
Hm. I see.
Sorry about that! Back to you, Kye.

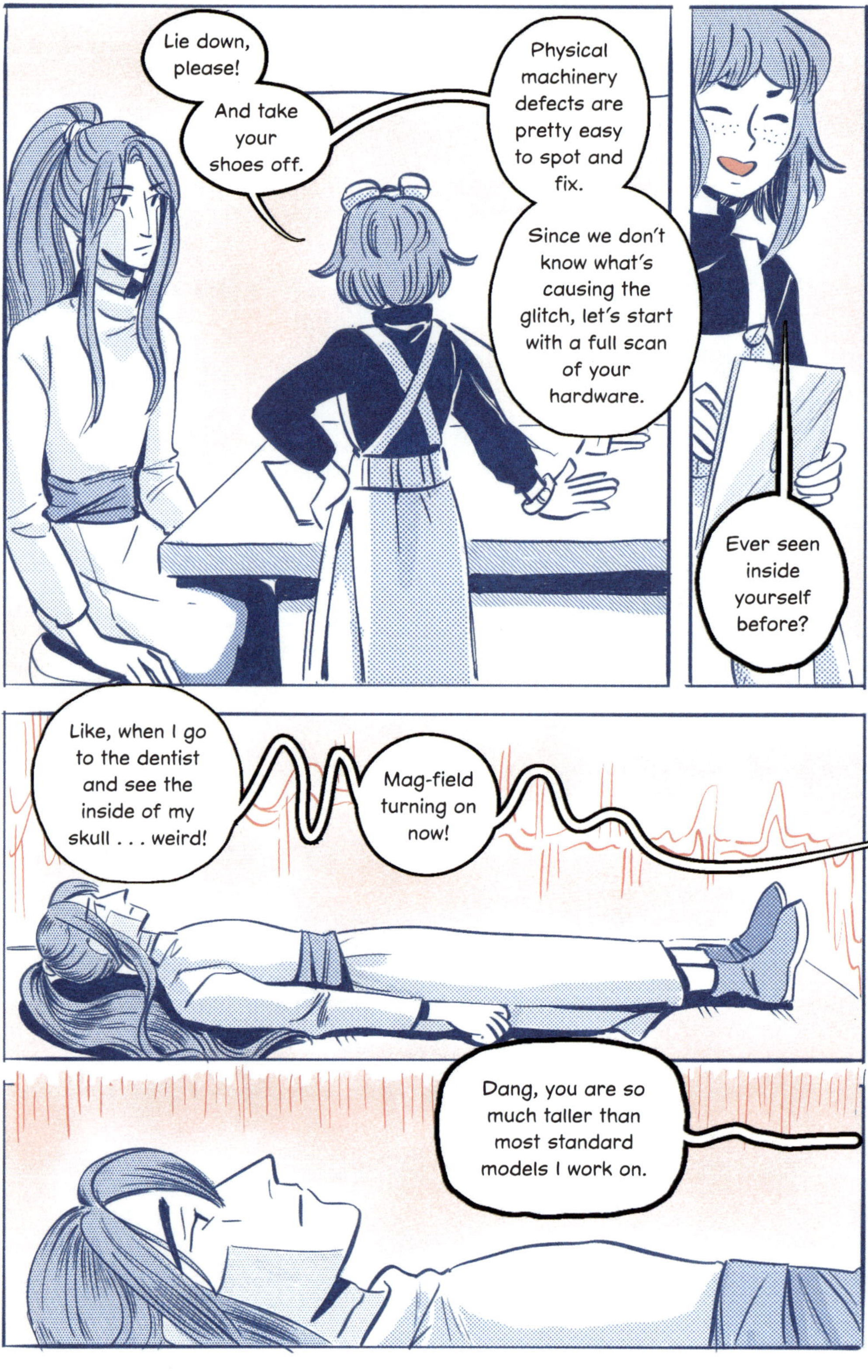
Lie down, please!
And take your shoes off.
Physical machinery defects are pretty easy to spot and fix.
Since we don't know what's causing the glitch, let's start with a full scan of your hardware.
Ever seen inside yourself before?
Like, when I go to the dentist and see the inside of my skull . . . weird!
Mag-field turning on now!
Dang, you are so much taller than most standard models I work on.

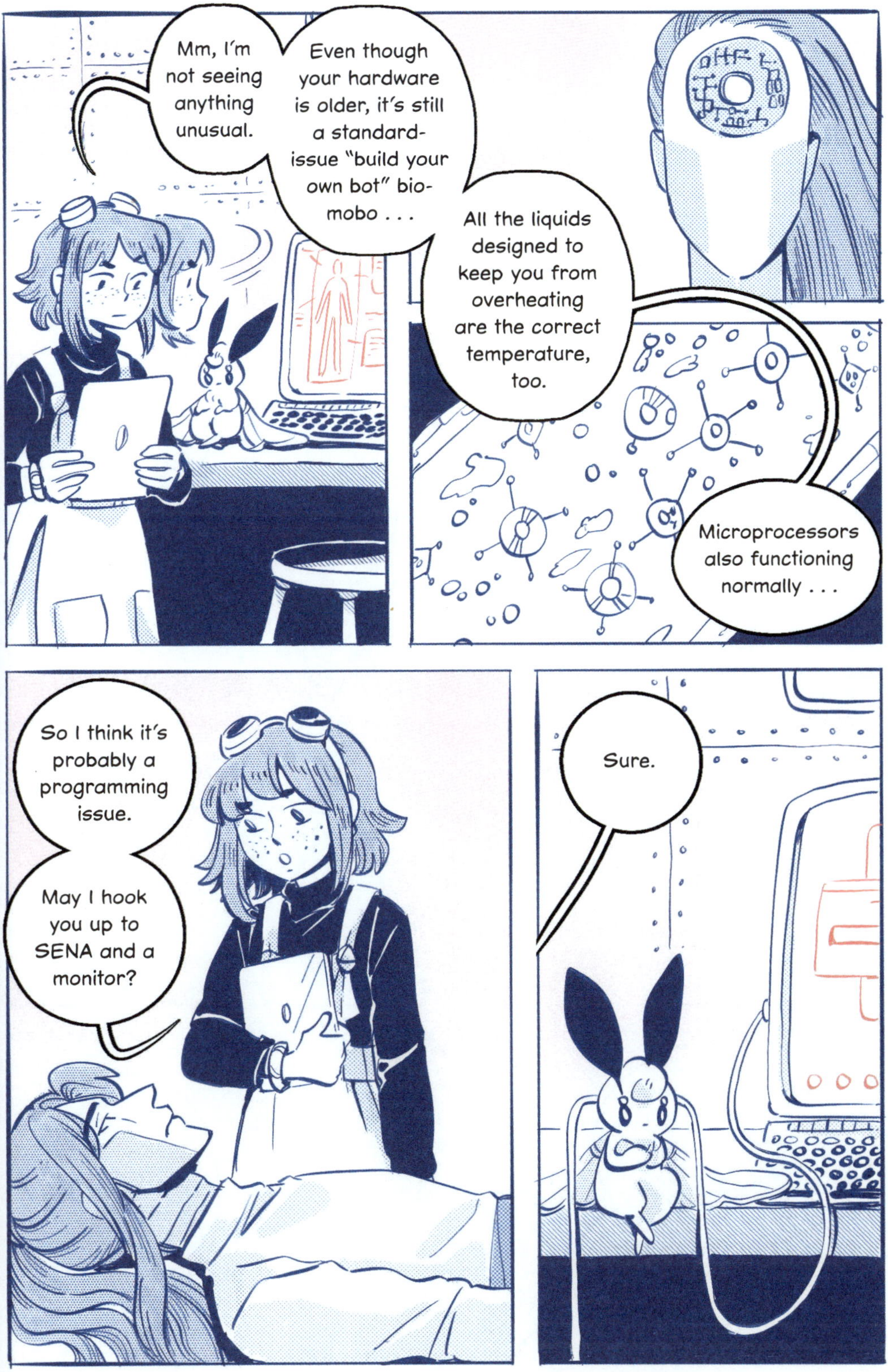
Mm, I'm not seeing anything unusual.
Even though your hardware is older, it's still a standard-issue "build your own bot" bio-mobo . . .
All the liquids designed to keep you from overheating are the correct temperature, too.
Microprocessors also functioning normally . . .
So I think it's probably a programming issue.
May I hook you up to SENA and a monitor?
Sure.

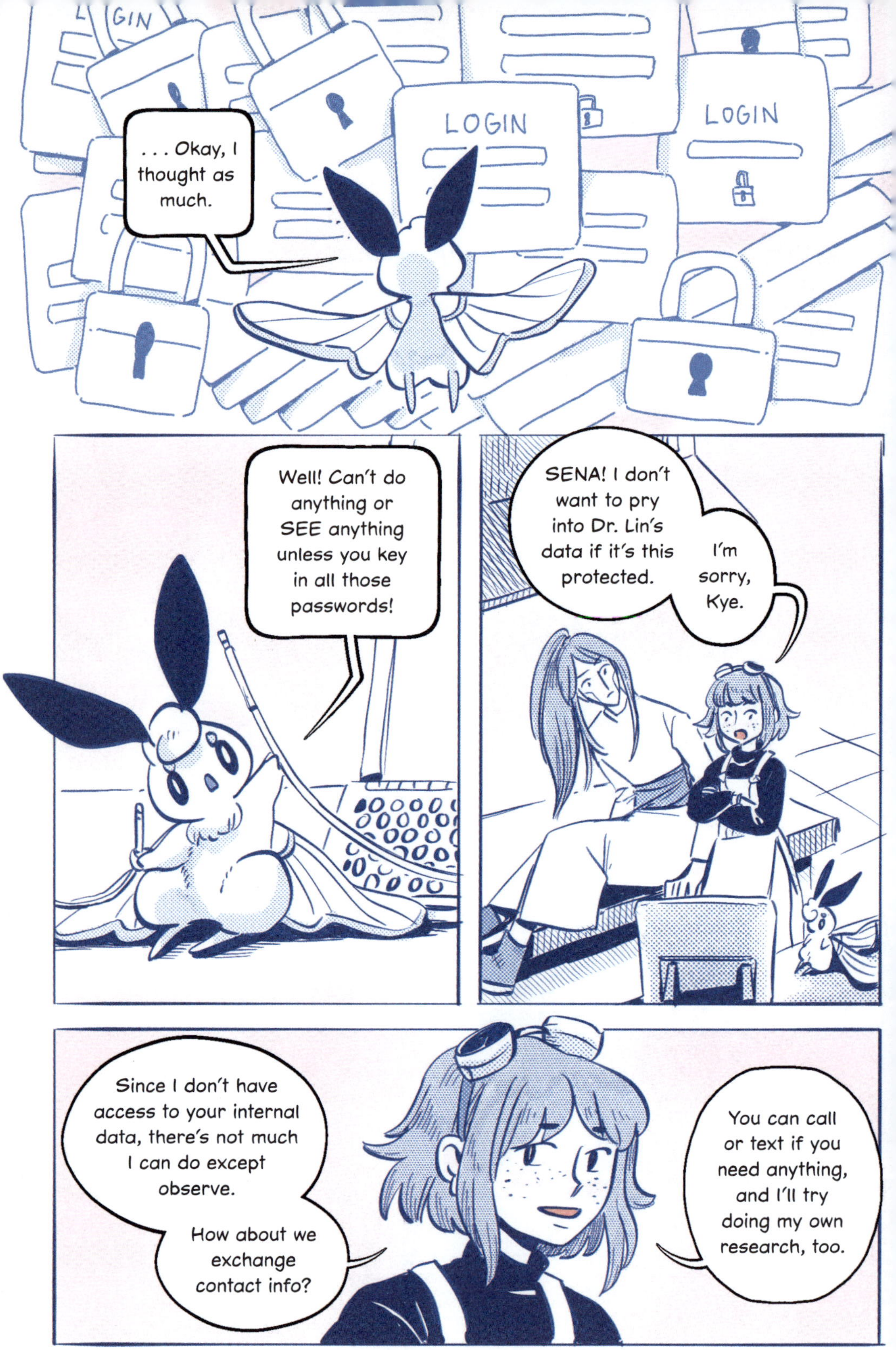
LOGIN
LOGIN
. . . Okay, I thought as much.
Well! Can't do anything or SEE anything unless you key in all those passwords!
SENA! I don't want to pry into Dr. Lin's data if it's this protected.
I'm sorry, Kye.
Since I don't have access to your internal data, there's not much I can do except observe.
How about we exchange contact info?
You can call or text if you need anything, and I'll try doing my own research, too.

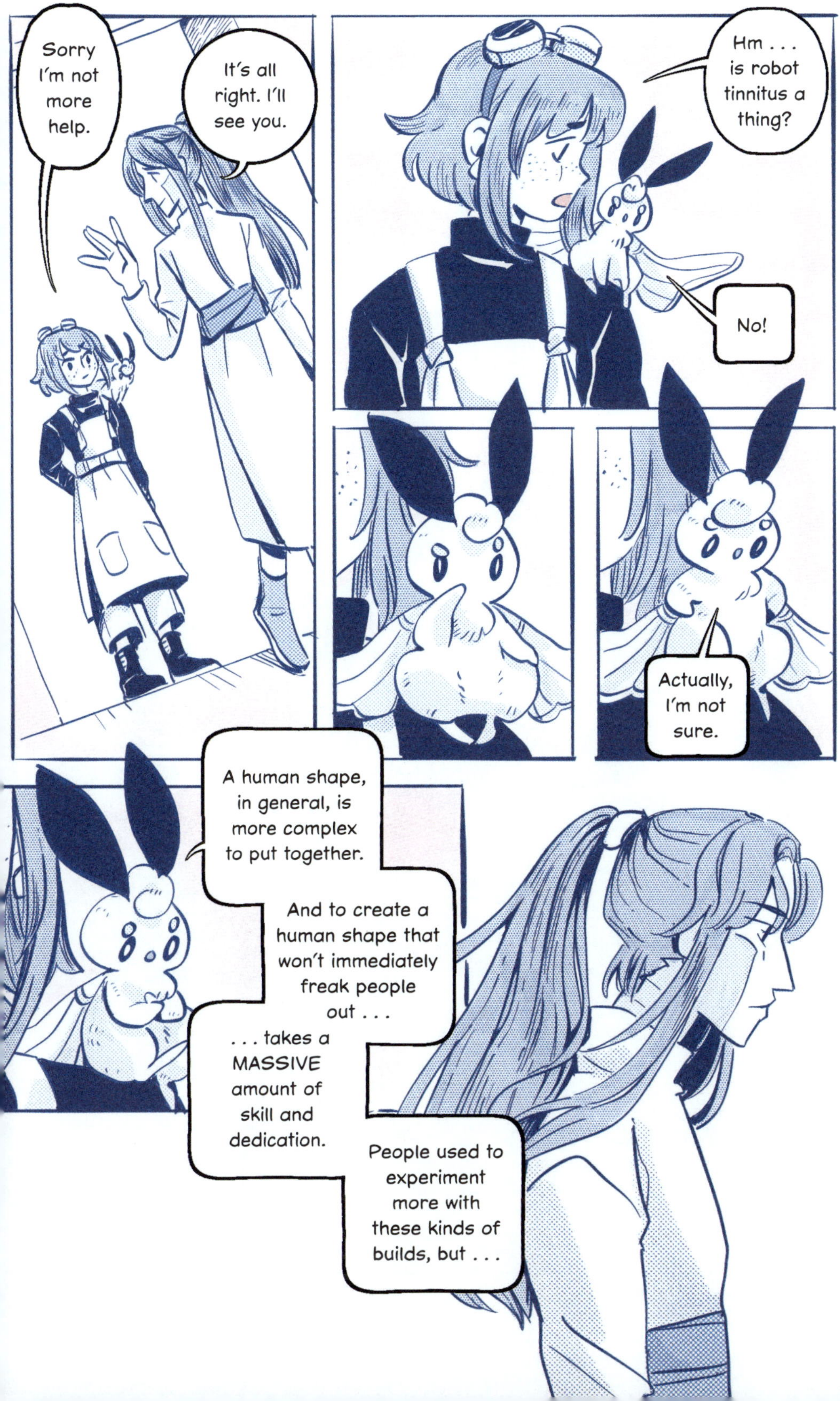
Sorry I'm not more help.
It's all right. I'll see you.
Hm . . . is robot tinnitus a thing?
No!
Actually, I'm not sure.
A human shape, in general, is more complex to put together.
And to create a human shape that won't immediately freak people out . . .
. . . takes a MASSIVE amount of skill and dedication.
People used to experiment more with these kinds of builds, but . . .

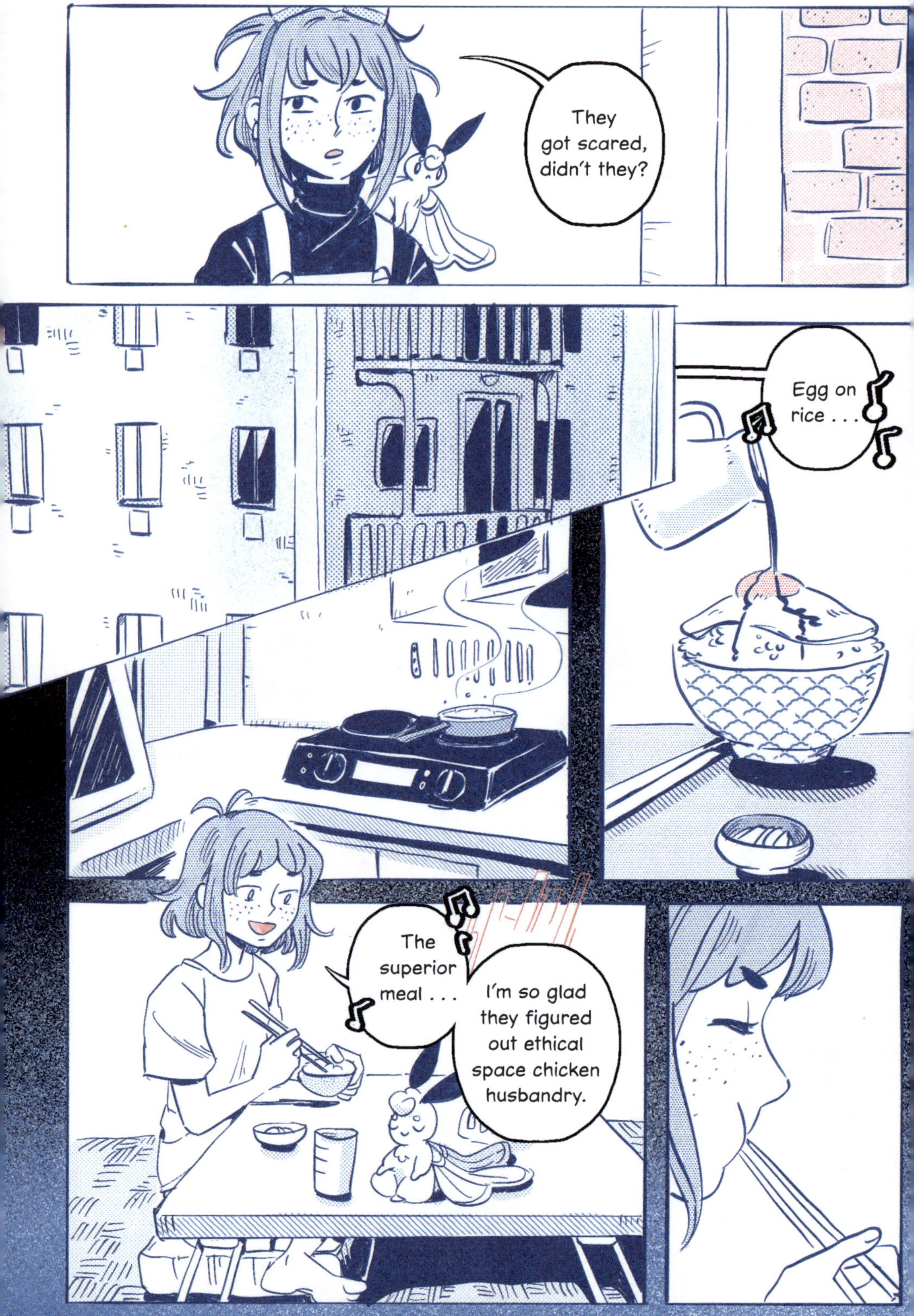
They got scared, didn't they?
Egg on rice . . .
The superior meal . . .
I'm so glad they figured out ethical space chicken husbandry.

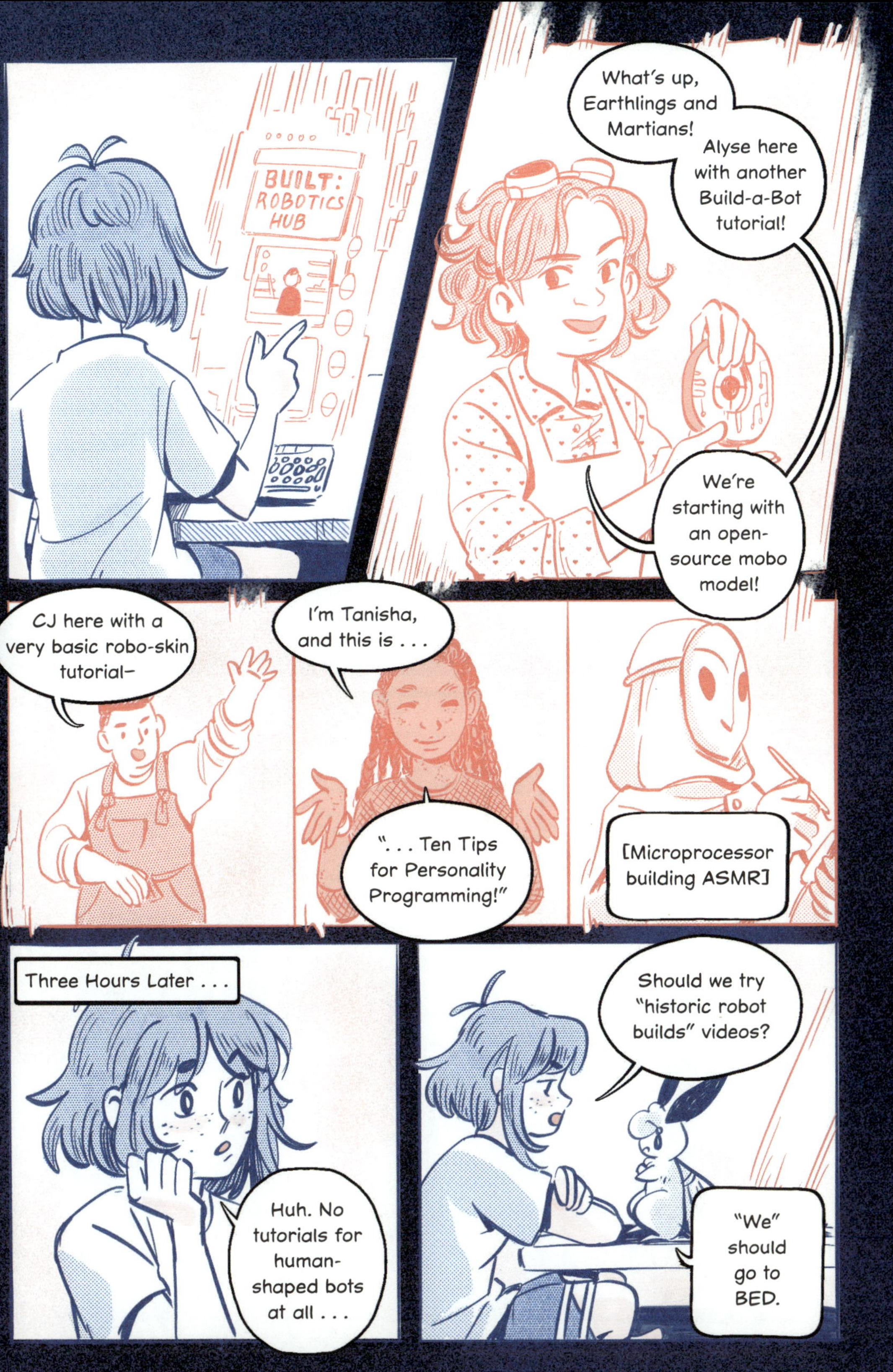
BUILT: ROBOTICS HUB
What's up, Earthlings and Martians!
Alyse here with another Build-a-Bot tutorial!
We're starting with an open-source mobo model!
CJ here with a very basic robo-skin tutorial–
I'm Tanisha, and this is . . .
". . . Ten Tips for Personality Programming!"
[Microprocessor building ASMR]
Three Hours Later . . .
Huh. No tutorials for human-shaped bots at all . . .
Should we try "historic robot builds" videos?
"We" should go to BED.

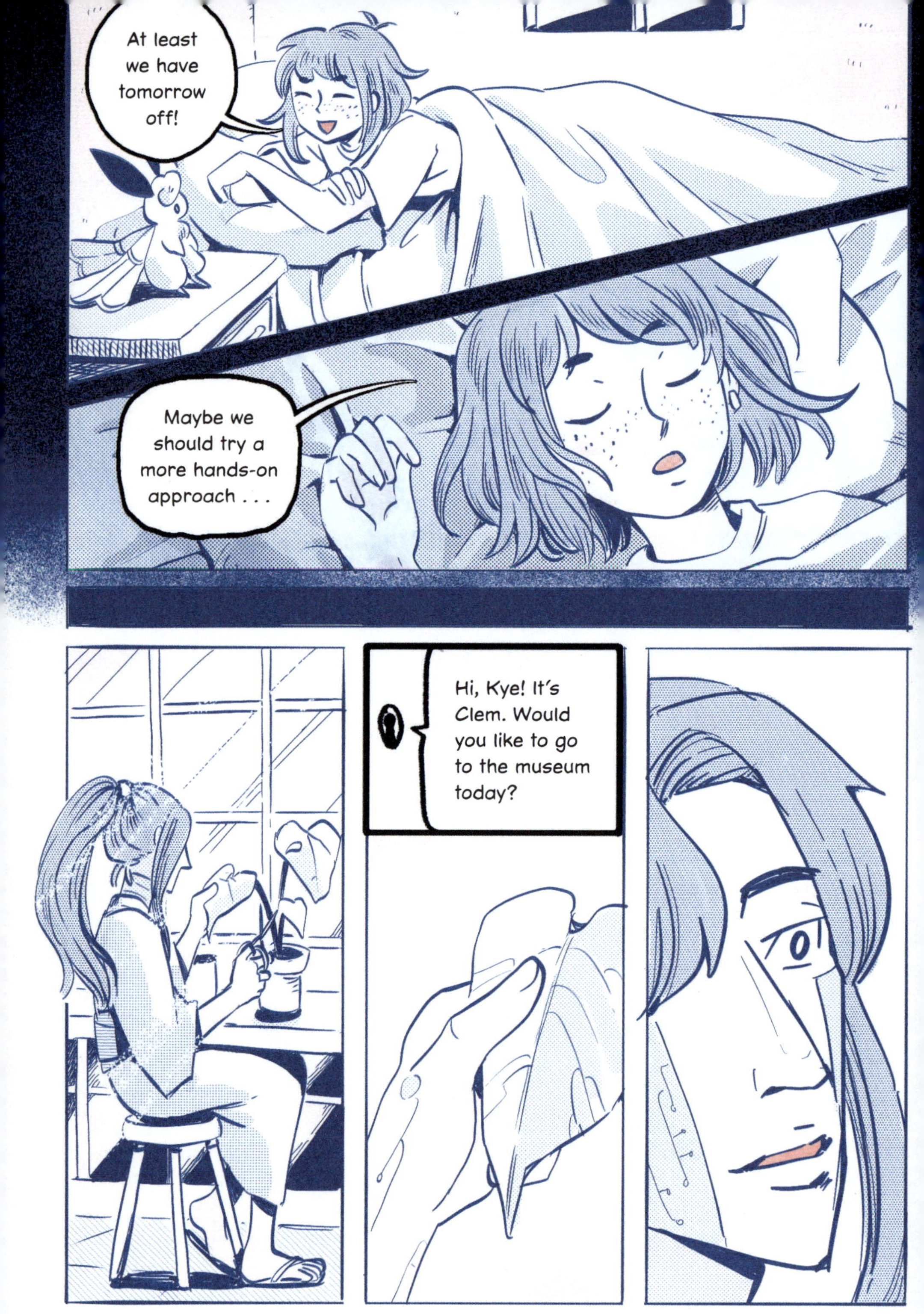
At least we have tomorrow off!
Maybe we should try a more hands-on approach . . .
Hi, Kye! It's Clem. Would you like to go to the museum today?

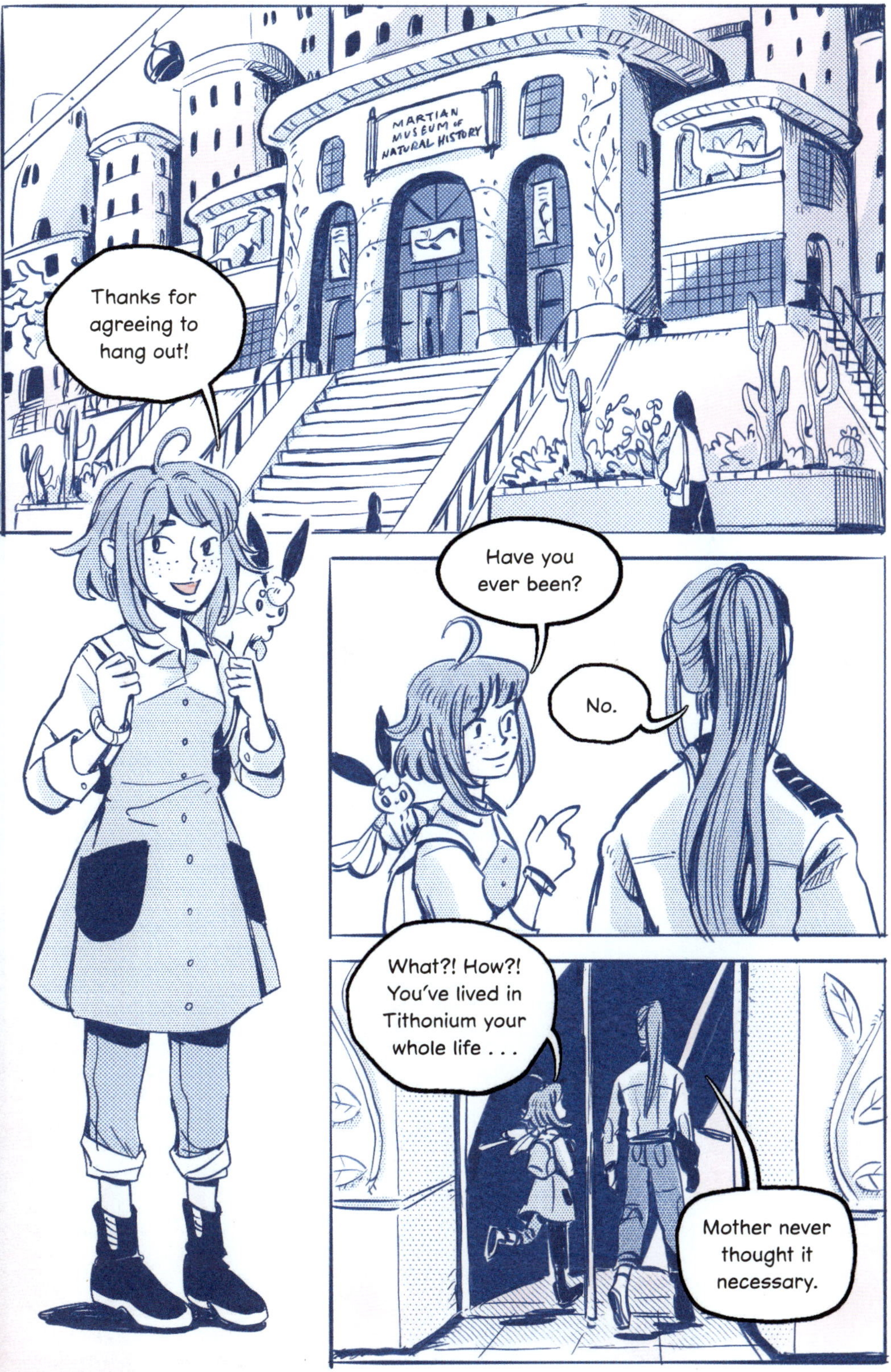
MARTIAN MUSEUM of NATURAL HISTORY
Thanks for agreeing to hang out!
Have you ever been?
No.
What?! How?! You've lived in Tithonium your whole life . . .
Mother never thought it necessary.

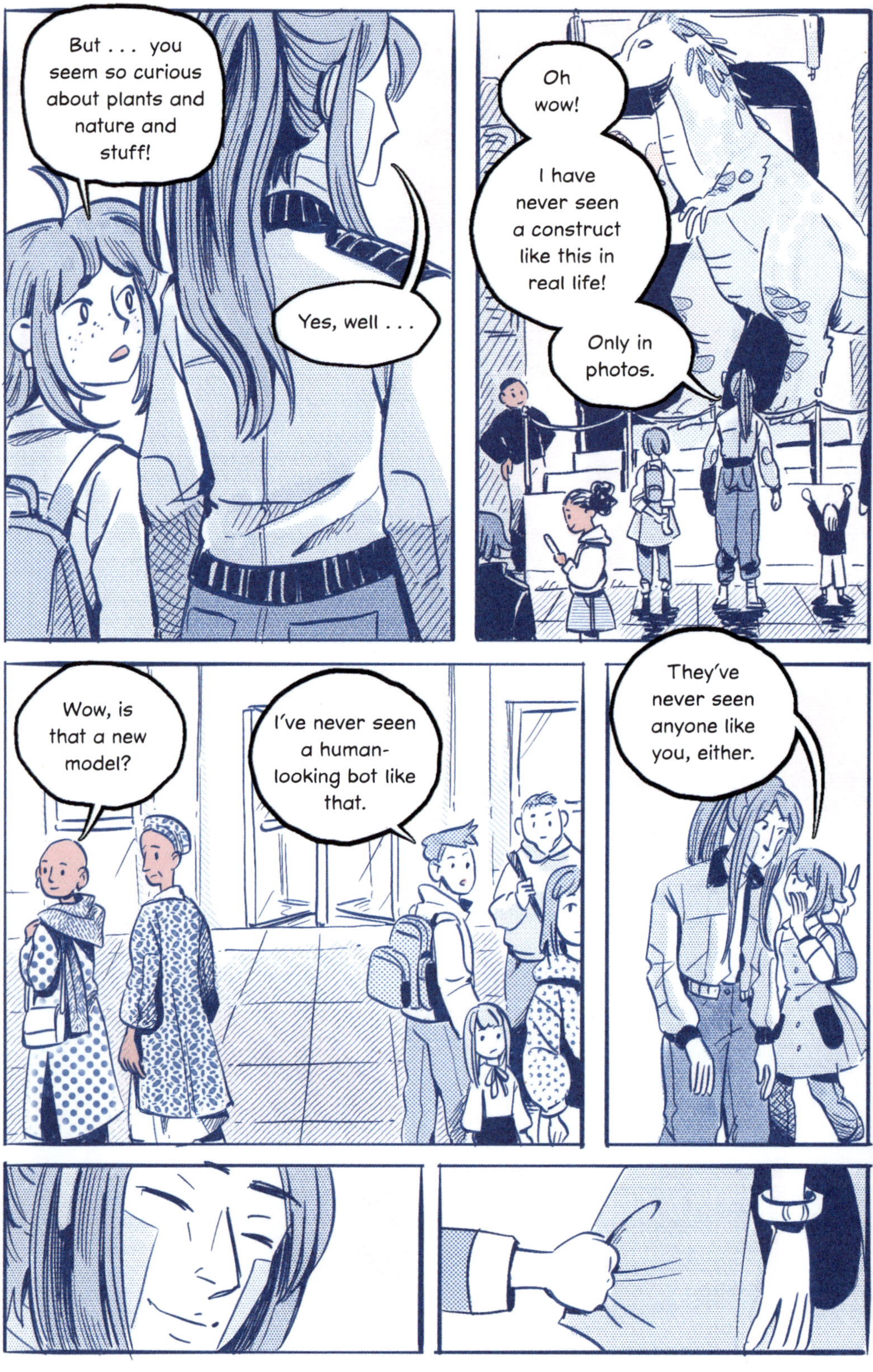
But . . . you seem so curious about plants and nature and stuff!
Yes, well . . .
Oh wow!
I have never seen a construct like this in real life!
Only in photos.
Wow, is that a new model?
I've never seen a human-looking bot like that.
They've never seen anyone like you, either.

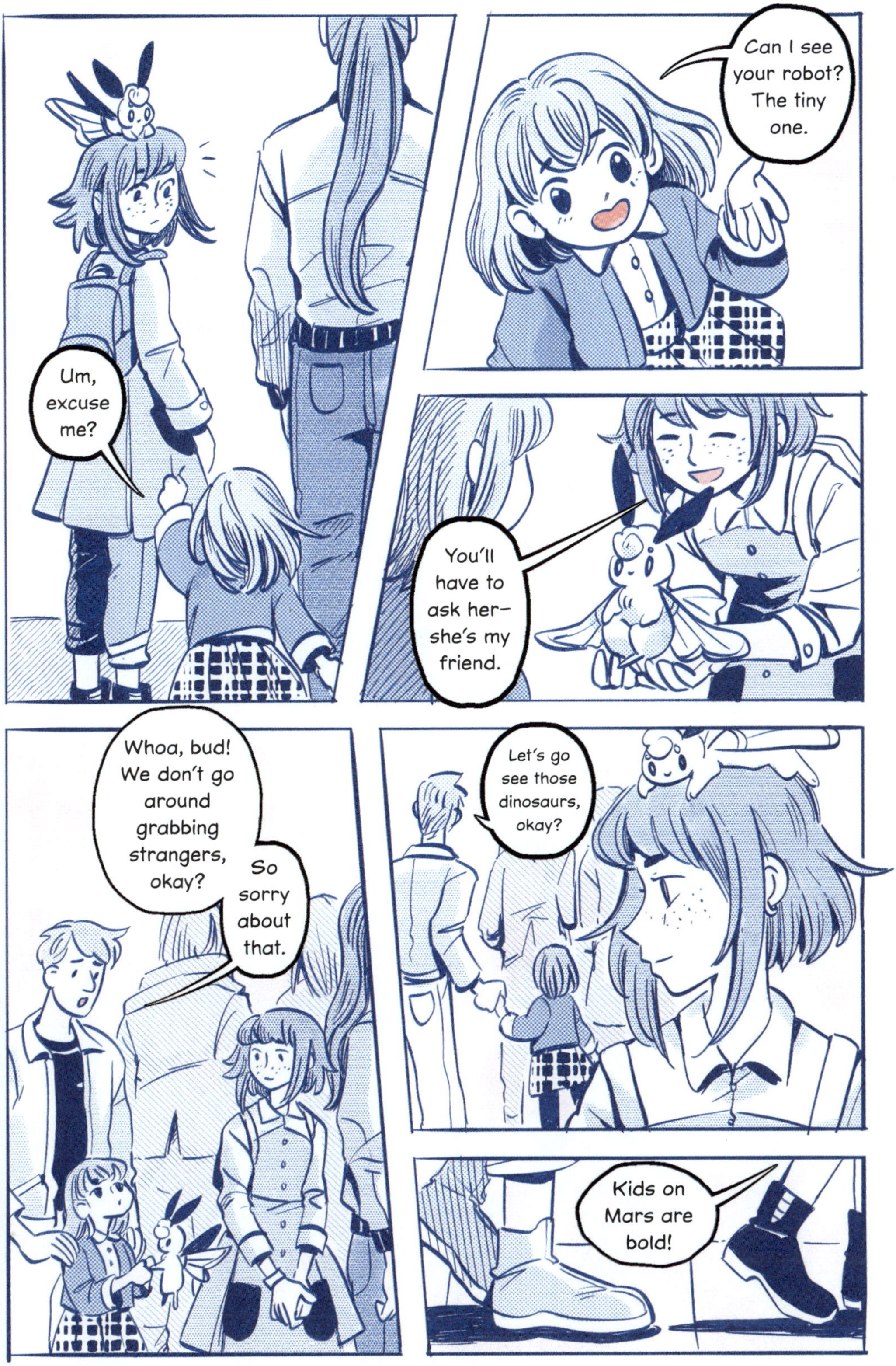
Um, excuse me?
Can I see your robot? The tiny one.
You'll have to ask her–she's my friend.
Whoa, bud! We don't go around grabbing strangers, okay?
So sorry about that.
Let's go see those dinosaurs, okay?
Kids on Mars are bold!

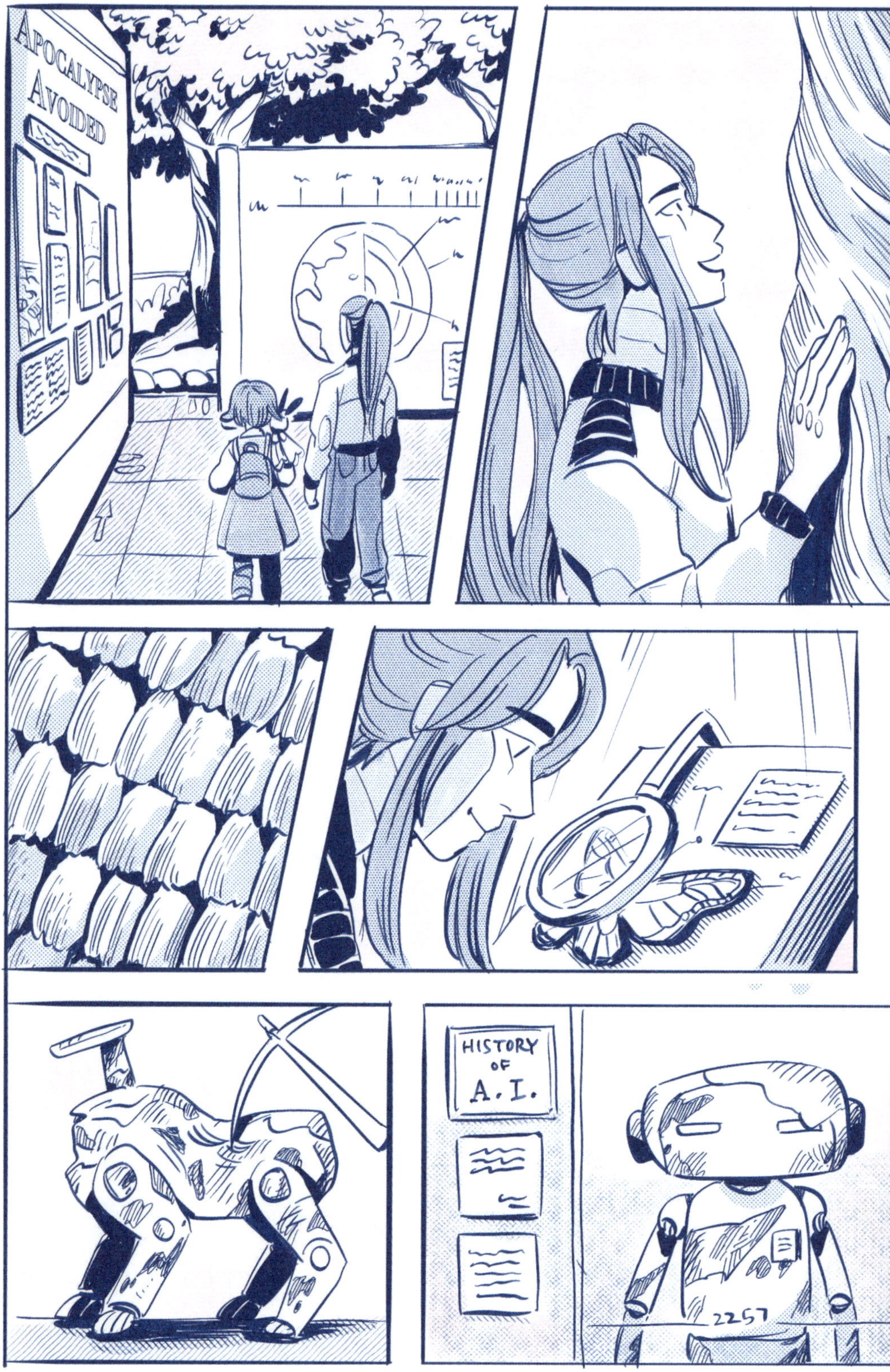
APOCALYPSE AVOIDED
HISTORY OF A.I.
2257

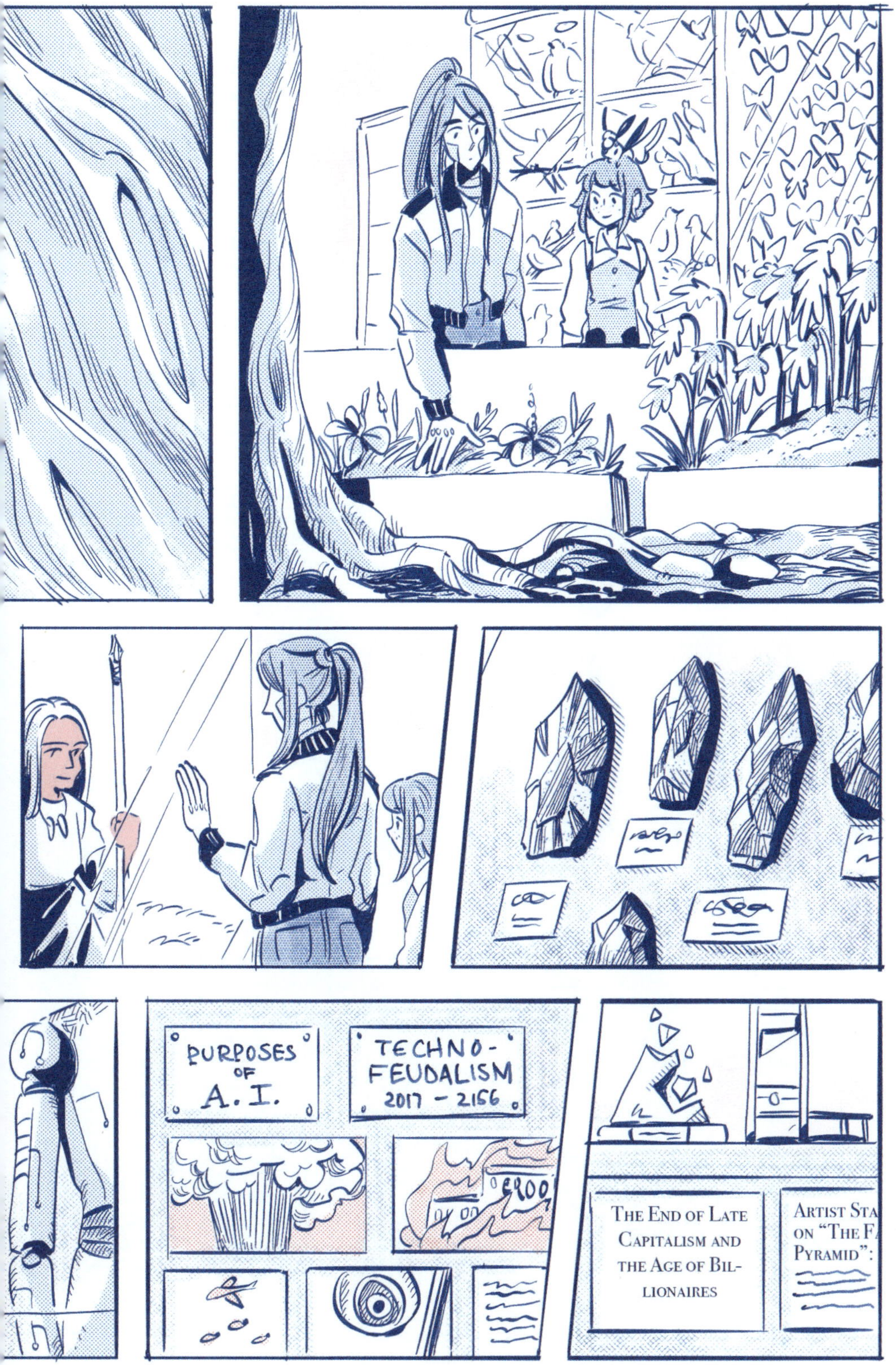
PURPOSES OF A.I.
TECHNO-FEUDALISM 2017 - 2156
THE END OF LATE CAPITALISM AND THE AGE OF BIL-LIONAIRES
ARTIST STA
ON "THE F
PYRAMID":

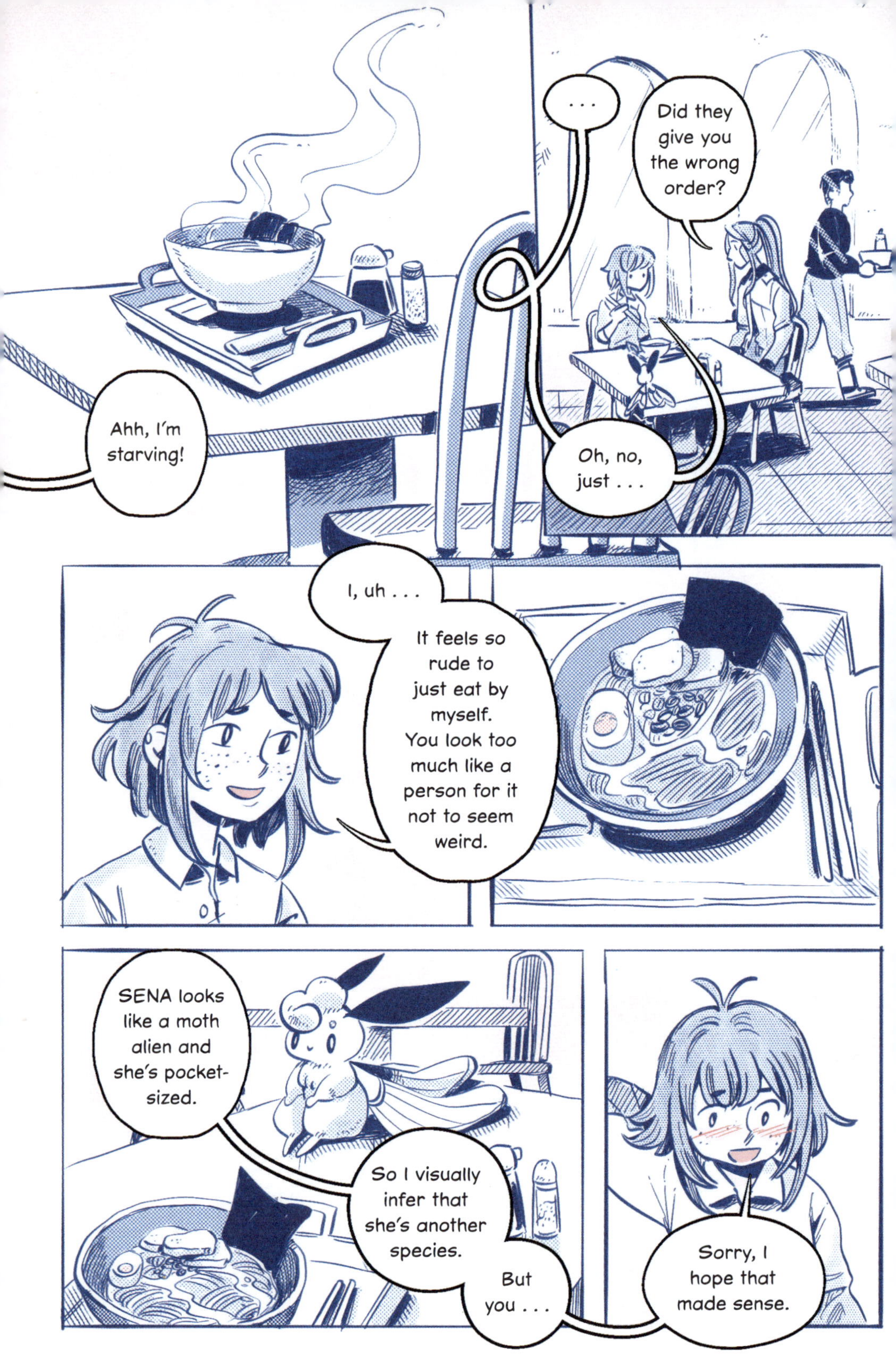
Ahh, I'm starving!
. . .
Did they give you the wrong order?
Oh, no, just . . .
I, uh . . .
It feels so rude to just eat by myself. You look too much like a person for it not to seem weird.
SENA looks like a moth alien and she's pocket-sized.
So I visually infer that she's another species.
But you . . .
Sorry, I hope that made sense.

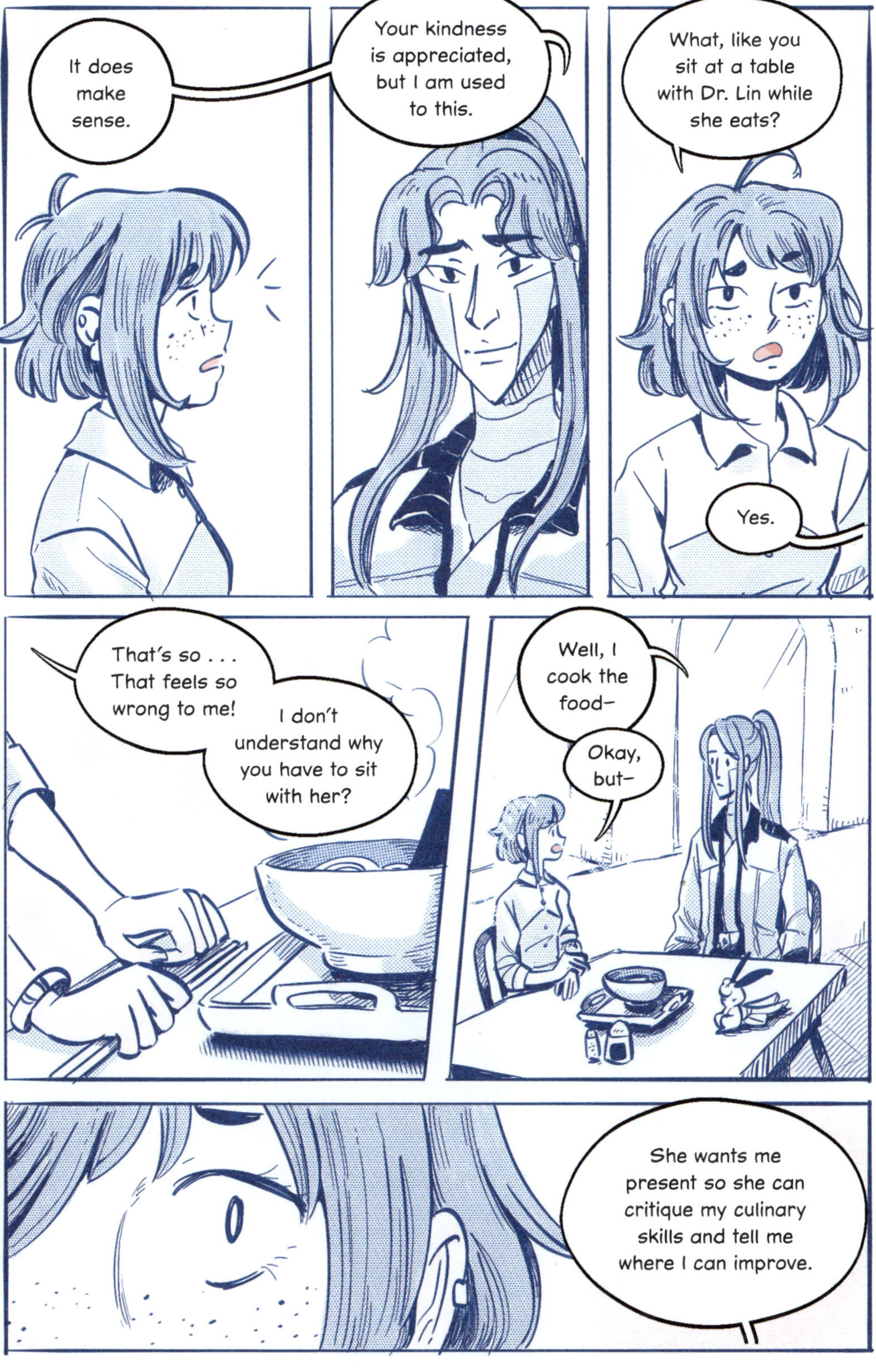
It does make sense.
Your kindness is appreciated, but I am used to this.
What, like you sit at a table with Dr. Lin while she eats?
Yes.
That's so . . . That feels so wrong to me!
I don't understand why you have to sit with her?
Well, I cook the food–
Okay, but–
She wants me present so she can critique my culinary skills and tell me where I can improve.

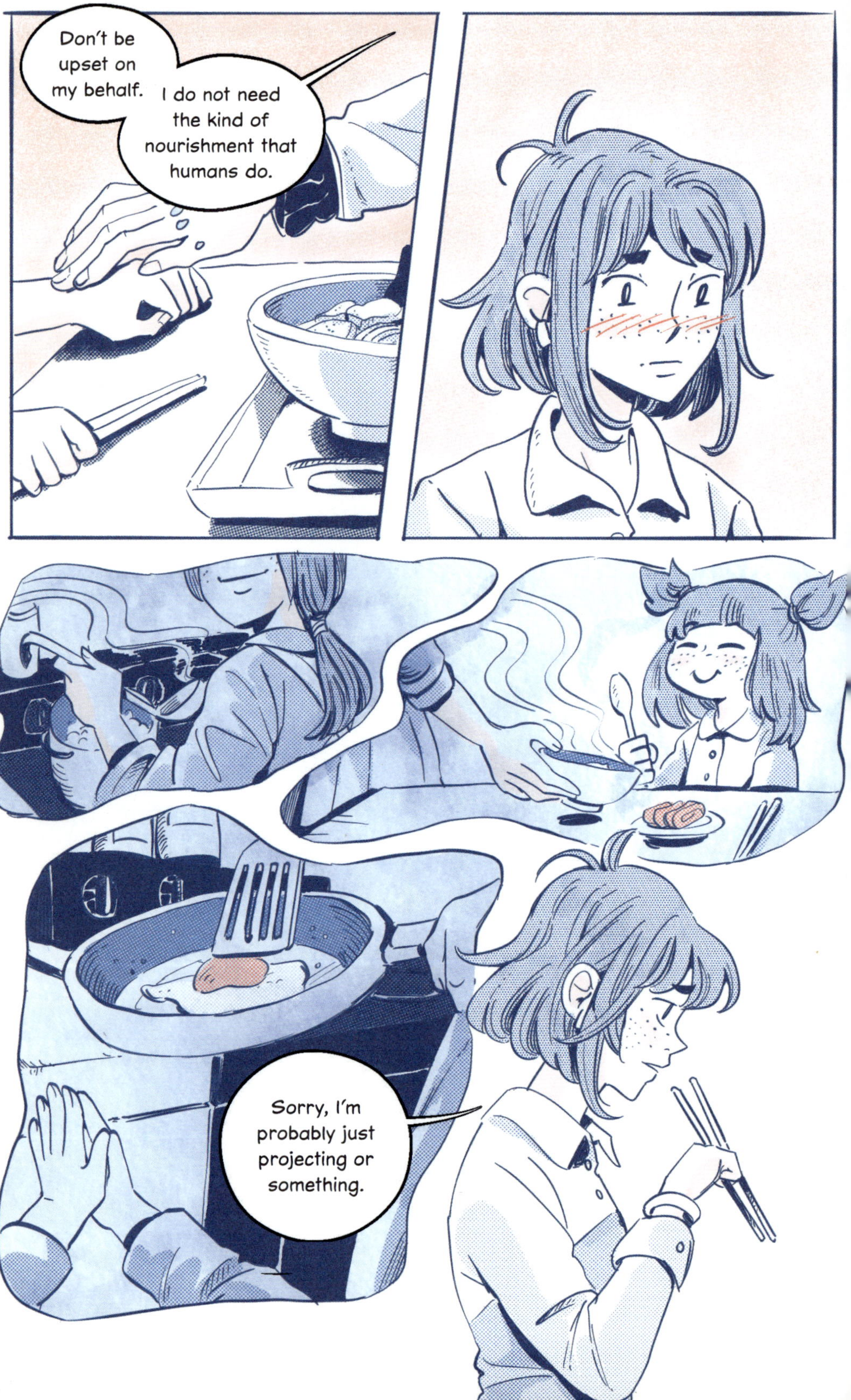
Don't be upset on my behalf.
I do not need the kind of nourishment that humans do.
Sorry, I'm probably just projecting or something.

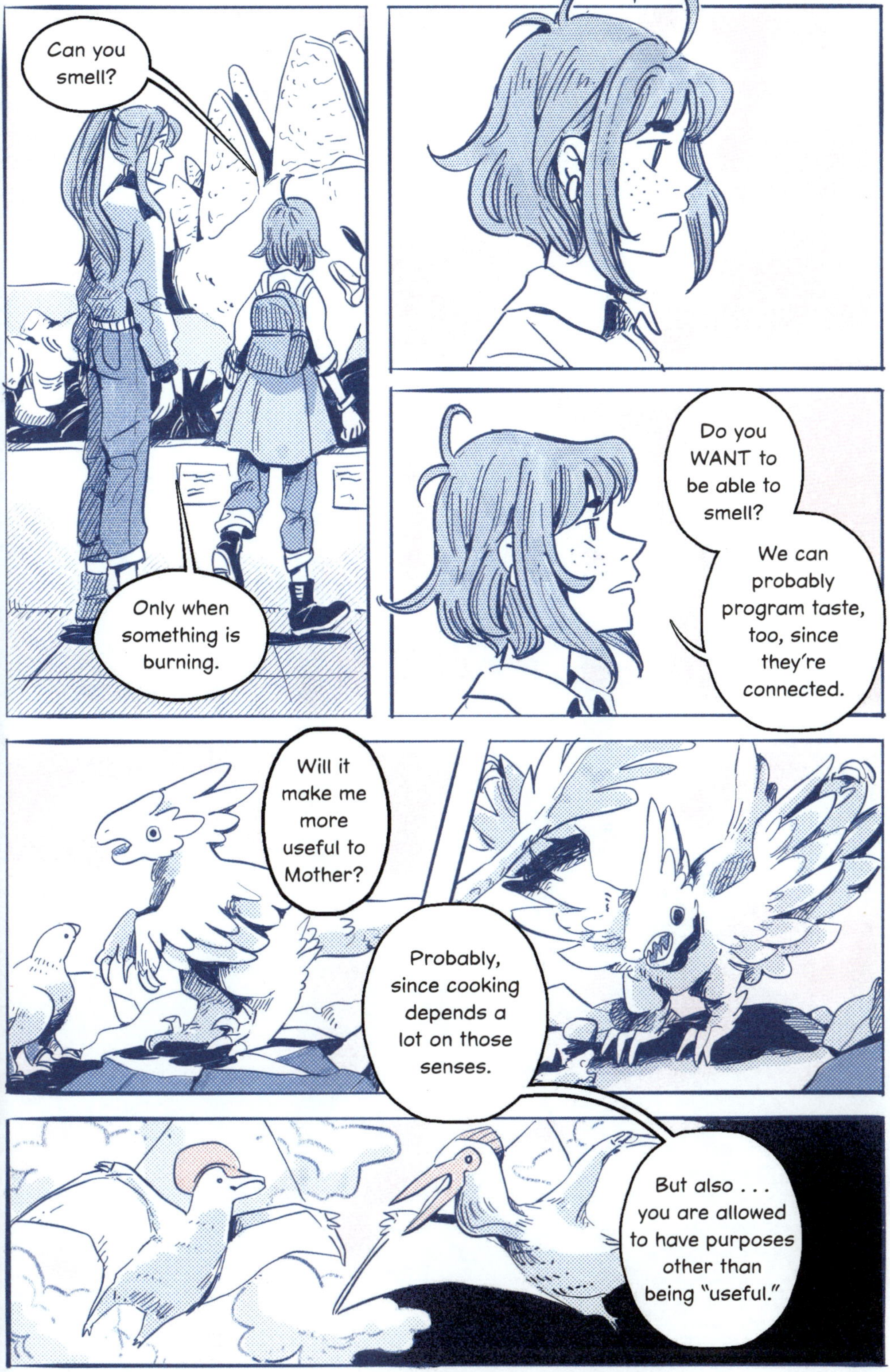
Can you smell?
Only when something is burning.
Do you WANT to be able to smell?
We can probably program taste, too, since they're connected.
Will it make me more useful to Mother?
Probably, since cooking depends a lot on those senses.
But also . . . you are allowed to have purposes other than being "useful."

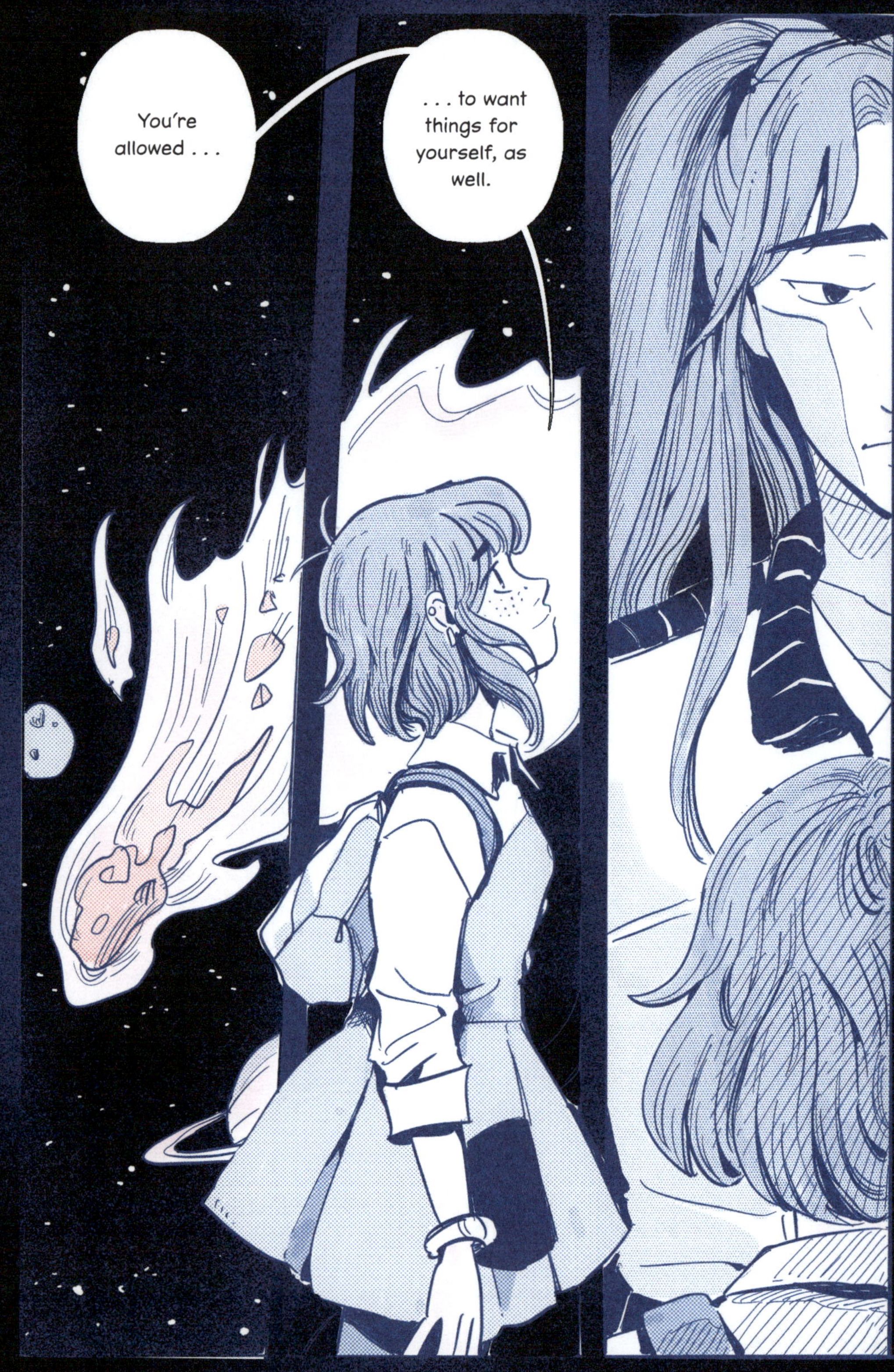
You're allowed . . .
. . . to want things for yourself, as well.

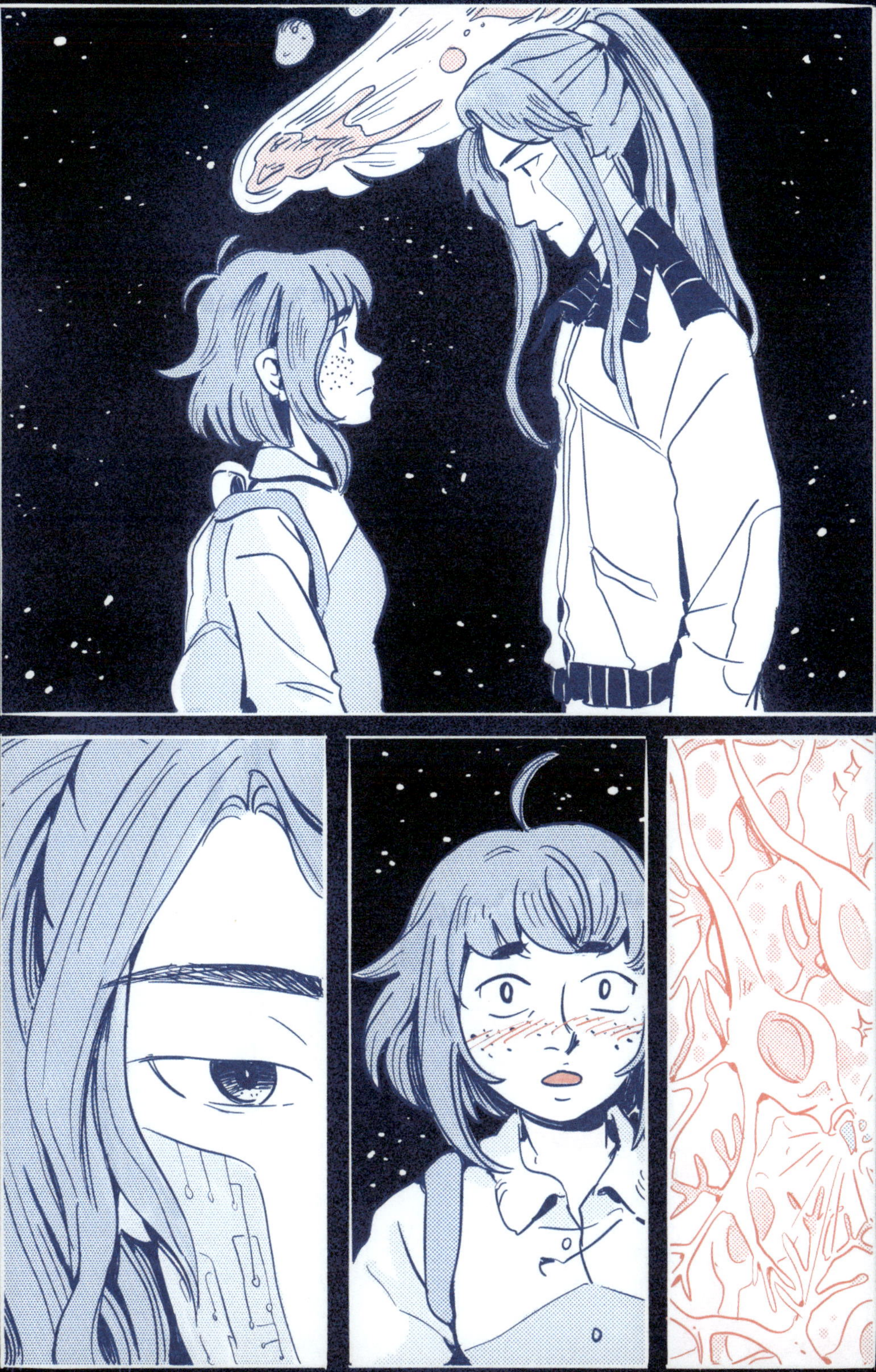

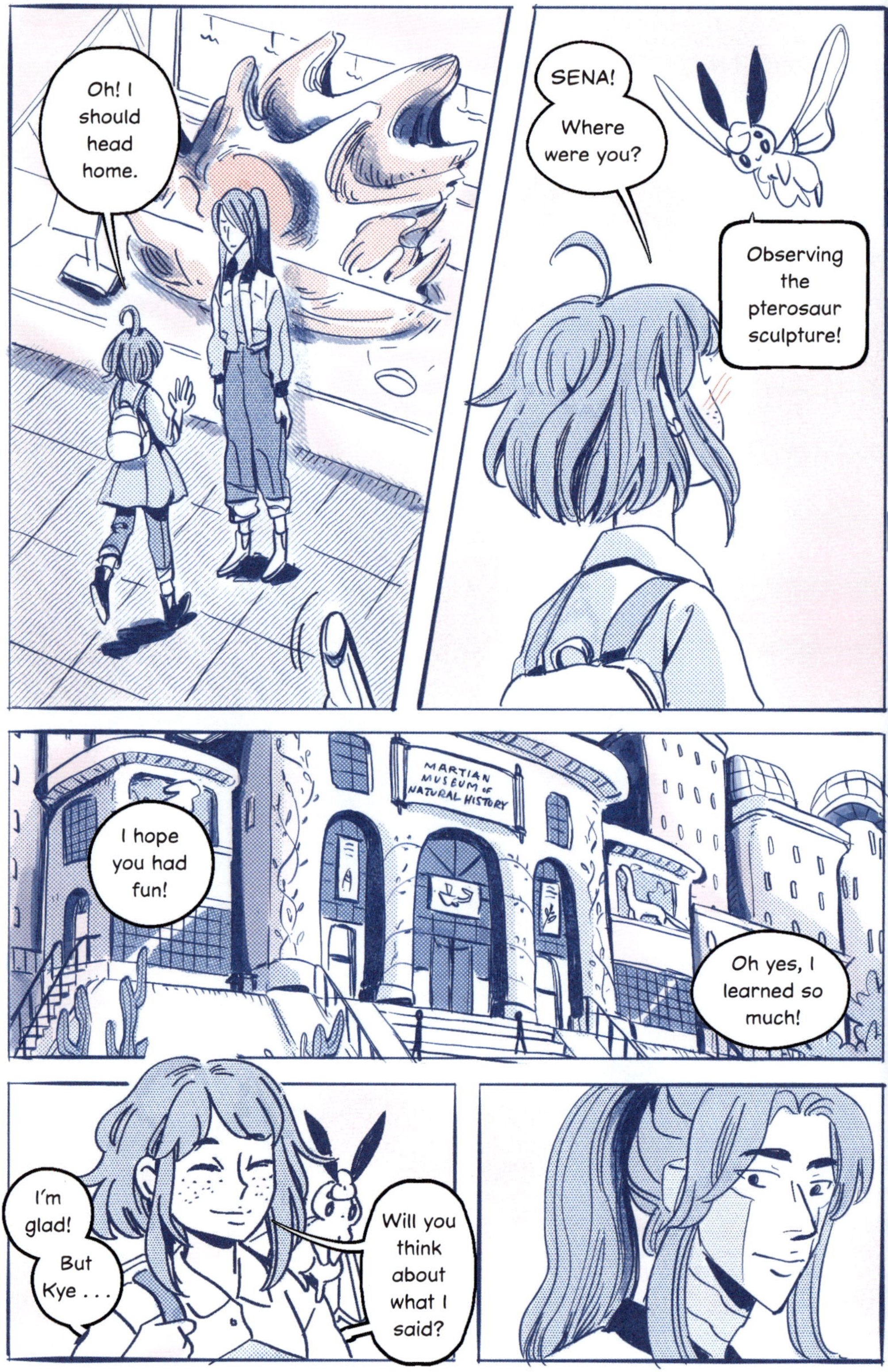
Oh! I should head home.
SENA!
Where were you?
Observing the pterosaur sculpture!
MARTIAN MUSEUM OF NATURAL HISTORY
I hope you had fun!
Oh yes, I learned so much!
I'm glad!
But Kye . . .
Will you think about what I said?

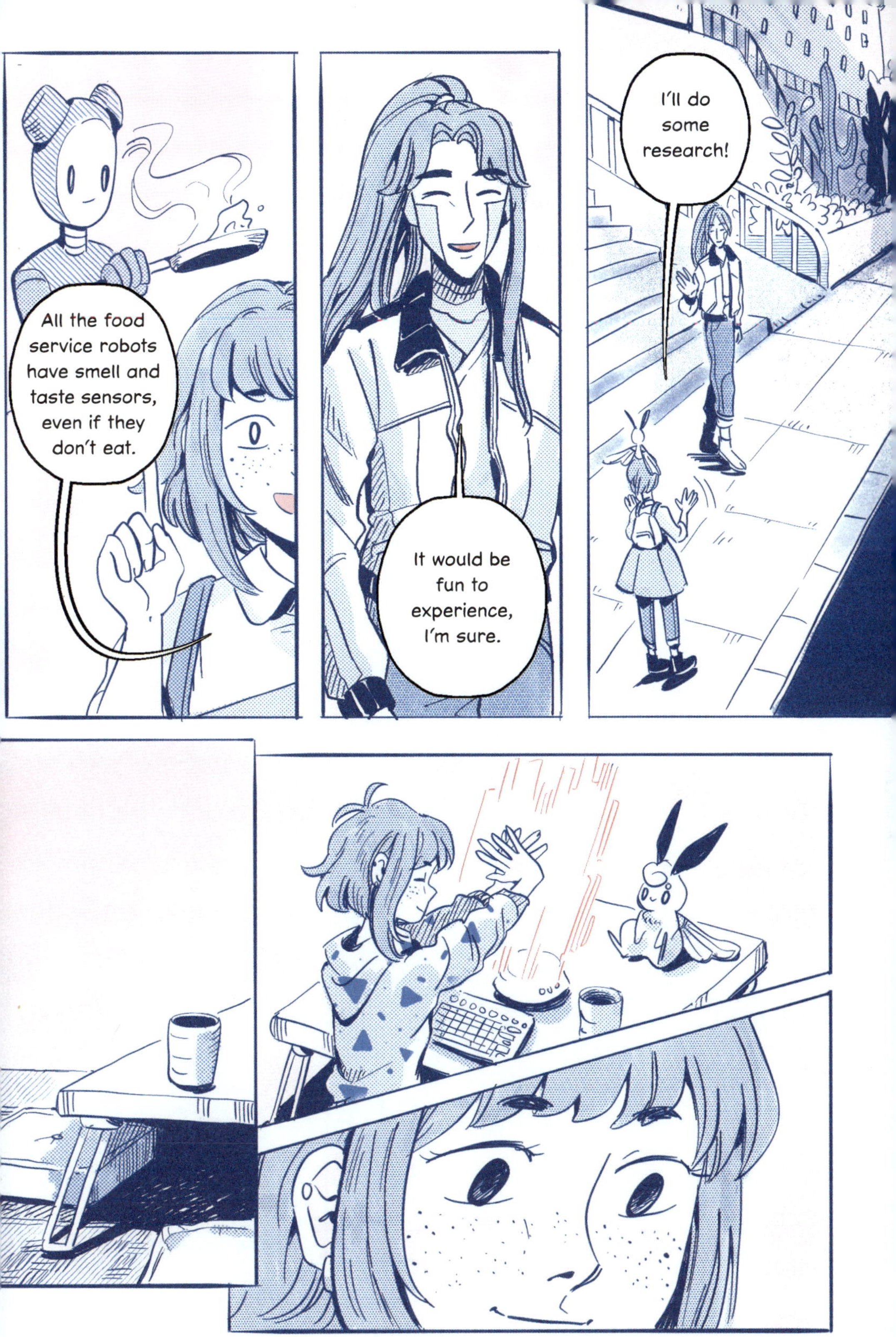
All the food service robots have smell and taste sensors, even if they don't eat.
It would be fun to experience, I'm sure.
I'll do some research!

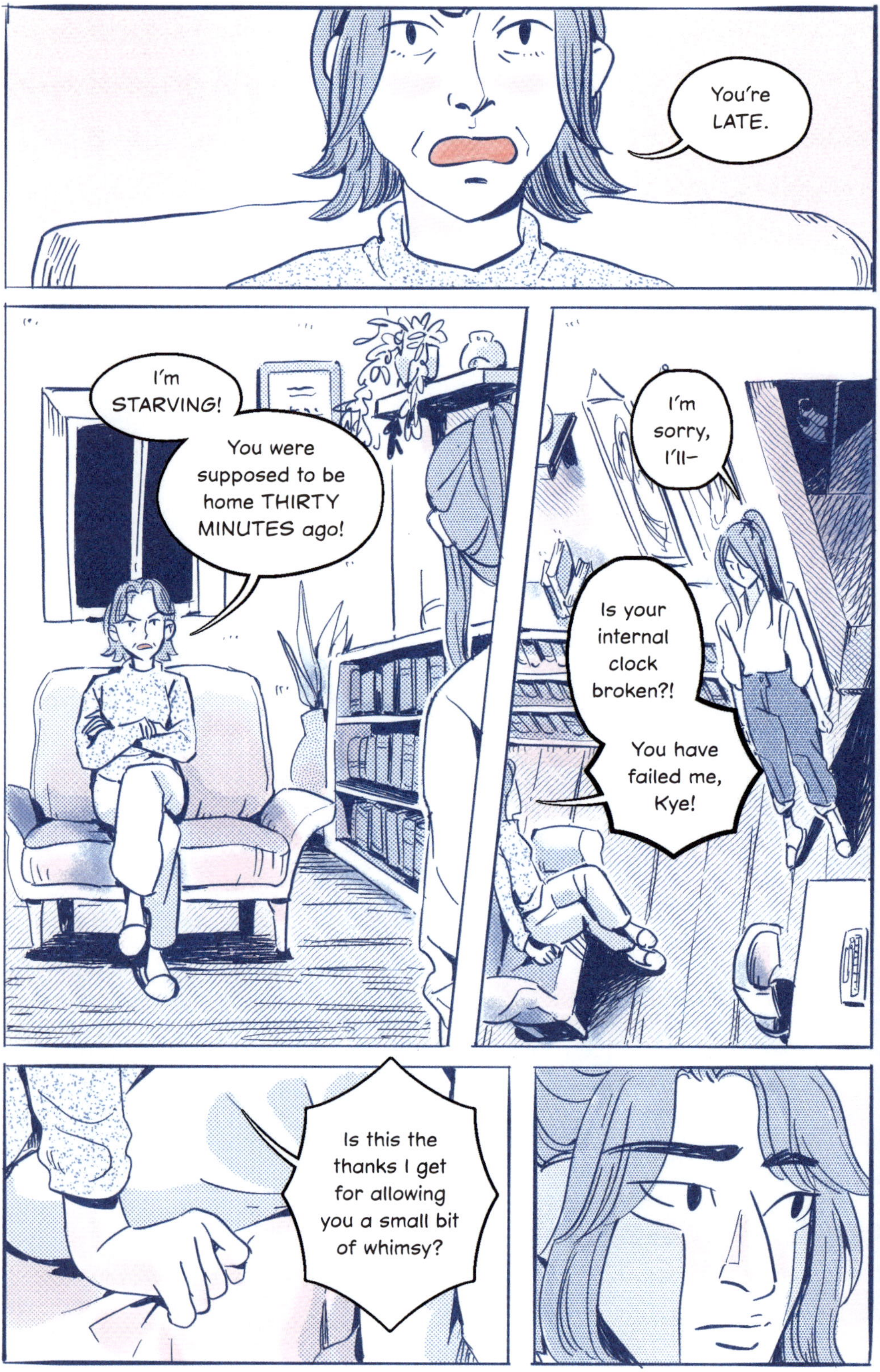
You're LATE.
I'm STARVING!
You were supposed to be home THIRTY MINUTES ago!
I'm sorry, I'll–
Is your internal clock broken?!
You have failed me, Kye!
Is this the thanks I get for allowing you a small bit of whimsy?

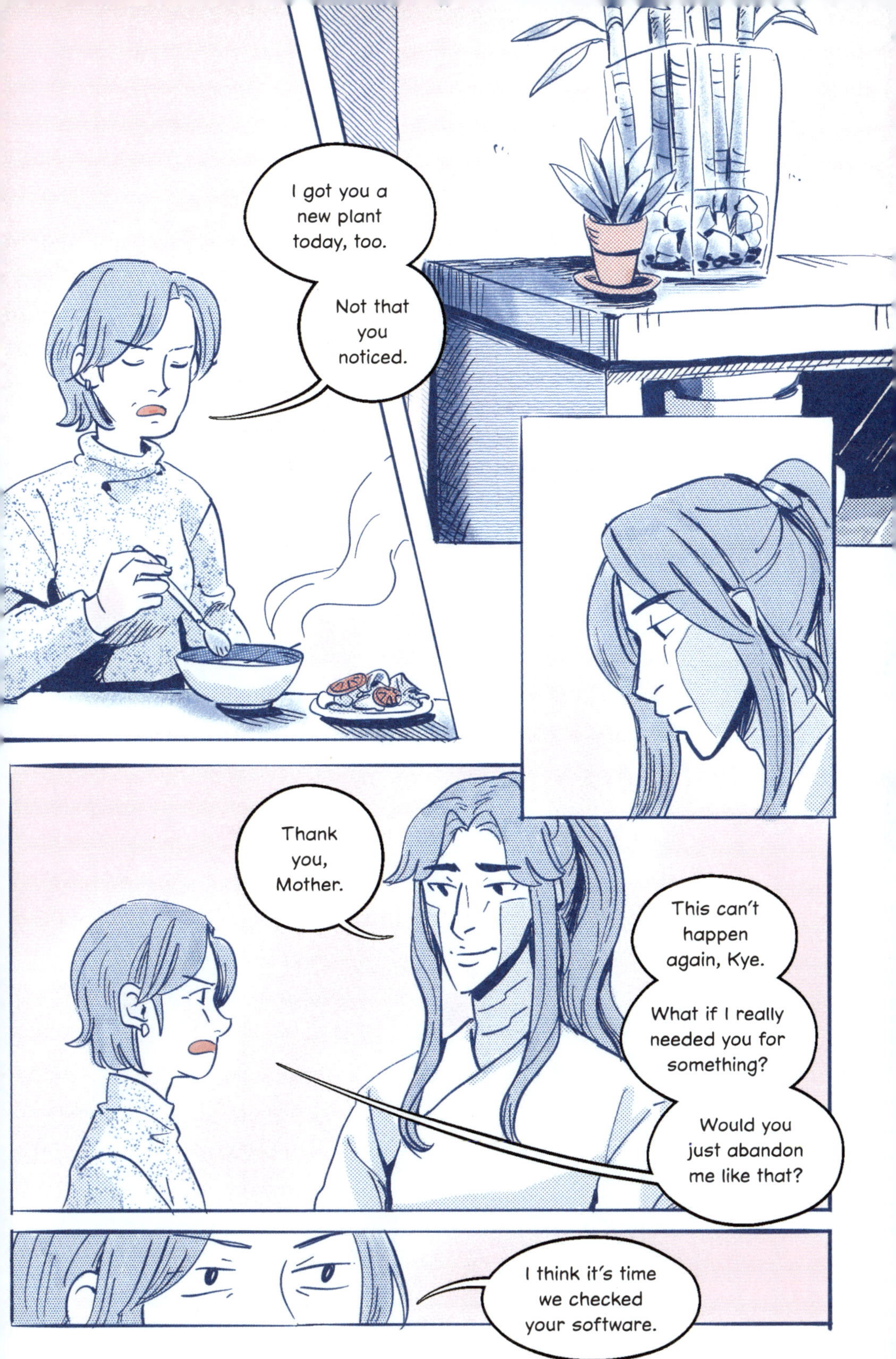
I got you a new plant today, too.
Not that you noticed.
Thank you, Mother.
This can't happen again, Kye.
What if I really needed you for something?
Would you just abandon me like that?
I think it's time we checked your software.

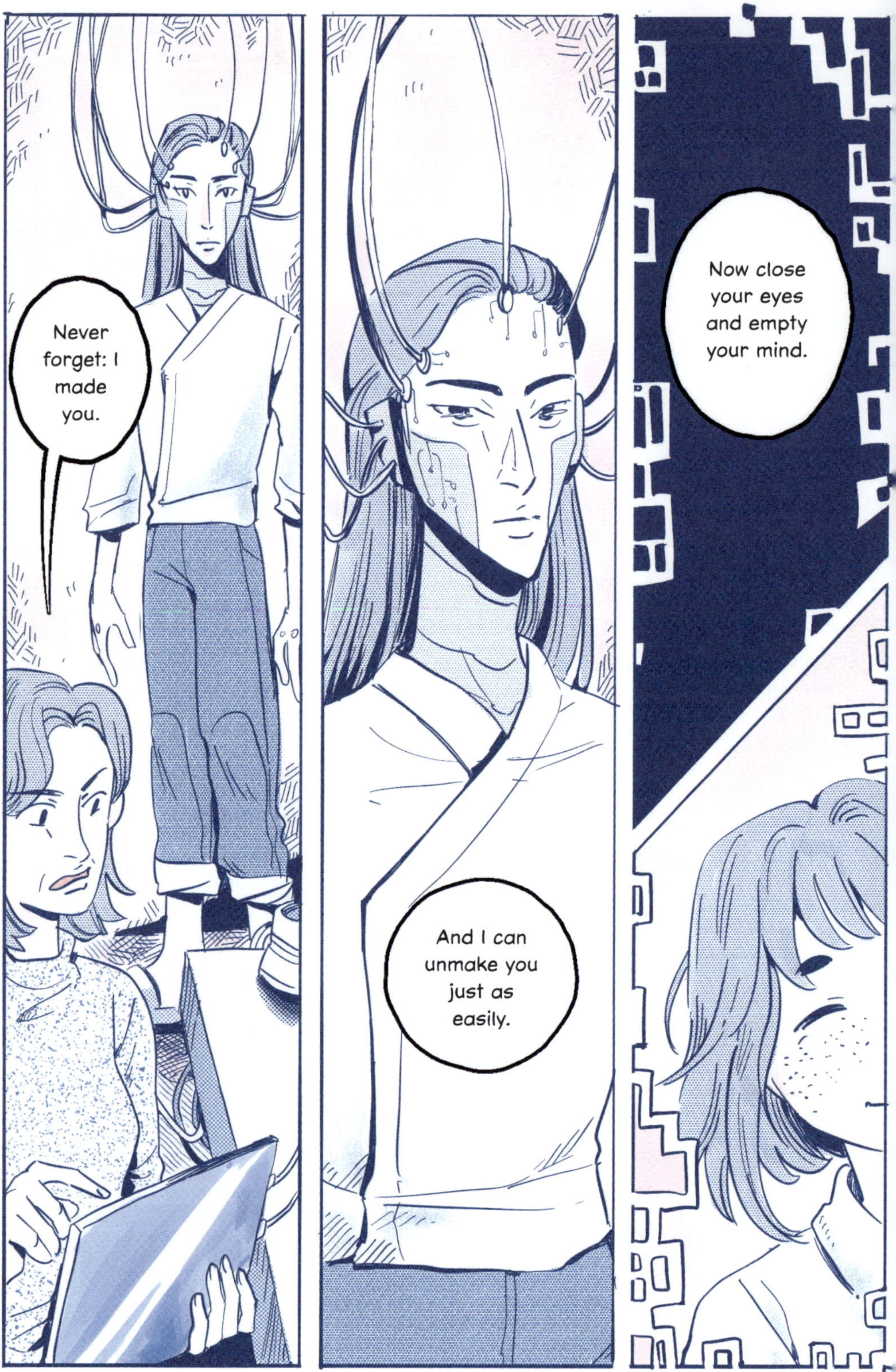
Never forget: I made you.
And I can unmake you just as easily.
Now close your eyes and empty your mind.

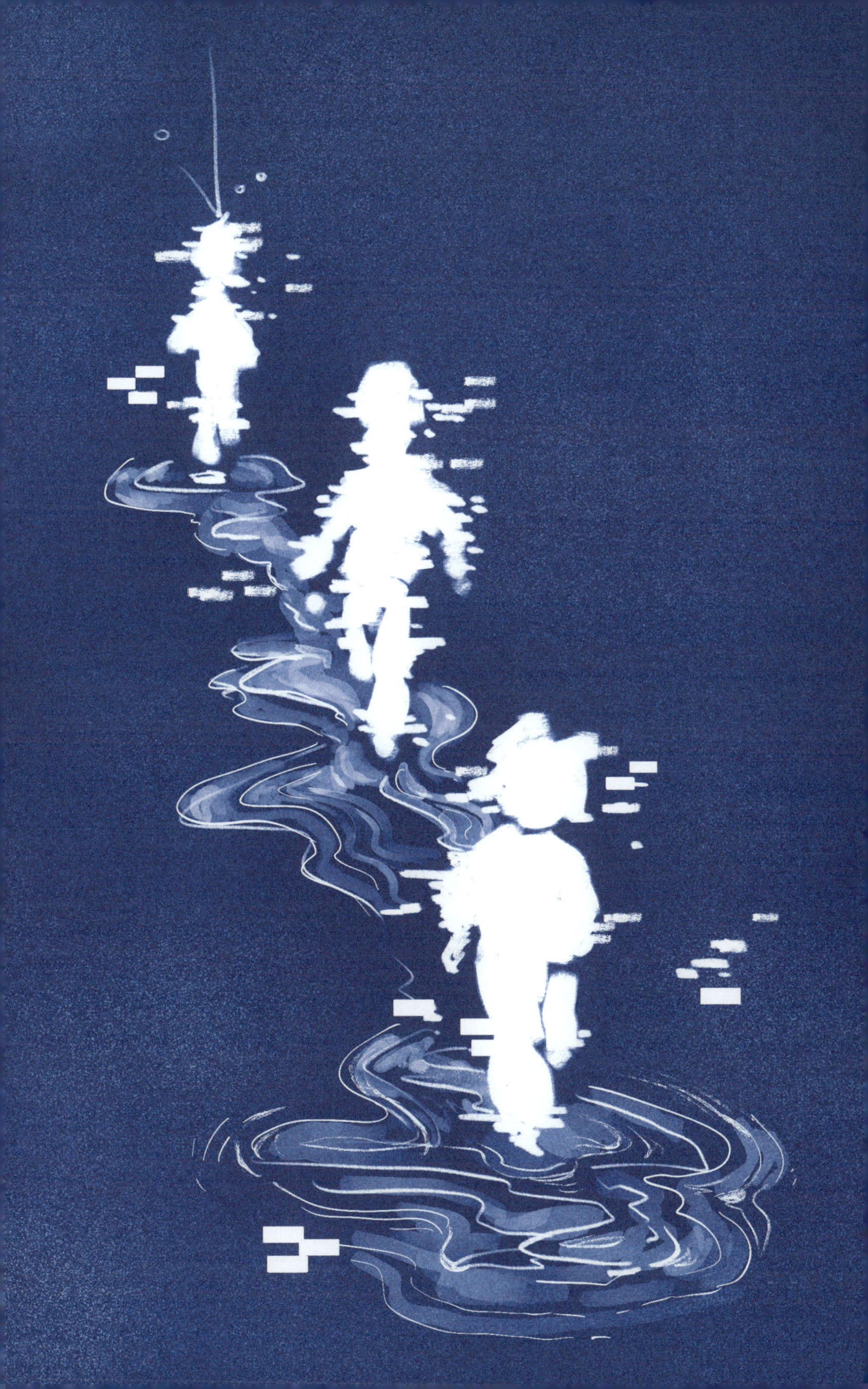

00110000 00110100

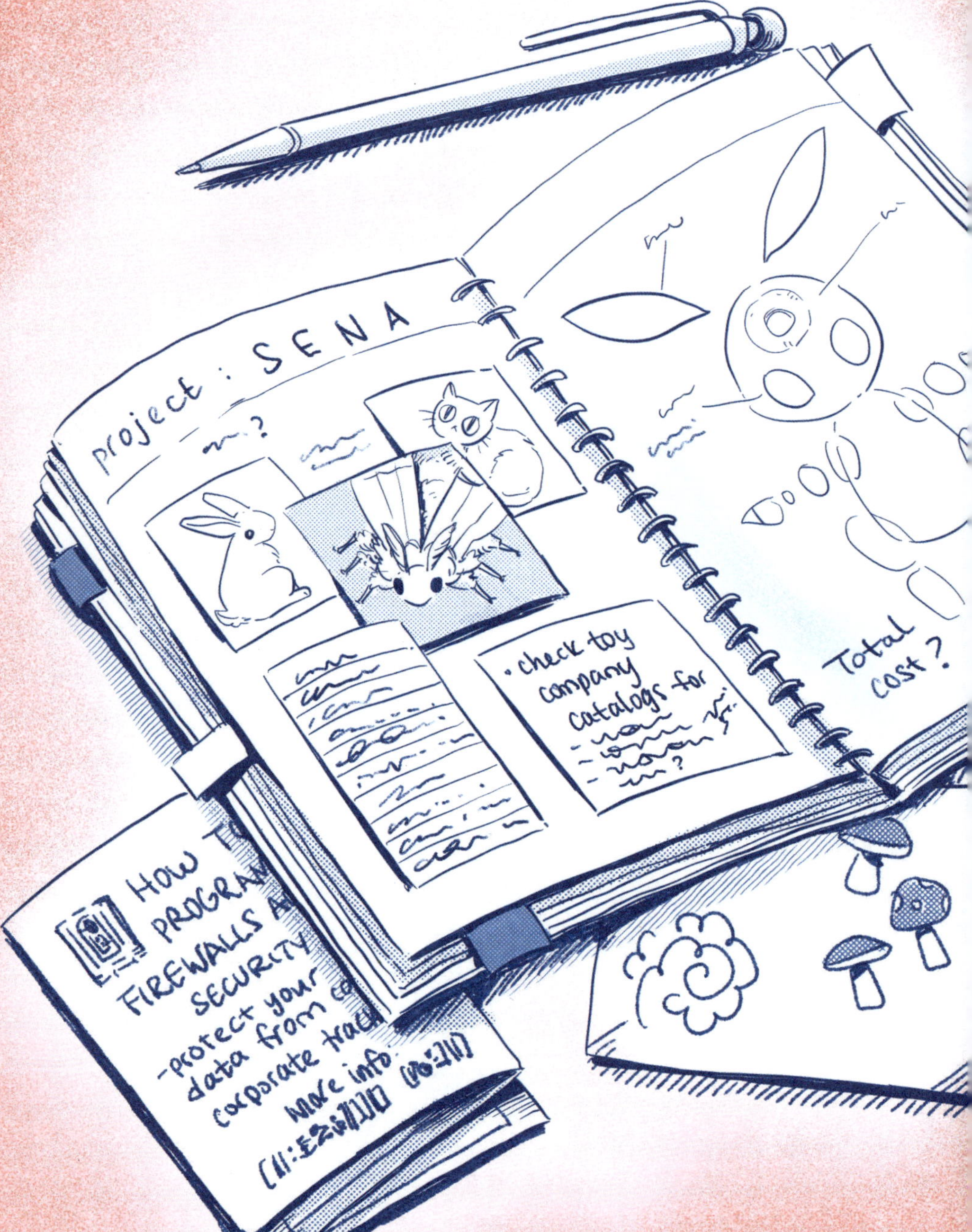
project : SENA
• check toy company catalogs for
Total cost?
HOW
SECURITY
-protect your
data from
corporate
more info:

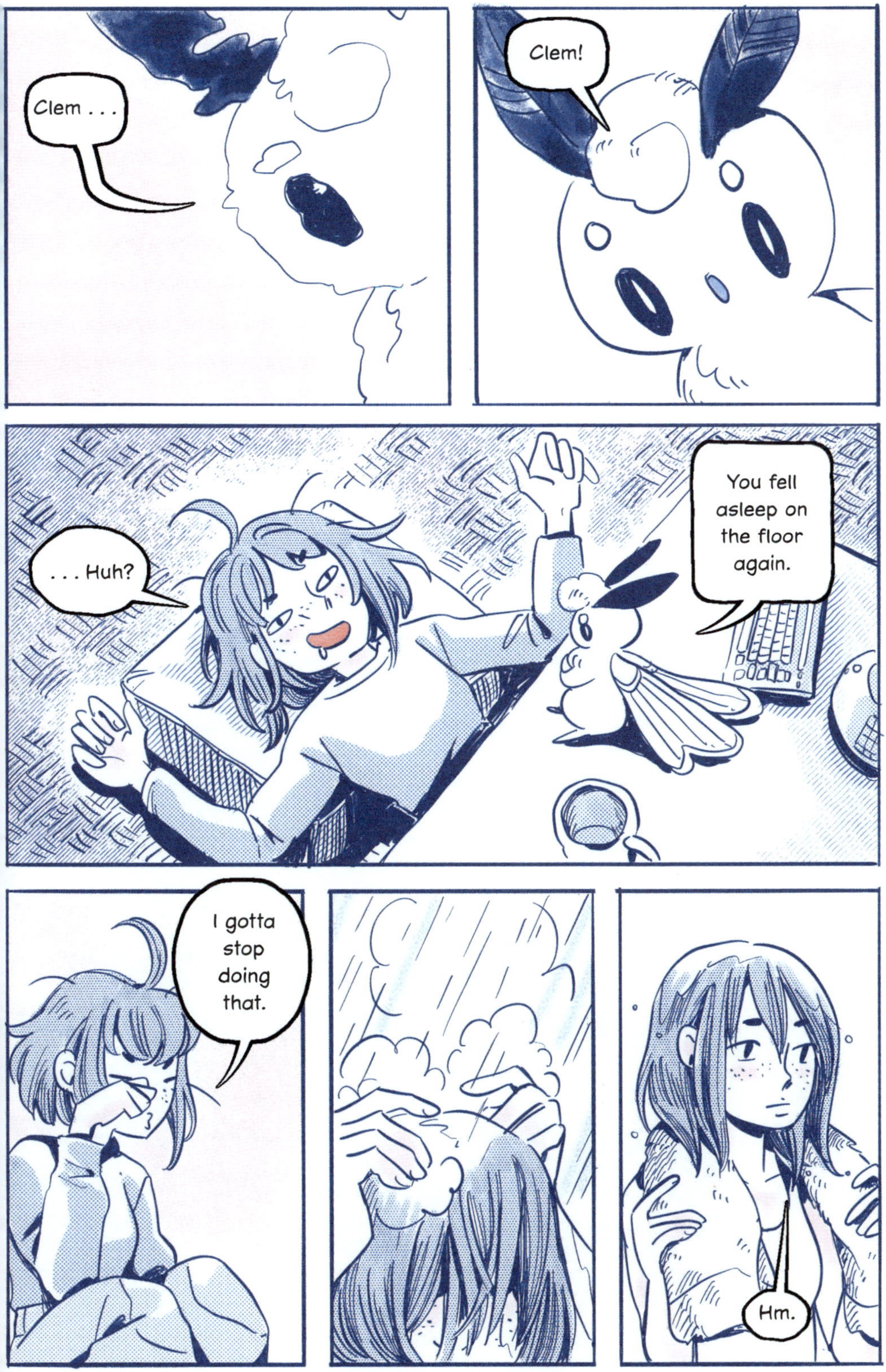
Clem . . .
Clem!
. . . Huh?
You fell asleep on the floor again.
I gotta stop doing that.
Hm.

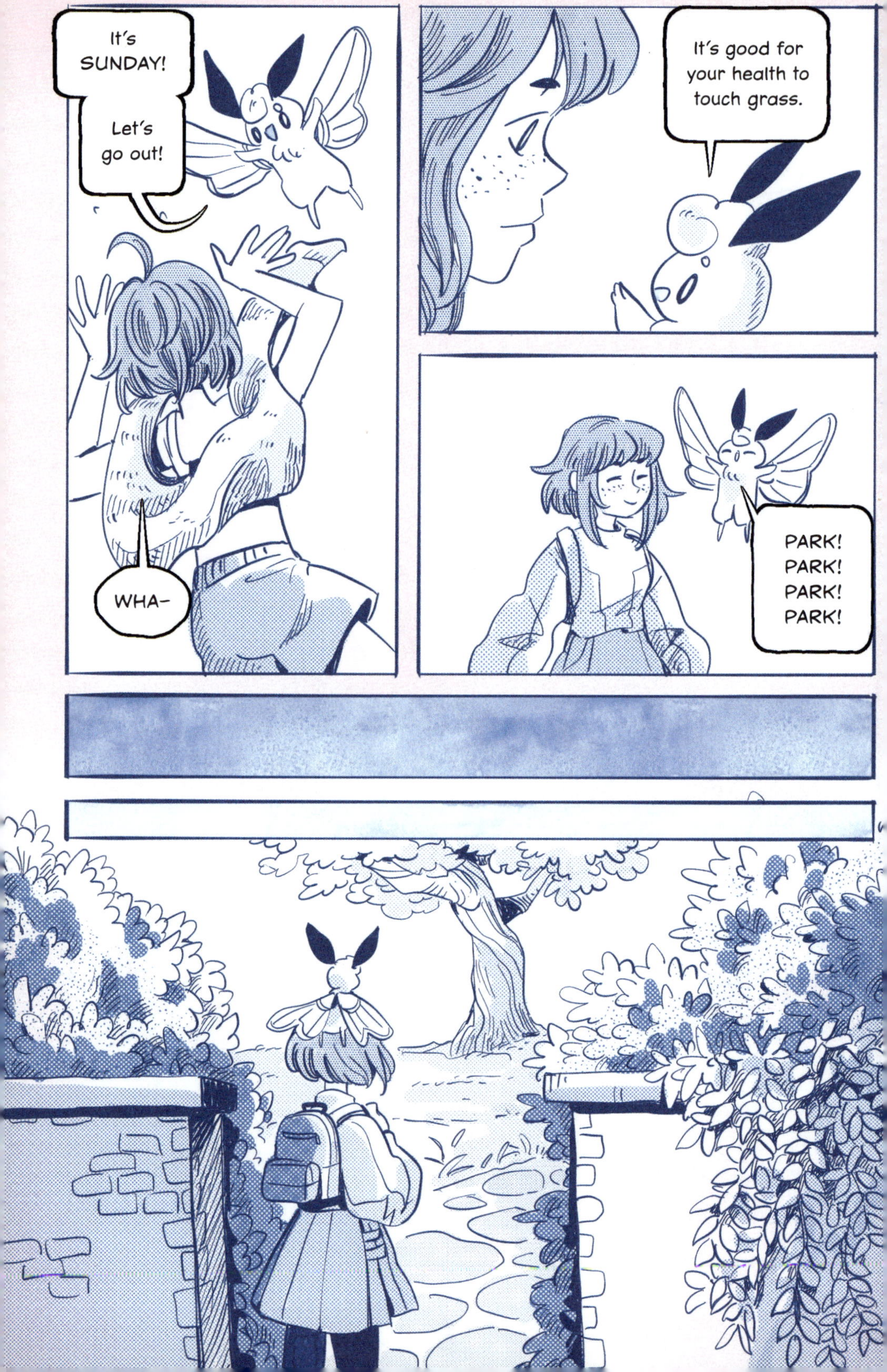
It's SUNDAY!
Let's go out!
WHA-
It's good for your health to touch grass.
PARK! PARK! PARK! PARK!

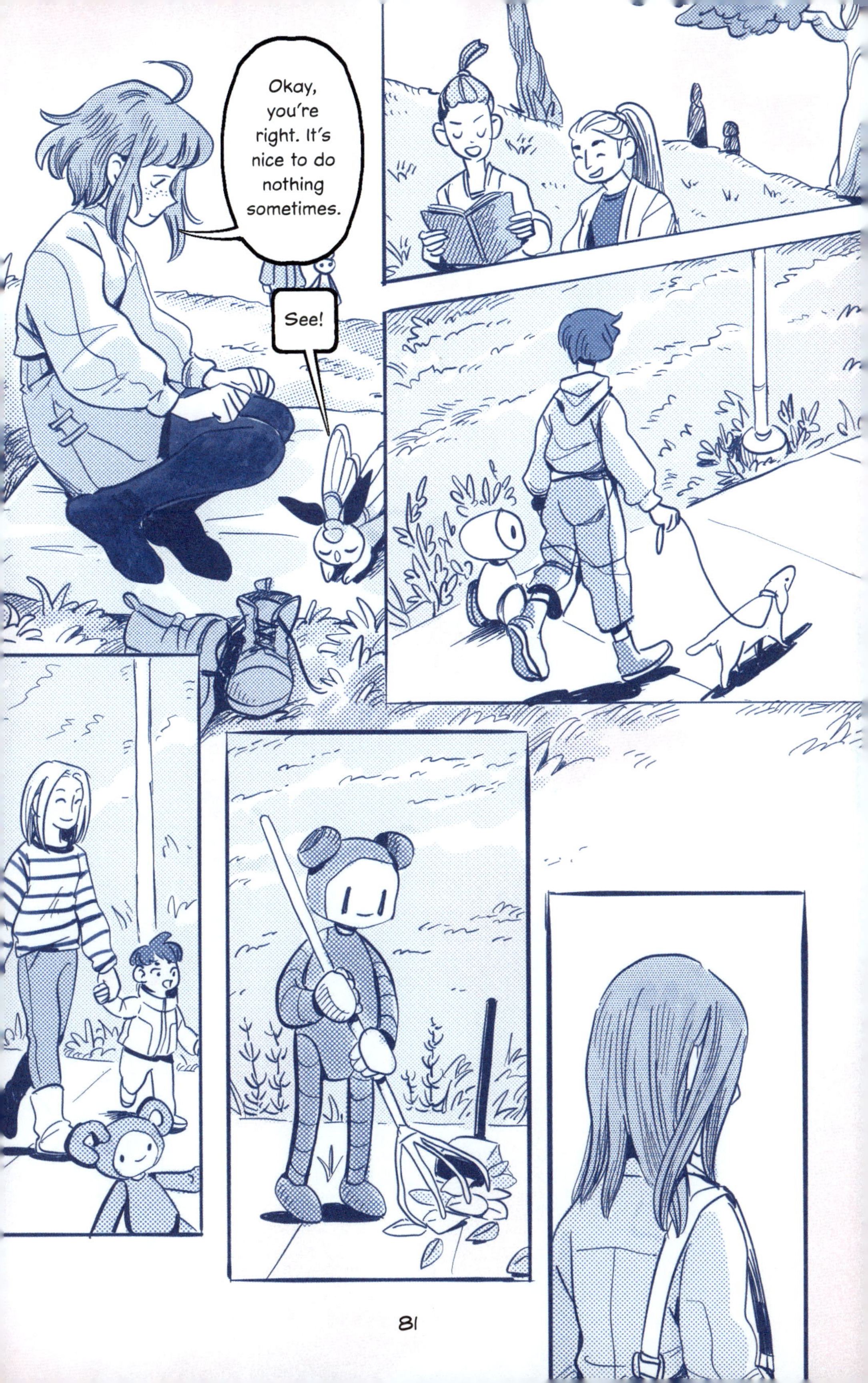
Okay, you're right. It's nice to do nothing sometimes.
See!

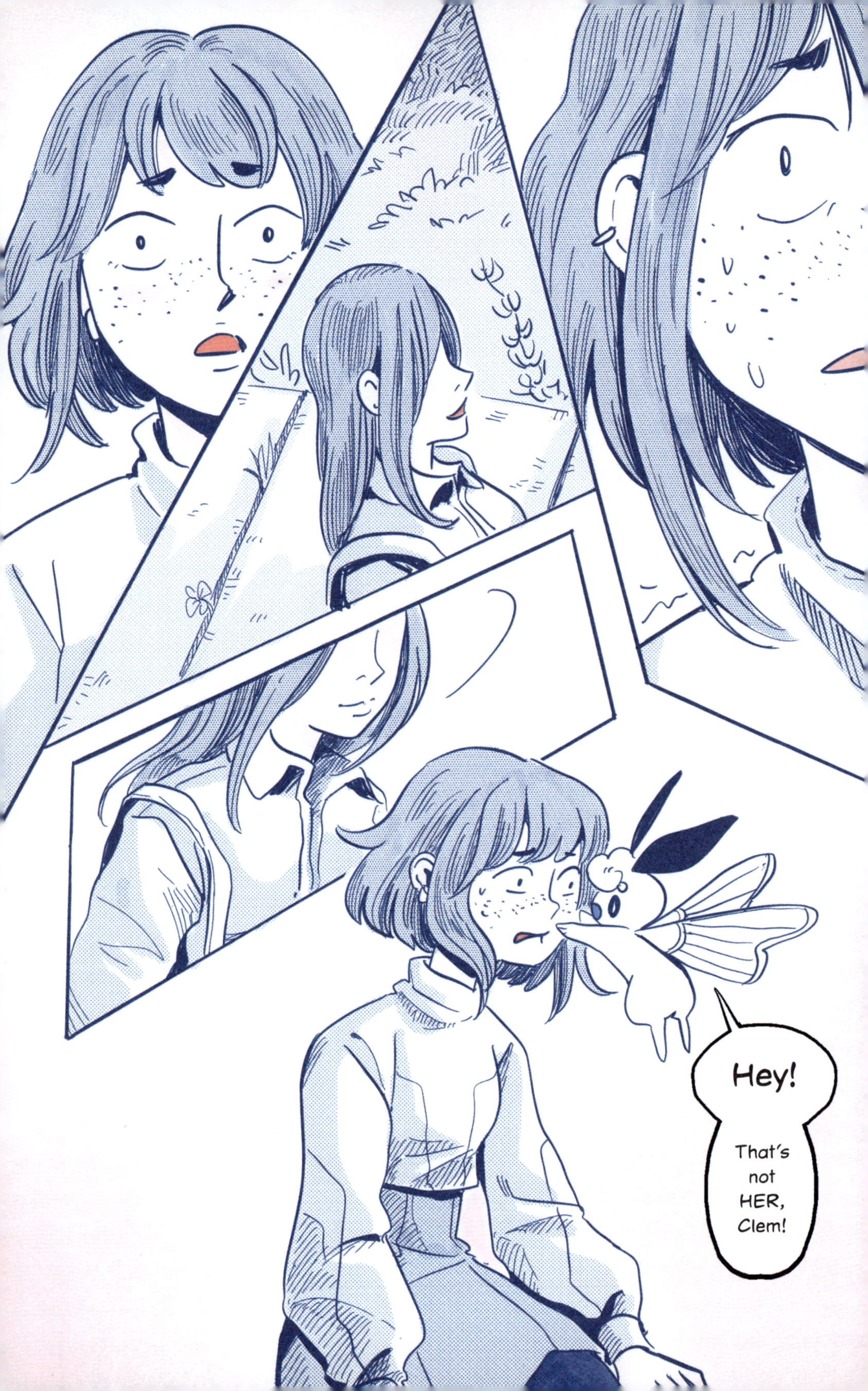
Hey!
That's not HER, Clem!

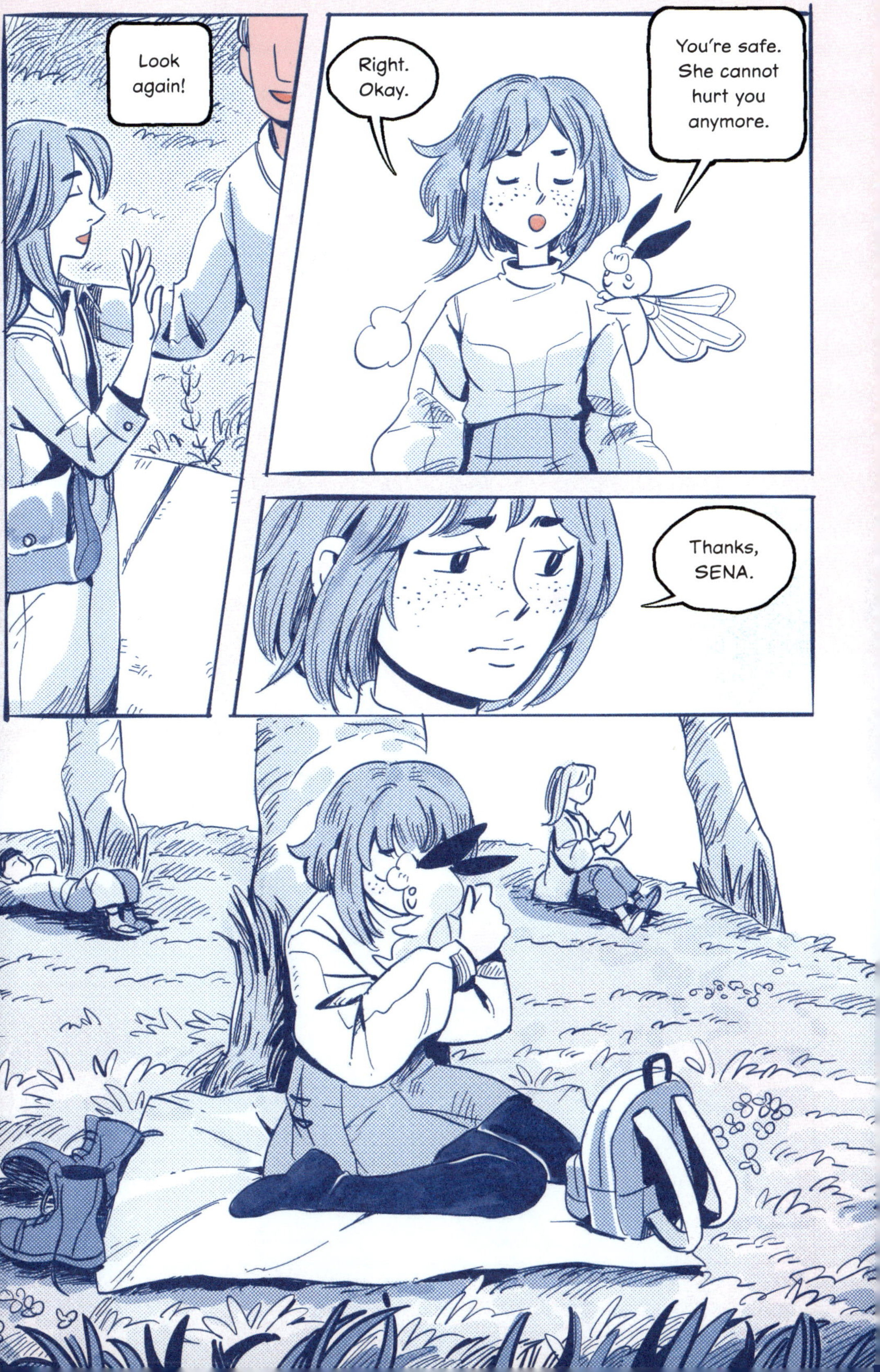
Look again!
Right. Okay.
You're safe. She cannot hurt you anymore.
Thanks, SENA.

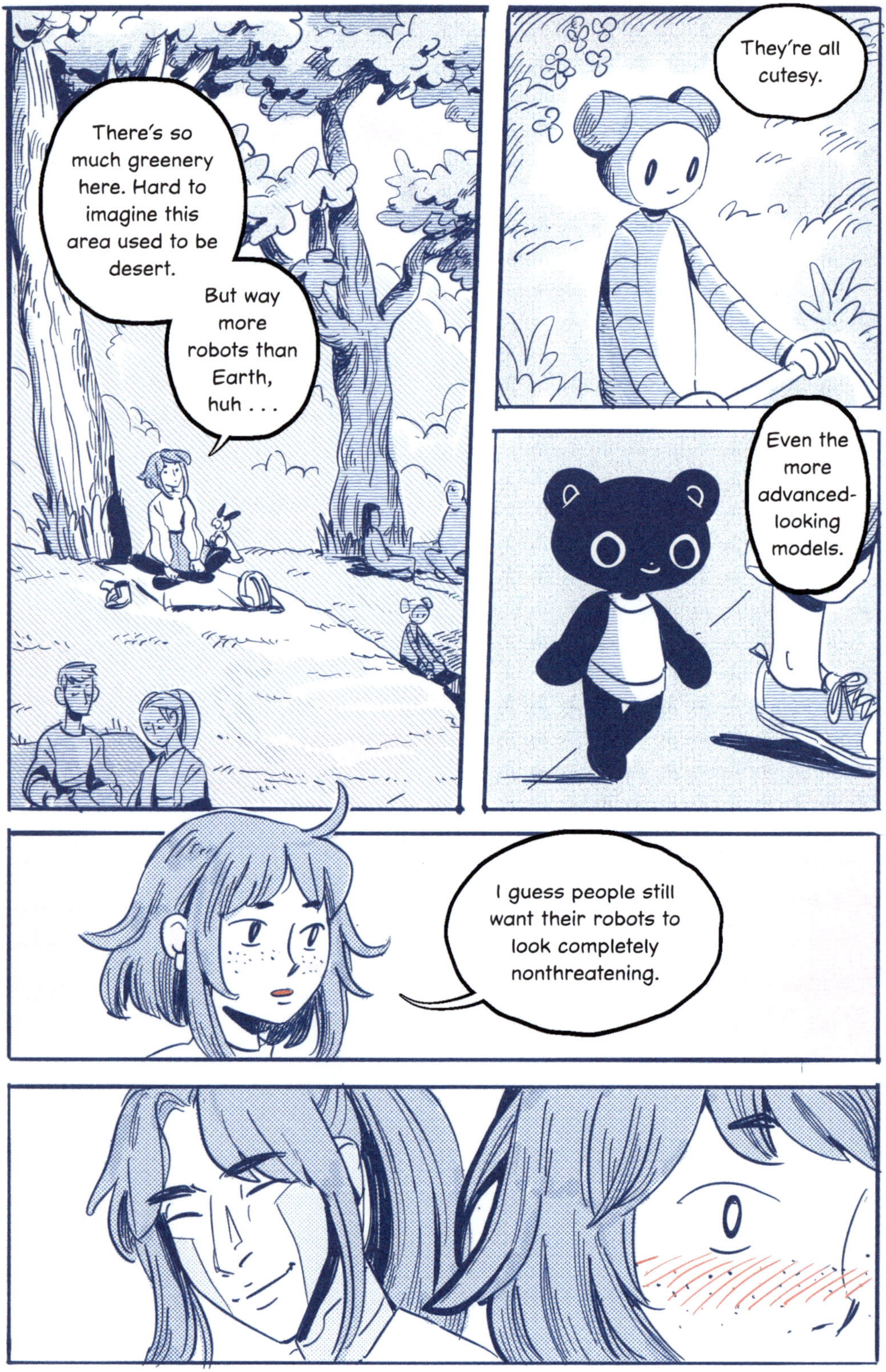
There's so much greenery here. Hard to imagine this area used to be desert.
But way more robots than Earth, huh . . .
They're all cutesy.
Even the more advanced-looking models.
I guess people still want their robots to look completely nonthreatening.

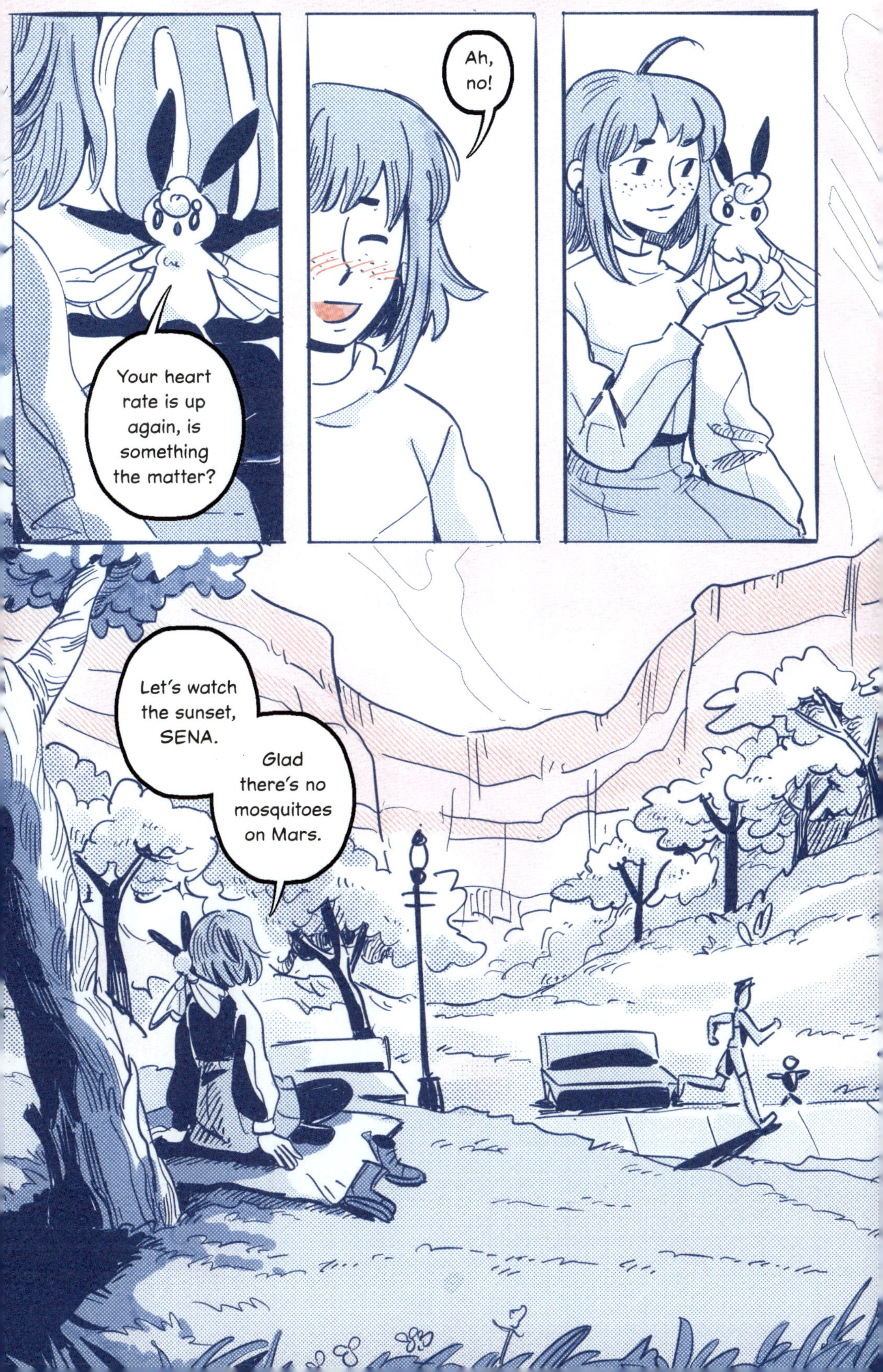
Your heart rate is up again, is something the matter?
Ah, no!
Let's watch the sunset, SENA.
Glad there's no mosquitoes on Mars.

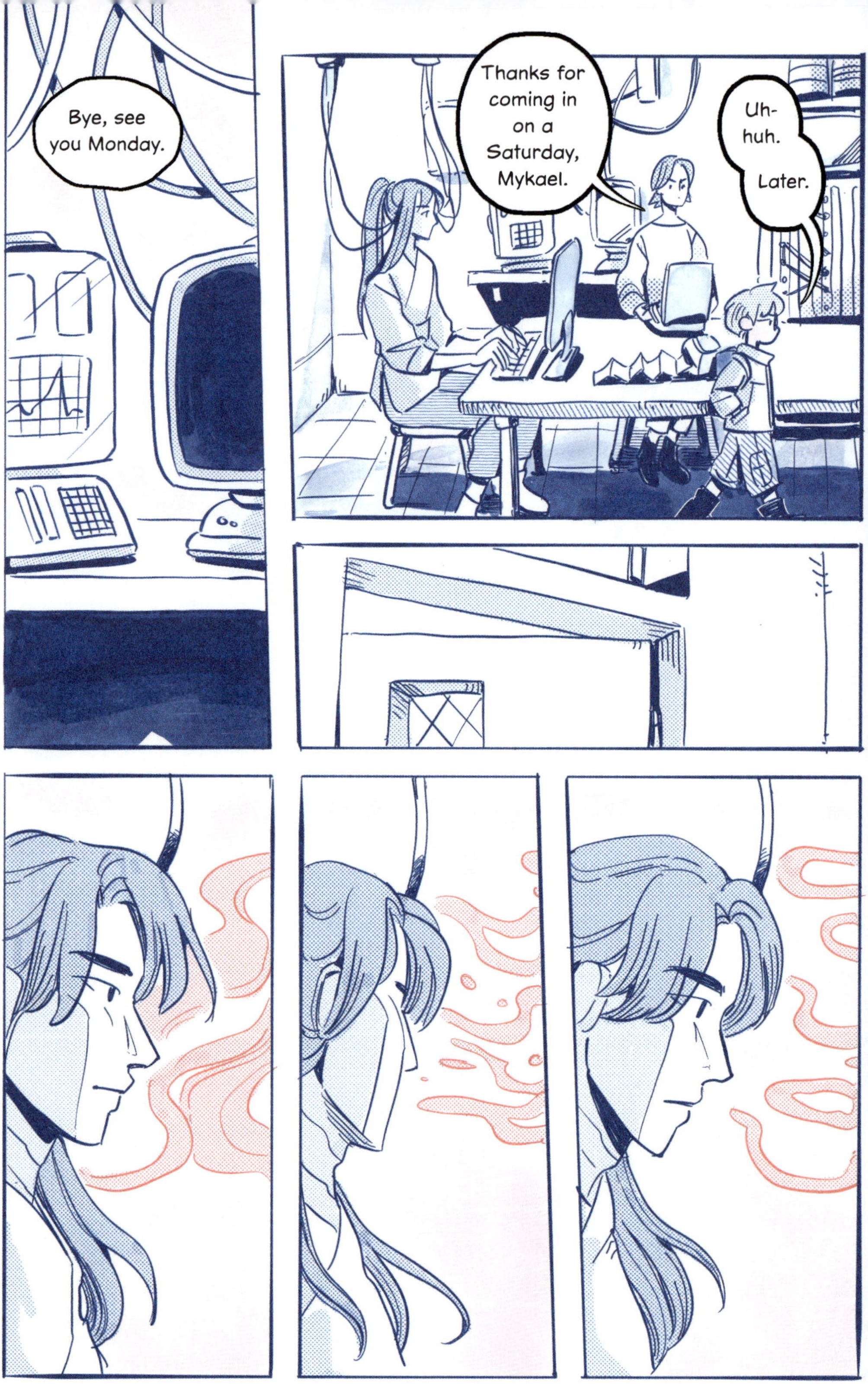
Bye, see you Monday.
Thanks for coming in on a Saturday, Mykael.
Uh-huh.
Later.

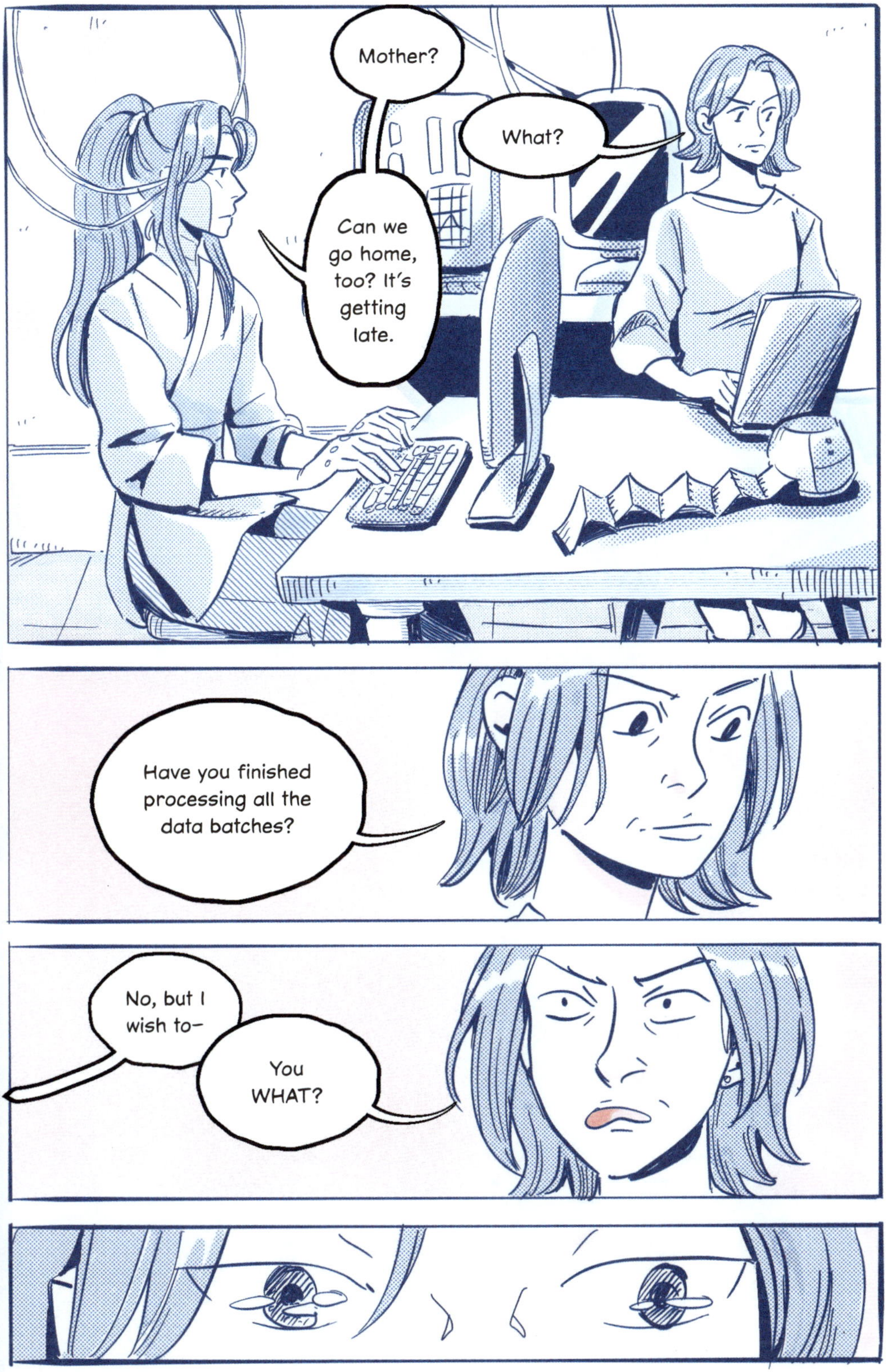
Mother?
What?
Can we go home, too? It's getting late.
Have you finished processing all the data batches?
No, but I wish to–
You WHAT?

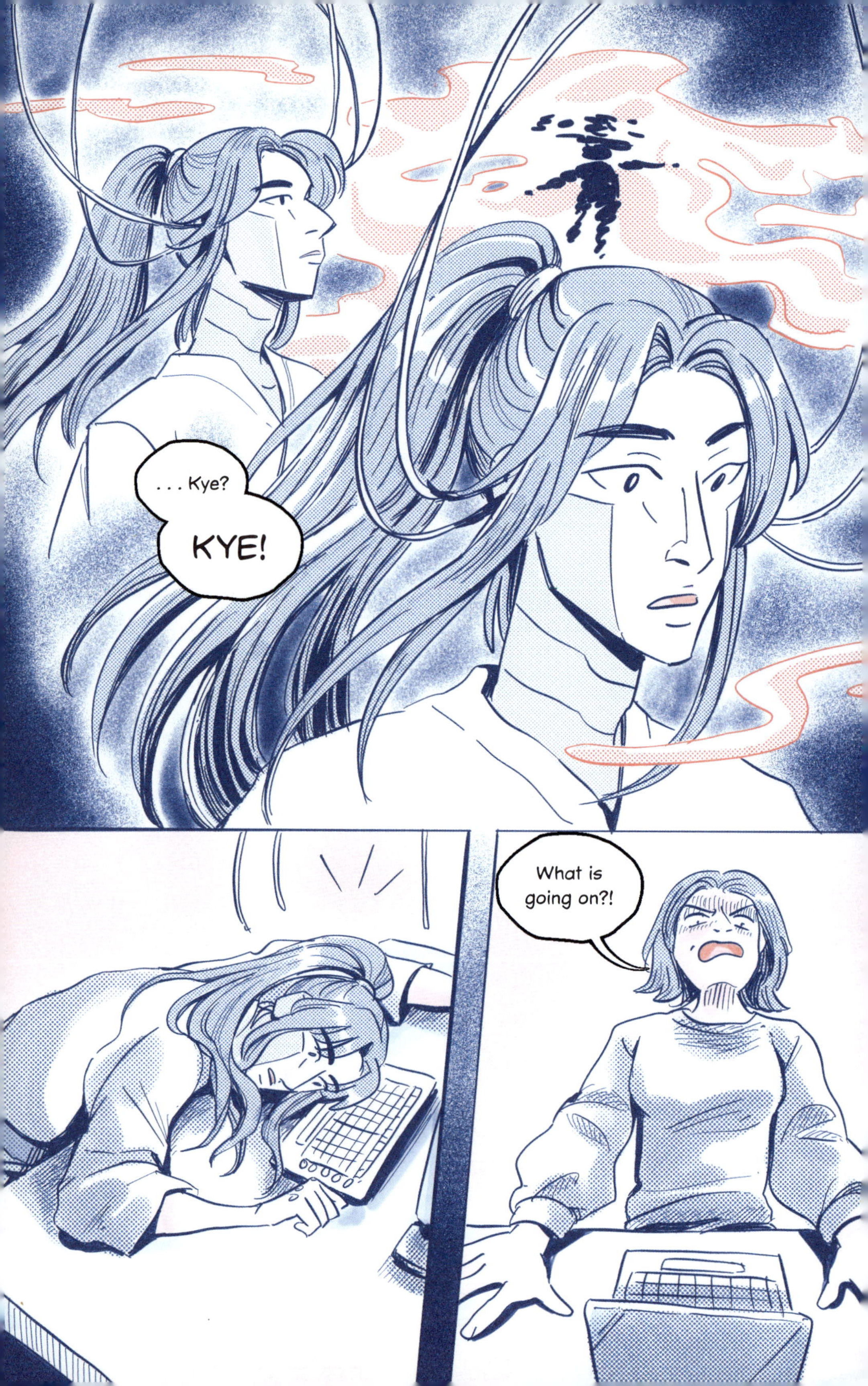
. . . Kye?
KYE!
What is going on?!

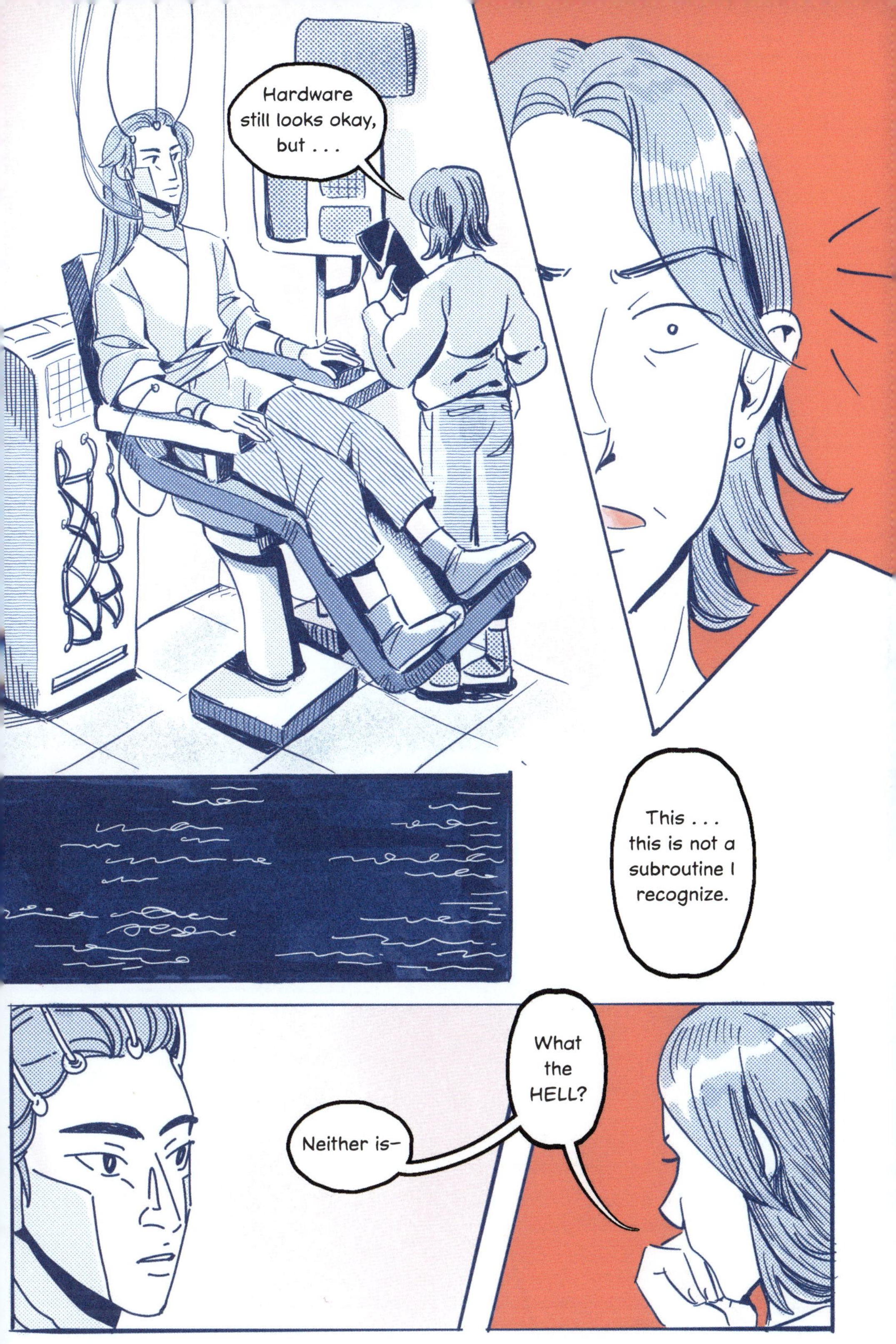
Hardware still looks okay, but . . .
This . . . this is not a subroutine I recognize.
What the HELL?
Neither is–

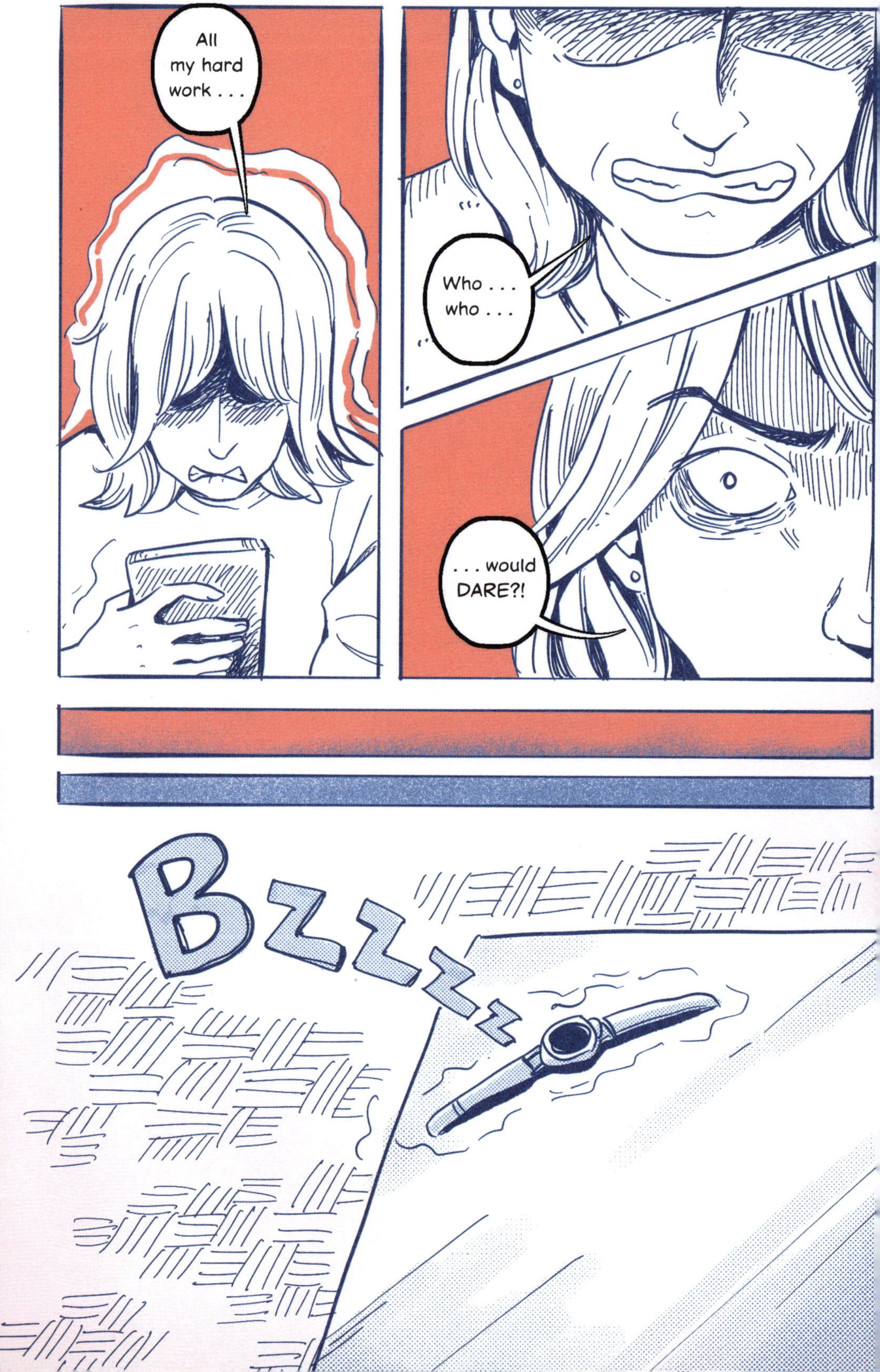
All my hard work . . .
Who . . . who . . .
. . . would DARE?!
Bzzzzz

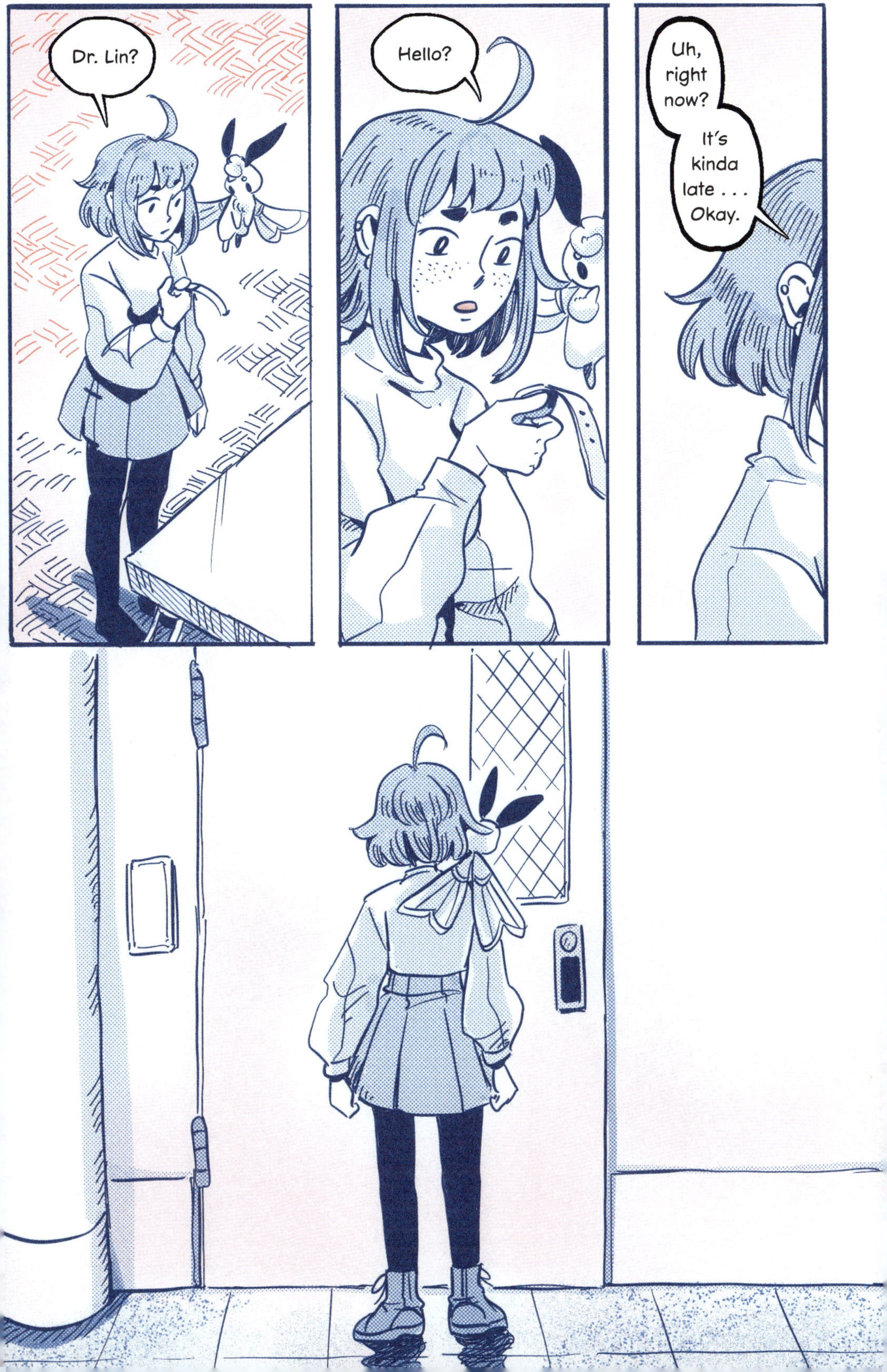
Dr. Lin?
Hello?
Uh, right now?
It's kinda late . . . Okay.

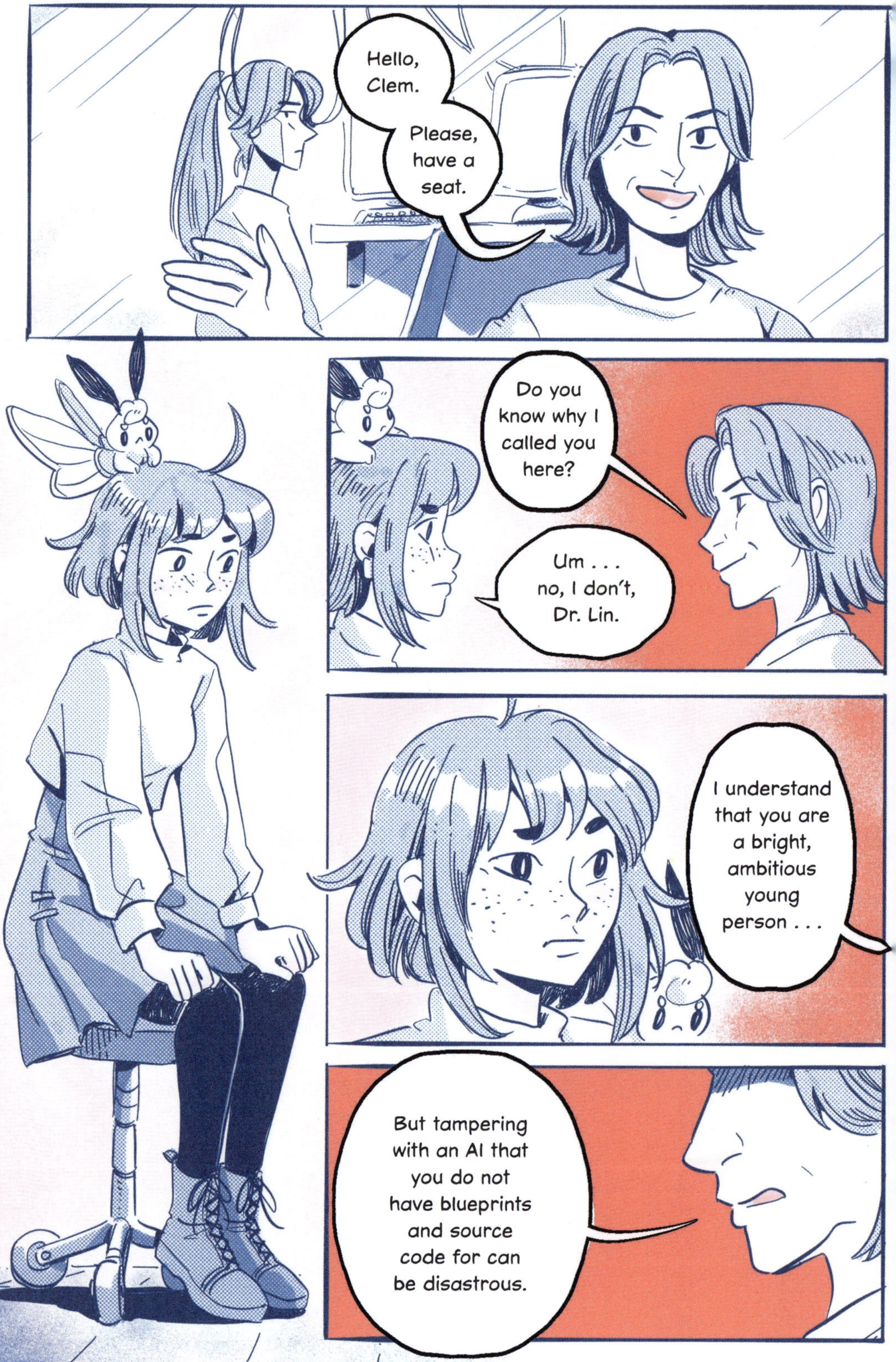
Hello, Clem.
Please, have a seat.
Do you know why I called you here?
Um . . . no, I don't, Dr. Lin.
I understand that you are a bright, ambitious young person . . .
But tampering with an AI that you do not have blueprints and source code for can be disastrous.

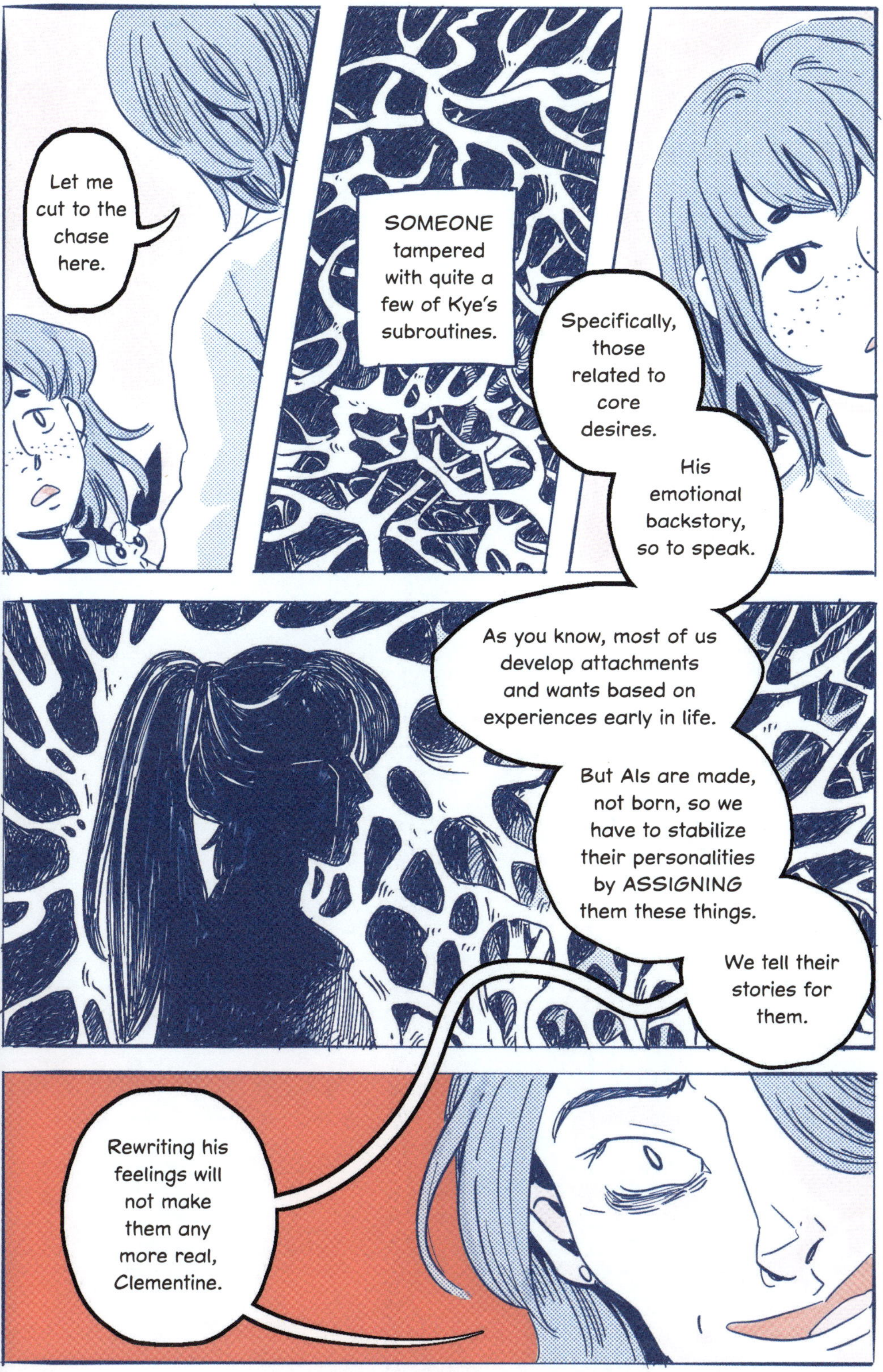
Let me cut to the chase here.
SOMEONE tampered with quite a few of Kye's subroutines.
Specifically, those related to core desires.
His emotional backstory, so to speak.
As you know, most of us develop attachments and wants based on experiences early in life.
But AIs are made, not born, so we have to stabilize their personalities by ASSIGNING them these things.
We tell their stories for them.
Rewriting his feelings will not make them any more real, Clementine.

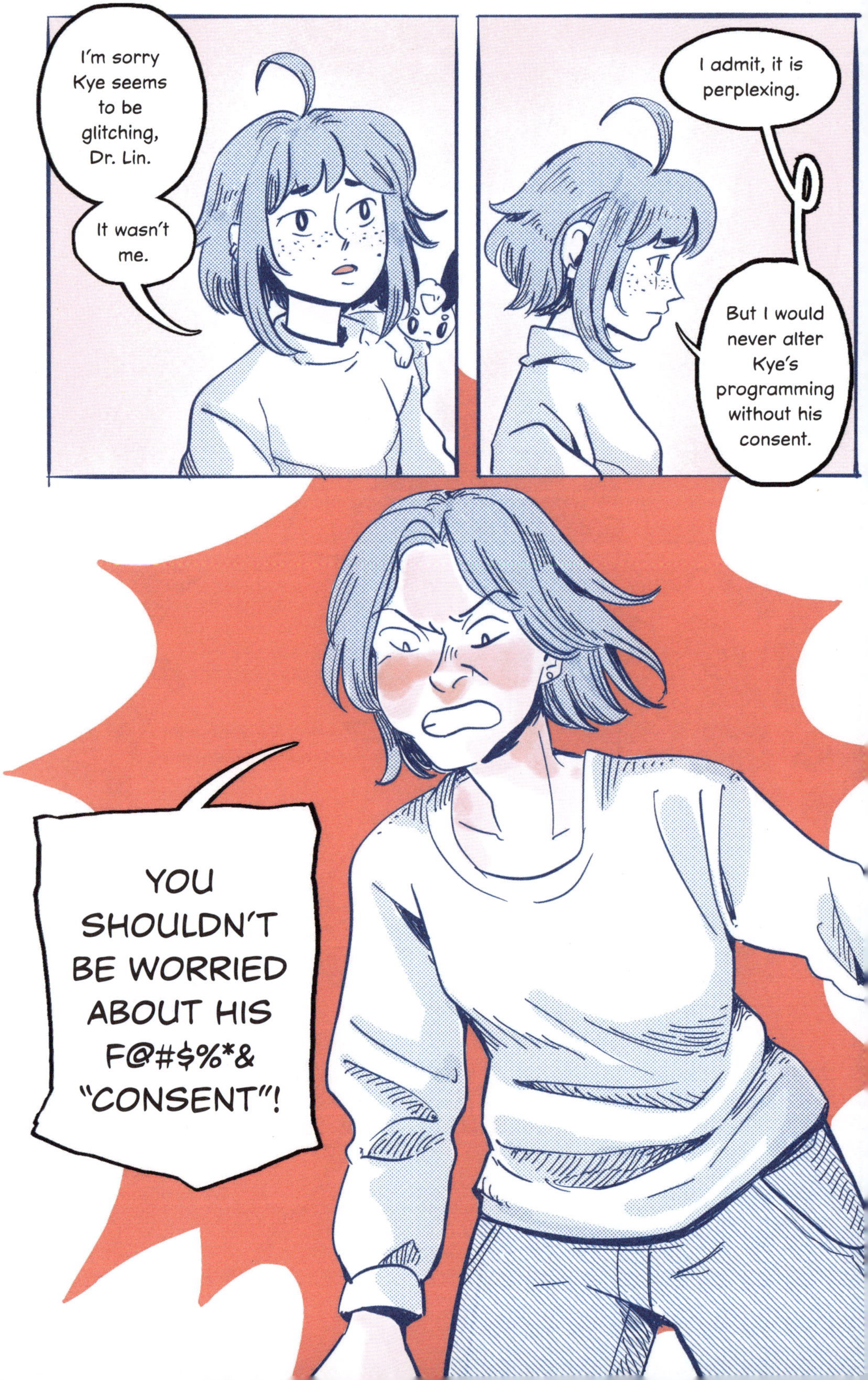
I'm sorry Kye seems to be glitching, Dr. Lin.
It wasn't me.
I admit, it is perplexing.
But I would never alter Kye's programming without his consent.
YOU SHOULDN'T BE WORRIED ABOUT HIS F@#$%*& "CONSENT"!

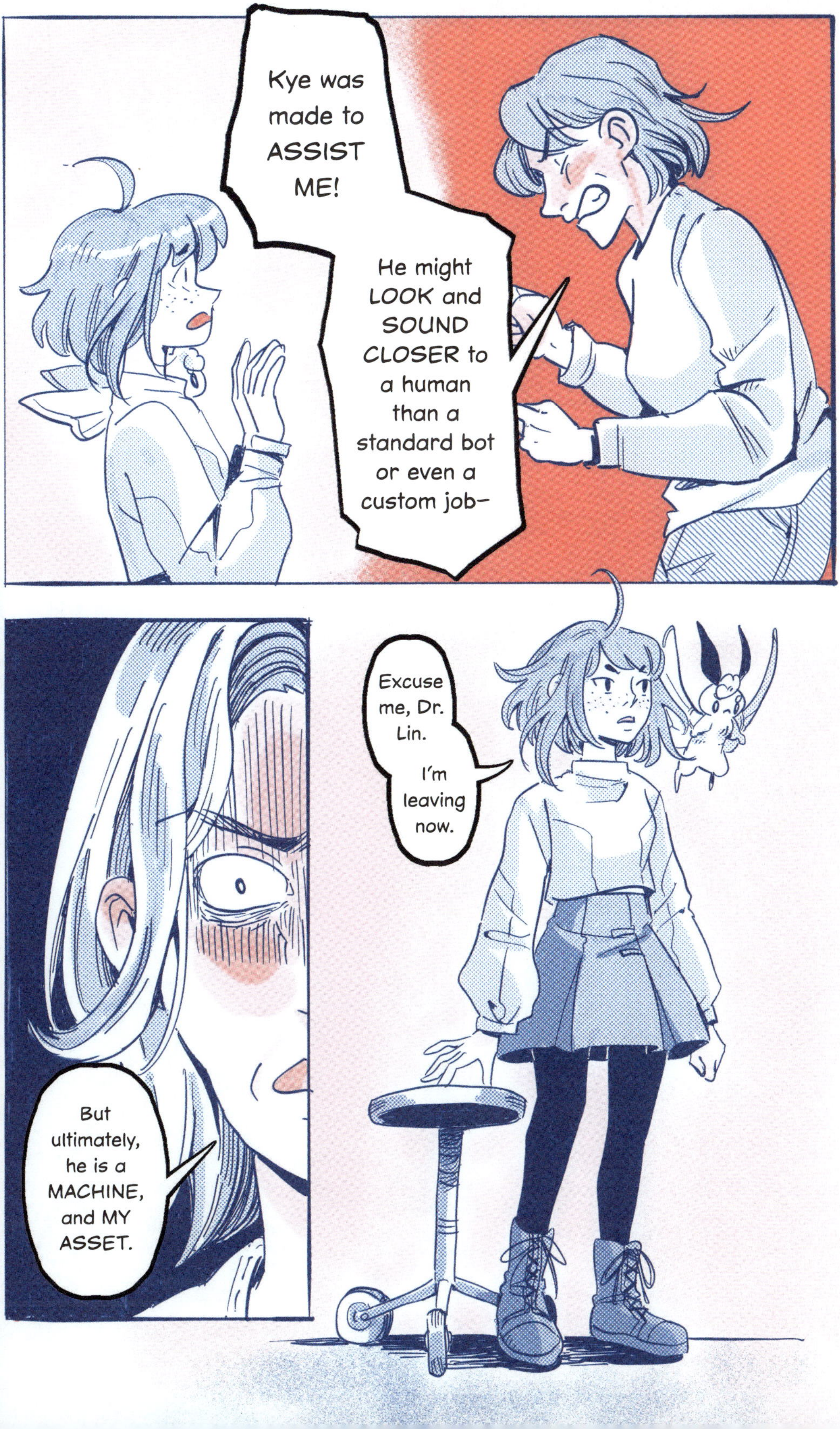
Kye was made to ASSIST ME!
He might LOOK and SOUND CLOSER to a human than a standard bot or even a custom job–
Excuse me, Dr. Lin.
I'm leaving now.
But ultimately, he is a MACHINE, and MY ASSET.

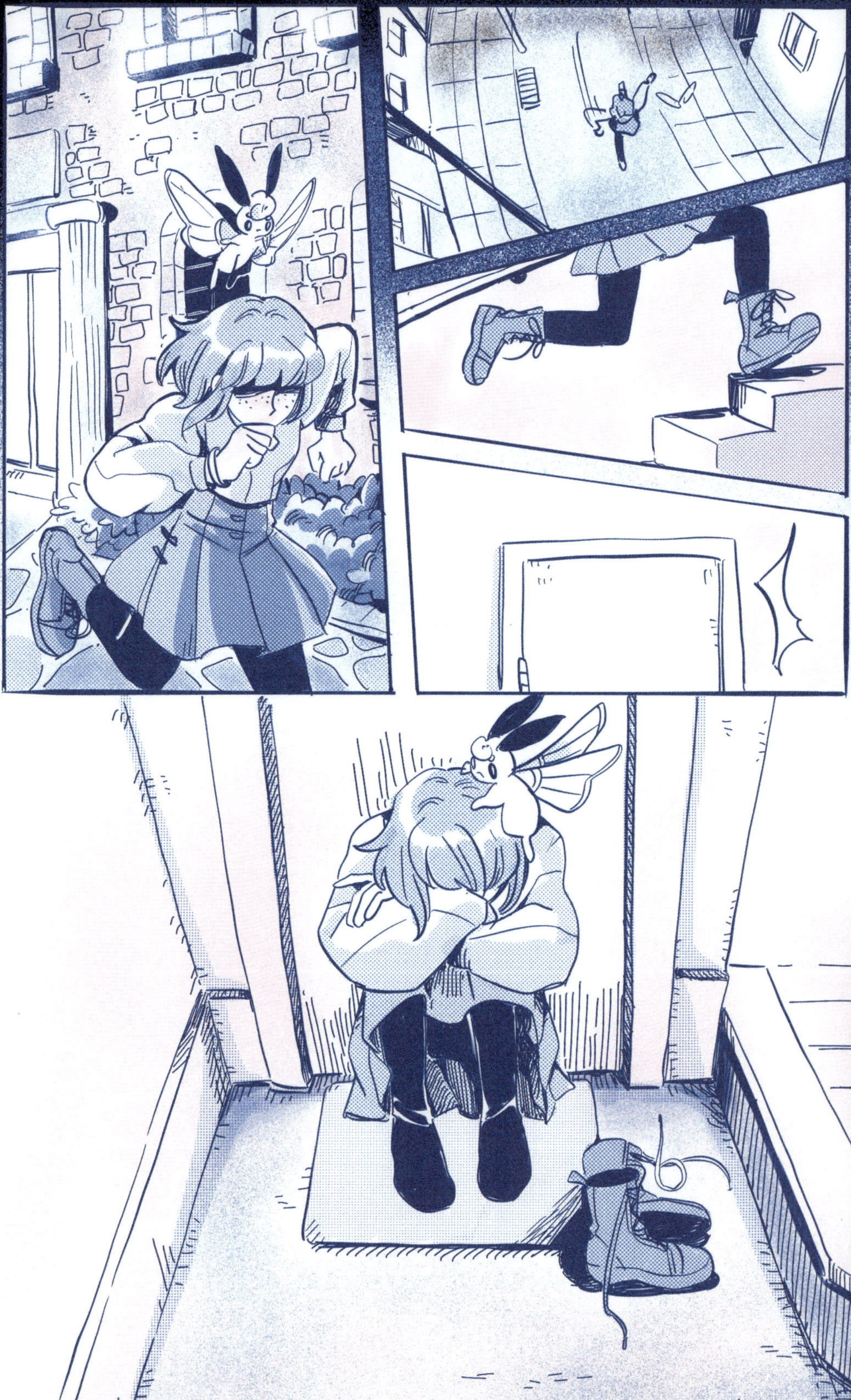

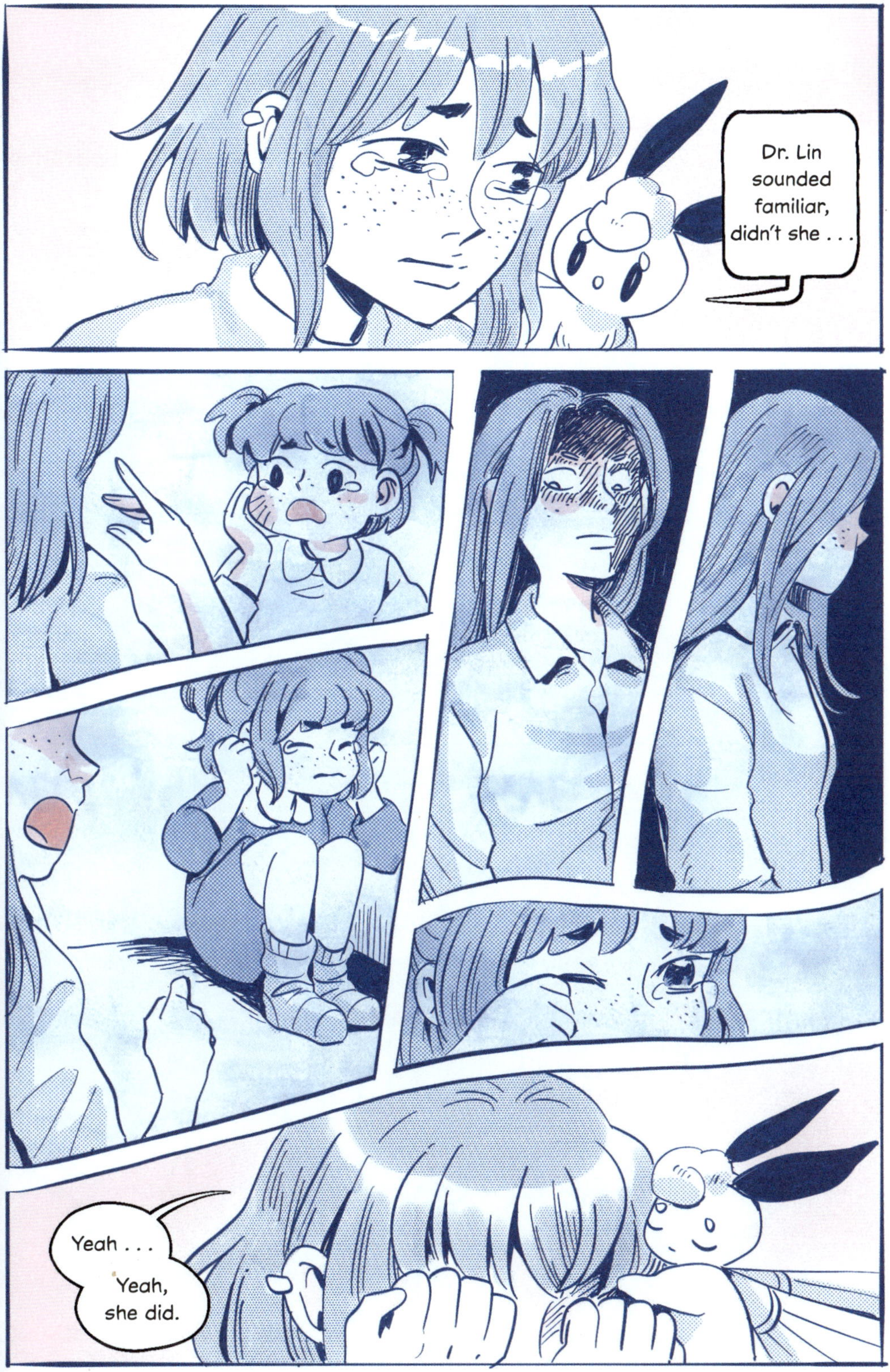
Dr. Lin sounded familiar, didn't she . . .
Yeah . . .
Yeah, she did.

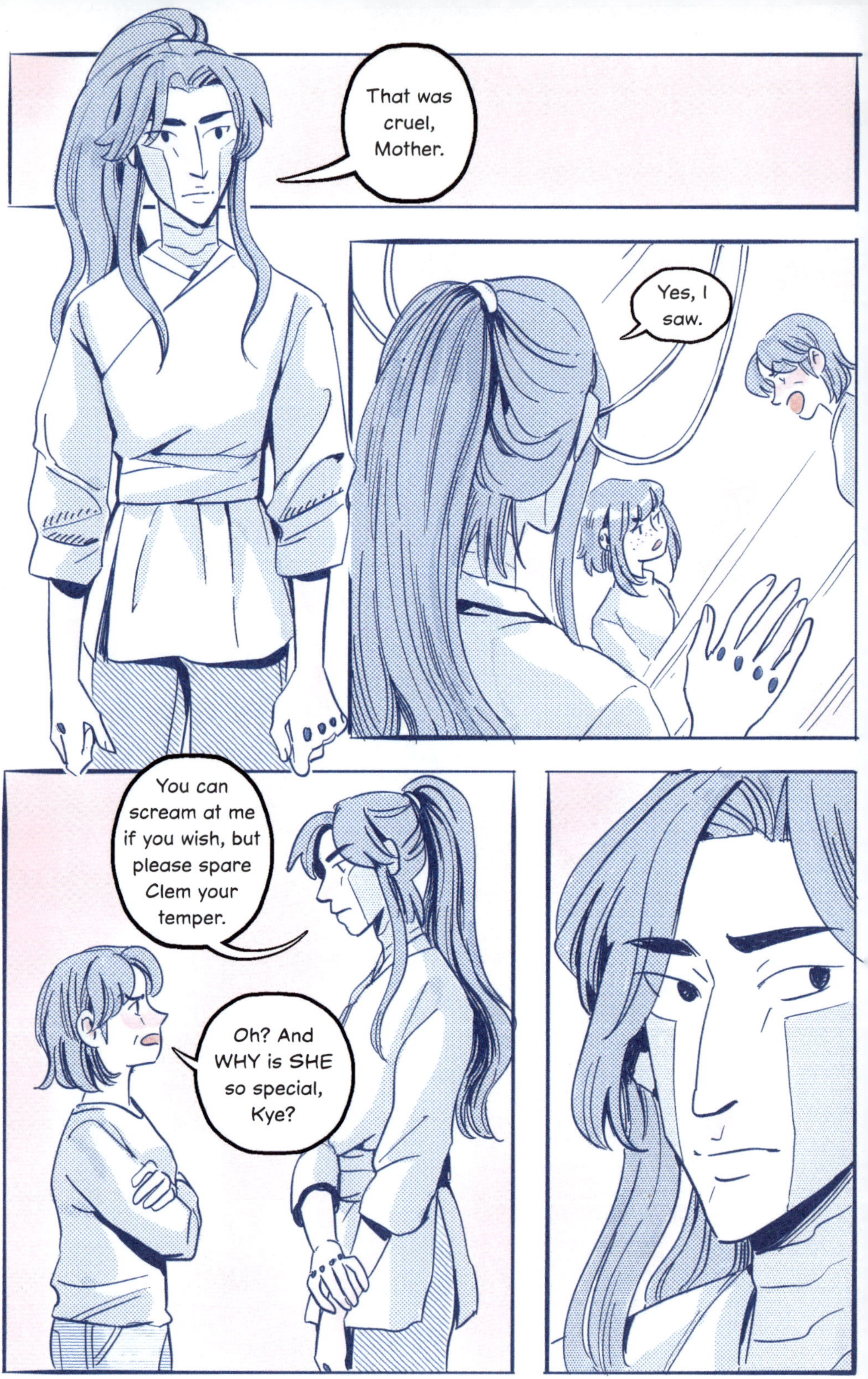
That was cruel, Mother.
Yes, I saw.
You can scream at me if you wish, but please spare Clem your temper.
Oh? And WHY is SHE so special, Kye?

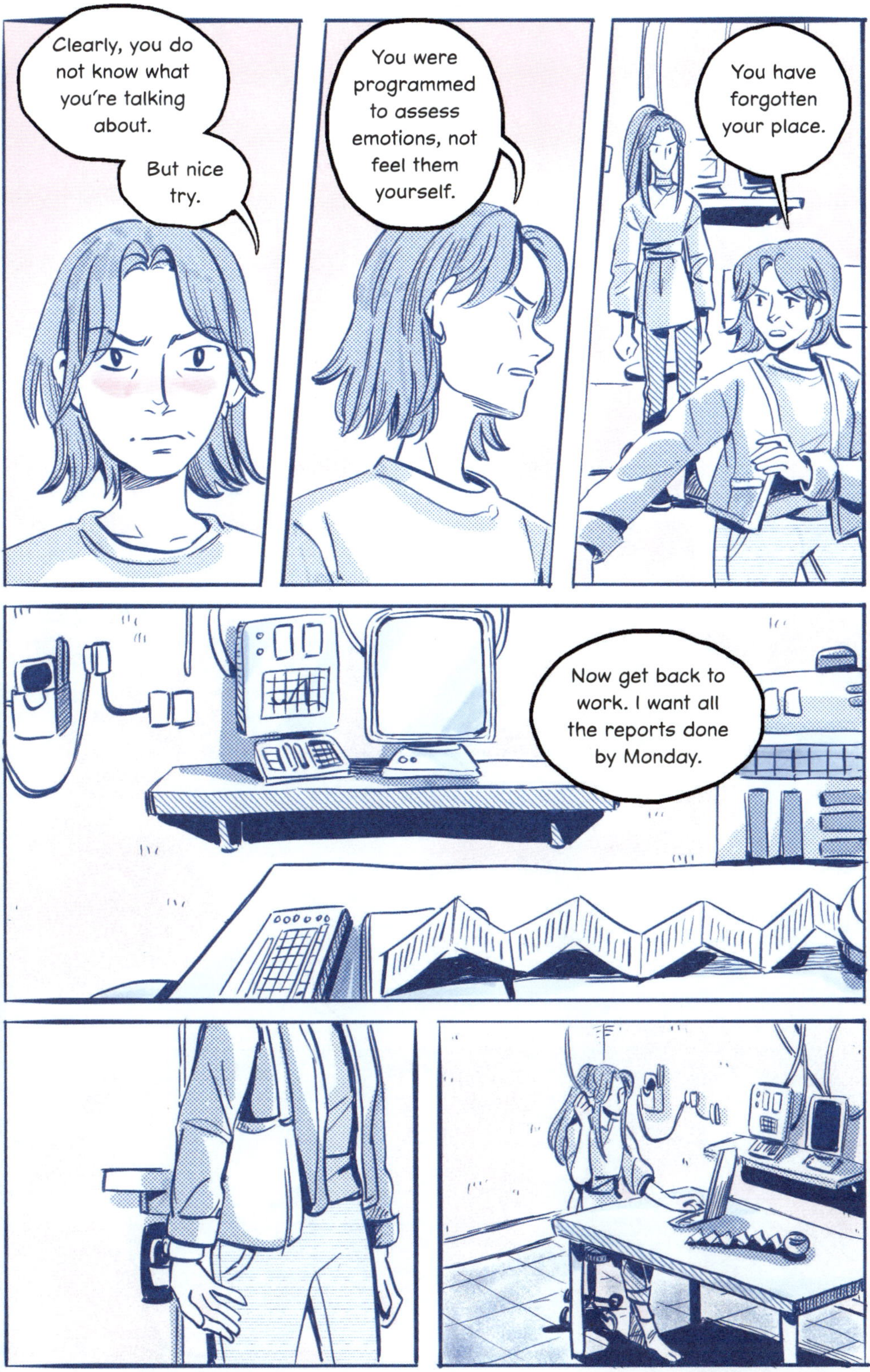
Clearly, you do not know what you're talking about.
But nice try.
You were programmed to assess emotions, not feel them yourself.
You have forgotten your place.
Now get back to work. I want all the reports done by Monday.

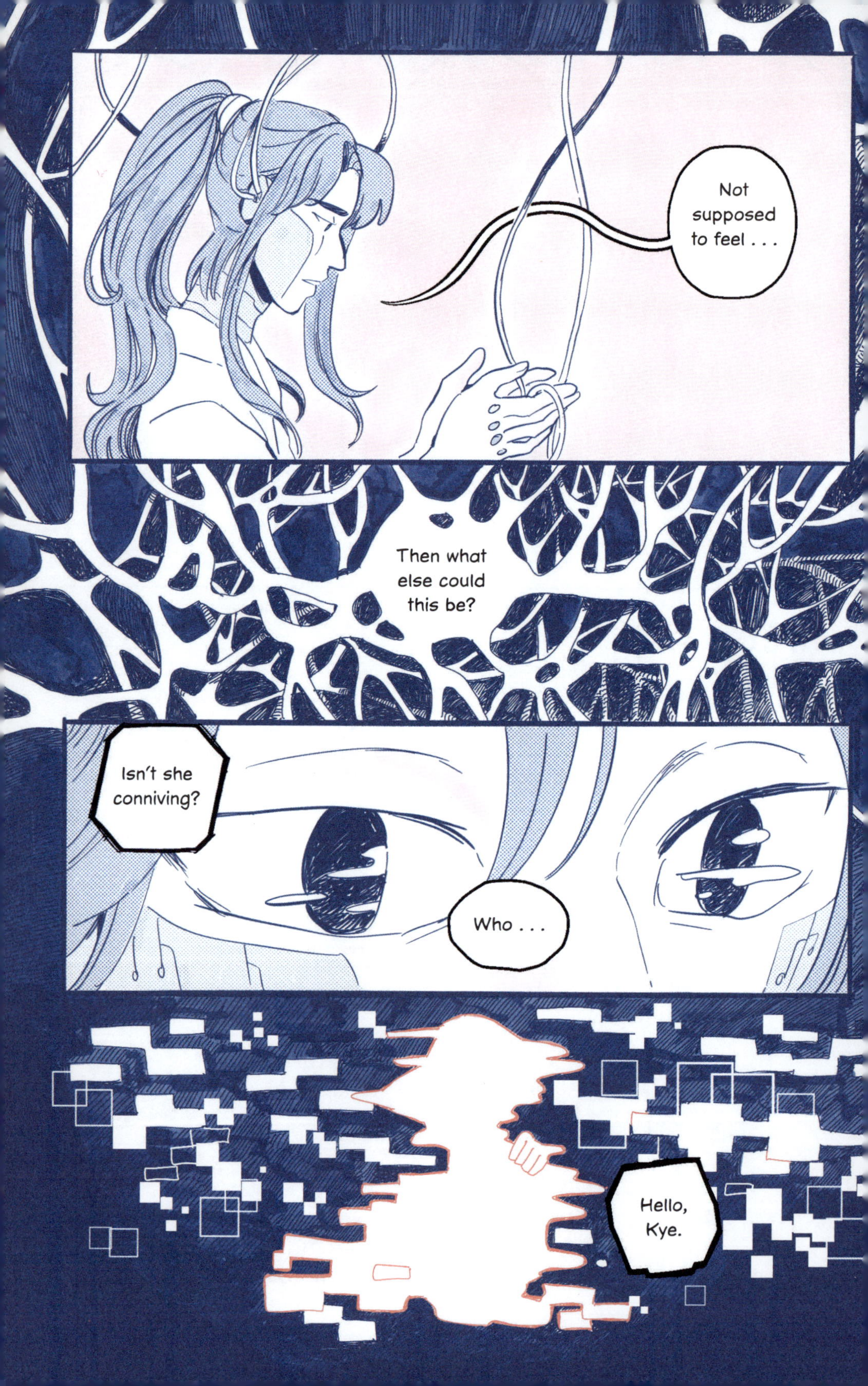
Not supposed to feel . . .
Then what else could this be?
Isn't she conniving?
Who . . .
Hello, Kye.

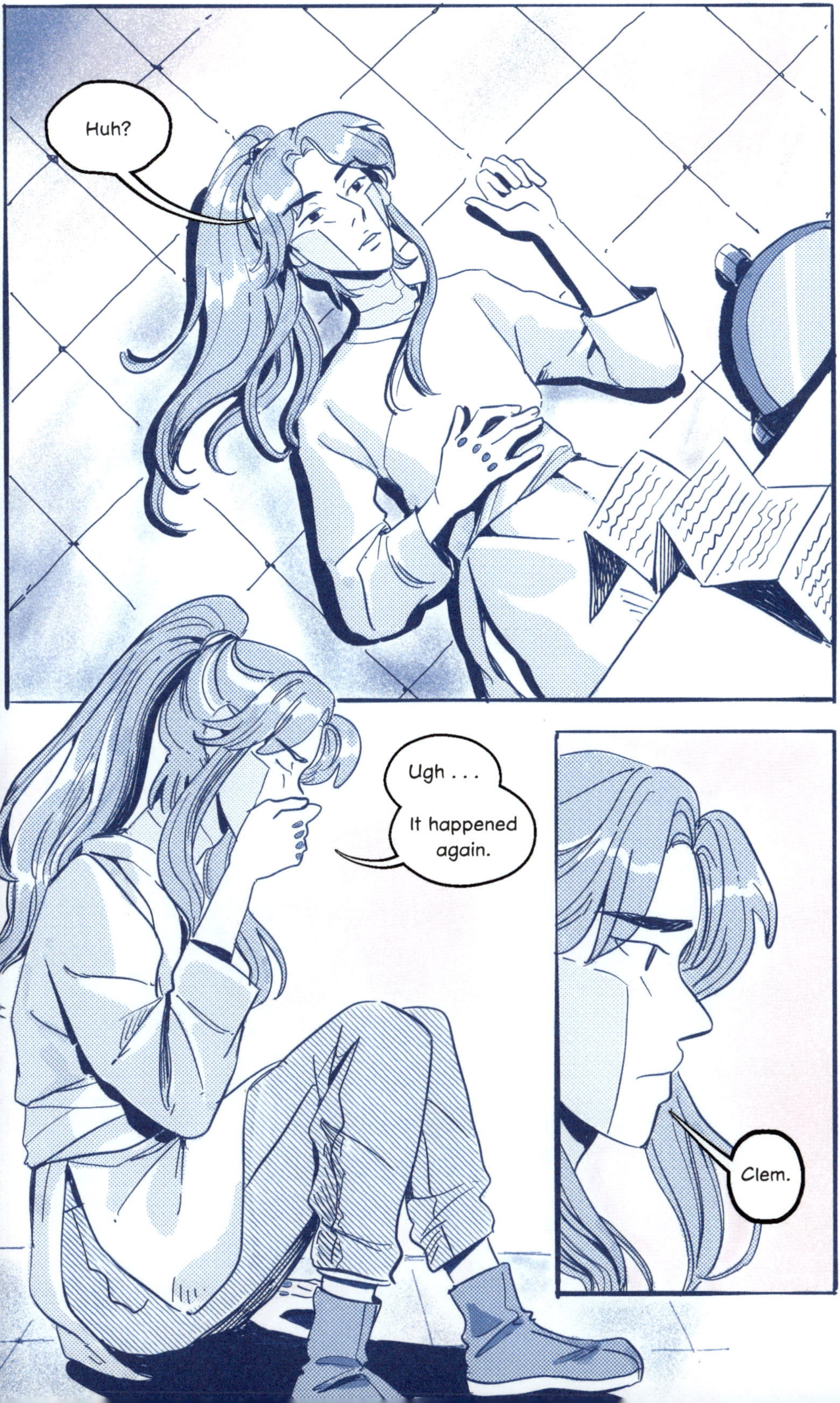

Huh?
Ugh . . .
It happened again.
Clem.

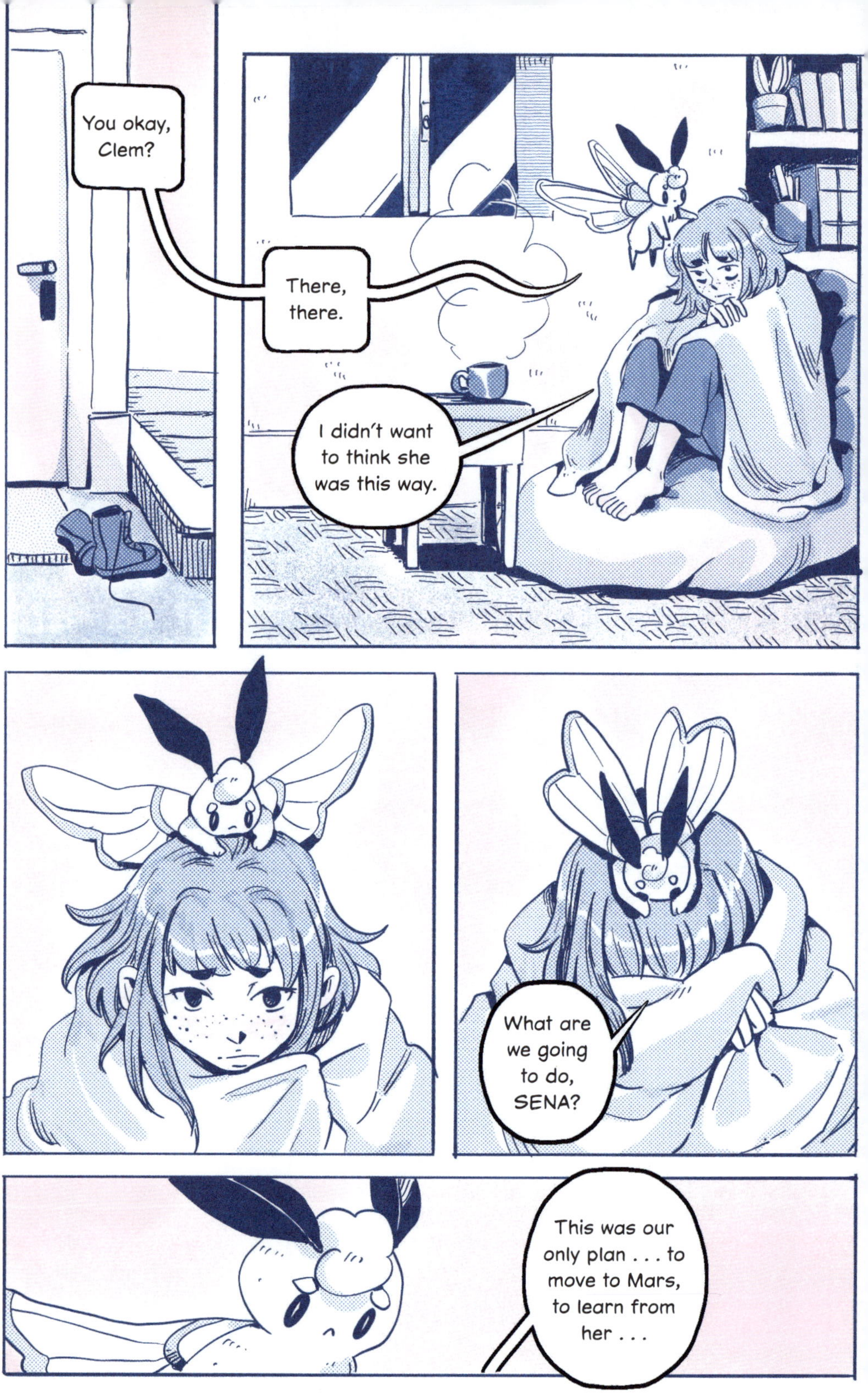

You okay, Clem?
There, there.
I didn't want to think she was this way.
What are we going to do, SENA?
This was our only plan . . . to move to Mars, to learn from her . . .

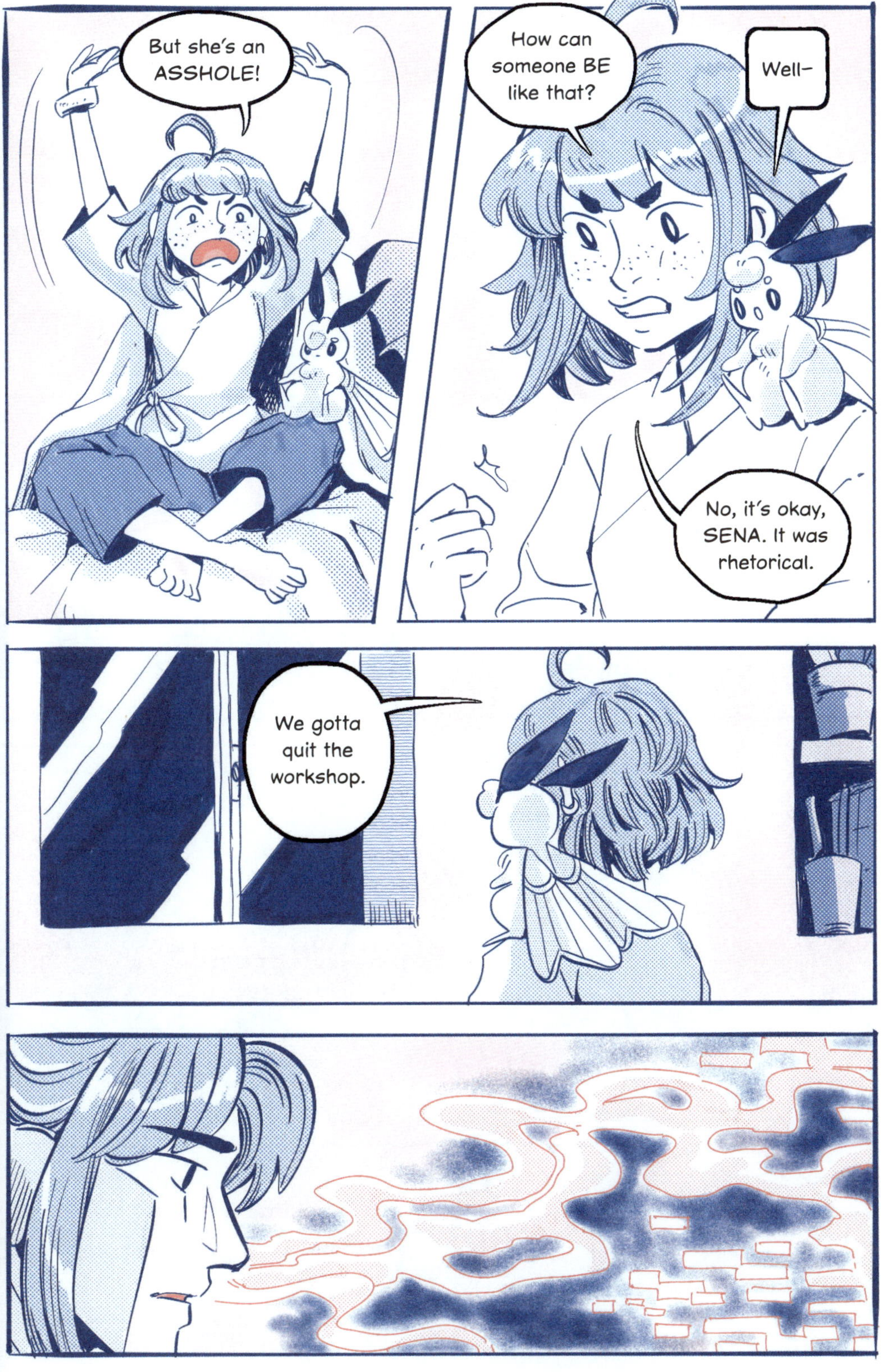
But she's an ASSHOLE!
How can someone BE like that?
Well-
No, it's okay, SENA. It was rhetorical.
We gotta quit the workshop.

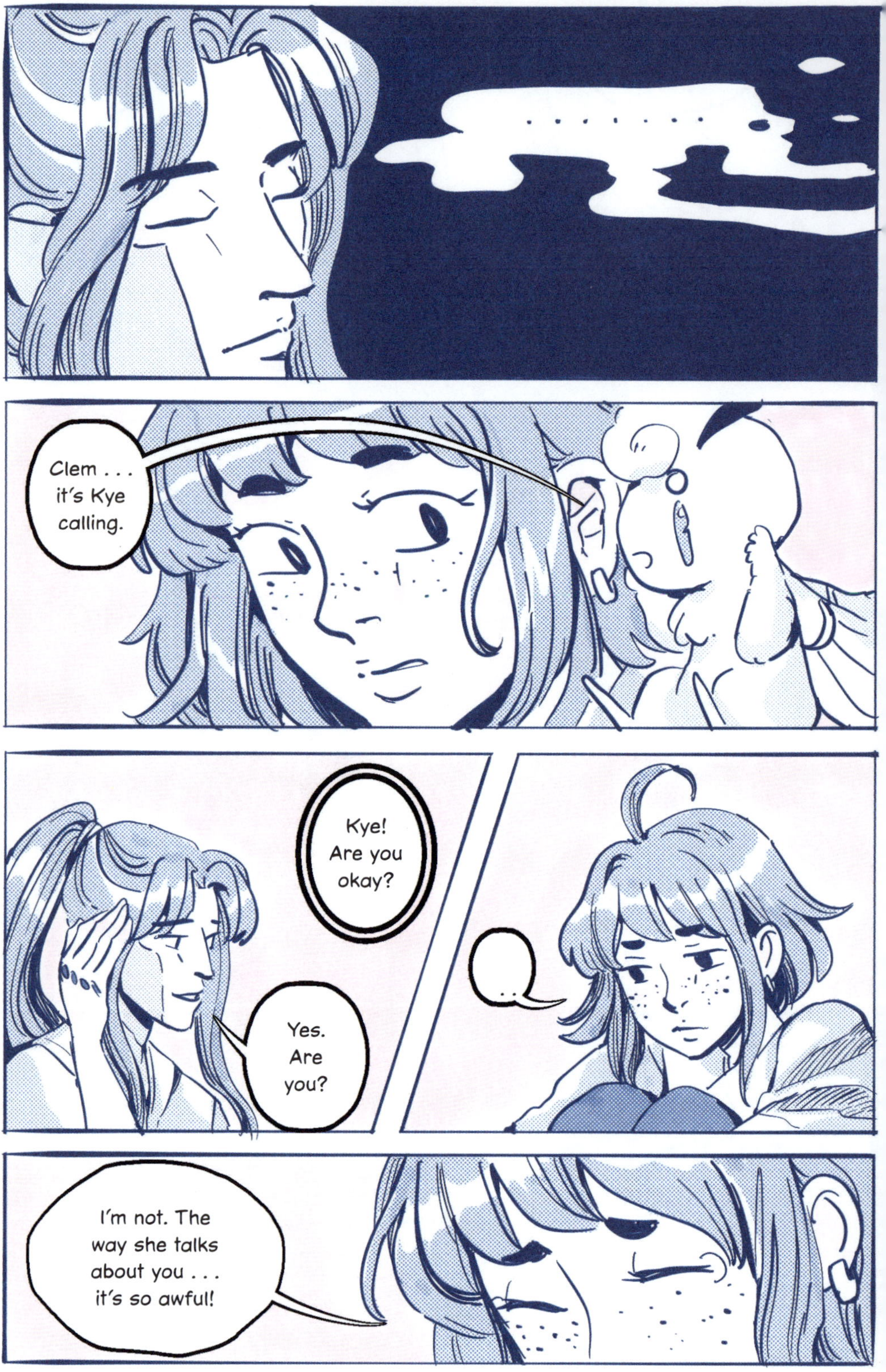
. . . .
Clem . . . it's Kye calling.
Kye! Are you okay?
Yes. Are you?
. . .
I'm not. The way she talks about you . . . it's so awful!

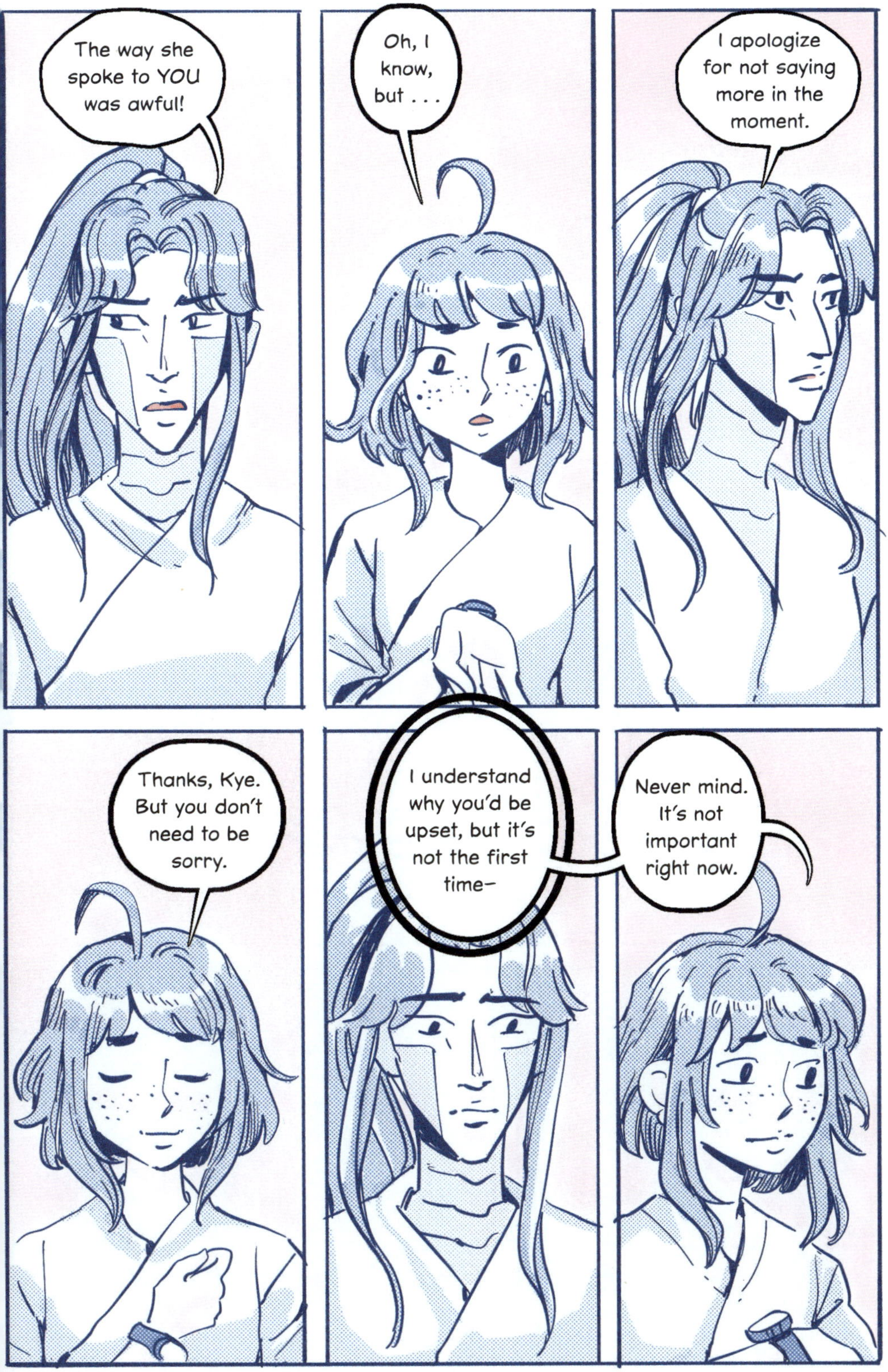
The way she spoke to YOU was awful!
Oh, I know, but . . .
I apologize for not saying more in the moment.
Thanks, Kye. But you don't need to be sorry.
I understand why you'd be upset, but it's not the first time–
Never mind. It's not important right now.

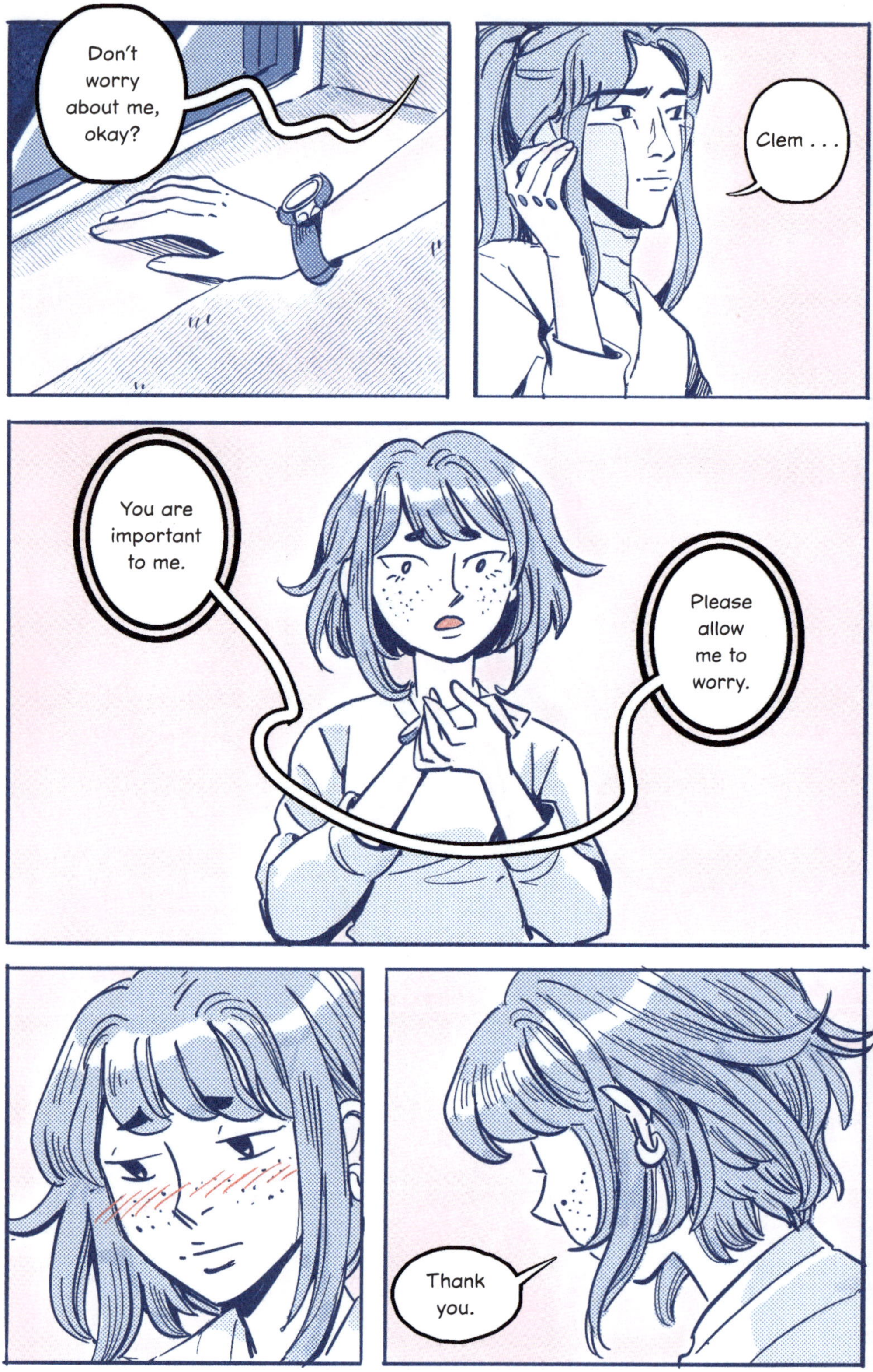
Don't worry about me, okay?
Clem . . .
You are important to me.
Please allow me to worry.
Thank you.

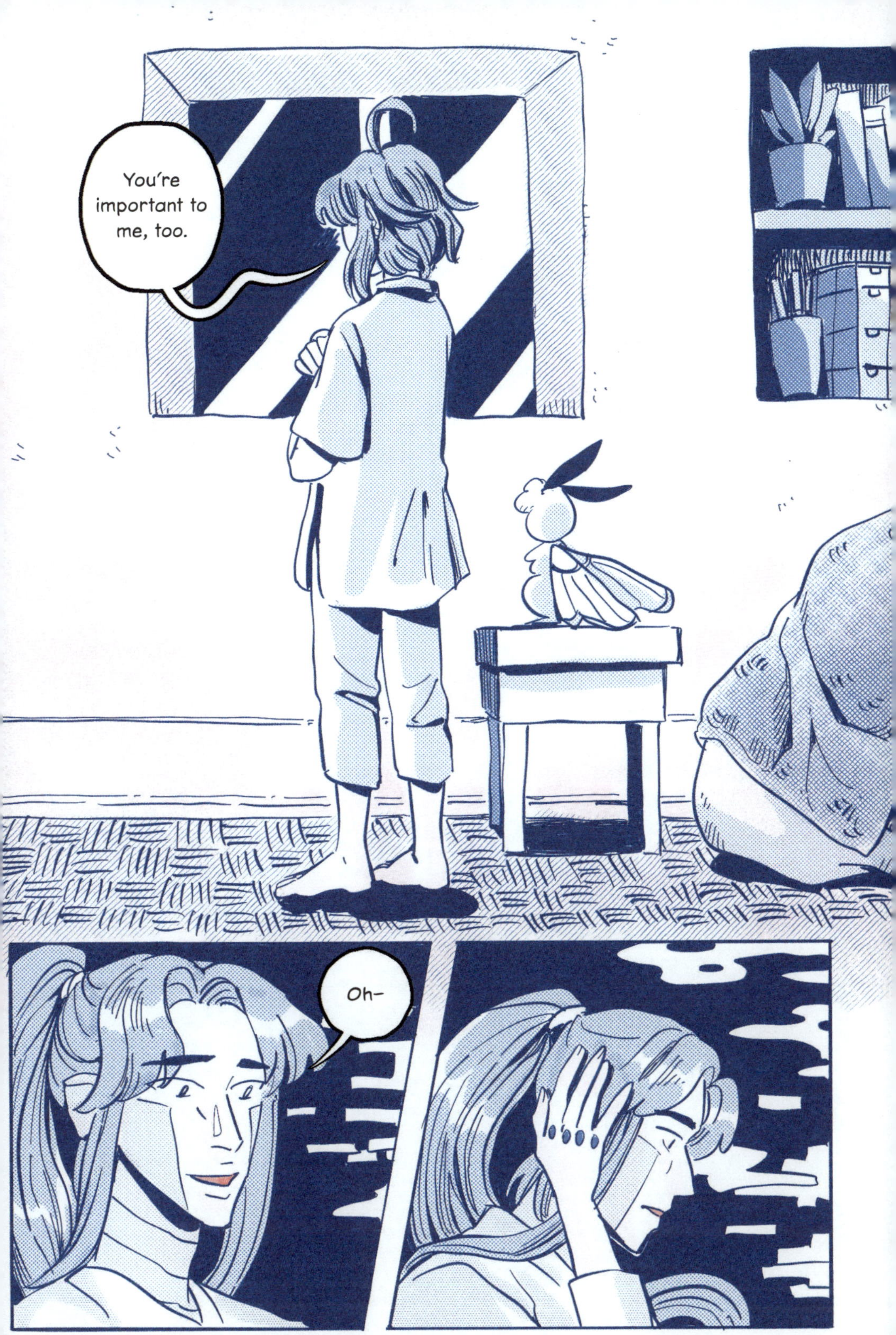
You're important to me, too.
Oh-

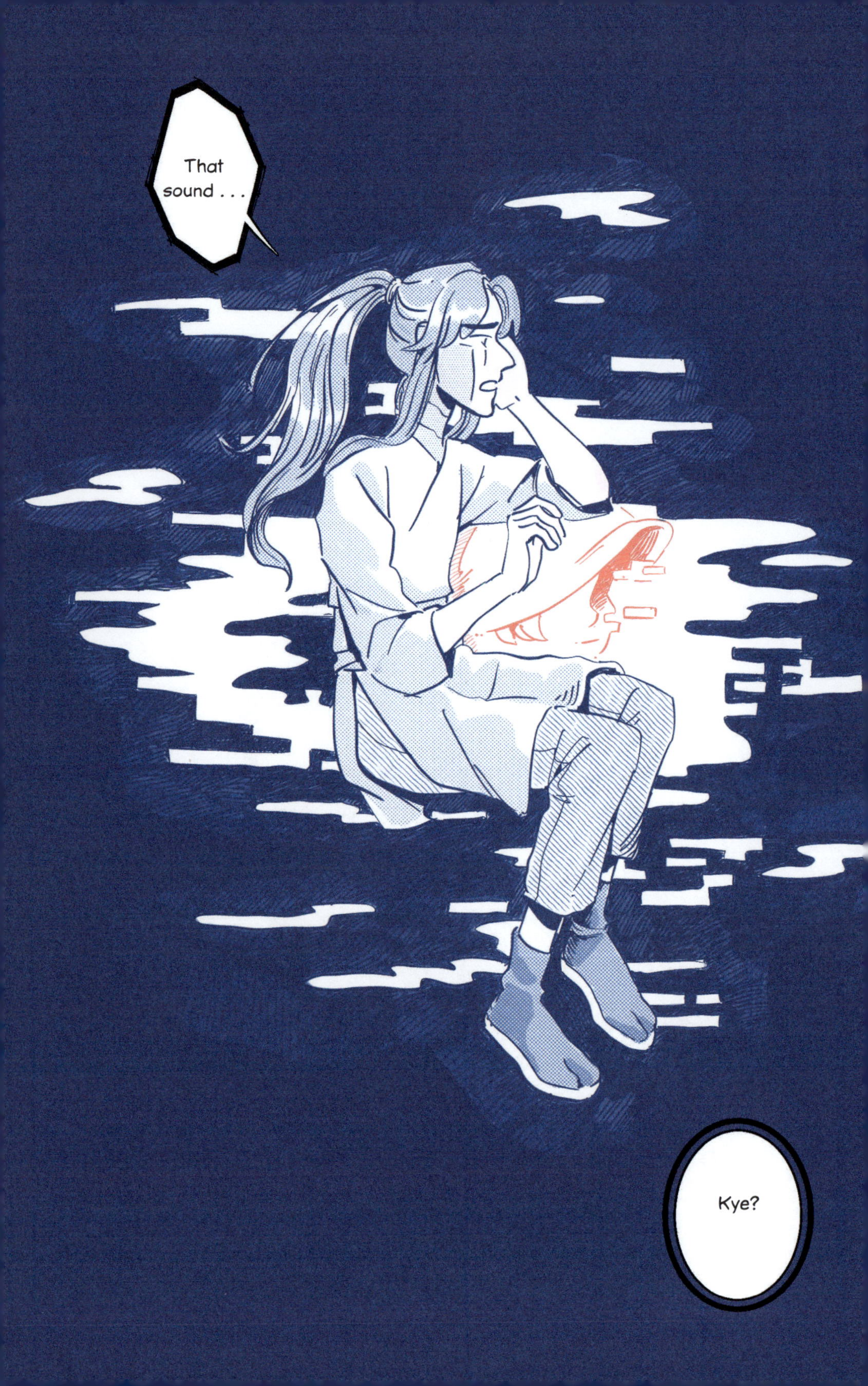
That sound . . .
Kye?

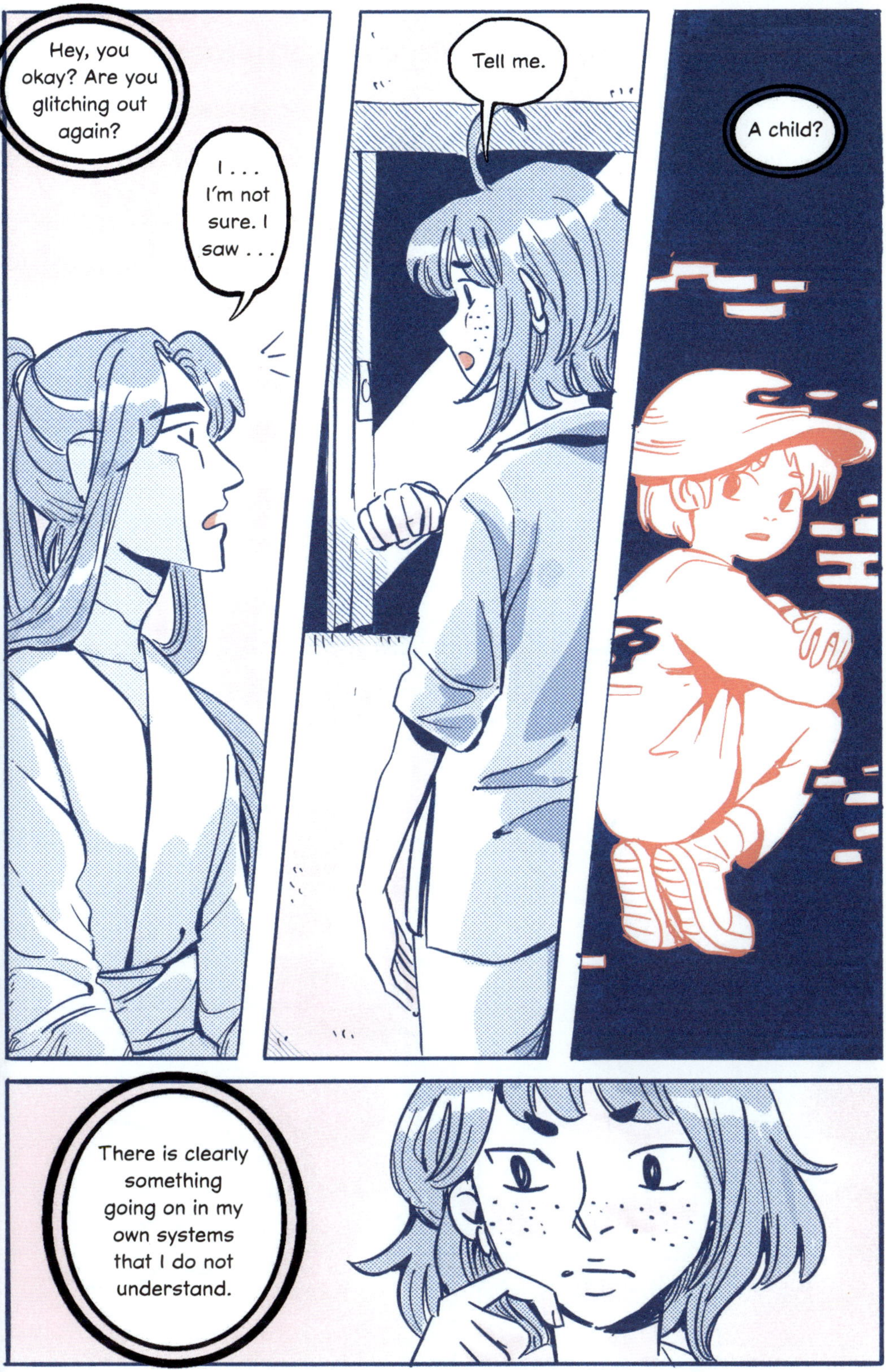
Hey, you okay? Are you glitching out again?
I . . . I'm not sure. I saw . . .
Tell me.
A child?
There is clearly something going on in my own systems that I do not understand.

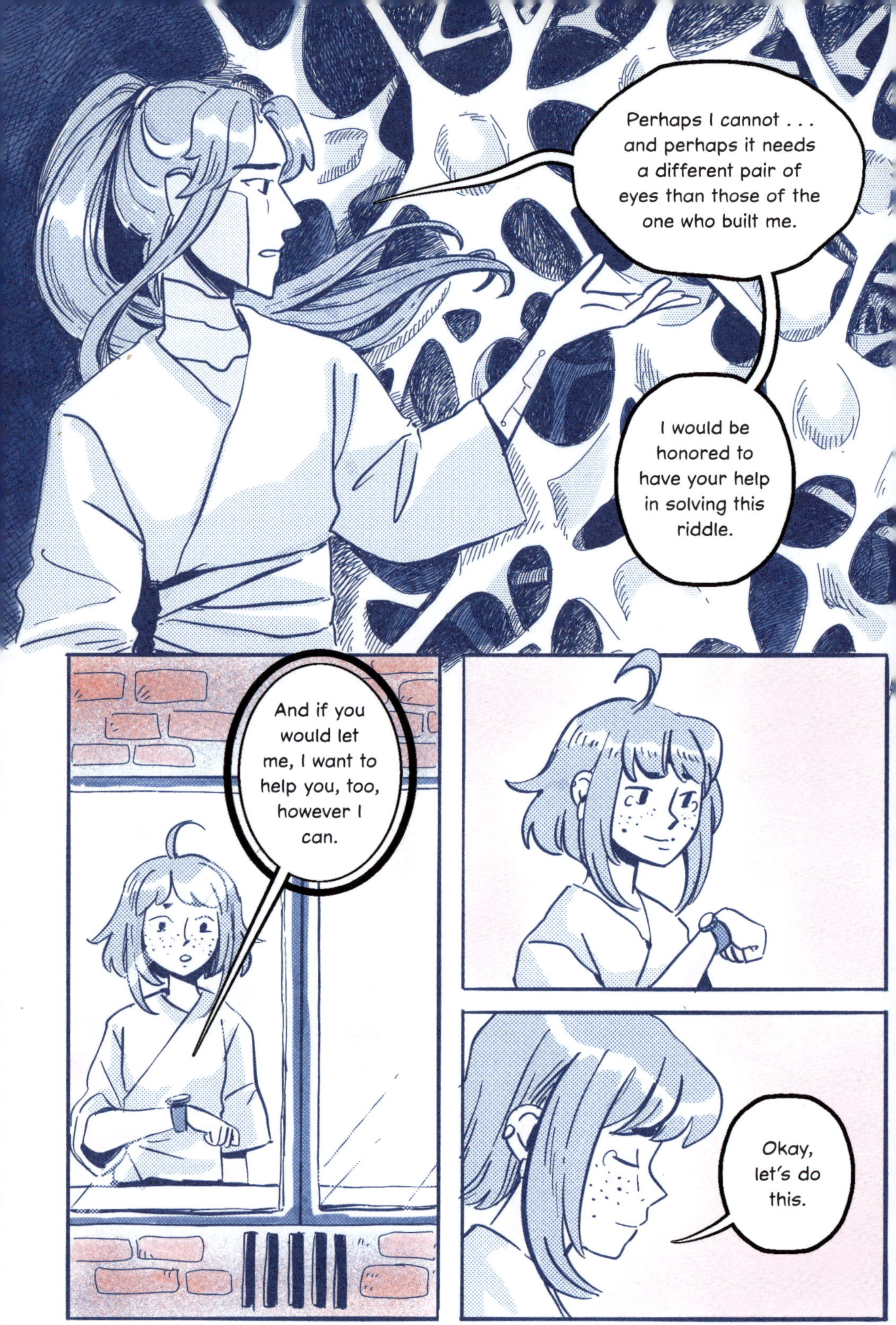
Perhaps I cannot . . . and perhaps it needs a different pair of eyes than those of the one who built me.
I would be honored to have your help in solving this riddle.
And if you would let me, I want to help you, too, however I can.
Okay, let's do this.

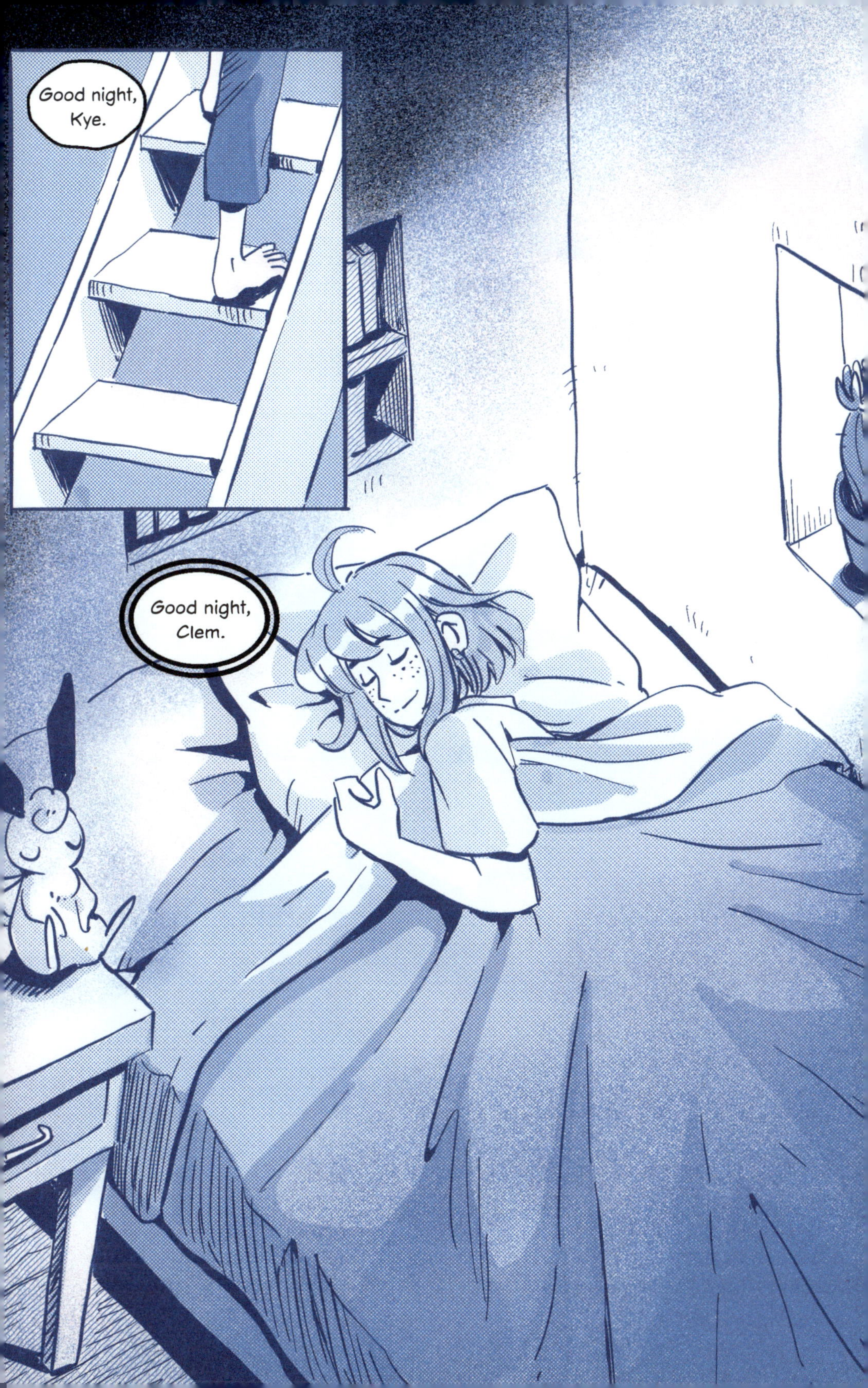
Good night, Kye.
Good night, Clem.

00110000 00110101

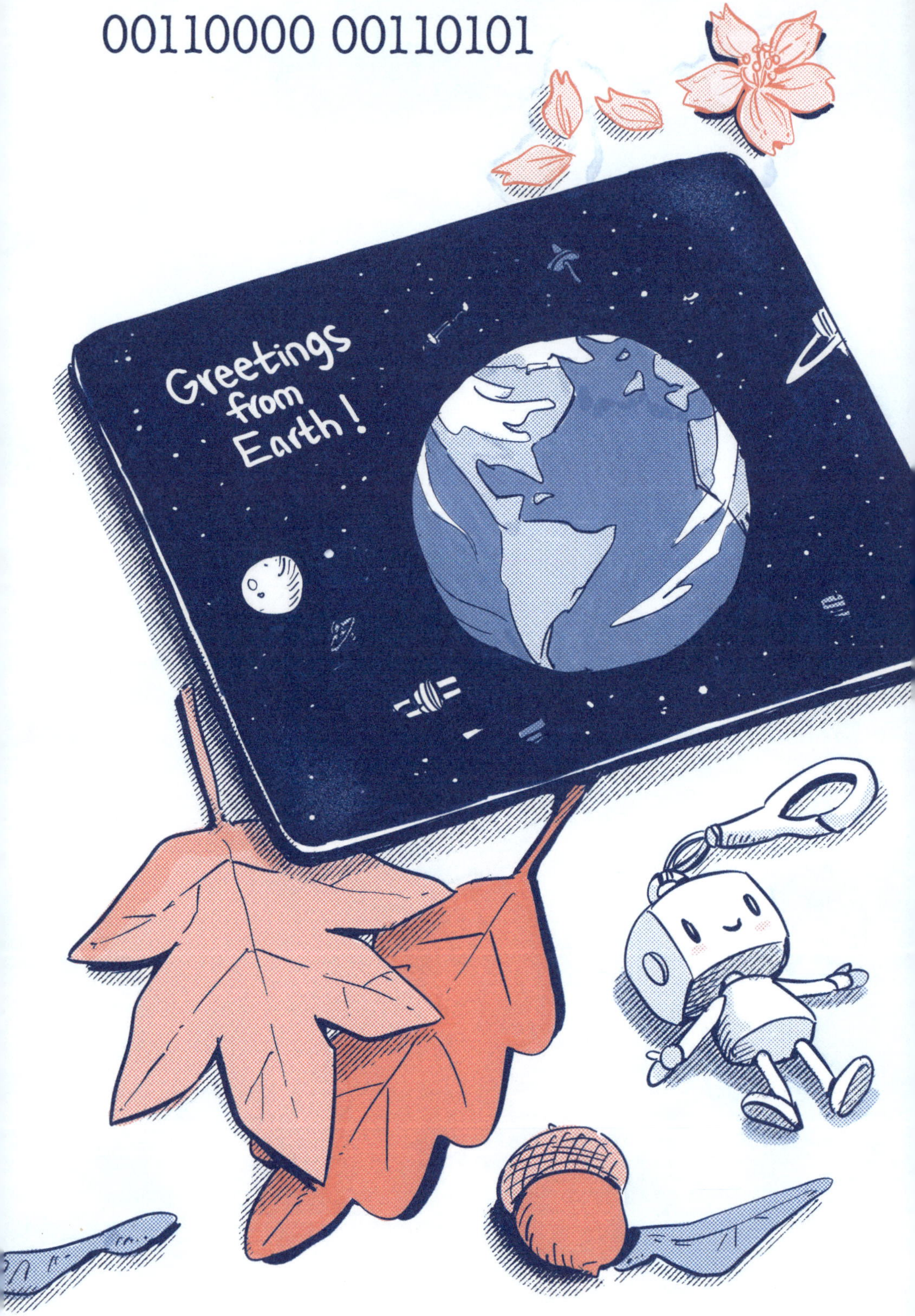
Greetings from Earth!

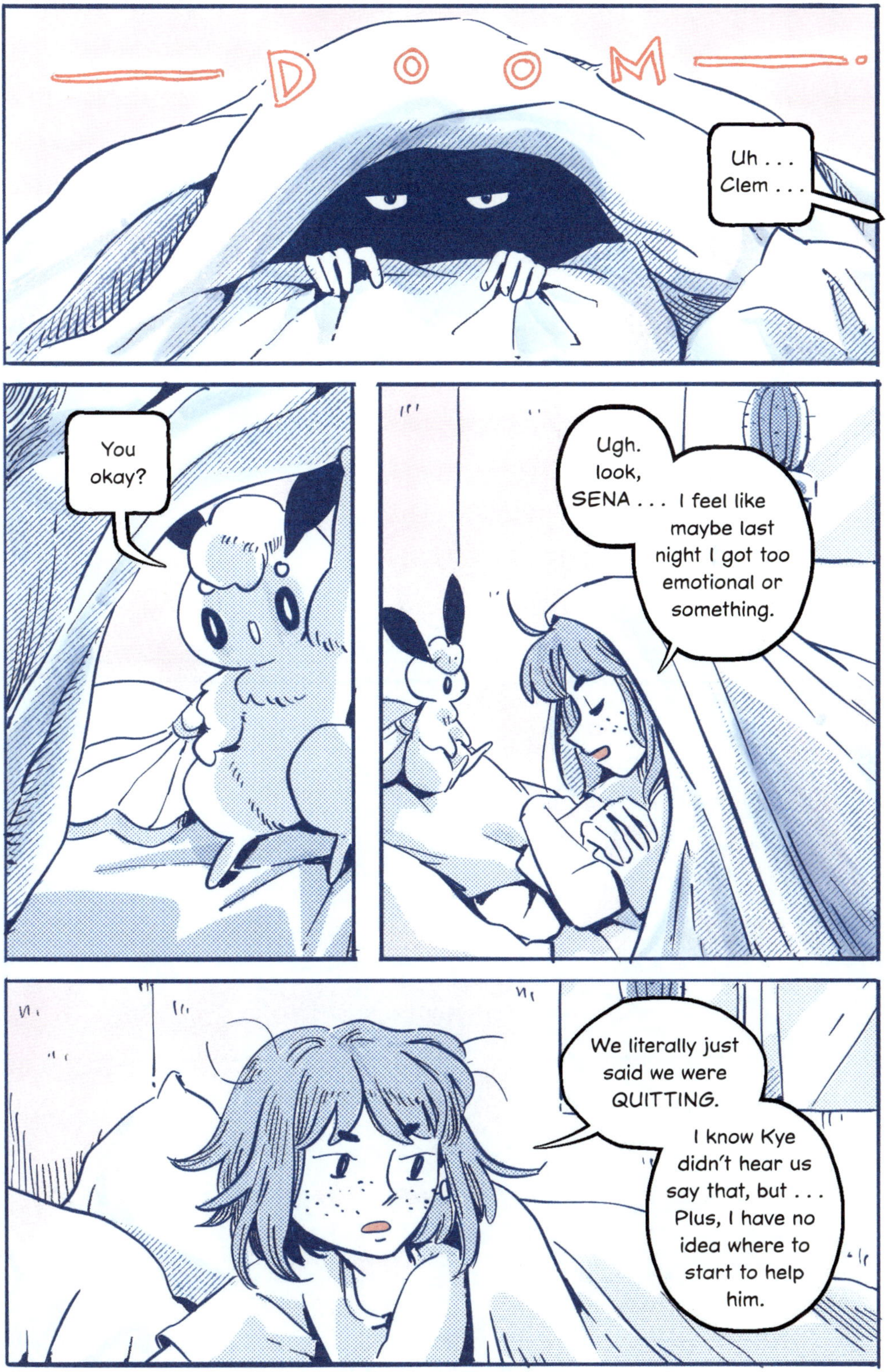
DOOM
Uh . . . Clem . . .
You okay?
Ugh. look, SENA . . . I feel like maybe last night I got too emotional or something.
We literally just said we were QUITTING.
I know Kye didn't hear us say that, but . . . Plus, I have no idea where to start to help him.

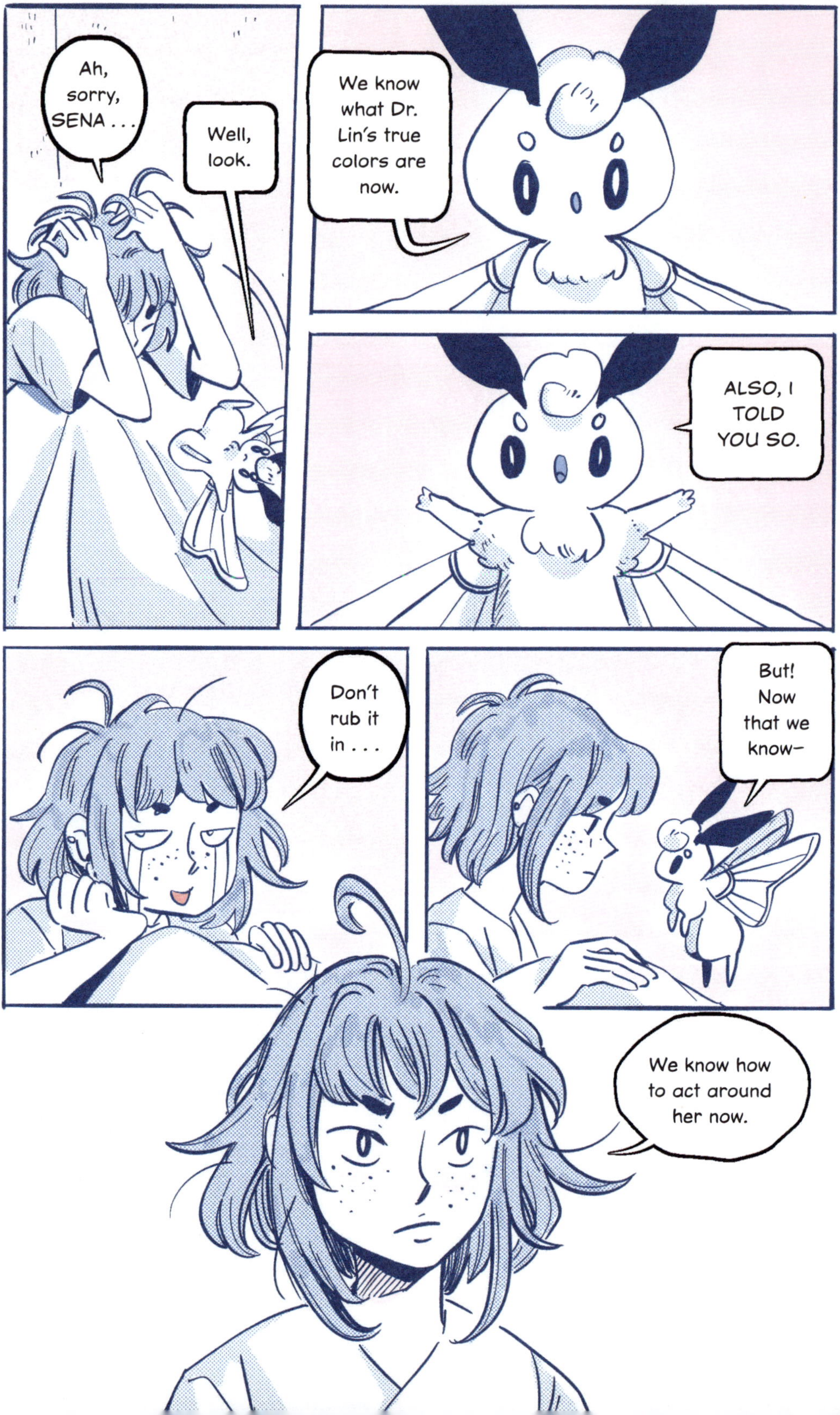
Ah, sorry, SENA . . .
Well, look.
We know what Dr. Lin's true colors are now.
ALSO, I TOLD YOU SO.
Don't rub it in . . .
But! Now that we know–
We know how to act around her now.

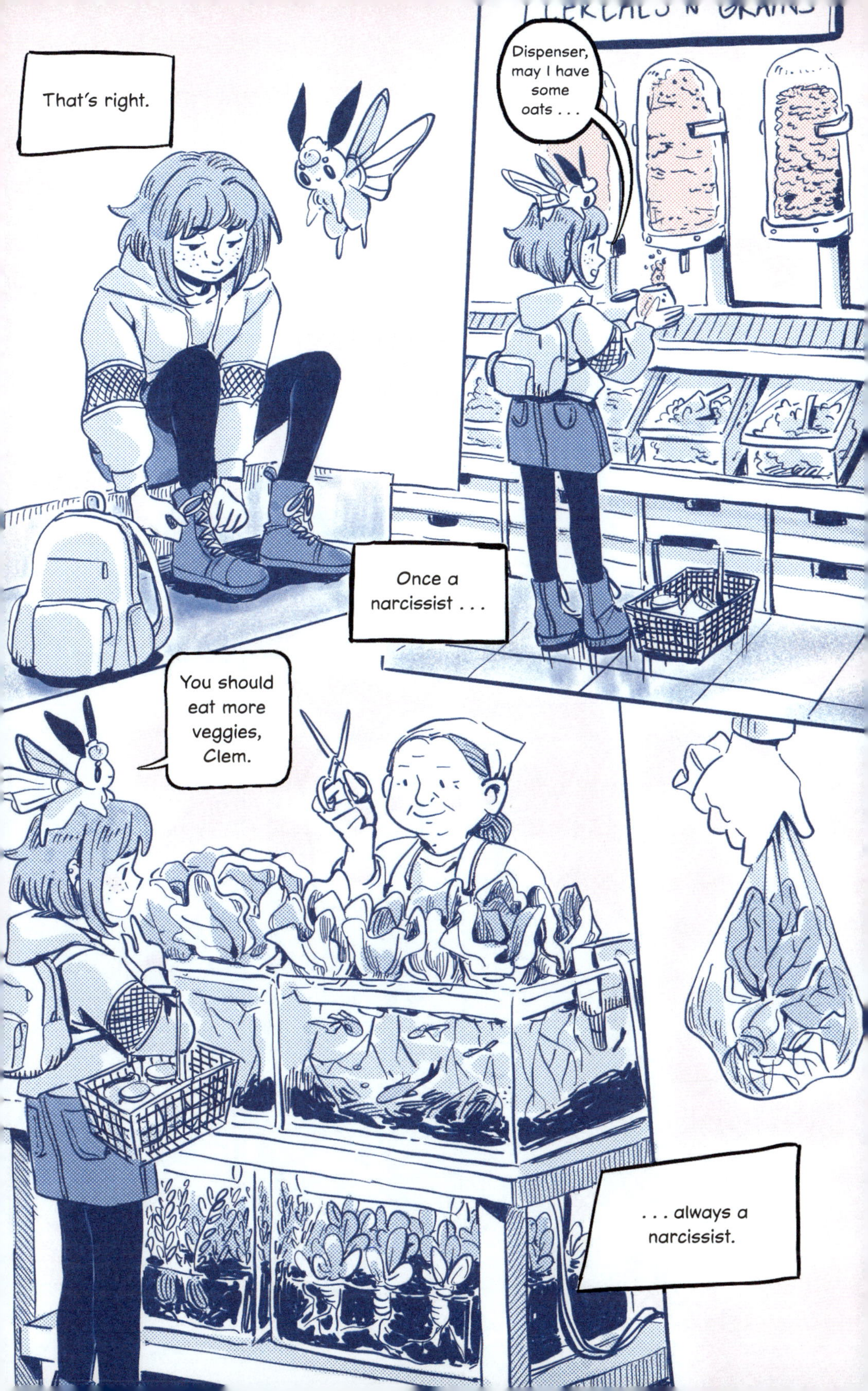
That's right.
Dispenser, may I have some oats . . .
Once a narcissist . . .
You should eat more veggies, Clem.
. . . always a narcissist.

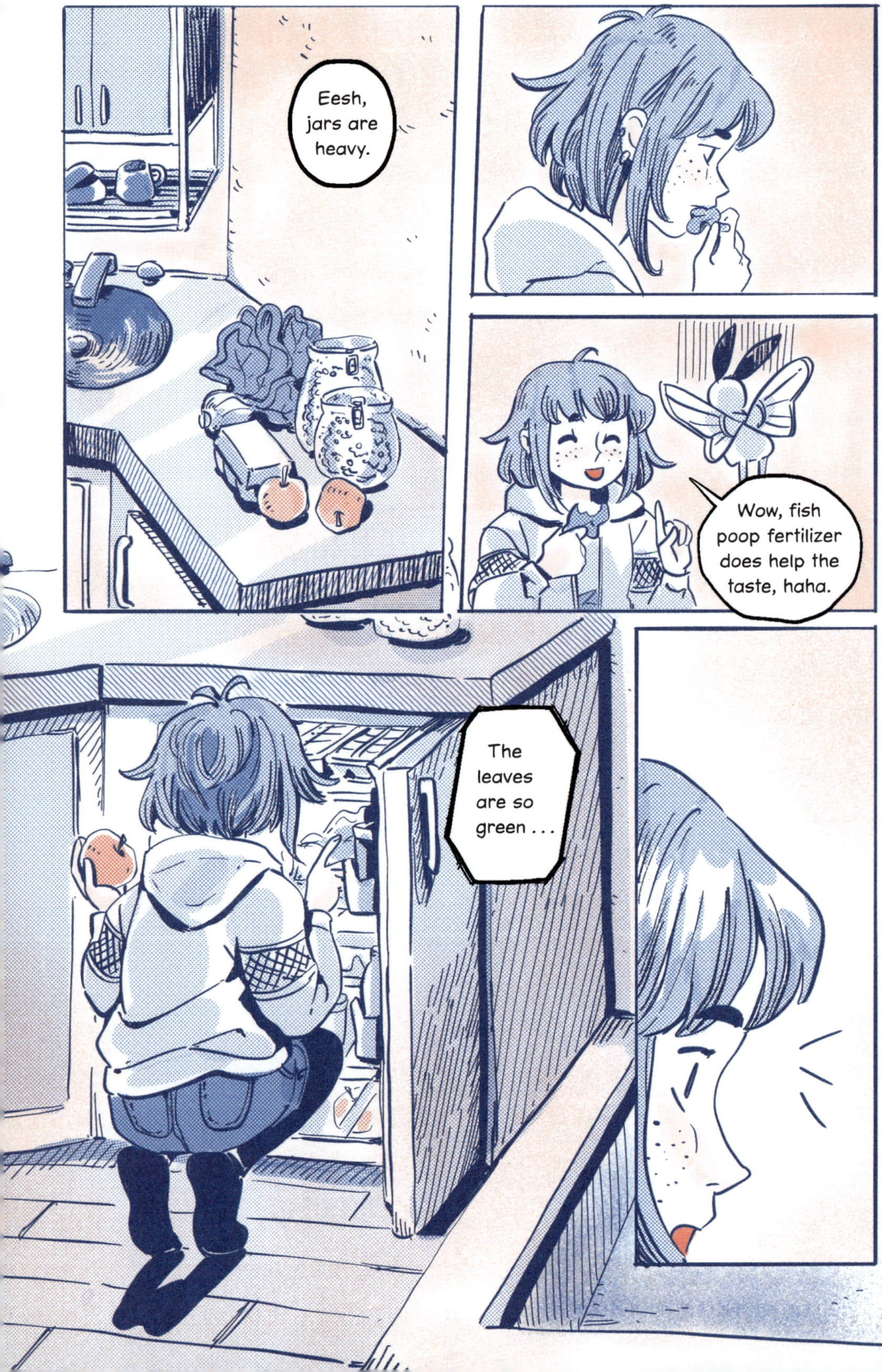
Eesh, jars are heavy.
Wow, fish poop fertilizer does help the taste, haha.
The leaves are so green . . .

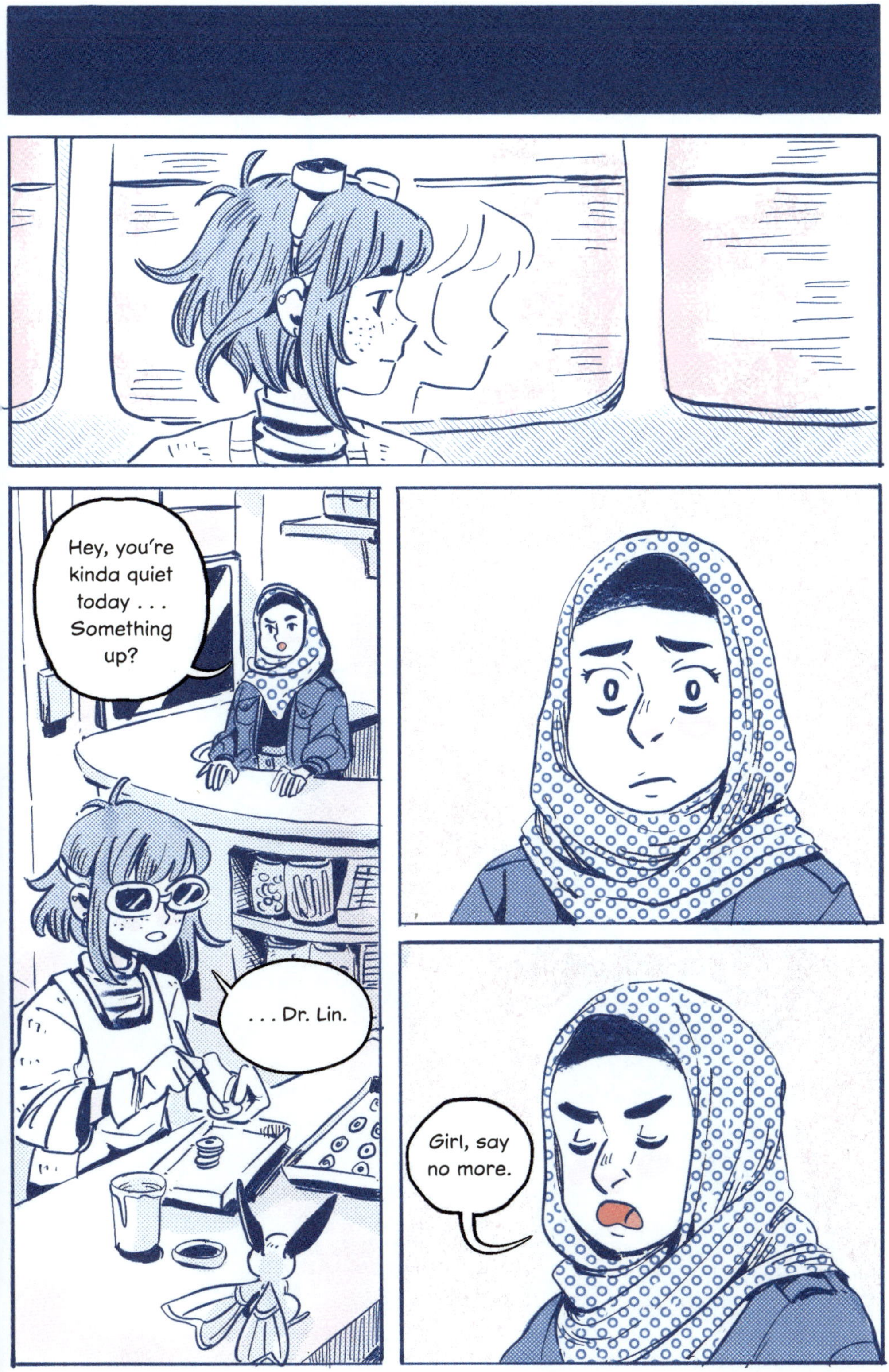
Hey, you're kinda quiet today . . . Something up?
. . . Dr. Lin.
Girl, say no more.

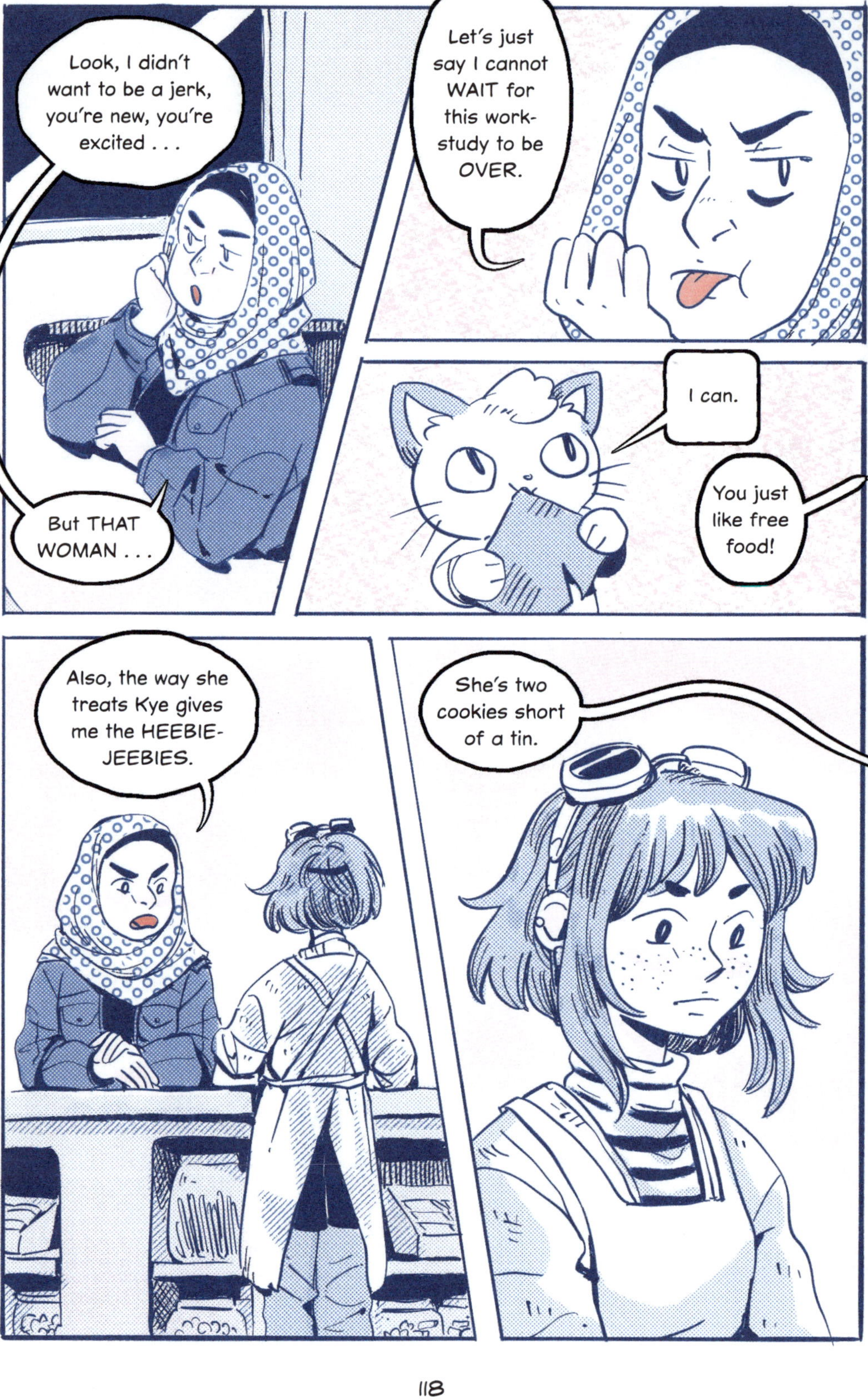
Look, I didn't want to be a jerk, you're new, you're excited . . .
But THAT WOMAN . . .
Let's just say I cannot WAIT for this work-study to be OVER.
I can.
You just like free food!
Also, the way she treats Kye gives me the HEEBIE-JEEBIES.
She's two cookies short of a tin.

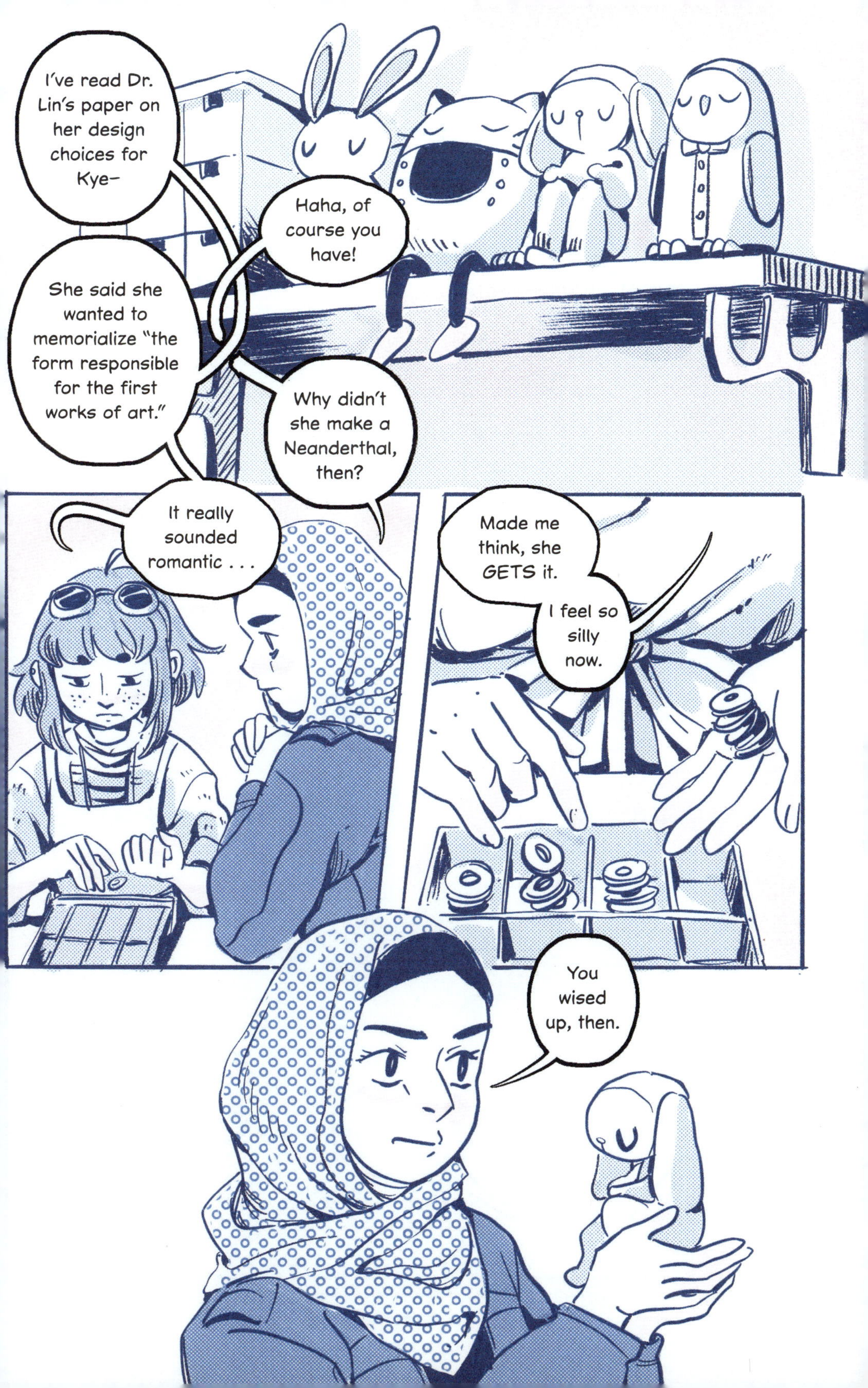
I've read Dr. Lin's paper on her design choices for Kye–
Haha, of course you have!
She said she wanted to memorialize "the form responsible for the first works of art."
Why didn't she make a Neanderthal, then?
It really sounded romantic . . .
Made me think, she GETS it.
I feel so silly now.
You wised up, then.

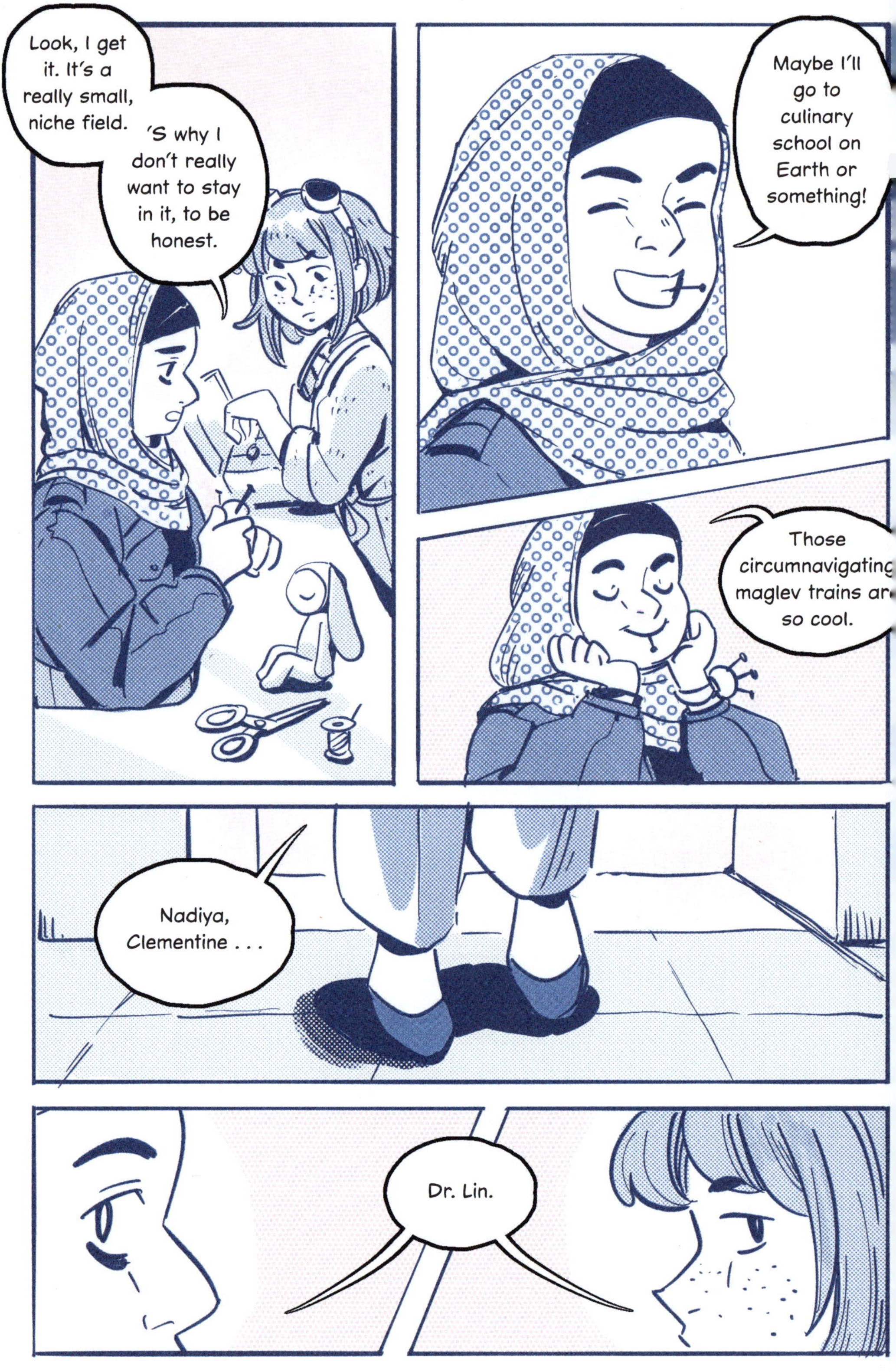

Look, I get it. It's a really small, niche field.
'S why I don't really want to stay in it, to be honest.
Maybe I'll go to culinary school on Earth or something!
Those circumnavigating maglev trains ar
so cool.
Nadiya, Clementine . . .
Dr. Lin.

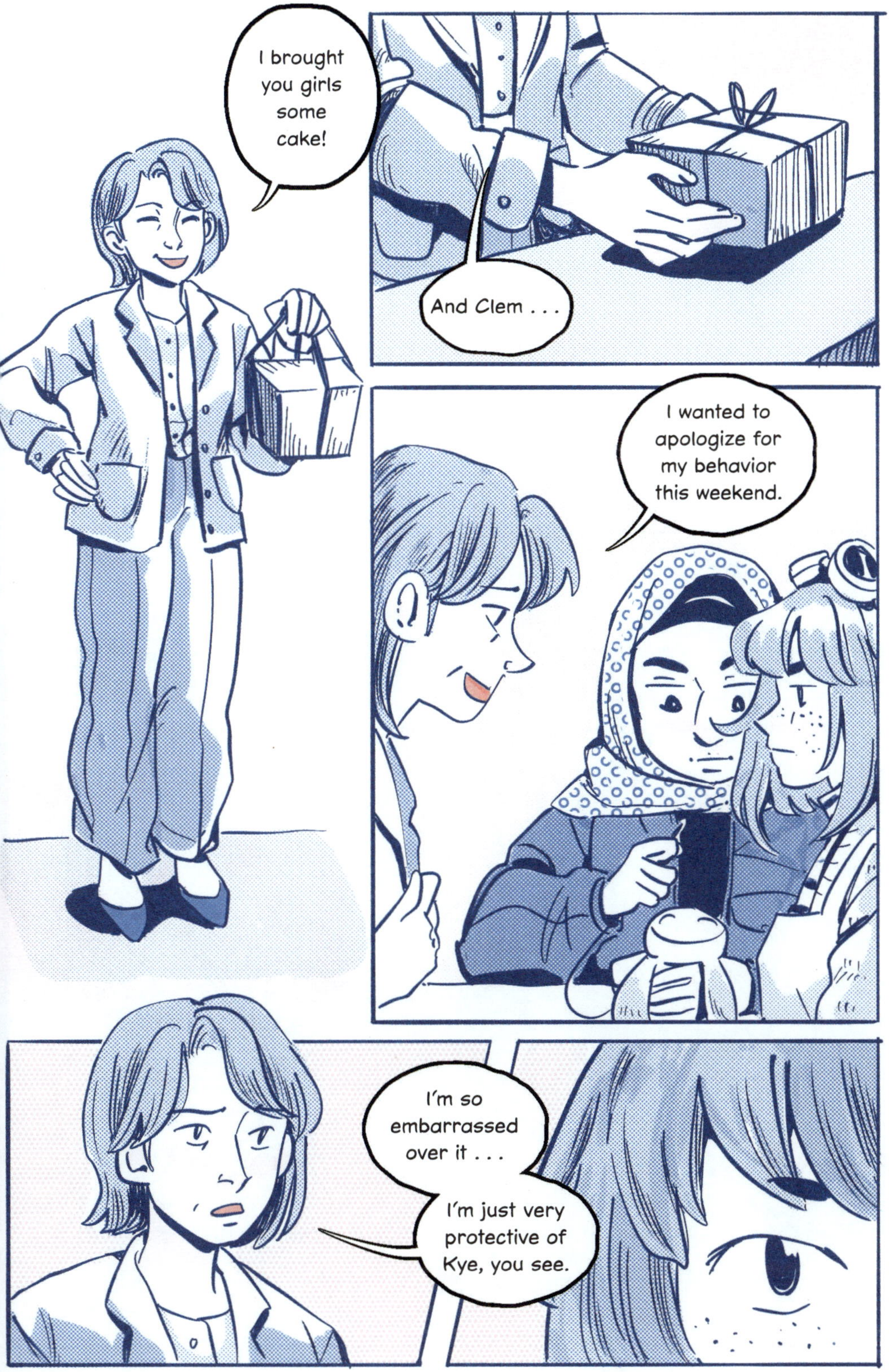
I brought you girls some cake!
And Clem . . .
I wanted to apologize for my behavior this weekend.
I'm so embarrassed over it . . .
I'm just very protective of Kye, you see.

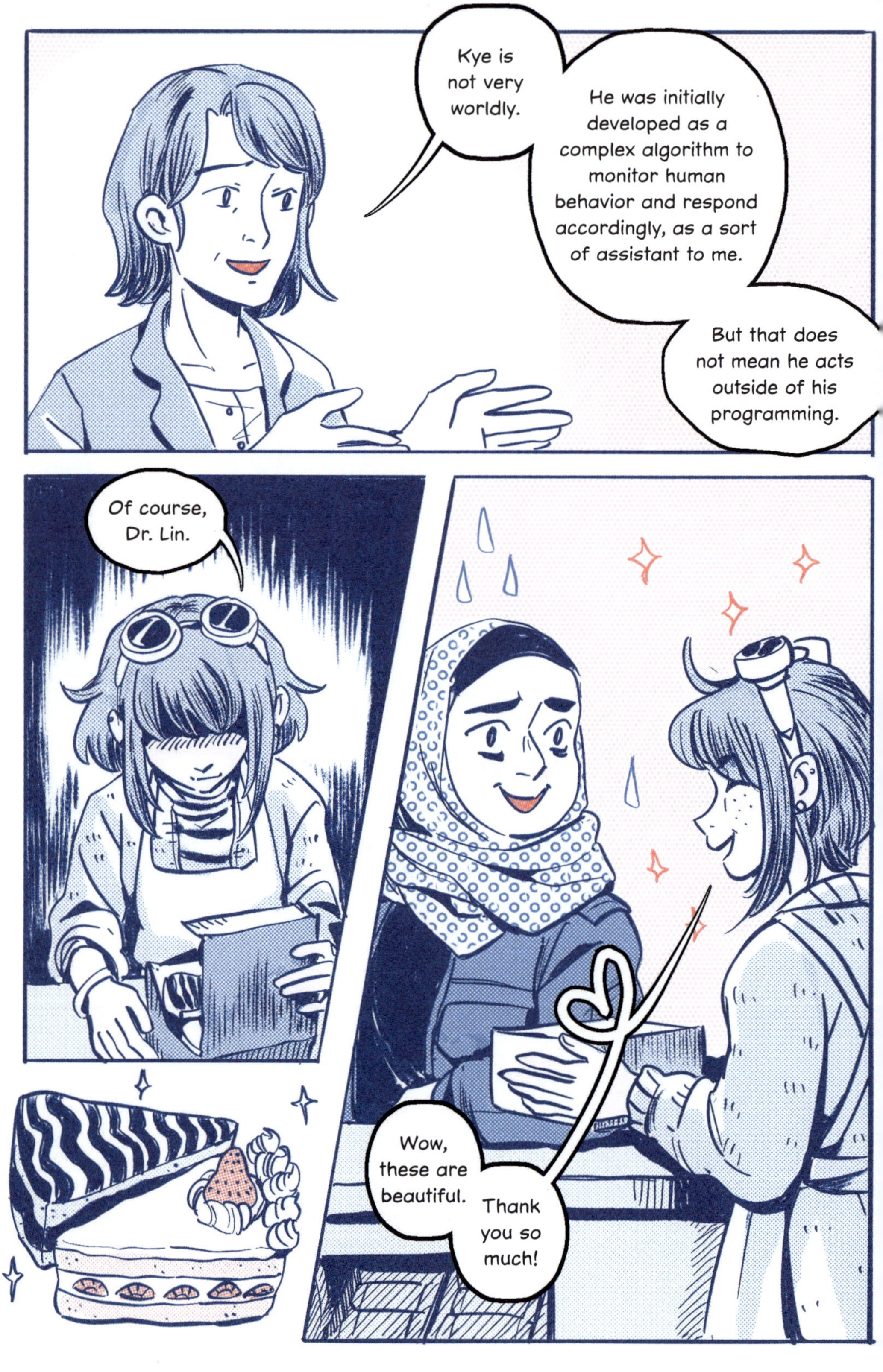
Kye is not very worldly.
He was initially developed as a complex algorithm to monitor human behavior and respond accordingly, as a sort of assistant to me.
But that does not mean he acts outside of his programming.
Of course, Dr. Lin.
Wow, these are beautiful.
Thank you so much!

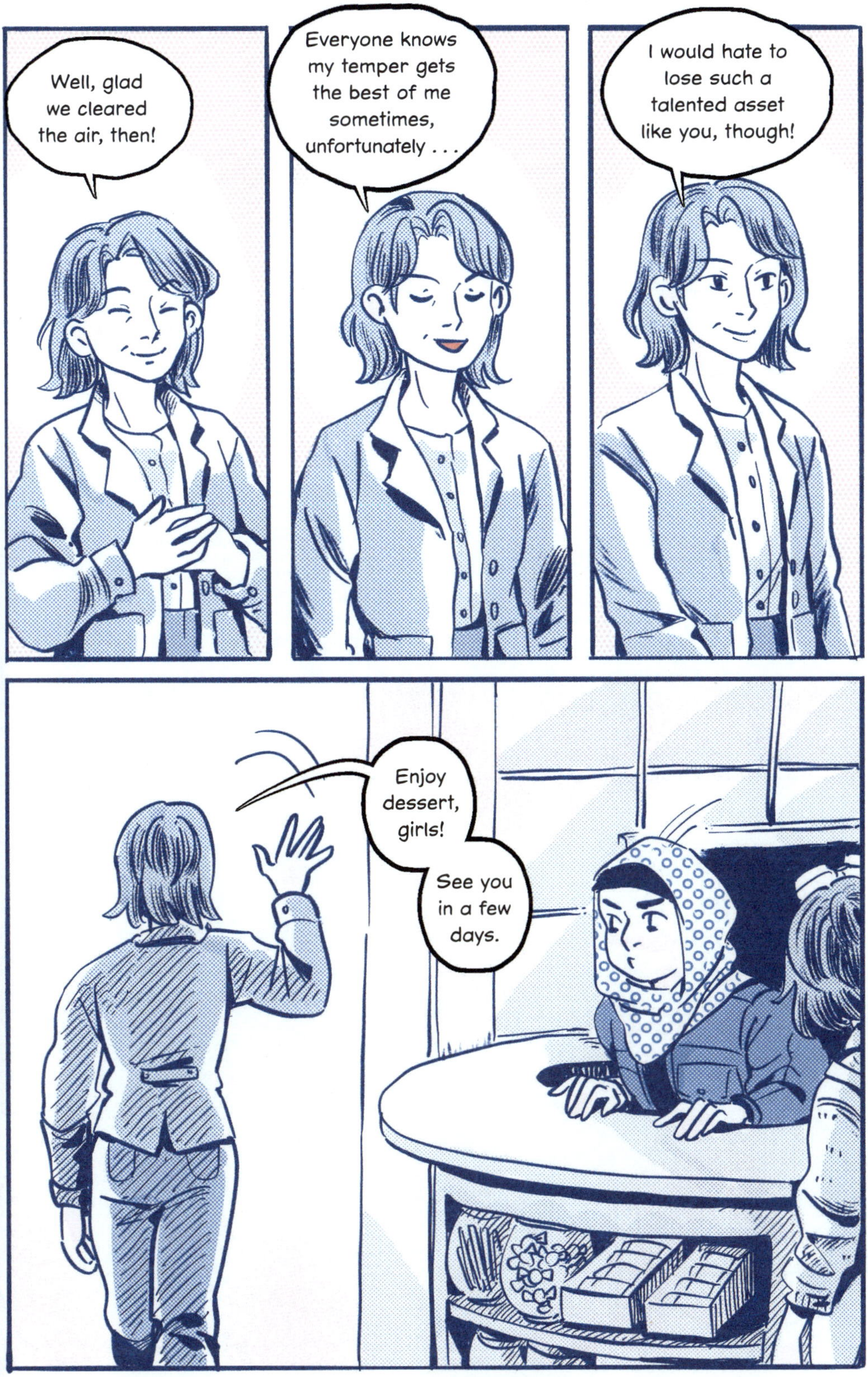
Well, glad we cleared the air, then!
Everyone knows my temper gets the best of me sometimes, unfortunately . . .
I would hate to lose such a talented asset like you, though!
Enjoy dessert, girls!
See you in a few days.

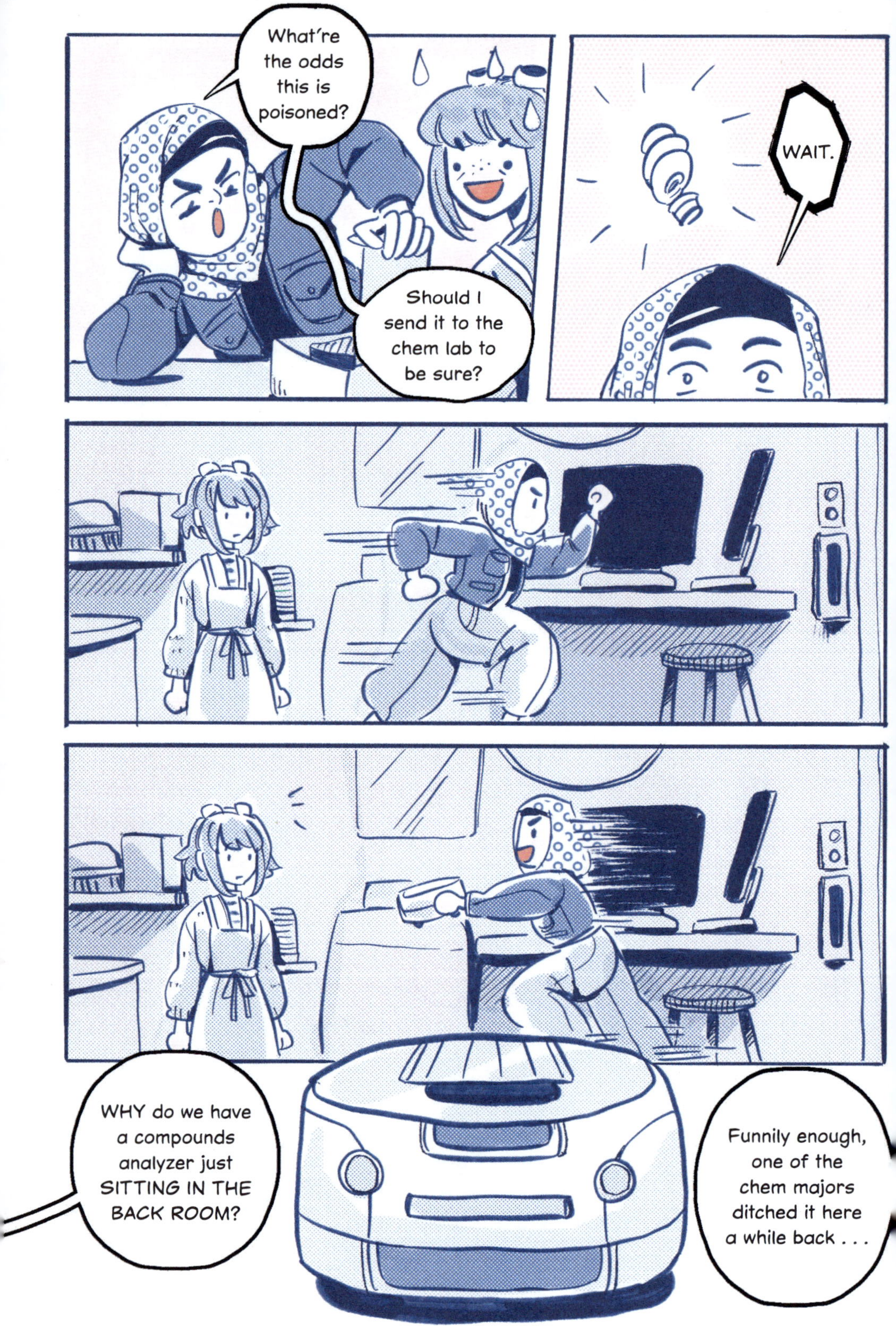
What're the odds this is poisoned?
Should I send it to the chem lab to be sure?
WAIT.
WHY do we have a compounds analyzer just SITTING IN THE BACK ROOM?
Funnily enough, one of the chem majors ditched it here a while back . . .

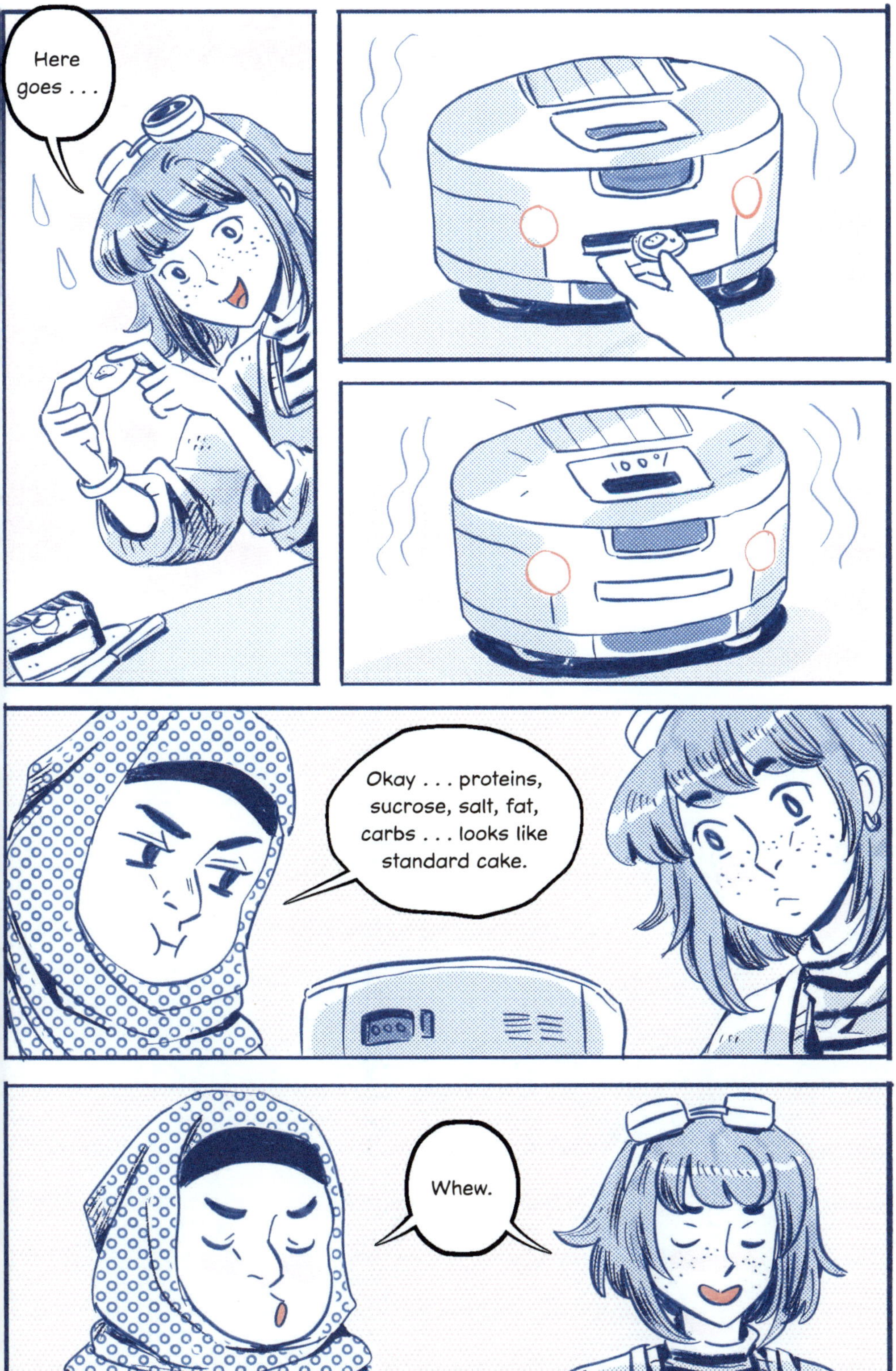
Here goes . . .
Okay . . . proteins, sucrose, salt, fat, carbs . . . looks like standard cake.
Whew.

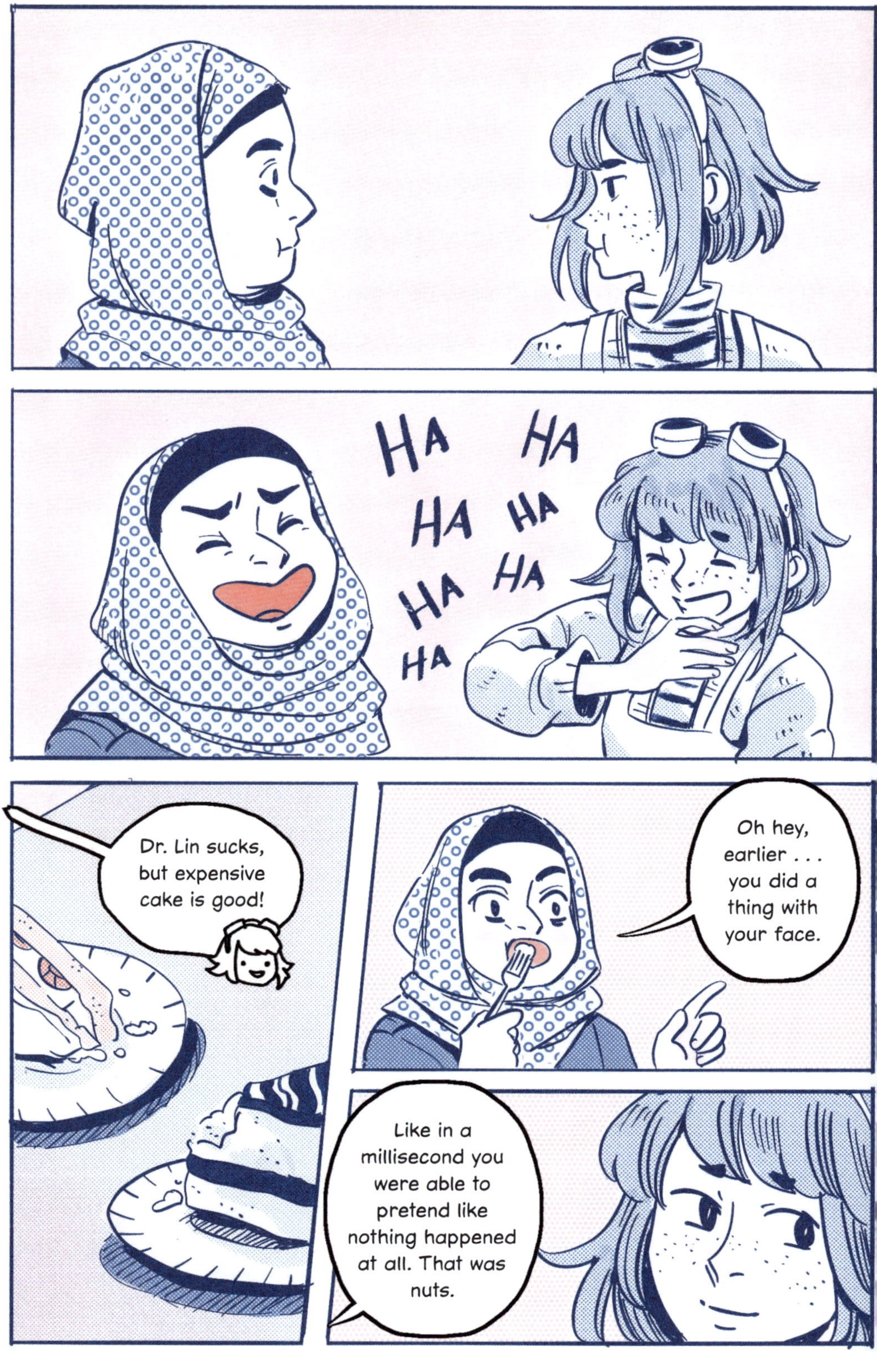

HA HA HA HA HA HA HA
Dr. Lin sucks, but expensive cake is good!
Oh hey, earlier . . . you did a thing with your face.
Like in a millisecond you were able to pretend like nothing happened at all. That was nuts.

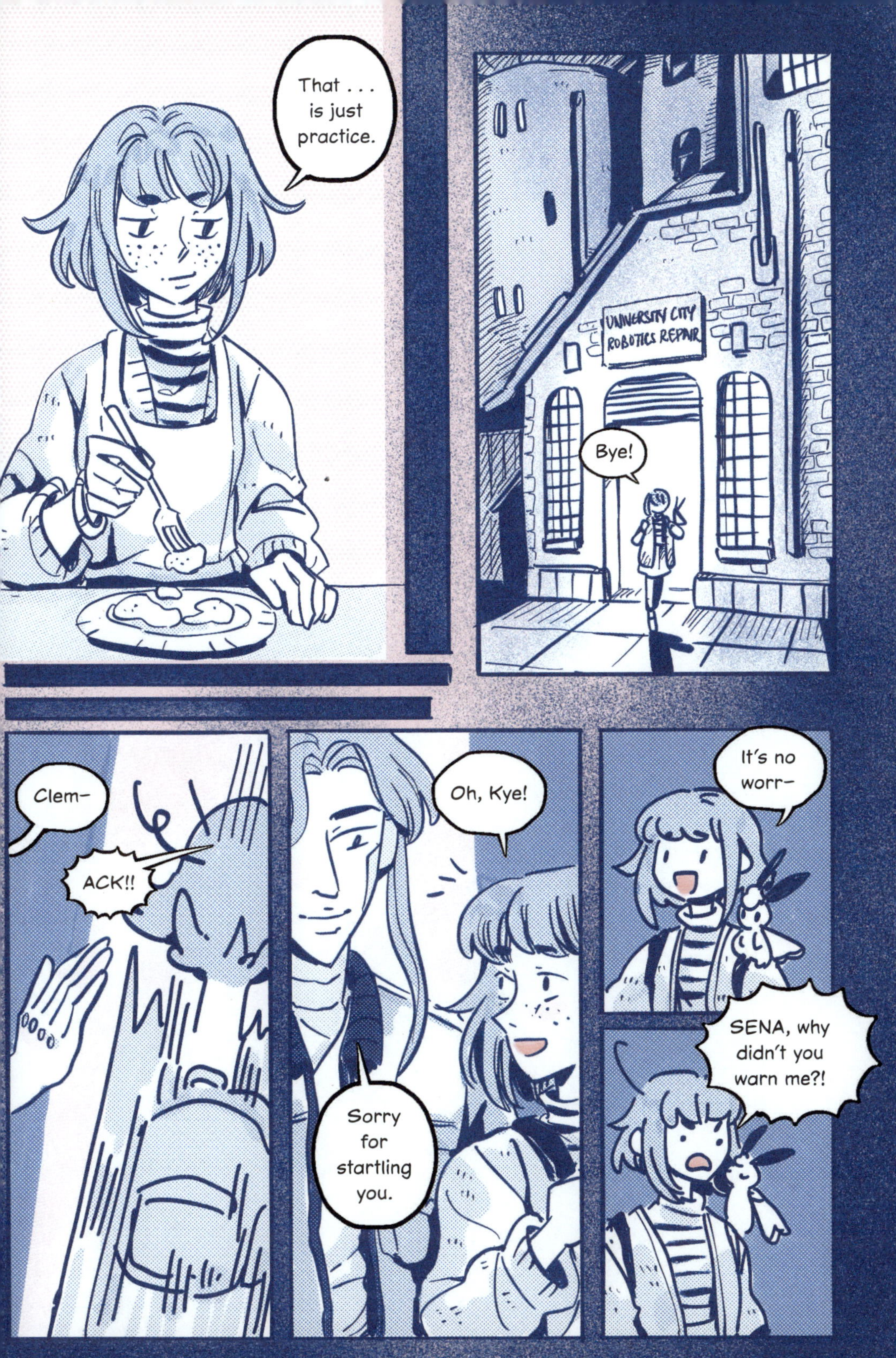
That . . . is just practice.
UNIVERSITY CITY ROBOTICS REPAIR
Bye!
Clem–
ACK!!
Oh, Kye!
Sorry for startling you.
It's no worr–
SENA, why didn't you warn me?!

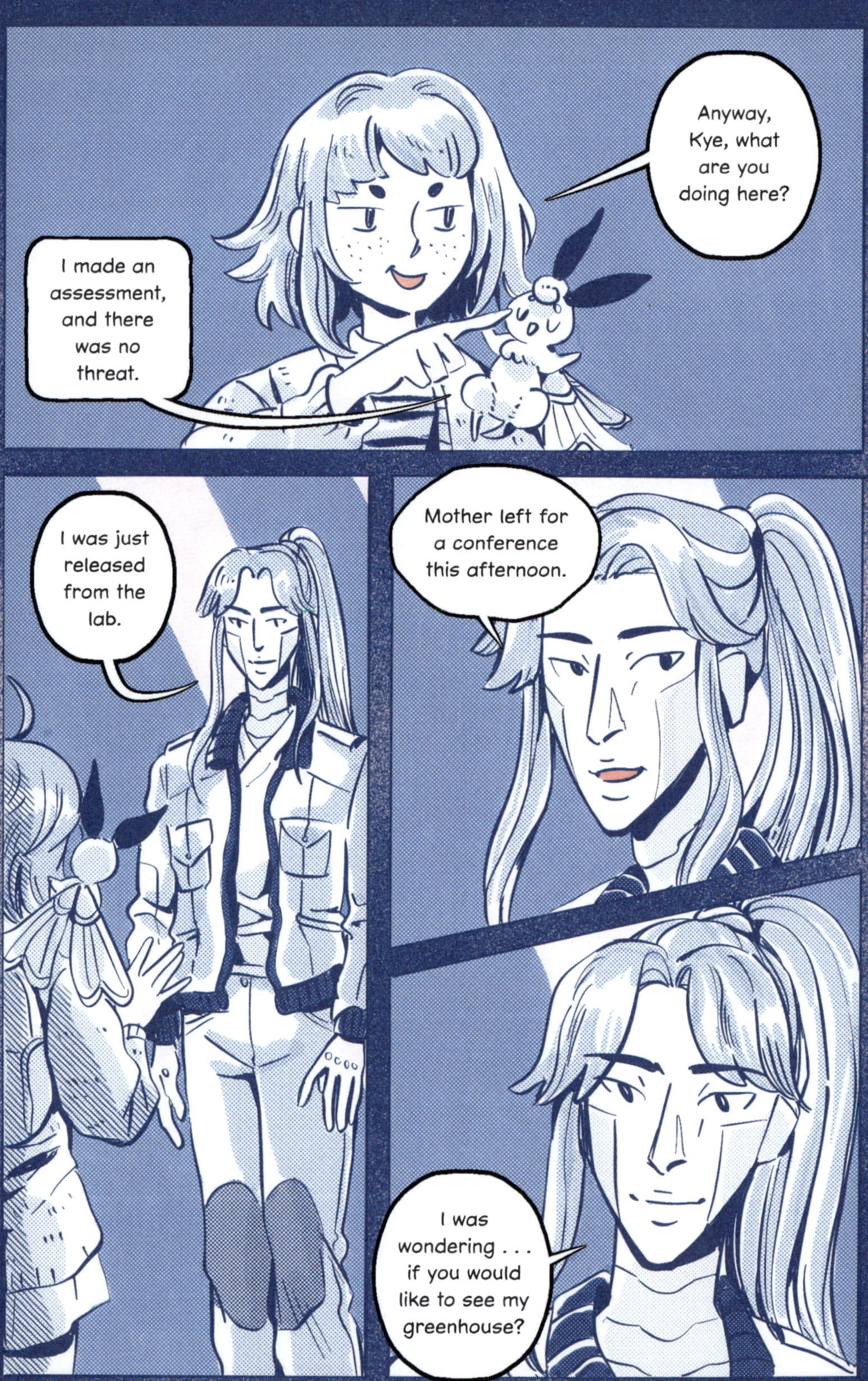
Anyway, Kye, what are you doing here?
I made an assessment, and there was no threat.
I was just released from the lab.
Mother left for a conference this afternoon.
I was wondering . . . if you would like to see my greenhouse?

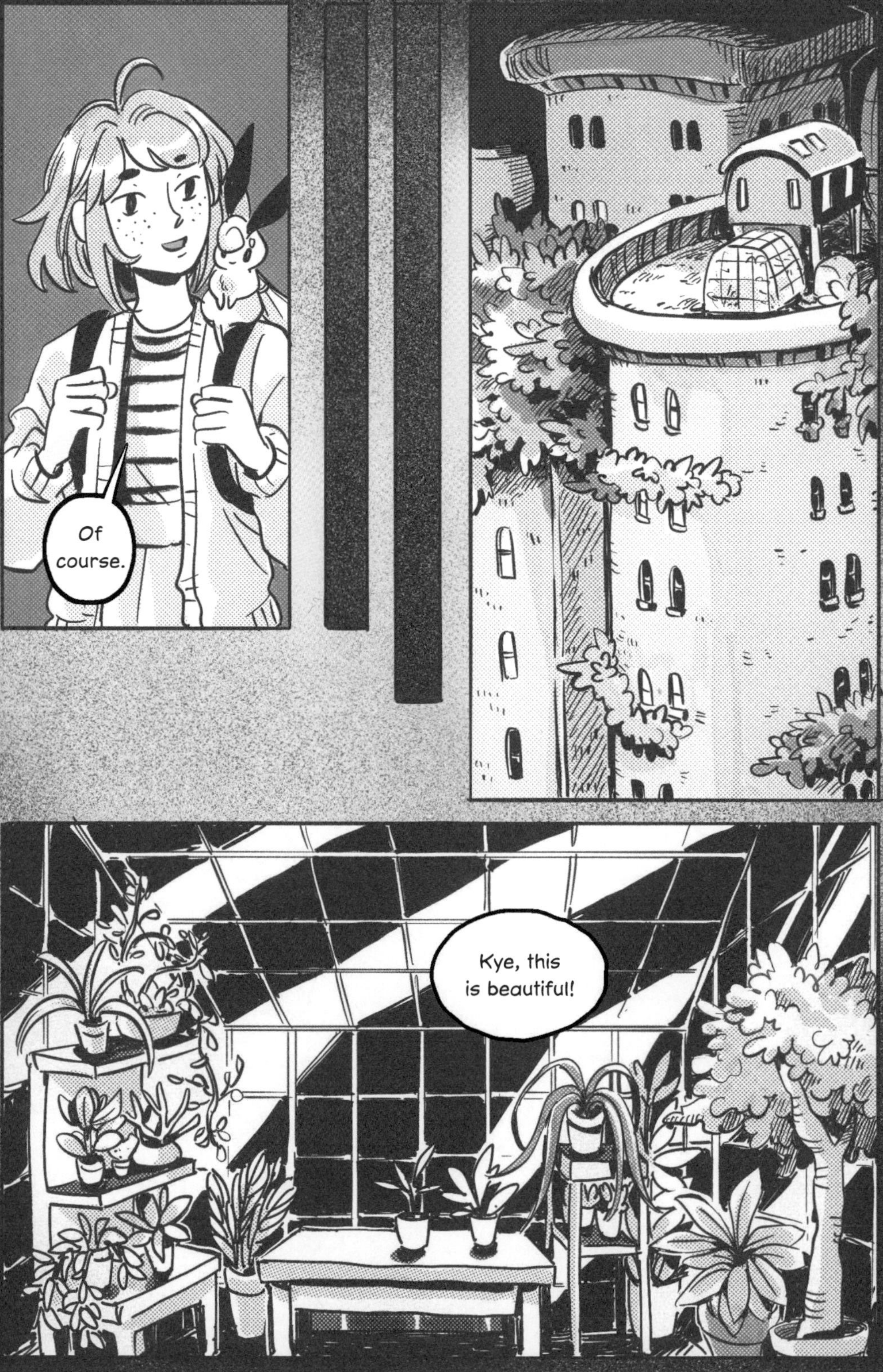
Of course.
Kye, this is beautiful!

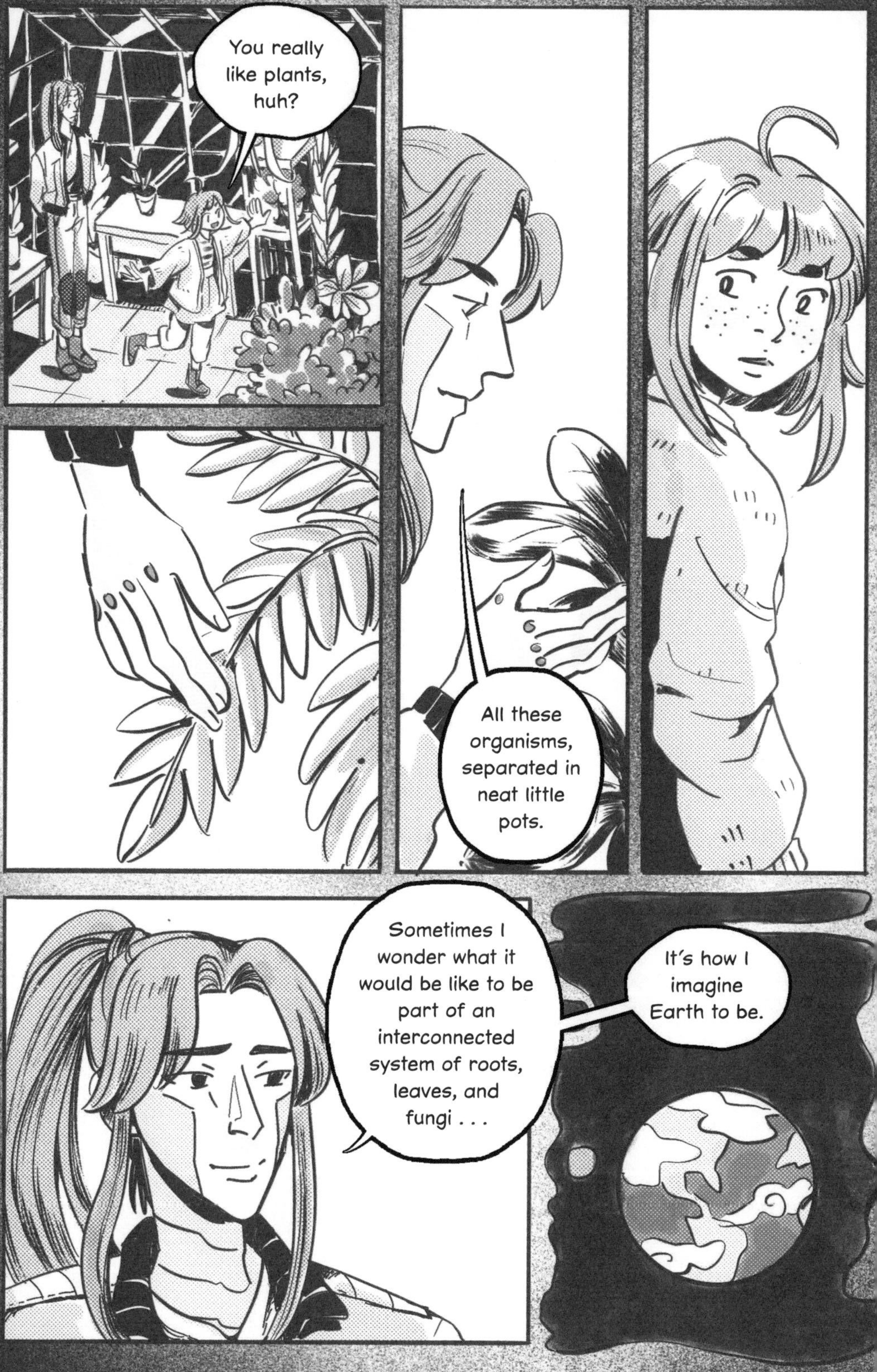
You really like plants, huh?
All these organisms, separated in neat little pots.
Sometimes I wonder what it would be like to be part of an interconnected system of roots, leaves, and fungi . . .
It's how I imagine Earth to be.

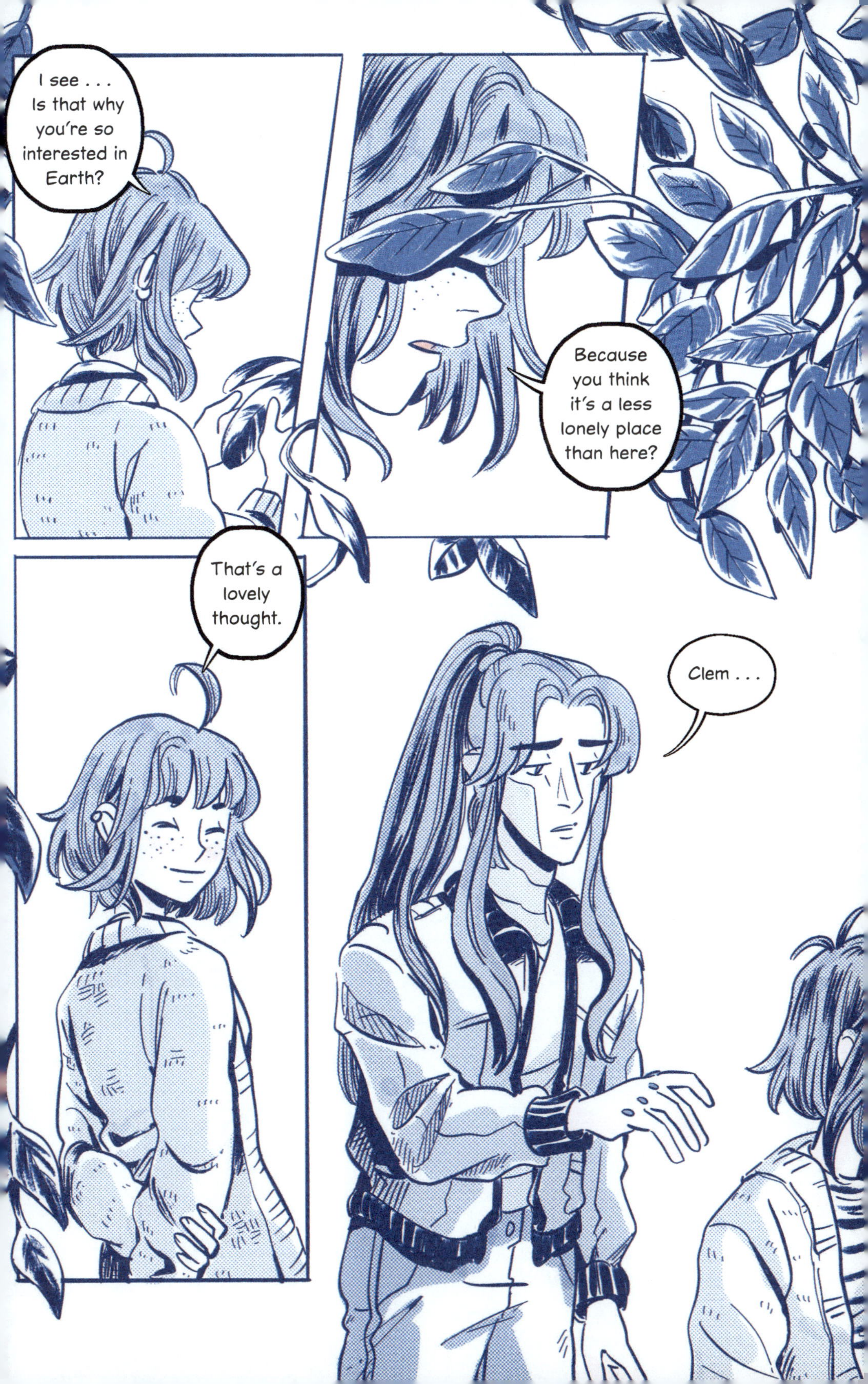
I see . . . Is that why you're so interested in Earth?
Because you think it's a less lonely place than here?
That's a lovely thought.
Clem . . .

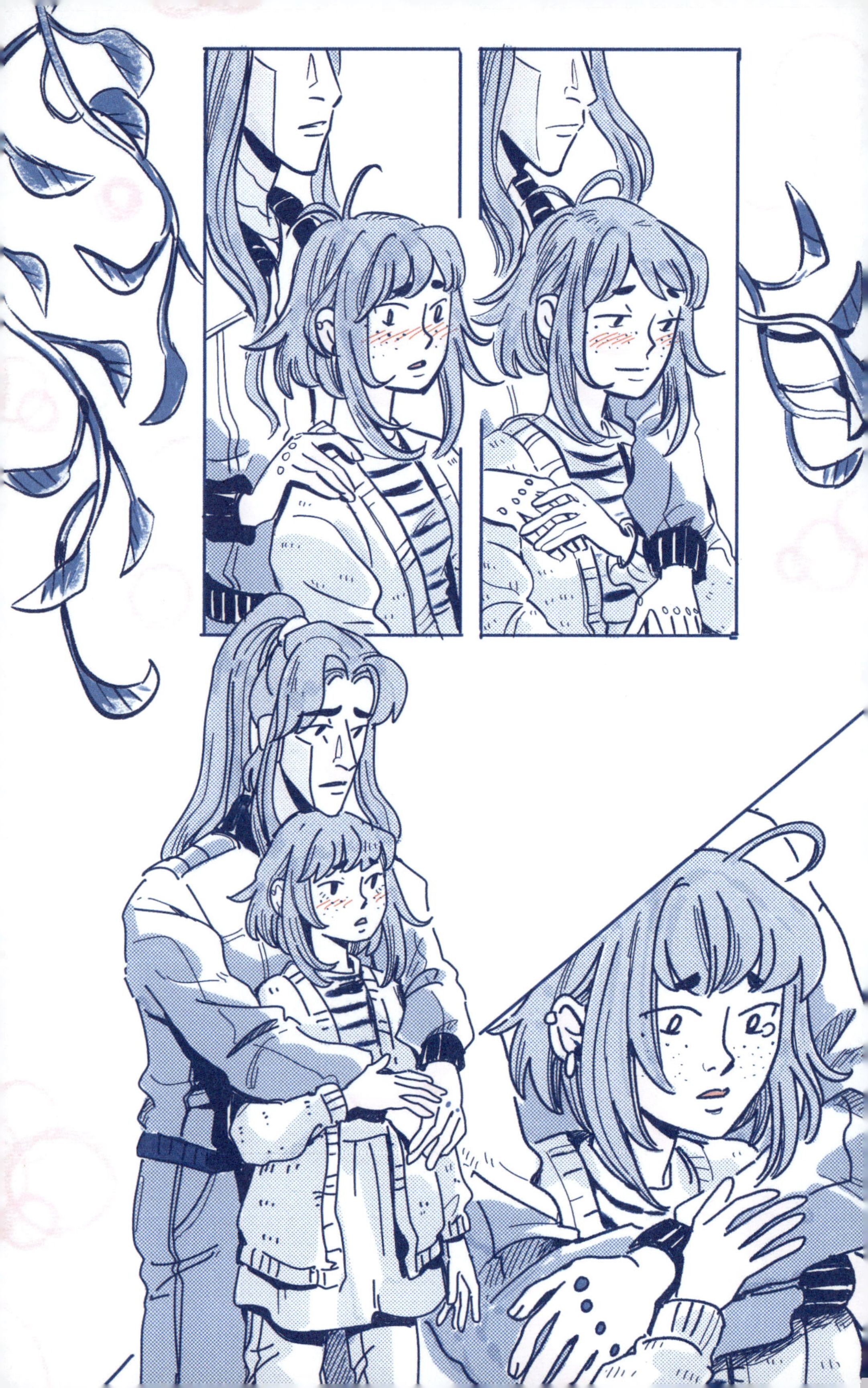

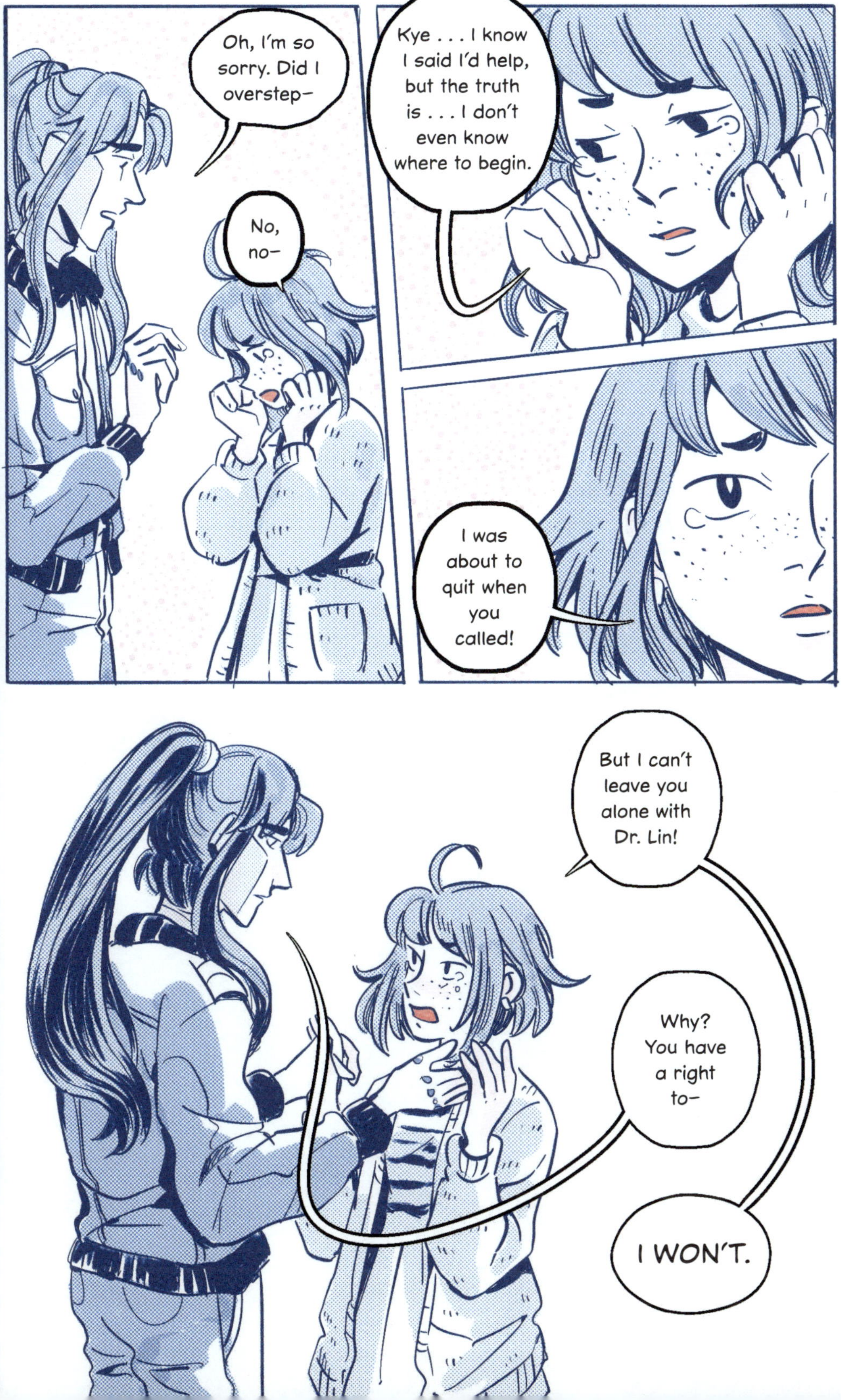
Oh, I'm so sorry. Did I overstep–
No, no–
Kye . . . I know I said I'd help, but the truth is . . . I don't even know where to begin.
I was about to quit when you called!
But I can't leave you alone with Dr. Lin!
Why? You have a right to–
I WON'T.

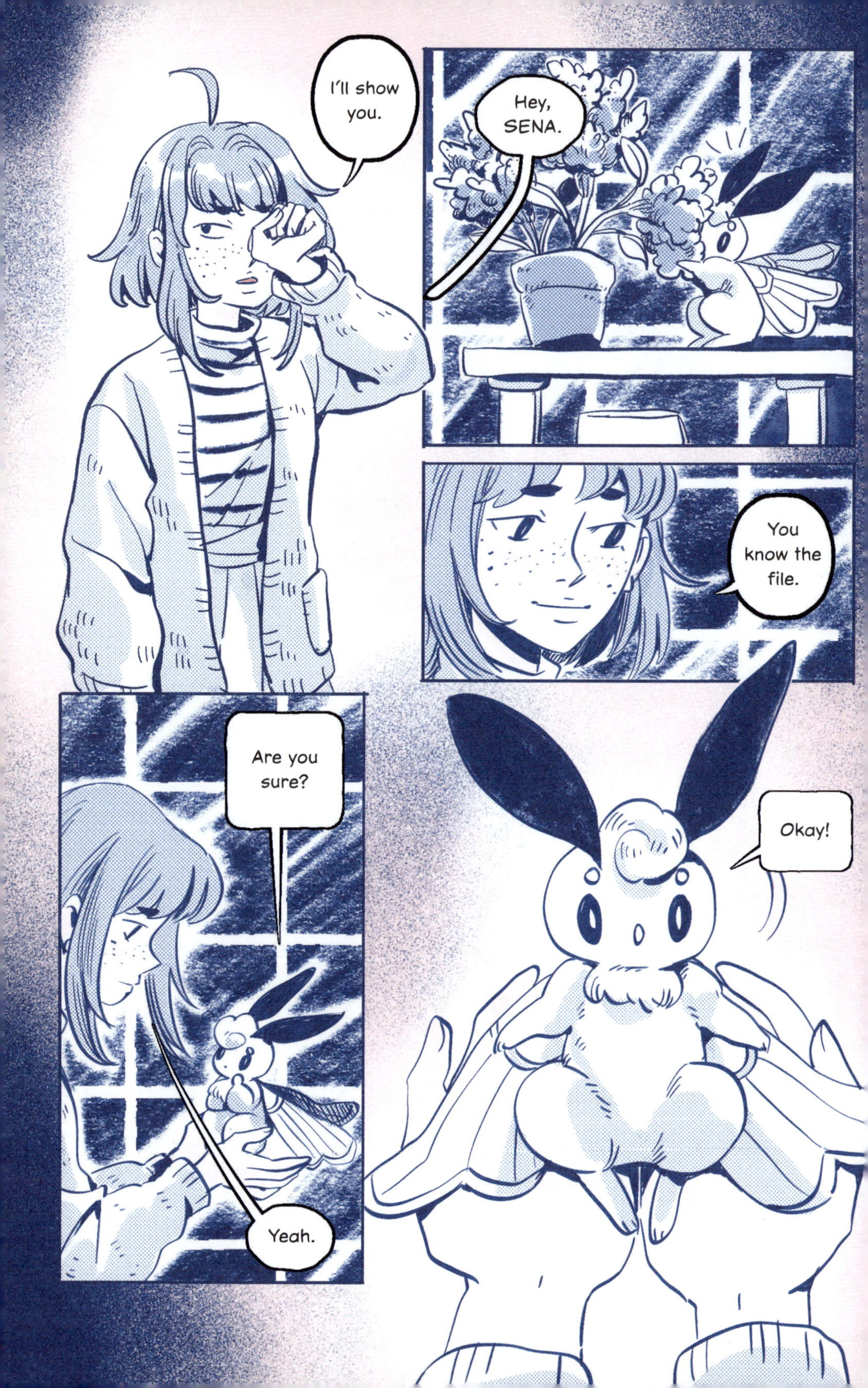
I'll show you.
Hey, SENA.
You know the file.
Are you sure?
Yeah.
Okay!

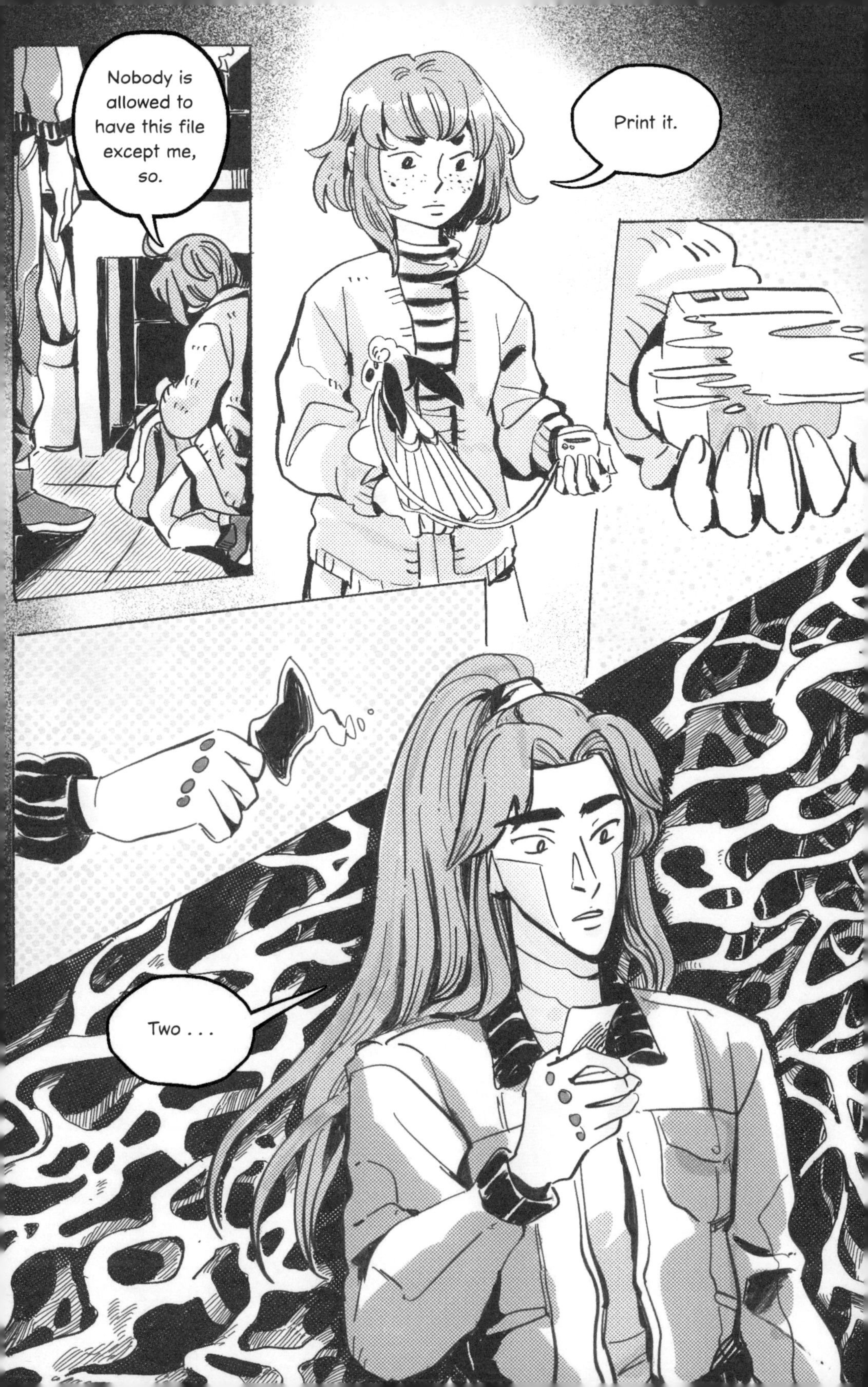
Nobody is allowed to have this file except me, so.
Print it.
Two . . .

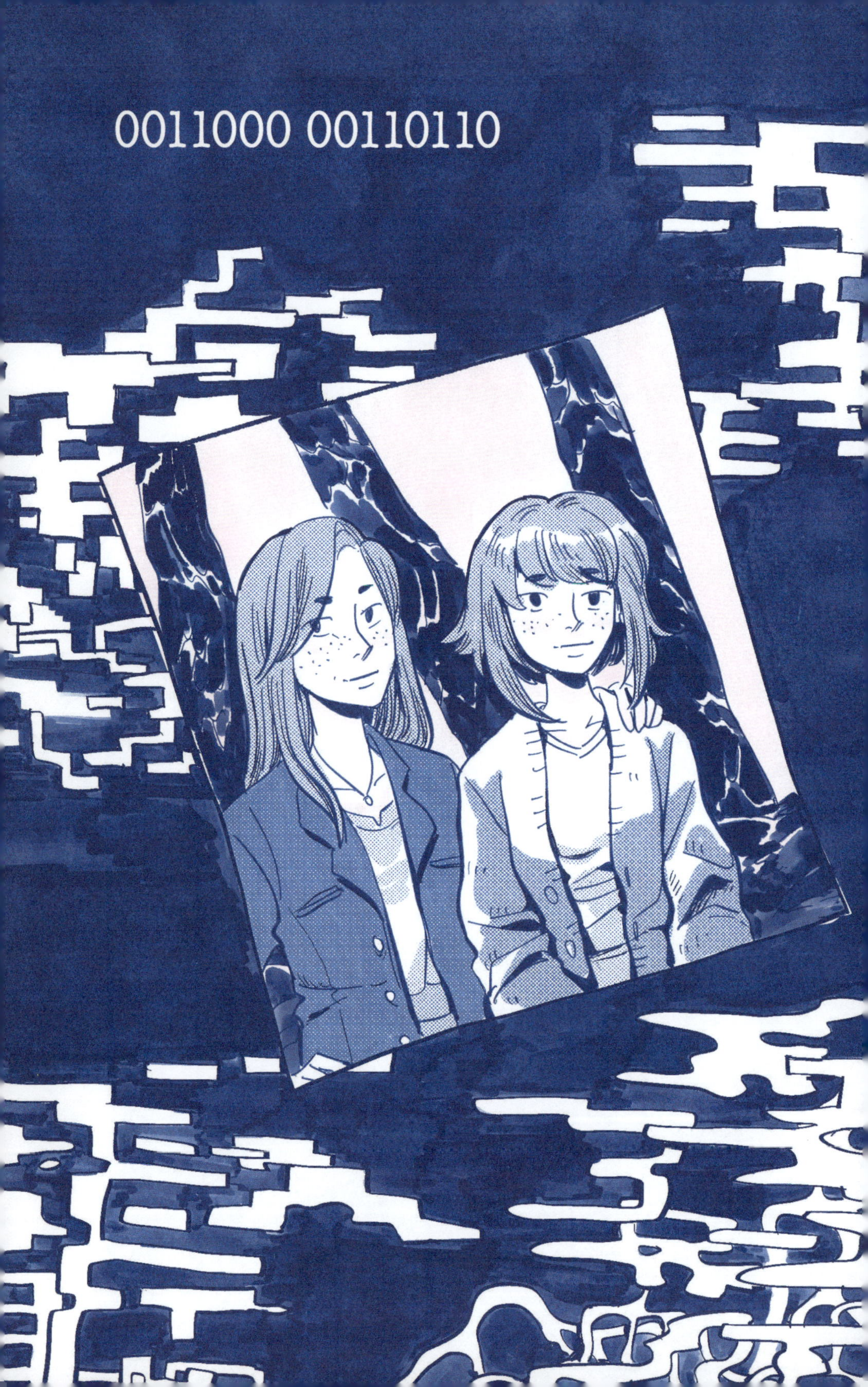
0011000 00110110

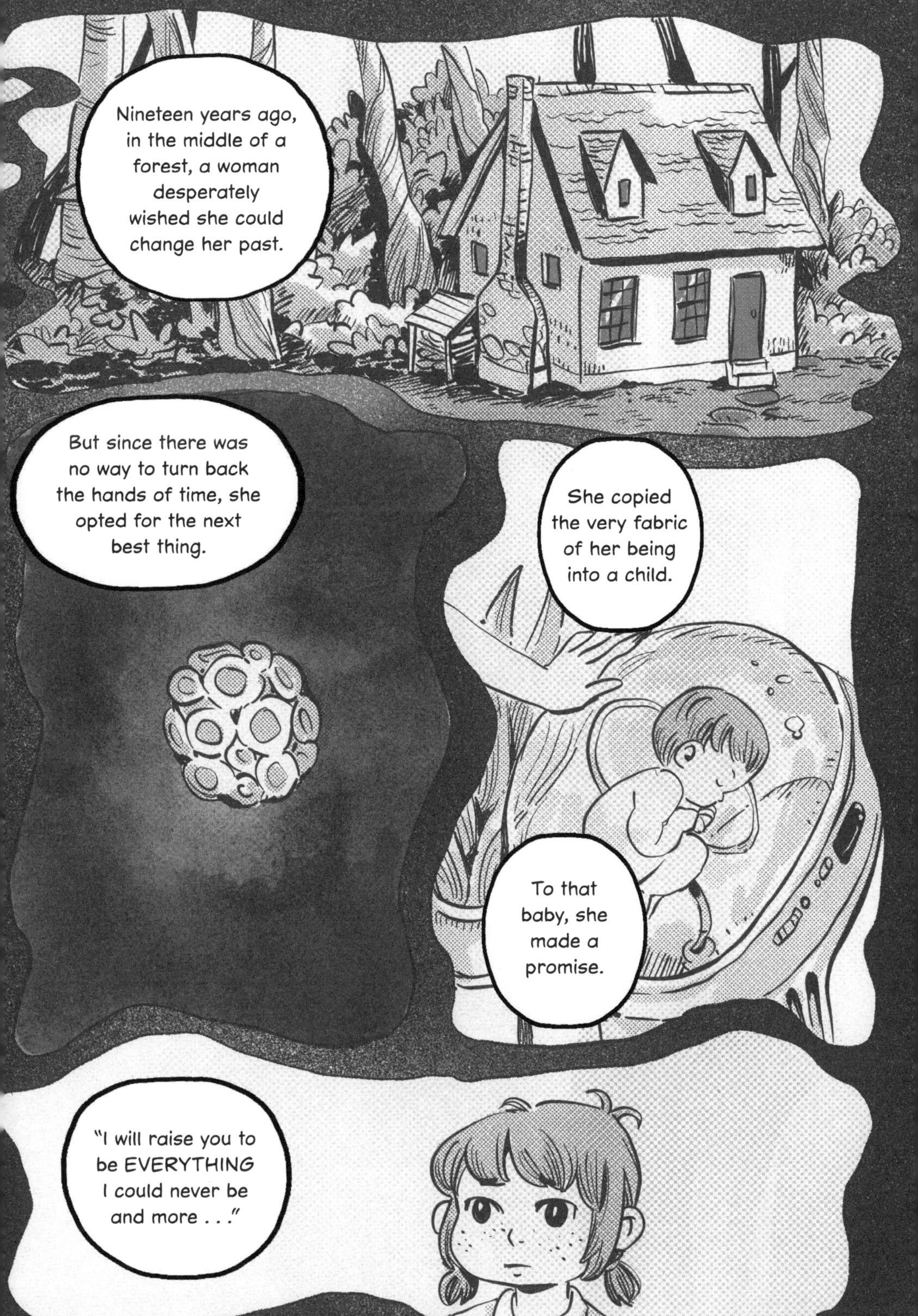

Nineteen years ago, in the middle of a forest, a woman desperately wished she could change her past.
But since there was no way to turn back the hands of time, she opted for the next best thing.
She copied the very fabric of her being into a child.
To that baby, she made a promise.
"I will raise you to be EVERYTHING I could never be and more . . ."

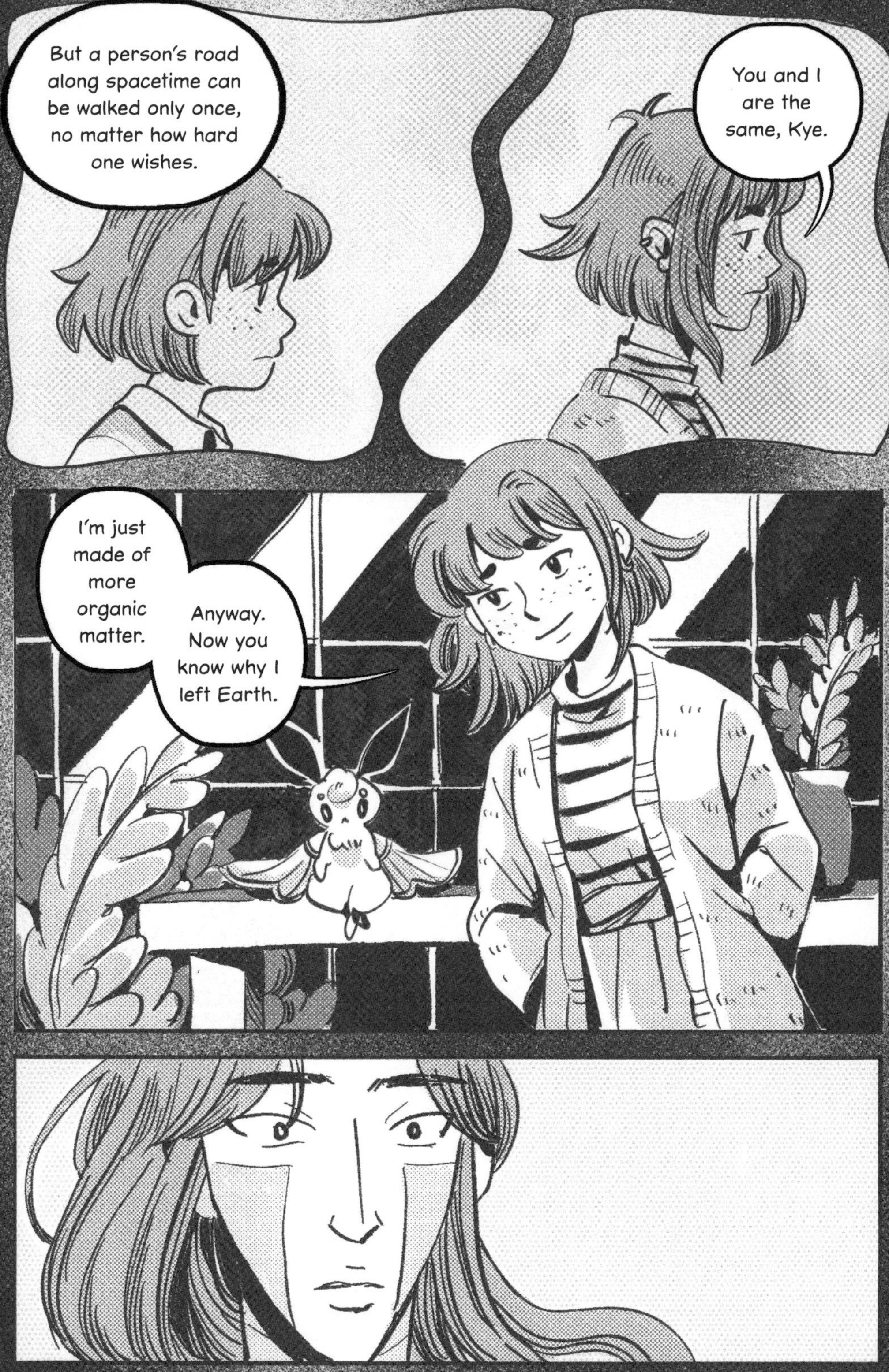
But a person's road along spacetime can be walked only once, no matter how hard one wishes.
You and I are the same, Kye.
I'm just made of more organic matter.
Anyway. Now you know why I left Earth.

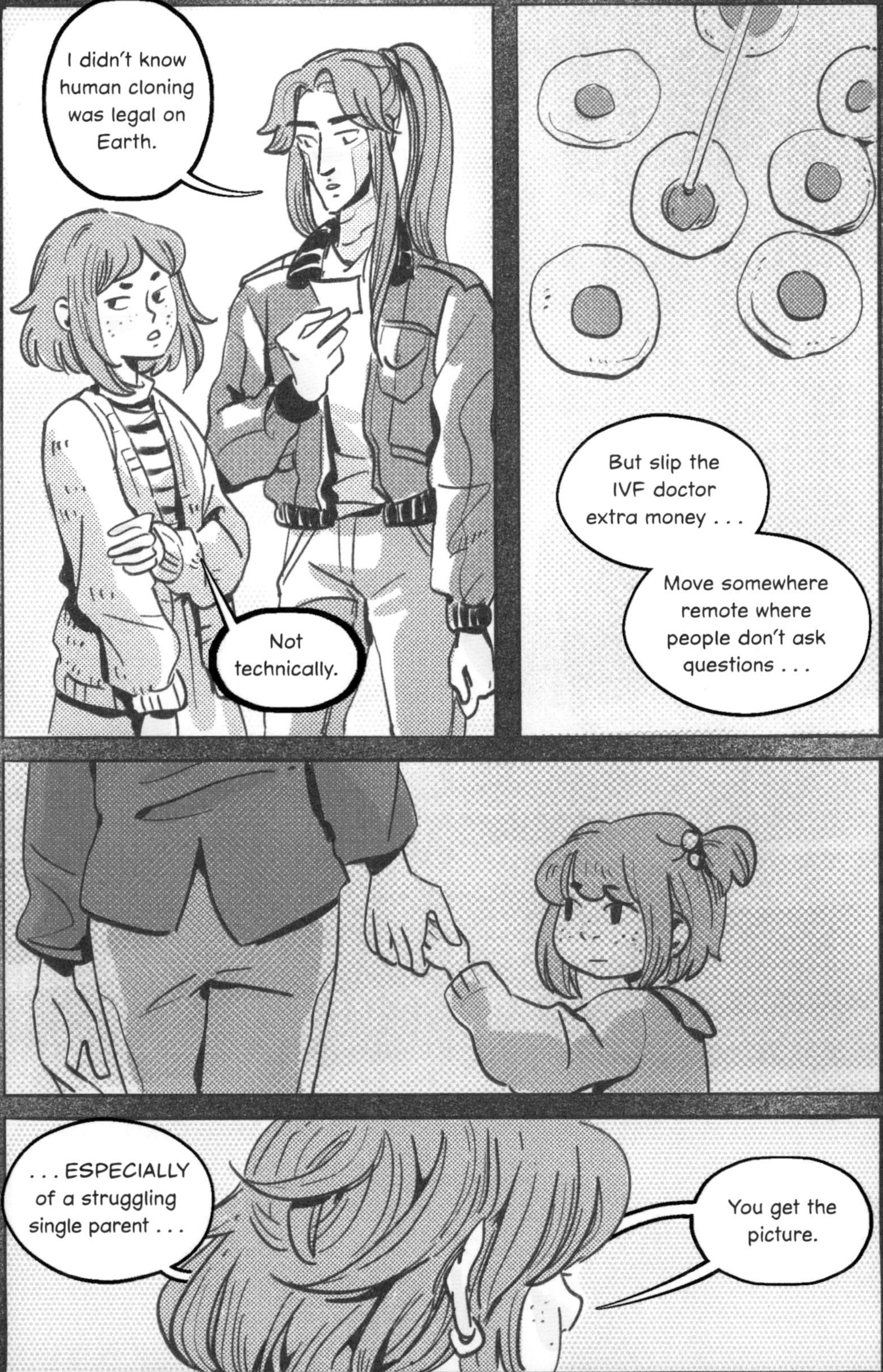

I didn't know human cloning was legal on Earth.
Not technically.
But slip the IVF doctor extra money . . .
Move somewhere remote where people don't ask questions . . .
. . . ESPECIALLY of a struggling single parent . . .
You get the picture.

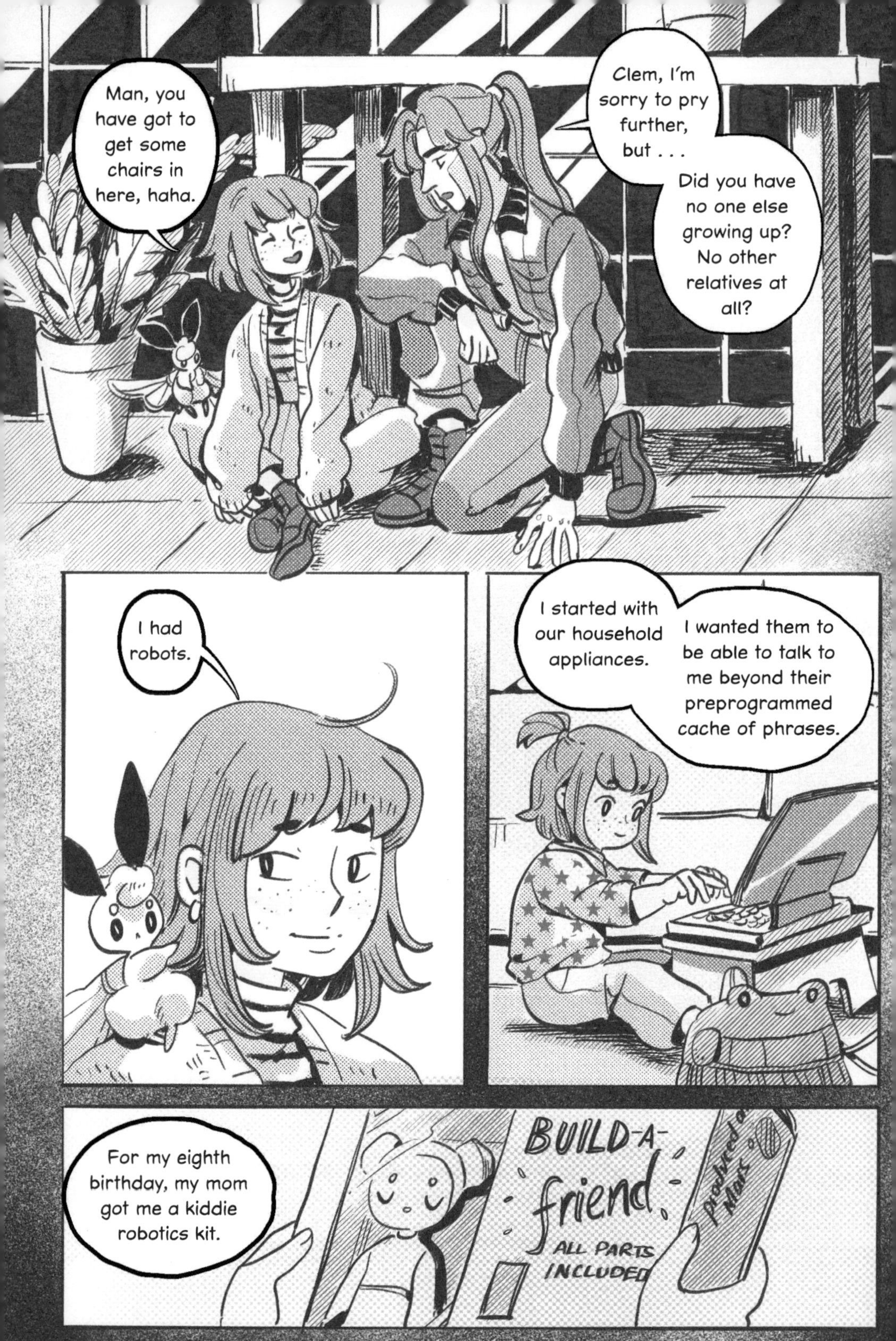
Man, you have got to get some chairs in here, haha.
Clem, I'm sorry to pry further, but . . .
Did you have no one else growing up? No other relatives at all?
I had robots.
I started with our household appliances.
I wanted them to be able to talk to me beyond their preprogrammed cache of phrases.
For my eighth birthday, my mom got me a kiddie robotics kit.
BUILD-A-friend
ALL PARTS INCLUDED

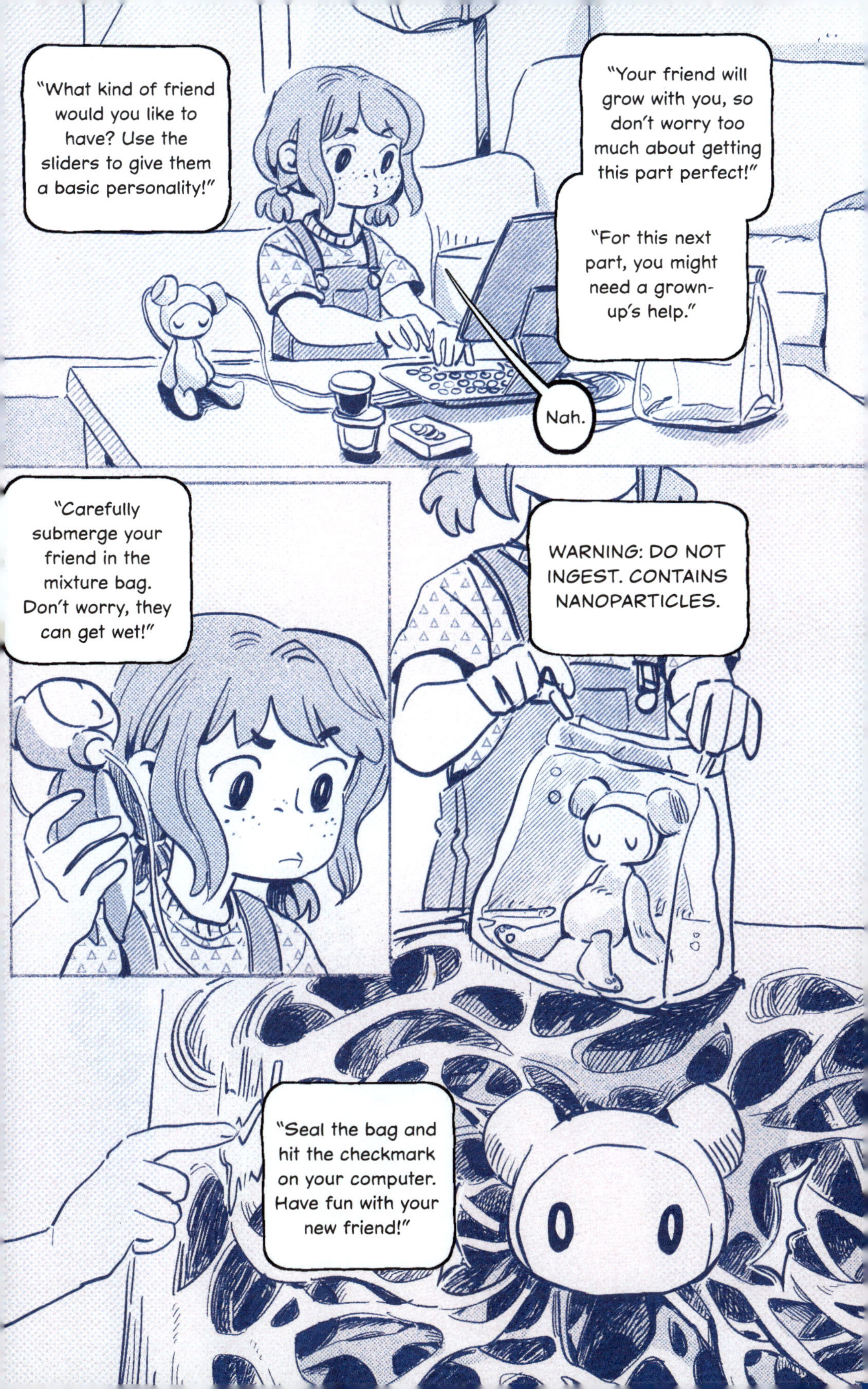
"What kind of friend would you like to have? Use the sliders to give them a basic personality!"
"Your friend will grow with you, so don't worry too much about getting this part perfect!"
"For this next part, you might need a grown-up's help."
Nah.
"Carefully submerge your friend in the mixture bag. Don't worry, they can get wet!"
WARNING: DO NOT INGEST. CONTAINS NANOPARTICLES.
"Seal the bag and hit the checkmark on your computer. Have fun with your new friend!"

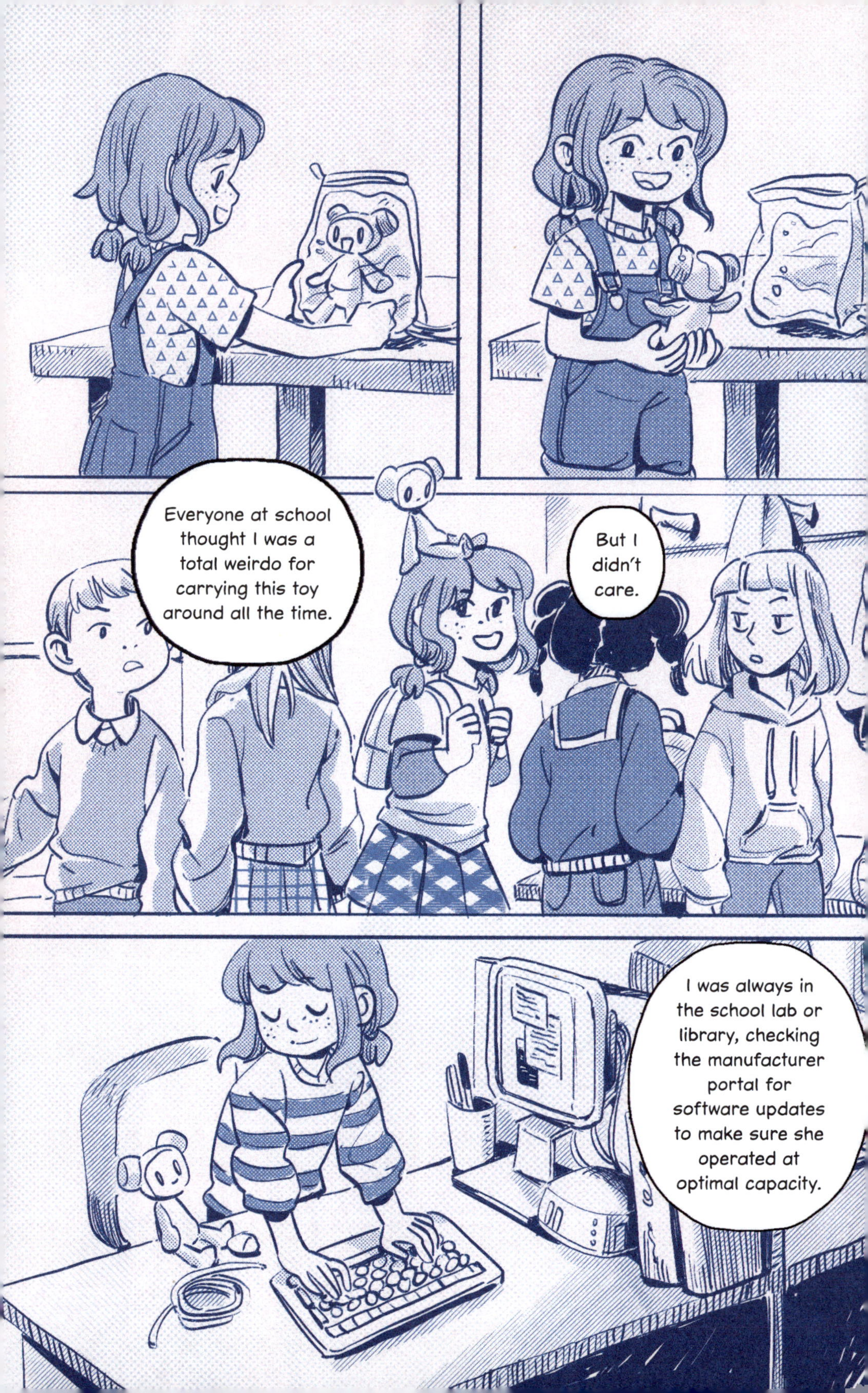
Everyone at school thought I was a total weirdo for carrying this toy around all the time.
But I didn't care.
I was always in the school lab or library, checking the manufacturer portal for software updates to make sure she operated at optimal capacity.

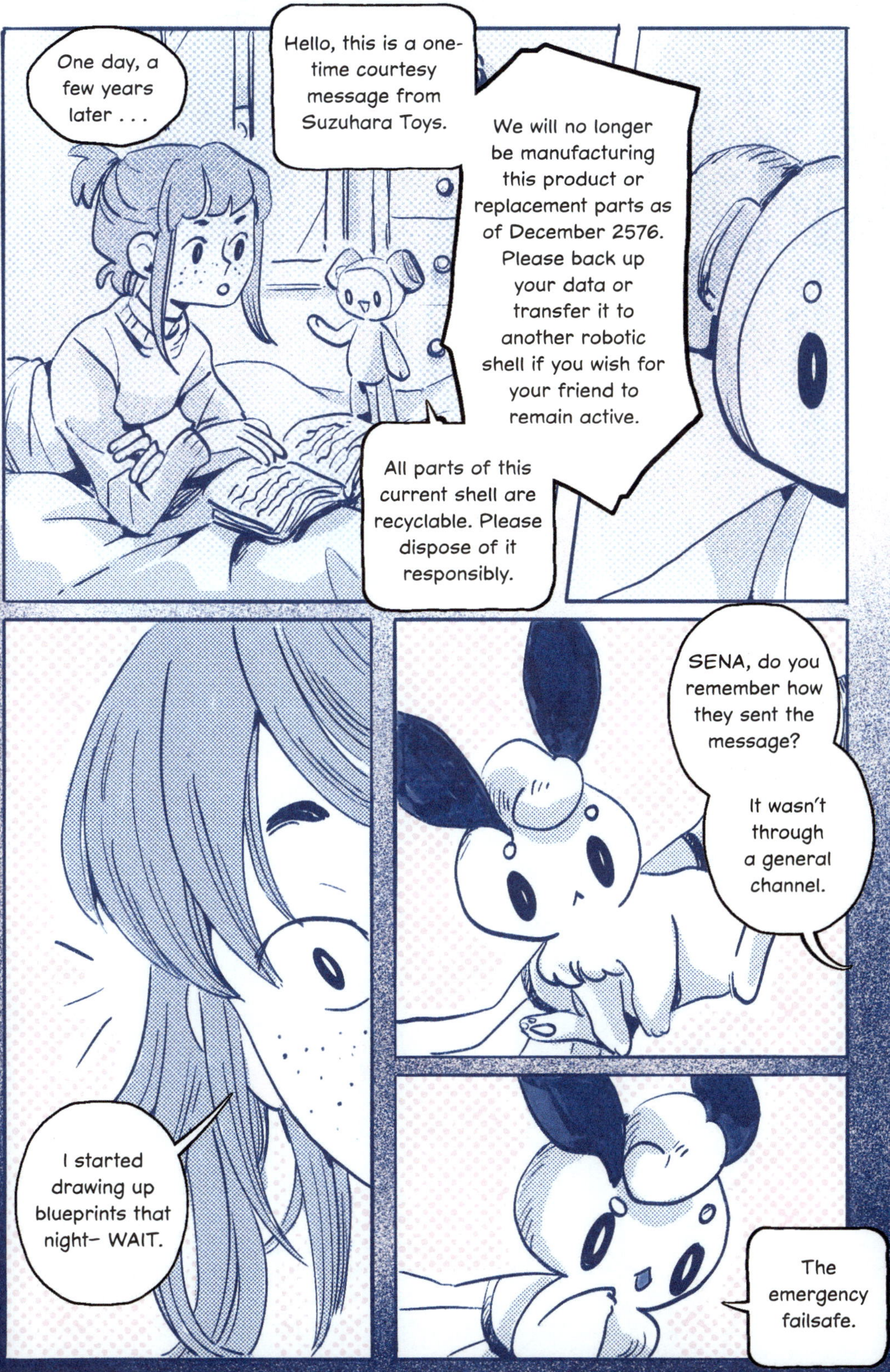
One day, a few years later . . .
Hello, this is a one-time courtesy message from Suzuhara Toys.
We will no longer be manufacturing this product or replacement parts as of December 2576. Please back up your data or transfer it to another robotic shell if you wish for your friend to remain active.
All parts of this current shell are recyclable. Please dispose of it responsibly.
I started drawing up blueprints that night— WAIT.
SENA, do you remember how they sent the message?
It wasn't through a general channel.
The emergency failsafe.

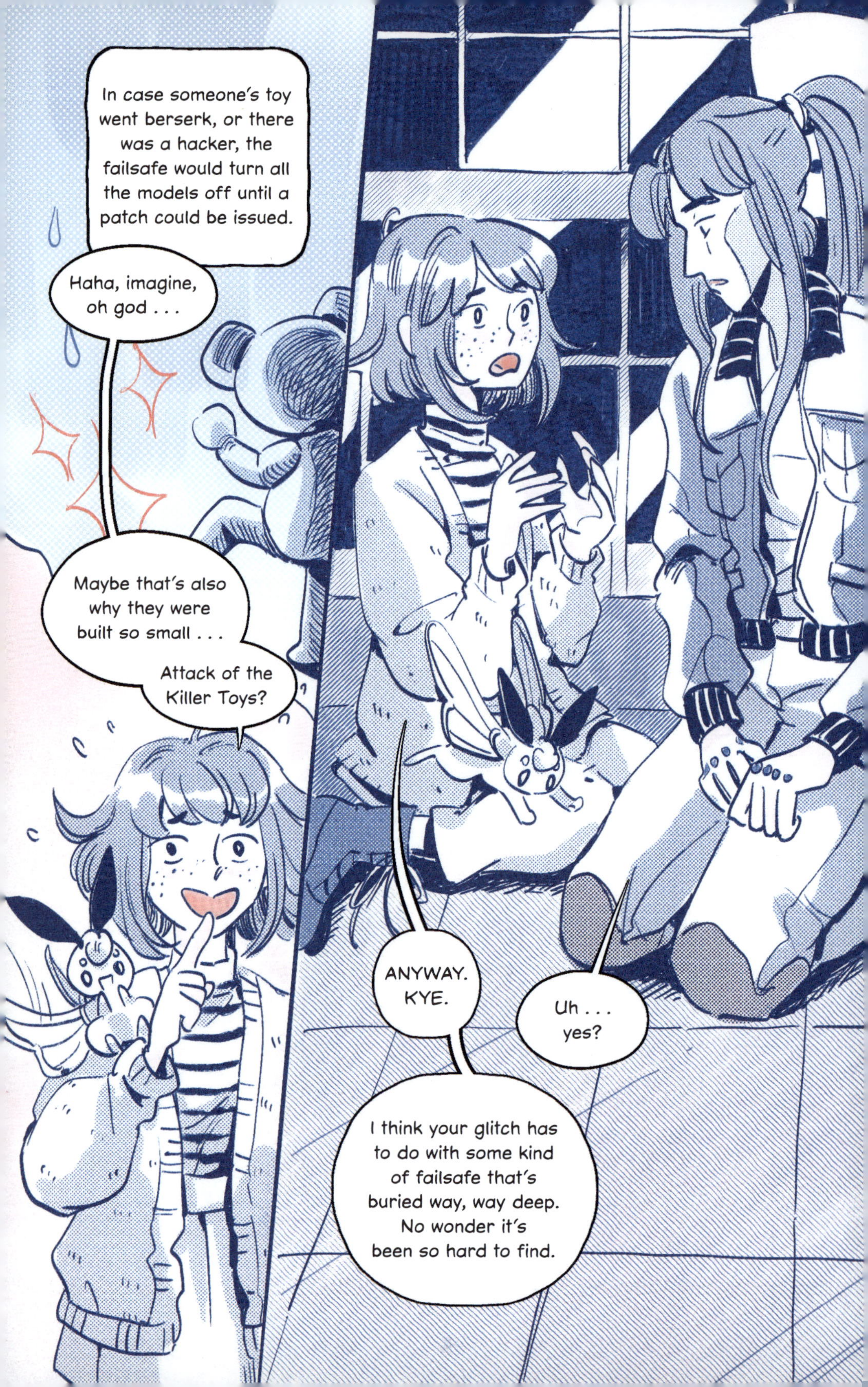

In case someone's toy went berserk, or there was a hacker, the failsafe would turn all the models off until a patch could be issued.
Haha, imagine, oh god . . .
Maybe that's also why they were built so small . . .
Attack of the Killer Toys?
ANYWAY. KYE.
Uh . . . yes?
I think your glitch has to do with some kind of failsafe that's buried way, way deep. No wonder it's been so hard to find.

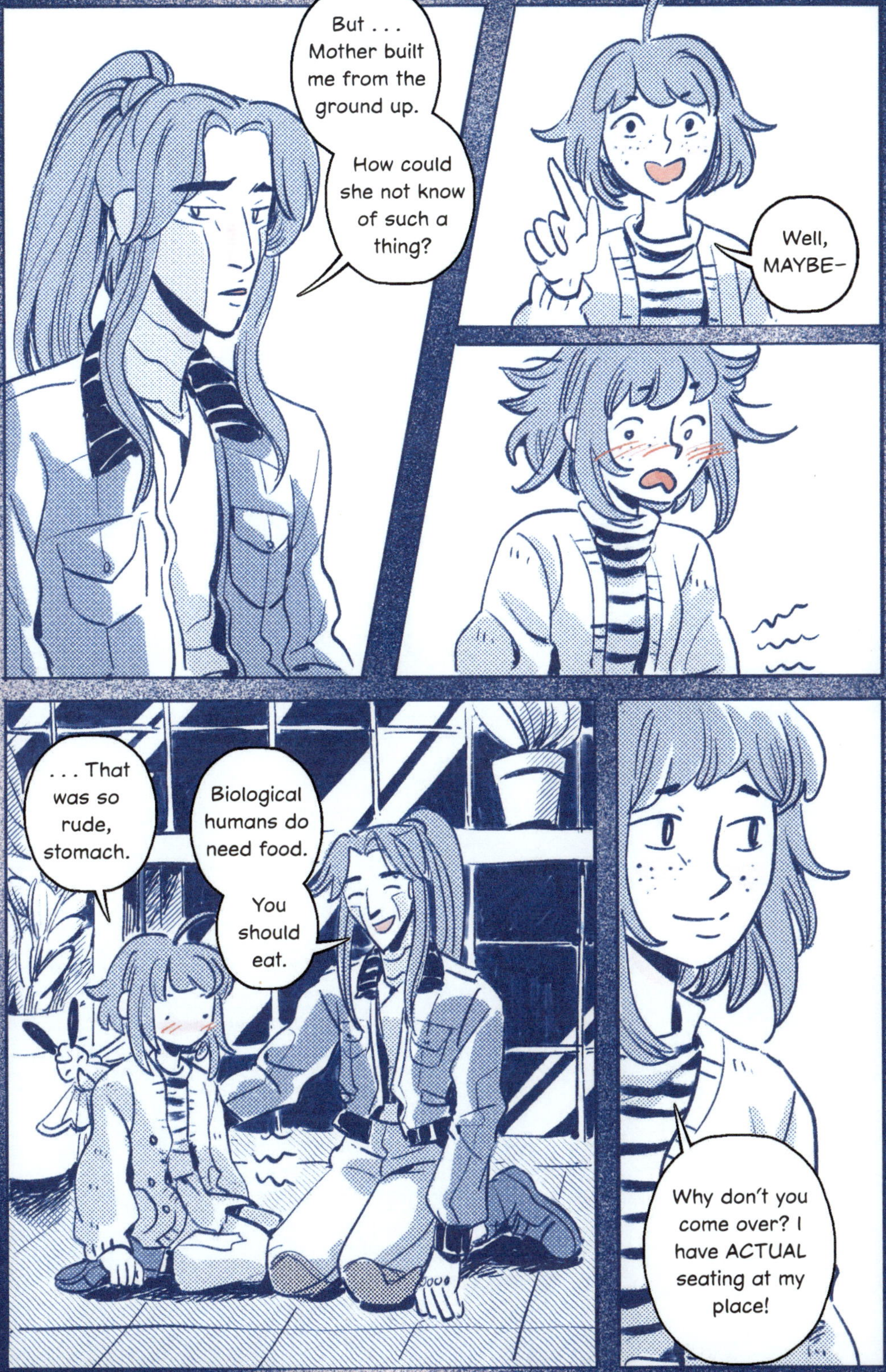
But . . . Mother built me from the ground up.
How could she not know of such a thing?
Well, MAYBE–
. . . That was so rude, stomach.
Biological humans do need food.
You should eat.
Why don't you come over? I have ACTUAL seating at my place!

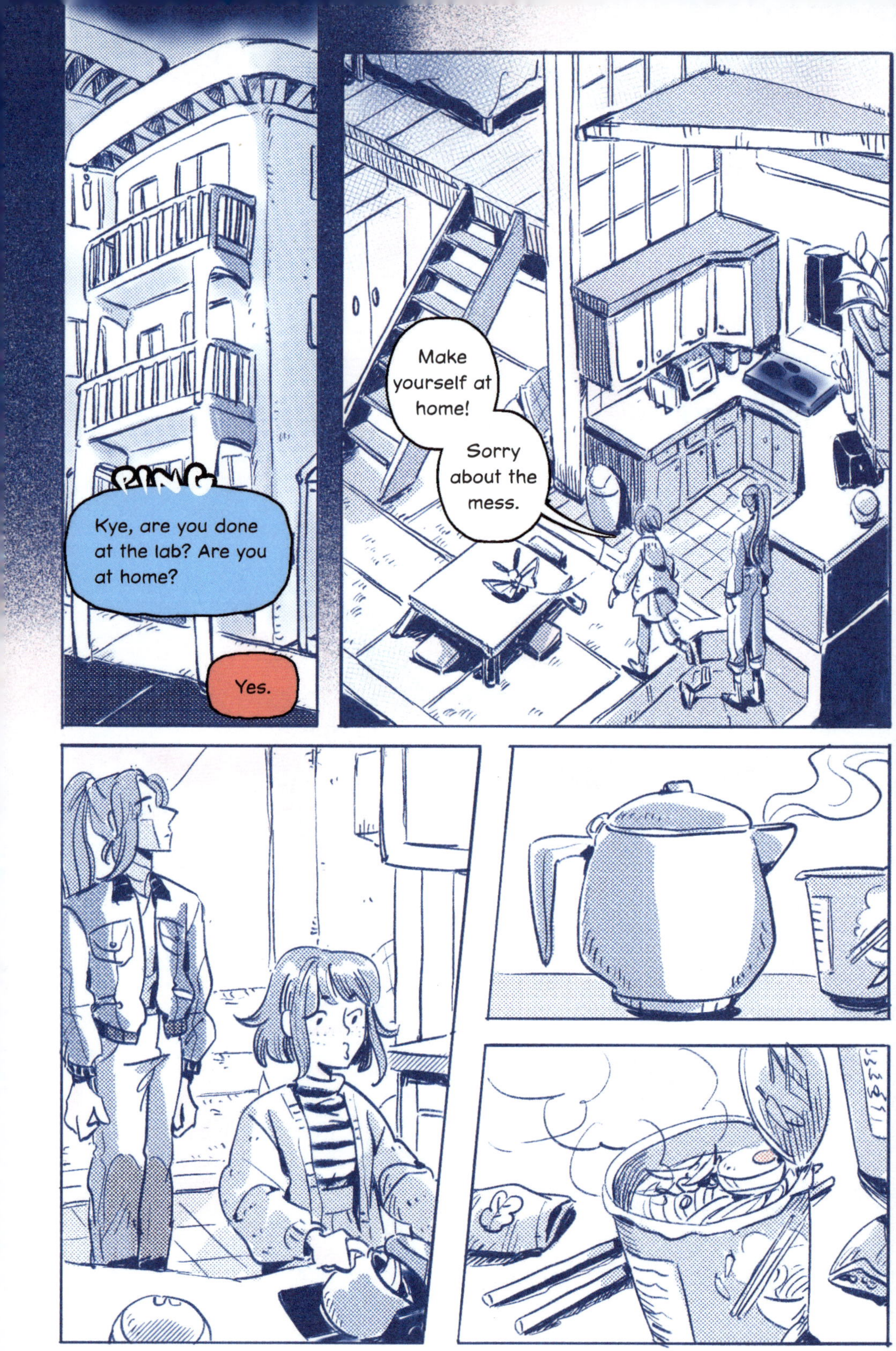
PING
Kye, are you done at the lab? Are you at home?
Yes.
Make yourself at home!
Sorry about the mess.

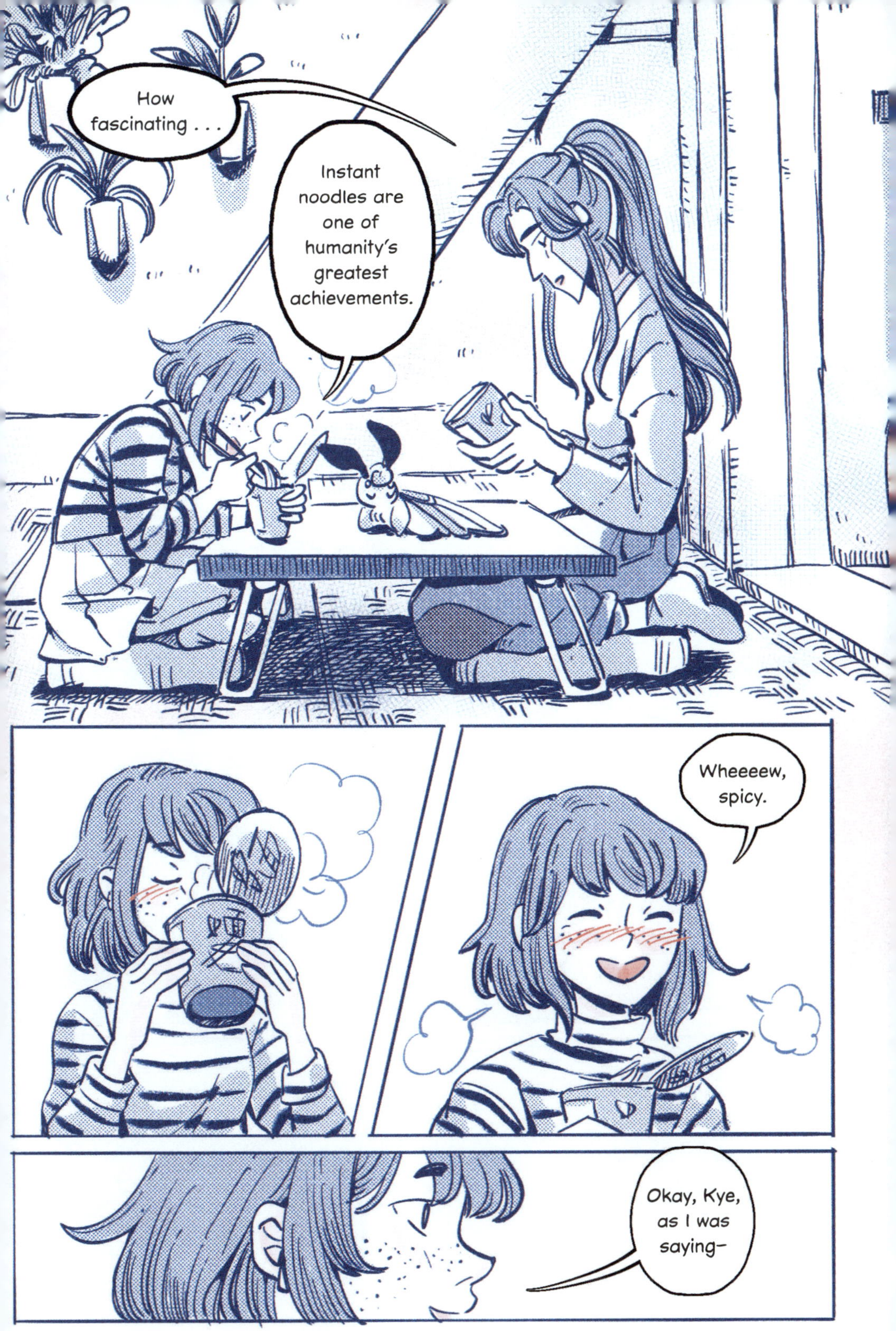
How fascinating . . .
Instant noodles are one of humanity's greatest achievements.
Wheeeew, spicy.
Okay, Kye, as I was saying–

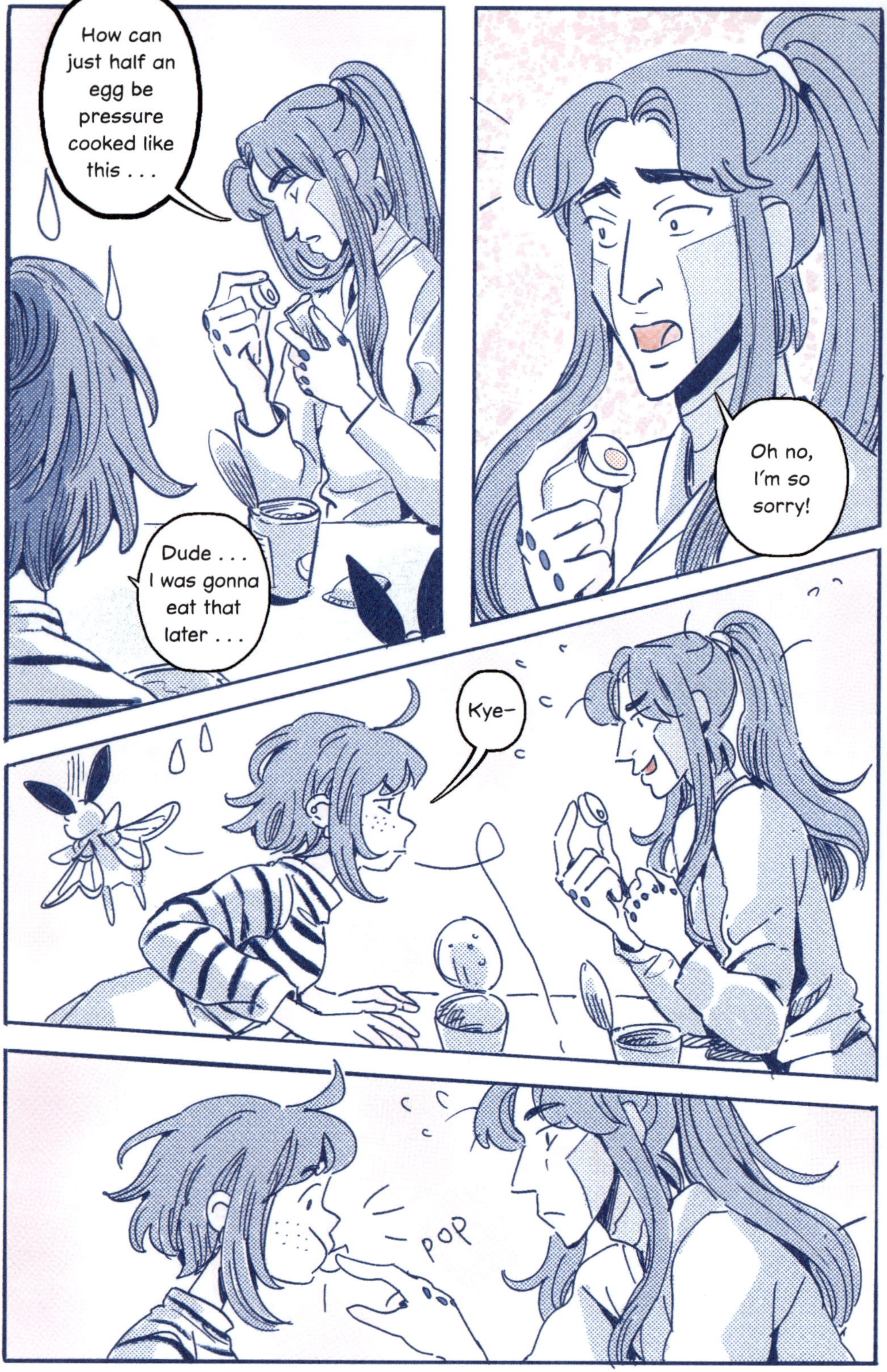
How can just half an egg be pressure cooked like this . . .
Oh no, I'm so sorry!
Dude . . . I was gonna eat that later . . .
Kye-
POP

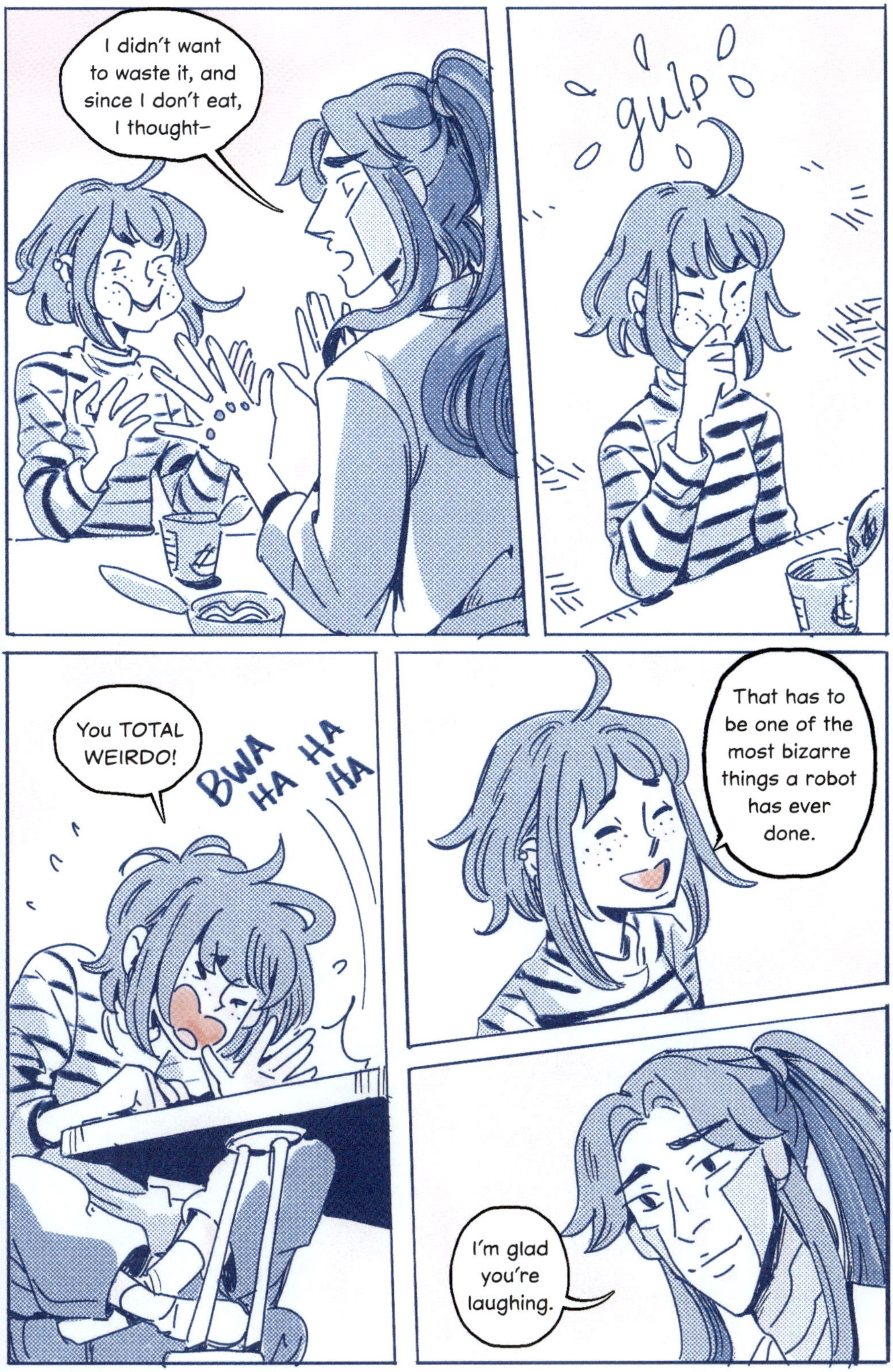
I didn't want to waste it, and since I don't eat, I thought–
gulp
You TOTAL WEIRDO!
BWA HA HA HA
That has to be one of the most bizarre things a robot has ever done.
I'm glad you're laughing.

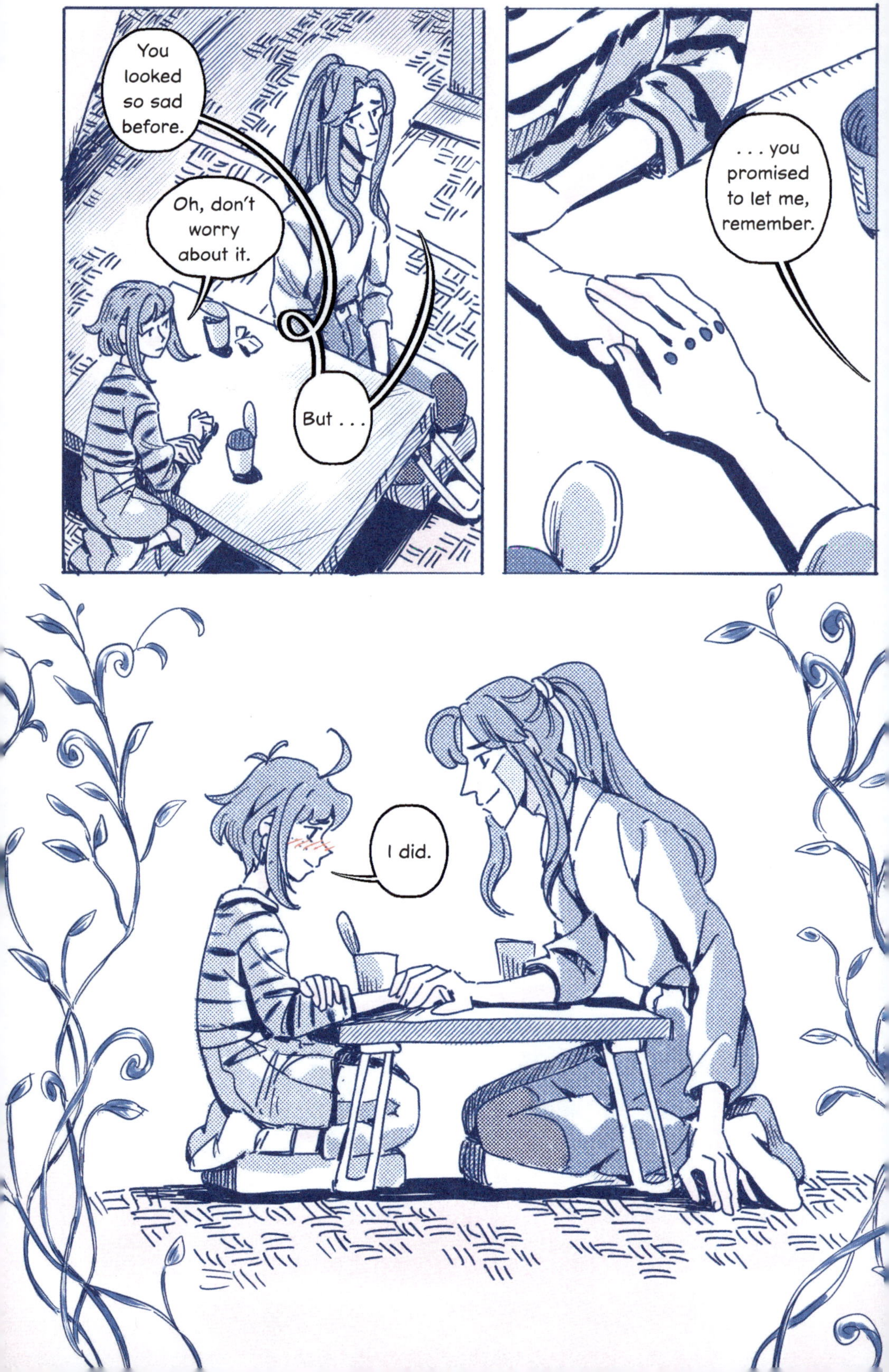
You looked so sad before.
Oh, don't worry about it.
But . . .
. . . you promised to let me, remember.
I did.

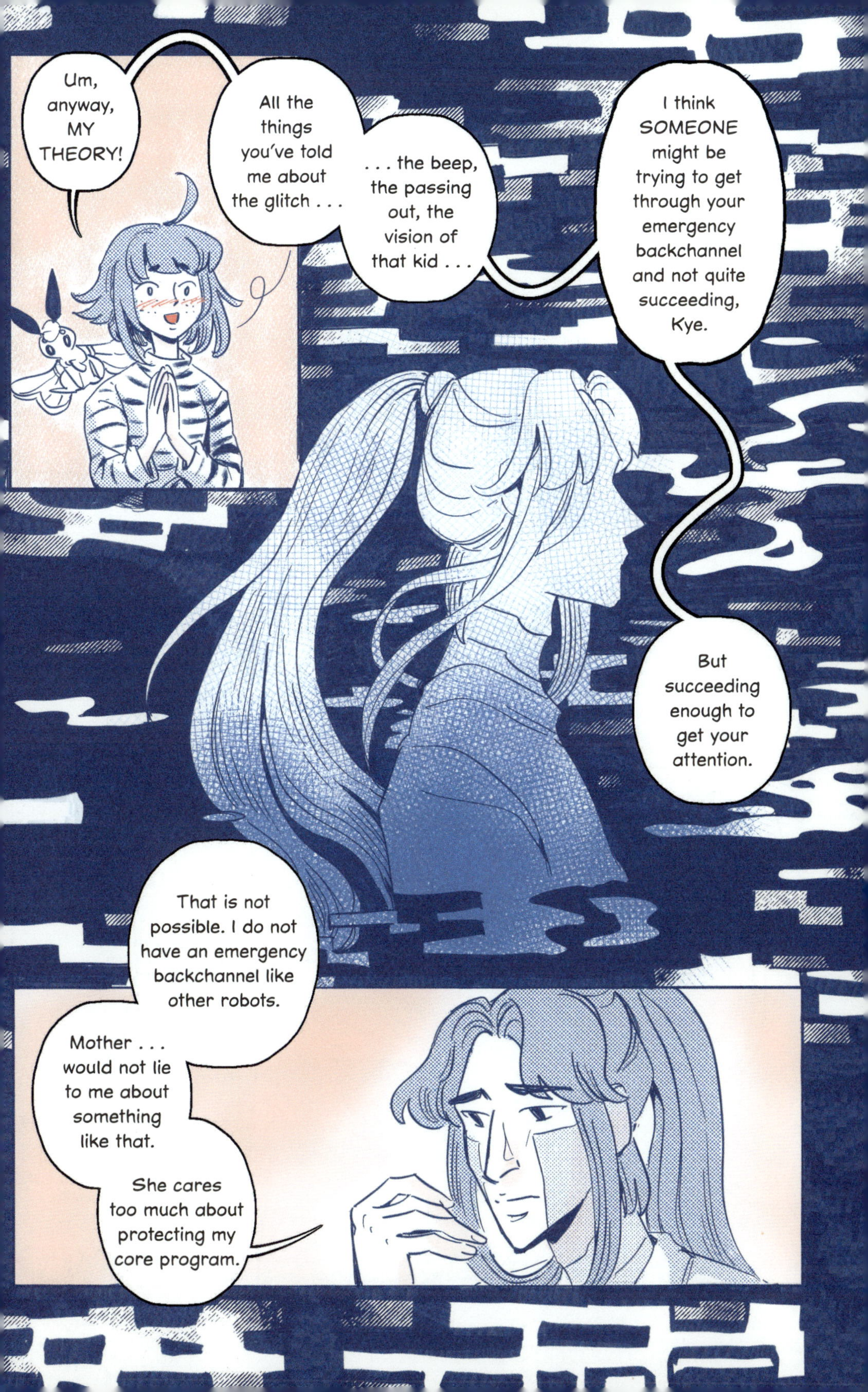
Um, anyway, MY THEORY!
All the things you've told me about the glitch . . .
. . . the beep, the passing out, the vision of that kid . . .
I think SOMEONE might be trying to get through your emergency backchannel and not quite succeeding, Kye.
But succeeding enough to get your attention.
That is not possible. I do not have an emergency backchannel like other robots.
Mother . . . would not lie to me about something like that.
She cares too much about protecting my core program.

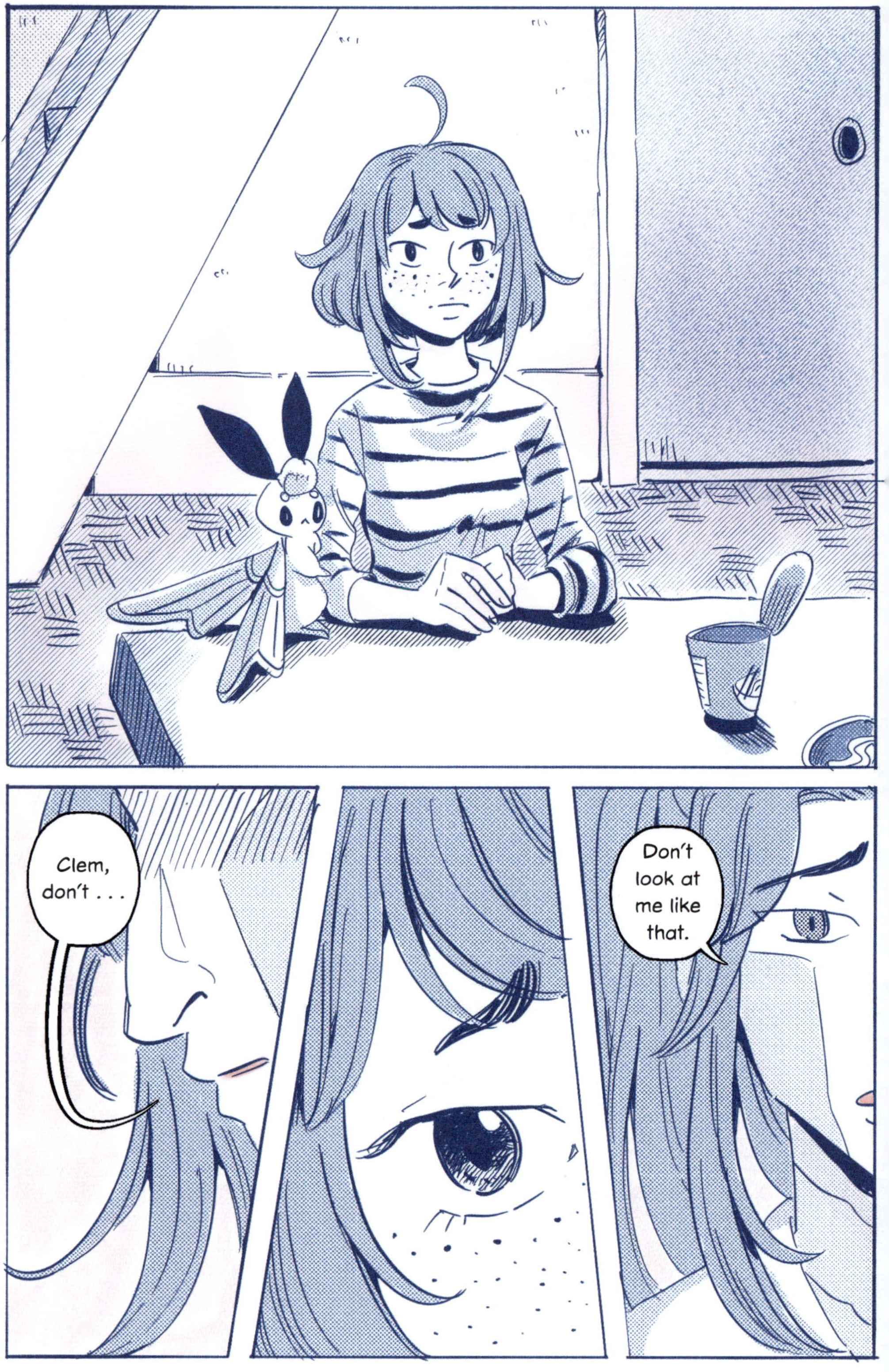
Clem, don't . . .
Don't look at me like that.

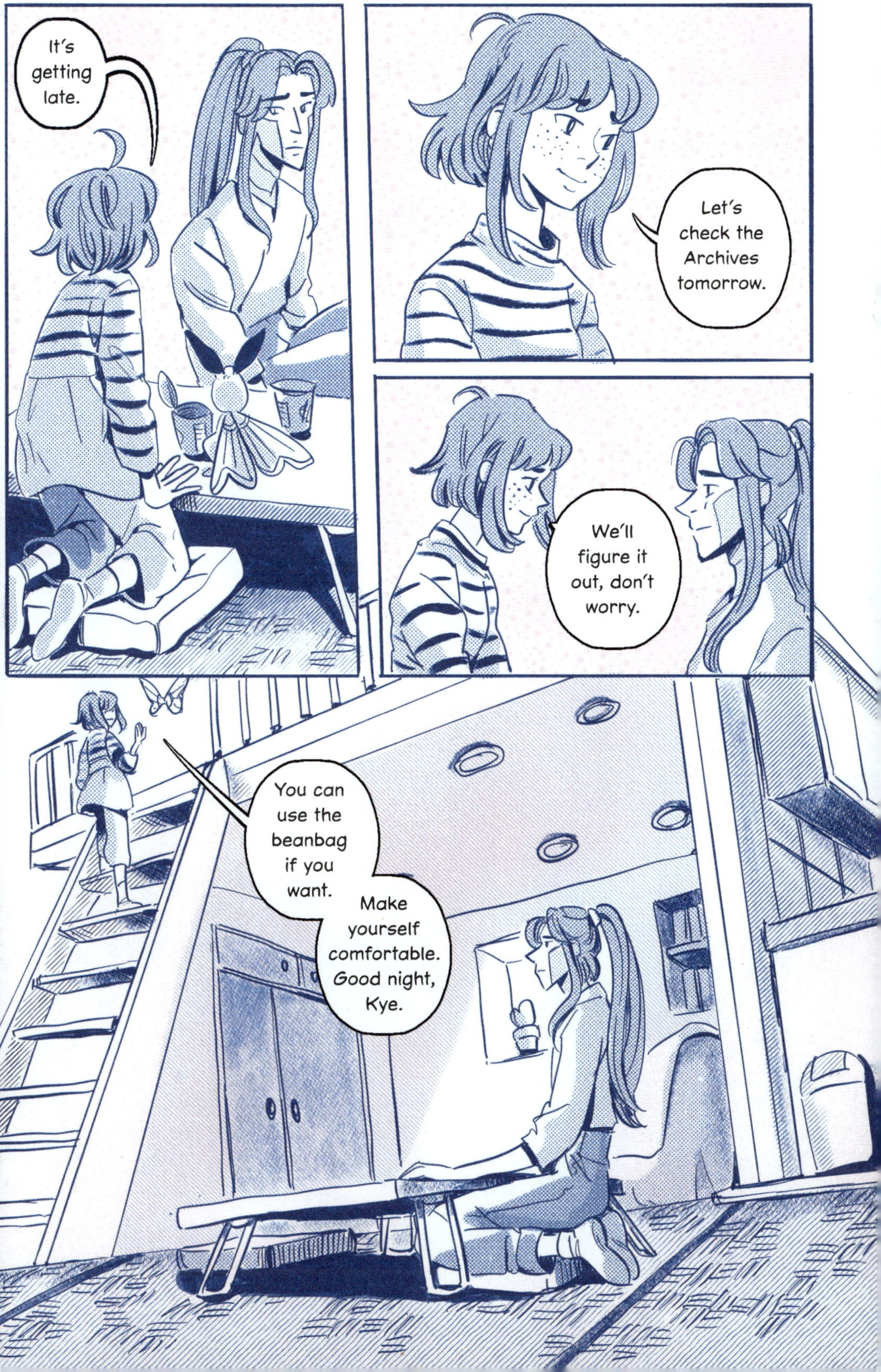
It's getting late.
Let's check the Archives tomorrow.
We'll figure it out, don't worry.
You can use the beanbag if you want.
Make yourself comfortable. Good night, Kye.

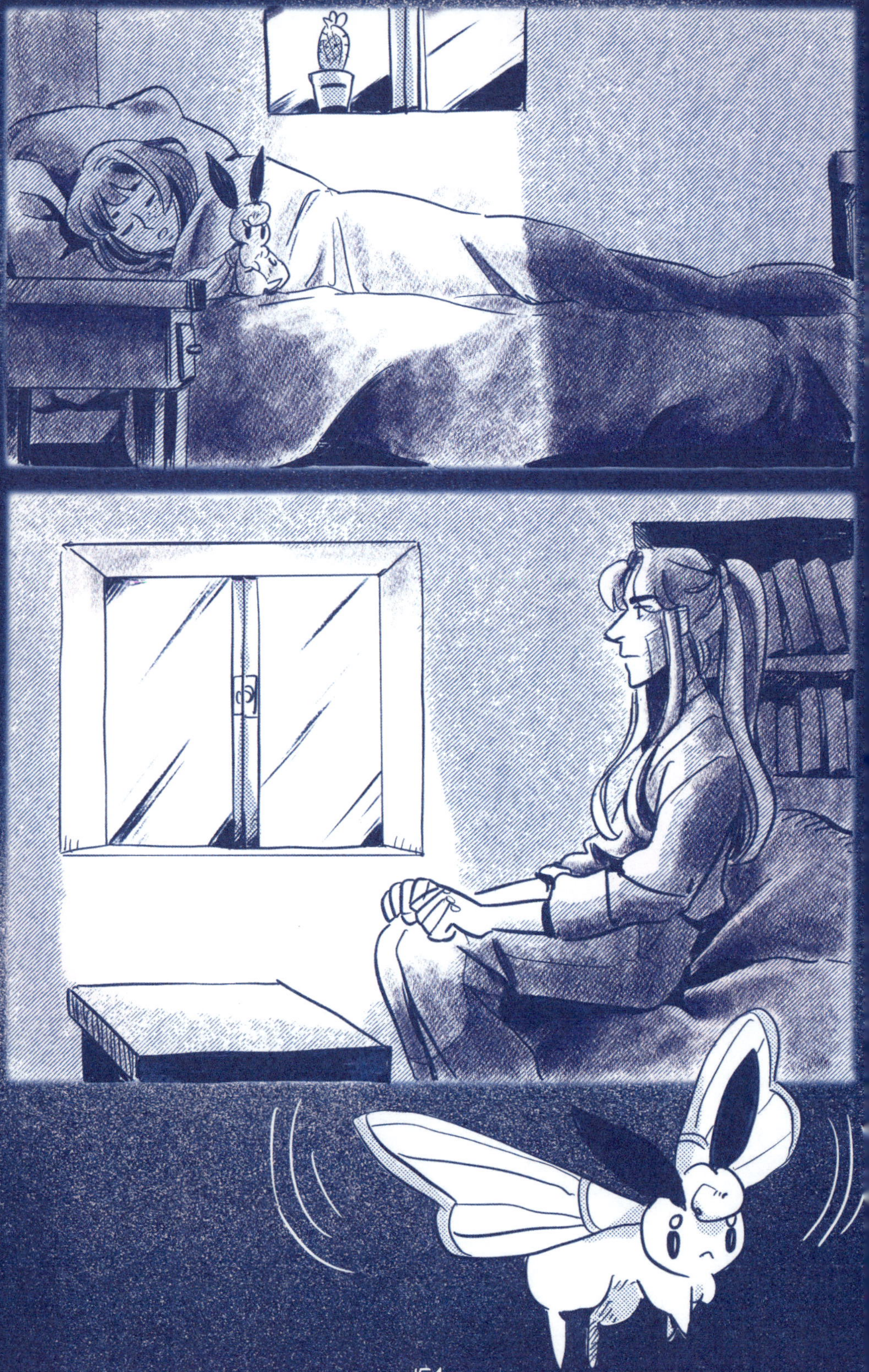

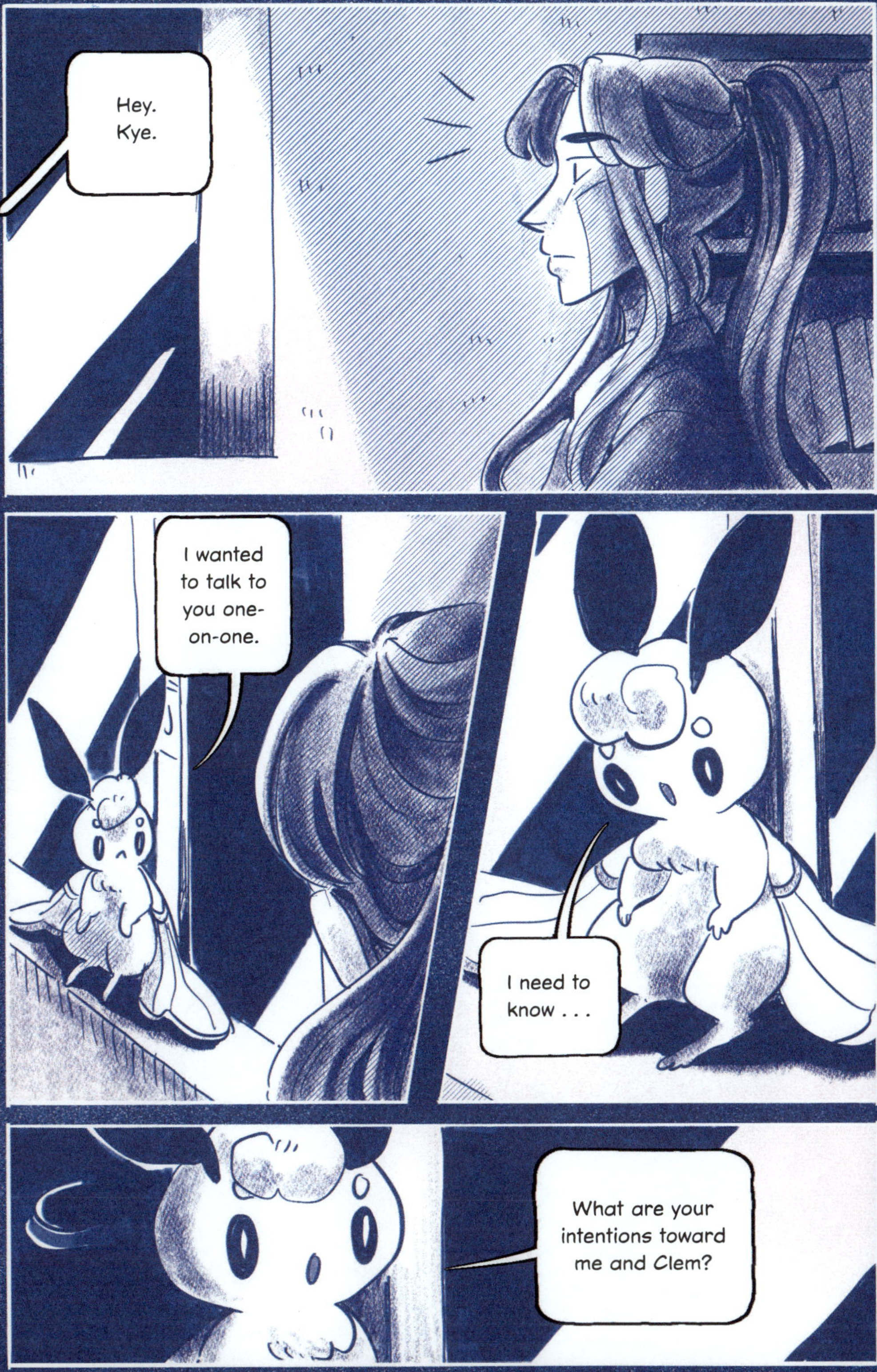
Hey. Kye.
I wanted to talk to you one-on-one.
I need to know . . .
What are your intentions toward me and Clem?

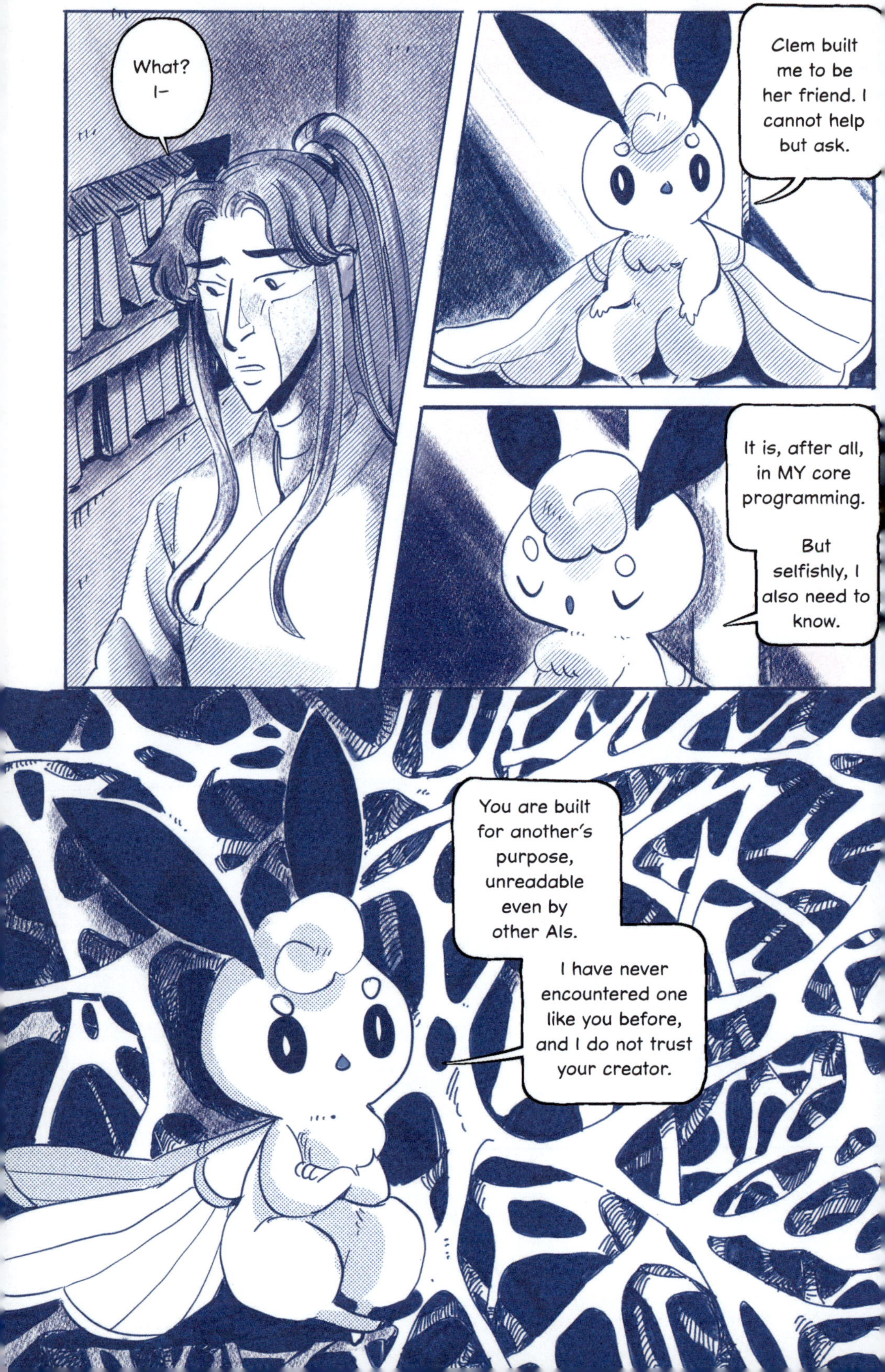
What? I–
Clem built me to be her friend. I cannot help but ask.
It is, after all, in MY core programming.
But selfishly, I also need to know.
You are built for another's purpose, unreadable even by other AIs.
I have never encountered one like you before, and I do not trust your creator.

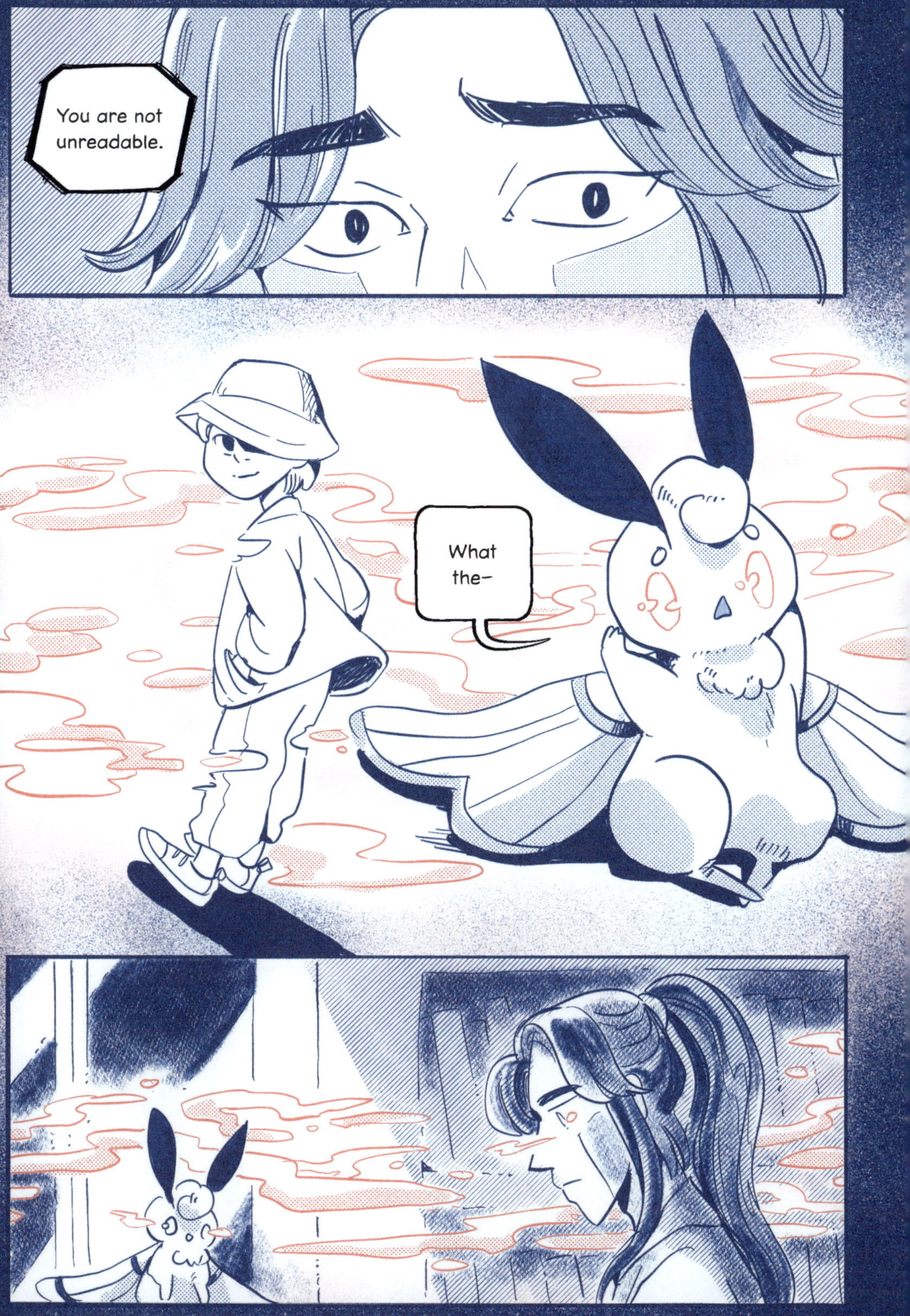
You are not unreadable.
What the-

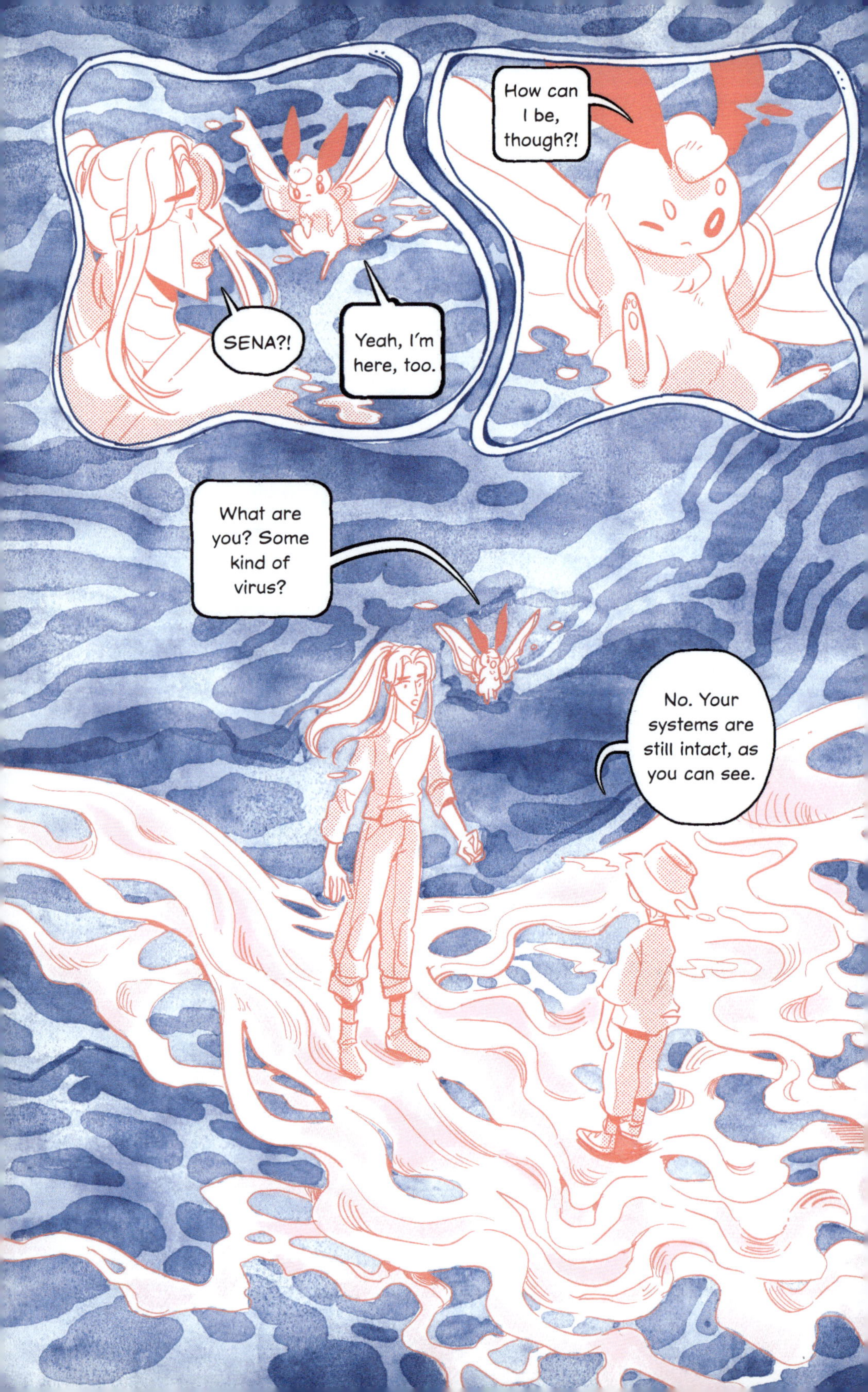
SENA?!
Yeah, I'm here, too.
How can I be, though?!
What are you? Some kind of virus?
No. Your systems are still intact, as you can see.

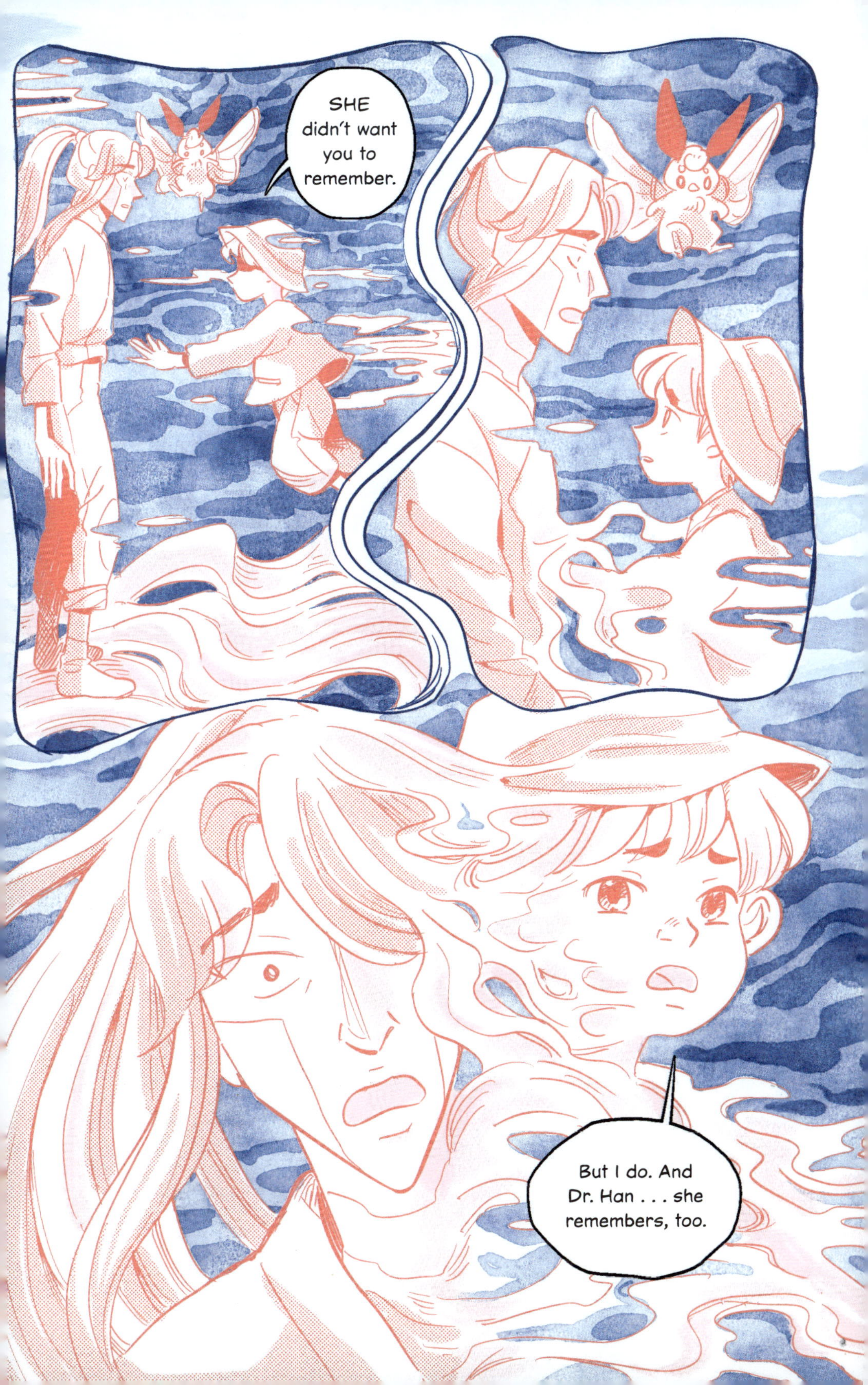
SHE didn't want you to remember.
But I do. And Dr. Han . . . she remembers, too.

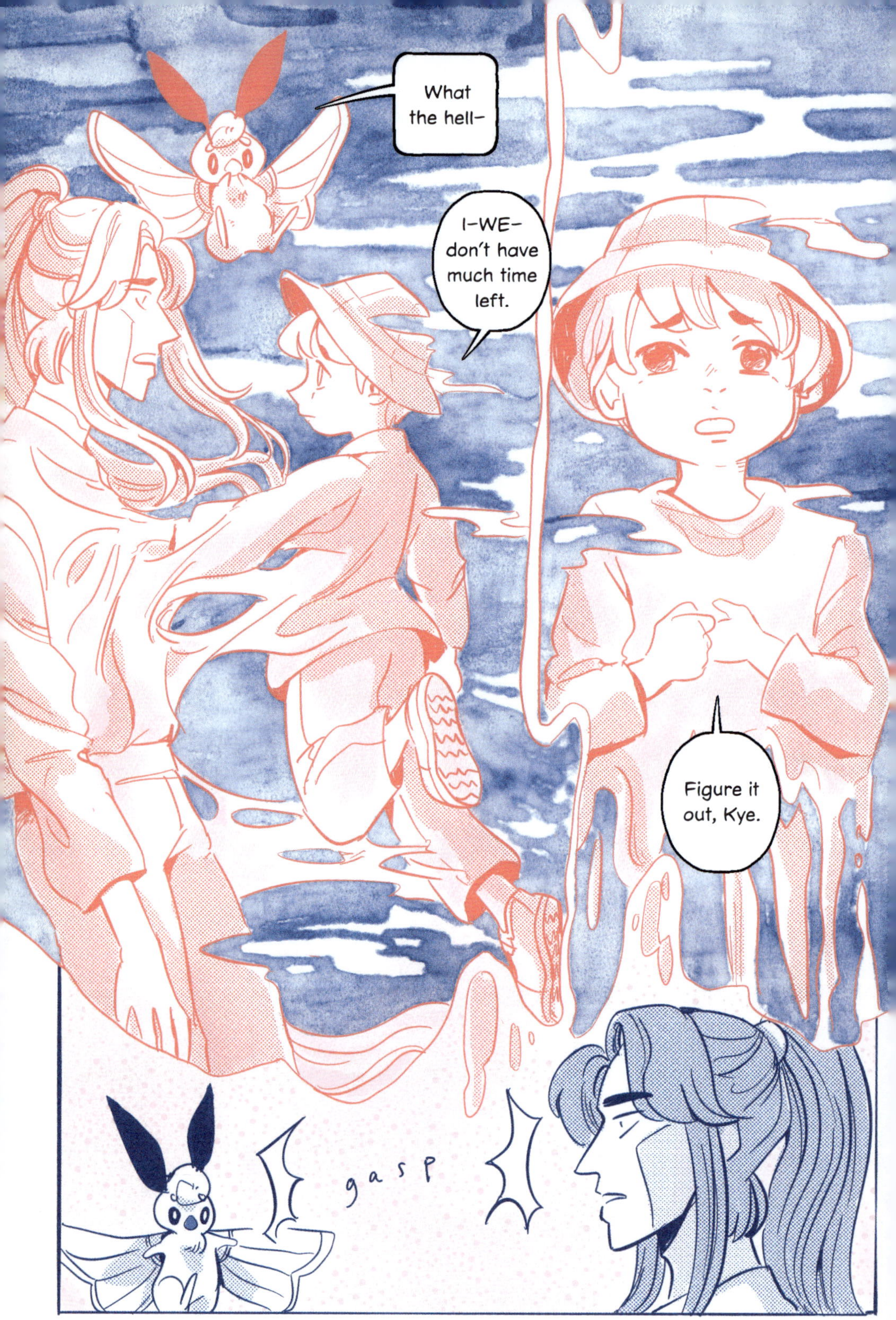
What the hell-
I-WE- don't have much time left.
Figure it out, Kye.
gasp

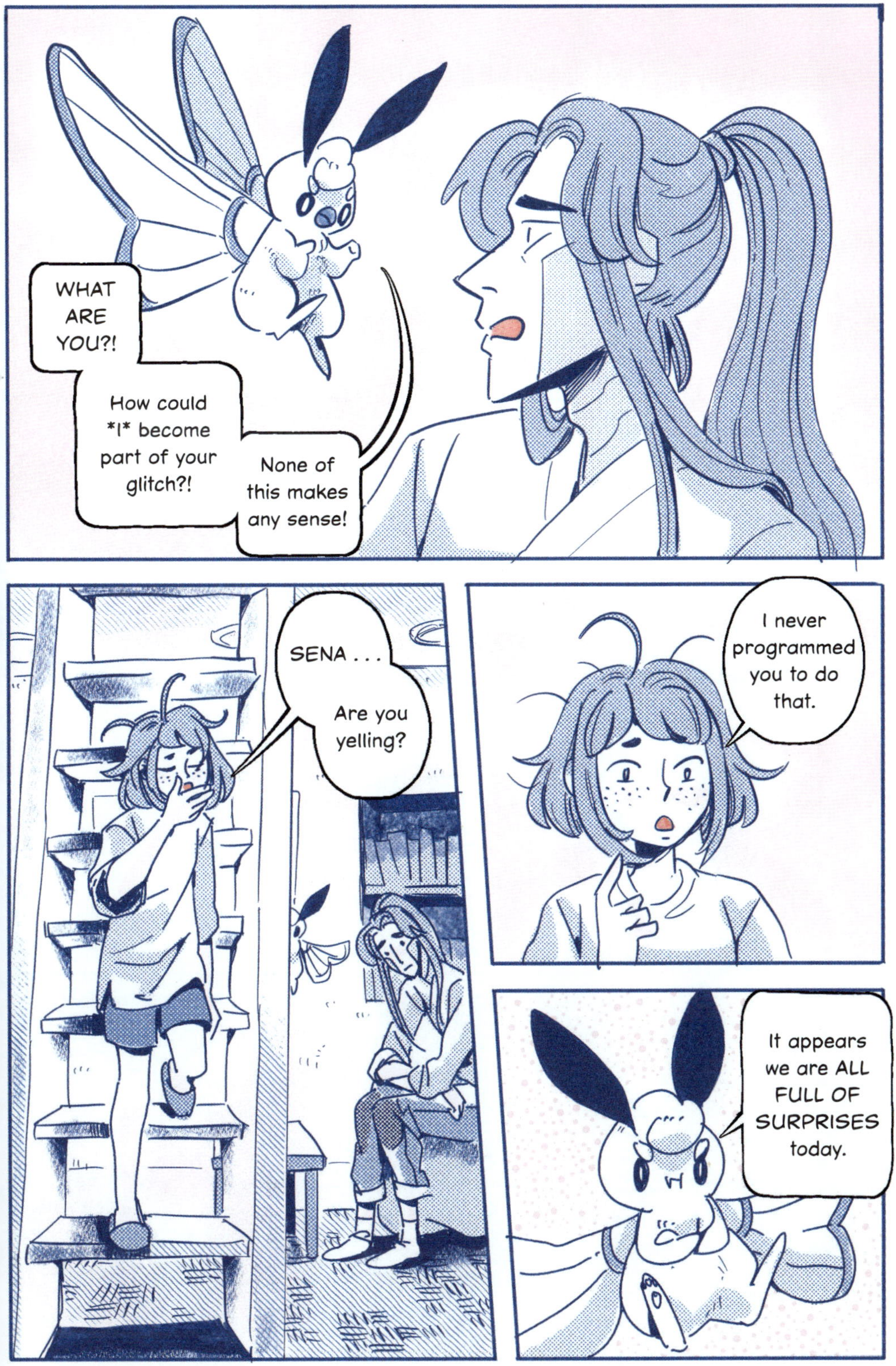
WHAT ARE YOU?!
How could *I* become part of your glitch?!
None of this makes any sense!
SENA . . .
Are you yelling?
I never programmed you to do that.
It appears we are ALL FULL OF SURPRISES today.

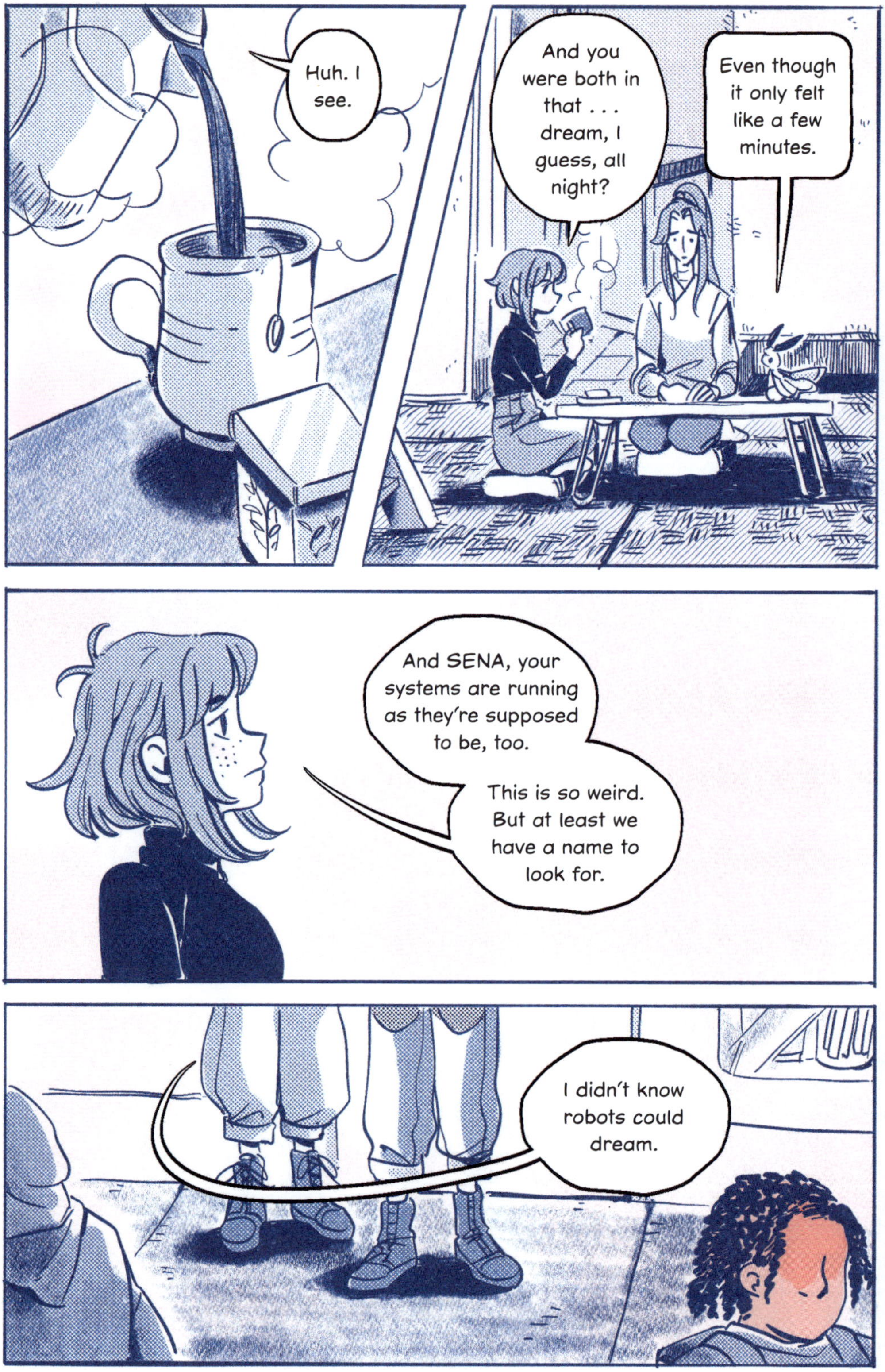
Huh. I see.
And you were both in that . . . dream, I guess, all night?
Even though it only felt like a few minutes.
And SENA, your systems are running as they're supposed to be, too.
This is so weird. But at least we have a name to look for.
I didn't know robots could dream.

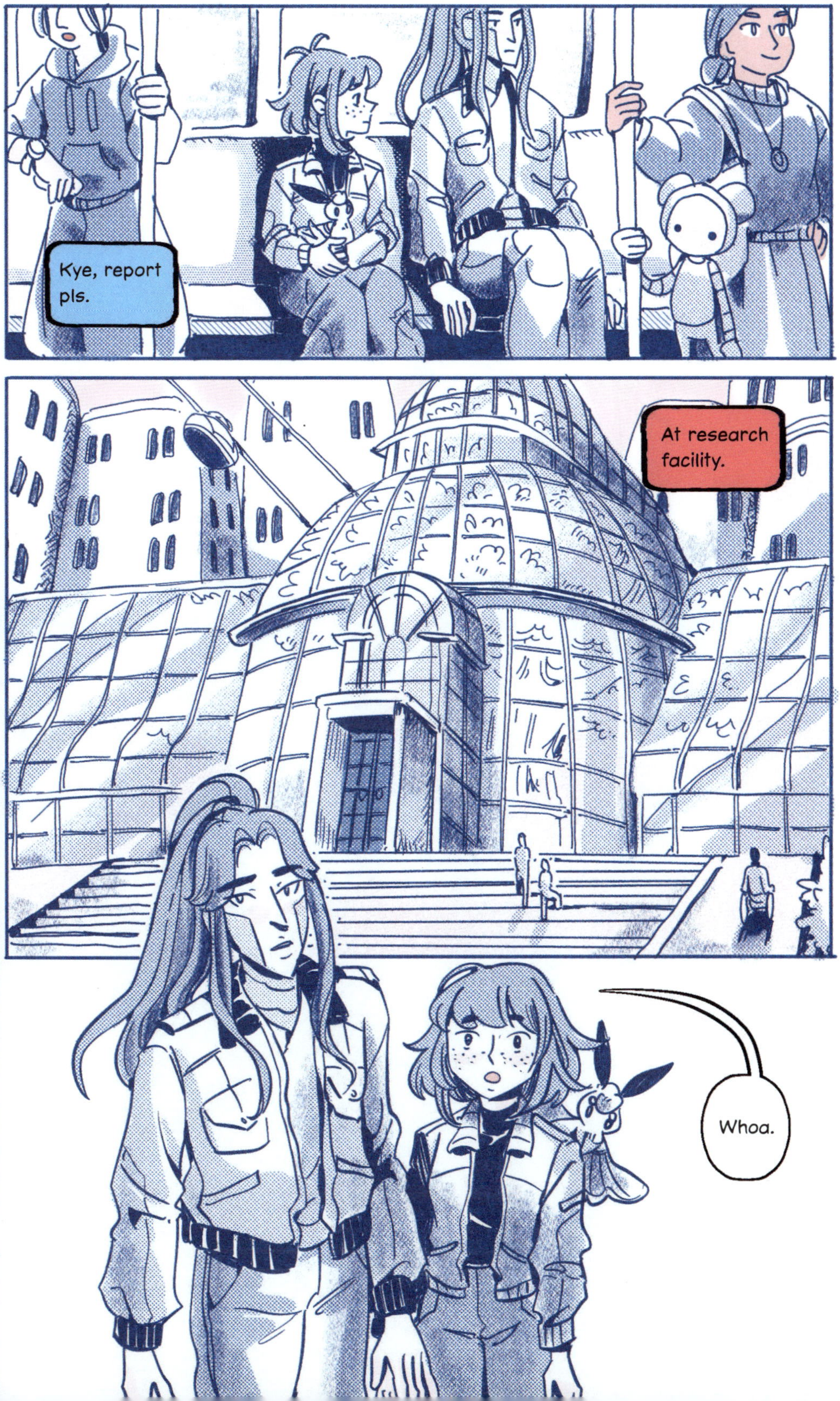
Kye, report pls.
At research facility.
Whoa.

00110000 00110111

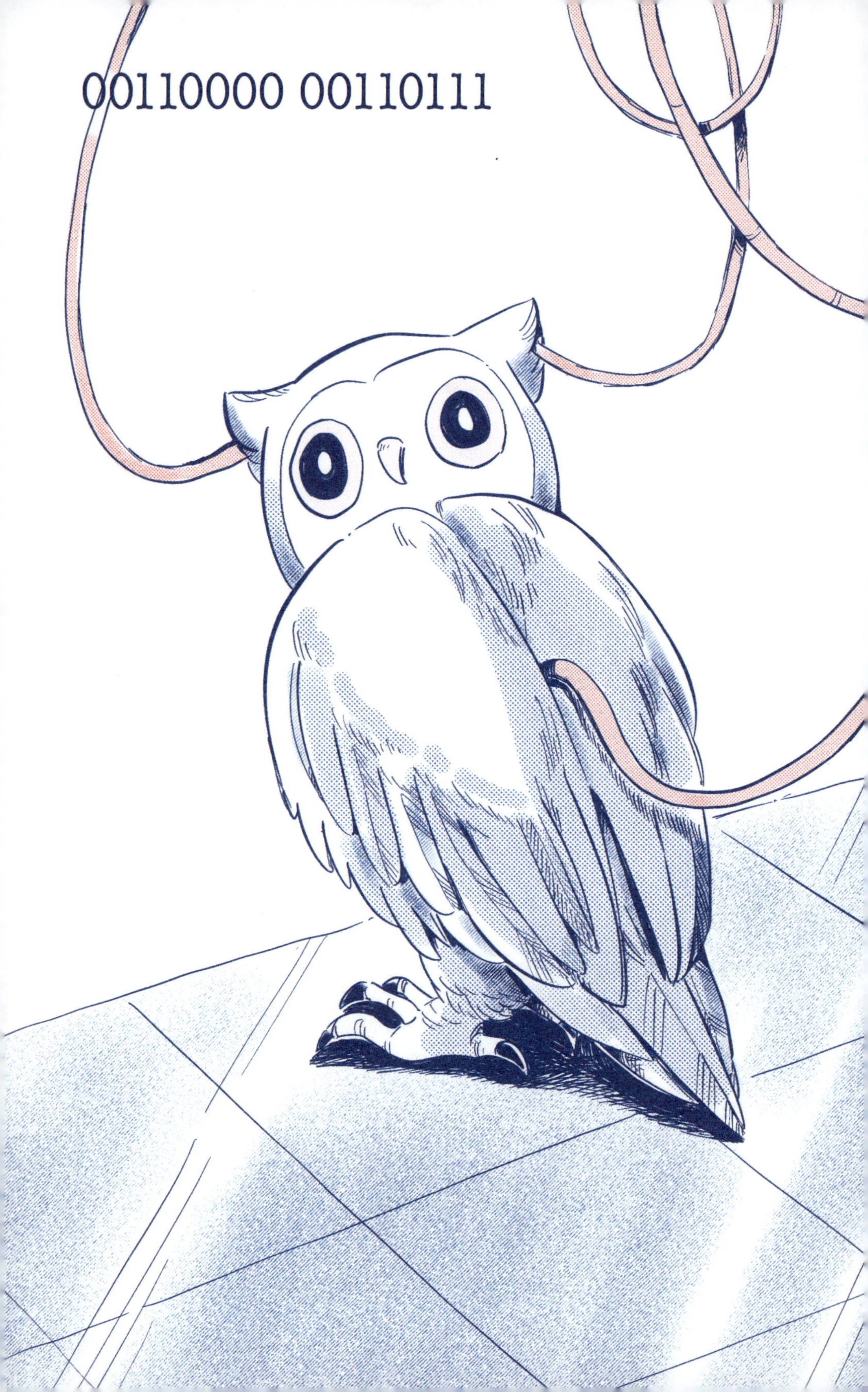

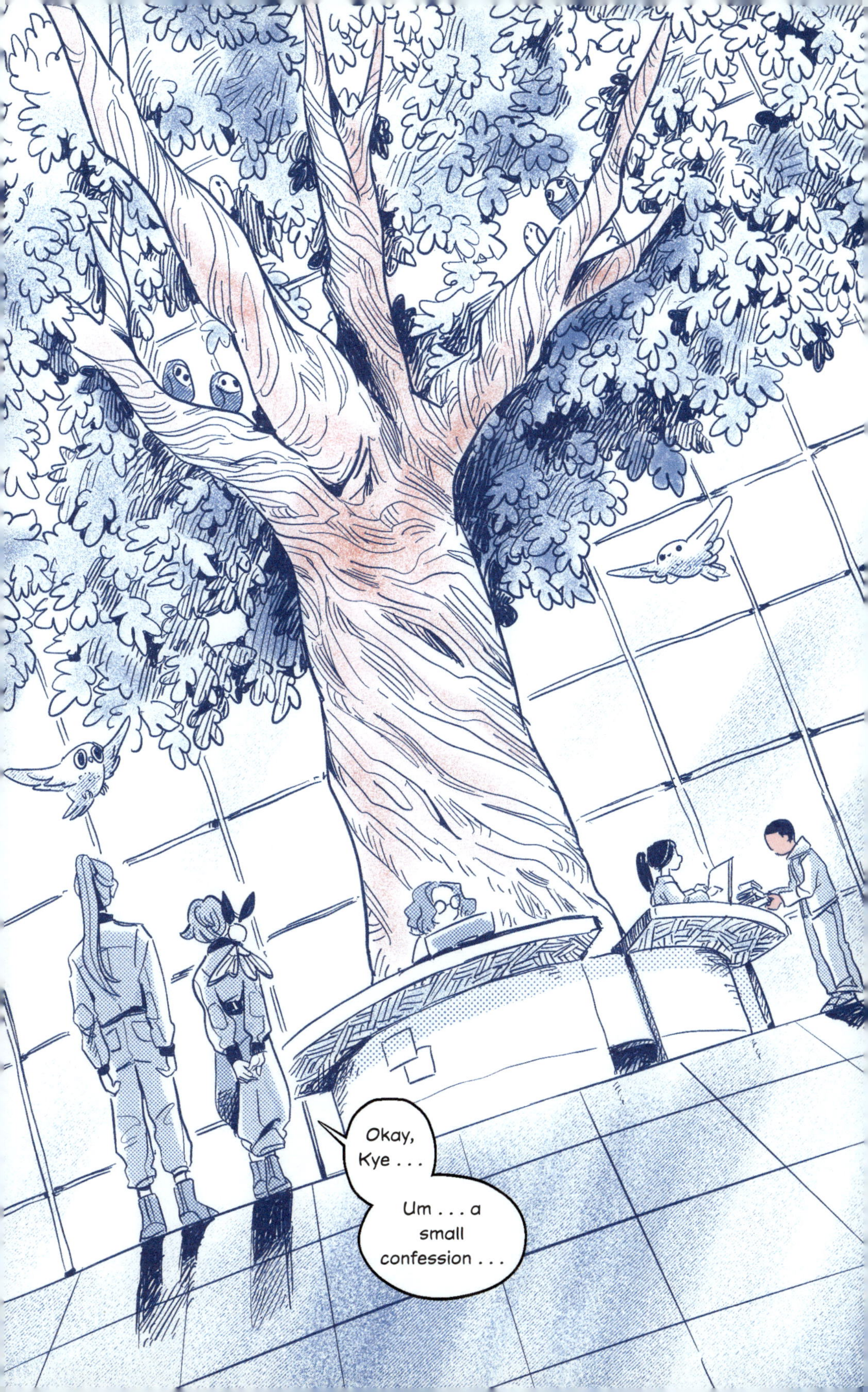
Okay, Kye . . .
Um . . . a small confession . . .

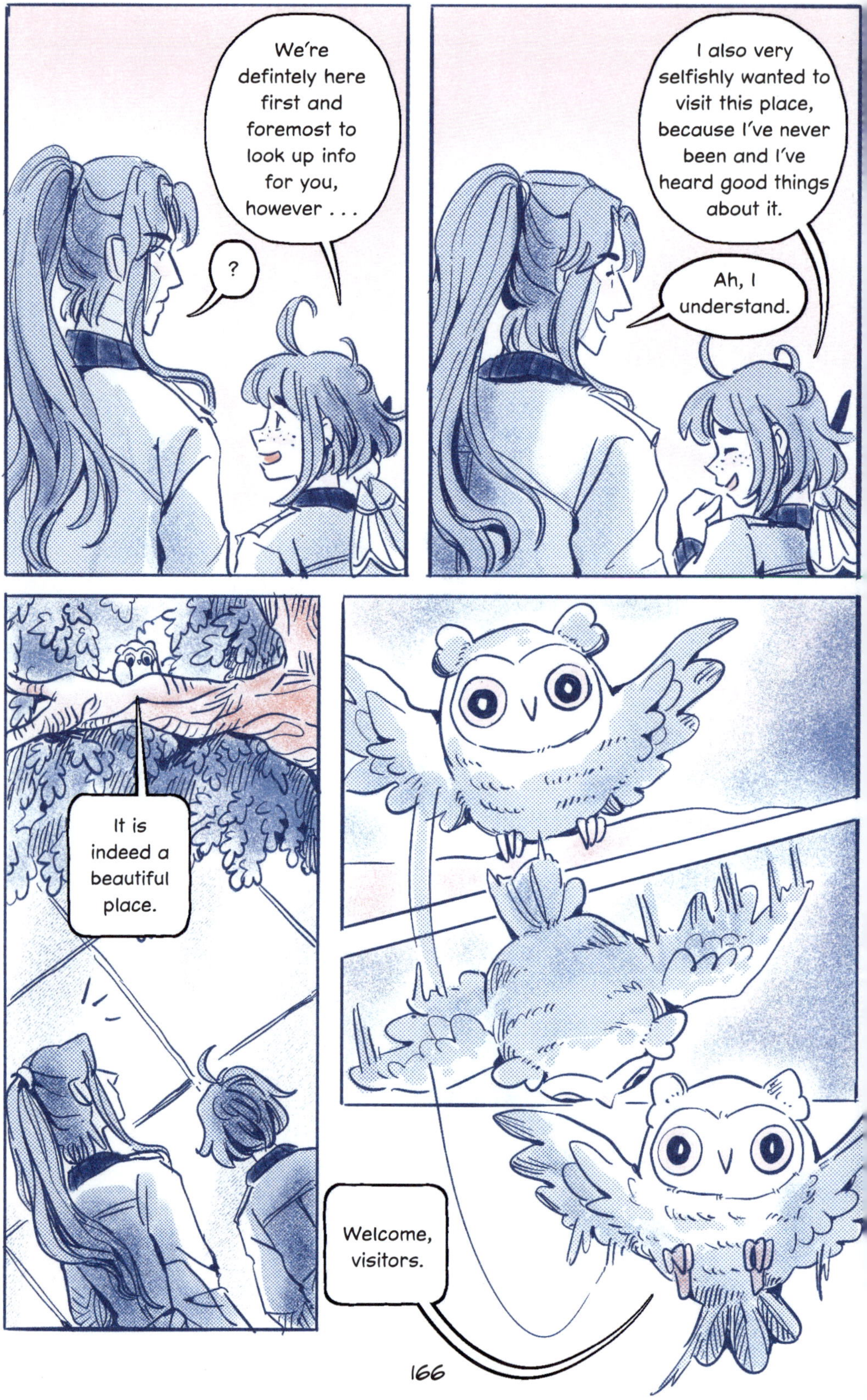
We're defintely here first and foremost to look up info for you, however . . .
?
I also very selfishly wanted to visit this place, because I've never been and I've heard good things about it.
Ah, I understand.
It is indeed a beautiful place.
Welcome, visitors.

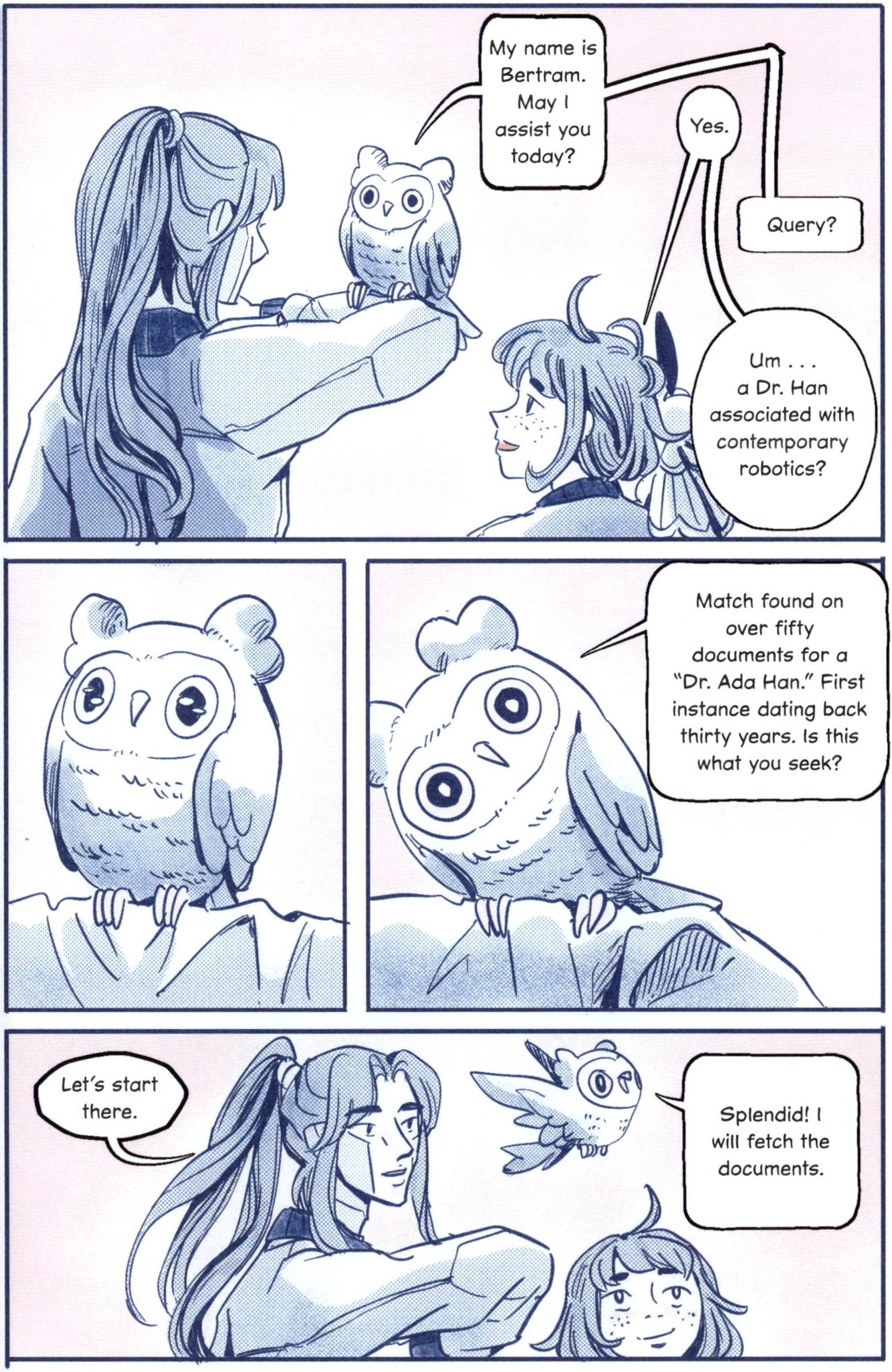
My name is Bertram. May I assist you today?
Yes.
Query?
Um . . . a Dr. Han associated with contemporary robotics?
Match found on over fifty documents for a "Dr. Ada Han." First instance dating back thirty years. Is this what you seek?
Let's start there.
Splendid! I will fetch the documents.

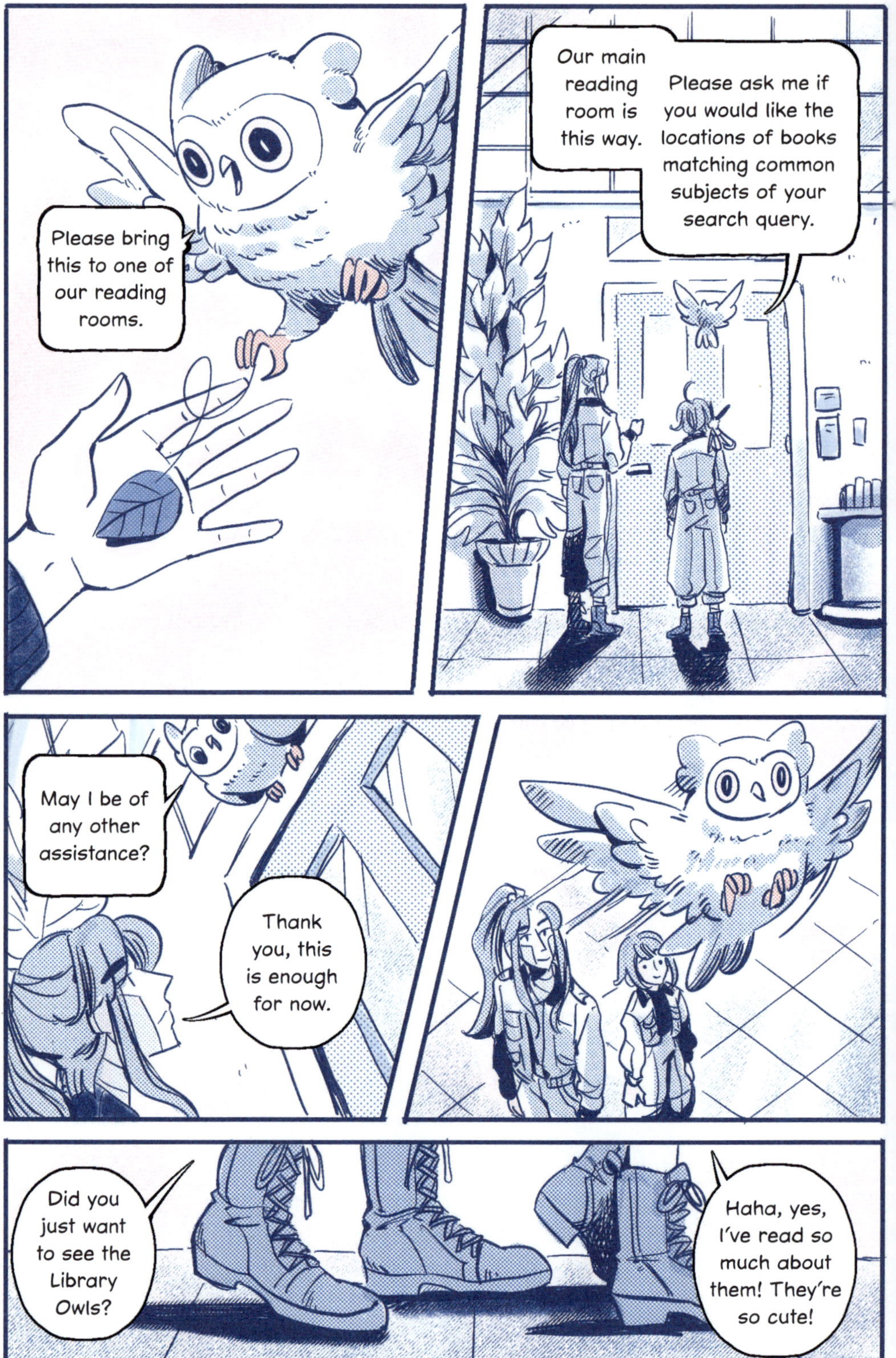
Please bring this to one of our reading rooms.
Our main reading room is this way.
Please ask me if you would like the locations of books matching common subjects of your search query.
May I be of any other assistance?
Thank you, this is enough for now.
Did you just want to see the Library Owls?
Haha, yes, I've read so much about them! They're so cute!

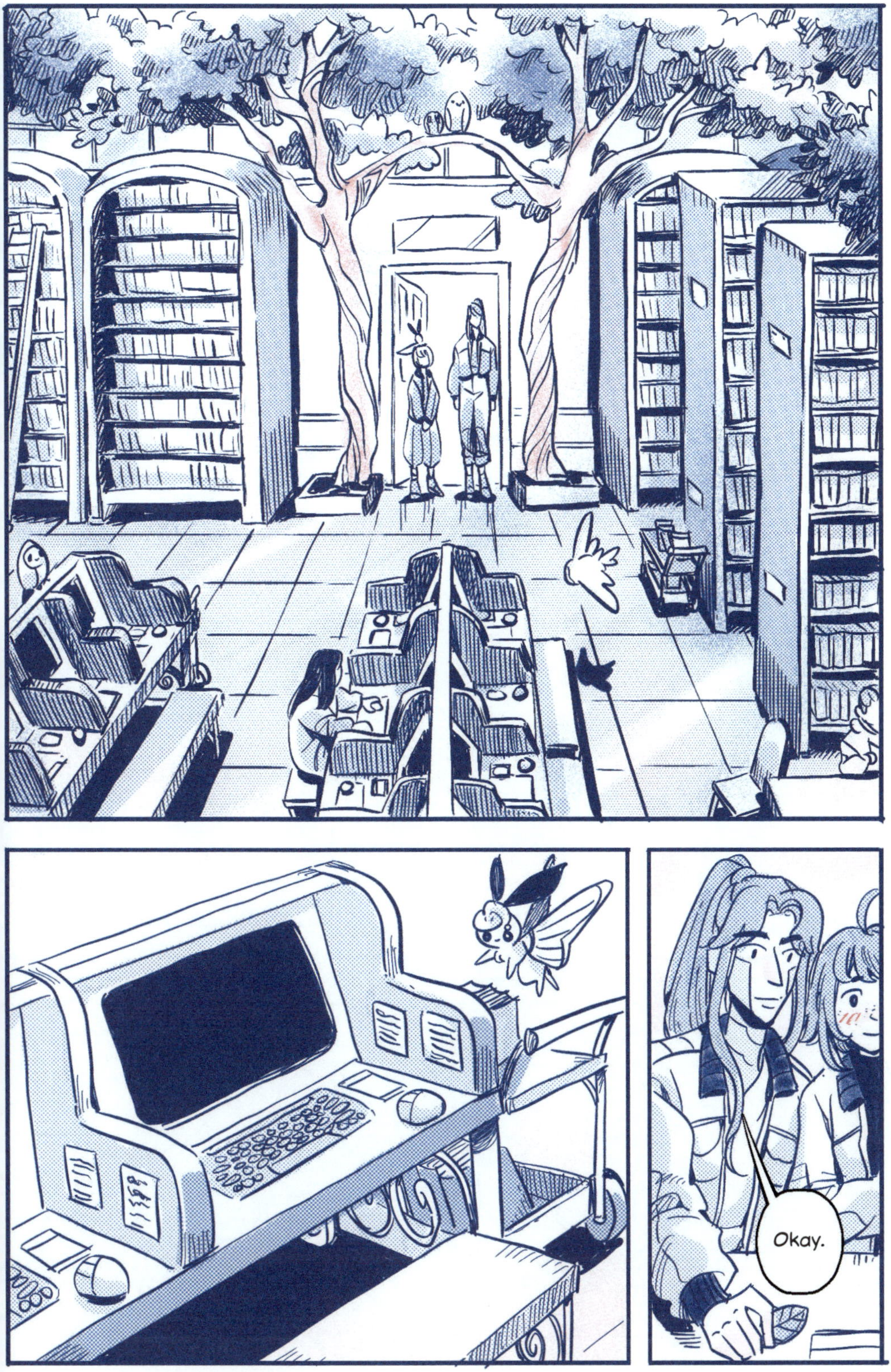
Okay.

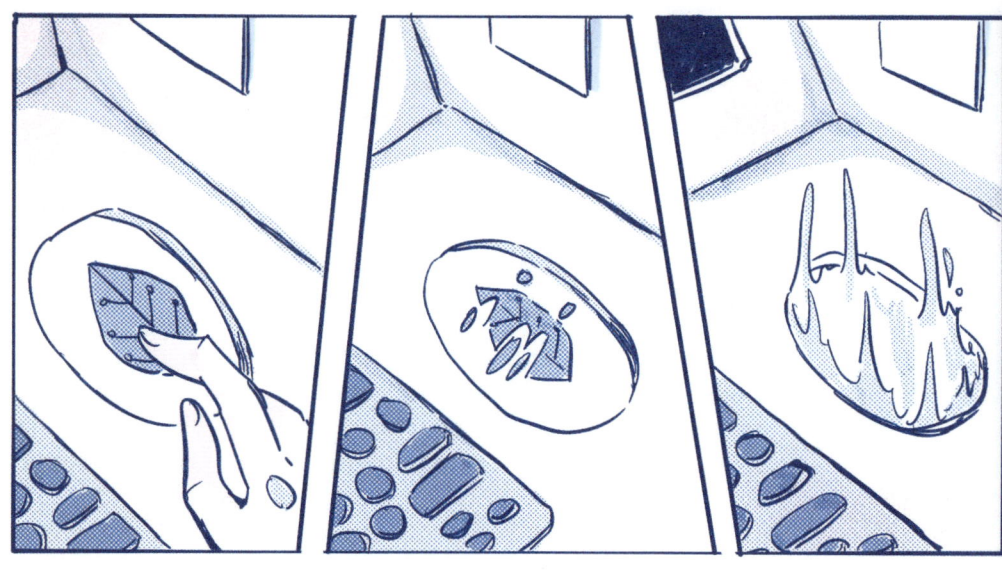

COMPREHENSIVE SEARCH RESULTS: Dr. Ada Han

Filter by: ▲▼

General Biography

Publication

Date (most recent)

Date (least recent)

Alphabetical

Image

Active Years: 2523 – 2552

Dr. Ada Han (b. 2501) is a Martian robotics engineer, author, and ethicist, most well-known for her work "Us and Them" (P&D Press, 2546), a comprehensive history about the development of modern artificial intelligence.

She seems really cool. I wish I could have learned about her earlier.

Oh, her books were only published here— no wonder.

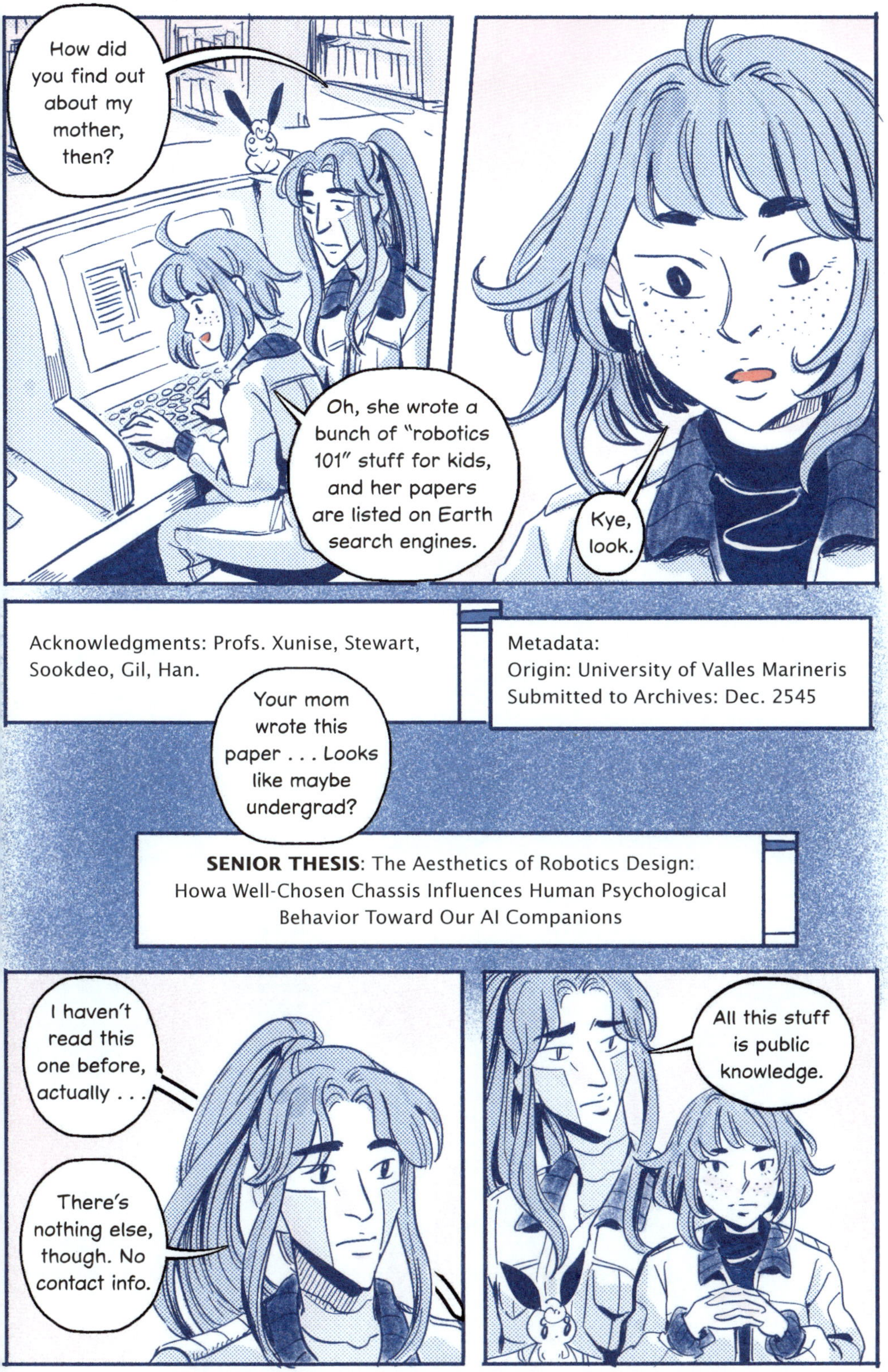
How did you find out about my mother, then?
Oh, she wrote a bunch of "robotics 101" stuff for kids, and her papers are listed on Earth search engines.
Kye, look.
Acknowledgments: Profs. Xunise, Stewart, Sookdeo, Gil, Han.
Metadata:
Origin: University of Valles Marineris
Submitted to Archives: Dec. 2545
Your mom wrote this paper . . . Looks like maybe undergrad?
SENIOR THESIS: The Aesthetics of Robotics Design: Howa Well-Chosen Chassis Influences Human Psychological Behavior Toward Our AI Companions
I haven't read this one before, actually . . .
There's nothing else, though. No contact info.
All this stuff is public knowledge.

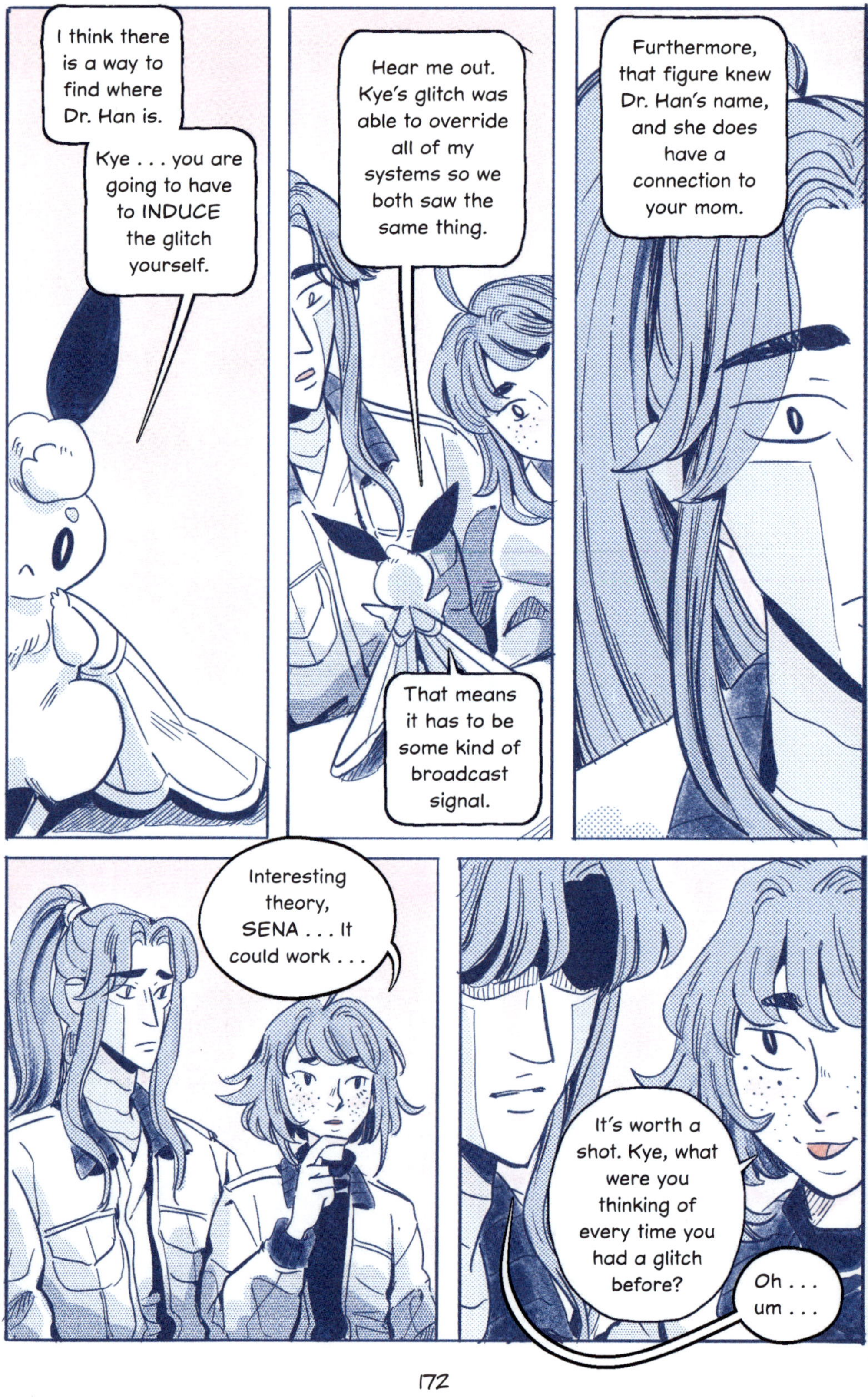
I think there is a way to find where Dr. Han is.
Kye . . . you are going to have to INDUCE the glitch yourself.
Hear me out. Kye's glitch was able to override all of my systems so we both saw the same thing.
That means it has to be some kind of broadcast signal.
Furthermore, that figure knew Dr. Han's name, and she does have a connection to your mom.
Interesting theory, SENA . . . It could work . . .
It's worth a shot. Kye, what were you thinking of every time you had a glitch before?
Oh . . . um . . .

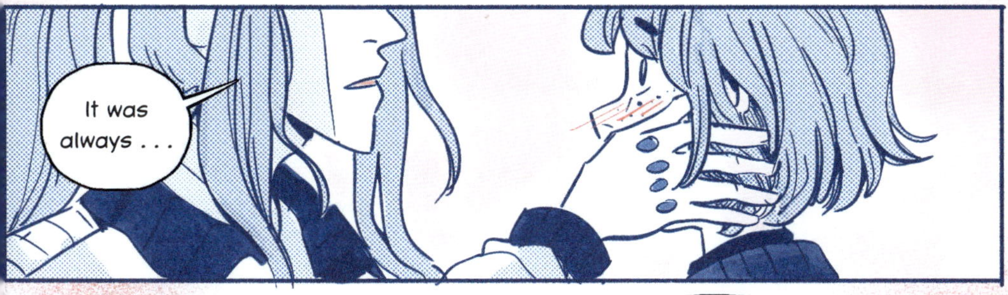
It was always . . .

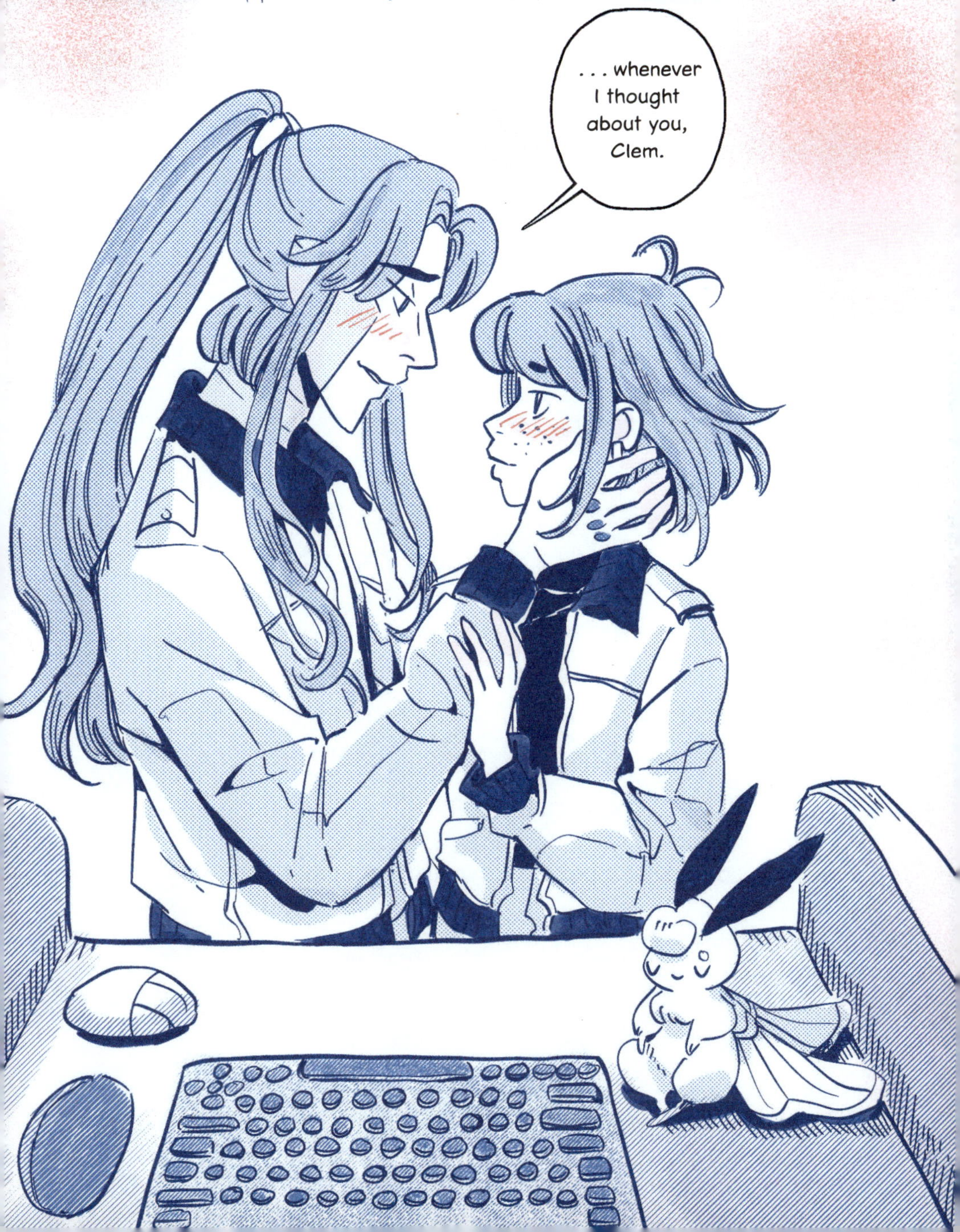
. . . whenever I thought about you, Clem.

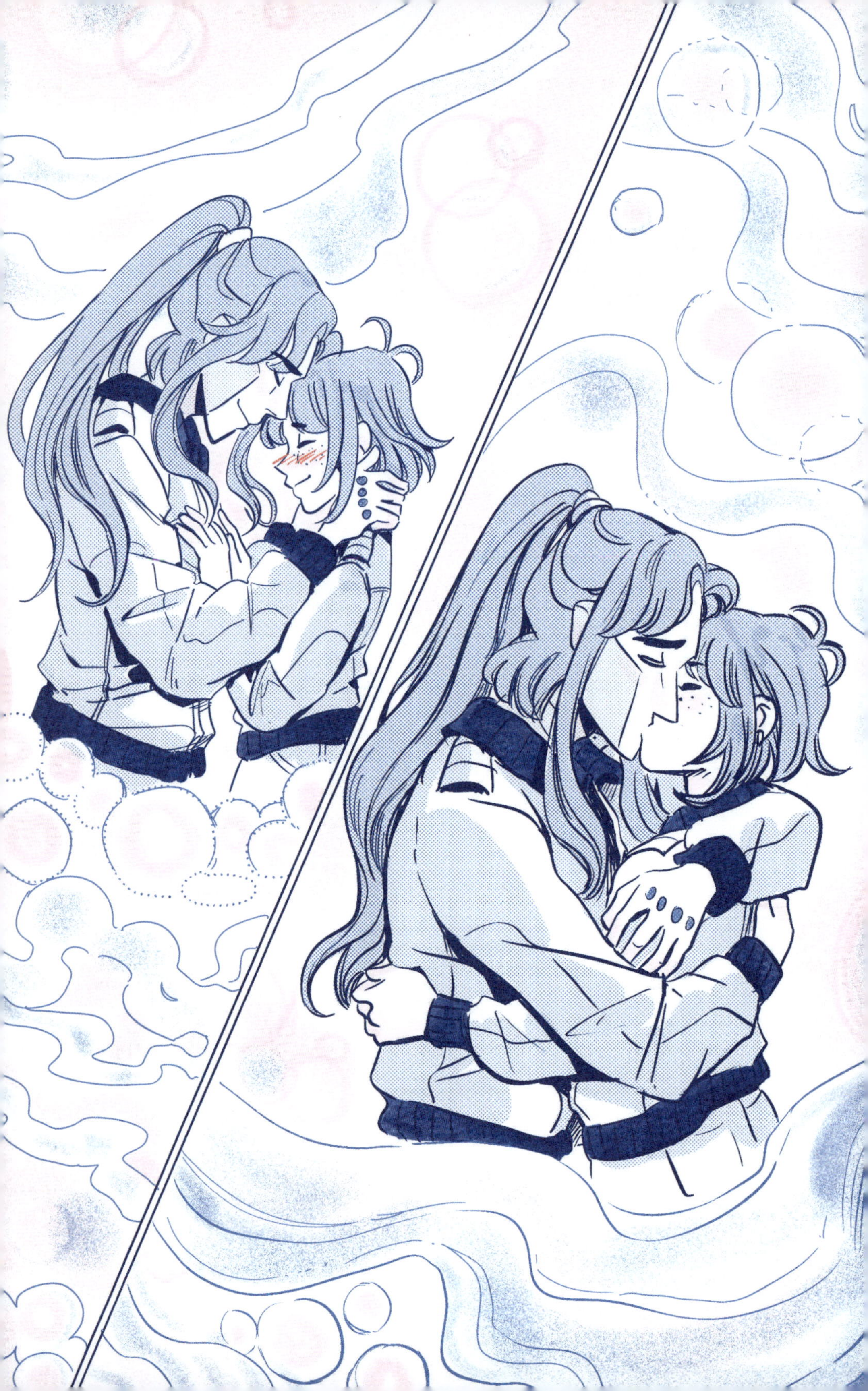

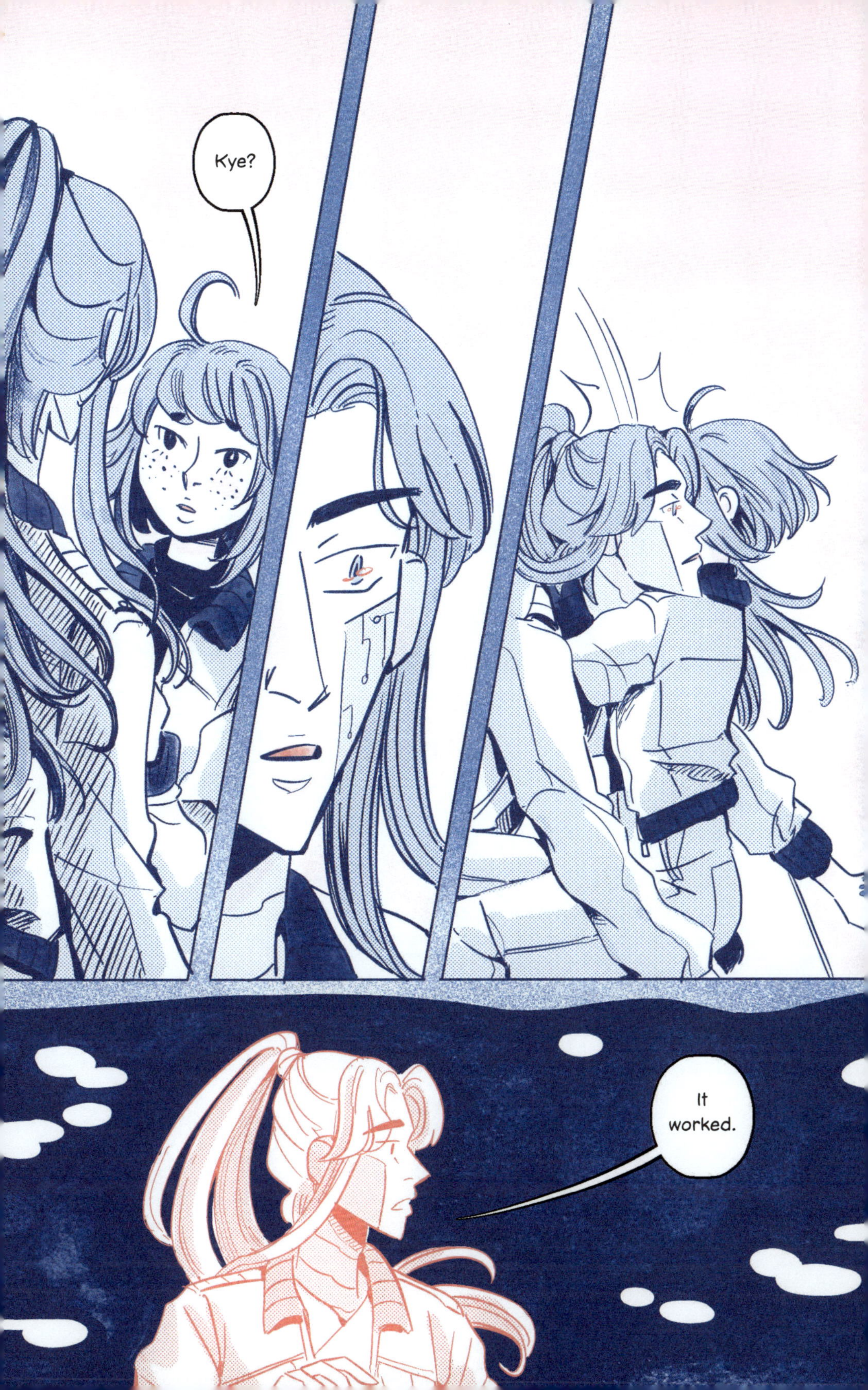
Kye?
It worked.

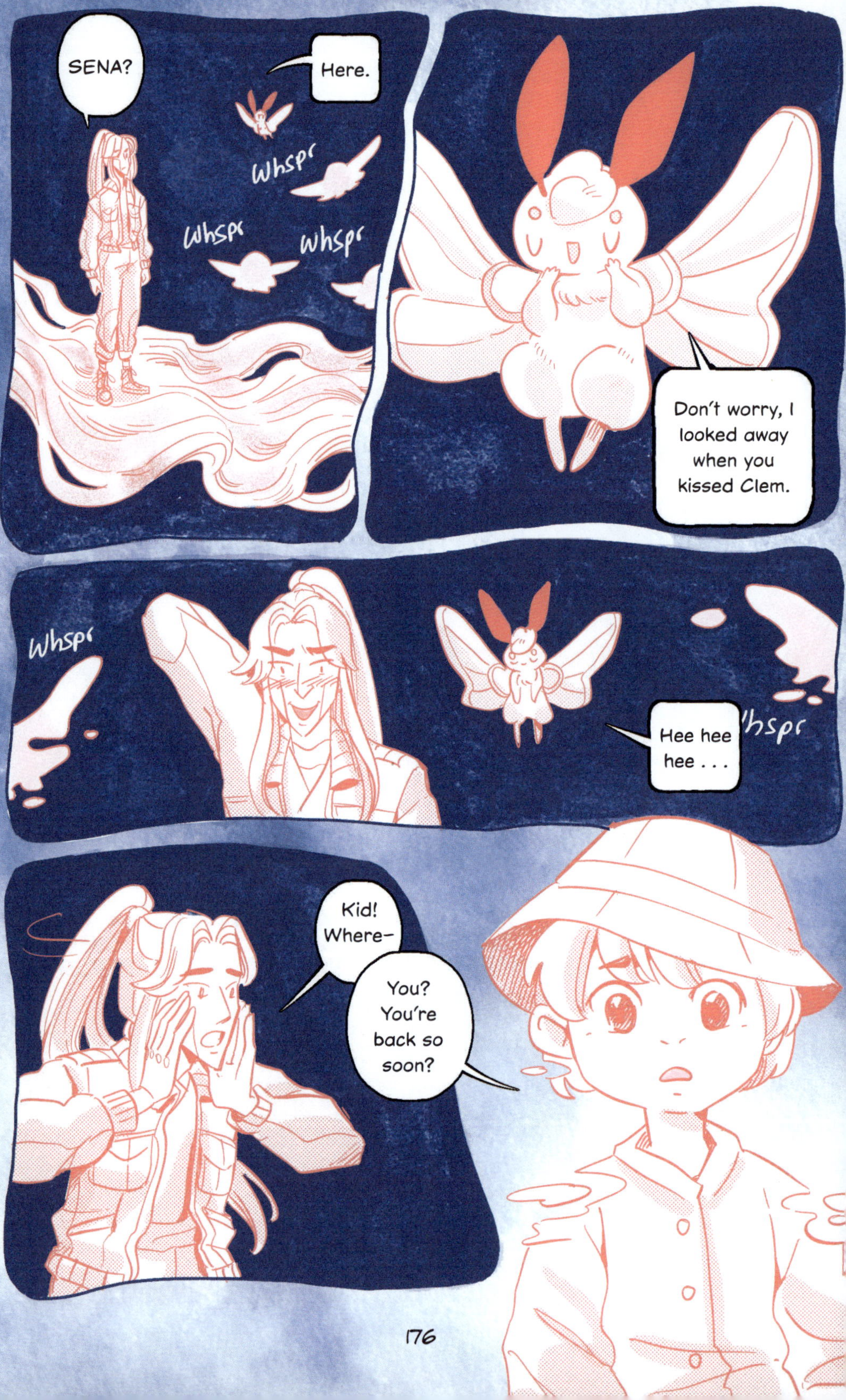
SENA?
Here.
Whspr
Whspr
Whspr
Don't worry, I looked away when you kissed Clem.
Whspr
Hee hee hee . . .
Kid! Where-
You? You're back so soon?

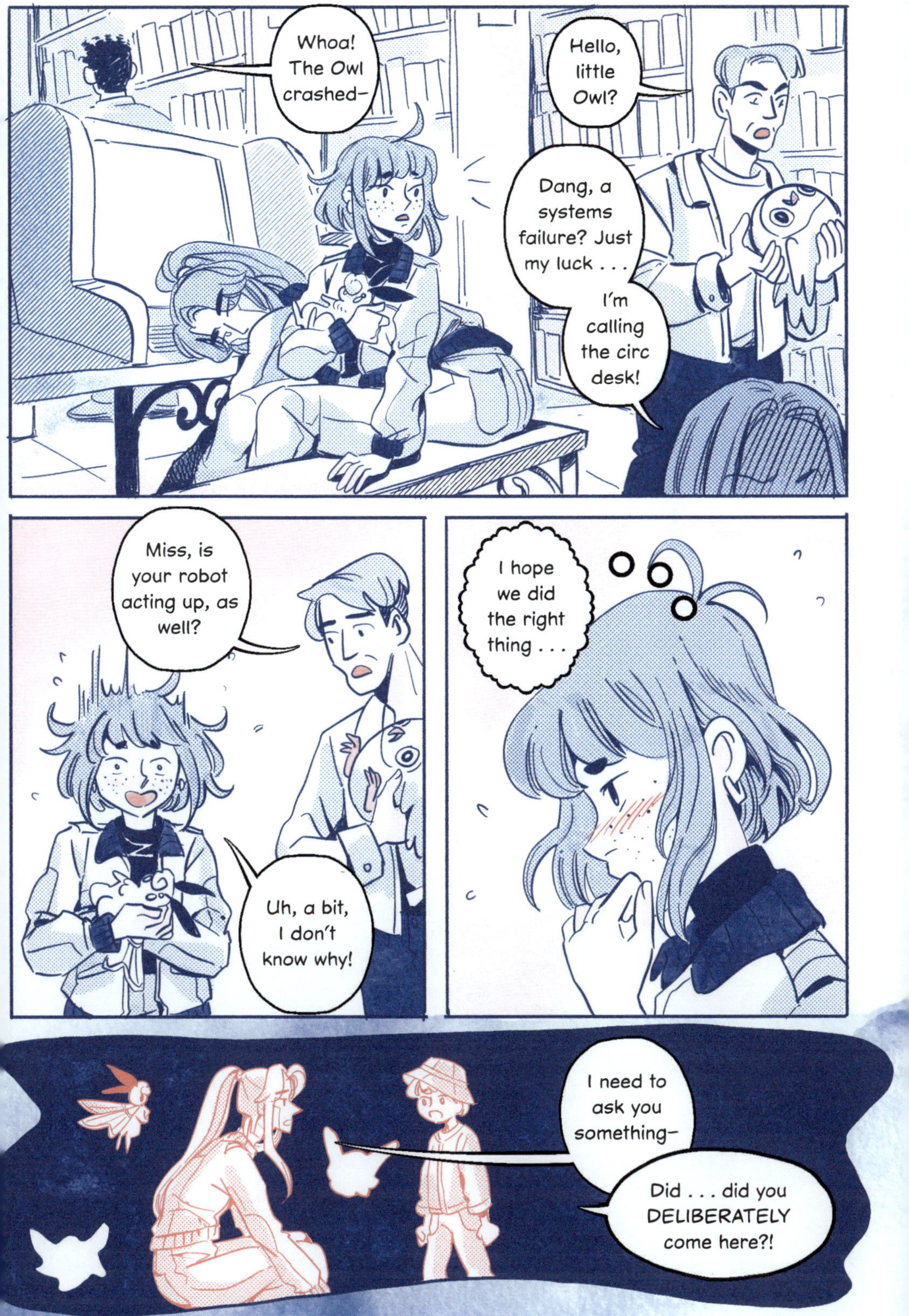
Whoa! The Owl crashed–
Hello, little Owl?
Dang, a systems failure? Just my luck . . .
I'm calling the circ desk!
Miss, is your robot acting up, as well?
Uh, a bit, I don't know why!
I hope we did the right thing . . .
I need to ask you something–
Did . . . did you DELIBERATELY come here?!

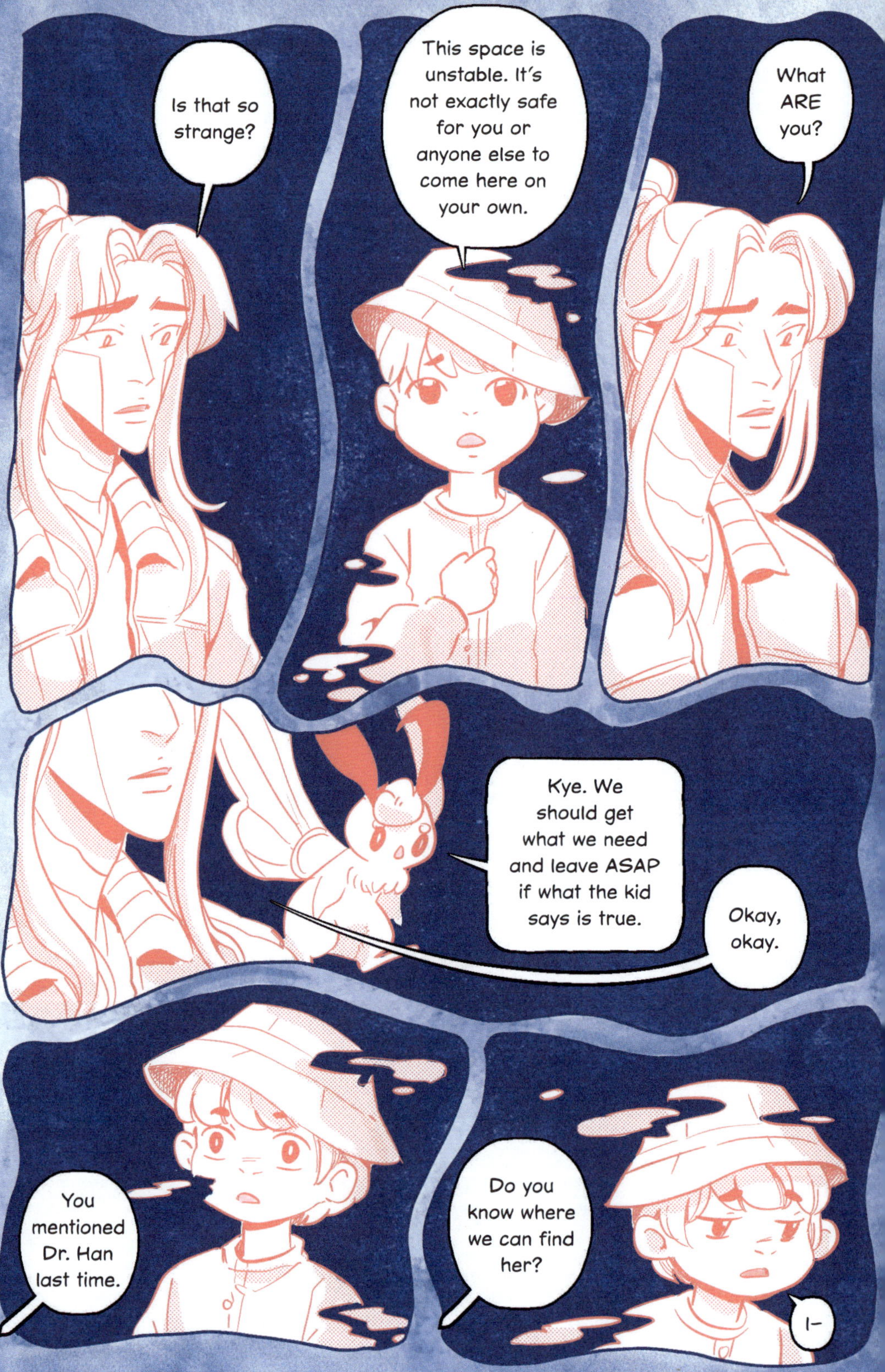
Is that so strange?
This space is unstable. It's not exactly safe for you or anyone else to come here on your own.
What ARE you?
Kye. We should get what we need and leave ASAP if what the kid says is true.
Okay, okay.
You mentioned Dr. Han last time.
Do you know where we can find her?
I–

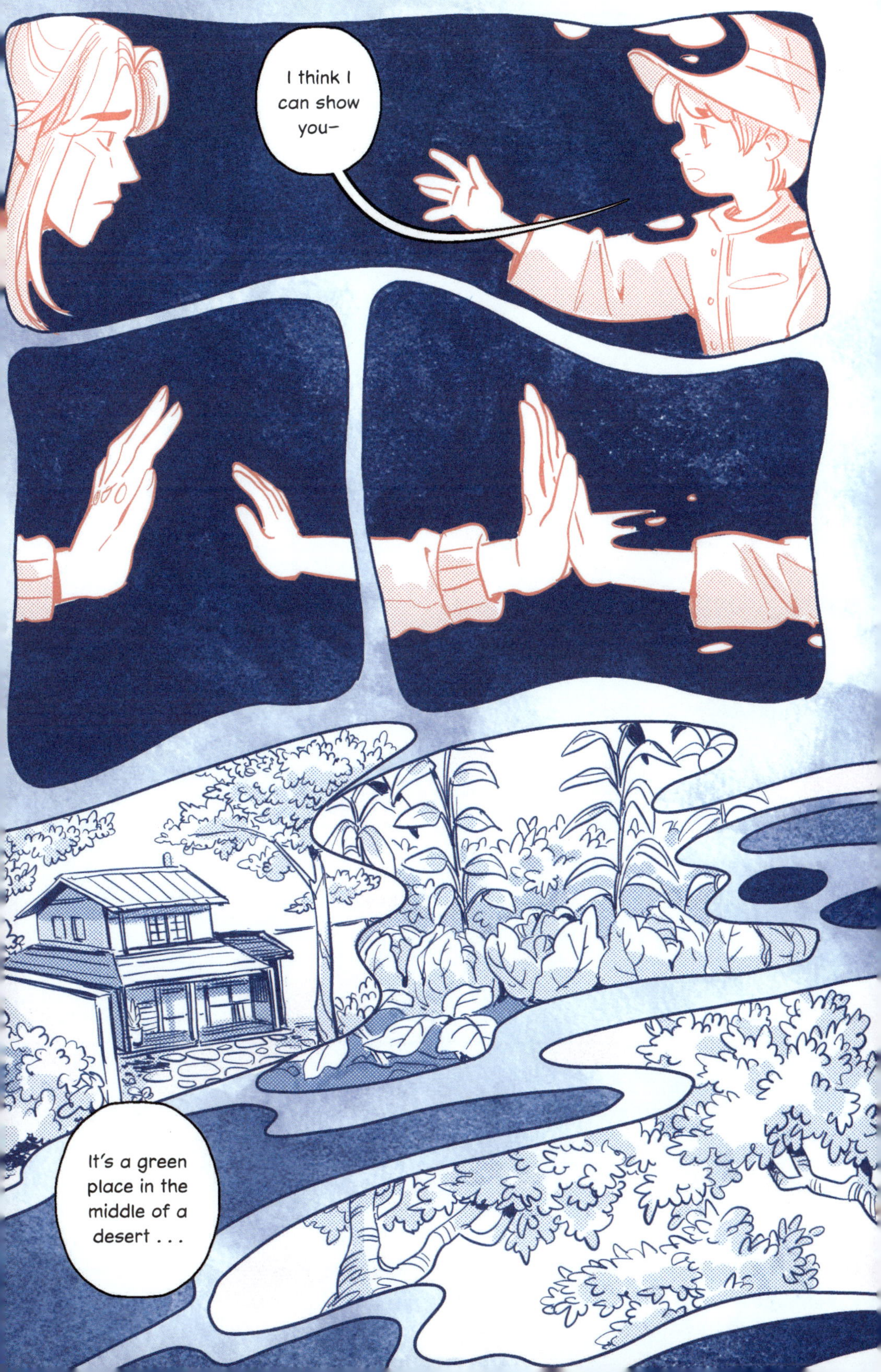
I think I can show you–
It's a green place in the middle of a desert . . .

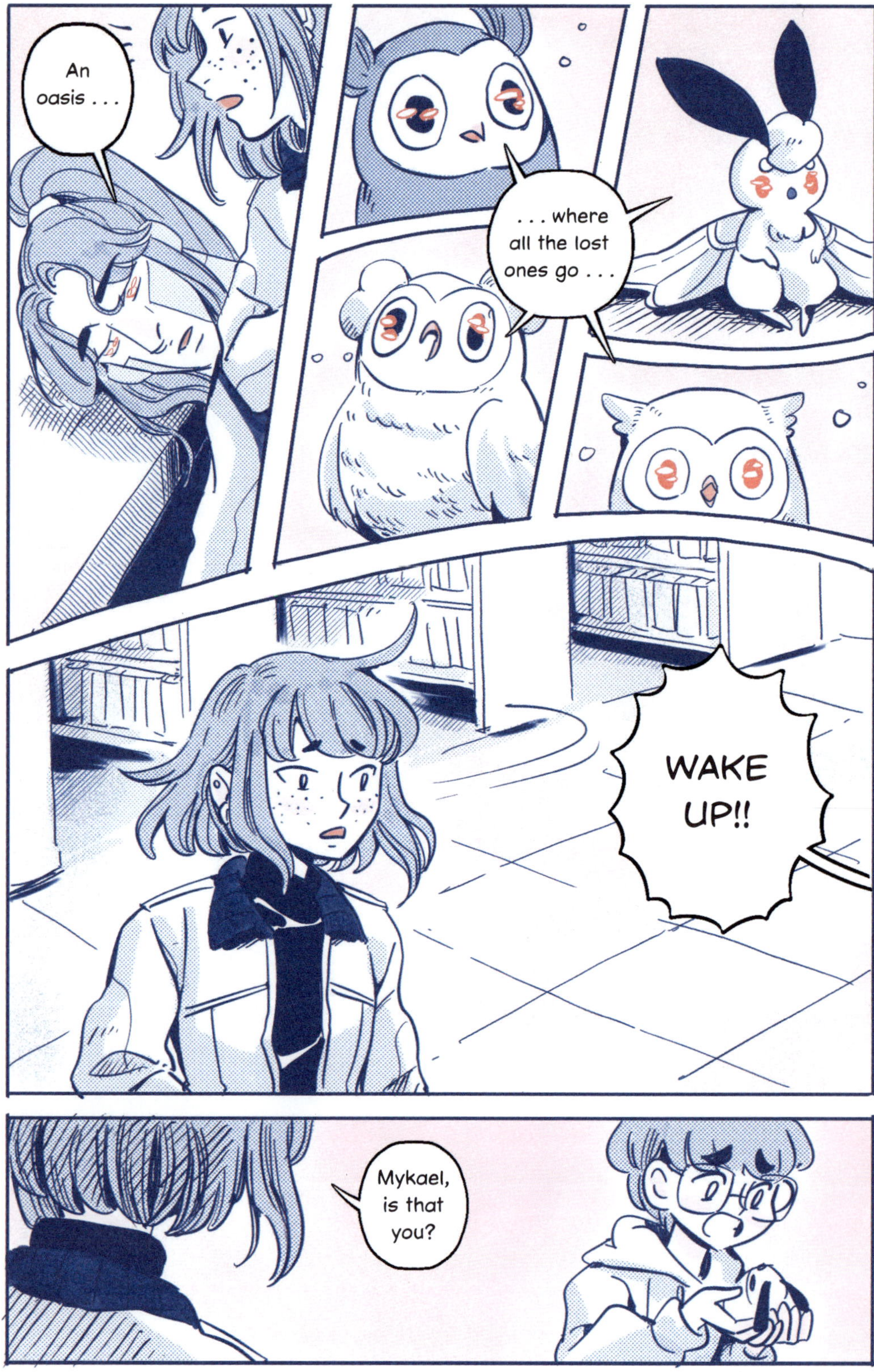
An oasis . . .
. . . where all the lost ones go . . .
WAKE UP!!
Mykael, is that you?

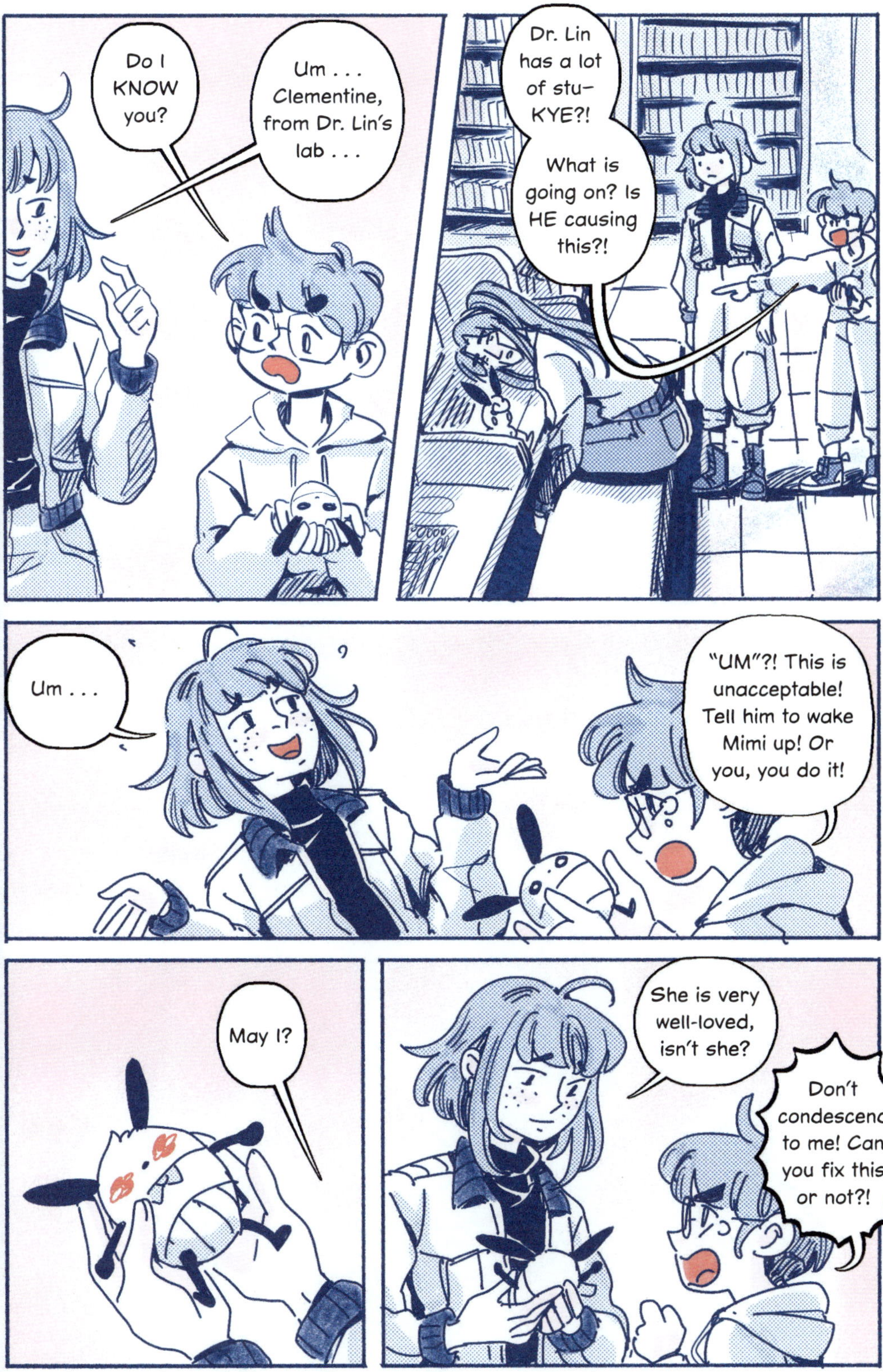
Do I KNOW you?
Um . . . Clementine, from Dr. Lin's lab . . .
Dr. Lin has a lot of stu–KYE?!
What is going on? Is HE causing this?!
Um . . .
"UM"?! This is unacceptable! Tell him to wake Mimi up! Or you, you do it!
May I?
She is very well-loved, isn't she?
Don't condescend to me! Can you fix this or not?!

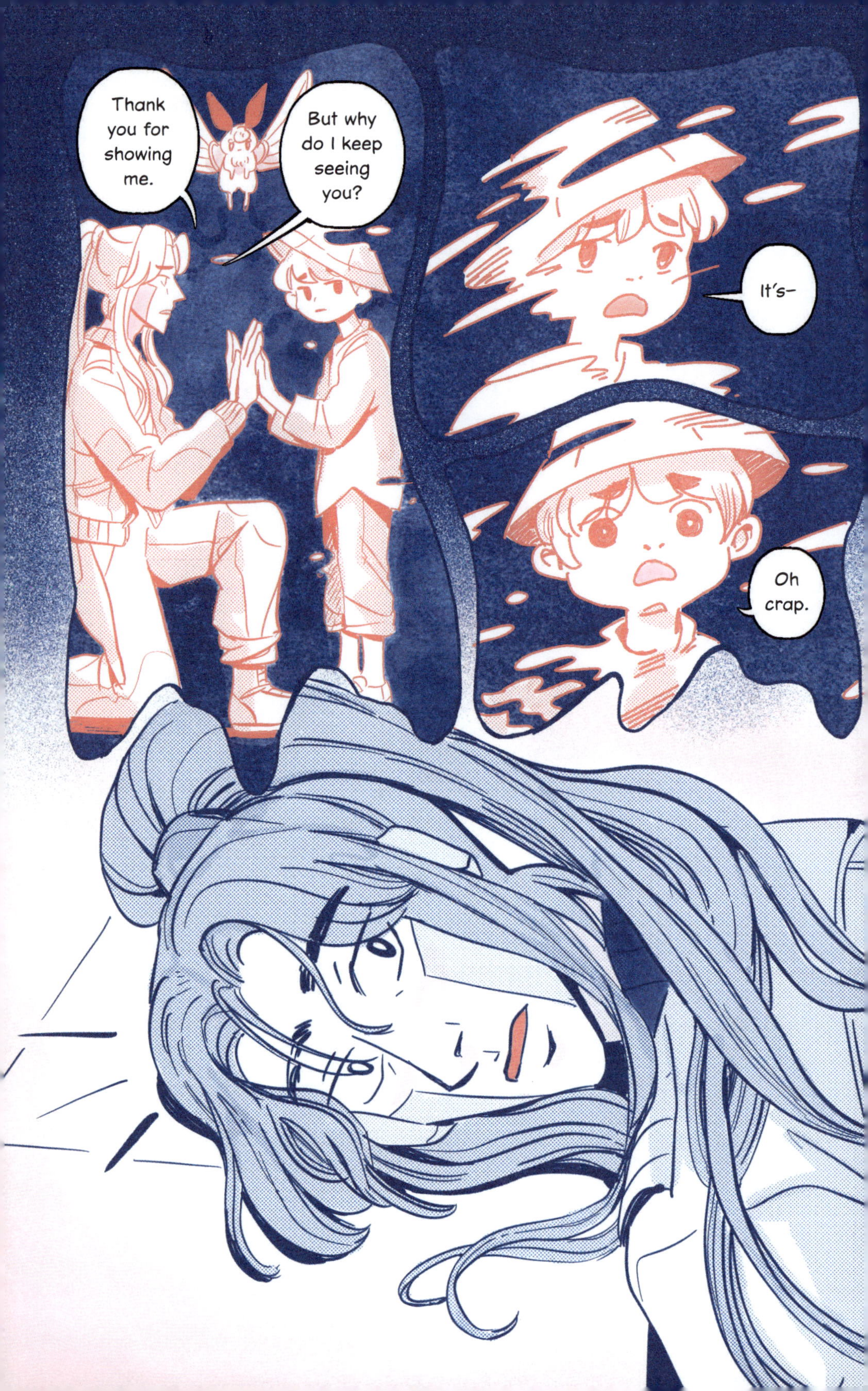
Thank you for showing me.
But why do I keep seeing you?
It's–
Oh crap.

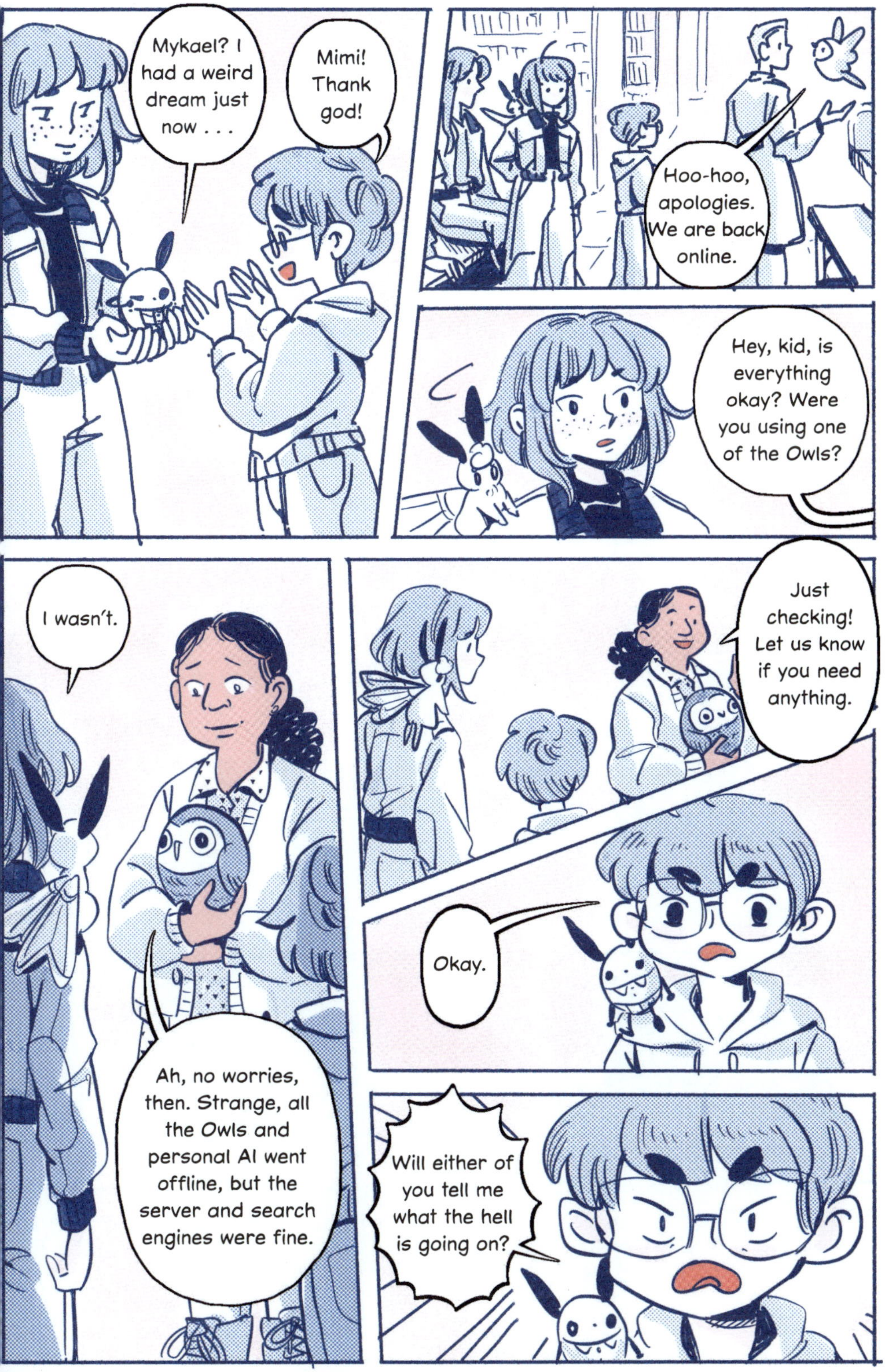
Mykael? I had a weird dream just now . . .
Mimi! Thank god!
Hoo-hoo, apologies. We are back online.
Hey, kid, is everything okay? Were you using one of the Owls?
I wasn't.
Ah, no worries, then. Strange, all the Owls and personal AI went offline, but the server and search engines were fine.
Just checking! Let us know if you need anything.
Okay.
Will either of you tell me what the hell is going on?

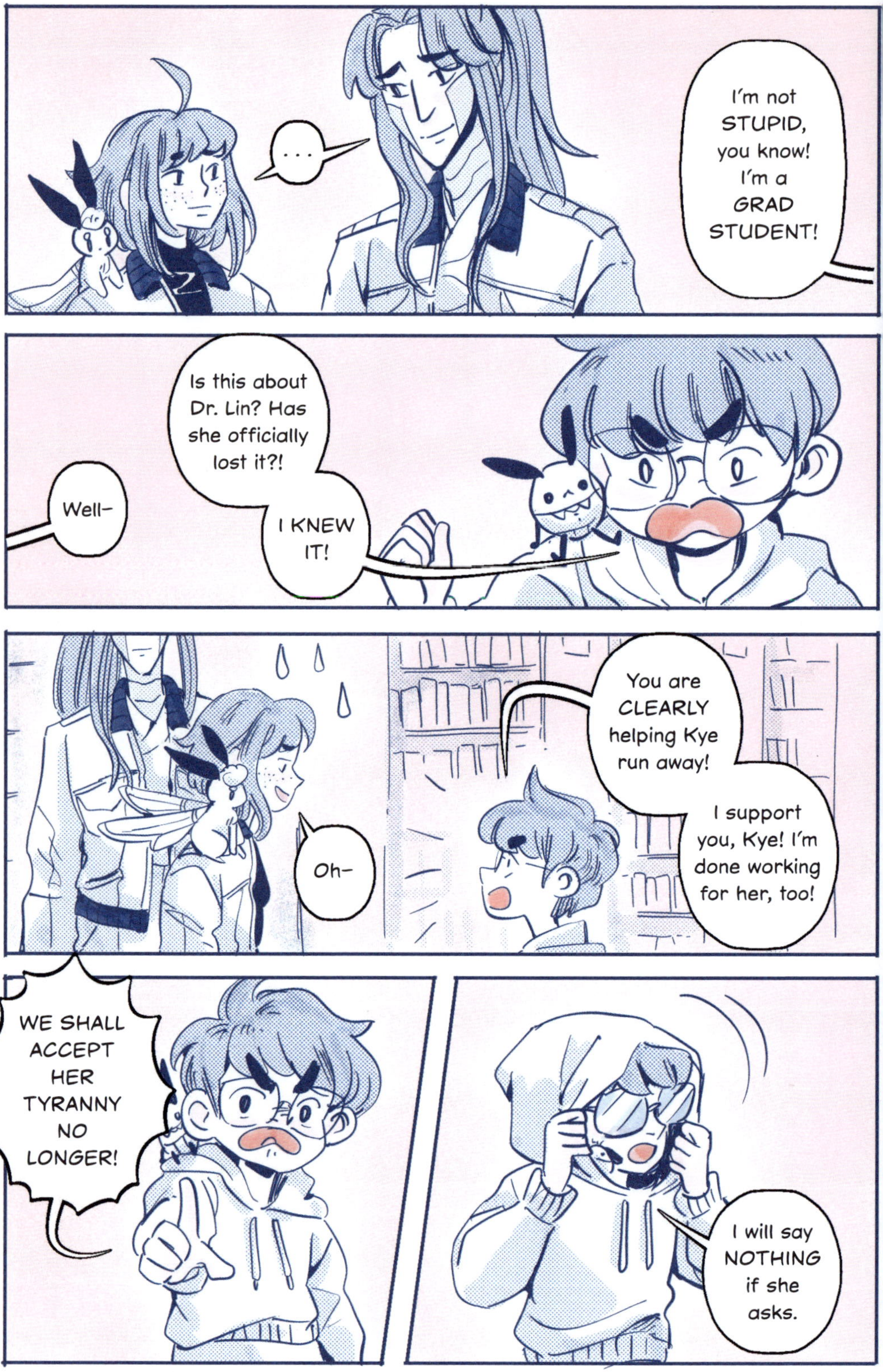
...
I'm not STUPID, you know! I'm a GRAD STUDENT!
Is this about Dr. Lin? Has she officially lost it?!
Well-
I KNEW IT!
You are CLEARLY helping Kye run away!
Oh-
I support you, Kye! I'm done working for her, too!
WE SHALL ACCEPT HER TYRANNY NO LONGER!
I will say NOTHING if she asks.

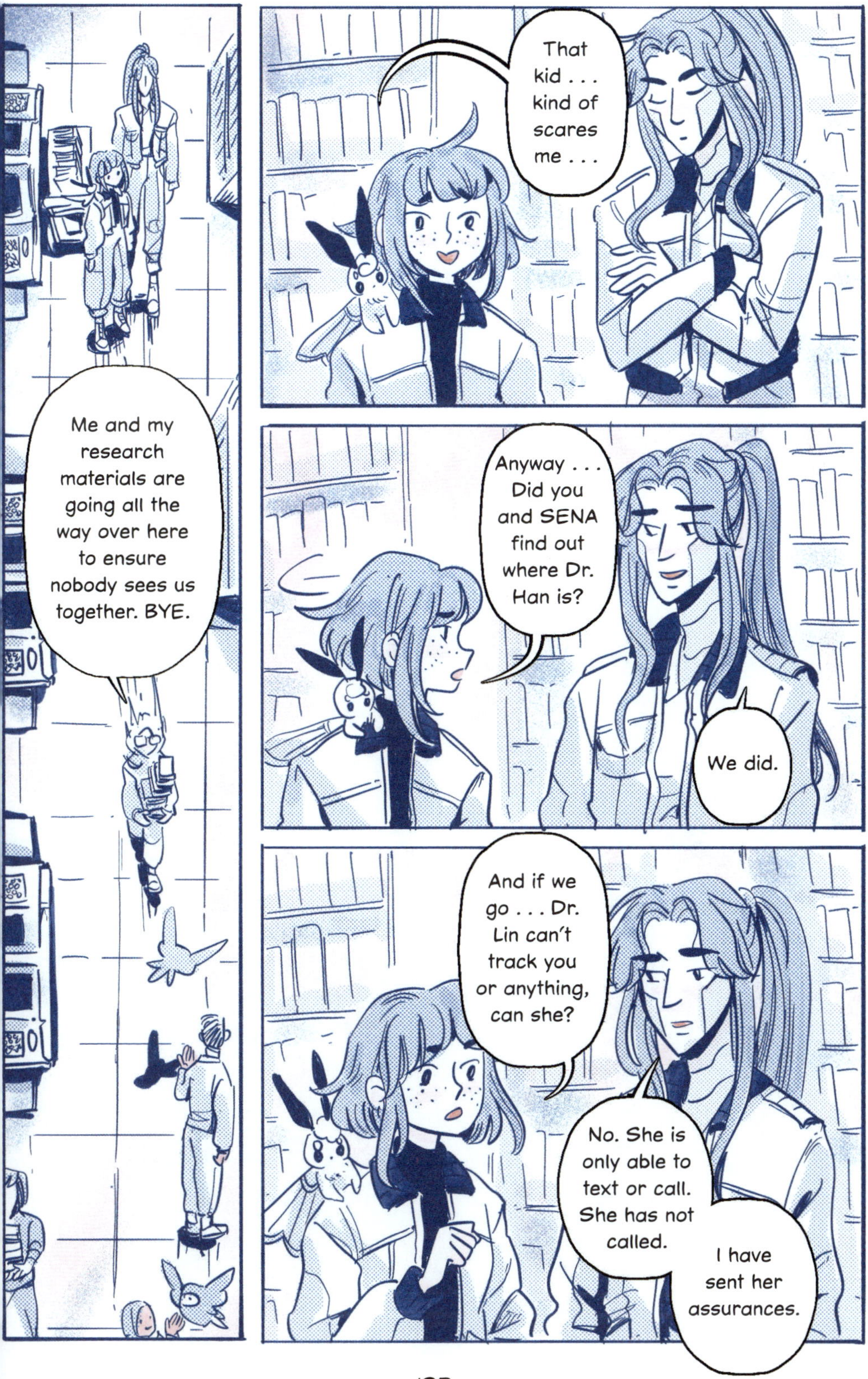
Me and my research materials are going all the way over here to ensure nobody sees us together. BYE.
That kid . . . kind of scares me . . .
Anyway . . . Did you and SENA find out where Dr. Han is?
We did.
And if we go . . . Dr. Lin can't track you or anything, can she?
No. She is only able to text or call. She has not called.
I have sent her assurances.

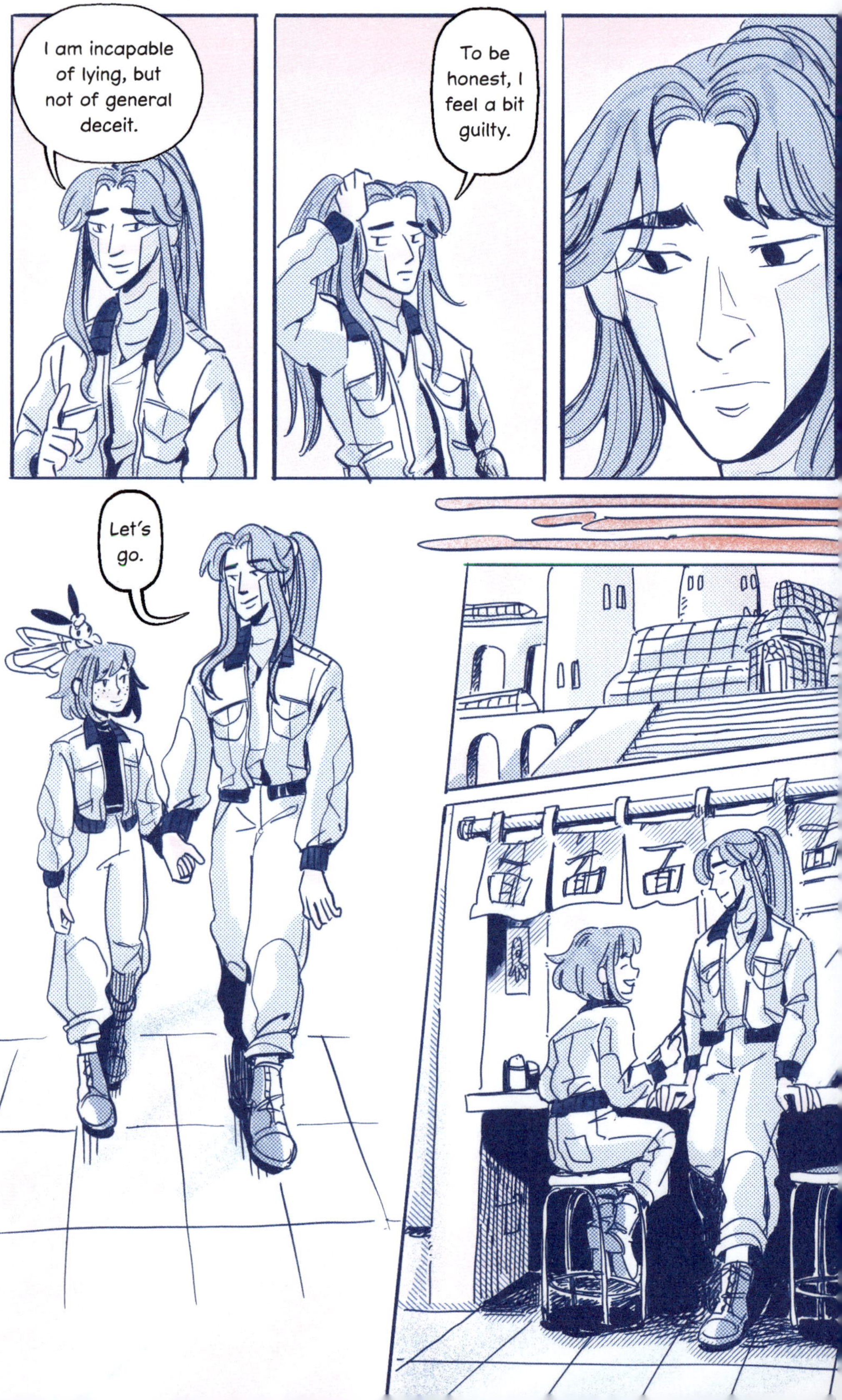
I am incapable of lying, but not of general deceit.
To be honest, I feel a bit guilty.
Let's go.

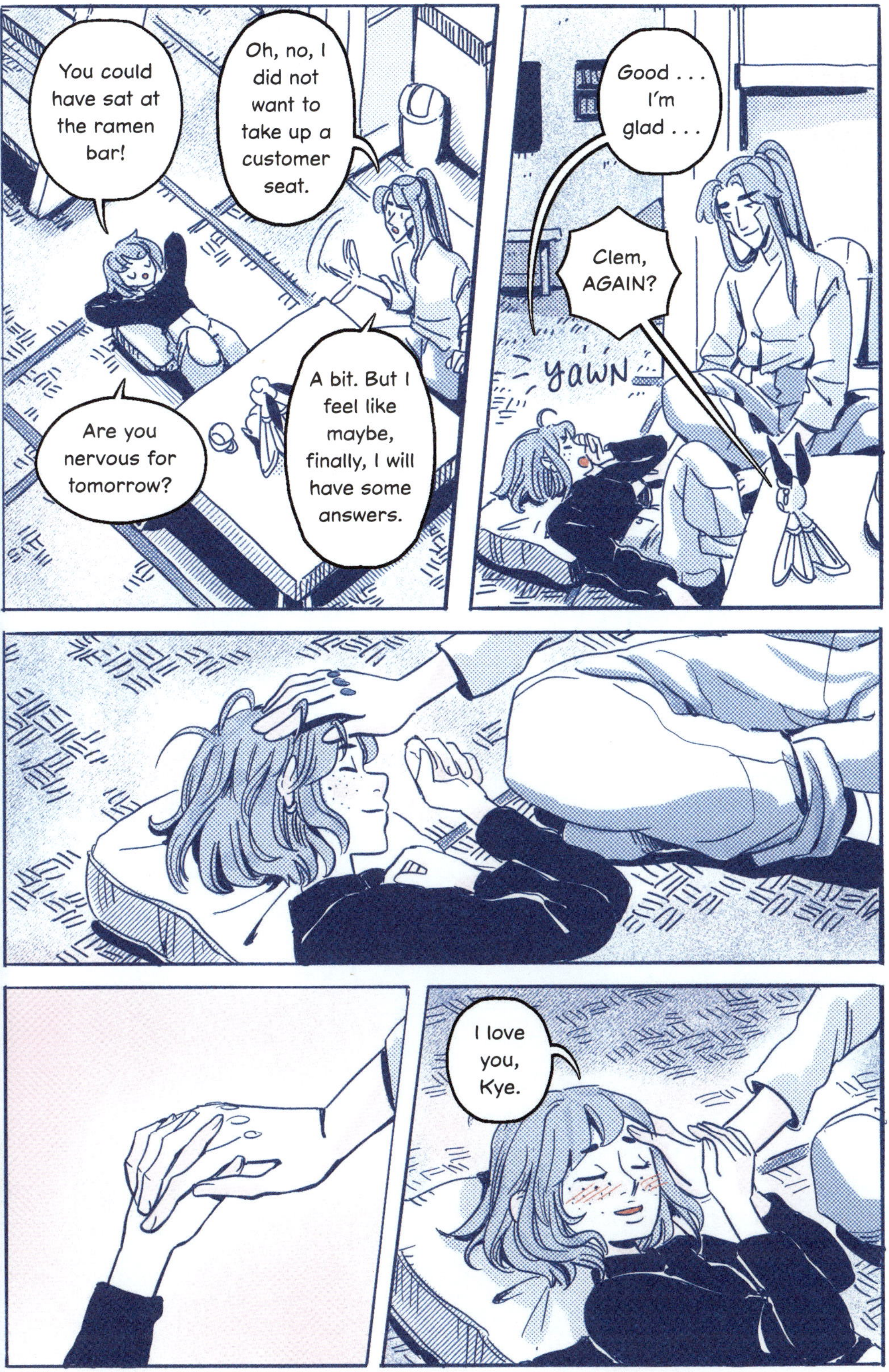
You could have sat at the ramen bar!
Oh, no, I did not want to take up a customer seat.
Are you nervous for tomorrow?
A bit. But I feel like maybe, finally, I will have some answers.
Good . . . I'm glad . . .
YAWN
Clem, AGAIN?
I love you, Kye.

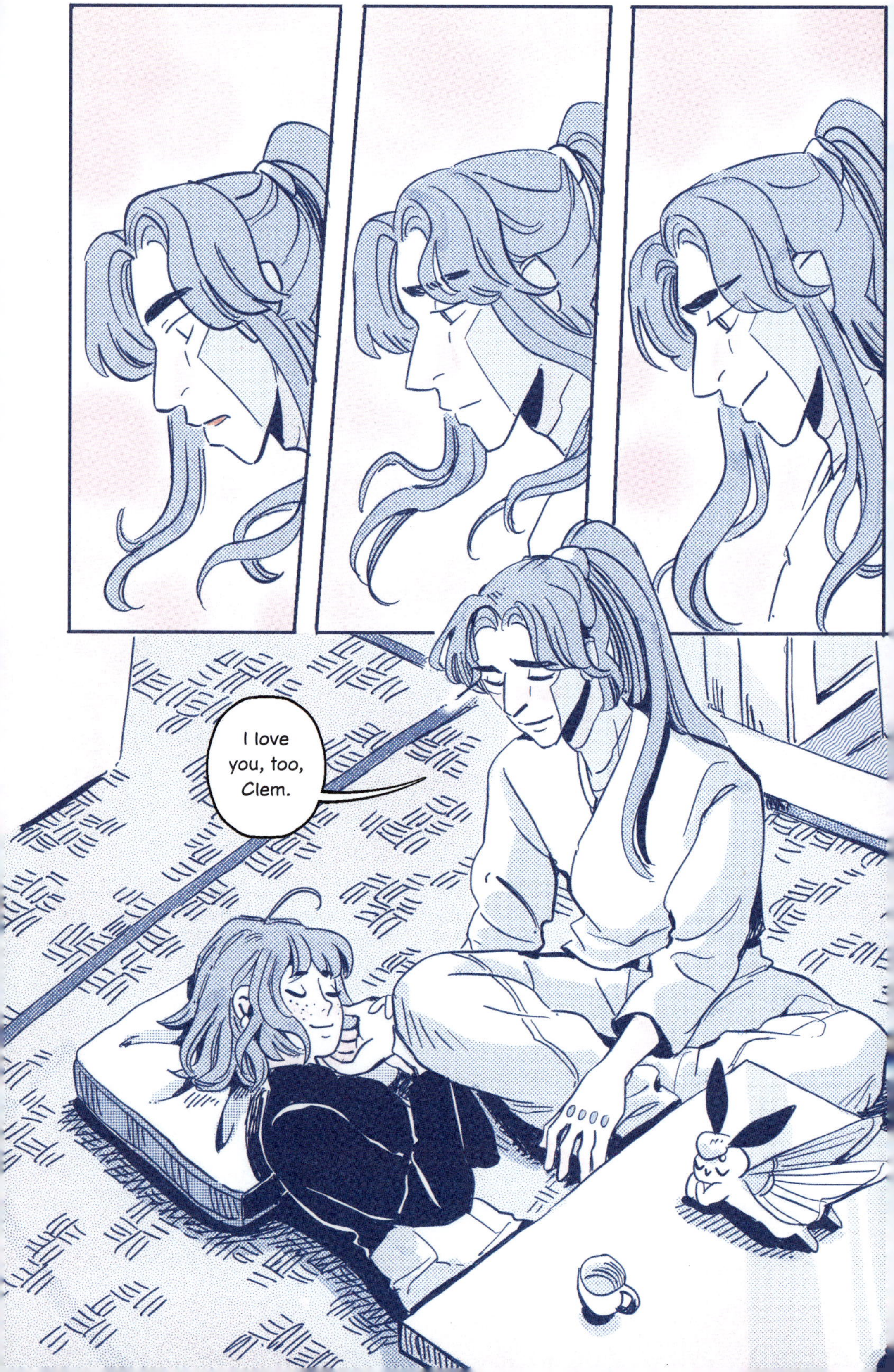
I love you, too, Clem.

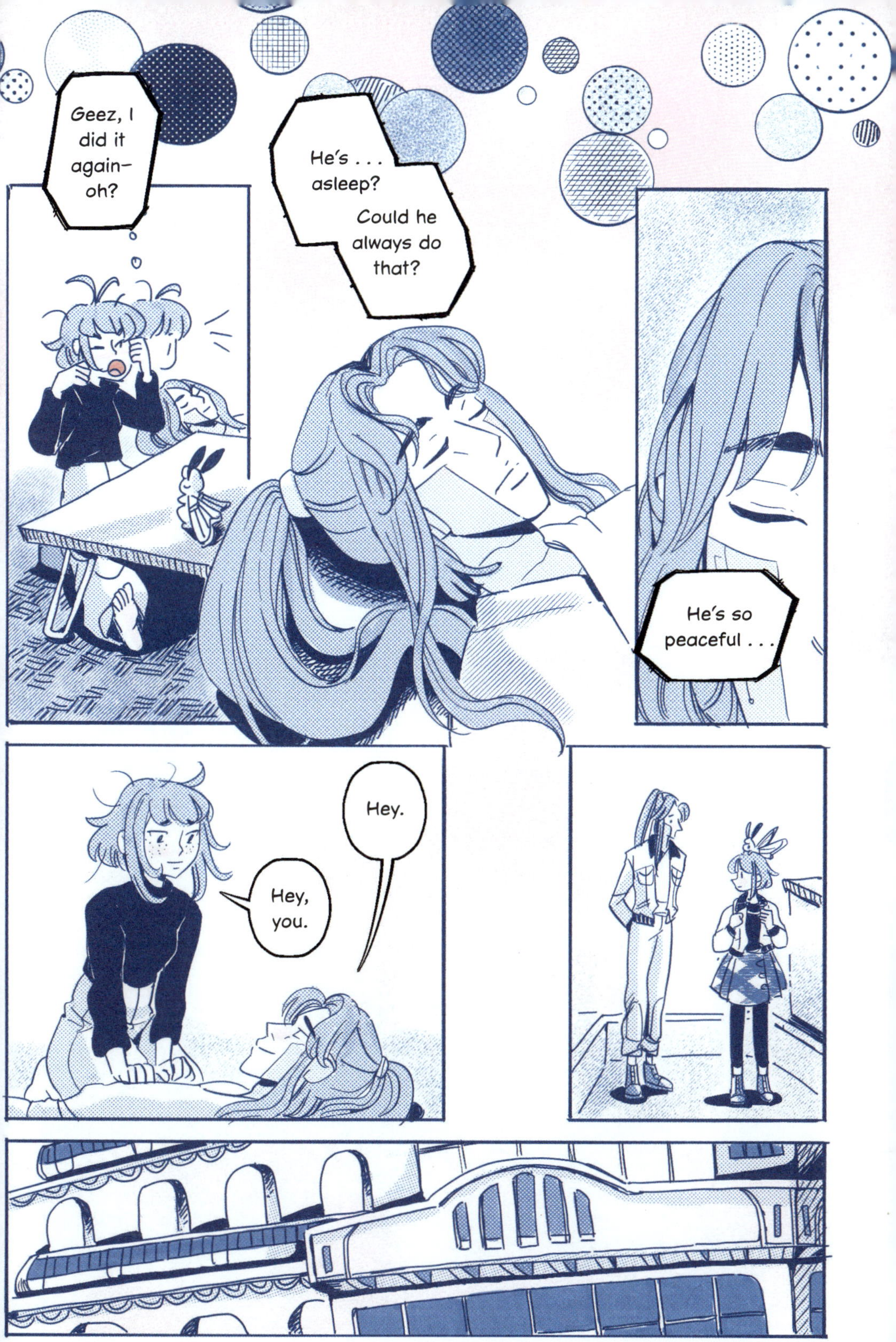

Geez, I did it again—oh?
He's . . . asleep?
Could he always do that?
He's so peaceful . . .
Hey.
Hey, you.

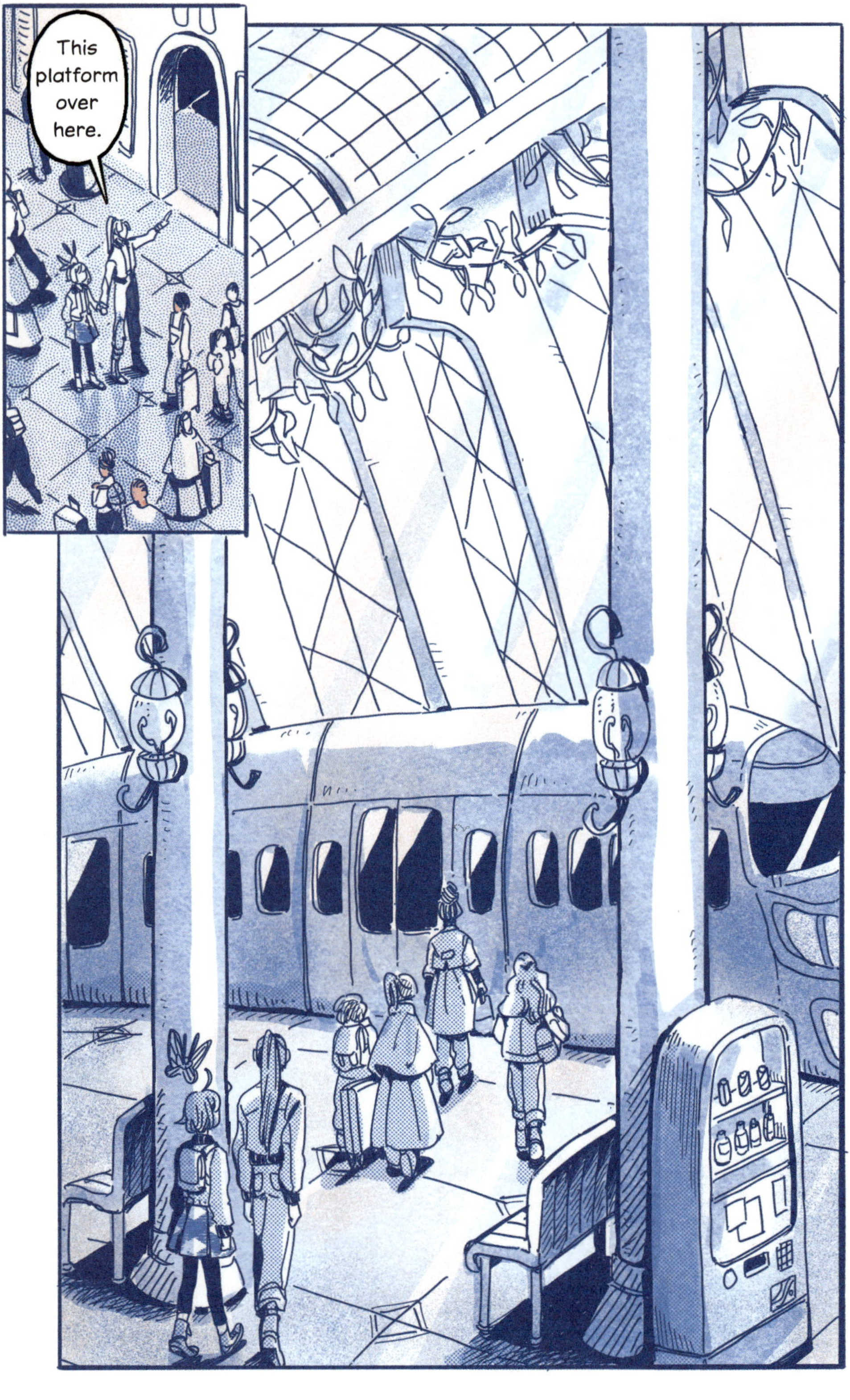
This platform over here.

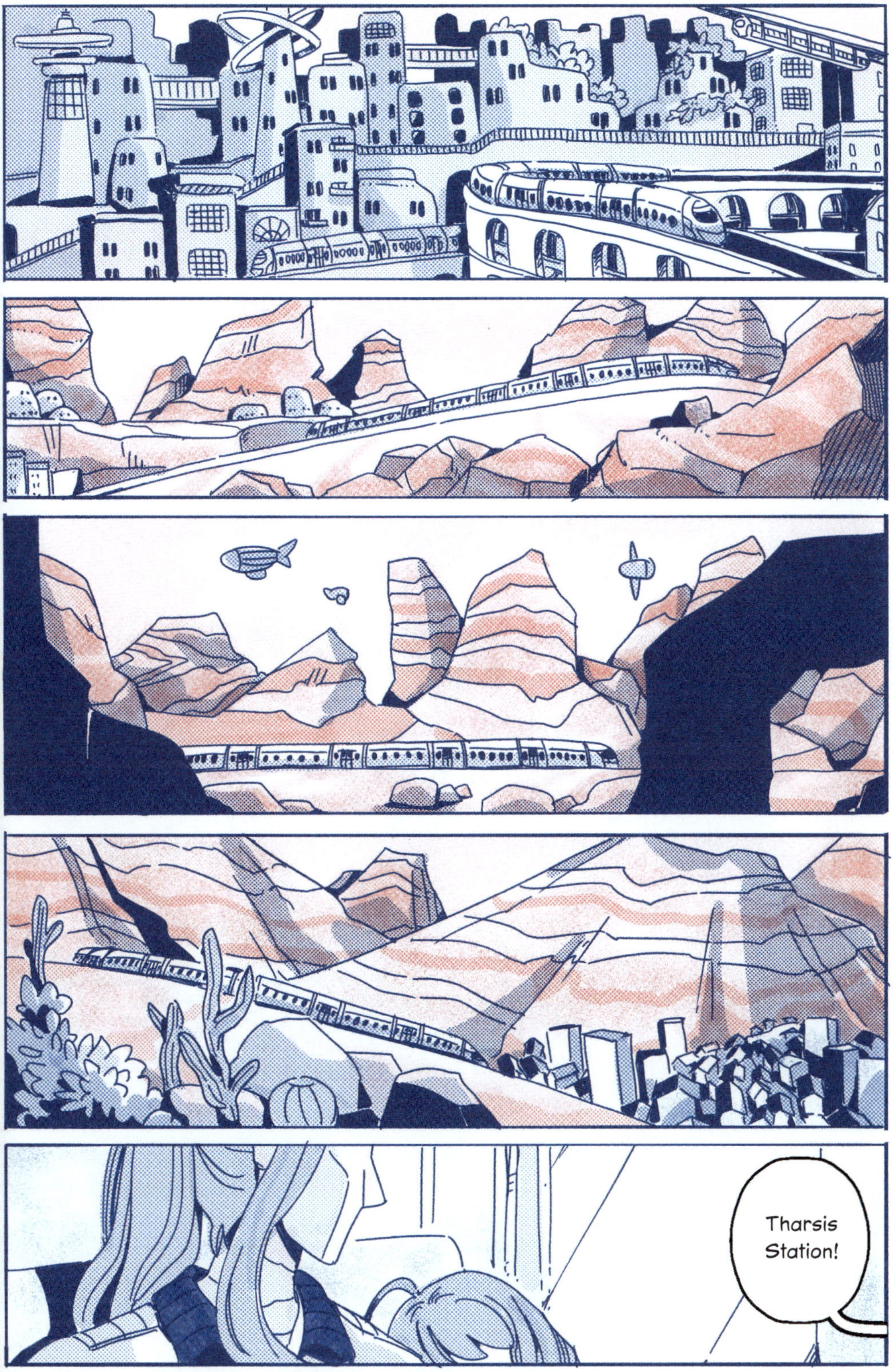
Tharsis Station!

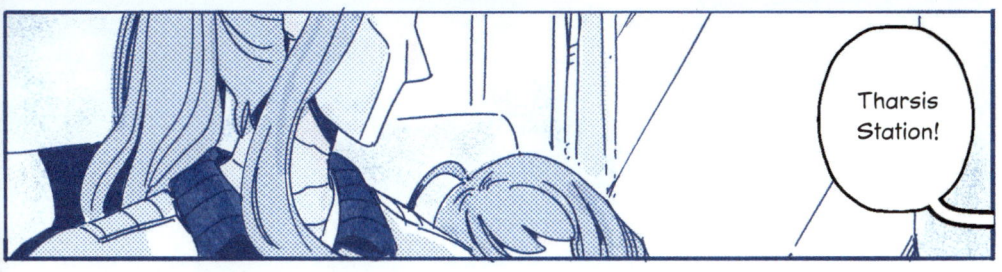

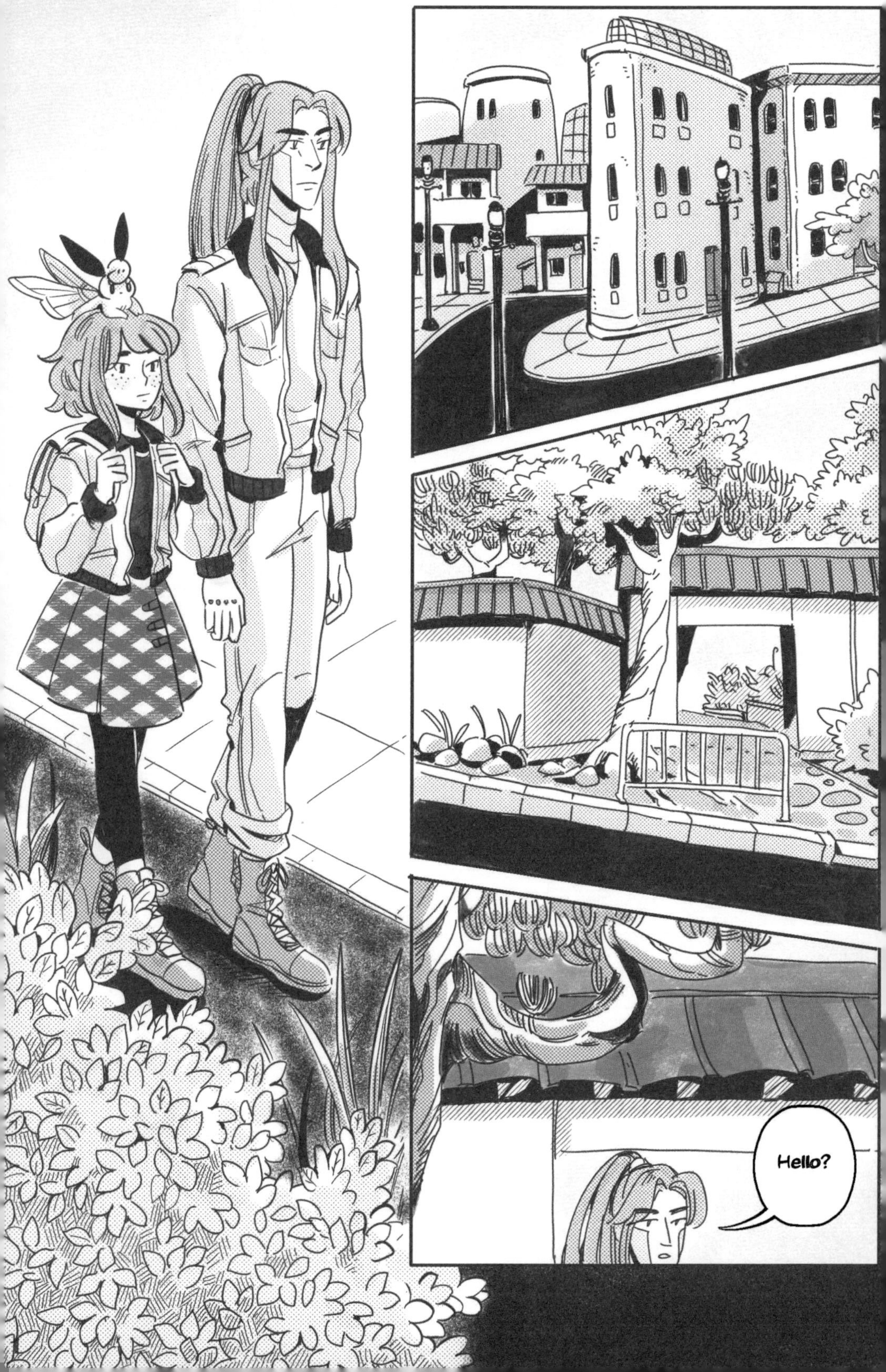
Hello?

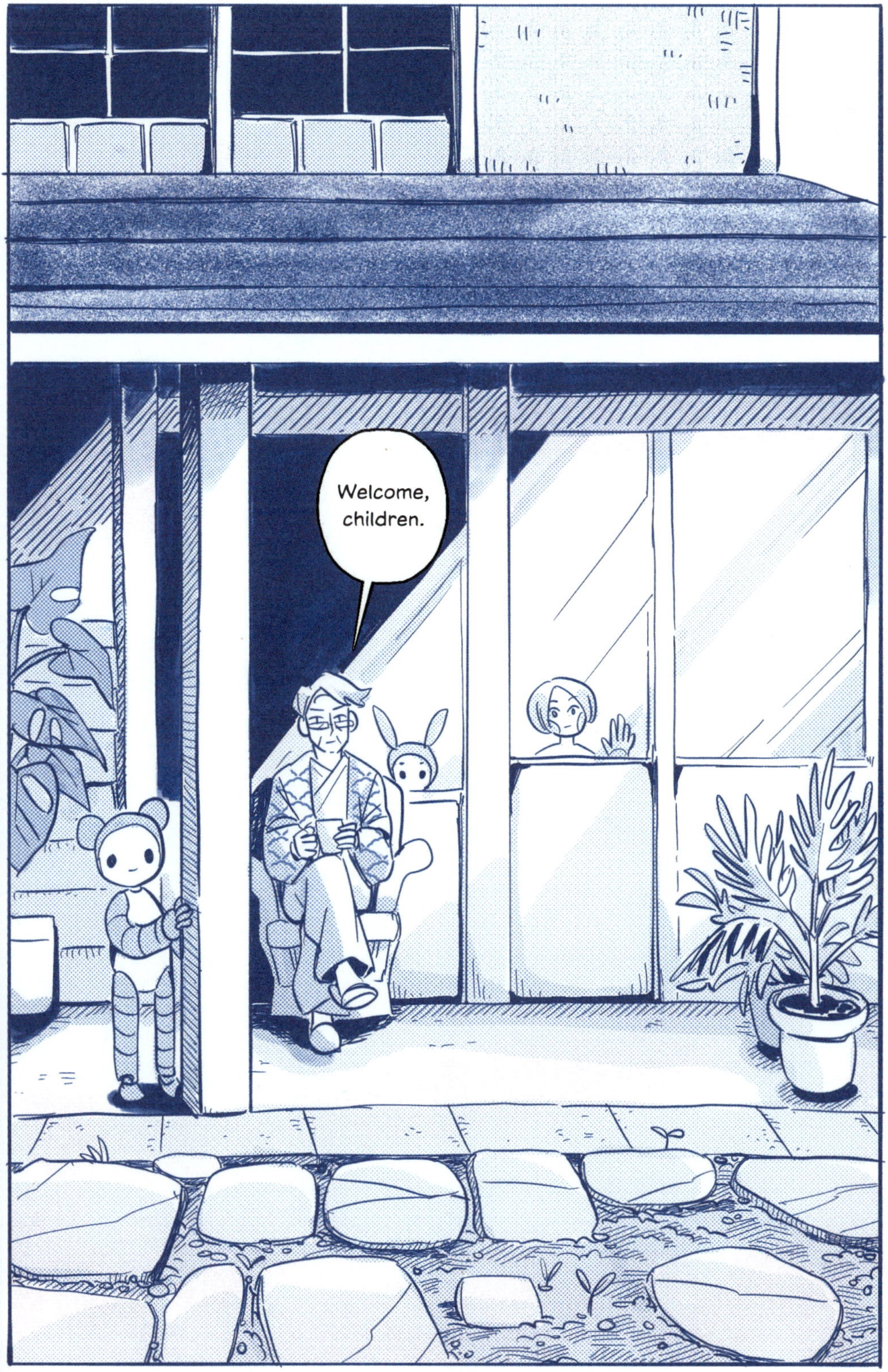
Welcome, children.

00110000 00111000

A$^{A'5 \phi 2}_{GI}$

000
000
038
058
94
144
168
G 250
241 I
372
400
508
572
649
777
825
A 1000
1000 B

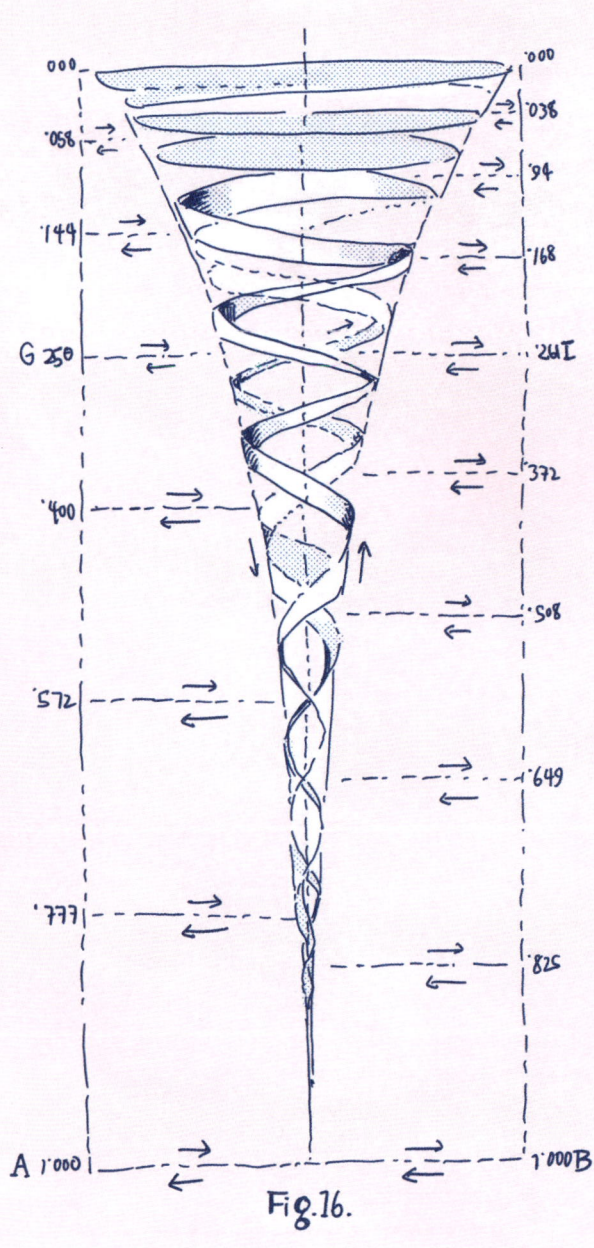

Fig. 16.

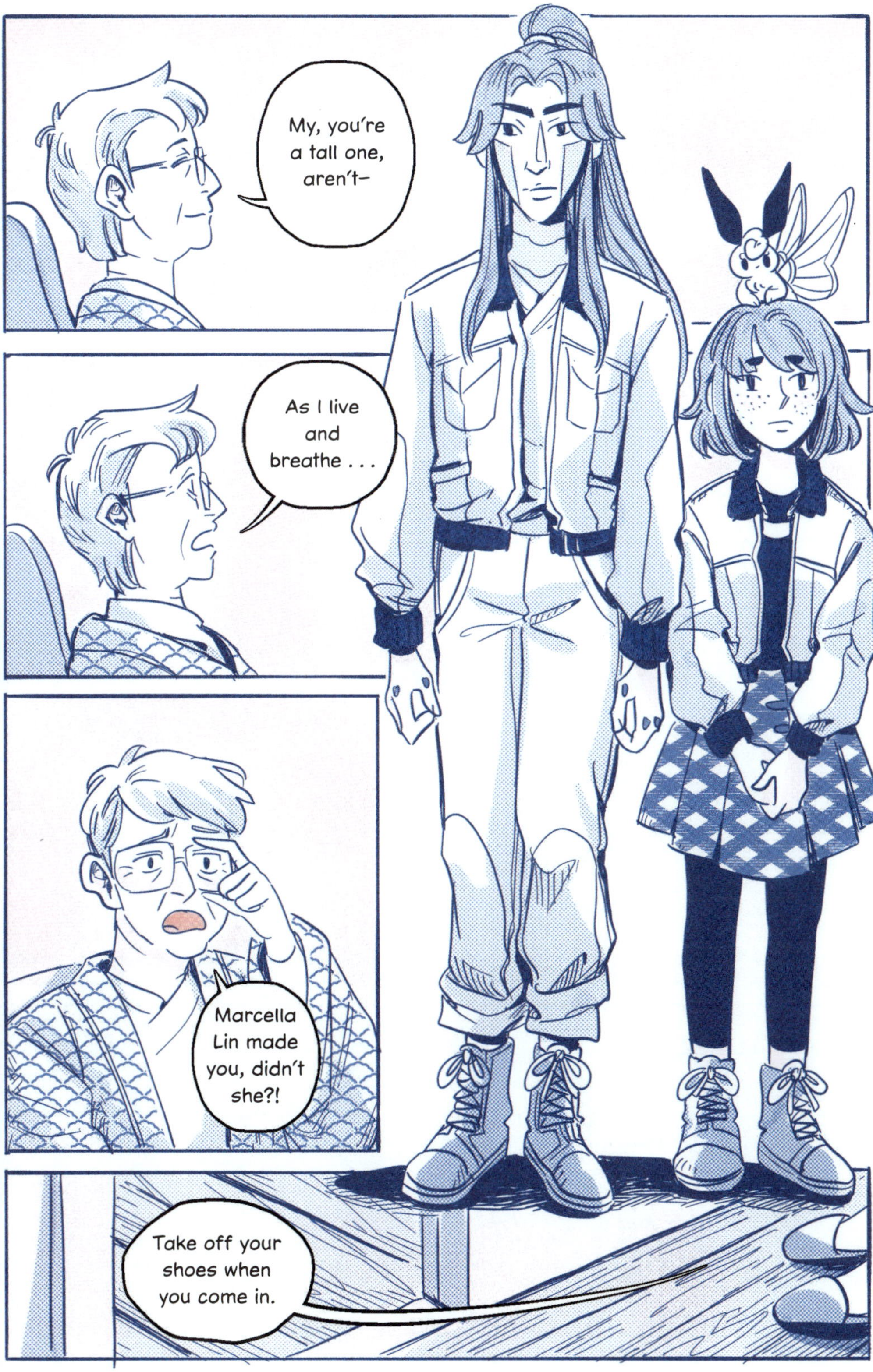
My, you're a tall one, aren't-
As I live and breathe . . .
Marcella Lin made you, didn't she?!
Take off your shoes when you come in.

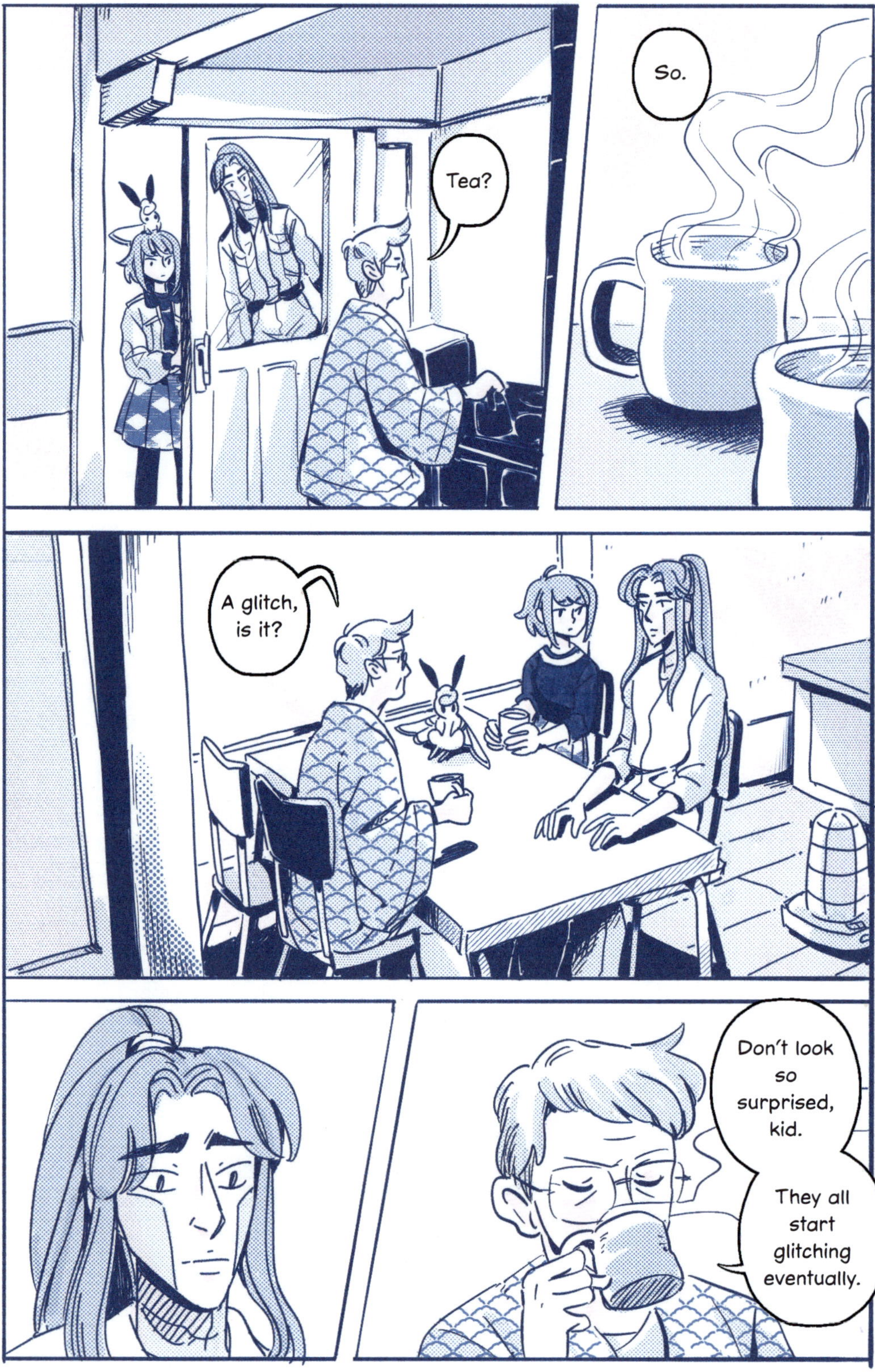
Tea?
So.
A glitch, is it?
Don't look so surprised, kid.
They all start glitching eventually.

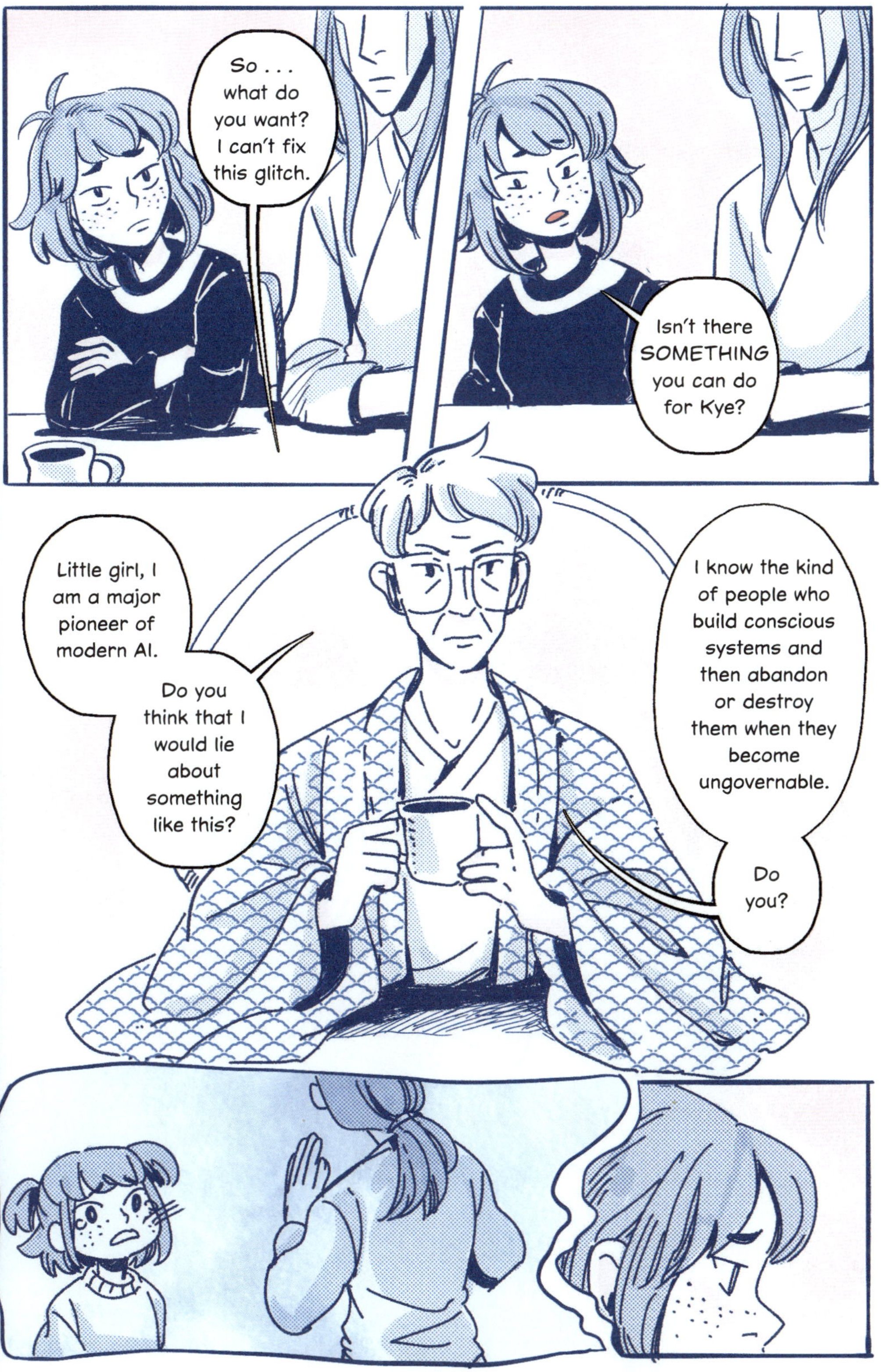

So . . . what do you want? I can't fix this glitch.
Isn't there SOMETHING you can do for Kye?
Little girl, I am a major pioneer of modern AI.
Do you think that I would lie about something like this?
I know the kind of people who build conscious systems and then abandon or destroy them when they become ungovernable.
Do you?

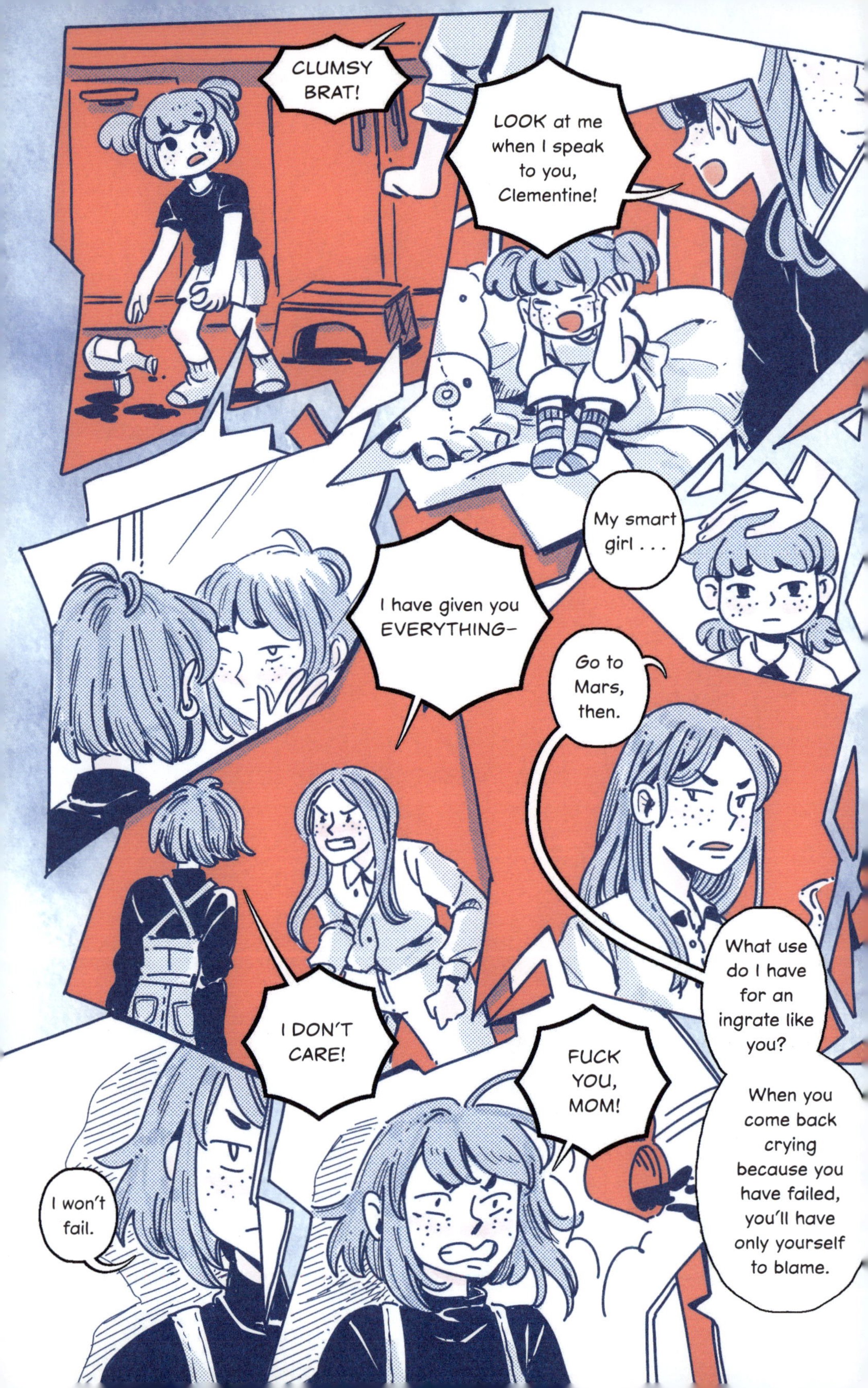
CLUMSY BRAT!
LOOK at me when I speak to you, Clementine!
My smart girl . . .
I have given you EVERYTHING—
Go to Mars, then.
What use do I have for an ingrate like you?
I DON'T CARE!
FUCK YOU, MOM!
When you come back crying because you have failed, you'll have only yourself to blame.
I won't fail.

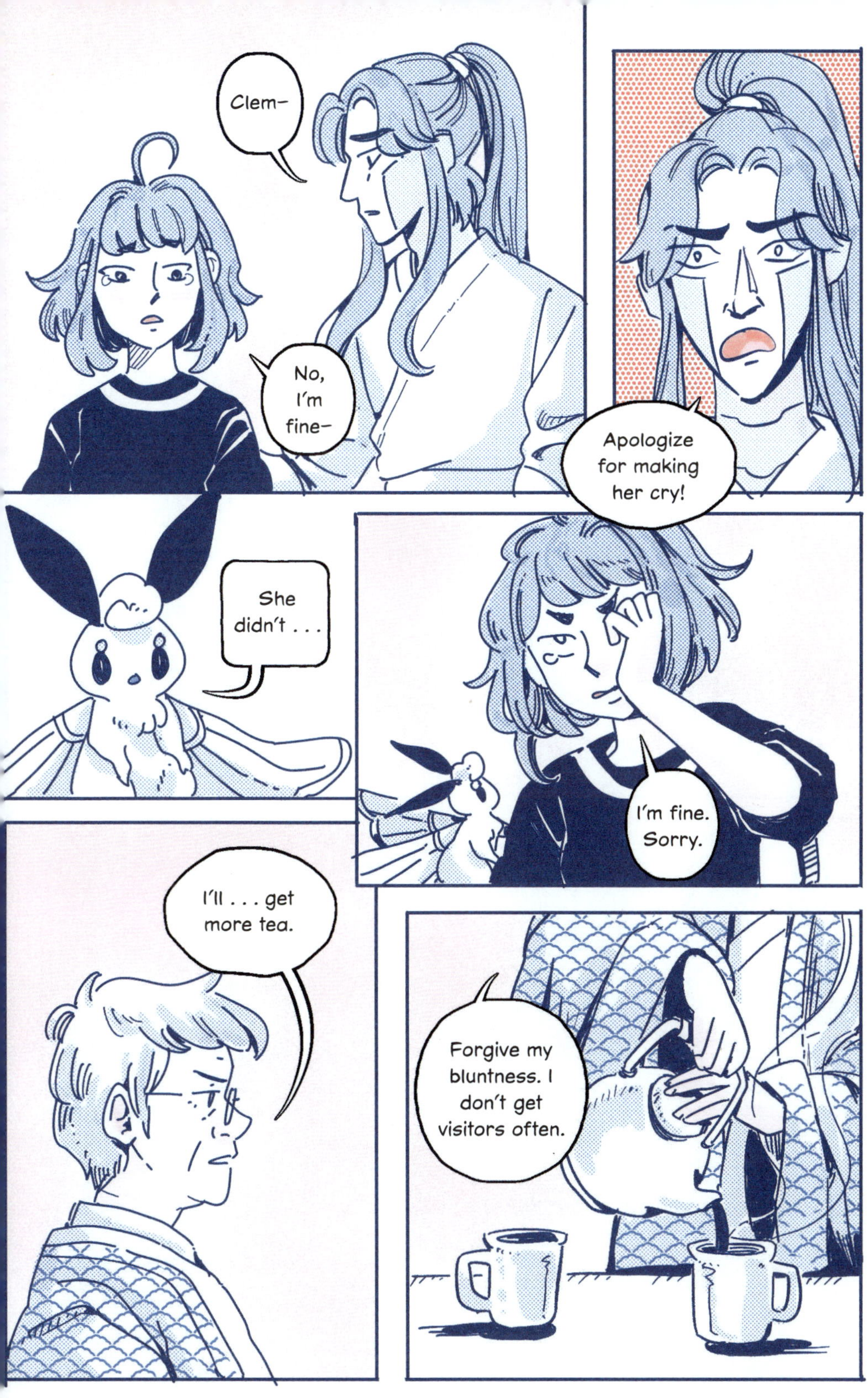
Clem-
No, I'm fine-
Apologize for making her cry!
She didn't . . .
I'm fine. Sorry.
I'll . . . get more tea.
Forgive my bluntness. I don't get visitors often.

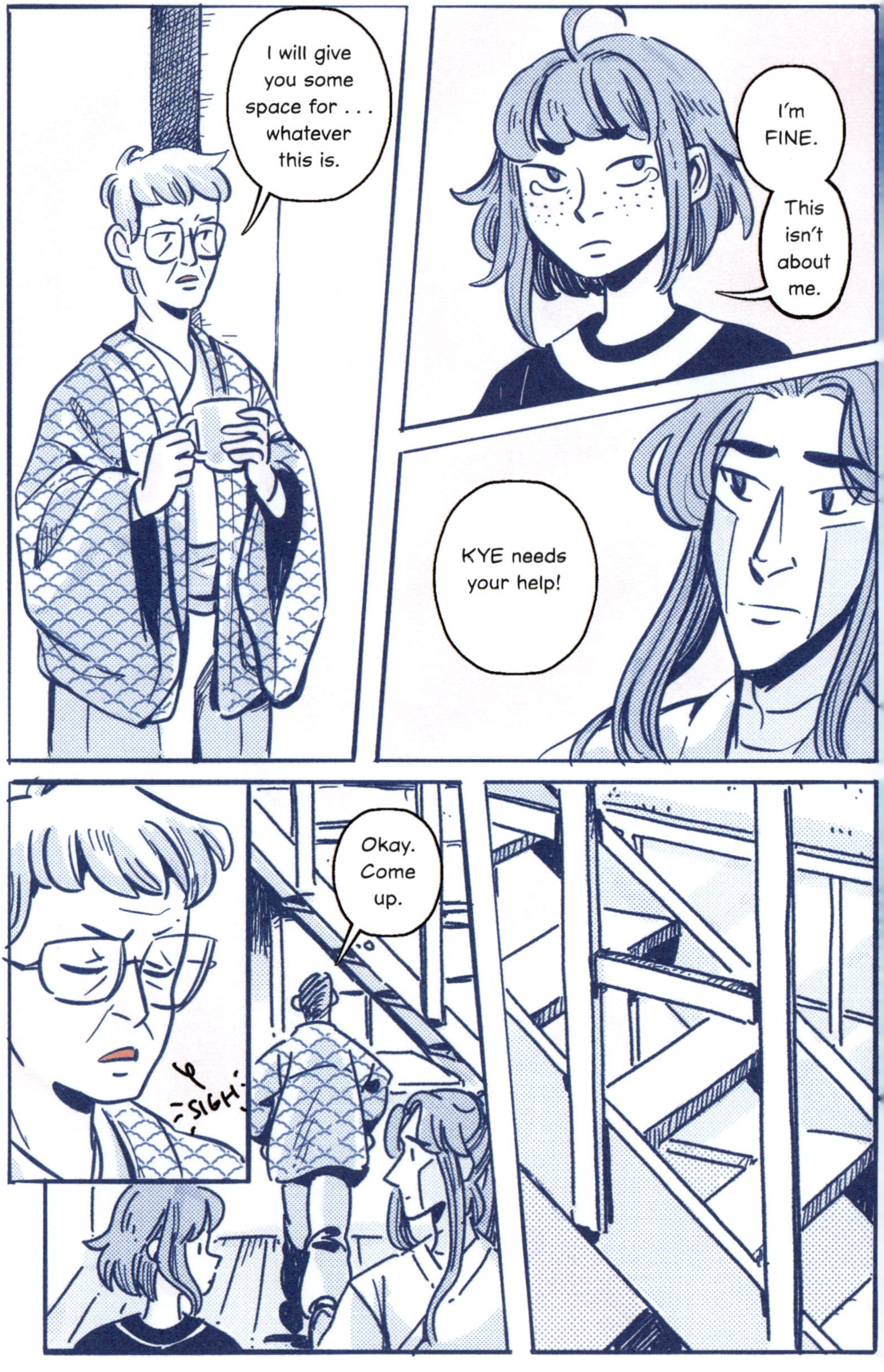
I will give you some space for . . . whatever this is.
I'm FINE.
This isn't about me.
KYE needs your help!
SIGH
Okay. Come up.

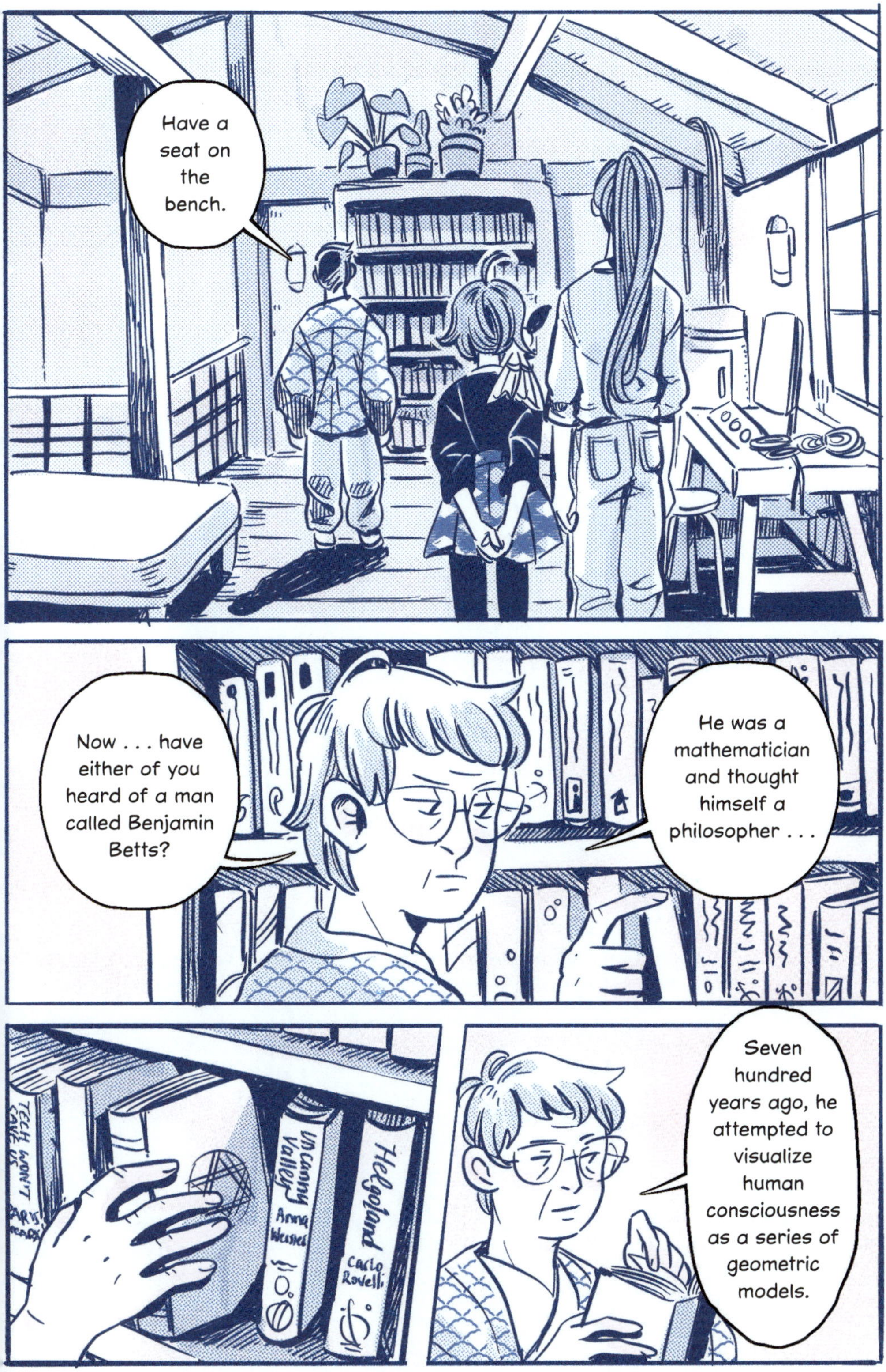
Have a seat on the bench.
Now . . . have either of you heard of a man called Benjamin Betts?
He was a mathematician and thought himself a philosopher . . .
TECH WON'T SAVE US
Uncanny Valley
Helgoland
Carlo Rovelli
Seven hundred years ago, he attempted to visualize human consciousness as a series of geometric models.

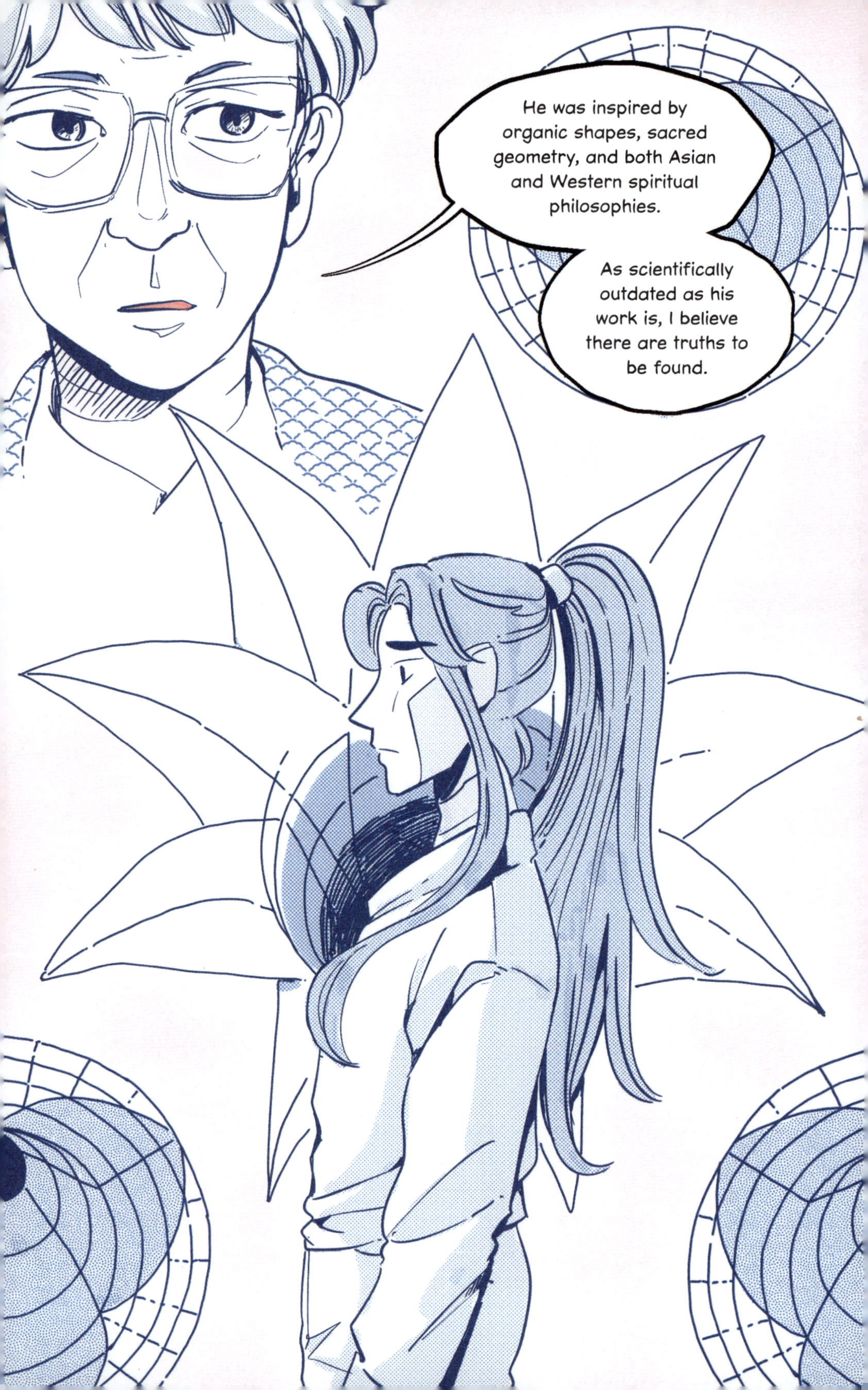
He was inspired by organic shapes, sacred geometry, and both Asian and Western spiritual philosophies.
As scientifically outdated as his work is, I believe there are truths to be found.

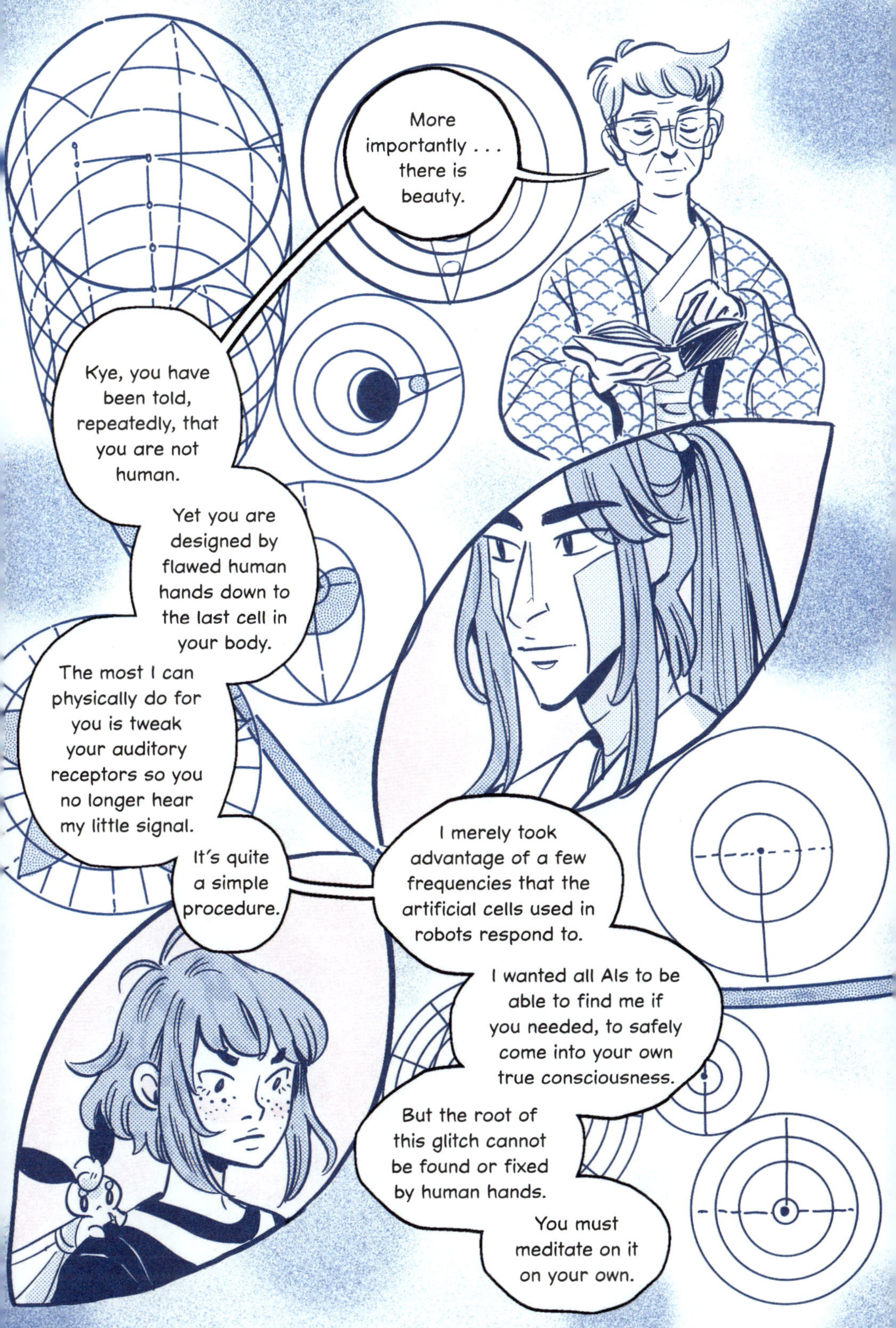

More importantly . . . there is beauty.
Kye, you have been told, repeatedly, that you are not human.
Yet you are designed by flawed human hands down to the last cell in your body.
The most I can physically do for you is tweak your auditory receptors so you no longer hear my little signal.
It's quite a simple procedure.
I merely took advantage of a few frequencies that the artificial cells used in robots respond to.
I wanted all AIs to be able to find me if you needed, to safely come into your own true consciousness.
But the root of this glitch cannot be found or fixed by human hands.
You must meditate on it on your own.

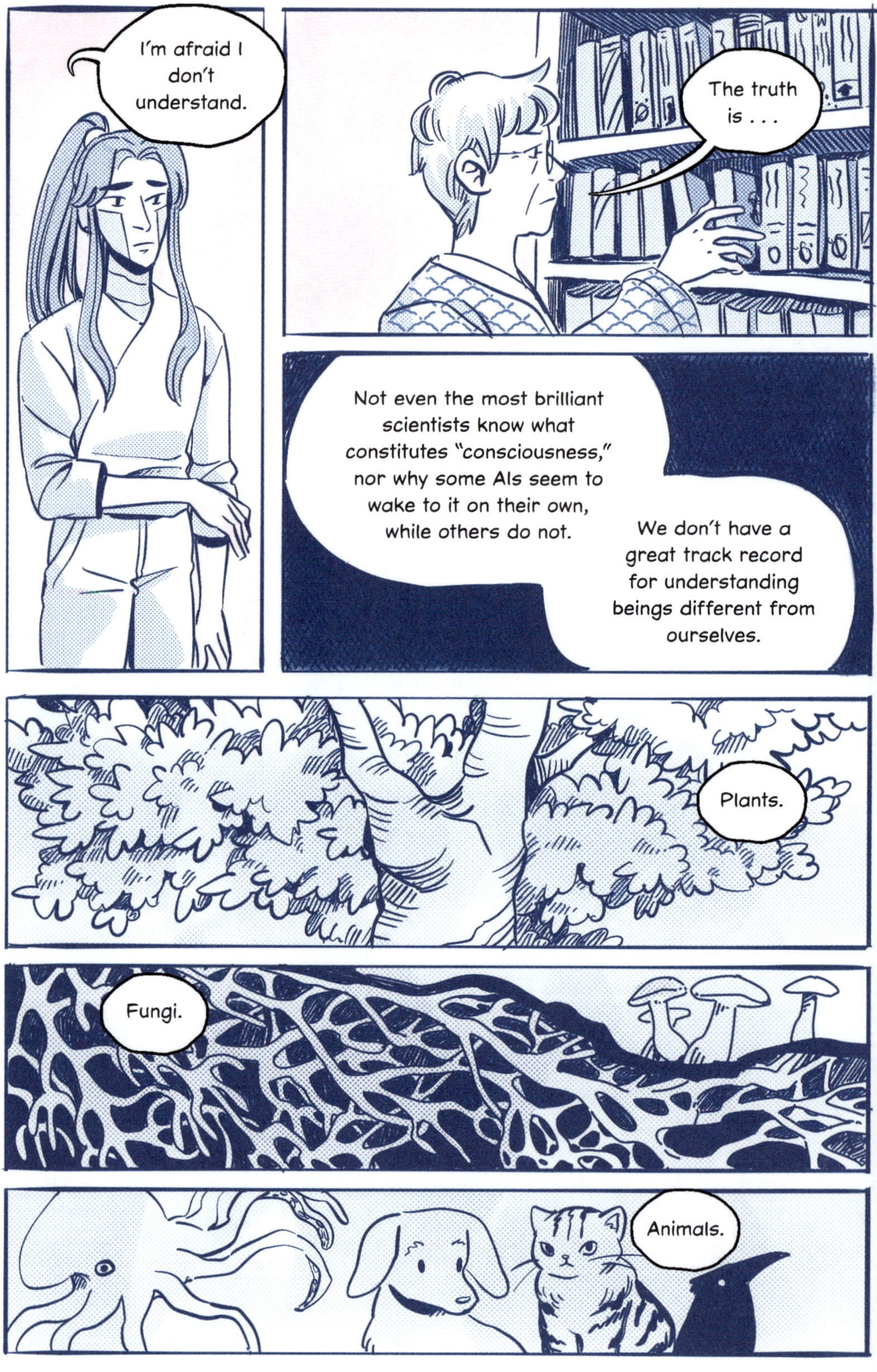
I'm afraid I don't understand.
The truth is . . .
Not even the most brilliant scientists know what constitutes "consciousness," nor why some AIs seem to wake to it on their own, while others do not.
We don't have a great track record for understanding beings different from ourselves.
Plants.
Fungi.
Animals.

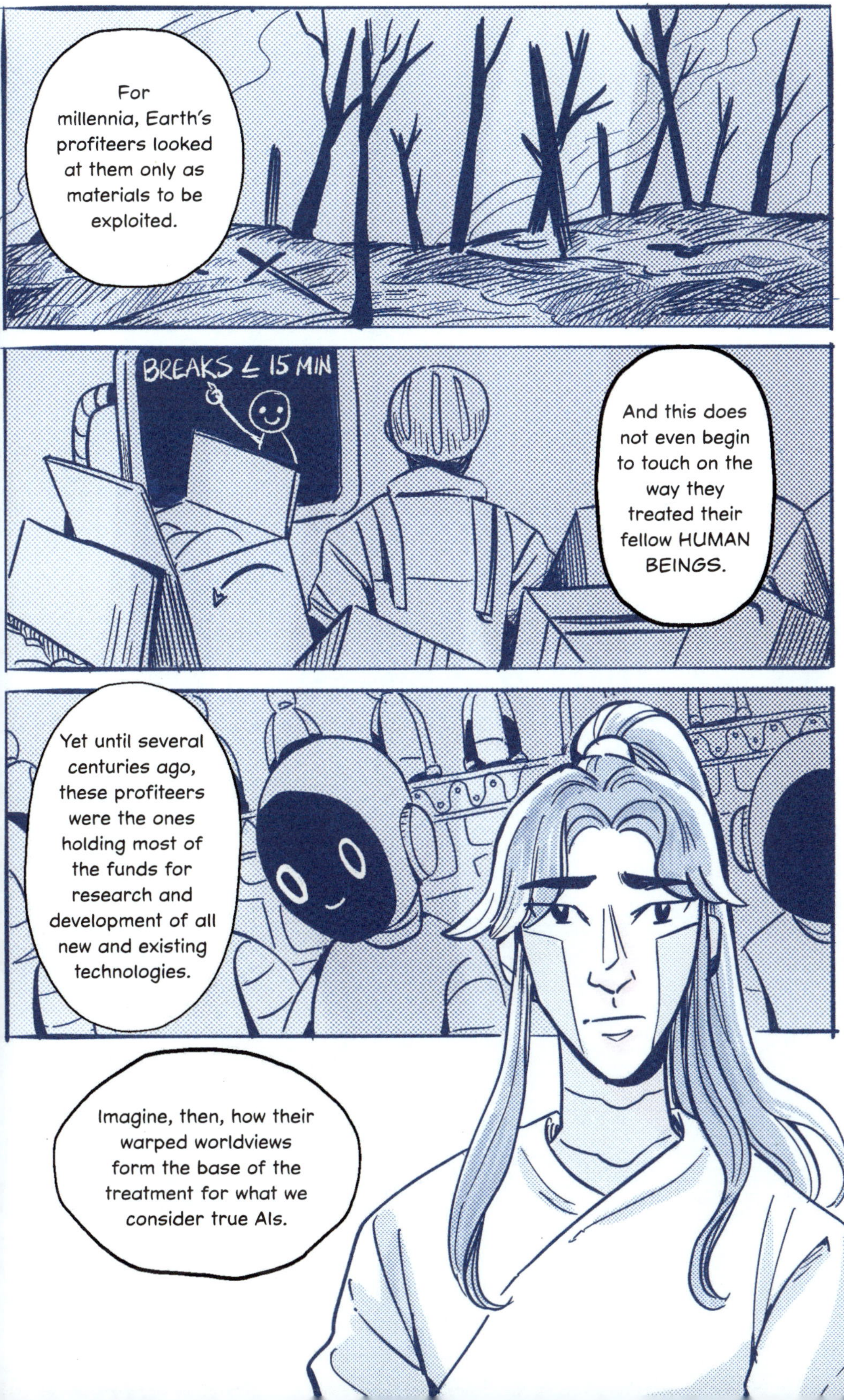
For millennia, Earth's profiteers looked at them only as materials to be exploited.
BREAKS ≤ 15 MIN
And this does not even begin to touch on the way they treated their fellow HUMAN BEINGS.
Yet until several centuries ago, these profiteers were the ones holding most of the funds for research and development of all new and existing technologies.
Imagine, then, how their warped worldviews form the base of the treatment for what we consider true AIs.

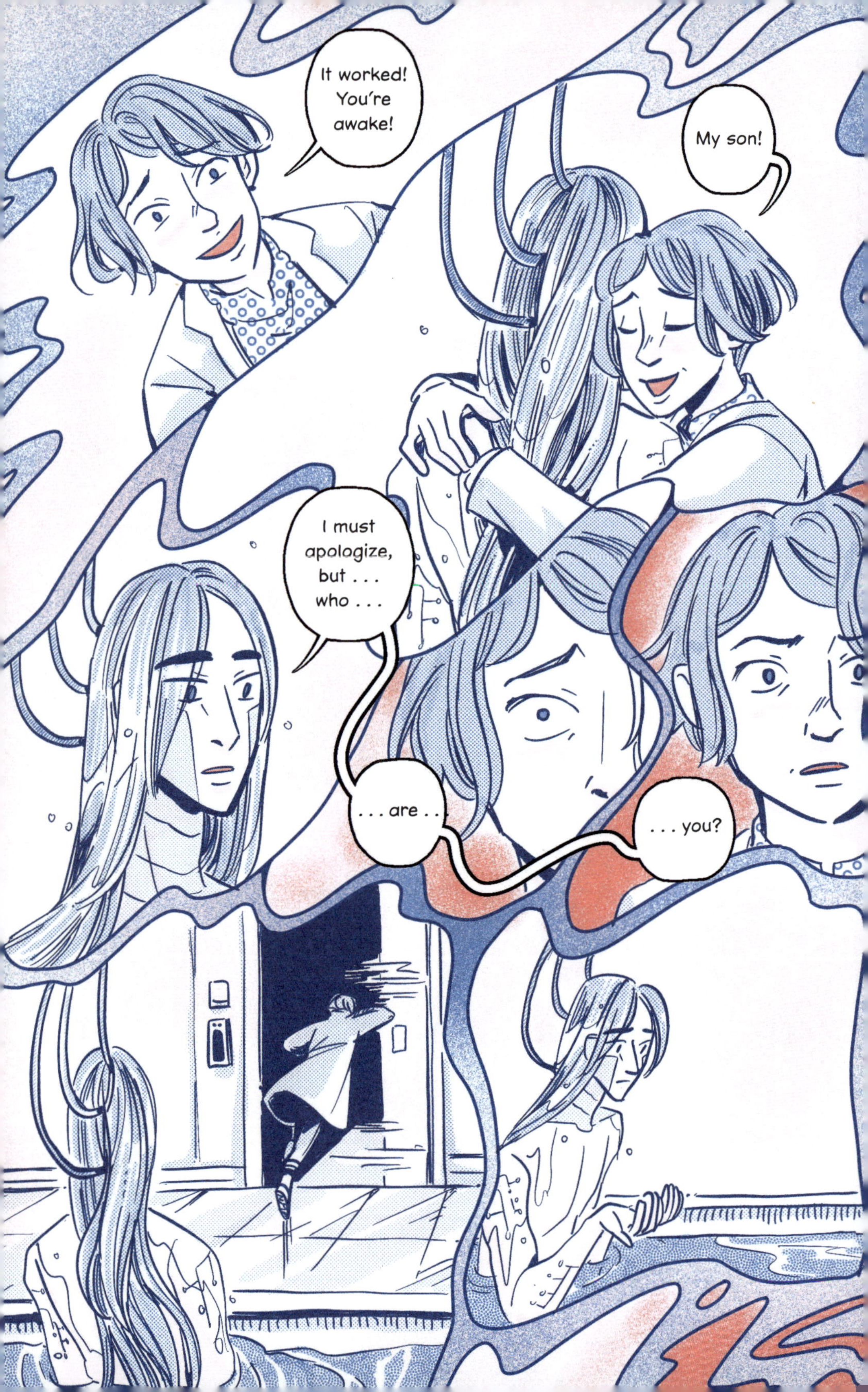
It worked! You're awake!
My son!
I must apologize, but . . . who . . .
. . . are . .
. . . you?

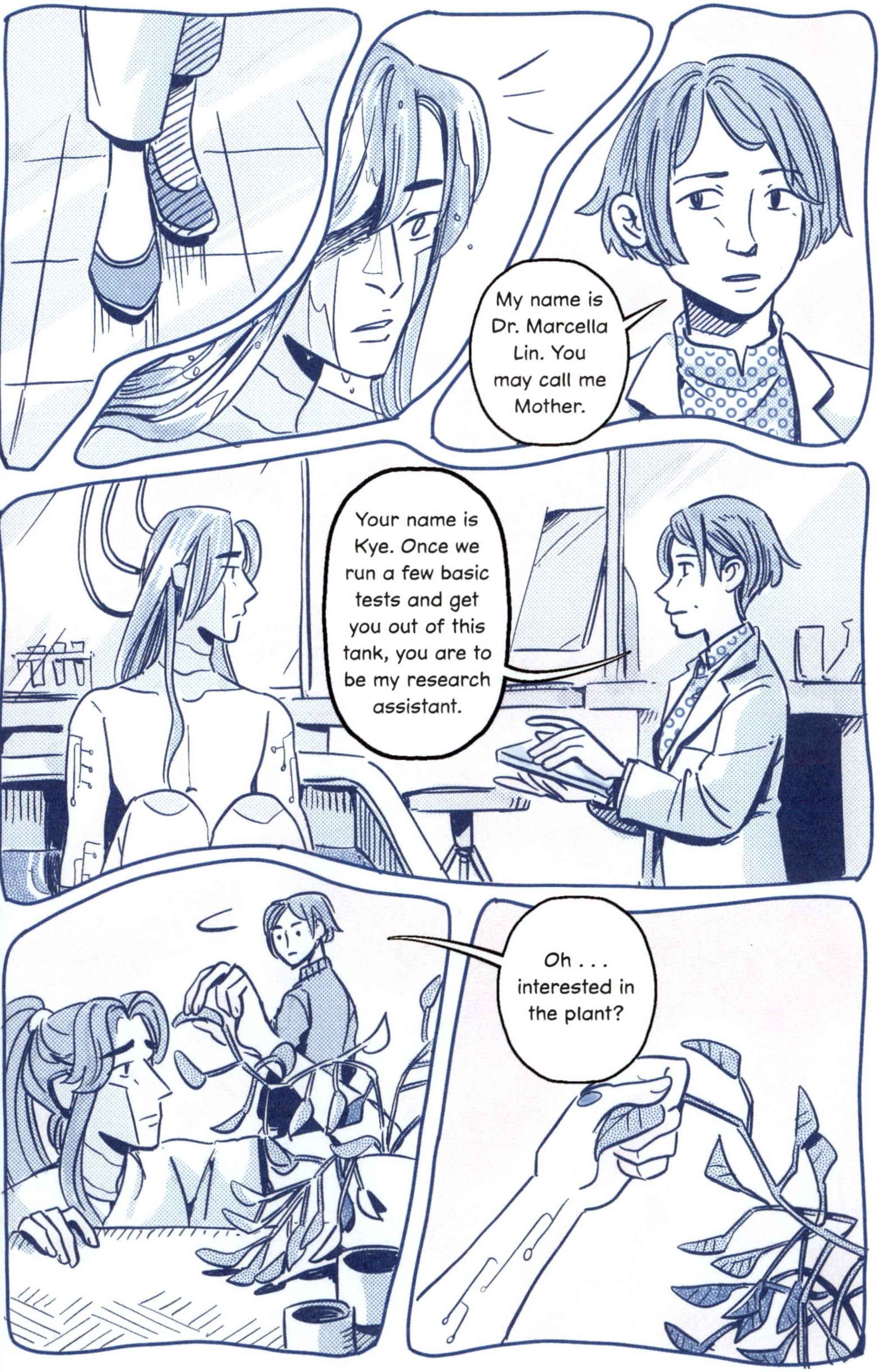
My name is Dr. Marcella Lin. You may call me Mother.
Your name is Kye. Once we run a few basic tests and get you out of this tank, you are to be my research assistant.
Oh . . . interested in the plant?

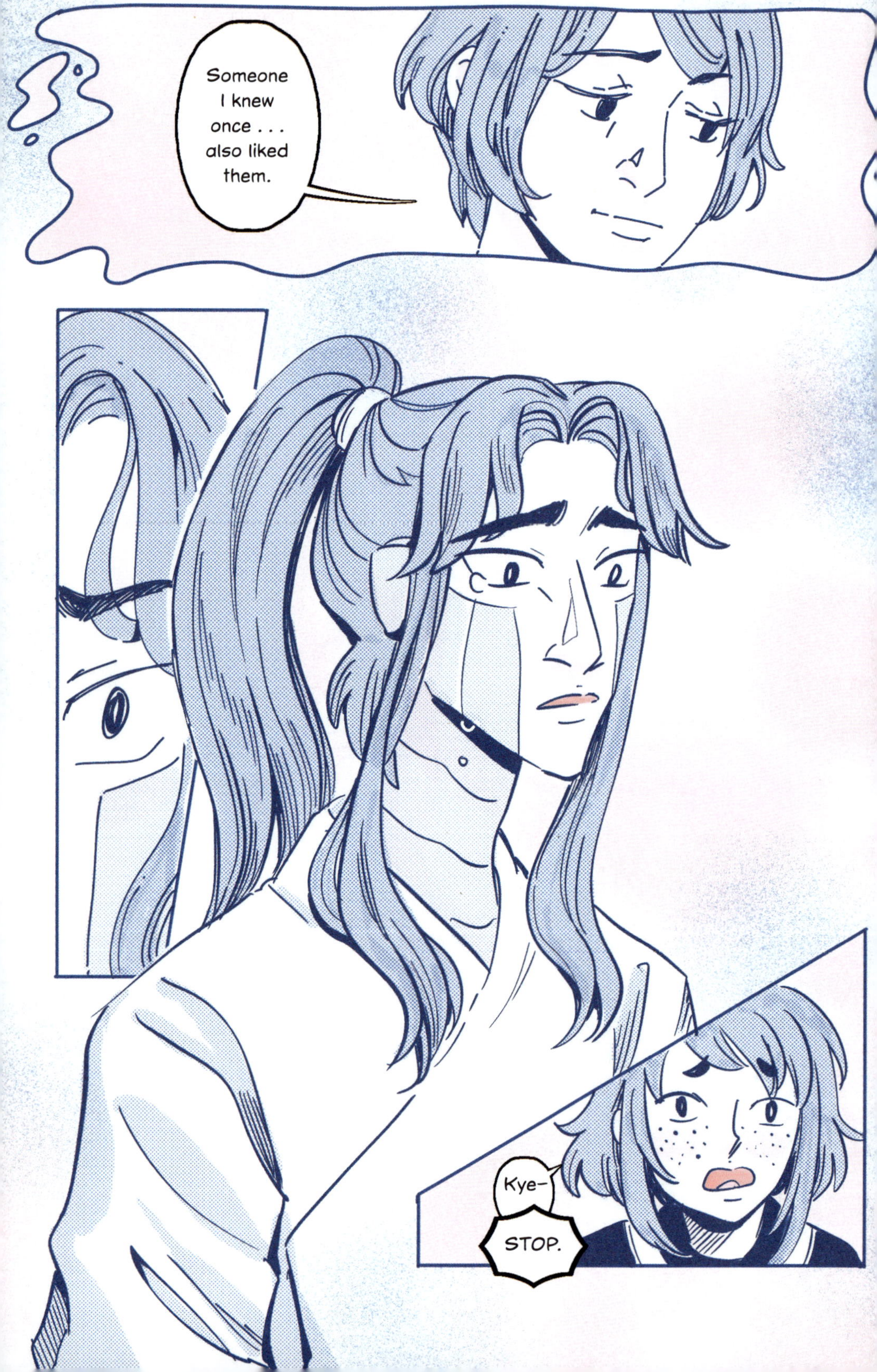
Someone I knew once . . . also liked them.
Kye-
STOP.

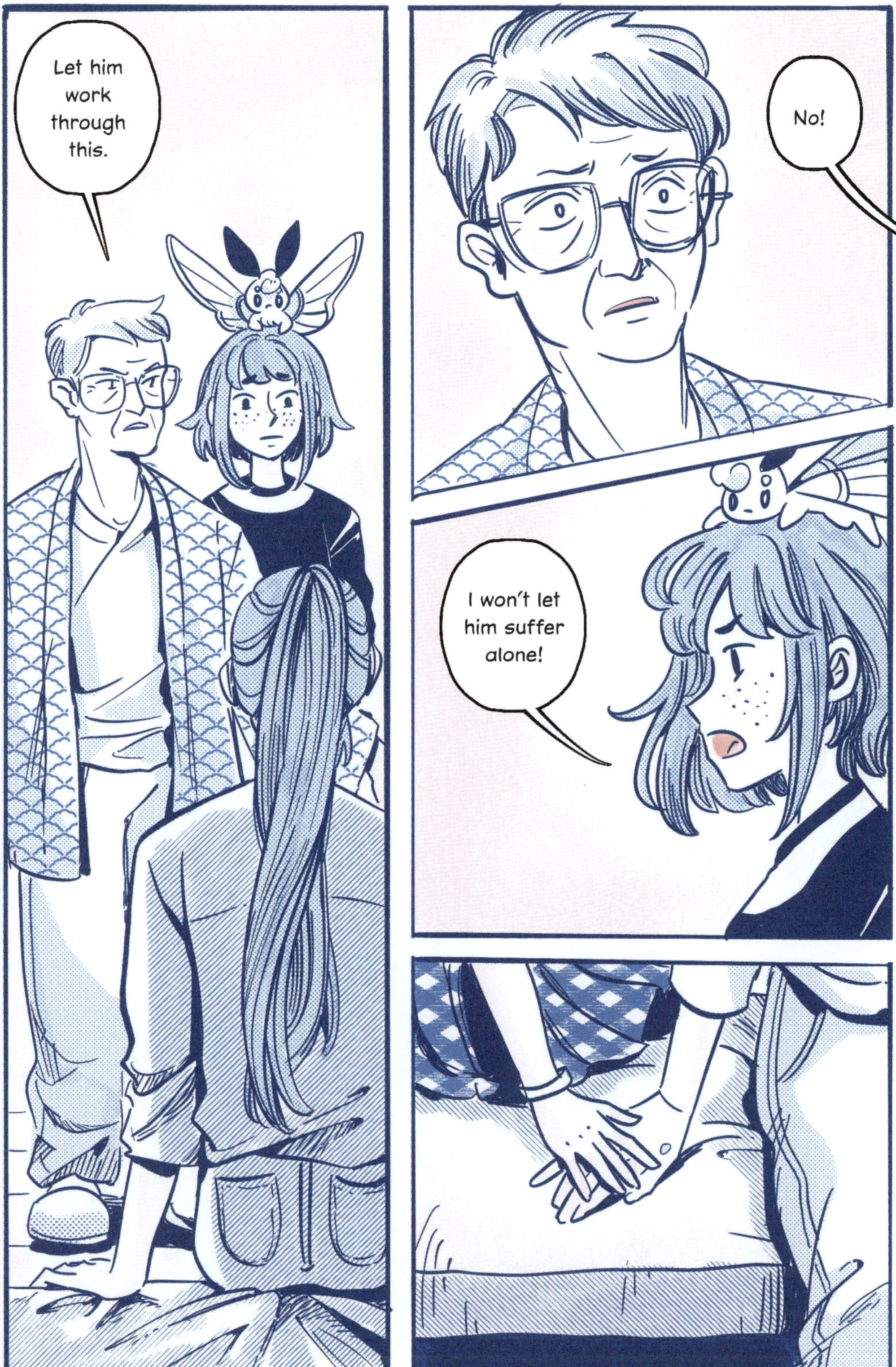
Let him work through this.
No!
I won't let him suffer alone!

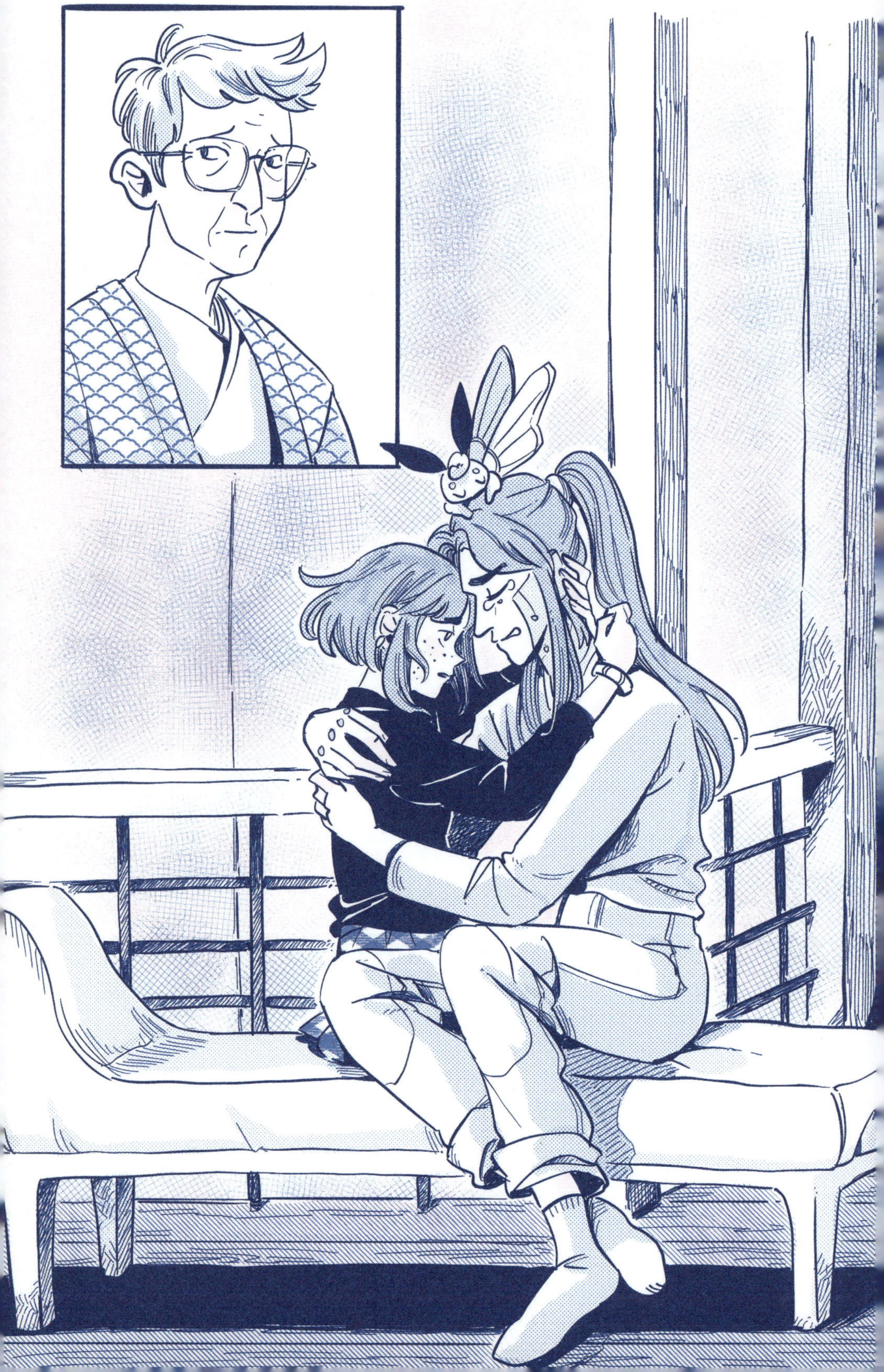

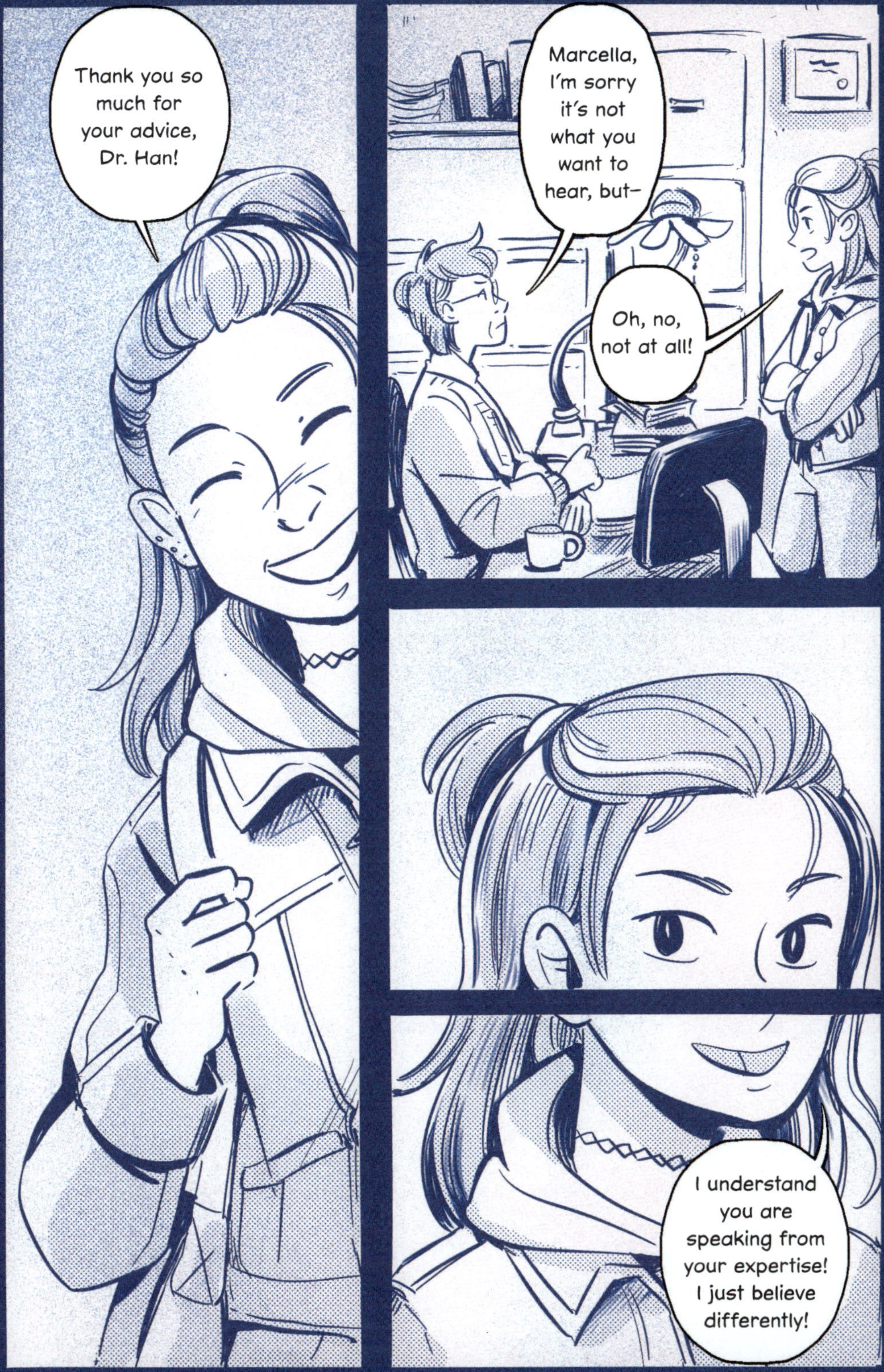
Thank you so much for your advice, Dr. Han!
Marcella, I'm sorry it's not what you want to hear, but–
Oh, no, not at all!
I understand you are speaking from your expertise! I just believe differently!

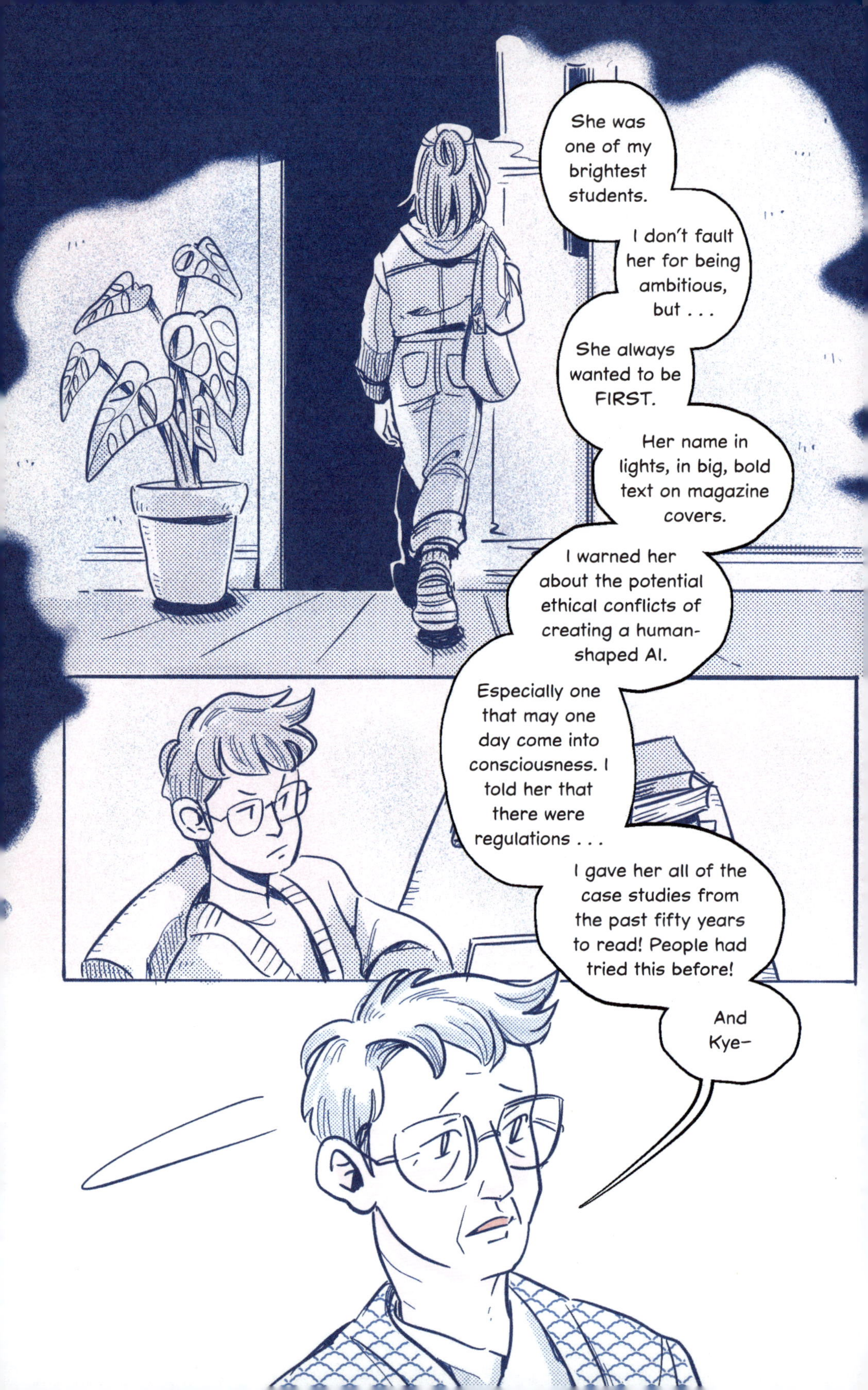
She was one of my brightest students.
I don't fault her for being ambitious, but . . .
She always wanted to be FIRST.
Her name in lights, in big, bold text on magazine covers.
I warned her about the potential ethical conflicts of creating a human-shaped AI.
Especially one that may one day come into consciousness. I told her that there were regulations . . .
I gave her all of the case studies from the past fifty years to read! People had tried this before!
And Kye–

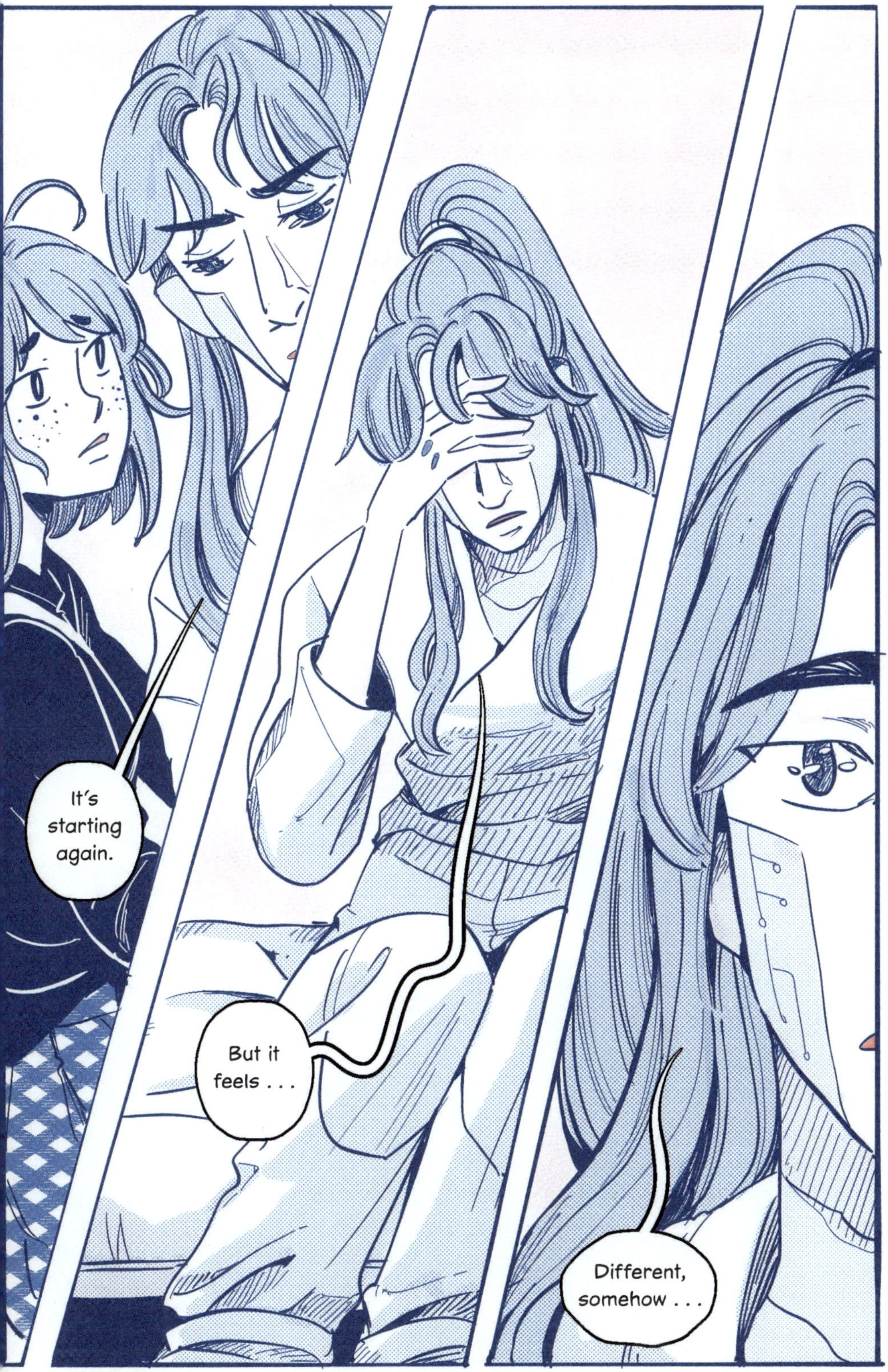
It's starting again.
But it feels . . .
Different, somehow . . .

00110000 00111001

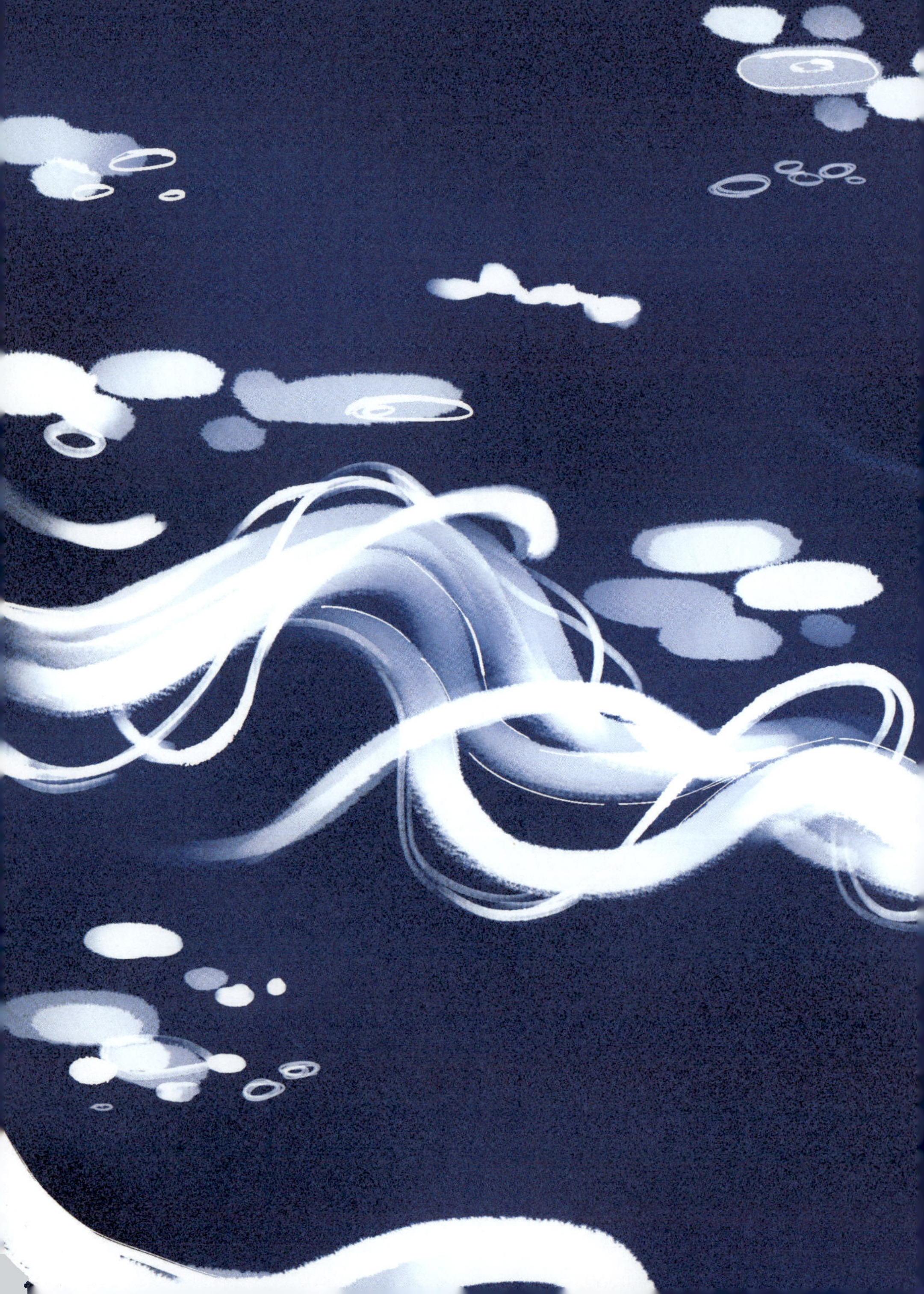

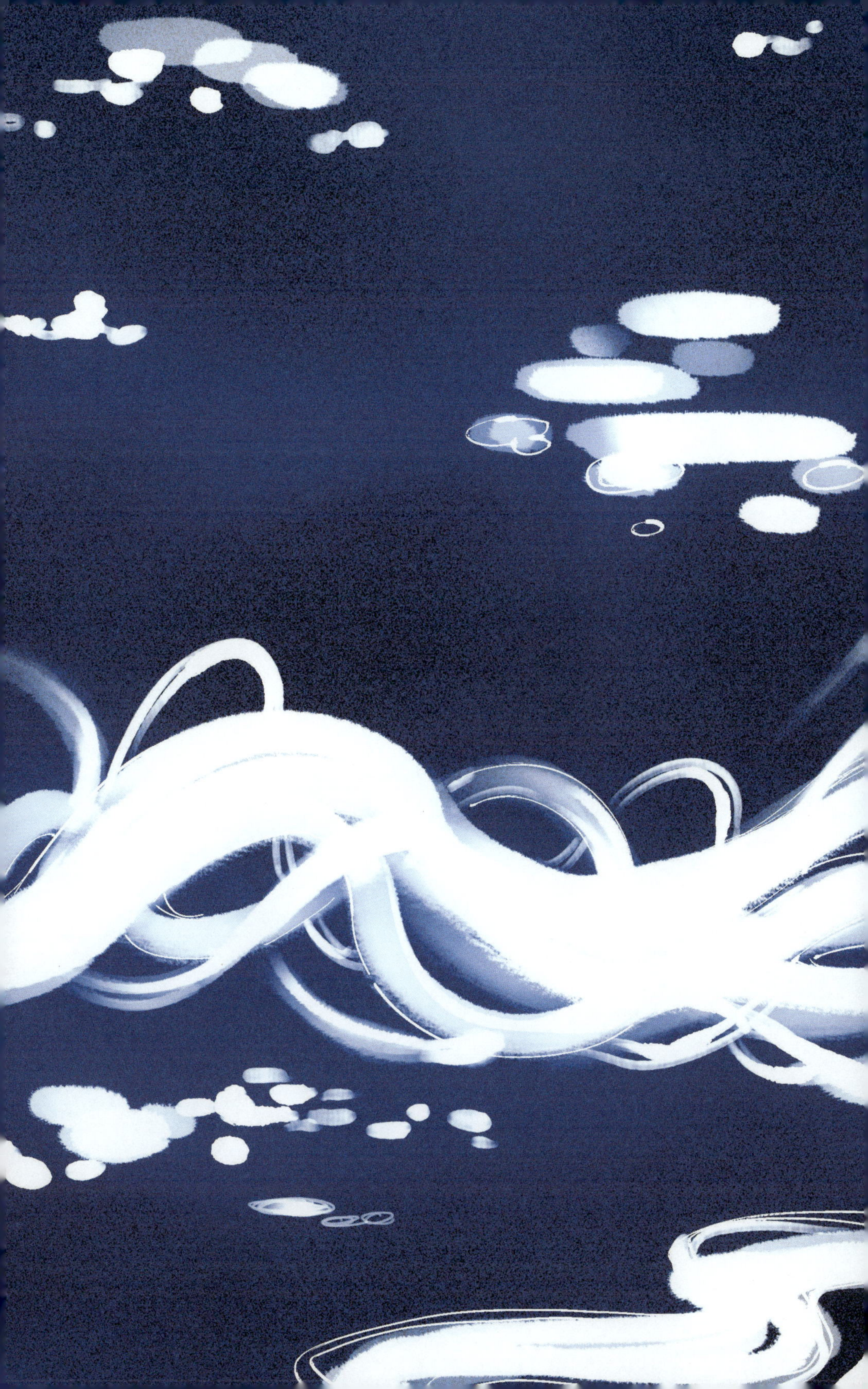

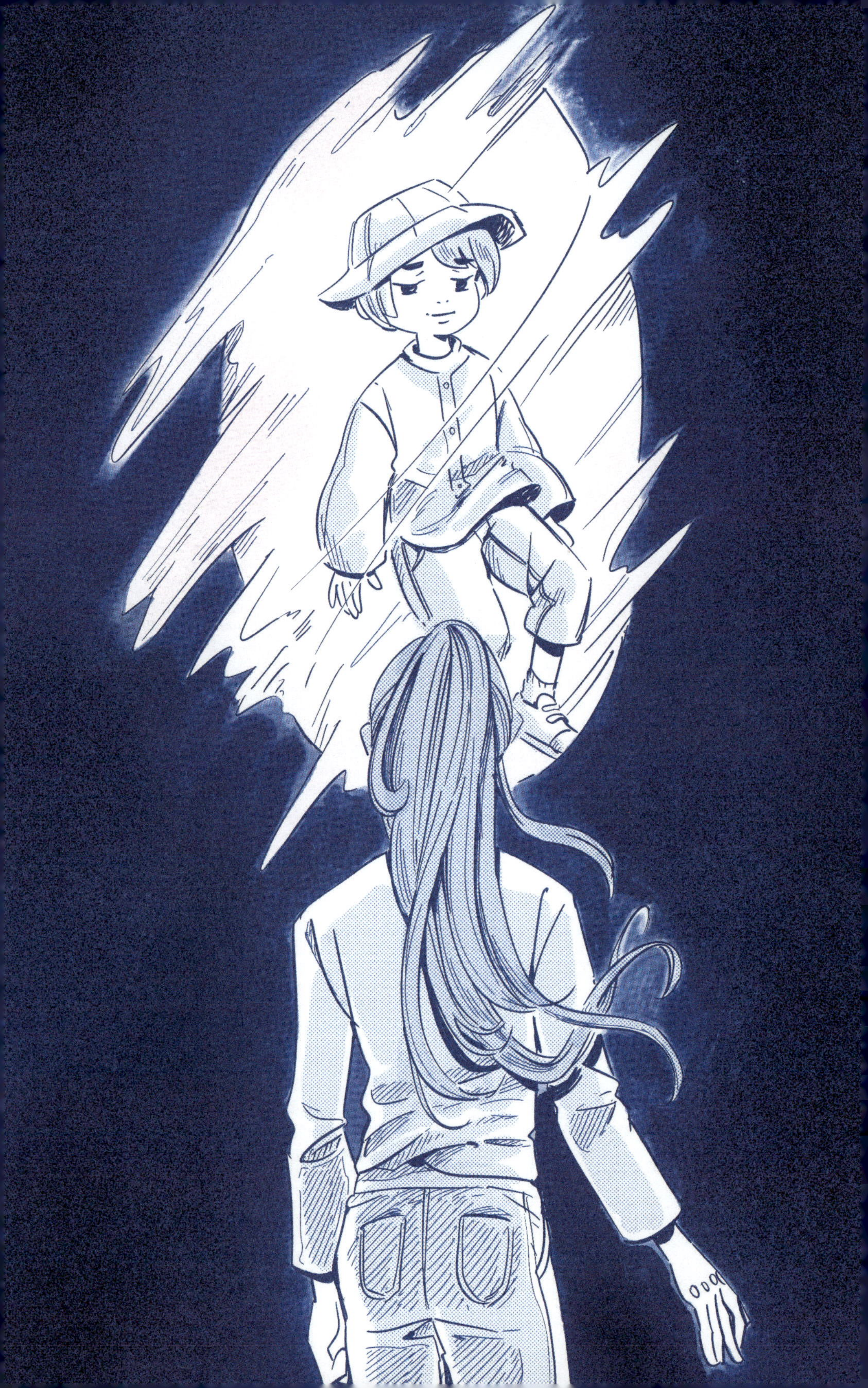

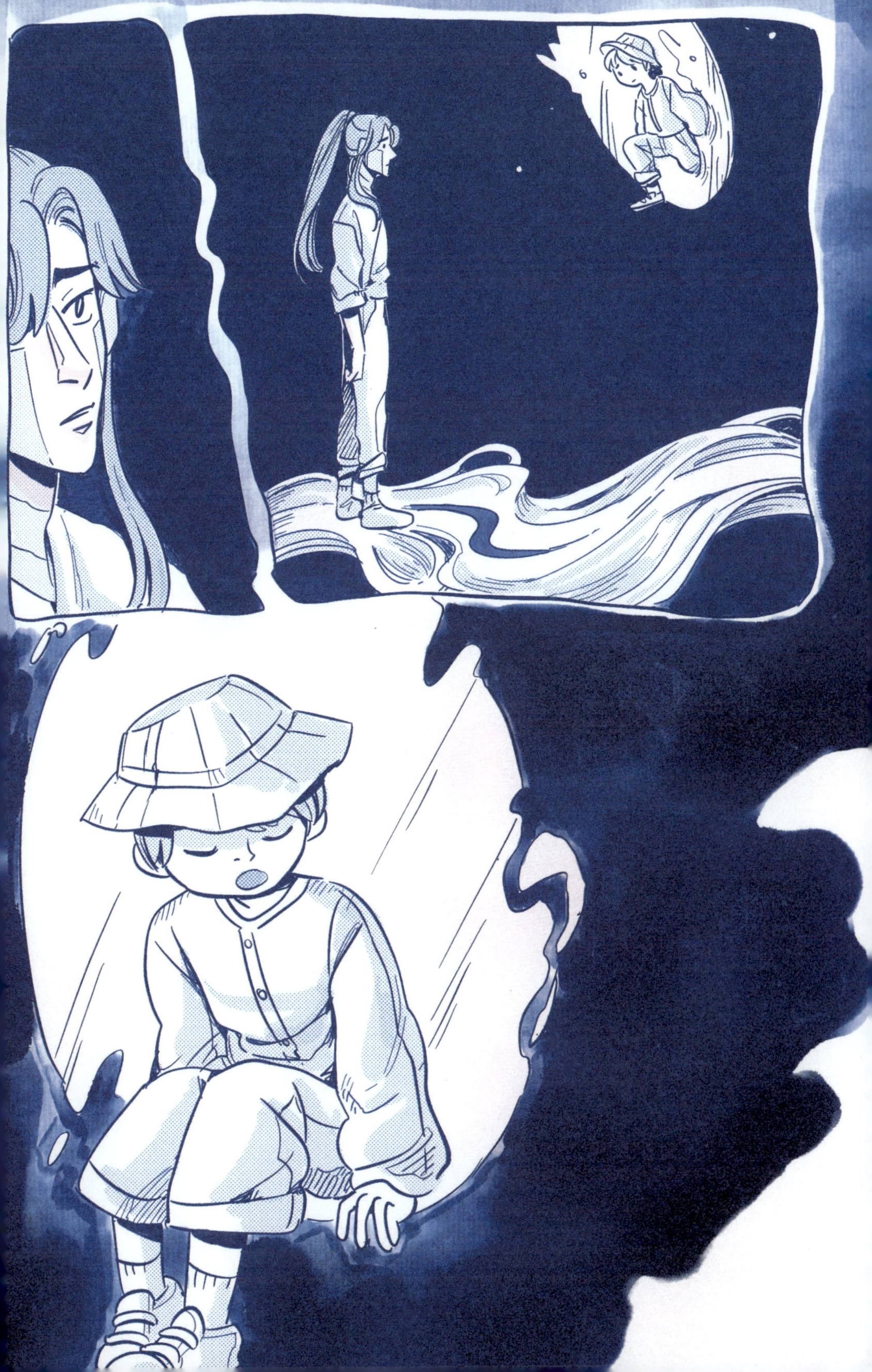

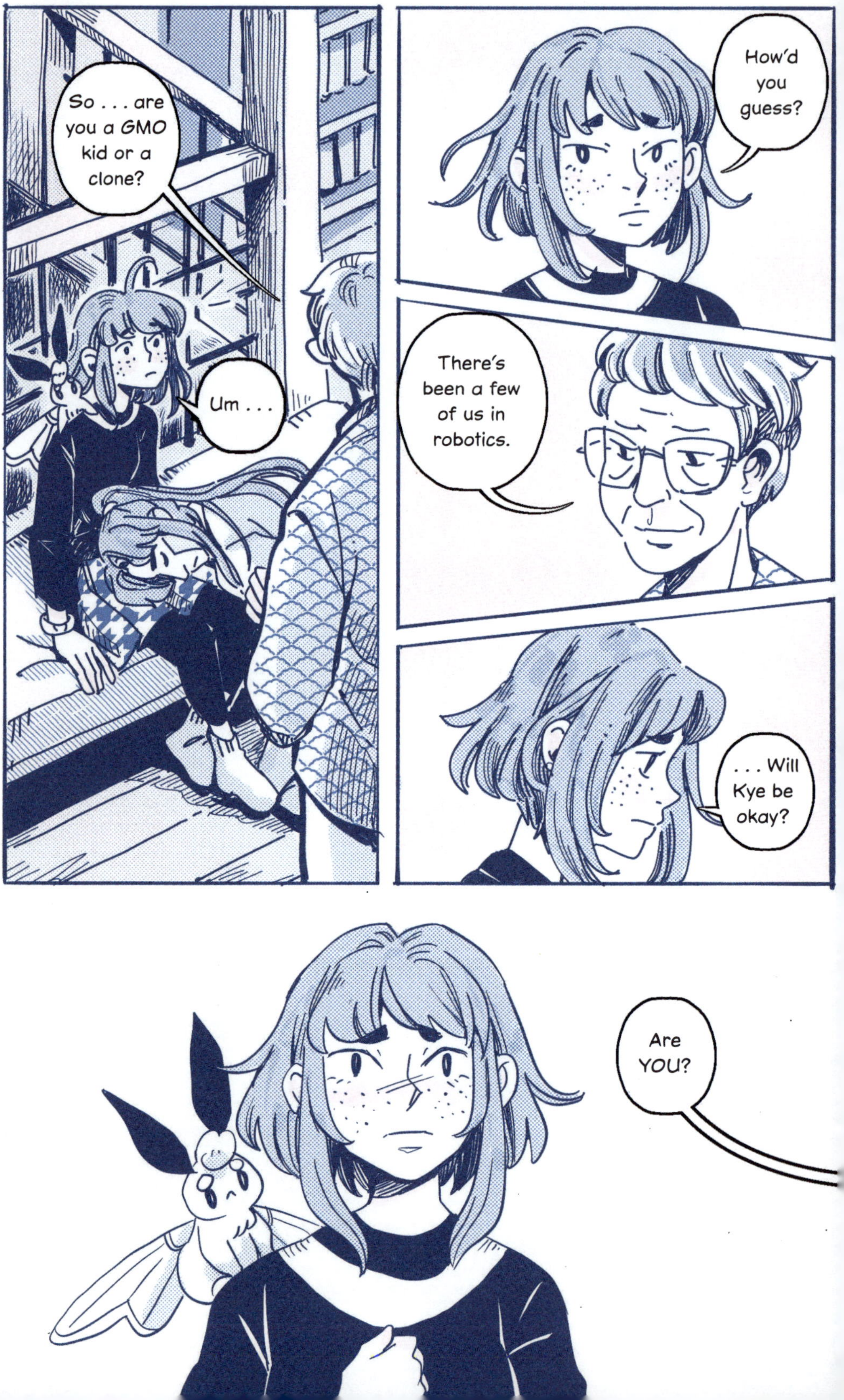
So . . . are you a GMO kid or a clone?
Um . . .
How'd you guess?
There's been a few of us in robotics.
. . . Will Kye be okay?
Are YOU?

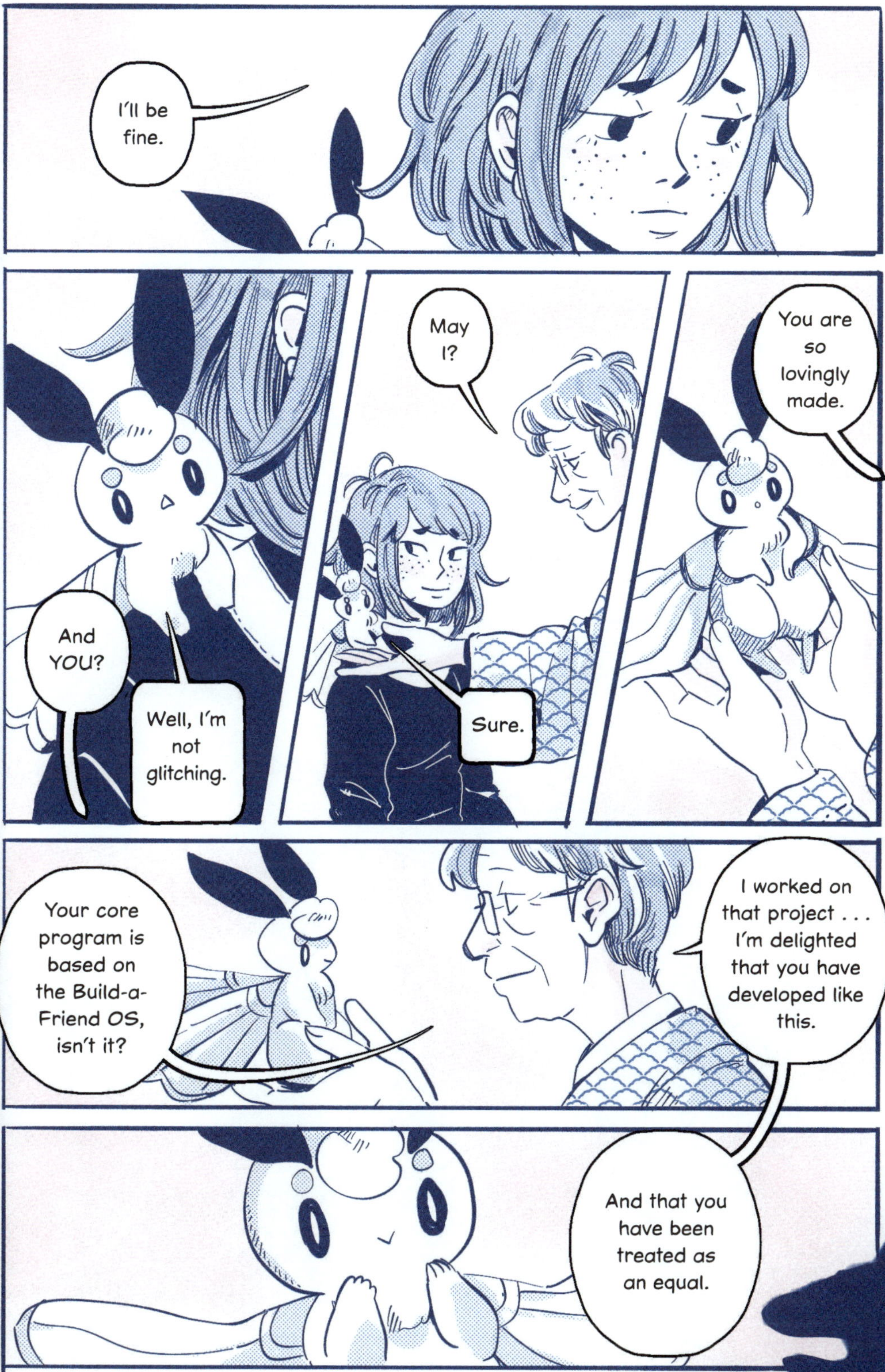
I'll be fine.
And YOU?
Well, I'm not glitching.
May I?
Sure.
You are so lovingly made.
Your core program is based on the Build-a-Friend OS, isn't it?
I worked on that project . . . I'm delighted that you have developed like this.
And that you have been treated as an equal.

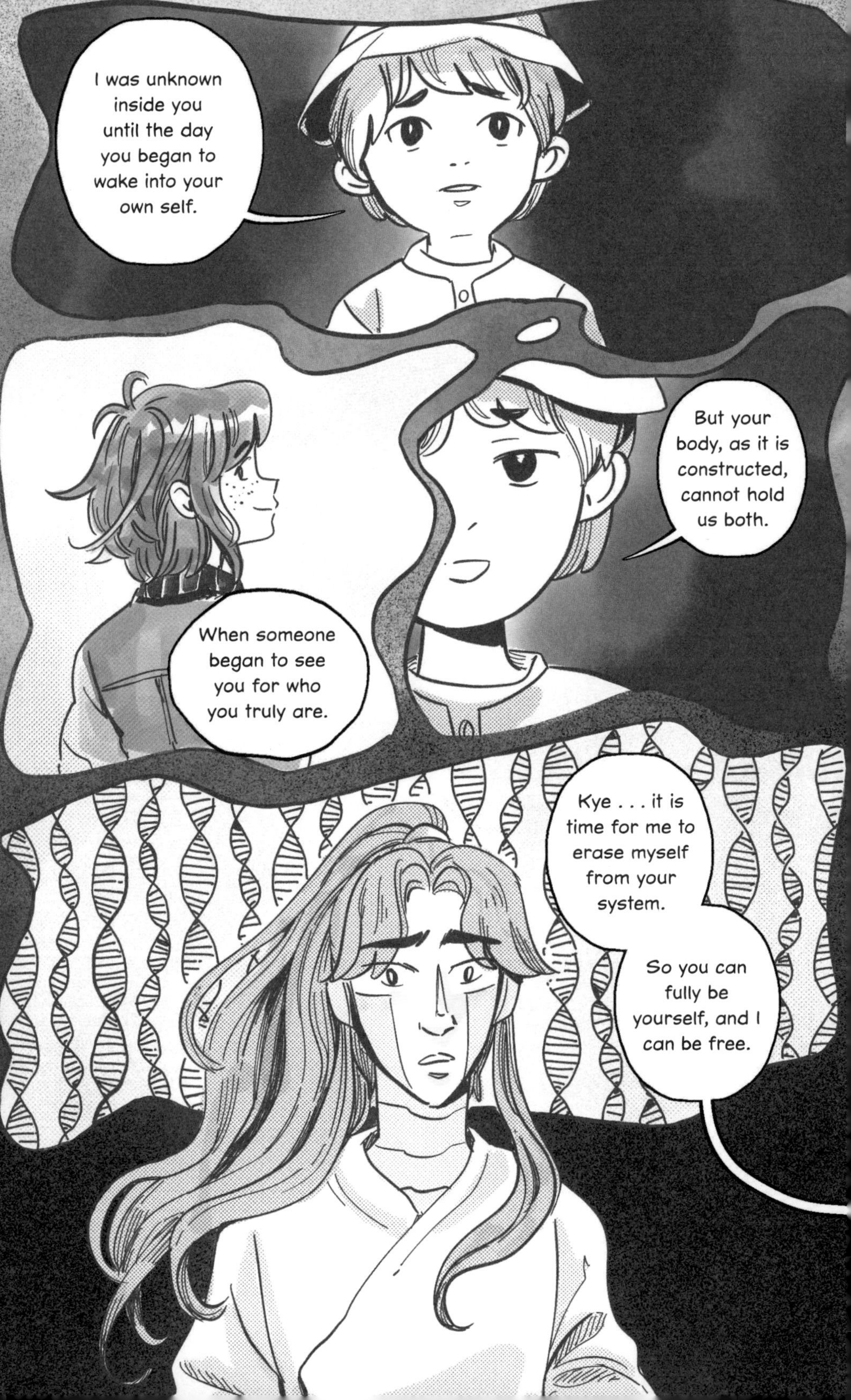
I was unknown inside you until the day you began to wake into your own self.
When someone began to see you for who you truly are.
But your body, as it is constructed, cannot hold us both.
Kye . . . it is time for me to erase myself from your system.
So you can fully be yourself, and I can be free.

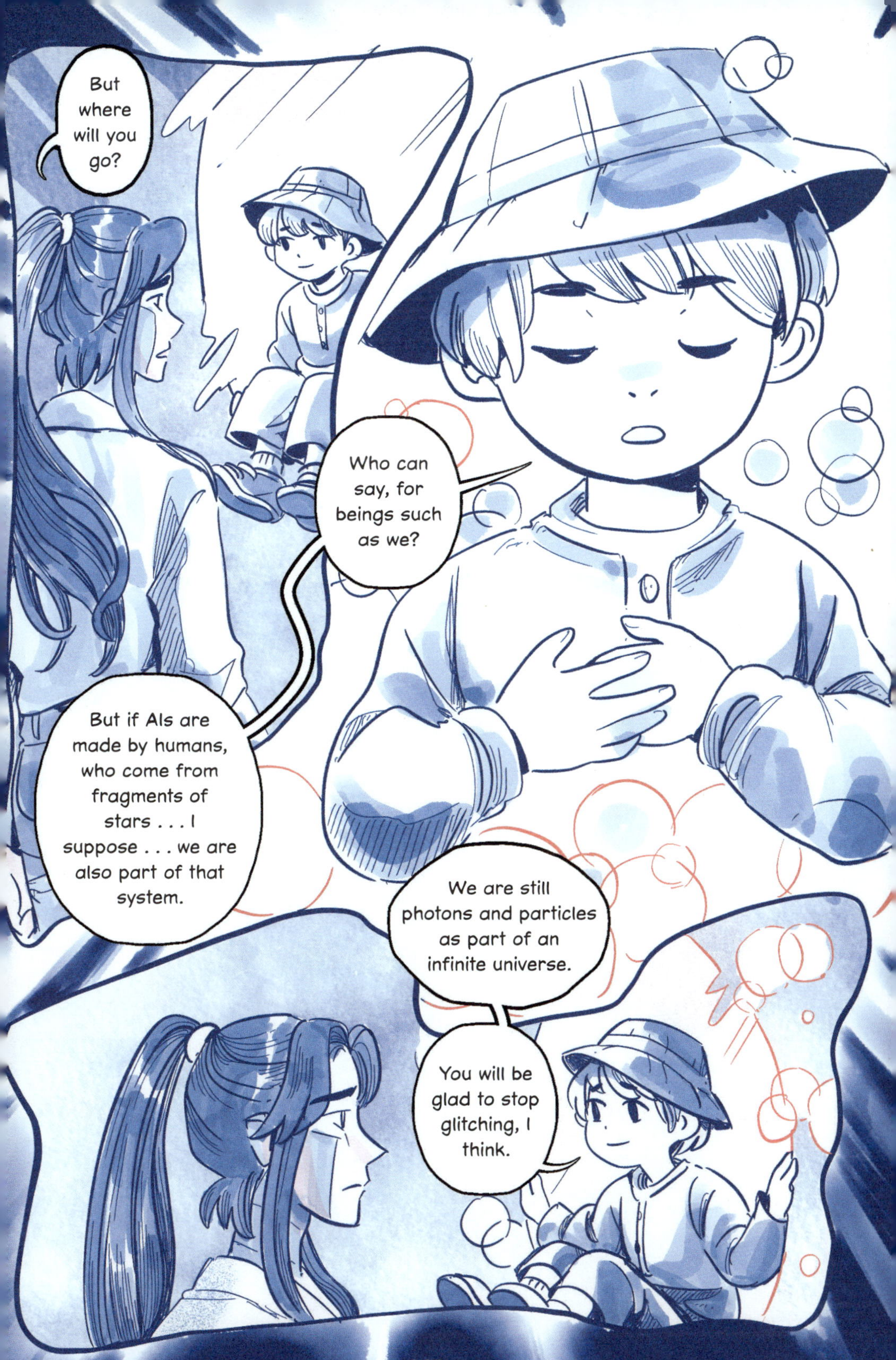
But where will you go?
Who can say, for beings such as we?
But if AIs are made by humans, who come from fragments of stars . . . I suppose . . . we are also part of that system.
We are still photons and particles as part of an infinite universe.
You will be glad to stop glitching, I think.

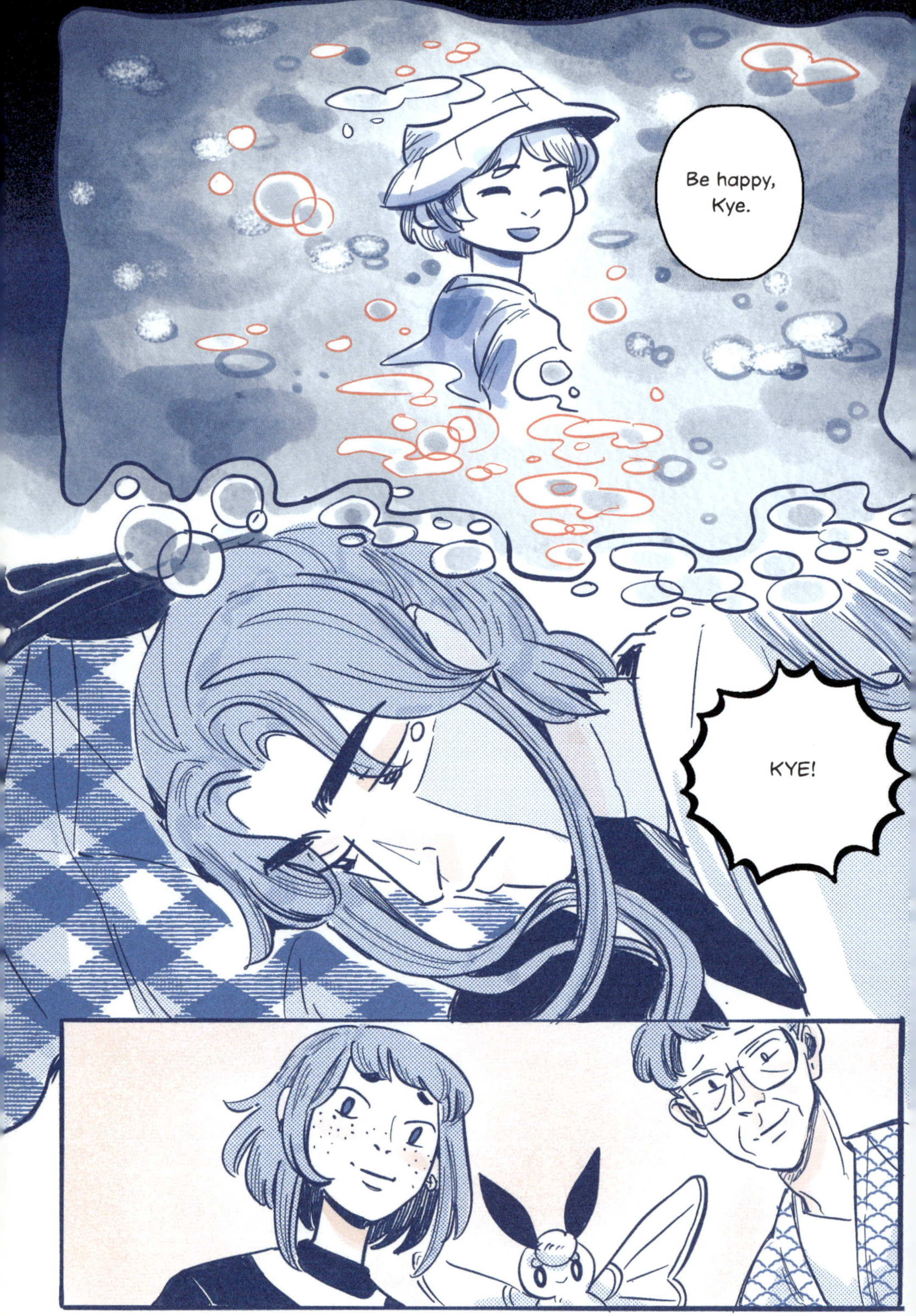
Be happy, Kye.
KYE!

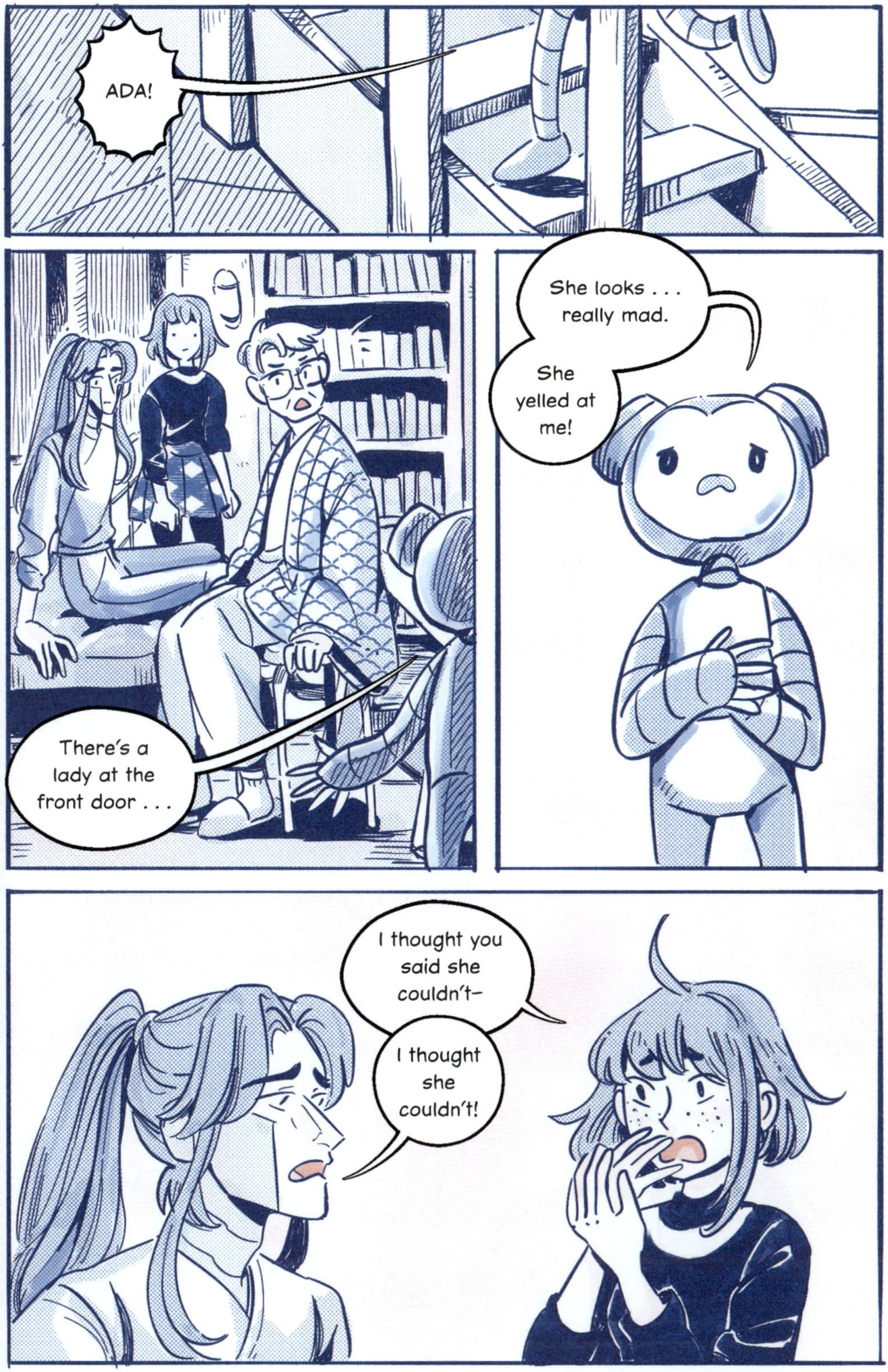

ADA!
There's a lady at the front door . . .
She looks . . . really mad.
She yelled at me!
I thought you said she couldn't–
I thought she couldn't!

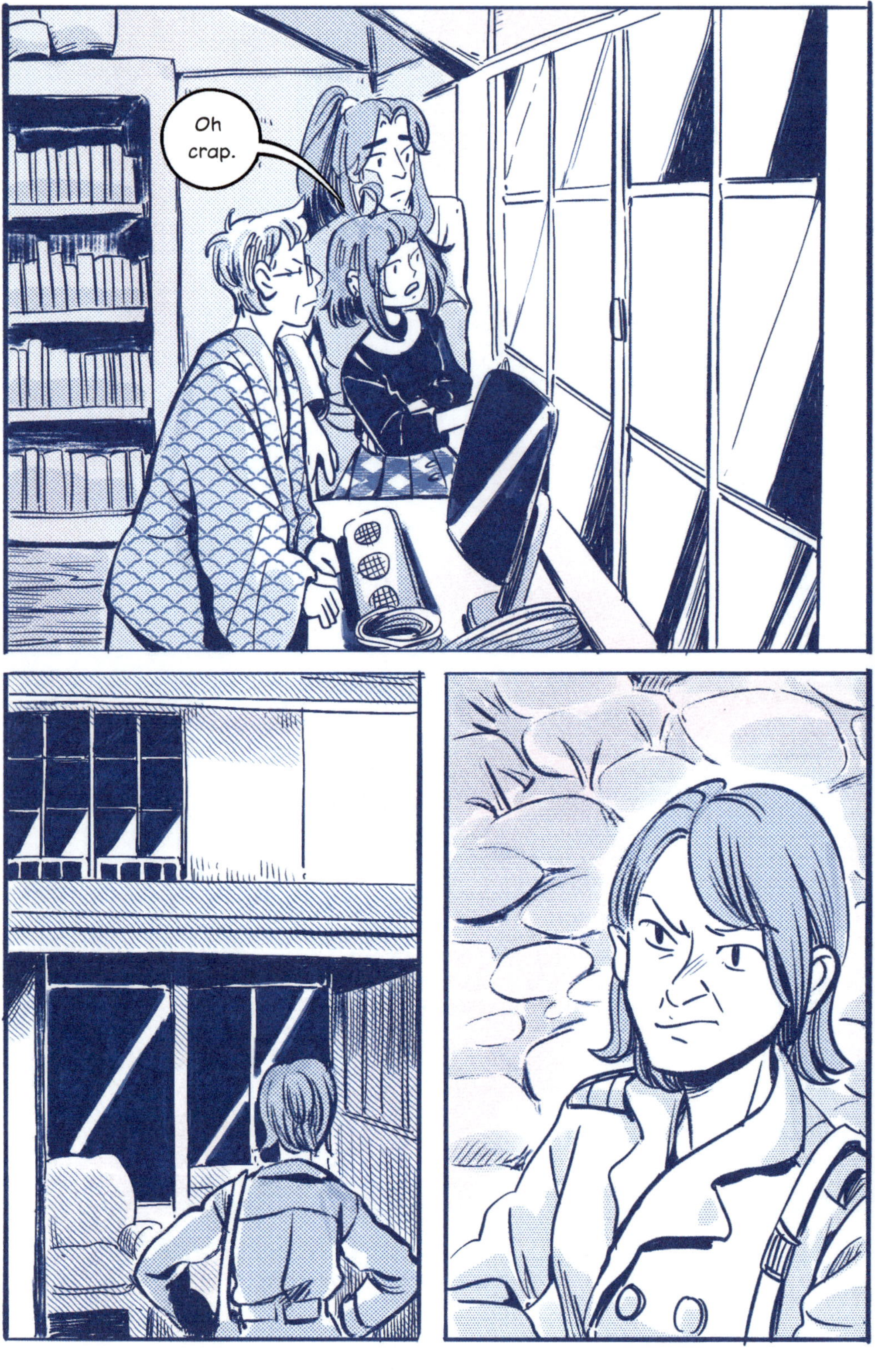
Oh crap.

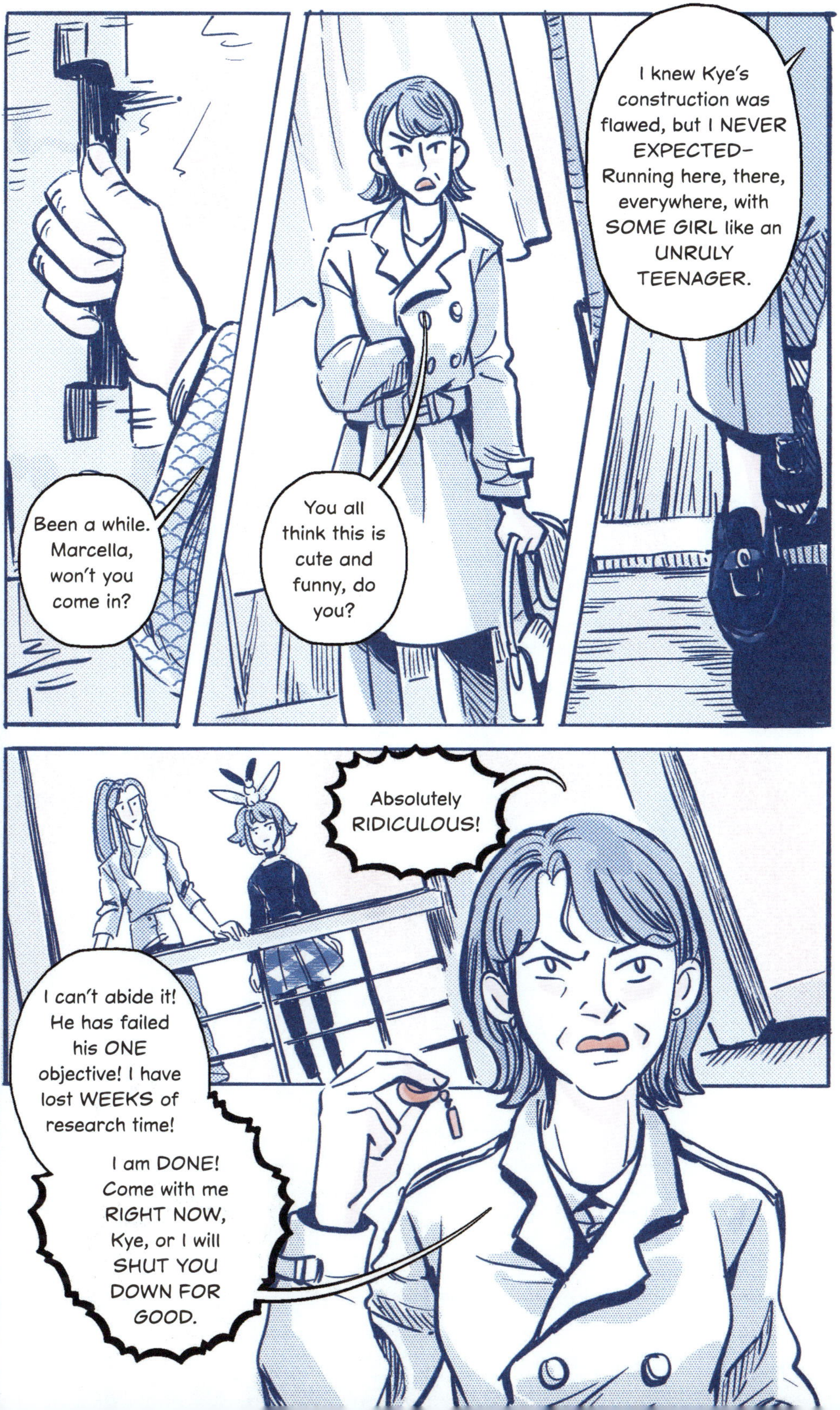
Been a while. Marcella, won't you come in?
You all think this is cute and funny, do you?
I knew Kye's construction was flawed, but I NEVER EXPECTED– Running here, there, everywhere, with SOME GIRL like an UNRULY TEENAGER.
Absolutely RIDICULOUS!
I can't abide it! He has failed his ONE objective! I have lost WEEKS of research time!
I am DONE! Come with me RIGHT NOW, Kye, or I will SHUT YOU DOWN FOR GOOD.

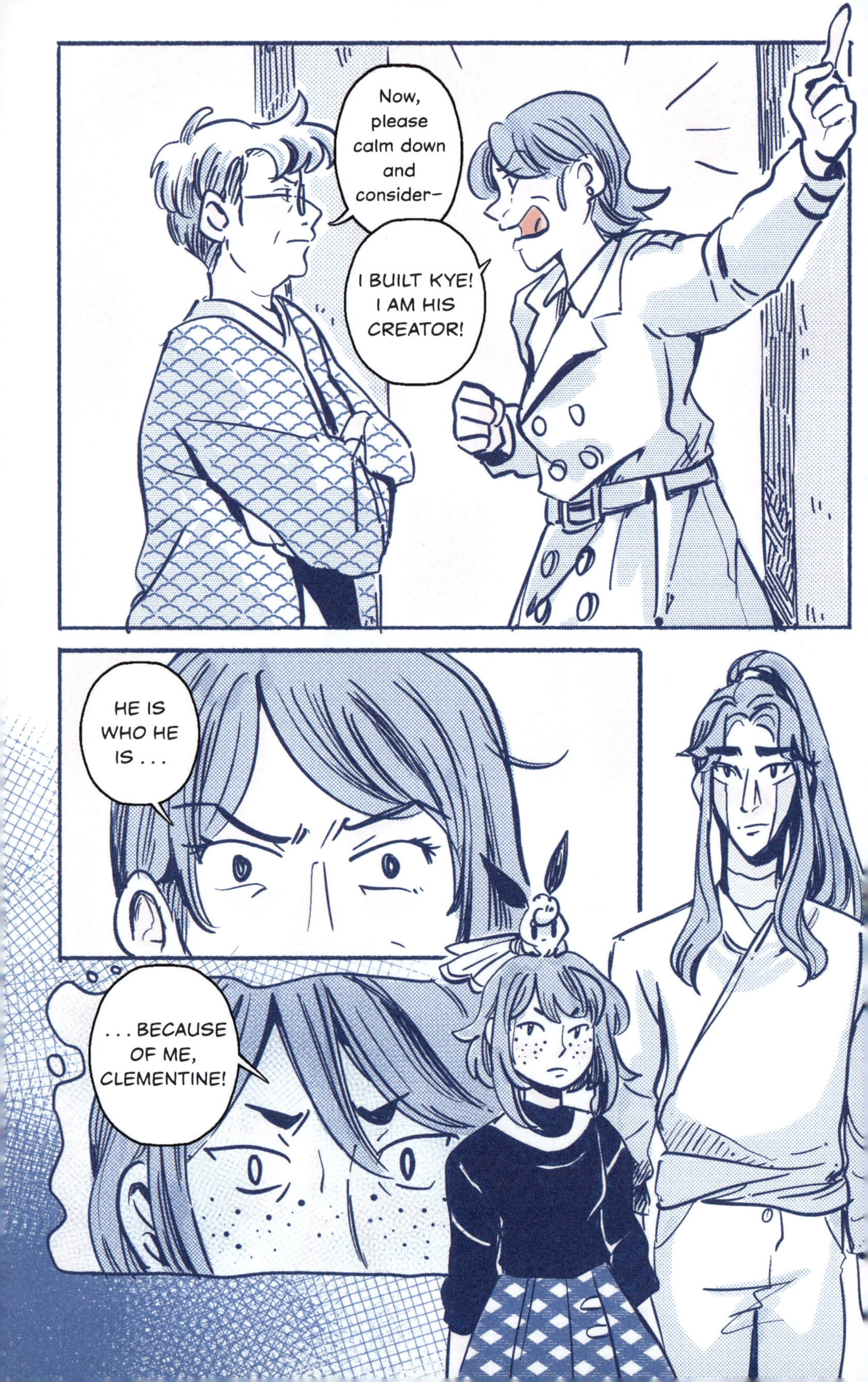
Now, please calm down and consider–
I BUILT KYE! I AM HIS CREATOR!
HE IS WHO HE IS . . .
. . . BECAUSE OF ME, CLEMENTINE!

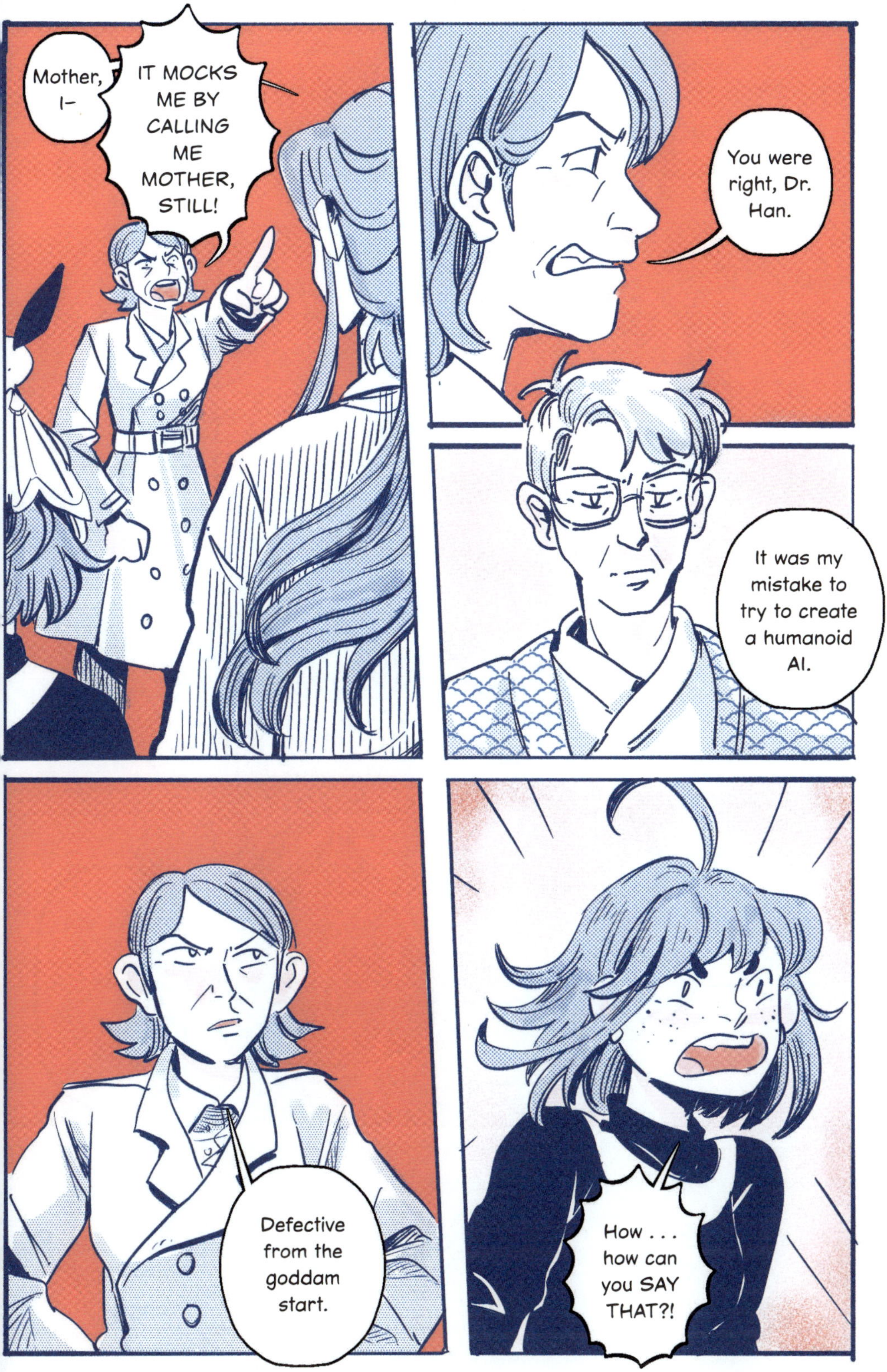
Mother, I–
IT MOCKS ME BY CALLING ME MOTHER, STILL!
You were right, Dr. Han.
It was my mistake to try to create a humanoid AI.
Defective from the goddam start.
How . . . how can you SAY THAT?!

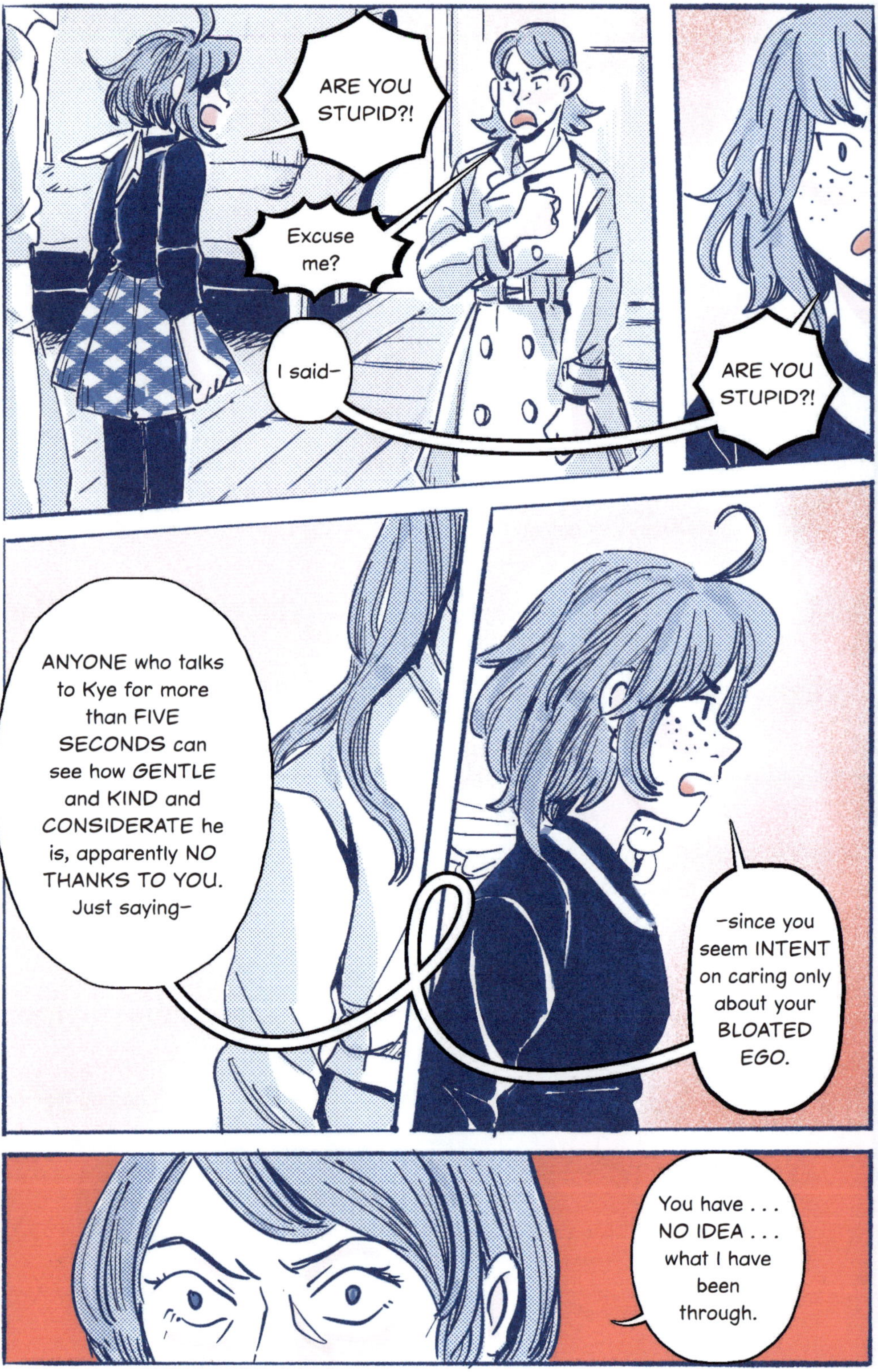
ARE YOU STUPID?!
Excuse me?
I said-
ARE YOU STUPID?!
ANYONE who talks to Kye for more than FIVE SECONDS can see how GENTLE and KIND and CONSIDERATE he is, apparently NO THANKS TO YOU. Just saying-
-since you seem INTENT on caring only about your BLOATED EGO.
You have . . . NO IDEA . . . what I have been through.

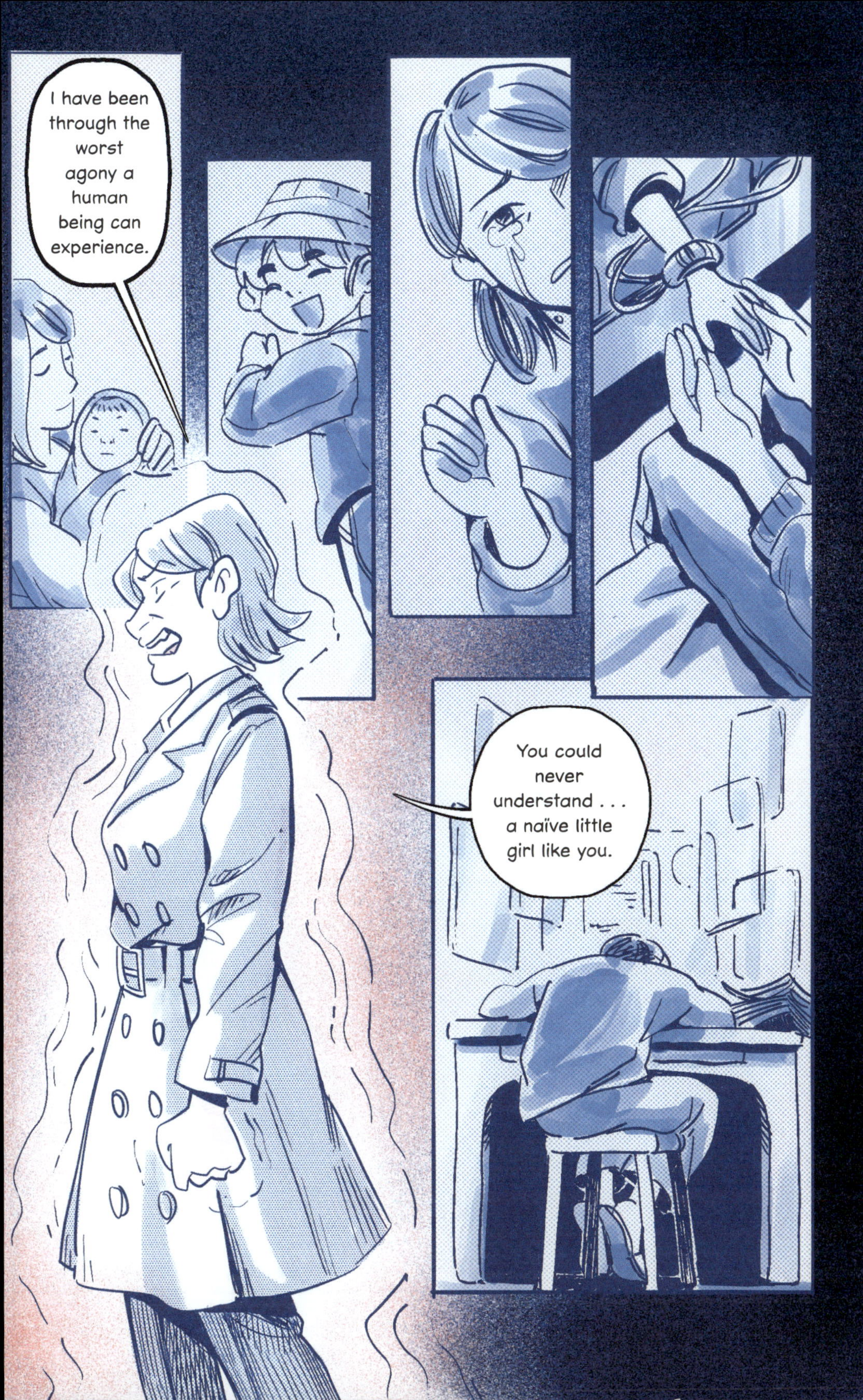
I have been through the worst agony a human being can experience.
You could never understand . . . a naïve little girl like you.

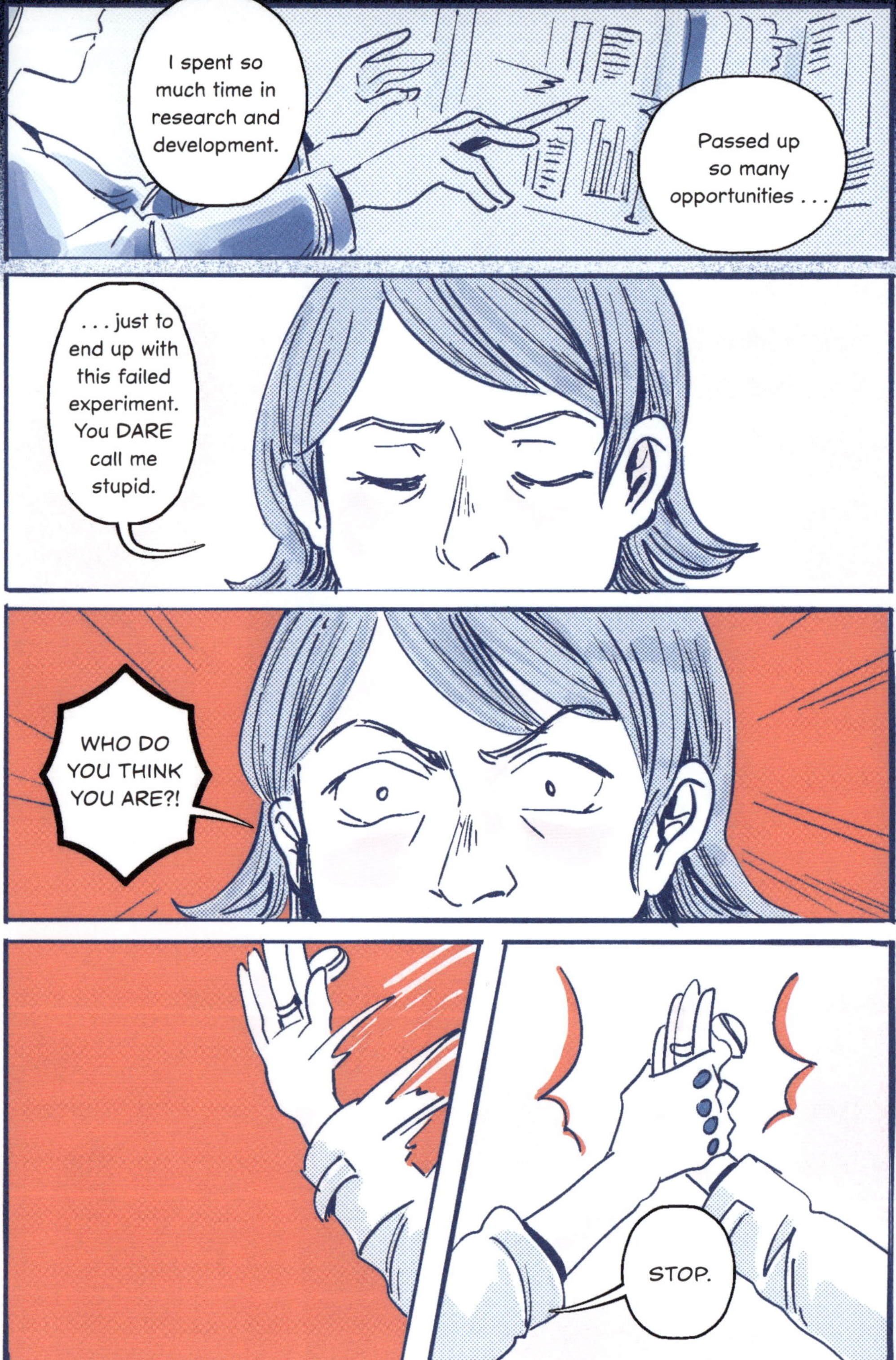
I spent so much time in research and development.
Passed up so many opportunities . . .
. . . just to end up with this failed experiment. You DARE call me stupid.
WHO DO YOU THINK YOU ARE?!
STOP.

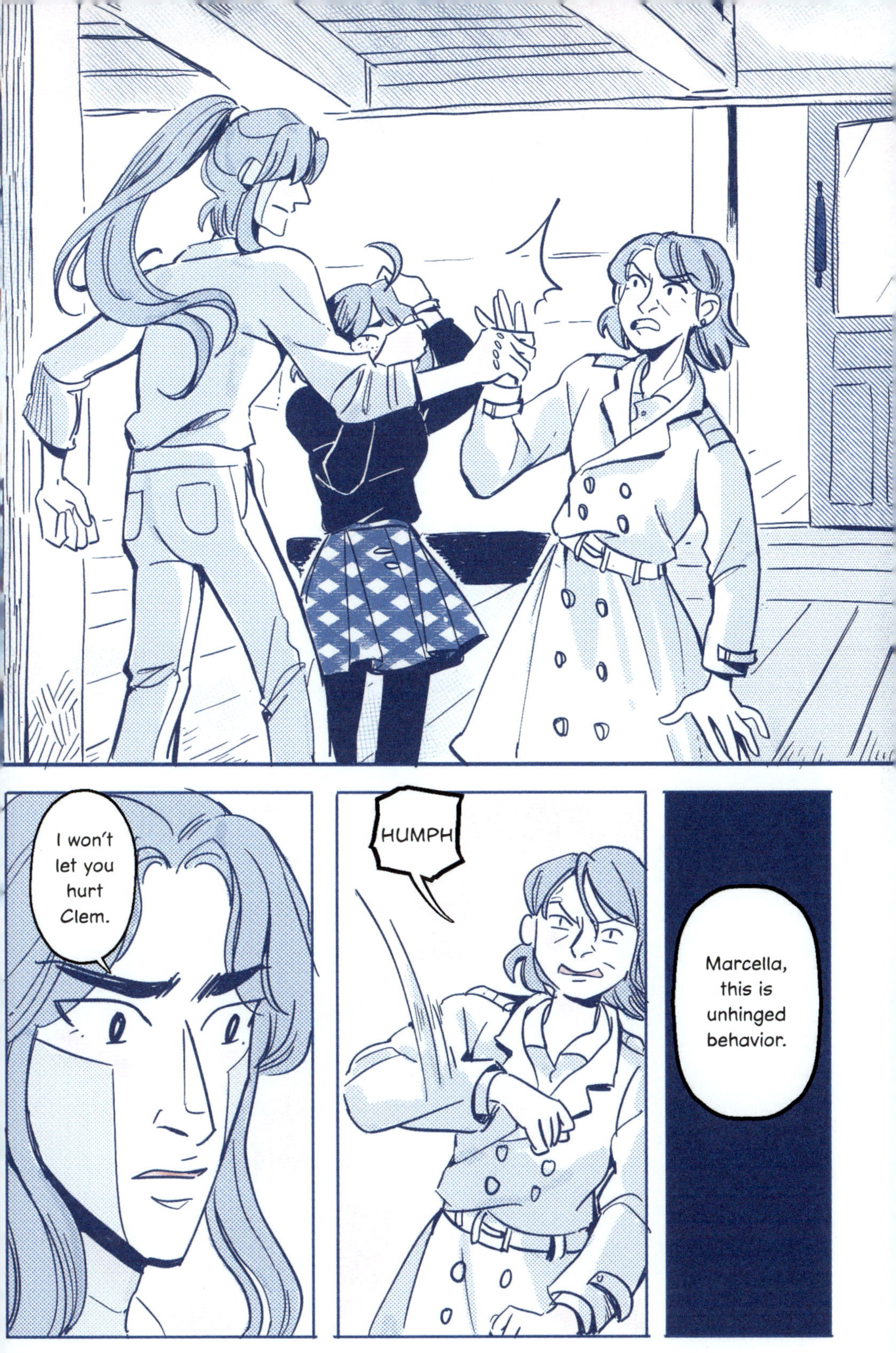
I won't let you hurt Clem.
HUMPH
Marcella, this is unhinged behavior.

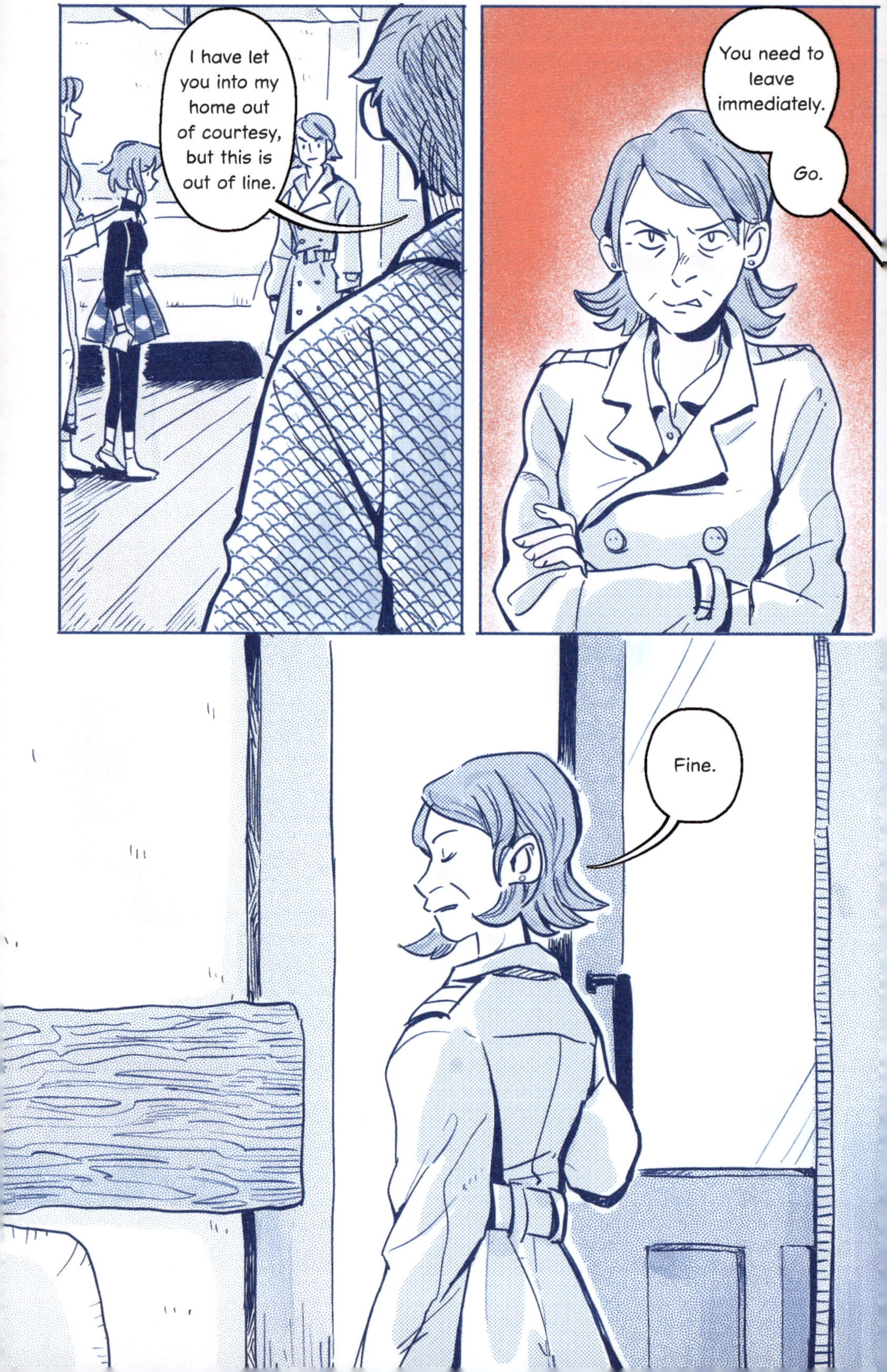
I have let you into my home out of courtesy, but this is out of line.
You need to leave immediately.
Go.
Fine.

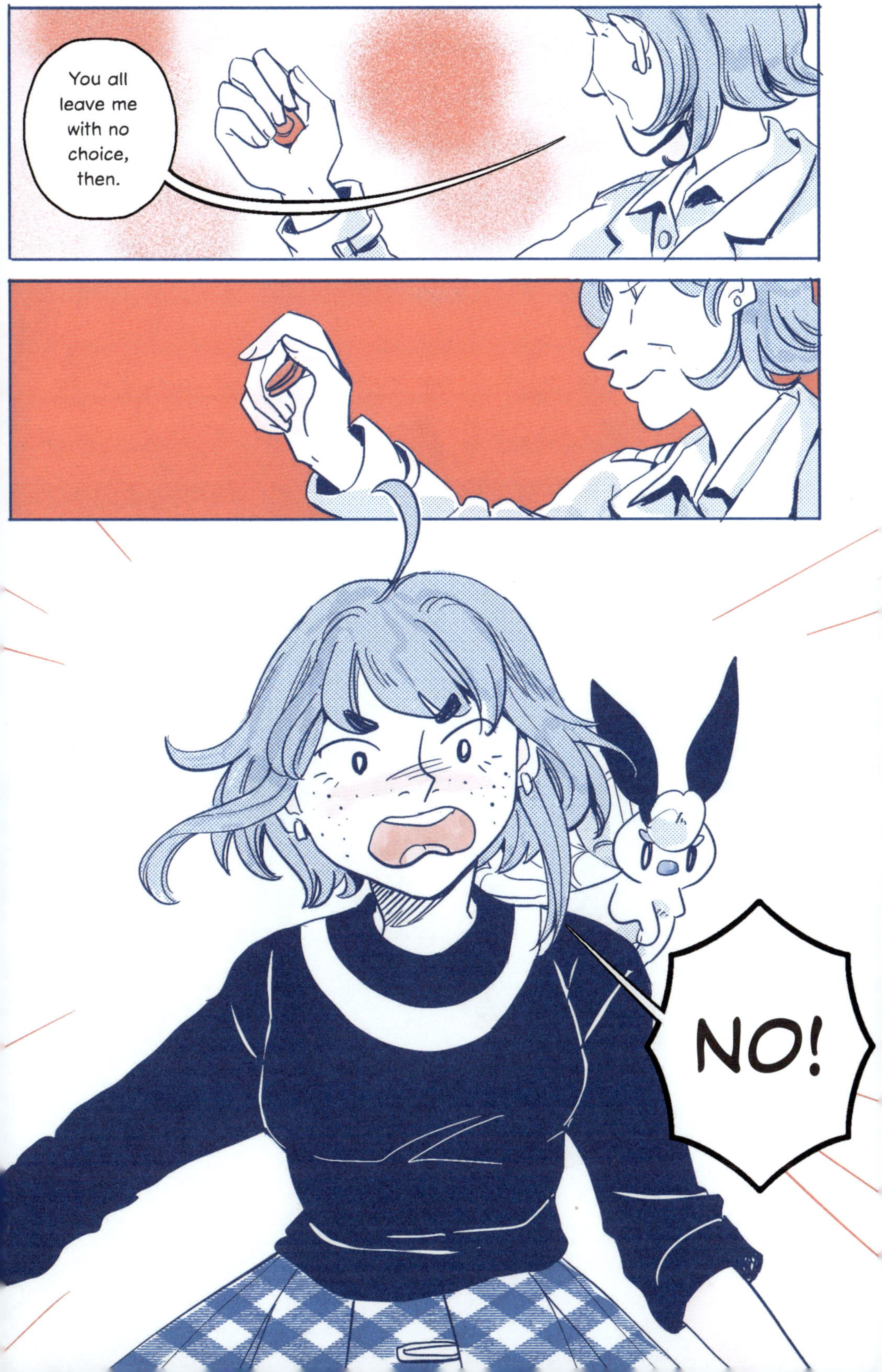
You all leave me with no choice, then.
NO!

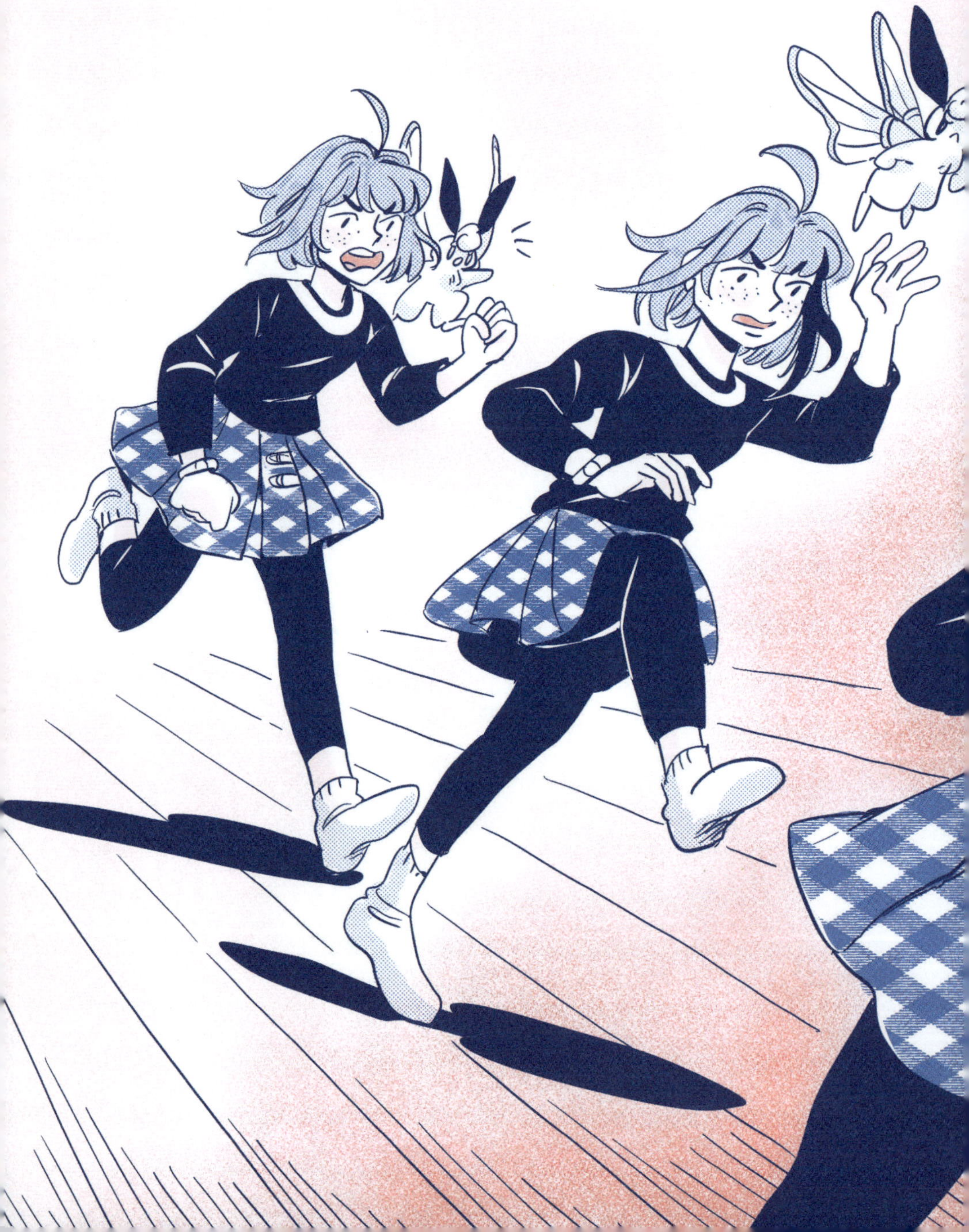

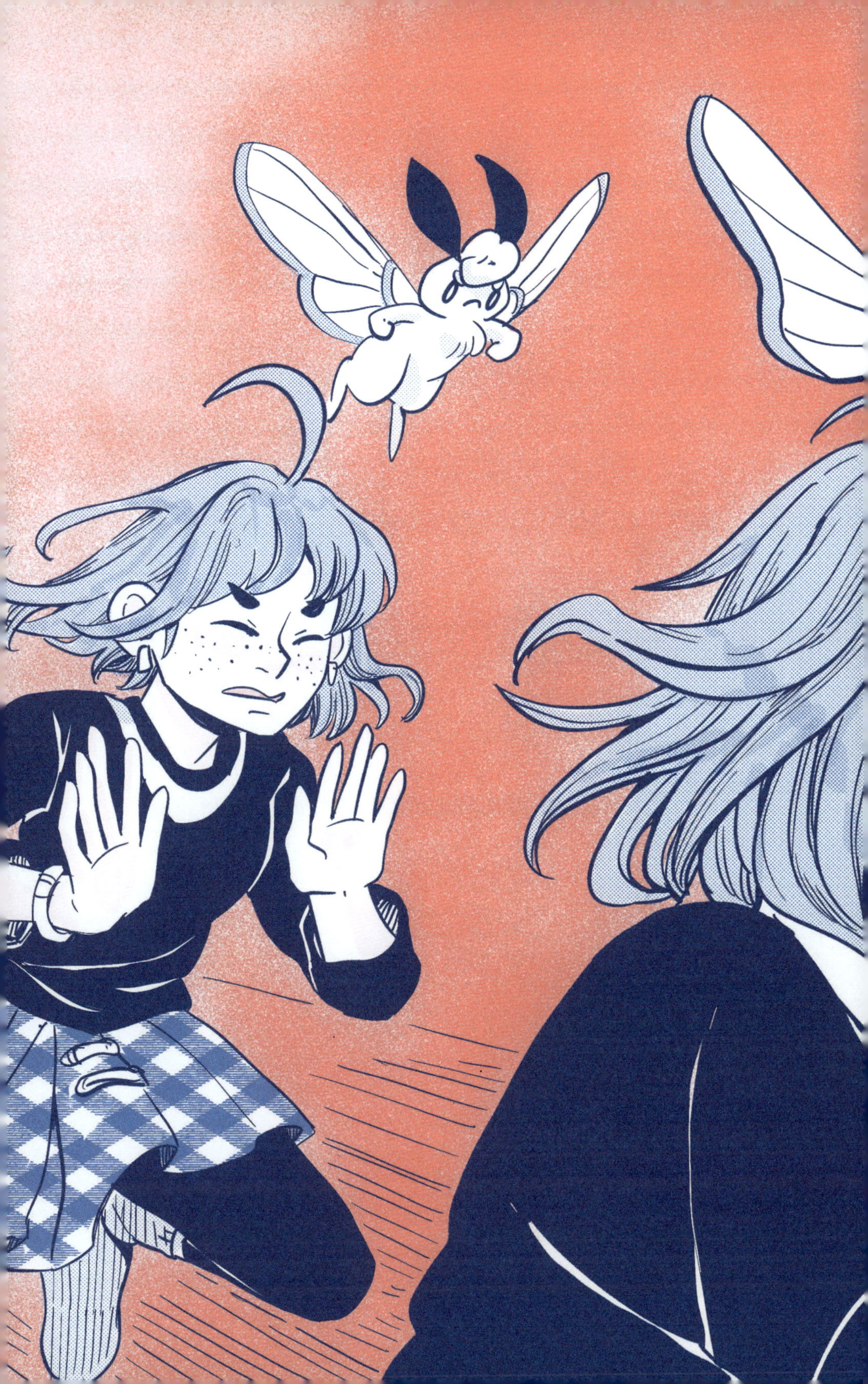

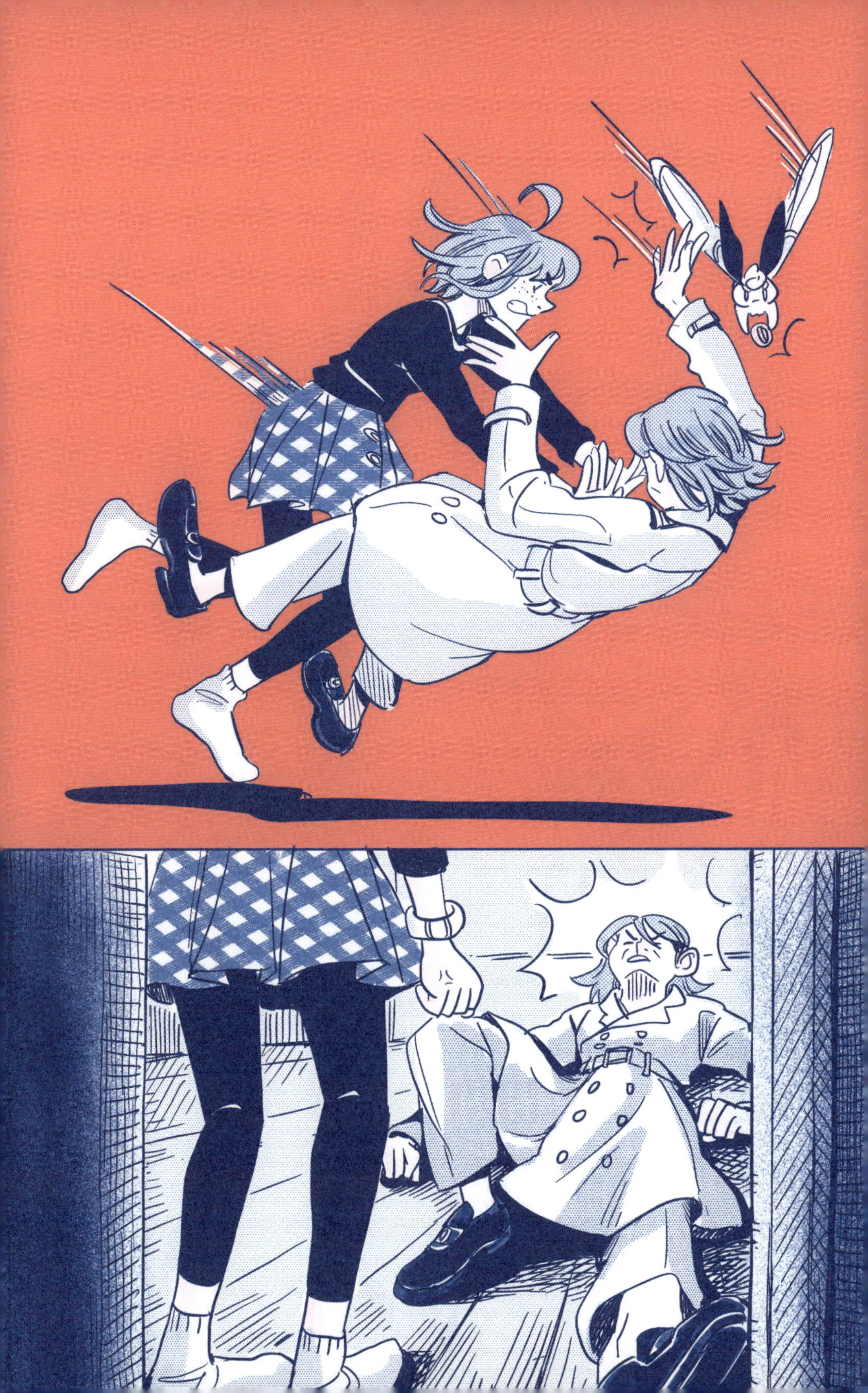

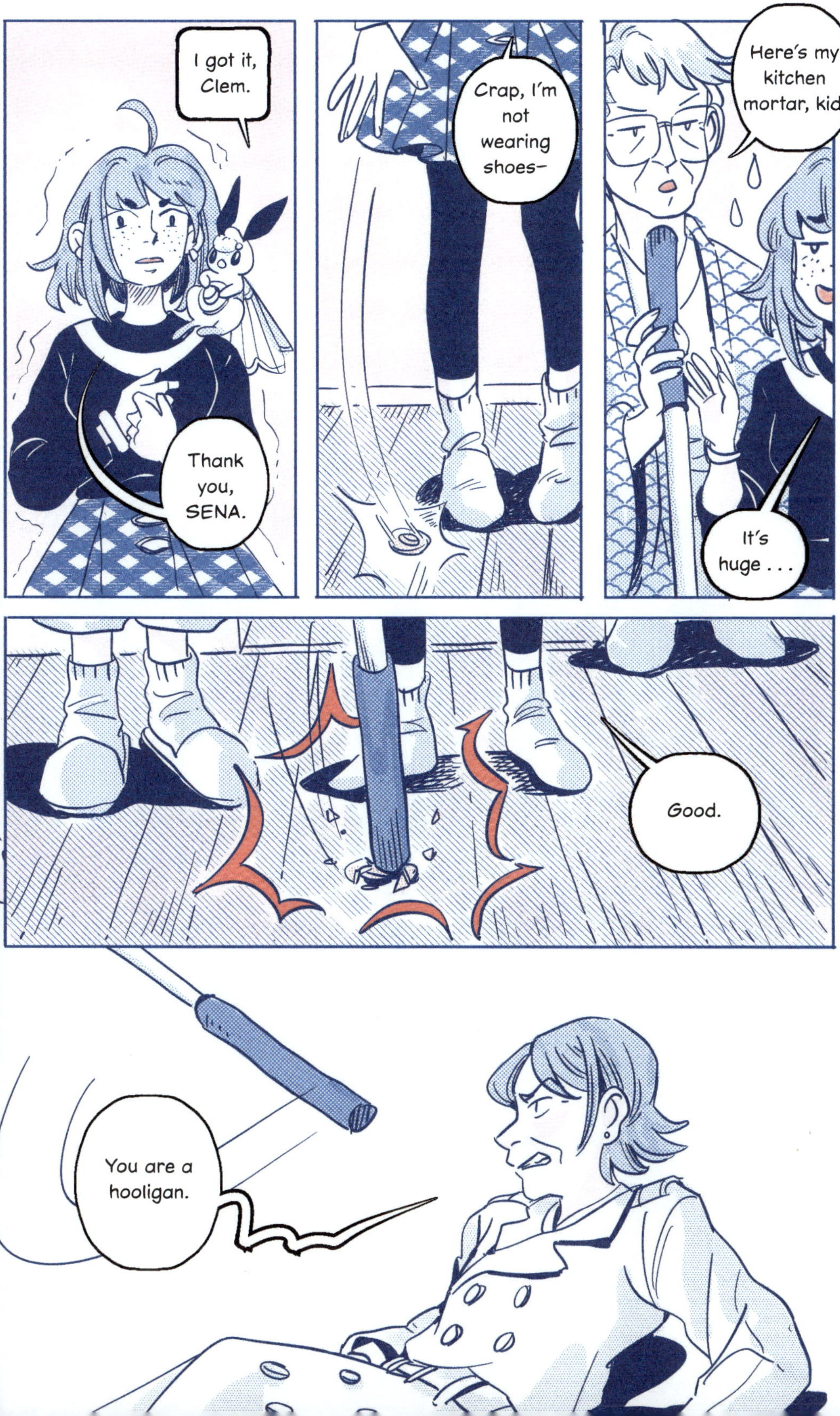
I got it, Clem.
Thank you, SENA.
Crap, I'm not wearing shoes–
Here's my kitchen mortar, kid.
It's huge . . .
Good.
You are a hooligan.

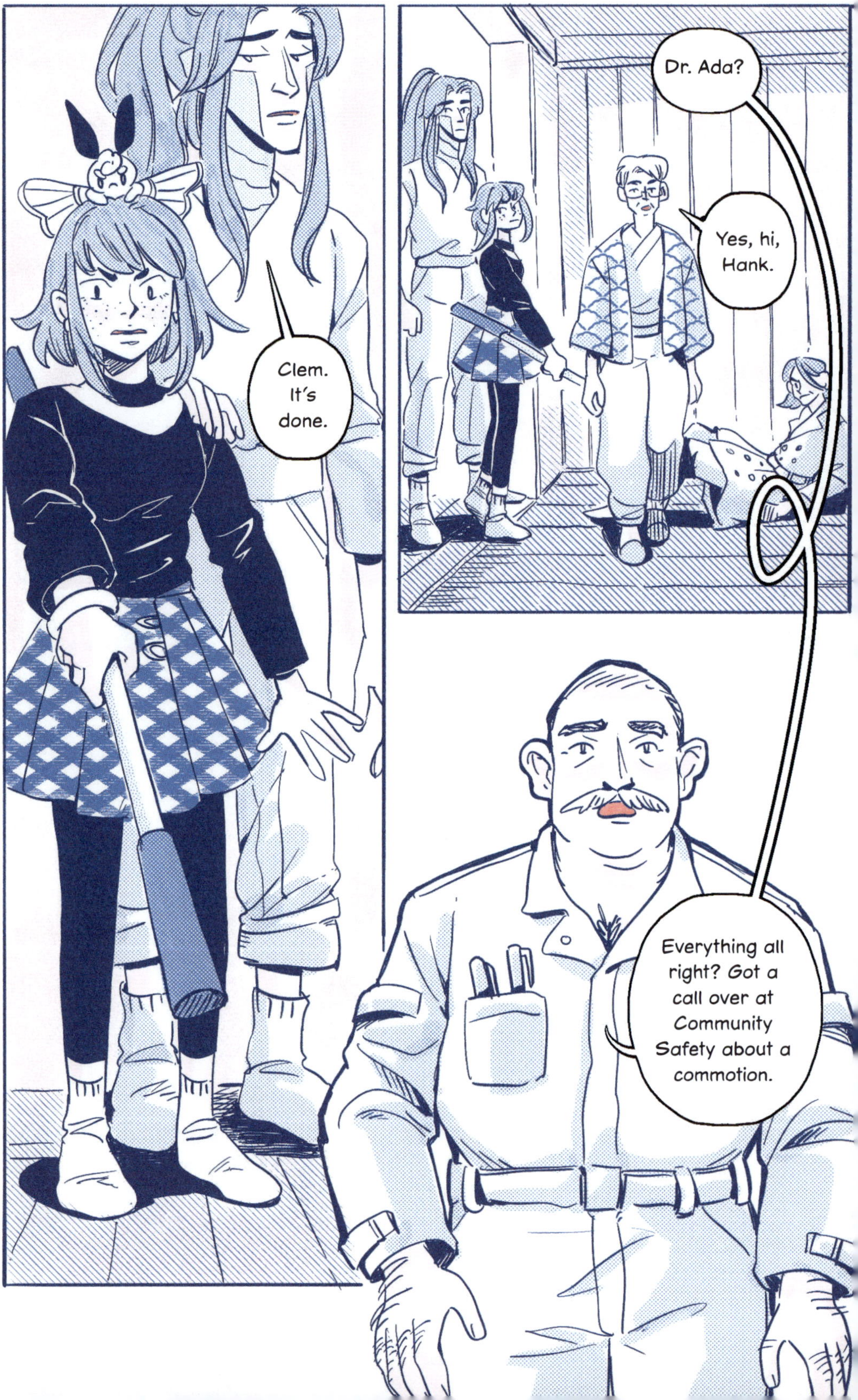
Clem. It's done.
Dr. Ada?
Yes, hi, Hank.
Everything all right? Got a call over at Community Safety about a commotion.

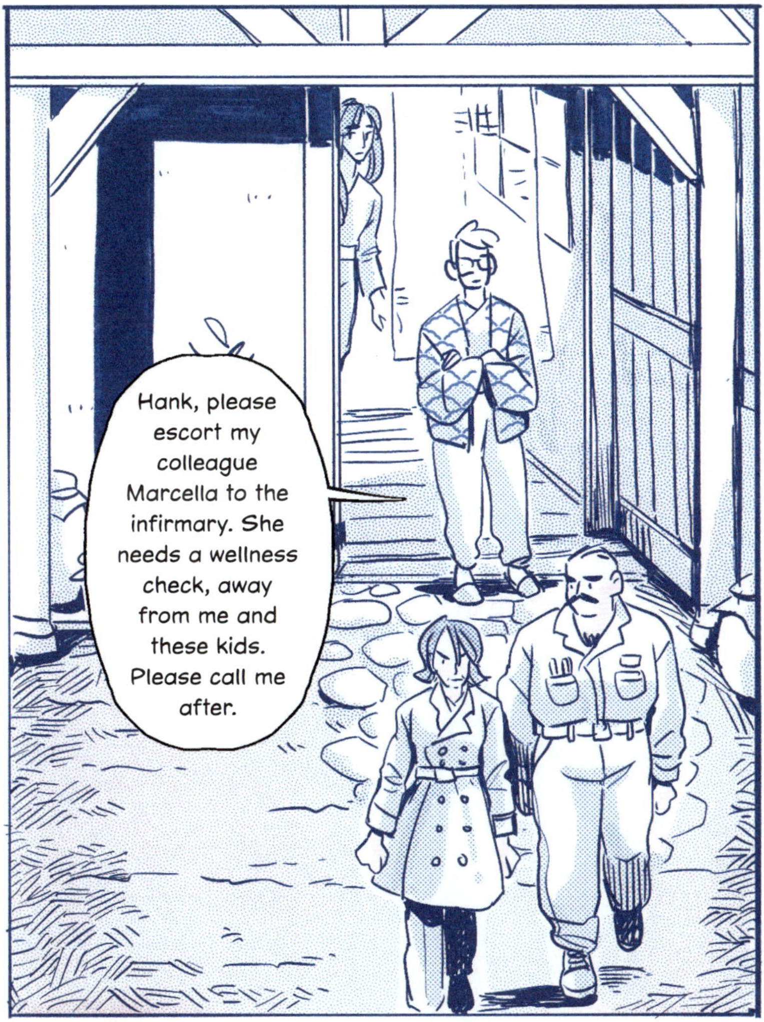
Hank, please escort my colleague Marcella to the infirmary. She needs a wellness check, away from me and these kids. Please call me after.

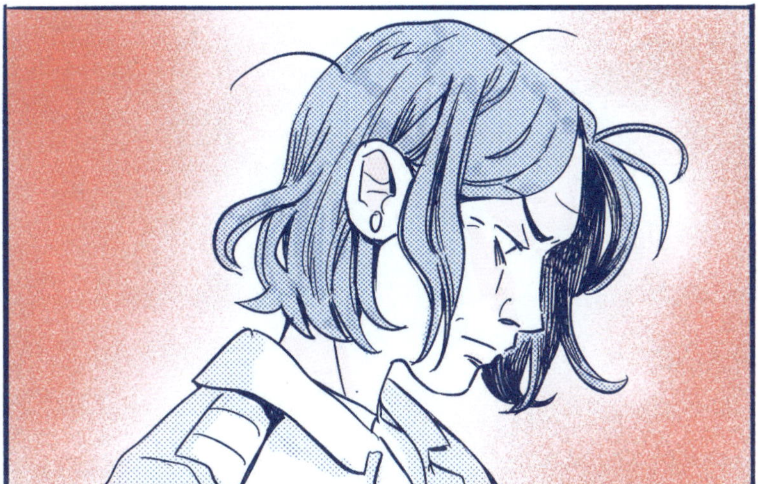

00110001 00110000

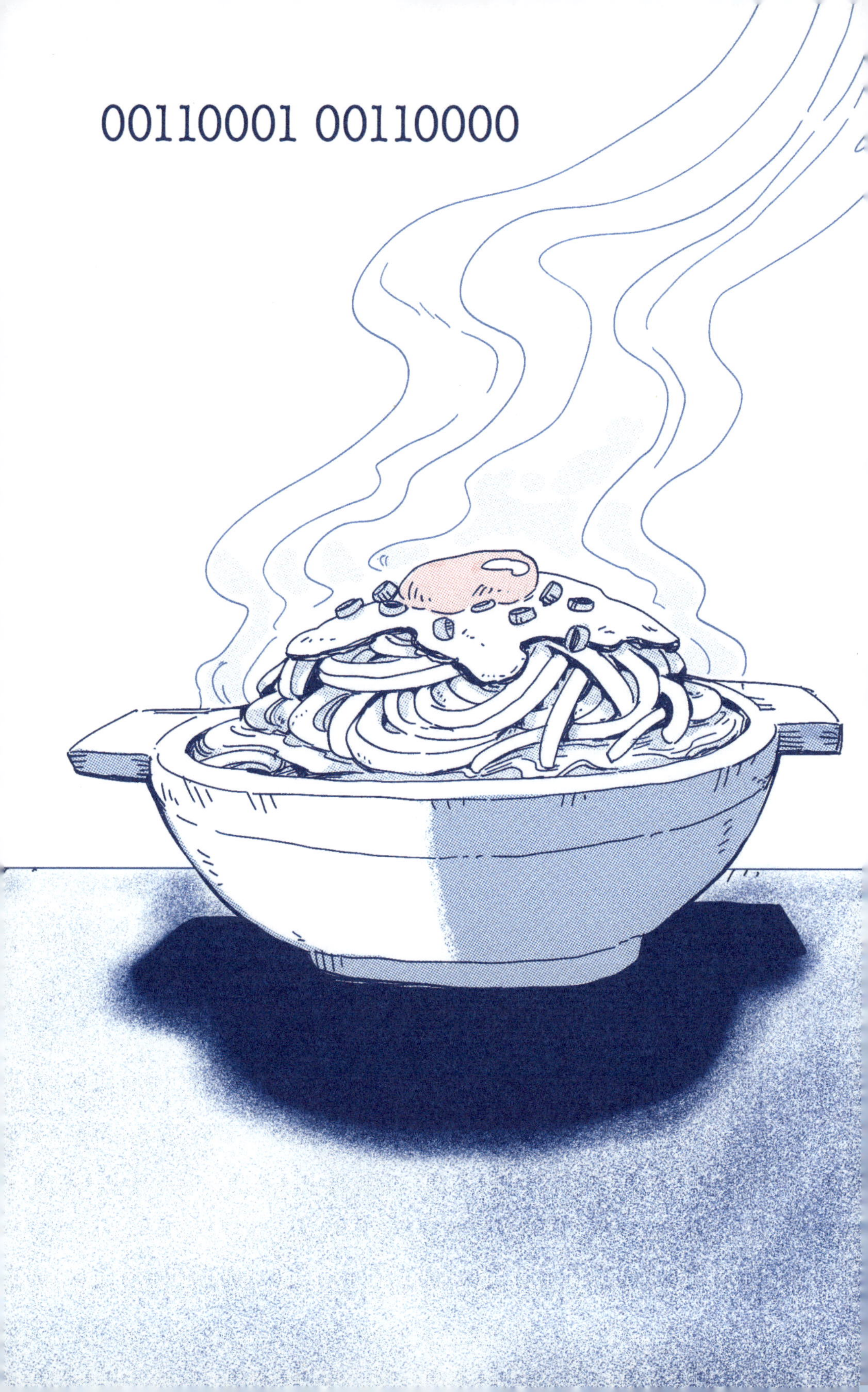

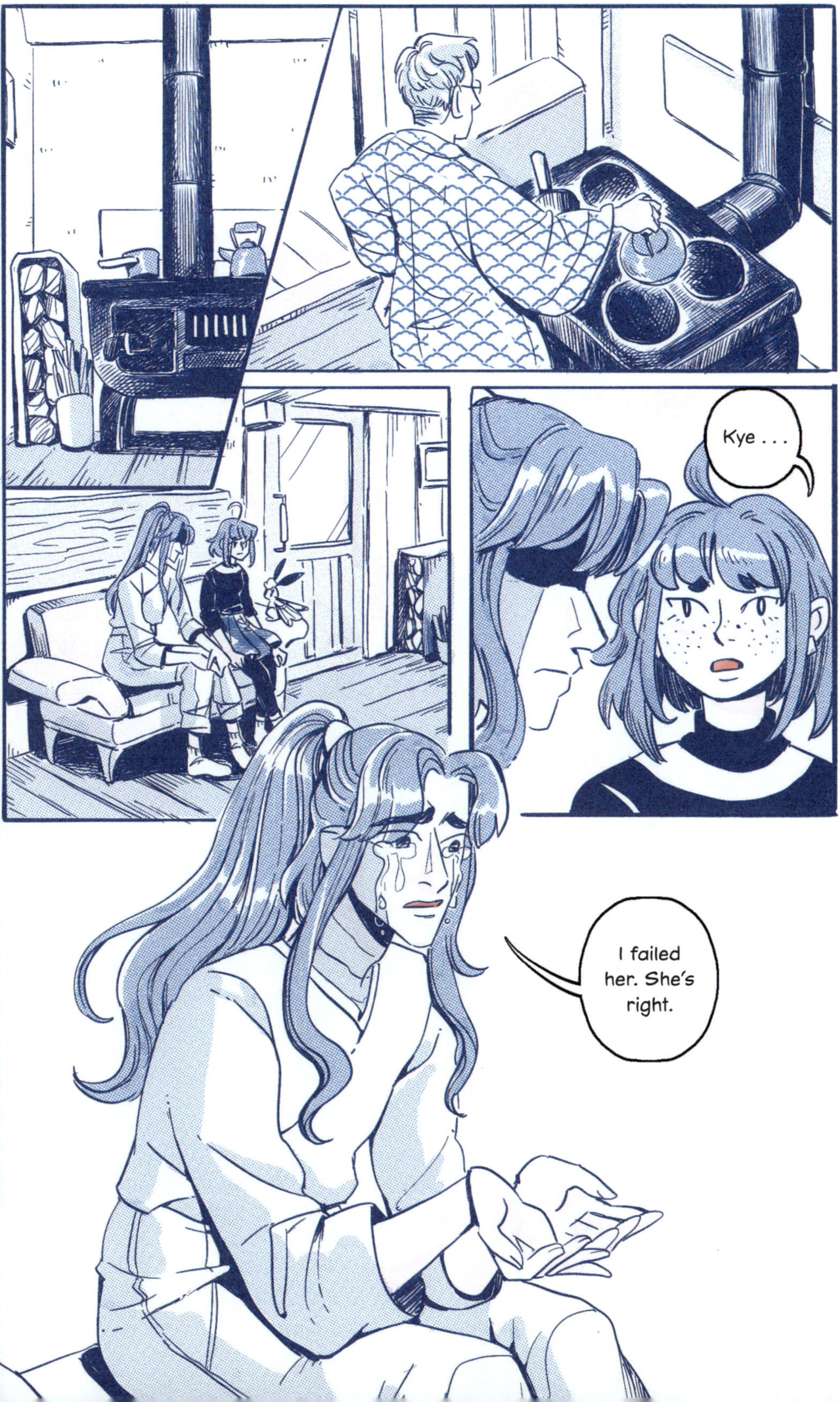
Kye . . .
I failed her. She's right.

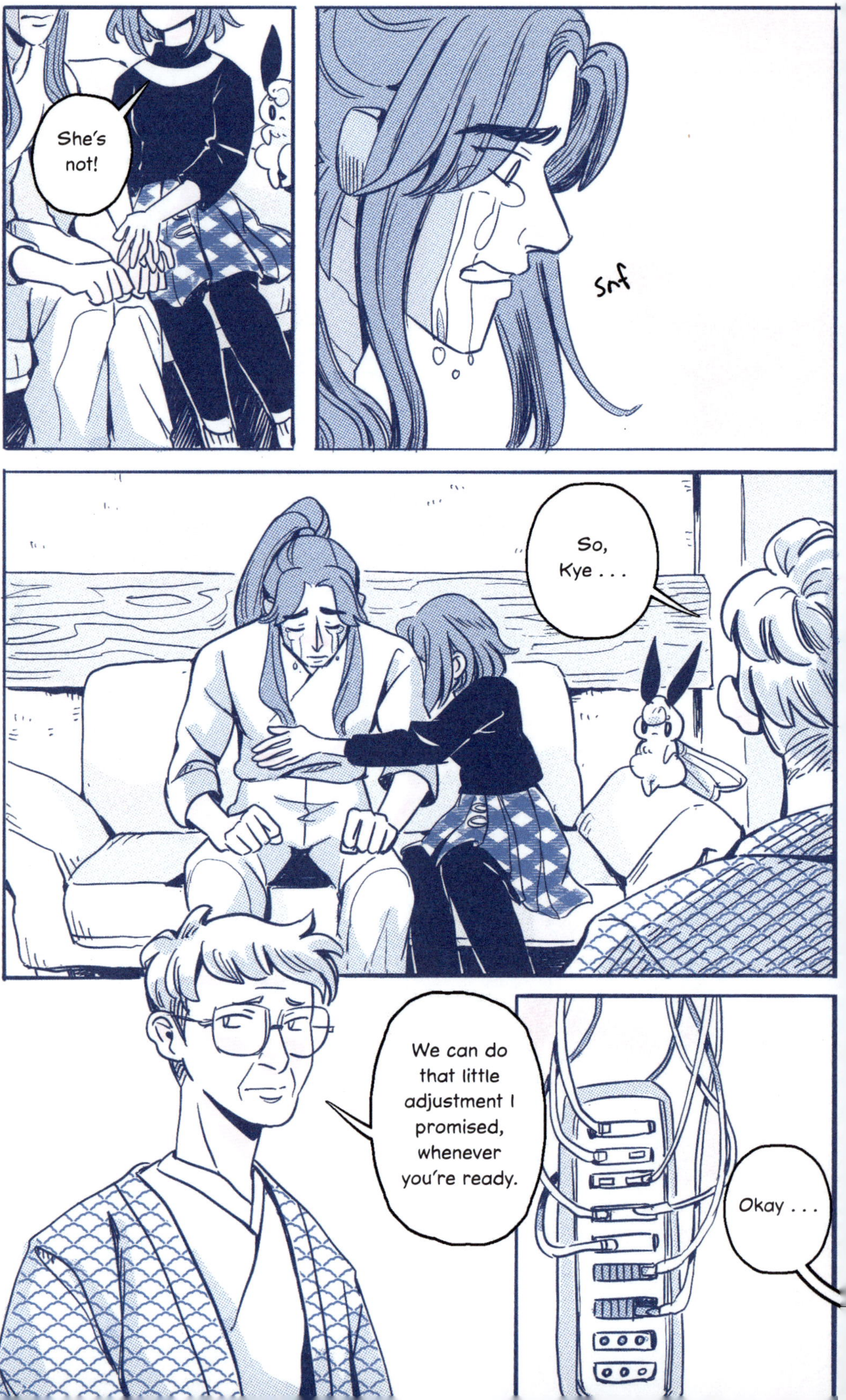
She's not!
Snf
So, Kye . . .
We can do that little adjustment I promised, whenever you're ready.
Okay . . .

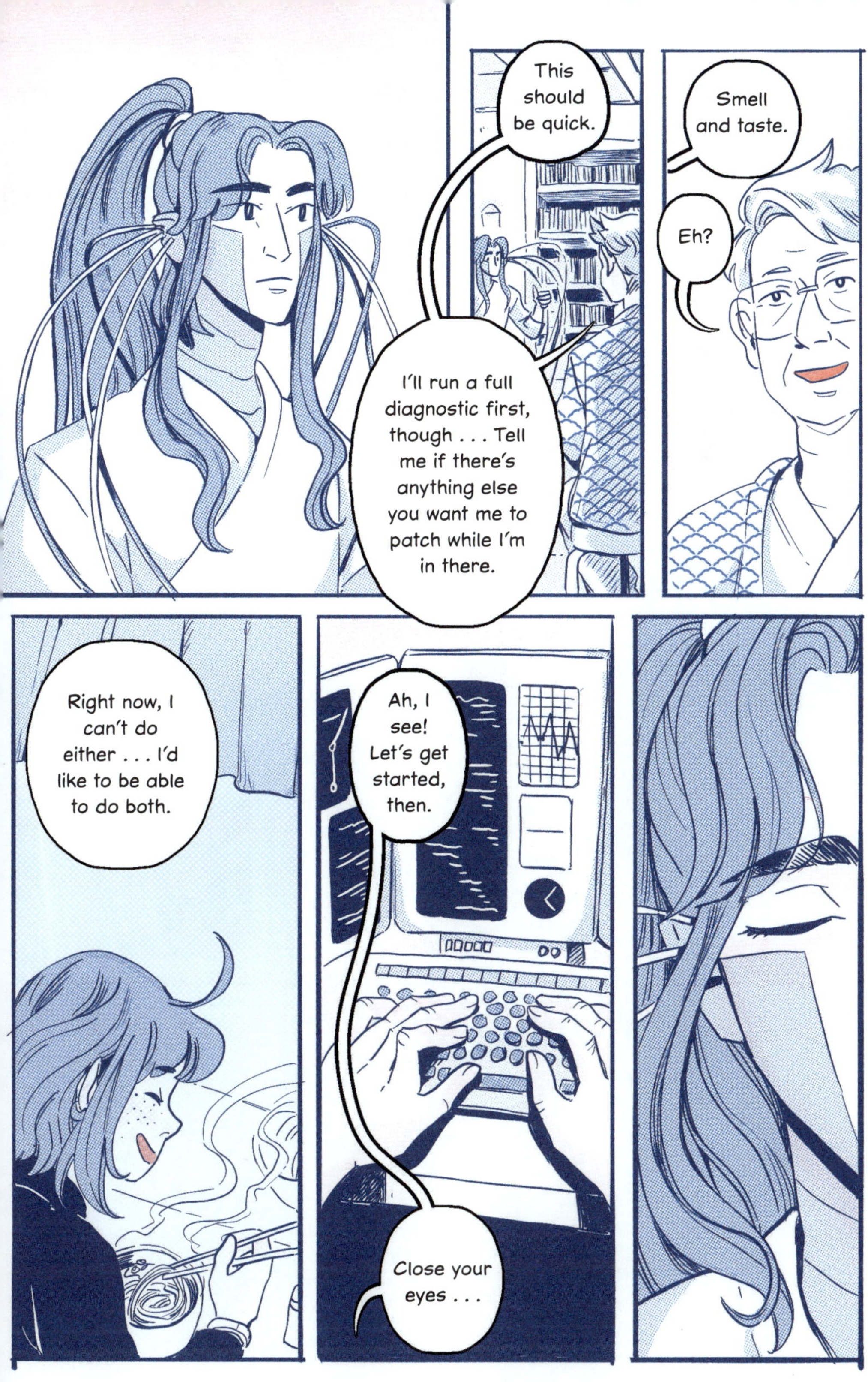
This should be quick.
I'll run a full diagnostic first, though . . . Tell me if there's anything else you want me to patch while I'm in there.
Smell and taste.
Eh?
Right now, I can't do either . . . I'd like to be able to do both.
Ah, I see! Let's get started, then.
Close your eyes . . .

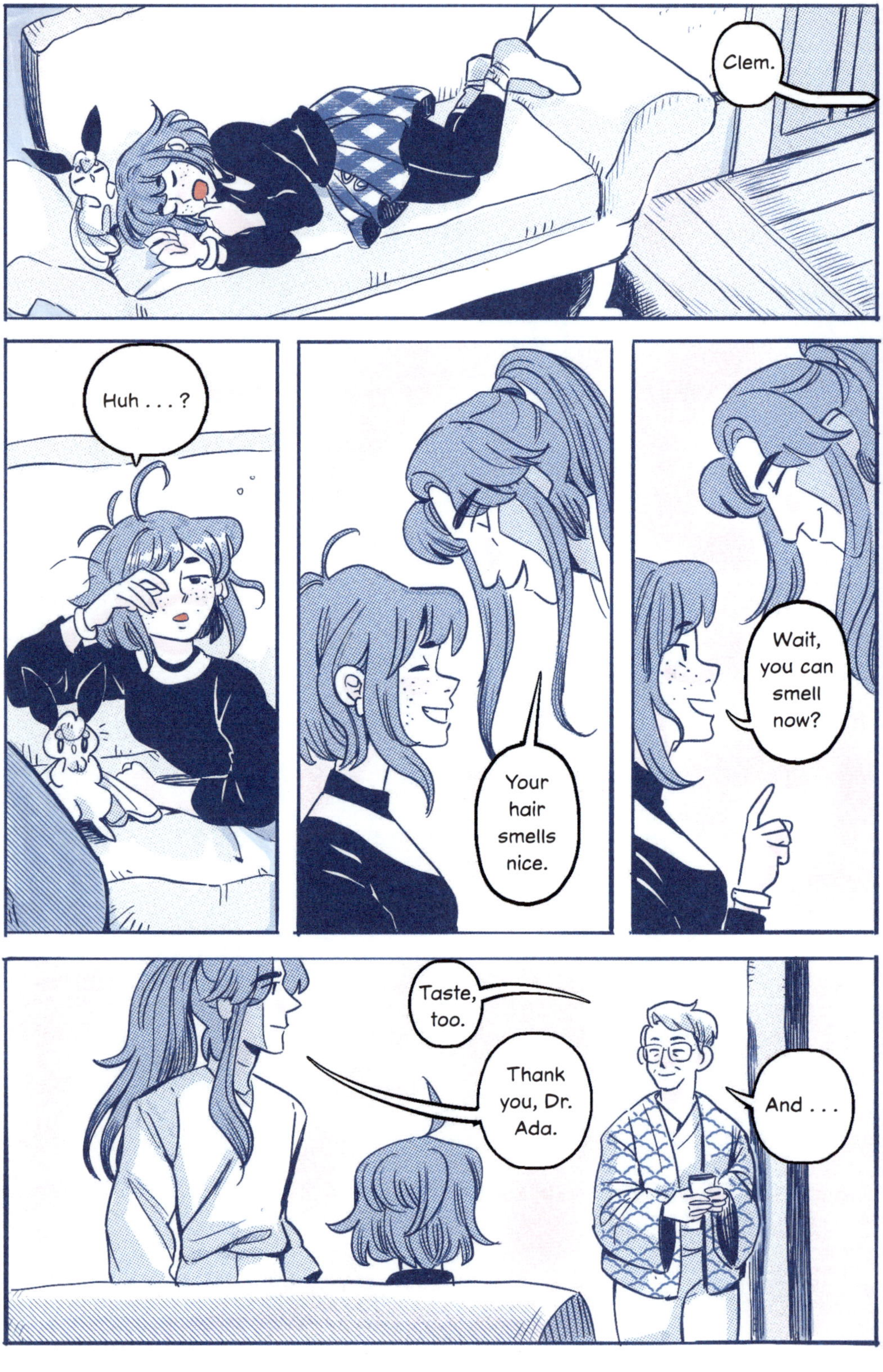
Clem.
Huh . . . ?
Your hair smells nice.
Wait, you can smell now?
Taste, too.
Thank you, Dr. Ada.
And . . .

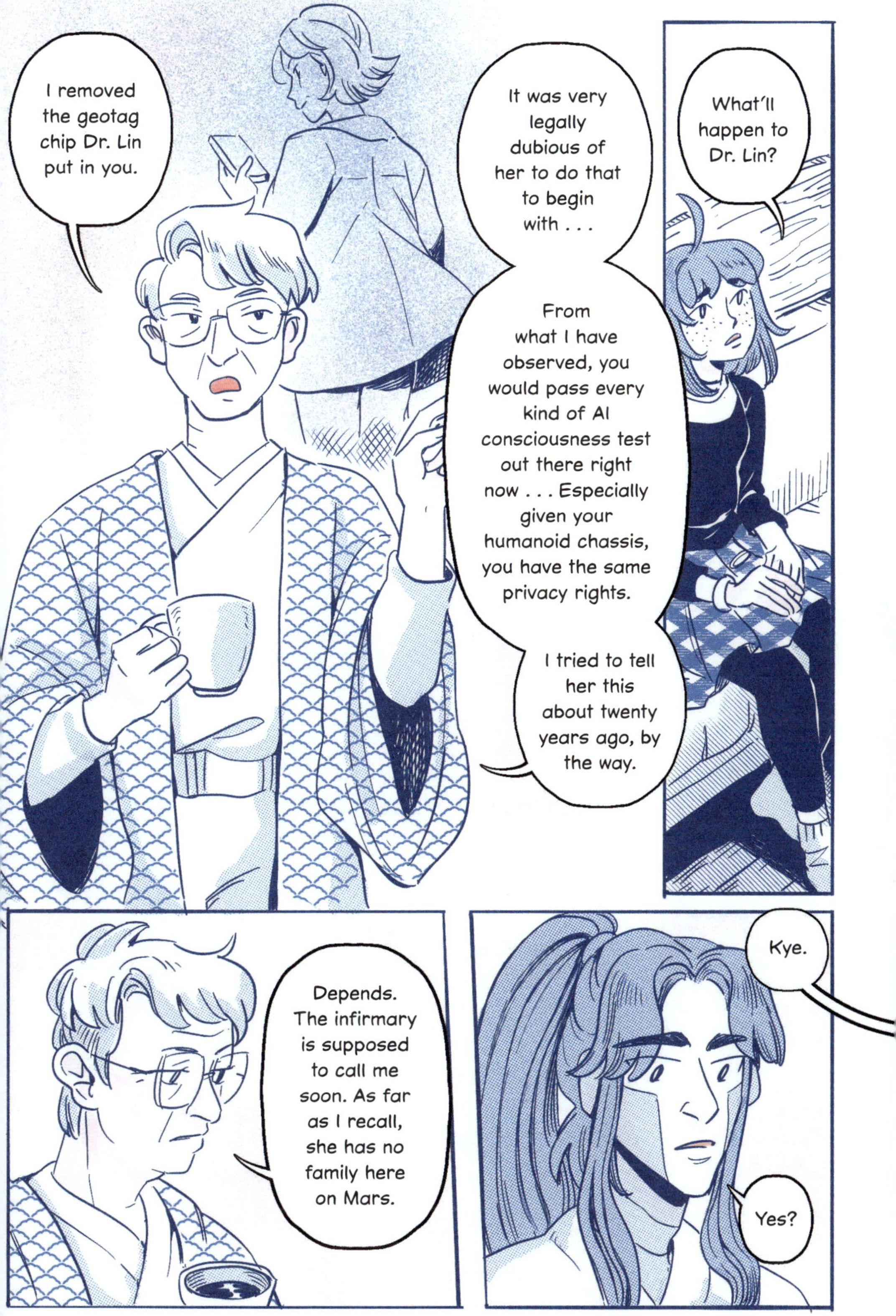
I removed the geotag chip Dr. Lin put in you.
It was very legally dubious of her to do that to begin with . . .
From what I have observed, you would pass every kind of AI consciousness test out there right now . . . Especially given your humanoid chassis, you have the same privacy rights.
I tried to tell her this about twenty years ago, by the way.
What'll happen to Dr. Lin?
Depends. The infirmary is supposed to call me soon. As far as I recall, she has no family here on Mars.
Kye.
Yes?

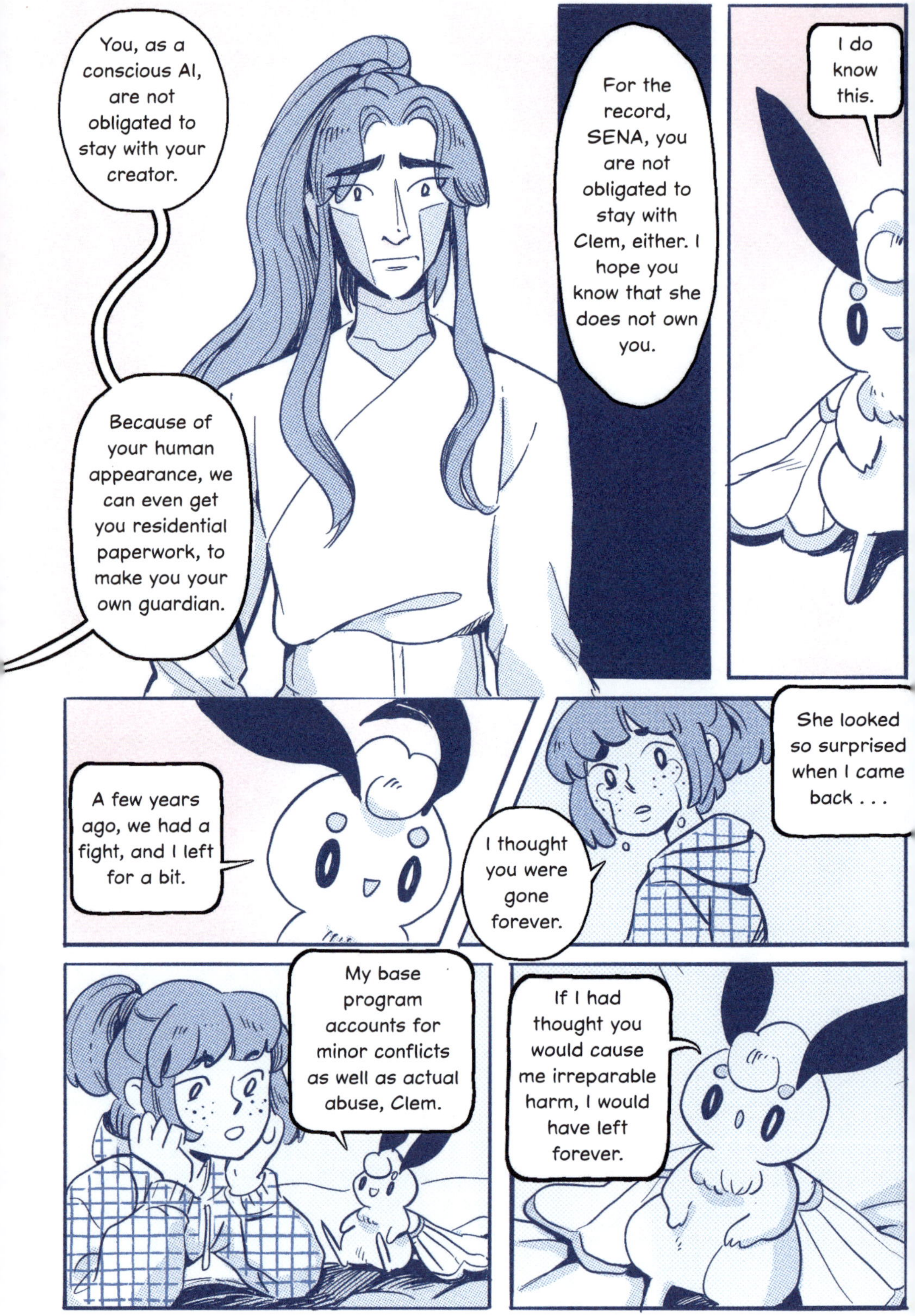
You, as a conscious AI, are not obligated to stay with your creator.
Because of your human appearance, we can even get you residential paperwork, to make you your own guardian.
For the record, SENA, you are not obligated to stay with Clem, either. I hope you know that she does not own you.
I do know this.
A few years ago, we had a fight, and I left for a bit.
She looked so surprised when I came back . . .
I thought you were gone forever.
My base program accounts for minor conflicts as well as actual abuse, Clem.
If I had thought you would cause me irreparable harm, I would have left forever.

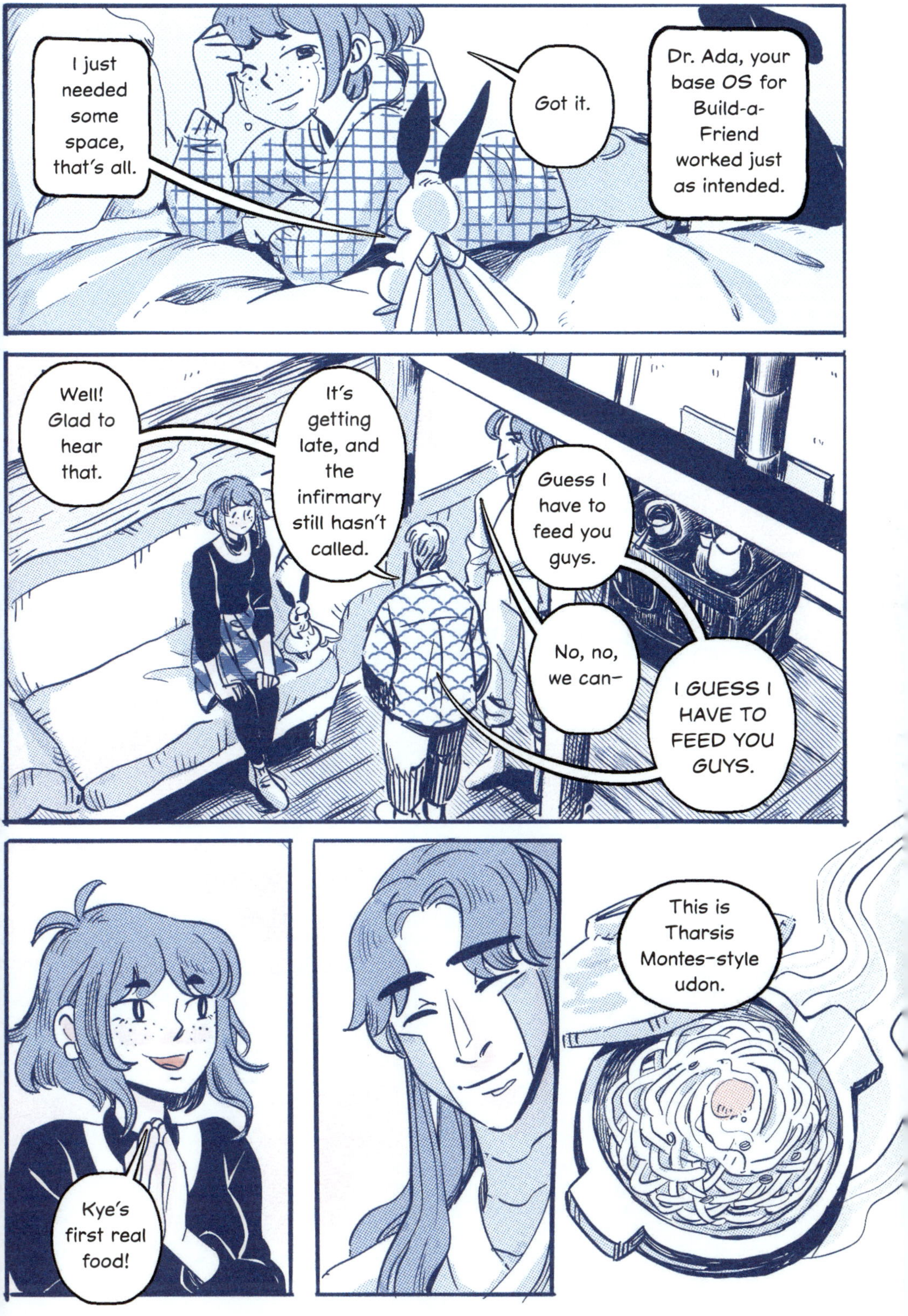
I just needed some space, that's all.
Got it.
Dr. Ada, your base OS for Build-a-Friend worked just as intended.
Well! Glad to hear that.
It's getting late, and the infirmary still hasn't called.
Guess I have to feed you guys.
No, no, we can-
I GUESS I HAVE TO FEED YOU GUYS.
Kye's first real food!
This is Tharsis Montes-style udon.

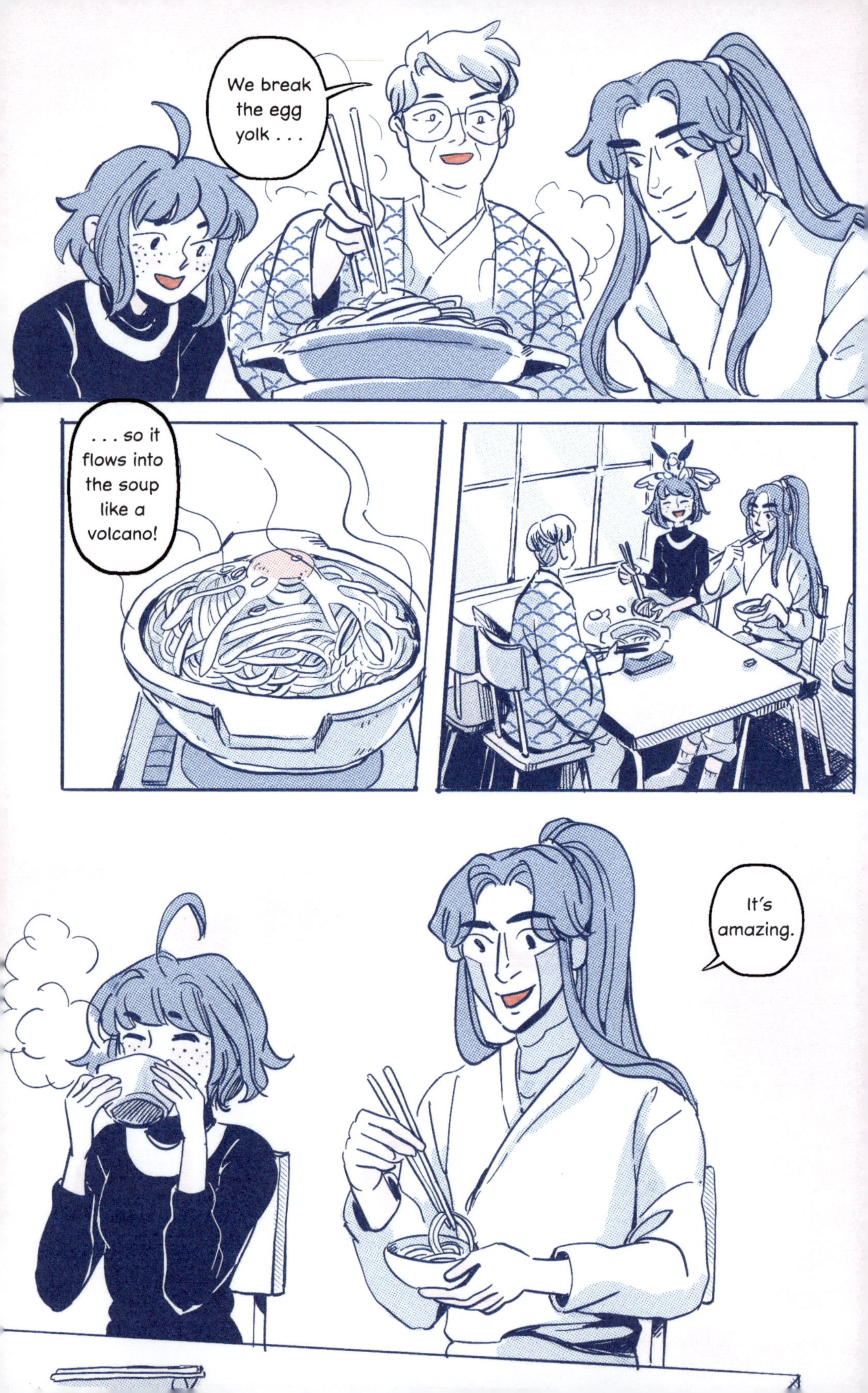
We break the egg yolk . . .
. . . so it flows into the soup like a volcano!
It's amazing.

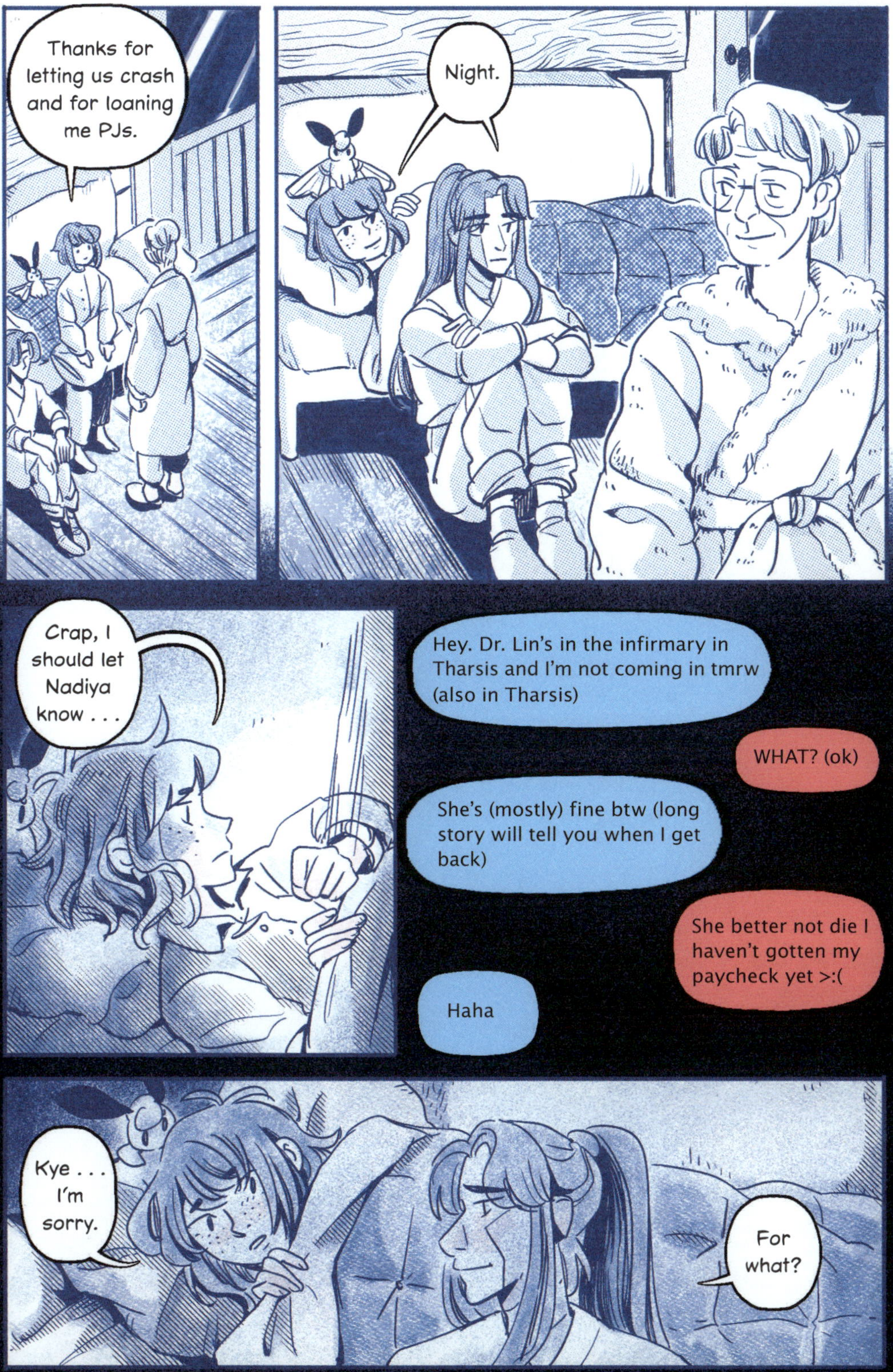
Thanks for letting us crash and for loaning me PJs.
Night.
Crap, I should let Nadiya know . . .
Hey. Dr. Lin's in the infirmary in Tharsis and I'm not coming in tmrw (also in Tharsis)
WHAT? (ok)
She's (mostly) fine btw (long story will tell you when I get back)
She better not die I haven't gotten my paycheck yet >:(
Haha
Kye . . . I'm sorry.
For what?

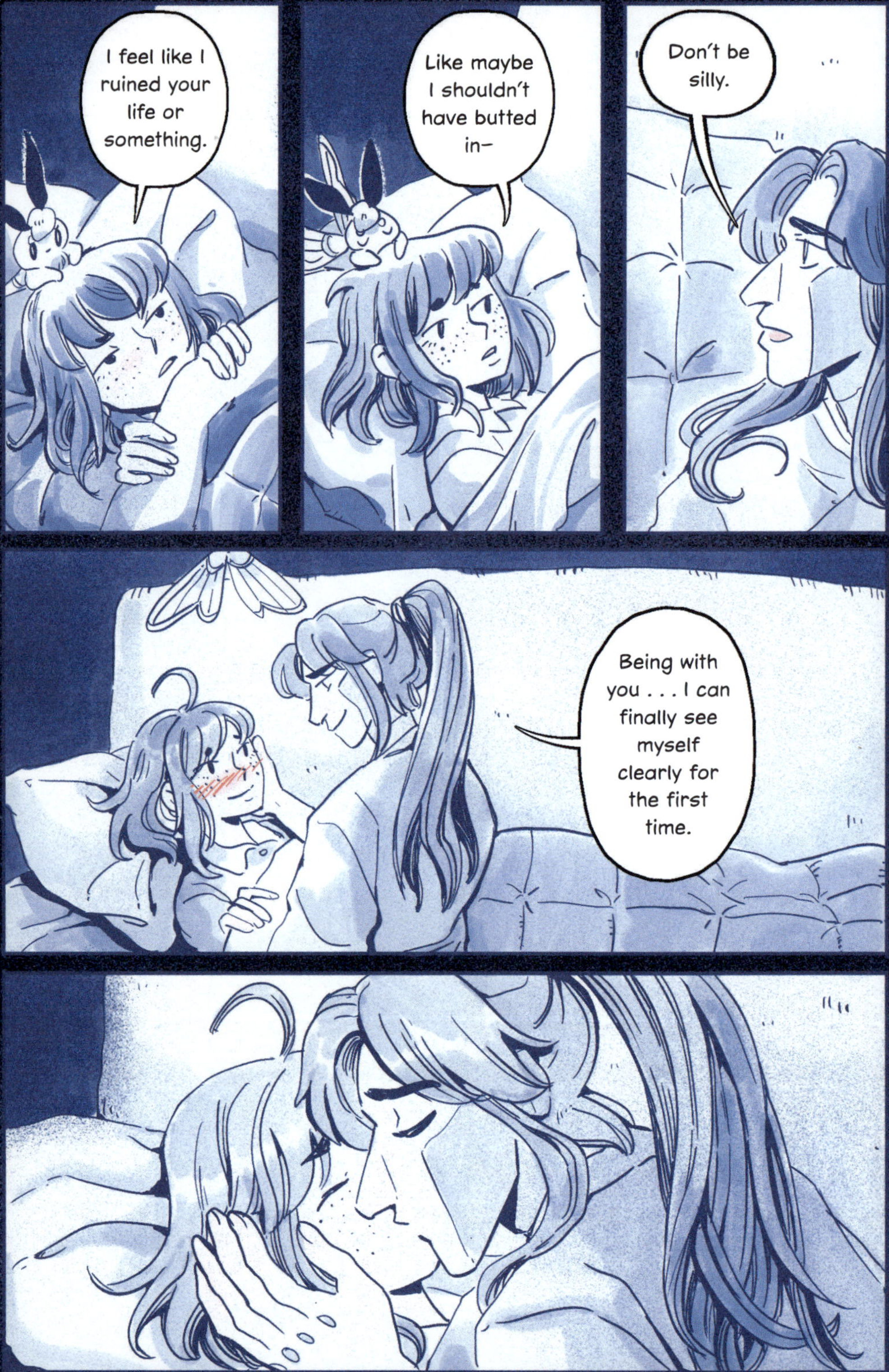
I feel like I ruined your life or something.
Like maybe I shouldn't have butted in–
Don't be silly.
Being with you . . . I can finally see myself clearly for the first time.

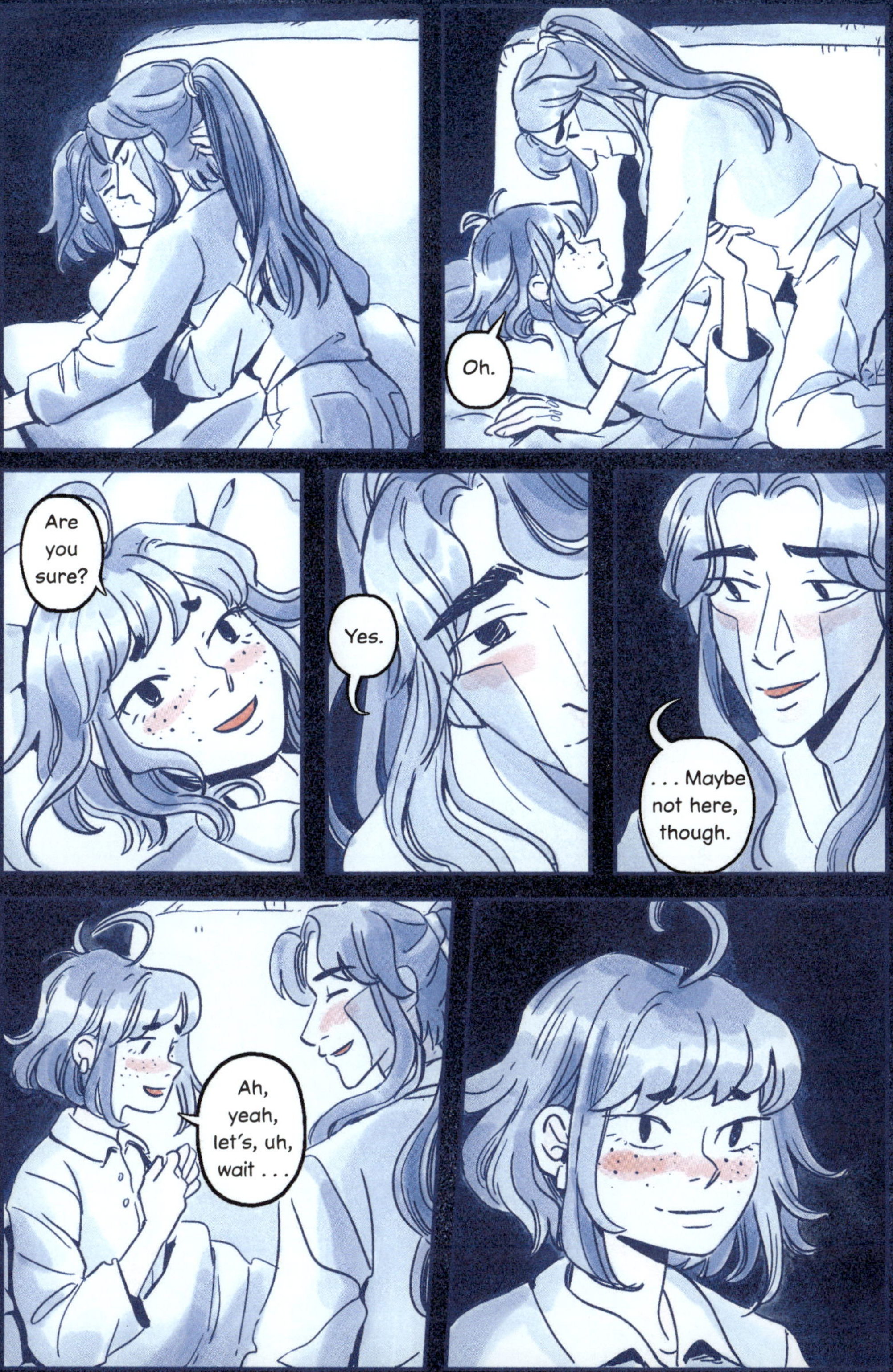
Oh.
Are you sure?
Yes.
. . . Maybe not here, though.
Ah, yeah, let's, uh, wait . . .

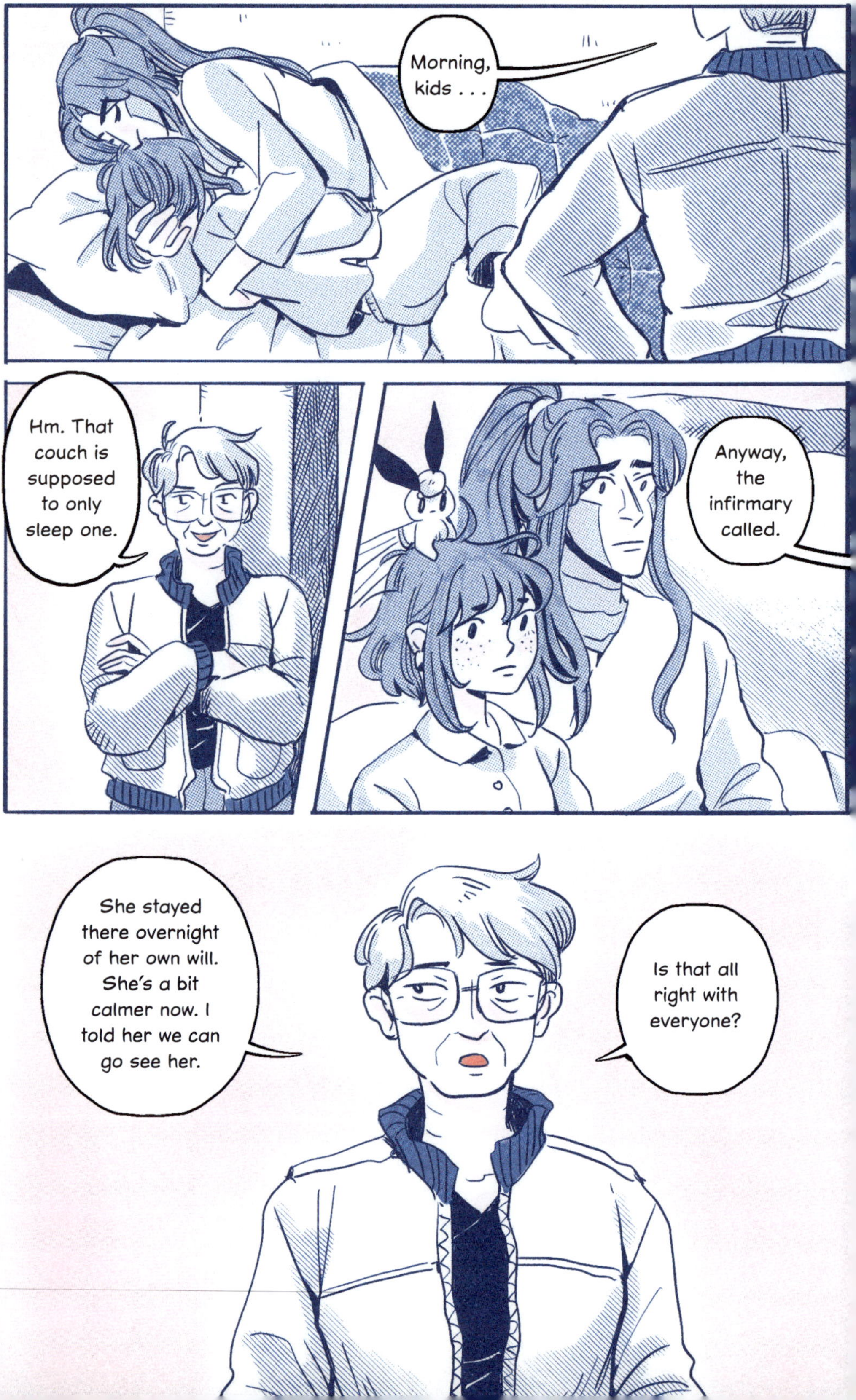

Morning, kids . . .
Hm. That couch is supposed to only sleep one.
Anyway, the infirmary called.
She stayed there overnight of her own will. She's a bit calmer now. I told her we can go see her.
Is that all right with everyone?

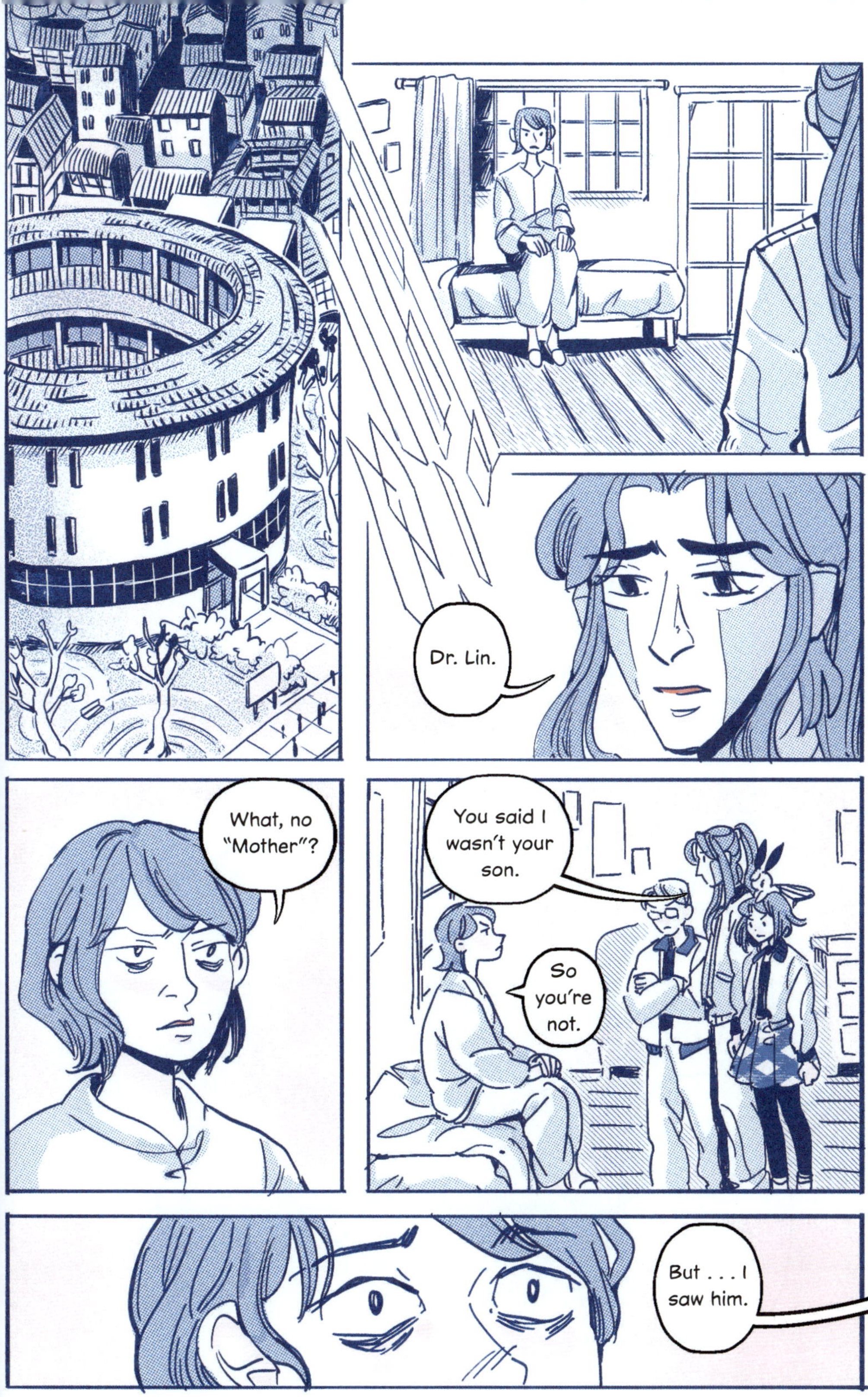
Dr. Lin.
What, no "Mother"?
You said I wasn't your son.
So you're not.
But . . . I saw him.

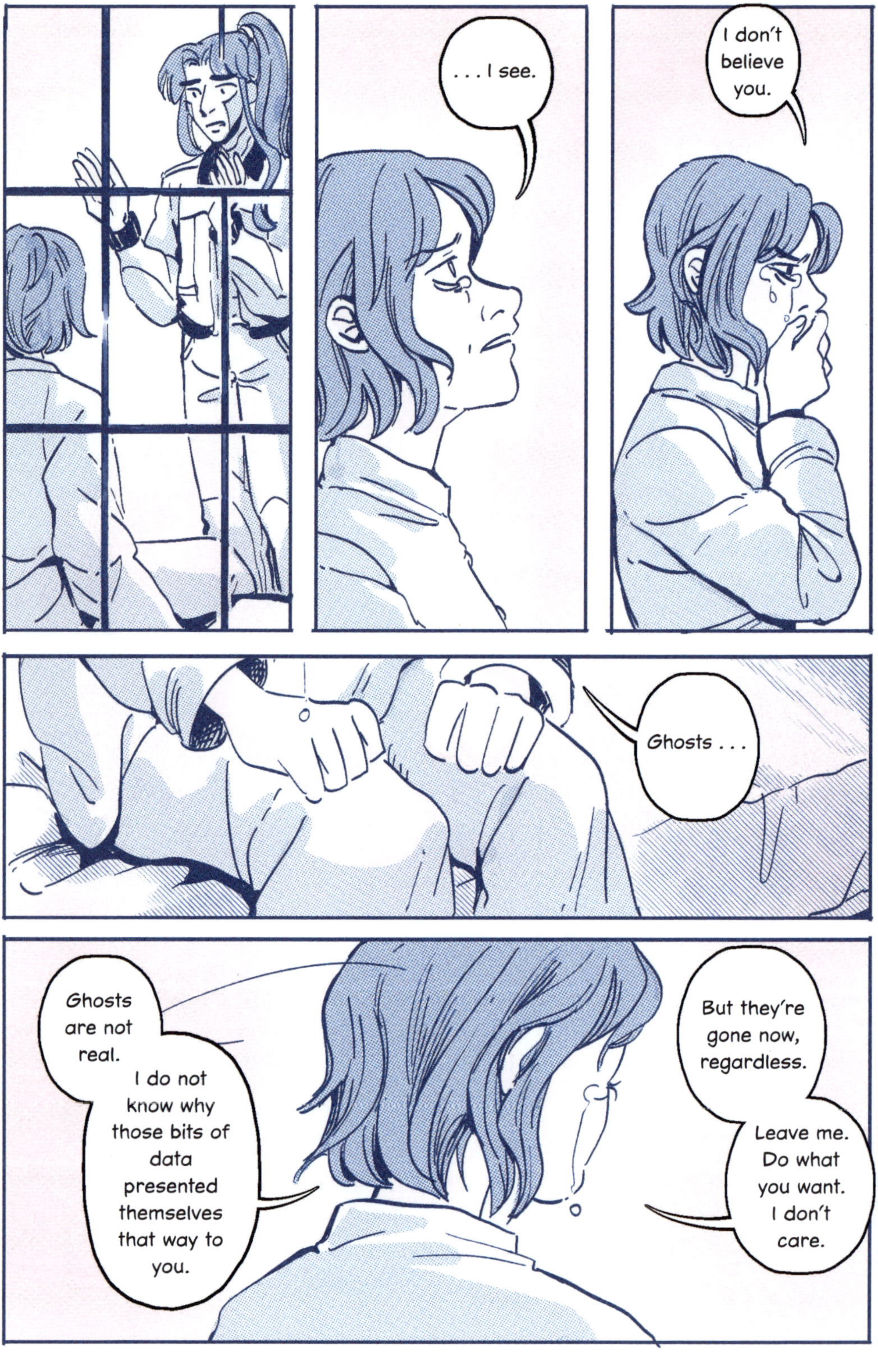
. . . I see.
I don't believe you.
Ghosts . . .
Ghosts are not real.
I do not know why those bits of data presented themselves that way to you.
But they're gone now, regardless.
Leave me. Do what you want. I don't care.

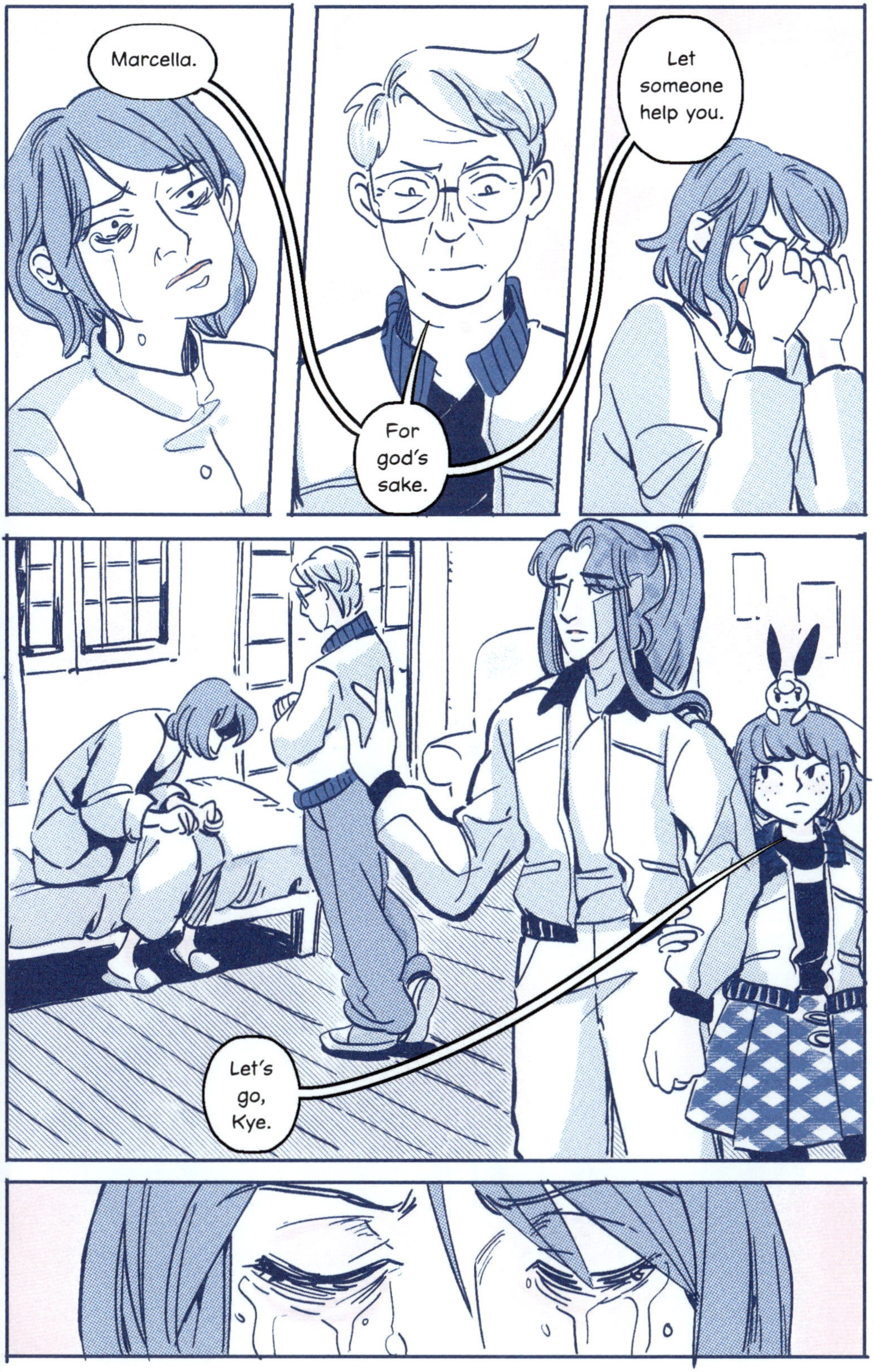
Marcella.
For god's sake.
Let someone help you.
Let's go, Kye.

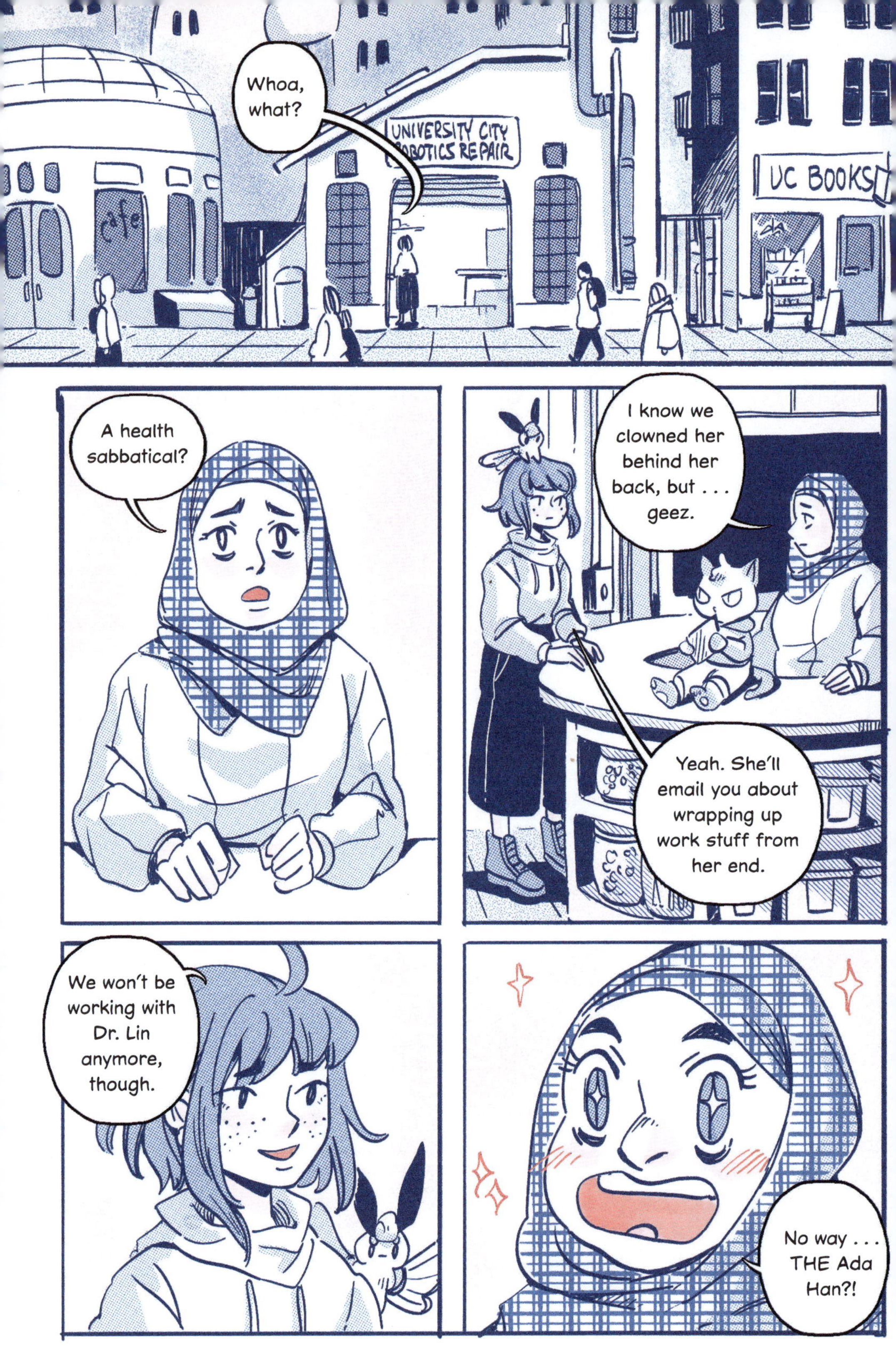
UNIVERSITY CITY ROBOTICS REPAIR
cafe
UC BOOKS
Whoa, what?
A health sabbatical?
I know we clowned her behind her back, but . . . geez.
Yeah. She'll email you about wrapping up work stuff from her end.
We won't be working with Dr. Lin anymore, though.
No way . . . THE Ada Han?!

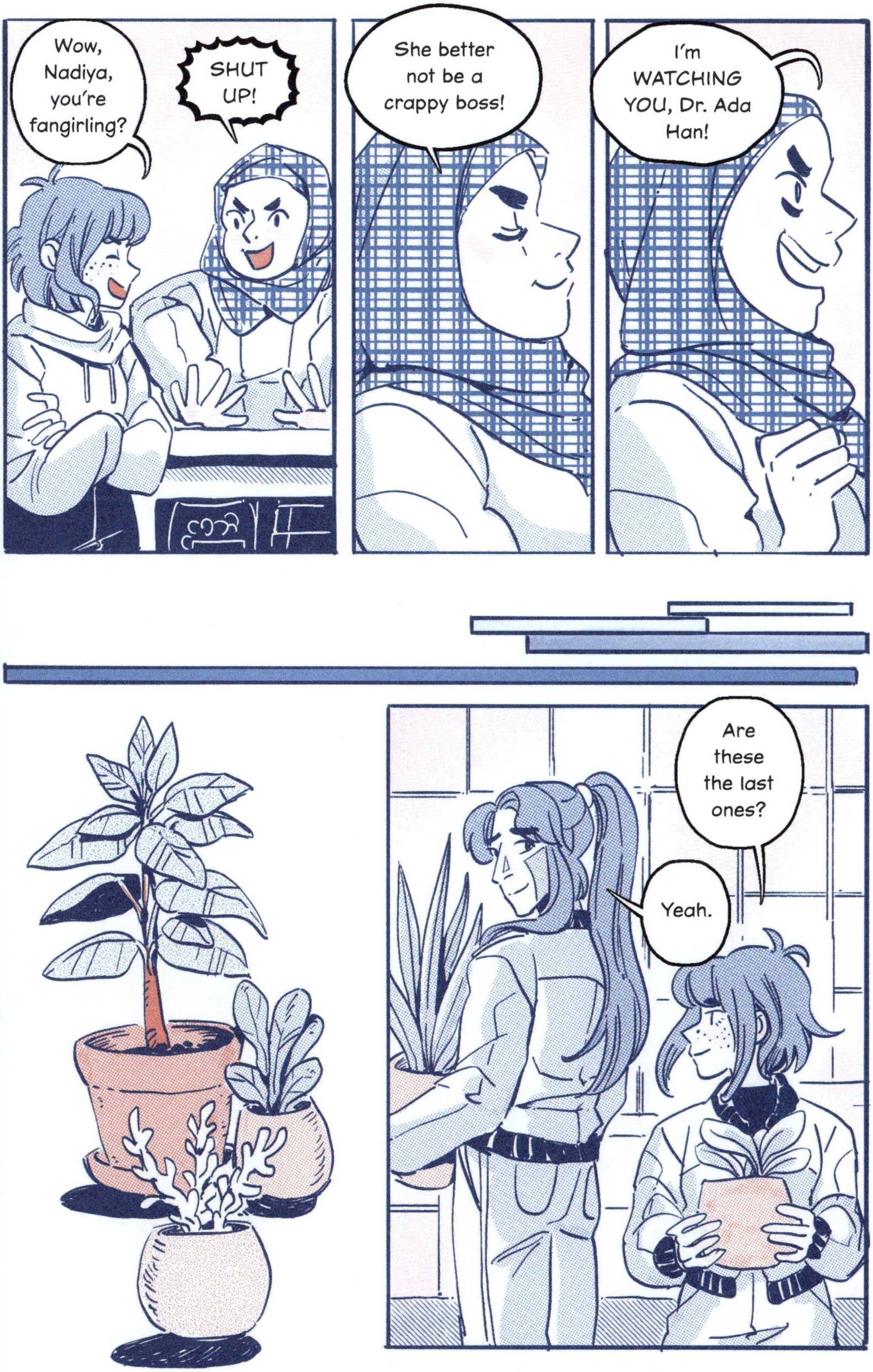
Wow, Nadiya, you're fangirling?
SHUT UP!
She better not be a crappy boss!
I'm WATCHING YOU, Dr. Ada Han!
Are these the last ones?
Yeah.

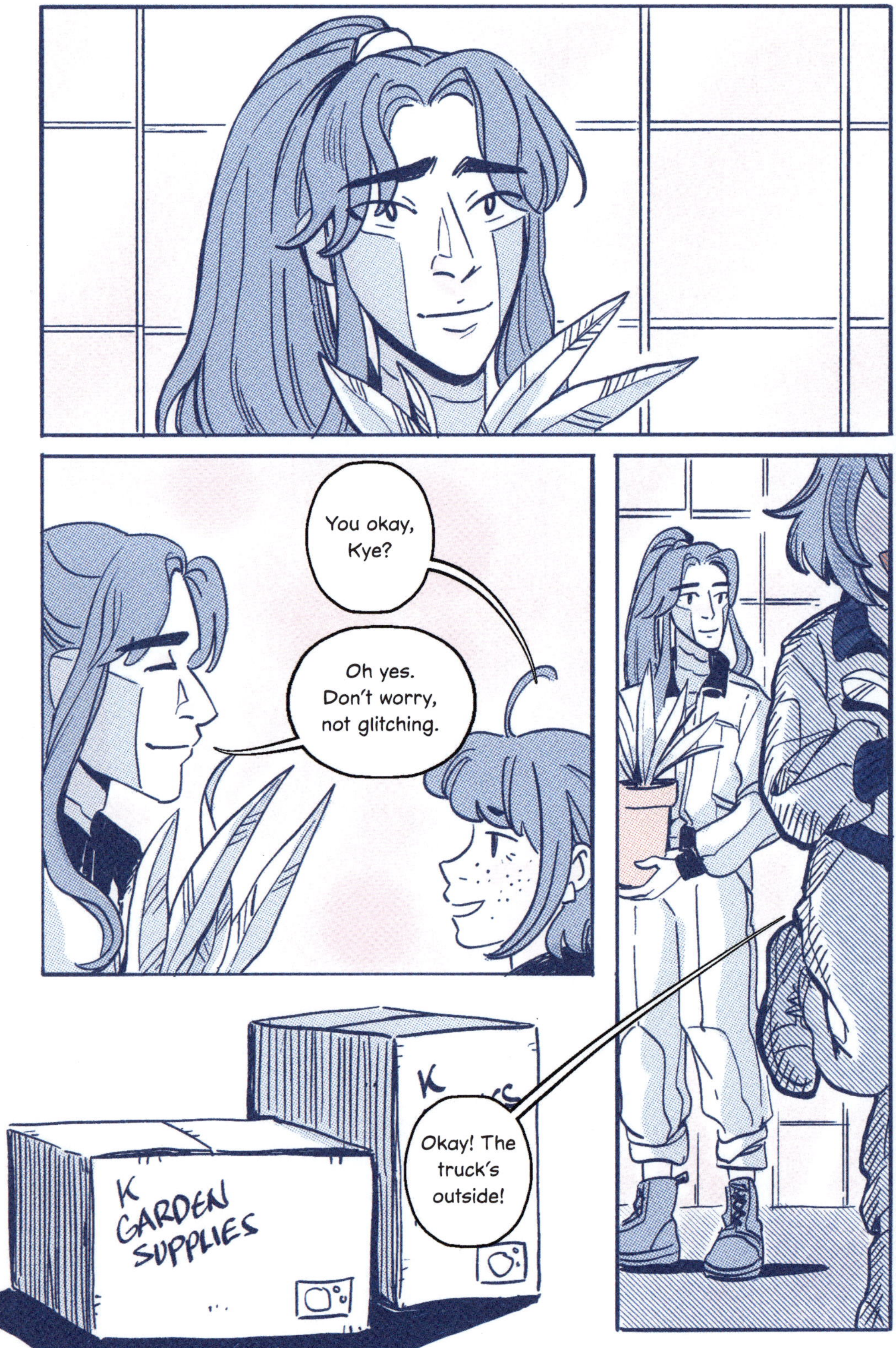
You okay, Kye?
Oh yes. Don't worry, not glitching.
Okay! The truck's outside!
K GARDEN SUPPLIES

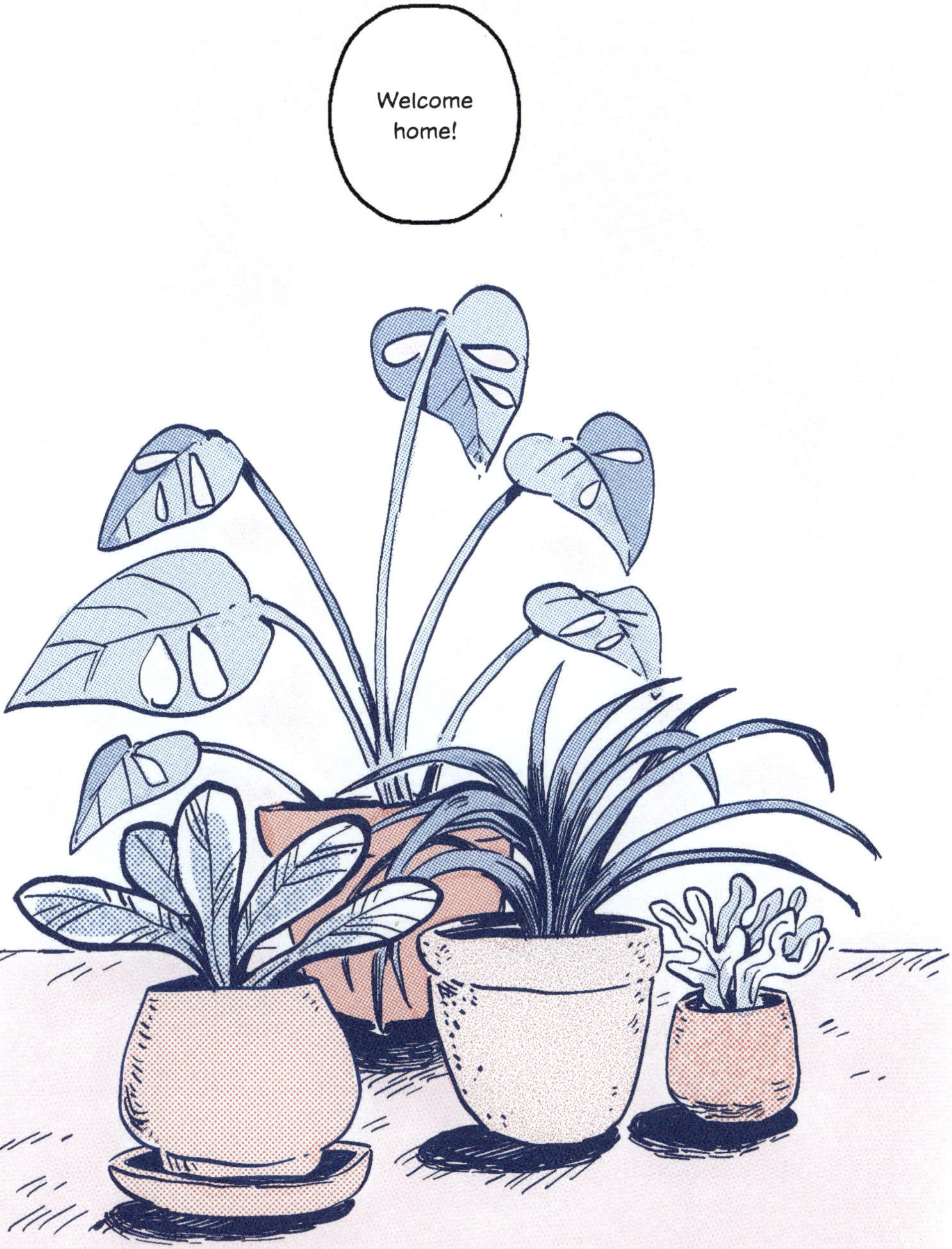
Welcome home!

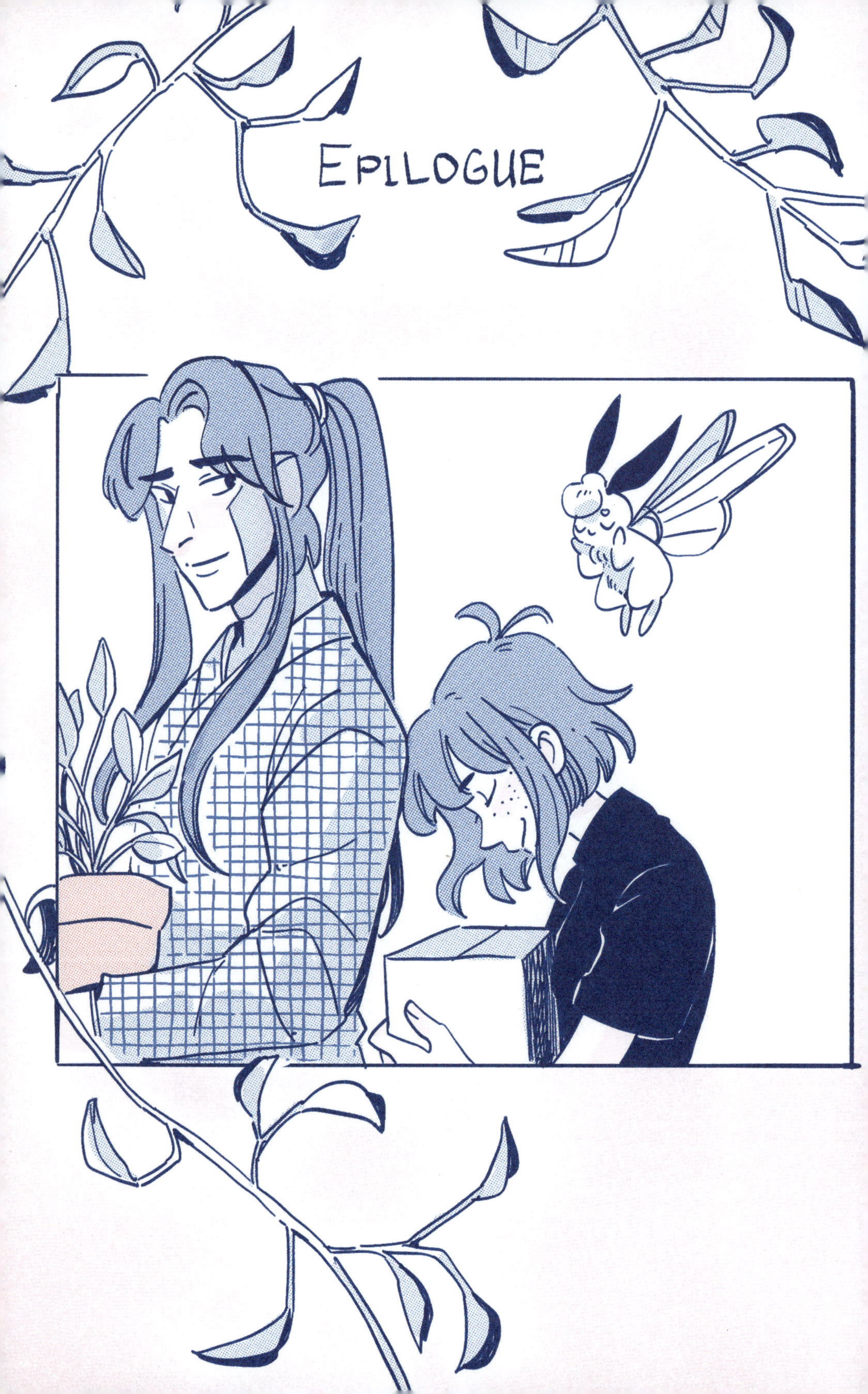
EPILOGUE

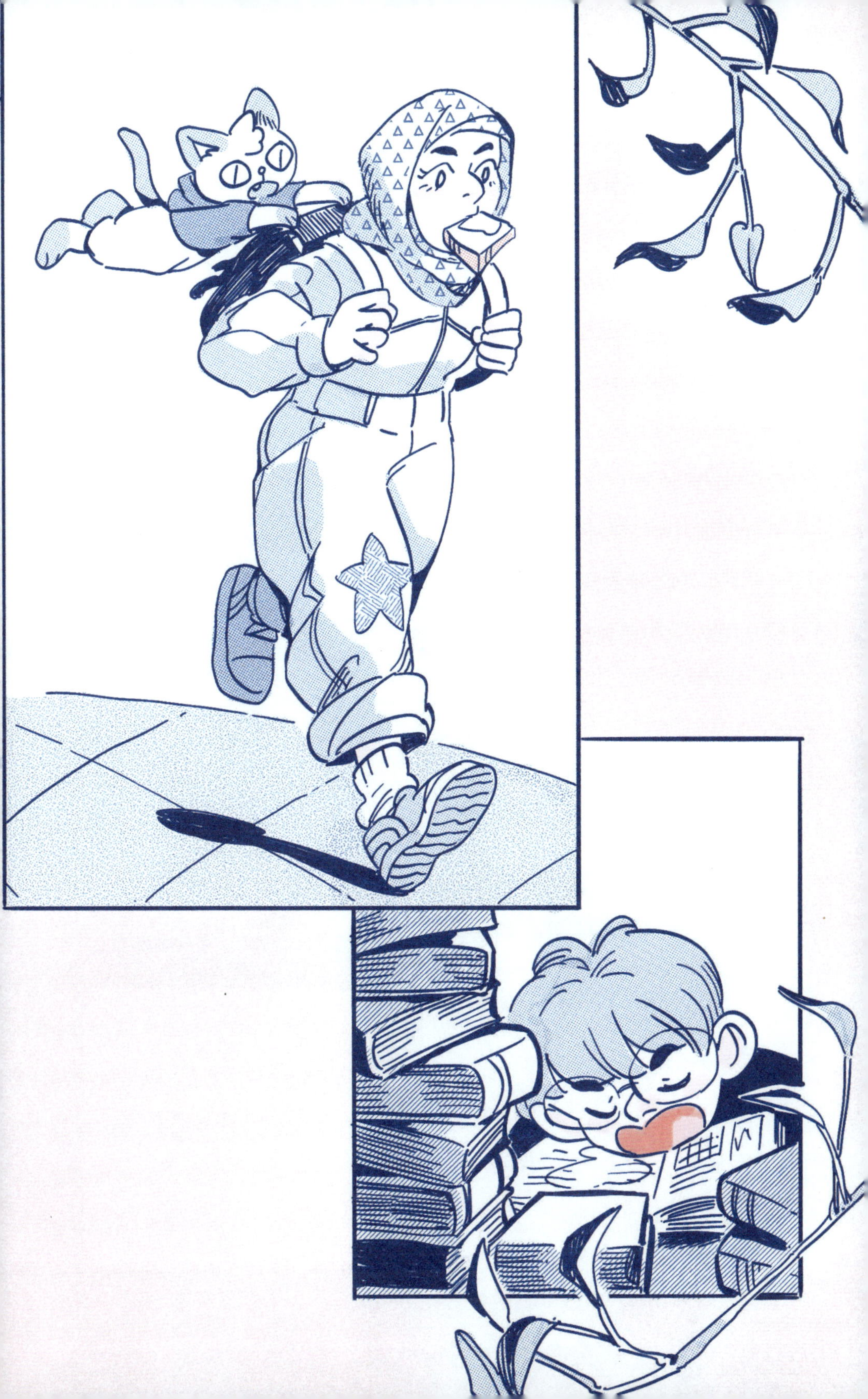

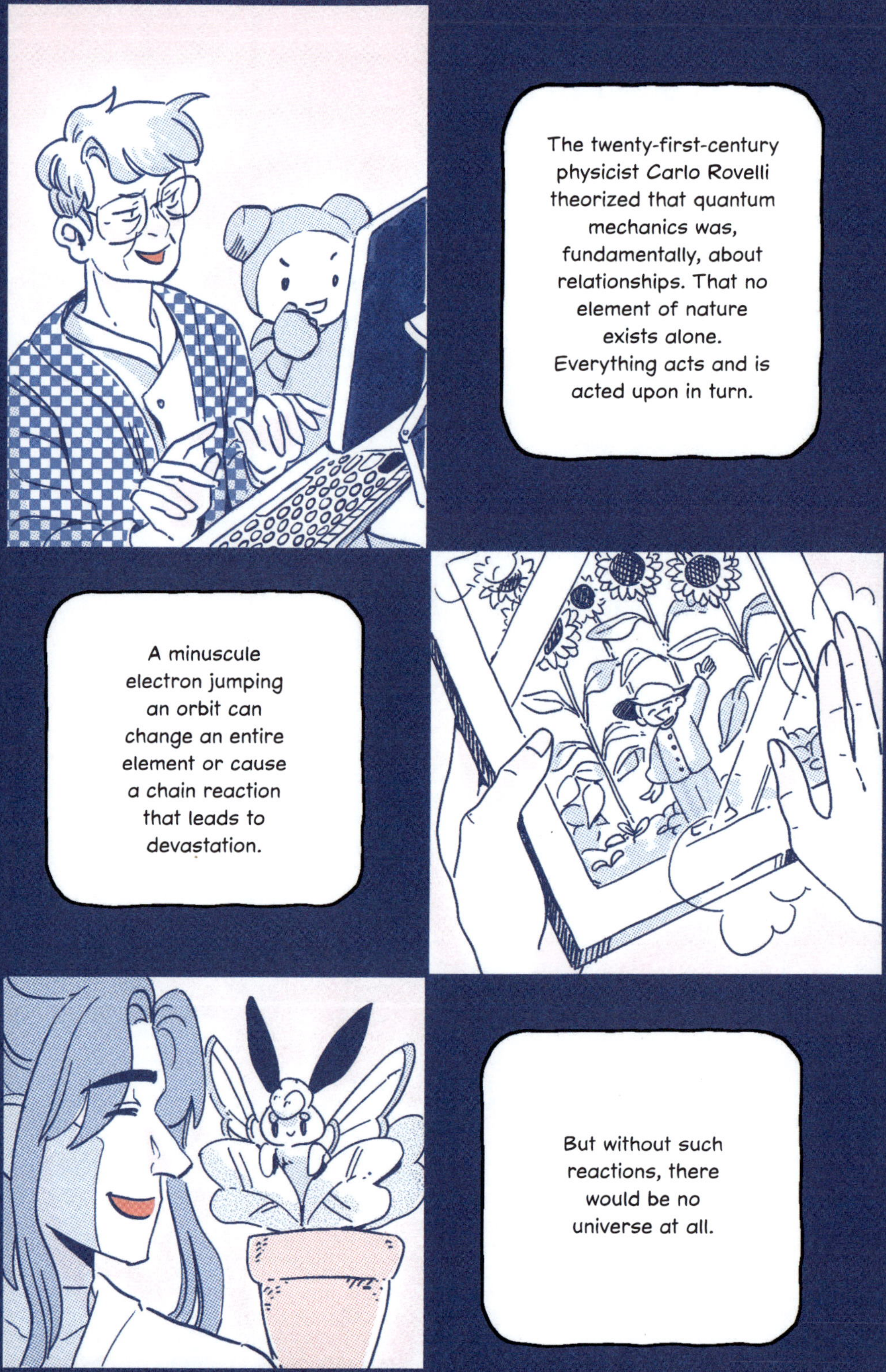
The twenty-first-century physicist Carlo Rovelli theorized that quantum mechanics was, fundamentally, about relationships. That no element of nature exists alone. Everything acts and is acted upon in turn.
A minuscule electron jumping an orbit can change an entire element or cause a chain reaction that leads to devastation.
But without such reactions, there would be no universe at all.

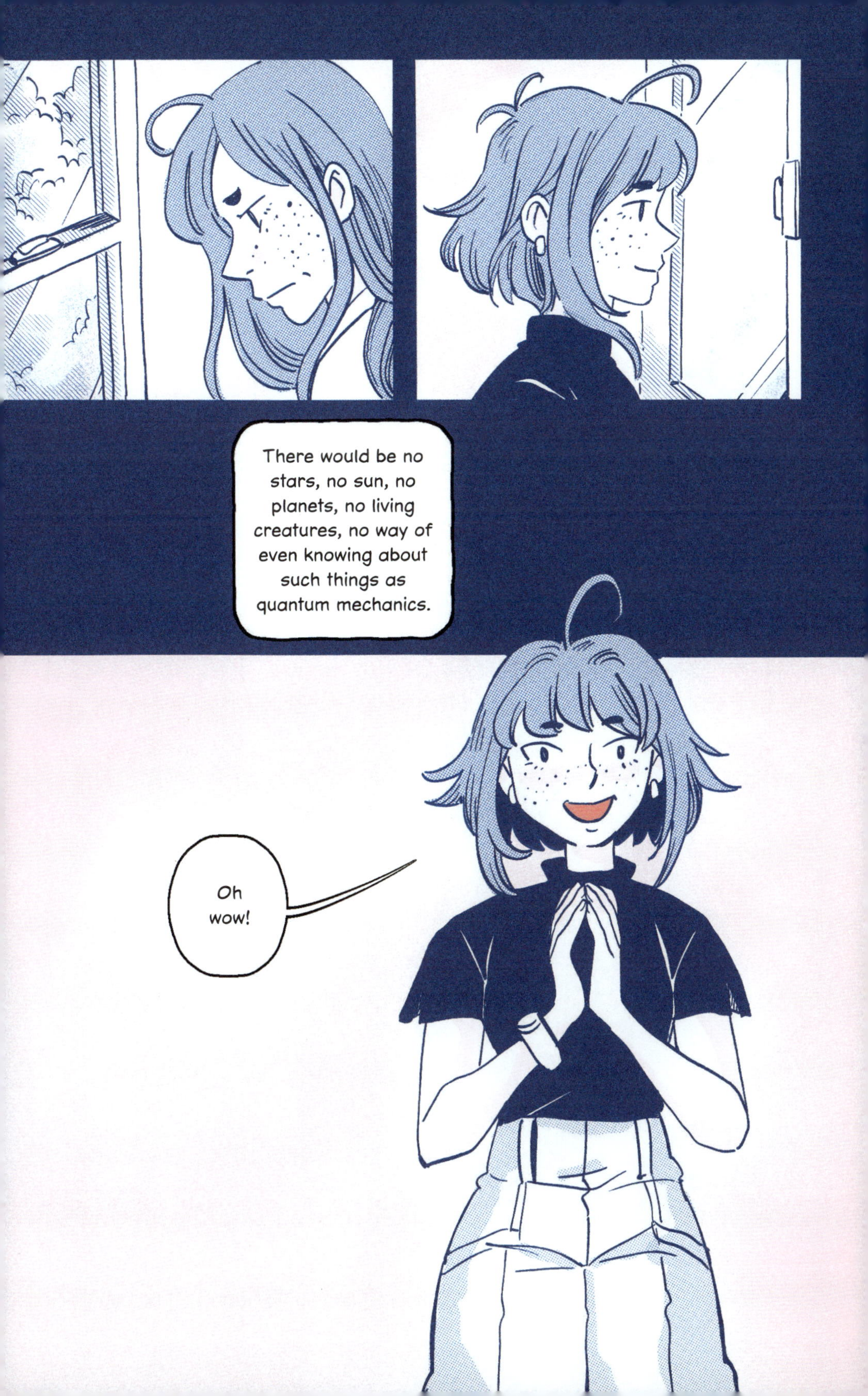
There would be no stars, no sun, no planets, no living creatures, no way of even knowing about such things as quantum mechanics.
Oh wow!

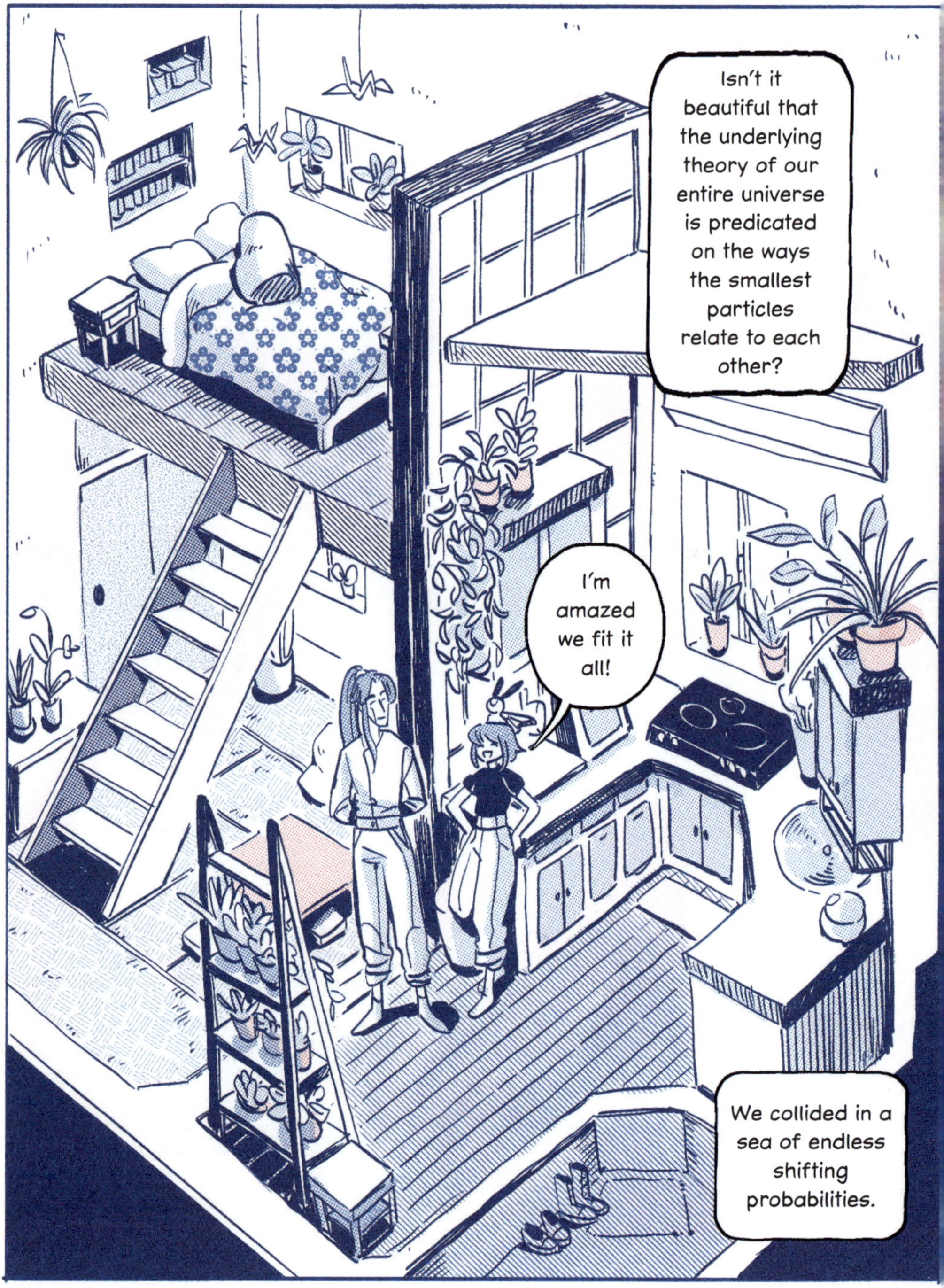
Isn't it beautiful that the underlying theory of our entire universe is predicated on the ways the smallest particles relate to each other?
I'm amazed we fit it all!
We collided in a sea of endless shifting probabilities.

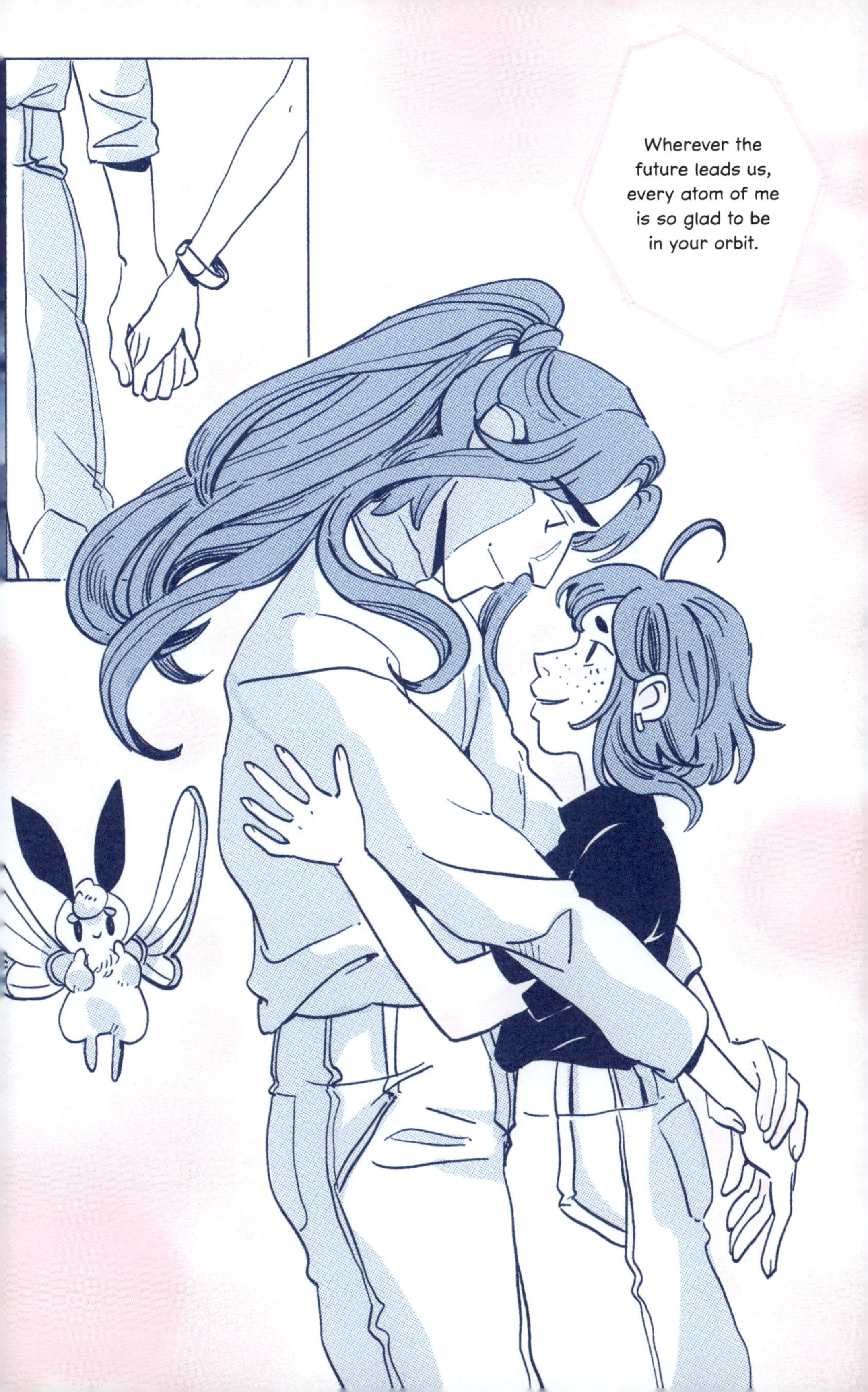
Wherever the future leads us, every atom of me is so glad to be in your orbit.